nese Literature: A Reader

# 中国文学选读

唐建清 李 彦 选编

南京大学出版社

**图书在版编目(CIP)数据**

中国文学选读 / 唐建清,李彦选编. —南京:南京大学
出版社,2009.12(2016.7重印)
ISBN 978 - 7 - 305 - 06589 - 7

Ⅰ.中… Ⅱ.①唐…②李… Ⅲ.文学欣赏-中国-对外
汉语教学-教材 Ⅳ.H195.4

中国版本图书馆 CIP 数据核字(2009)第 219436 号

出版发行 南京大学出版社
社 址 南京市汉口路 22 号 邮 编 210093
出 版 人 金鑫荣

书 名 中国文学选读
选 编 唐建清 李 彦
责任编辑 王 洁 编辑热线 025 - 83594933
照 排 南京紫藤制版印务中心
印 刷 南京理工大学资产经营有限公司
开 本 787×960 1/16 印张 30 字数 516 千
版 次 2009 年 12 月第 1 版 2016 年 7 月第 3 次印刷
ISBN 978 - 7 - 305 - 06589 - 7
定 价 60.00 元

网址:http://www.njupco.com
官方微博:http://weibo.com/njupco
官方微信:njupress
销售咨询热线:(025)83594756

# Preface

As one of the cradles of human civilization, China has produced a vast library of great literature over the past five thousand years. Like that of many other nations, Chinese literature is the essence of Chinese thought, the treasure of Chinese culture; it is the record of our forefathers' struggles against heaven and earth, providing vivid depictions of the material and spiritual lives of Chinese in both ancient and modern times.

In the long history of Chinese literature, a series of masterful figures emerged in genres such as poetry, fiction, and drama. Unlike the ruling emperors, these writers, sitting on the "throne" of Chinese characters, write about China in pride and elegance with their brushes. Because of their writings, Chinese history becomes more vivid and interesting. And these writers have become immortal with their writings.

Over the course of history, many works of literature have been lost to political upheavals or to the ravages of time. Even so, a great amount of masterpieces of Chinese literature, whether poems, stories, essays, novels, or dramas, have been handed down to the present. *The Book of Songs*, *Li Sao*, poetry of the Tang and Song dynasties, drama from the Yuan, and novels from the Ming and Qing dynasties all exhibit their own unique styles. These works cover a wide range of subjects, reflect on and respond to such eternal themes as love and death, nature and humankind, society and individual life, etc. With gripping images and ornate prose, their messages have profound implications and offer long-standing appeal to even modern audiences. Many lines of poetry, aphorisms from essays, and romantic or heroic stories from fiction or drama are still on everyone's lips in China today, and have become prized gems in the treasure house of Chinese as well as world literature.

As the saying goes, the best way to come to know a country and its people is to read its literature. In studying Chinese literature, the reader will come to better understand Chinese traditions and society, as well as the cultural mindset, values, and lifestyles of the Chinese people.

*Chinese Literature: A Reader* is a product of the joint efforts of Professor Jianqing Tang and Professor Yan Li over a two-year span at the Confucius Institute, an institution co-sponsored by two renowned universities in China and Canada: Nanjing University and the University of Waterloo. Professor Tang has taught literature for over twenty years, and Professor Li is herself a fiction writer. Based on their experiences teaching foreign students, the two authors have selected works from the vast ocean of Chinese literature that they deem most appropriate and valuable to the students' learning. As such, the writers included in this textbook are all fitting representatives of significant periods in Chinese literary history. The selected texts are also accessible to foreign readers, and cover all important genres and schools of thought in Chinese literature. With its simple explanatory language, this book can become a gateway to understanding Chinese literature as well as China for both foreign students and international readers.

Cheng Aimin

Oct. 6th, 2009

# Contents

**Chapter One  *Shi Jing* and *Li Sao*** ···················································· 1

  1. General Description  ···················································· 1

  2. Introduction to *Shi Jing*  ···················································· 3

  3. Selections from *Shi Jing*  ···················································· 5

  4. Introduction to Qu Yuan ···················································· 18

  5. Selected Works from Qu Yuan  ···················································· 20

  6. Further Readings  ···················································· 27

  7. Topics for Discussion  ···················································· 32

**Chapter Two  Historical Narratives** ···················································· 33

  1. General Description  ···················································· 33

  2. Introduction to *Shi Ji*  ···················································· 34

  3. Selections from *Shi Ji*  ···················································· 36

  4. Further Readings  ···················································· 55

  5. Topics for Discussion  ···················································· 59

**Chapter Three  Literature in the Wei and Jin Period** ···················································· 61

  1. General Description  ···················································· 61

  2. Introduction to the Works of Tao Yuanming ···················································· 62

  3. Selected Works from Tao Yuanming  ···················································· 63

  4. Further Readings  ···················································· 70

  5. Topics for Discussion  ···················································· 75

**Chapter Four  Poetry in the Tang Dynasty** ················· 77

    1. General Description ····························· 77

    2. Introduction to the Poems of Li Bai ··············· 79

    3. Selected Poems of Li Bai ························· 80

    4. Introduction to the Poems of Du Fu ··············· 85

    5. Selected Poems of Du Fu ························· 86

    6. Further Readings ······························· 92

    7. Topics for Discussion ··························· 95

**Chapter Five  Ci in the Song Dynasty** ··················· 97

    1. General Description ····························· 97

    2. Introduction to the Ci of Su Shi ················· 99

    3. Selected Works of Su Shi ························ 100

    4. Introduction to the Ci of Li Qingzhao ············ 104

    5. Selected Works of Li Qingzhao ·················· 106

    6. Further Readings ······························ 110

    7. Topics for Discussion ·························· 112

**Chapter Six  Essays in the Tang and Song Dynasties** ······· 113

    1. General Description ···························· 113

    2. Introduction to the Works of Liu Zongyuan ········ 115

    3. Selected Works of Liu Zongyuan ················· 116

    4. Introduction to the Works of Ouyang Xiu ········· 121

    5. Selected Works of Ouyang Xiu ·················· 122

    6. Further Readings ······························ 126

    7. Topics for Discussion ·························· 134

**Chapter Seven  Drama in the Yuan Dynasty** ·············· 135

    1. General Description ···························· 135

    2. Introduction to *Dou E Yuan* ··················· 137

    3. Selection from *Dou E Yuan* ··················· 139

中国文学选读

    4. Introduction to *The Western Chamber* ·············· 146

    5. Selection from *The Western Chamber* ·············· 148

    6. Further Readings ······························ 164

    7. Topics for Discussion ························· 179


**Chapter Eight   Novels of the Ming and Qing Dynasties** ·············· 181

    1. General Description ························· 181

    2. Introduction to *Dream of the Red Chamber* ············ 184

    3. Selection from *Dream of the Red Chamber* ············ 187

    4. Further Readings ························· 201

    5. Topics for Discussion ························· 270


**Chapter Nine   Modern Chinese Literature** ·············· 271

    1. General Description ························· 271

    2. Introduction to the Stories of Lu Xun ·············· 273

    3. Selected Works of Lu Xun ·················· 274

    4. Introduction to the Poems of Xu Zhimo ············ 309

    5. Selected Poems of Xu Zhimo ·················· 310

    6. Further Readings ························· 315

    7. Topics for Discussion ························· 362


**Chapter Ten   Contemporary Chinese Literature** ·············· 363

    1. General Description ························· 363

    2. Introduction to the Works of Zhang Jie ············ 364

    3. Selection from Zhang Jie's Works ·············· 365

    4. Introduction to the Works of Zhang Chengzhi ·········· 390

    5. Selection from Zhang Chengzhi's Works ············ 391

    6. Further Readings ························· 415

    7. Topics for Discussion ························· 464

**Appendix** ················································· 465

  Ⅰ Glossary ··············································· 465

  Ⅱ Chronological Table and Major Literary Events ··········· 469

  Ⅲ Acknowledgments ································· 471

中国文学选读

Chapter One

# *Shi Jing* and *Li Sao*

## General Description

Chinese literature has a long history with a past that can be traced back to ancient times, to a time before written characters. The original literature was of myths, legends and songs, created orally and passed on from generation to generation.

Poetry was the first form of literature, with early poetry being combined with music to produce chants and songs that could be easily remembered and passed on.

The first era of Chinese literature began prior to the Qin Dynasty. It covers the period of the Xia(夏), Shang(商) and Zhou(周) Dynasties(2100BC～221BC). In terms of literary development, the Pre-Qin(先秦)can broadly be divided into three sections. First period: Xia Dynasty—Shang Dynasty(2100BC～1100BC). Second period: Western Zhou(西周 1100BC)—Spring and Autumn(春秋 770BC～476BC). Third period: Warring States(战国 475BC～221BC).

In comparison to the oral literature that had previously existed, the literature of the Pre-Qin period advanced with the addition of written characters, and included prose as well as poetry. Naturally, due to the length of time that has passed, the authorship of many of the works created in the Pre-Qin cannot possibly be unequivocally confirmed.

The most recognized literary achievements of the Pre-Qin period were *Shi Jing* (《诗经》 *Book of Songs or Book of Odes*), *Chu Ci*(《楚辞》 *Songs of Chu* or *Songs of the South*) and essays from various scholars.

This chapter includes selections from *Shi Jing*, the first and last chapters of *Li Sao*, and a genuine masterpiece, *The Spirit of the Mountains*, by Qu Yuan. The supplementary piece is by Zhuangzi.

中国文学选读

## Introduction to *Shi Jing*

*Shi Jing* is the earliest collection of Chinese poems in existence. Originally called "Shi(诗)" or "300 Poems", it actually consists of 305 poems spanning 500 years from the early Zhou Dynasty(1100BC) to the Mid-Spring and Autumn period(600BC), with the final list of poems drawn up around that time. Throughout history there have been many terms used to describe *Shi Jing* such as Xian Shi(献诗 presenting poems), Cai Shi(采诗 collecting poems) and Shan Shi(删诗 editing poems). It was believed that the collection, included in the "Six Classics(六经 Liu Jing)", had been compiled by Confucius(孔子) who once said, "If one does not learn poetry, one cannot speak well." This indicates that during the time of Confucius, *Shi Jing* was not just a collection of poems, it was also looked upon as the equivalent of knowledge of the humanities by intellectuals. Learning and using *Shi Jing* became a mandatory part of an aristocratic cultural education.

*Shi Jing* is composed of Liu Yi(六艺 six kinds) referred to as Feng(风), Ya (雅), Song(颂), Fu(赋), Bi(比) and Xing(兴). The first three categories signify the contents of the poems. So, Feng, Ya, and Song are categories of the various musical hymns and tunes that were developed in different areas. Fu, Bi and Xing on the other hand, indicate the literary styles employed.

"Feng", also called "Guo Feng(国风)", are folk songs or ballads from different areas, with romantic love and prominent themes. The ballads came from 15 areas and total 160 poems, accounting for a major portion of *Shi Jing*.

"Ya" songs are imperial court music and are typically divided into the 31 titles of Da Ya(大雅 major festal odes—for more solemn ceremonies) and the 74 titles of Xiao Ya(小雅 minor festal odes—for court festivities). Most of these works were created by the aristocracy.

"Song" pieces are religious hymns and eulogies. There are 40 titles of Zhou Song (周颂), Lu Song(鲁颂) and Shang Song(商颂). Ya and Song are special works written for the court or for temple sacrificial feasts.

Fu, Bi, and Xing refer to the methods of depiction, approach, or style. "Fu"

孔子及其弟子

means description and with it the poets directly express emotional thoughts and feelings in a straightforward narrative. "Bi" means explicit comparison and uses obvious daily expressions to convey nonfigurative phrases and make them clearly understandable. "Xing" is implied comparison and is commonly used at the beginning of a poem to trigger what follows. These three major styles are often interactively employed and applied to create the artistic images in poetry.

*Shi Jing* poems are normally written with four-character lines and constructed in four-line groups. Occasionally, though, you will see two-character lines or eight-character lines in the poems. The two-beat tempo contains a very powerful rhythm which can usually be discovered in the four-character lines. The distinctive rhythm is short, sharp and clear. Overlapping lines and repeated characters strengthen the tune's back-and-forth nature, enhancing the poetic melody. This basic and straightforward method is a fundamental component of *Shi Jing*.

Although *Shi Jing* does contain a few short epic narratives, it is mainly a collection of expressive works, so we can accurately describe *Shi Jing* as a compilation of lyrical poems. It can therefore be said to have paved the way for lyrical poems to become the dominant form of Chinese poetry.

The issues addressed in *Shi Jing*, including a penchant for realism, strong political and moral awareness, sincerity, and a positive attitude towards life are essential spirits that have a direct impact later on Chinese poetic sensibilities, and can be summed up as the "Feng Ya(风雅)" spirit.

中国文学选读

## Selections from *Shi Jing*

### 1. Cooing and Wooing

By riverside are cooing
    A pair of turtledoves;
A good young man is wooing
    A fair maiden he loves.

Water flows left and right
    Of cress long here, short there;
The youth yearns day and night
    For the good maiden fair.

His yearning grows so strong,
    He cannot fall asleep,
But tosses all night long,
    So deep in love, so deep!

Now gather left and right
    Cress long or short and tender!
O lute, play music bright
    For the bride sweet and slender!

Feast friends at left and right
    On cress cooked till tender!
O bells and drums, delight
    The bride so sweet and slender!

                    (translated by Xu Yuanchong)

# 国风·关雎

关关雎鸠，在河之洲。窈窕淑女，君子好逑。

参差荇菜，左右流之；窈窕淑女，寤寐求之。

求之不得，寤寐思服；悠哉悠哉，辗转反侧。

参差荇菜，左右采之；窈窕淑女，琴瑟友之。

参差荇菜，左右芼之；窈窕淑女，钟鼓乐之。


## 2. Jiang Chung Tzu

I beg of you, Chung Tzu,

Do not climb into our homestead,

Do not break the willows we have planted.

Not that I mind about the willows,

But I am afraid of my father and mother.

Chung Tzu I dearly love;

But of what my father and mother say

Indeed I am afraid.


I beg of you, Chung Tzu,

Do not climb over our wall,

Do not break the mulberry trees we have planted.

Not that I mind about the mulberry trees,

But I am afraid of my brothers.

Chung Tzu I dearly love;

But of what my brothers say

Indeed I am afraid.


I beg of you, Chung Tzu,

Do not climb into our garden,

Do not break the hardwood we have planted.

Not that I mind about the hardwood,

But I am afraid of what people will say.

Chung Tzu I dearly love;

But of all that people will say

Indeed I am afraid.

(translated by Arthur Waley)

## 国风·将仲子

将仲子兮，无逾我里，无折我树杞。岂敢爱之？
畏我父母。仲可怀也，父母之言，亦可畏也。

将仲子兮，无逾我墙，无折我树桑。岂敢爱之？
畏我诸兄。仲可怀也，诸兄之言，亦可畏也。

将仲子兮，无逾我园，无折我树檀。岂敢爱之？
畏人之多言。仲可怀也，人之多言，亦可畏也。

### 3. The Reed

Green, green the reed,

　　Dew and frost gleam.

Where's she I need?

　　Beyond the stream.

Upstream I go;

　　The way is long.

Downstream I go;

　　She's there among.

White, white the reed,

　　Dew not yet dried.

Where's she I need?

On the other side.

Upstream I go;

Hard is the way.

Downstream I go;

She's far away.


Bright, bright the reed,

Dew and frost blend.

Where's she I need?

At river's end.

Upstream I go;

The way does wind.

Downstream I go;

She's far behind.

(translated by Xu Yuanchong)

## 国风·蒹葭

蒹葭苍苍，白露为霜。所谓伊人，在水一方。
溯洄从之，道阻且长；溯游从之，宛在水中央。

蒹葭凄凄，白露未晞。所谓伊人，在水之湄。
溯洄从之，道阻且跻；溯游从之，宛在水中坻。

蒹葭采采，白露未已。所谓伊人，在水之涘。
溯洄从之，道阻且右；溯游从之，宛在水中沚。


## 4. Life of Peasants

In seventh moon Fire Star west goes;

In ninth to make dress we are told.

In days of first moon the wind blows;

In those of second weather's cold.

We have no garments warm to wear.

How can we get through the year?

In days of third we mend our plough with care;

In fourth our way afield we steer.

Our wives and children take the food

To southern fields; the overseer says, "Good!"

In seventh moon Fire Star west goes;

In ninth we make dress all day long.

By and by warm spring grows

And golden orioles sing their song.

The lasses take their baskets deep

And go along the small pathways

To gather tender mulberry leaves in heap.

When lengthen vernal days,

They pluck in heaps southernwood white,

Their heart in pitiable plight

Lest sons of lords take them by might.

In seventh moon Fire Star west goes;

In eighth we gather rush and reed.

In silkworm month with axe's blow

We cut mulberry sprigs with speed.

We lop off branches long and high

And bring young tender leaves in.

In seventh moon we hear shrikes cry;

In eighth moon we begin to spin.

We use a bright red dye

And a dark yellow one

To color robes of our lord's son.


In fourth moon grass begins to seed;

   In fifth cicadas cry.

In eighth moon to reap we proceed;

   In tenth down come leaves dry.

In days of first moon we go in chase

   For wild cats and foxes fleet

To make furs for the son of noble race.

   In days of second moon we meet

And manoeuvre with lance and sword.

We keep the smaller boars for our reward

And offer larger ones o'er to our lord.


In fifth moon locusts move their legs;

   In sixth the spinner shakes its wings.

In seventh in the field laying its eggs,

   In eighth under the leaves the cricket sings.

In ninth it moves indoors when chilled;

   In tenth it enters under the bed.

We clear the corners, chinks are filled,

   We smoke the house and rats run in dread.

We plaster northern window and door

   And tell our wives and lad and lass:

The old year will soon be no more.

   Let's dwell inside, alas!


In sixth moon we've wild plums and grapes to eat;

In seventh we cook beans and mallows nice.

In eighth moon down the dates we beat;

In tenth we reap the rice

And brew the vernal wine,

A cordial for the oldest-grown.

In seventh moon we eat melon fine;

In eighth moon the gourds are cut down.

In ninth we gather the hemp-seed;

Of fetid tree we make firewood;

We gather lettuce to feed

Our husbandmen as food.

In ninth moon we repair the threshing-floor;

In tenth we bring in harvest clean:

The millet early sown and late are put in store,

And wheat and hemp, paddy and bean.

There is no rest for husbandmen:

Once harvesting is done, alas!

We're sent to work in lord's house then.

By day for thatch we gather reed and grass;

At night we twist them into ropes,

Then hurry to mend the roofs again,

For we should not abandon the hopes

Of sowing in time our fields with grain.

In days of second moon we hew out ice;

In those of third we store it deep.

In those of fourth we offer early sacrifice

Of garlic, lamb and sheep.

In ninth moon frosty is the weather;

In tenth we sweep and clear the threshing-floor.

We drink two bottles of wine together

And kill a lamb before the door.

Then we go up

To the hall where

We raise our buffalo-horn cup

And wish our lord to live fore'er.

(translated by Xu Yuanchong)

## 国风·七月

七月流火，九月授衣。

一之日觱发，二之日栗烈。

无衣无褐，何以卒岁？

三之日于耜，四之日举趾。

同我妇子，馌彼南亩，田畯至喜！


七月流火，九月授衣。

春日载阳，有鸣仓庚。

女执懿筐，遵彼微行，爰求柔桑。

春日迟迟，采蘩祁祁。

女心伤悲，殆及公子同归。


七月流火，八月萑苇。

蚕月条桑，取彼斧斨。

以伐远扬，猗彼女桑。

七月鸣鵙，八月载绩。

载玄载黄，我朱孔阳，为公子裳。


四月秀葽，五月鸣蜩。

八月其获，十月陨箨。

中国文学选读

一之日于貉，取彼狐狸，为公子裘。

二之日其同，载缵武功。

言私其豵，献豣于公。


五月斯螽动股，六月莎鸡振羽。

七月在野，八月在宇。

九月在户，十月蟋蟀入我床下。

穹窒熏鼠，塞向墐户。

嗟我妇子，曰为改岁，入此室处。


六月食郁及薁，七月亨葵及菽。

八月剥枣，十月获稻。

为此春酒，以介眉寿。

七月食瓜，八月断壶。

九月叔苴，采荼薪樗，食我农夫。


九月筑场圃，十月纳禾稼。

黍稷重穋，禾麻菽麦。

嗟我农夫，我稼既同，上入执宫功。

昼尔于茅，宵尔索绹。

亟其乘屋，其始播百谷。


二之日凿冰冲冲，三之日纳于凌阴。

四之日其蚤，献羔祭韭。

九月肃霜，十月涤场。

朋酒斯飨，曰杀羔羊。

跻彼公堂，称彼兕觥：万寿无疆！


## 5. A Homesick Warrior

We gather fern

Which springs up here.

Why not return?

Now ends the year.

We left dear ones

To fight the Huns.

All night we wake

For the Huns' sake.


We gather fern

So tender here.

Why not return?

My heart feels drear.

Hard pressed by thirst

And hunger worst,

My heart is burning

For home I'm yearning.

Far from home, how

To send word now?


We gather fern

Which grows tough here.

Why not return?

The tenth month's near.

The war not won,

We cannot rest.

Consoled by none,

We feel distressed.


How gorgeous are

The cherry flowers!

中国文学选读

How great the car
 Of lord of ours!
It's driven by
 Four horses nice.
We can't but hie
 In one month thrice.

Driven by four
 Horses alined,
Our lord before,
 We march behind.
Four horses neigh,
 Quiver and bow
Ready each day
 To fight the foe.

On parting day
 Willows did sway.
I come back now;
 Snow bends the bough.
Long, long the way;
 Hard, hard the day.
Hunger and thirst
 Press me the worst.
My grief o'er flows.
 Who knows? Who knows?

(translated by Xu Yuanchong)

## 小雅·采薇

采薇采薇，薇亦作止。曰归曰归，岁亦莫止。
靡室靡家，玁狁之故。不遑启居，玁狁之故。

采薇采薇，薇亦柔止。曰归曰归，心亦忧止。
忧心烈烈，载饥载渴。我戍未定，靡使归聘。

采薇采薇，薇亦刚止。曰归曰归，岁亦阳止。
王事靡盬，不遑启处。忧心孔疚，我行不来！

彼尔维何，维常之华。彼路斯何，君子之车。
戎车既驾，四牡业业。岂敢定居，一月三捷。

驾彼四牡，四牡骙骙。君子所依，小人所腓。
四牡翼翼，象弭鱼服。岂不日戒，玁狁孔棘。

昔我往矣，杨柳依依。今我来思，雨雪霏霏。
行道迟迟，载饥载渴。我心伤悲，莫知我哀。

## 6. Hymn of Thanksgiving in Autumn

Sharp are plough-shares we wield;

　　We plough the southern field.

All kinds of grain we sow

　　Burst into life and grow.

Our wives come to the ground

　　With baskets square and round

Of millet and steamed bread,

　　With straw-hat on the head.

We weed with hoe in hand

中国文学选读

On the dry or wet land.

When weeds fall in decay,

Luxuriant millets sway.


When millet rustling fall,

We reap and pile them up all

High and thick as a wall.


Like comb teeth stacks are close;

Stores are opened in rows.

When all of them are full,

Wives and children repose.


We kill a tawny bull,

Whose horns crooked appear.

We follow fathers dear

To perform rites with cheer.

(translated by Xu Yuanchong)

## 周颂·良耜

畟畟良耜，俶载南亩。播厥百谷，实函斯活。

或来瞻女，载筐及筥，其饟伊黍。

其笠伊纠，其镈斯赵，以薅荼蓼。

荼蓼朽止，黍稷茂止。获之挃挃，积之栗栗。

其崇如墉，其比如栉，以开百室。百室盈止，妇子宁止。

杀时犉牡，有捄其角。以似以续，续古之人。

## Introduction to Qu Yuan

Qu Yuan(屈原 339~278BC?) was born into an aristocratic family and was an official during the reign of Chu Huai Wang(楚怀王). However he was slandered by corrupt officials and banished into exile by the King. He ended his life by jumping into the Miluo River in an expression of patriotism upon the fall of the Chu capital. The traditional Chinese Dragon Boat Festival(端午节 May 5th on the lunar calendar) is a commemoration of this great poet's life.

Qu Yuan is the most representative *Chu Ci* writer.

*Chu Ci* (《楚辞》*Songs of Chu*), from the Warring States Period (475BC~ 221BC), together with *Shi Jing*, constitutes the creative source of Chinese poetry known as the "Feng and Sao Style(风骚)". Chu culture came from an area located in the middle reaches of the Yangtze and Han River basins and was very different from characteristic Chinese culture in the northern part of China, especially with its embrace of sorcery and exotic romance.

Coming after *Shi Jing*, *Chu Ci* embodied a unique feature and became a new form of poetry, visibly different from the poetry of the Northern area, especially musically and linguistically.

*Li Sao* (《离骚》*The Lament*) is Qu Yuan's masterpiece. A long lyrical poem, with the air of an autobiography, it contains over 370 sentences and nearly 2500 words. There are many interpretations of the meaning of the title "Li Sao", one being "suffering hardship", another being "a sorrowful departure from his country". Most people, though, agree that it represents the thoughts of Qu Yuan during his tor-

屈原

中国文学选读

ment in exile.

This long poem can be divided into two parts. The first part describes the high expectations he has for himself and the ongoing conflicts between him and the aristocrats in the kingdom. The latter part uses the material of myth to present his inner thoughts in the form of fantasy. *Li Sao* is an expression of Qu Yuan's patriotism, loyalty and political ideals. It is written with an anguished voice that bares his sorrow at his unfair treatment.

*Li Sao* uses literary images of herbs and beauty to symbolize the longing and pursuit of aesthetics and a noble character.

In format, *Li Sao* is different from *Shi Jing*. *Shi Jing* is presented in short, brief four-character lines, with a chanted variation. In *Li Sao* the sentences are of uneven length and the format is more free and lively with the use of flamboyant vocabulary to broaden the writing range. Also, Qu Yuan adapted the local Chu dialect and made extensive use of local words such as "Xi(兮)", a sound in the local dialect. This unique approach enhances the poem, making it rich with local color.

Most of the poems in *Shi Jing* are folk songs, forming a collective creation. *Li Sao* on the other hand is the work of one individual, an individual who initiated a new era in writing.

"The Spirit of the Mountains"(《山鬼》) is a famous poem from Qu Yuan's collected poems, *Nine Songs* (《九歌》). Using an internal monologue with mythological constructs the poet paints the image of an innocent and devoted female character.

# Selected Works from Qu Yuan

## 1. Li Sao

A Prince am I of Ancestry renowned,

Illustrious Name my royal Sire hath found.

When Sirius did in Spring its Light display,

A Child was born, and Tiger marked the Day.

When first upon my Face my Lord's Eye glanced,

For me auspicious Names he straight advanced,

Denoting that in me Heaven's Marks divine

Should with the Virtues of the Earth combine.

With lavished innate Qualities in dued,

By Art and Skill my Talents I renewed;

Angelic Herbs and sweet Selineas too,

And Orchids late that by the Water grew,

I wove for Ornament; till creeping Time,

屈原与《离骚》

Like Water flowing, stole away my Prime.
Magnolias of the Glade I plucked at Dawn,
At Eve beside the Stream took Winter-thorn.
Without Delay the Sun and Moon sped fast,
In swift Succession Spring and Autumn passed;
The fallen Flowers lay scattered on the Ground,
The Dusk might fall before my Dream was found.
Had I not loved my Prime and spurned the Vile,
Why should I not have changed my former Style?
My Chariot drawn by Steeds of Race divine
I urged; to guide the King my sole Design.

Three ancient Kings there were so pure and true
That round them every fragrant Flower grew;
Cassia and Pepper of the Mountain-side
With Melilotus white in Clusters vied.
Two Monarchs then, who high Renown received,
Followed the kingly Way, their Goal achieved.
Two Princes proud by Lust their Reign abused,
Sought easier Path, and their own Steps confused.
The Faction for illicit Pleasure longed;
Dreadful their Way where hidden Perils thronged.
Danger against myself could not appal,
But feared I lest my Sovereign's Sceptre fall.

Forward and back I hastened in my Quest,
Followed the former Kings, and took no Rest.
The Prince my true Integrity defamed,
Gave Ear to Slander, high his Anger flamed;
Integrity I knew could not avail,
Yet still endured; my Lord I would not fail.

Celestial Spheres my Witness be on high,

I strove but for His Sacred Majesty.

Twas first to me he gave his plighted Word,

But soon repenting other Counsel heard.

For me Departure could arouse no Pain;

I grieved to see his royal Purpose vain.

. . . .

With Omens bright the Seer revealed the Way,

I then appointed an auspicious Day.

As Victuals rare some Jasper Twigs I bore,

And some prepared, Provision rich to store;

Then winged Horses to my Chariot brought

My Carriage bright with Jade and Ivory wrought.


How might two Hearts at Variance accord?

I roamed till Peace be to my Mind restored.

The Pillar of the Earth I stayed beside;

The Way was long, and winding far and wide.

In Twilight glowed the Clouds with wondrous Sheen,

And chirping flew the Birds of Jasper green.

I went at Dawn high Heaven's Ford to leave;

To Earth's Extremity I came at Eve.

On phoenix Wings the Dragon Pennons lay;

With Plumage bright they flew to lead the Way.


I crossed the Quicksand with its treach'rous Flood,

Beside the burning River, red as Blood;

To bridge the Stream my Dragons huge I bade,

Invoked the Emperor of the West to aid.


The Way was long, precipitous in View;

I bade my Train a different Path pursue.

There where the Heaven fell we turned a Space,

And marked the Western Sea as Meeting-place.

A thousand Chariots gathered in my Train,

With Axles full abreast we drove amain;

Eight Horses drew the Carriages behind;

The Pennons shook like Serpents in the Wind.

I lowered Flags, and from my Whip refrained;

My Train of towering Chariots I restrained.

I sang the Odes. I trod a sacred Dance,

In Revels wild my last Hour to enhance.

Ascending where celestial Heaven blazed,

On native Earth for the last Time we gazed;

My Slaves were sad, my Steeds all neighed in Grief,

And, gazing back, the Earth they would not leave.


Since in that Kingdom all my Virtue spurn,

Why should I for the royal City yearn?

Wide though the World, no Wisdom call be found.

I'll seek the Stream where once the Sage was drowned.

（translated by Yang Xianyi and Gladys Yang）

## 离骚（节选）

帝高阳之苗裔兮，朕皇考曰伯庸。

摄提贞于孟陬兮，惟庚寅吾以降。

皇览揆余初度兮，肇锡余以嘉名：

名余曰正则兮，字余曰灵均。


纷吾既有此内美兮，又重之以修能。

扈江离与辟芷兮，纫秋兰以为佩。

汨余若将不及兮，恐年岁之不吾与。

朝搴阰之木兰兮，夕揽洲之宿莽。
日月忽其不淹兮，春与秋其代序。
惟草木之零落兮，恐美人之迟暮。
不抚壮而弃秽兮，何不改乎此度？
乘骐骥以驰骋兮，来吾道夫先路！

昔三后之纯粹兮，固众芳之所在。
杂申椒与菌桂兮，岂维纫夫蕙茝？
彼尧舜之耿介兮，既遵道而得路。
何桀纣之猖披兮，夫唯捷径以窘步！
惟夫党人之偷乐兮，路幽昧以险隘。
岂余身之惮殃兮，恐皇舆之败绩。
忽奔走以先后兮，及前王之踵武。
荃不察余之中情兮，反信谗而齐怒。
余固知謇謇之为患兮，忍而不能舍也。
指九天以为正兮，夫唯灵修之故也。
曰黄昏以为期兮，羌中道而改路。
初既与余成言兮，后悔遁而有他。
余既不难夫离别兮，伤灵修之数化。
……
灵氛既告余以吉占兮，历吉日乎吾将行。
折琼枝以为羞兮，精琼爢以为粻。
为余驾飞龙兮，杂瑶象以为车。
何离心之可同兮，吾将远逝以自疏。
遭吾道夫昆仑兮，路修远以周流。
扬云霓之晻蔼兮，鸣玉鸾之啾啾。
朝发轫于天津兮，夕余至乎西极。
凤凰翼其承旗兮，高翱翔之翼翼。
忽吾行此流沙兮，遵赤水而容与。
麾蛟龙使梁津兮，诏西皇使涉予。
路修远以多艰兮，腾众车使径待。

中国文学选读

路不周以左转兮，指西海以为期。

屯余车其千乘兮，齐玉轪而并驰。
驾八龙之蜿蜿兮，载云旗之委蛇。
抑志而弭节兮，神高驰之邈邈。
奏九歌而舞韶兮，聊假日以为婾乐。
陟陛皇之赫戏兮，忽临睨夫旧乡。
仆夫悲余马怀兮，蜷局顾而不行。

乱曰：已矣哉！
国无人莫我知兮，又何怀乎故都？
既莫足与为美政兮，吾将从彭咸之所居。


## 2. The Spirit of the Mountains

A Presence lingers in the Mountain Glade,
In Ivy and Wistaria Leaves arrayed.
My laughing Lips with gay and sparking Glance
By sprightly Beauty ev'ry Heart entrance.
With Foxes Train, on tawny Leopards borne,
Jasmine and Cassia Flags my Steeds adorn.
Clad in Rock Orchids, in Azalea decked,
I pluck the fragrant Herbs for my Elect.
Where Reeds gloom darkly and obscure the Day,
Later am I come through steep and weary Way;
I stand alone upon the Mountain's Head,
While multitud'nous Clouds beneath are spread.
The Day is wild, with darking Gloom increased;
Spirits send Show'rs; Wind blusters from the East.
Delayed by me my love forgets to leave.
Now the Year wanes, who will my Garlands weave?

Within the Mountain magic Herbs I find,

Where clinging Vines the crumbling Boulders bind.

I mourn my Love, forgetting to return.

Kept from his Sight to see him still I yearn.

Midst fragrant Herbs within the Mountain Glade

I drink clear Springs, where Pine and Cedar shade.

You think of me, yet still in Doubt remain,

While Thunder rumbles, mixed with Show'rs of Rain.

At Night the Monkeys and Hyaenas moan,

By sobbing Winds the rustling Trees are blown,

In vain my absent Lord I mourn alone.

（translated by Yang Xianyi and Gladys Yang）

## 九歌·山鬼

若有人兮山之阿，被薜荔兮带女萝。

既含睇兮又宜笑，子慕予兮善窈窕。

乘赤豹兮从文狸，辛夷车兮结桂旗。

被石兰兮带杜衡，折芳馨兮遗所思。

余处幽篁兮终不见天，路险难兮独后来。


表独立兮山之上，云容容兮而在下。

杳冥冥兮羌昼晦，东风飘兮神灵雨。

留灵修兮憺忘归，岁既晏兮孰华予？

采三秀兮于山间，石磊磊兮葛蔓蔓。

怨公子兮怅忘归，君思我兮不得闲。

山中人兮芳杜若，饮石泉兮荫松柏。

君思我兮然疑作。

雷填填兮雨冥冥，猿啾啾兮又夜鸣。

风飒飒兮木萧萧，思公子兮徒离忧。

# Further Readings

## 1. Wandering in Absolute Freedom

In the North Sea there is a kind of fish by the name of *kun*, whose size covers thousands of *li*. The fish metamorphoses into a kind of bird by the name of *peng*, whose back covers thousands of *li*. When it rises in flight, its wings are like clouds that hang from the sky. When the wind blows over the sea, the *peng* moves to the South Sea, the Celestial Pond.

According to *Qi Xie*, a collection of mysterious stories, "On its journey to the South Sea, the *peng* flaps sprays for 3 000 *li* and soars to a height of 90 000 *li* at the windy time of June." The air, the dusts and the microbes float in the sky at the breath of the wind. Does the sky display the blueness as its true color? Or does it reach an unattainable distance? When the *peng* looks from above, it must have observed a similar sight.

If a mass of water is not deep enough, it will not be able to float large ships. When you pour a cup of water into a hole on the floor, a straw can sail on it as a boat, but a cup will get stuck in it, for the water is too shallow and the vessel is too large. If the wind is not strong enough, it will not be able to bear large wings. Therefore, the *peng* must have a strong wind under it as its support so as to soar to a height of 90,000 *li*. Only then can it brave the blue sky and clear all obstacles on its southward journey.

A cicada and a turtle-dove derided the *peng*, saying, "We fly upward until we alight on an elm or a sandal tree. Sometimes when we cannot make it, we just fall back to the ground. What's the sense of soaring to a height of 90,000 *li* on your journey to the south?" If you are going to the green suburbs, you only have to bring three meals and you will come back with a full stomach. If you are going 100 *li* away, you have to grind enough grain for the overnight stay. If you are going 1,000 *li* away, you have to bring enough grain to last you three months. How could these two little creatures know about all this?

Little learning does not come up to great learning; the short-lived does not come up to the long-lived. How do we know that this is the case? The fungi that sprout in the morning and die before evening do not know the alternation of night and day; cicadas do not know the alternation of spring and autumn. Those are cases of the short-lived. In the south of the state of Chu there is a miraculous tortoise, for whom each spring or autumn lasts 500 years; in the remote ages there was a huge toon tree, for which each spring or autumn lasted 8 000 years. Those are cases of the long-lived. But today, Pengzu, who lived over 700 years, is uniquely acknowledged for his longevity. Is it not lamentable that he is an object of envy to all!

Tang, the first king of the Shang Dynasty, asked his minister Ji a similar question. Tang asked Ji, "Are there limits up and down, east and west, north and south?" Ji answered, "There are limits beyond limits. In the remote and barren north, there is a dark sea, the Celestial Pond, where lives a kind of fish by the name of *kun*, whose size covers thousands of *li*. There also lives a kind of bird by the name of *peng*, whose back is like a lofty mountain and whose wings are like clouds that hang from the sky. Soaring like a whirlwind to a height of 90,000 *li*, the *peng* flies above the heavy clouds and against the blue sky on its southward journey toward the South Sea. A quail in the marsh laughed at the *peng*, saying, 'Where does he think he's going? I hop and skip and fly up, but I never fly up more than a dozen meters before I come down and hover above the reeds. That's the highest I ever fly! And where does he think he's going?'" Such is the difference between the small and the great.

—From *Zhuangzi*

(translated by Wang Rongpei)

## 逍遥游(节选)

北冥有鱼,其名为鲲。鲲之大,不知其几千里也;化而为鸟,其名为鹏。鹏之背,不知其几千里也;怒而飞,其翼若垂天之云。是鸟也,海运则将徙于南冥。南冥者,天池也。

《齐谐》者,志怪者也。《谐》之言曰:"鹏之徙于南冥也,水击三千里,抟扶摇而上者九万里,去以六月息者也。"野马也,尘埃也,生物之以息相吹也。天之苍苍,其正色邪? 其远而无所至极邪? 其视下也,亦若是则已矣。

中国文学选读

且夫水之积也不厚，则其负大舟也无力。覆杯水于坳堂之上，则芥为之舟。置杯焉则胶，水浅而舟大也。风之积也不厚，则其负大翼也无力。故九万里则风斯在下矣，而后乃今培风；背负青天而莫之夭阏者，而后乃今将图南。蜩与学鸠笑之曰："我决起而飞，抢榆枋，时则不至，而控于地而已矣；奚以之九万里而南为？"适莽苍者，三餐而反，腹犹果然；适百里者，宿舂粮；适千里者，三月聚粮。之二虫又何知！

小知不及大知，小年不及大年。奚以知其然也？朝菌不知晦朔，蟪蛄不知春秋，此小年也。楚之南有冥灵者，以五百岁为春，五百岁为秋；上古有大椿者，以八千岁为春，八千岁为秋，此大年也。而彭祖乃今以久特闻，众人匹之，不亦悲乎？

汤之问棘也是已。汤问棘曰："上下四方极乎？"棘曰："无极之外复无极也。穷发之北有冥海者，天池也。有鱼焉，其广数千里，未有知其修者，其名为鲲。有鸟焉，其名为鹏，背若泰山，翼若垂天之云，抟扶摇羊角而上者九万里，绝云气，负青天，然后图南，且适南冥也。斥鴳笑之曰："彼且奚适也？我腾跃而上，不过数仞而下，翱翔蓬蒿之间，此亦飞之至也。而彼且奚适也？"此小大之辩也。

——选自《庄子》

## 2. Perfect Happiness

Is there really perfect happiness in the world? Is there really some way by which we can enjoy life? If there is, what should we do and what should we depend on? What should we avoid and what should we adhere to? What should we follow and what should we evade? What should we like and what should we dislike?

What men in the world esteem is wealth, honors, longevity and good fame. What men in the world enjoy is a comfortable life, abundant food, fine clothes, beautiful colors and sweet music. What men in the world despise is poverty, disgrace, premature death, and bad fame. What men in the world worry about is lack of a comfortable life, lack of abundant food, lack of fine clothes, lack of beautiful colors and lack of sweet music. They are greatly worried and

庄子

upset when they are in lack of these pleasures. How foolish they are in their way of valuing life!

Men of wealth toil and moil to accumulate more riches than they can possibly consume. How superfluous they are in their way of valuing life! Men of distinction ponder over good and evil day and night. How irrelevant they are in their way of valuing life! Men are born into this world together with worry and care. In a muddled state of mind, men of longevity live a long life of worry and care. How distressing they are! How pointless they are in their way of valuing life! Men of martyrdom are eulogized by men in the world, but they have failed to preserve their lives. I do not know whether their merits are good or not. Perhaps I should think that their merits are good, but they have not been able to preserve their lives; perhaps I should think that their merits are not good, but they have preserved the lives of other people. Therefore, as the saying goes, "When your loyal admonitions are not accepted, you should withdraw and refrain from argument." As a result, Wu Zixu argued with the king and was put to death; if he had not argued with the king, he would not have gained his good fame. Is there really something that can be regarded as good?

As to what the people practice and enjoy, I do not know whether their happiness is genuine or not. As to what the people enjoy—what they pursue and go all the way to strive after and universally claim to be happiness—I do not know whether their happiness is genuine or not. Is there really something that can be regarded as happiness? In my opinion, genuine happiness lies in the refrainment from action while people regard it as sorrow and grief. Therefore, as the saying goes, "Perfect happiness is derived from the absence of happiness; perfect fame is derived from the absence of fame."

In this world of ours, it is impossible to decide what is right and what is wrong. Nevertheless, refrainment from action can help to solve this puzzle. In refrainment of action we are closest to perfect happiness and enjoyment of life. I shall try to put it this way. The heaven is clear because it does nothing; the earth is quiet because it does nothing. As neither the heaven nor the earth does anything, everything in the world is born out of them. Opaque and obscure, they seem to come from nowhere. Obscure and opaque, they seem to have left no trace whatsoever. Everything in the

中国文学选读

world is born with nothing having done anything. Therefore, as the saying goes, "The heaven and the earth do nothing and there is nothing they cannot do." However, who among the men can refrain from taking action?

Zhuangzi's wife died. When Huizi went to express his condolence, he saw that Zhuangzi was squatting on the ground, singing and beating time on a basin.

Huizi said, "Your wife has lived such a long time with you. She has born and reared children for you. Now that she has grown old and died, you are pitiless enough if you do not even shed a tear. Haven't you gone too far when you sing and beat time on a basin?"

Zhuangzi said, "By no means. When my wife just died, how could I refrain from sorrow? But if we trace her beginning, she did not have life before she was born. Neither did she have life, nor had she physical form at all. Neither did she have physical form, nor had she had vital energy at all. Amid what was opaque and obscure, transformation took place and she obtained her vital energy. Another transformation took place with her vital energy and she obtained her physical form. Yet another transformation took place with her physical form and she obtained life. Now that one more transformation has taken place and she has returned to death, this is like the succession of spring, summer, autumn and winter. My deceased wife is now lying peacefully between the heaven and the earth. If I were to weep over her death, I think, this would mean that I am ignorant of fate. That is why I stopped weeping."

—From *Zhuangzi*

(translated by Wang Rongpei)

## 至　乐

天下有至乐无有哉？有可以活身者无有哉？今奚为奚据？奚避奚处？奚就奚去？奚乐奚恶？夫天下之所尊者，富贵寿善也；所乐者，身安厚味美服好色音声也；所下者，贫贱夭恶也；所苦者，身不得安逸，口不得厚味，形不得美服，目不得好色，耳不得音声。若不得者，则大忧以惧，其为形也亦愚哉！夫富者，苦身疾作，多积财而不得尽用，其为形也亦外矣！夫贵者，夜以继日，思虑善否，其为形也亦疏矣！人之生也，与忧俱生。寿者惛惛，久忧不死，何之苦也！其为形也亦远矣！烈士为天下见善矣，未足以活身。吾未知善之诚善邪？诚不善邪？

若以为善矣，不足活身；以为不善矣，足以活人。故曰："忠谏不听，蹲循勿争。"故夫子胥争之，以残其形；不争，名亦不成。诚有善无有哉？今俗之所为与其所乐，吾又未知乐之果乐邪？果不乐邪？吾观夫俗之所乐，举群趣者，誙誙然如将不得已，而皆曰乐者，吾未之乐也，亦未之不乐也。果有乐无有哉？吾以无为诚乐矣，又俗之所大苦也。故曰："至乐无乐，至誉无誉。"天下是非果未可定也。虽然，无为可以定是非。至乐活身，唯无为几存。请尝试言之：天无为以之清，地无为以之宁。故两无为相合，万物皆化生。芒乎芴乎，而无从出乎！芴乎芒乎，而无有象乎！万物职职，皆从无为殖。故曰："天地无为也而无不为也。"人也孰能得无为哉！

庄子妻死，惠子吊之，庄子则方箕踞鼓盆而歌。惠子曰："与人居，长子、老、身死，不哭亦足矣，又鼓盆而歌，不亦甚乎！"庄子曰："不然。是其始死也，我独何能无概！然察其始而本无生；非徒无生也，而本无形；非徒无形也，而本无气。杂乎芒芴之间，变而有气，气变而有形，形变而有生。今又变而之死。是相与为春秋冬夏四时行也。人且偃然寝于巨室，而我噭噭然随而哭之，自以为不通乎命，故止也。"

——选自《庄子》

## Topics for Discussion

1. As a present day reader, are you touched and moved by the love poems from *Shi Jing*? If so, explain how.

2. What are the "Liu Yi(六艺)"? Provide examples to explain the usage of "Bi" and "Xing" in *Shi Jing*.

3. What differences are there in artistic styles between *Shi Jing* and *Li Sao*?

4. Why did Zhuangzi "beat the basin and sing" when his wife passed away?

Chapter Two

# Historical Narratives

## General Description

In addition to verse there was prose. There were two types of prose during the Pre-Qin period: narratives and essays. The main narrative texts were historical narratives, while the essays mainly depicted the philosophical points of view of various scholars of the time.

The Pre-Qin was the period that marked the beginning of a narrative literature of Chinese history. It was a time when court culture developed in ancient China and a time when states started to document events in their realms and annual chronicles began to be written. There were many essays written, such as *Zuo Zhuan* (《左传》 *Chronicle of Zuo*), *Guo Yu* (《国语》 *Collections of Historical Records from Numerous States*), and *Zhan Guo Ce* (《战国策》 *Warring States Records*), which showed the maturation of the narrative form.

During the Pre-Qin period historical prose adopted the narrative method in order to distinctly portray historical events and at the same time vividly reflect them with literary images. For example, written prose merged mythology and legend with historical events. It also fictionalized figures from history with a special emphasis on imaginatively describing the characteristics of those figures. Historiographers used "Chun Qiu Bi Fa(春秋笔法 the power of the pen)" to assess events and then enrich the narrative.

The works of *Shi Ji* (《史记》 *Records of the Grand Historian*) and *Han Shu* (《汉书》 *Book of Han*) marked the historical narrative climax of the Han Dynasty.

This chapter presents selections from *Shi Ji* as well as additional materials from *Zhan Guo Ce*.

## Introduction to *Shi Ji*

Sima Qian(司马迁 145~87BC?) was the greatest historian and literary scholar in ancient China. He was born and raised in a family of court historians. He enjoyed reading as a child and cherished travel as an adult. Upon his father's death, he succeeded to the position of court astrologer and continued his father's unfinished work recording historical events. He began to write *Shi Ji*, but it was not long before he was sentenced to jail by the Emperor Wu of Han(汉武帝) based upon a false accusation. He suffered tremendous physical and mental torment in jail and after his release he endured further humiliation. But, he gathered his strength and, over the next ten years, completed *Shi Ji*. Lu Xun once praised it as being "the highest achievement in historical writing, like *Li Sao*, but in an unrhymed form".

Sima Qian was profoundly influenced by Chinese history and reviewed many ancient written historical records. He became the first historiographer in Chinese history to create a brand new historical writing style called "Ji Zhuan Ti(纪传体)". This style, with its written layout and format, later became a commonly recognized standard for official Chinese historiography during the dynasties. It assisted historians that

司马迁

中国文学选读

followed with assuming the role of an unbiased recorder of historical events, and to do so with truthfulness and integrity, while maintaining a high standard of historical documentation.

*Shi Ji* contains 520 000 words and is comprised of 130 volumes of text that can be classified into several categories. There are 12 volumes of Ben Ji(本纪 imperial biographies) following the rise and fall of dynasties and emperors, 10 volumes of Biao (表 tables) which are timelines of events between the individual Lords, 8 volumes of Shu(书 treatises)—special treatises on economics, culture, astronomy and the calendar, 30 volumes of Shi Jia(世家)—biographies of feudal houses and eminent persons, and 70 volumes of Lie Zhuan(列传)—collective biographies of important figures from different levels and ranks.

*Shi Ji* chronicled significant historical events over a time frame of 3 000 years, from the Yellow Emperor(黄帝) to the Emperor Wu of Western Han, and did so in a way that broke through the limitations of what history or prose could typically describe. It focuses on the important figures and draws them into the center of the outlines, skillfully combining history with literature. The author's narrative skill and ability to characterize remarkable figures are especially evident in his biographies of Ben Ji, Shi Jia and Lie Zhuan. Ultimately *Shi Ji* became a fundamental model for Chinese biography and literature and had an enormous impact on the development of the art of Chinese narratives and biographical historical records.

# Selections from *Shi Ji*

## 1. Banquet in Hongmen

Liu Bang's army was at Bashang. Before he got in touch with Xiang Yu, his left marshal Cao Wushang sent a messenger to Xiang Yu to say: "The Lord of Pei wants to be king inside the Pass, with the Qin prince Ziying as his prime minister. He will keep all the booty for himself." In a rage, Xiang Yu swore: "Tomorrow I shall feast my men, and then we shall smash Liu Bang's army."

At this time Xiang Yu had four hundred thousand men at Hongmen near Xinfeng, and Liu Bang had only one hundred thousand at Bashang.

Fan Zeng also told Xiang Yu: "When the Lord of Pei was in the east, he hankered after wealth and beautiful women; but since entering the Pass he has taken no loot nor women. This shows he has great ambitions. I told a man to examine his halo, and it takes the shape of many colored dragons and tigers—the halo of an emperor. You must lose no time in attacking him!"

Xiang Yu's uncle, Xiang Bo, the left minister of Chu, was a friend of Zhang Liang, marquis of Liu, who served with Liu Bang. Xiang Bo galloped to Liu Bang's army by night to see Zhang Liang secretly, and told him what had happened. He urged Zhang Liang to go away with him.

"Otherwise you will perish," he warned him.

But Zhang Liang replied, "The King of Han sent me here with the Lord of Pei. It would not be right to leave him in this emergency. I must tell him."

He went in and told Liu Bang.

"What shall I do?" asked Liu Bang in great alarm.

"Who advised you to take this course?" inquired Zhang Liang.

"A fool of a scholar advised me to hold the Pass and not let the others in, for then I should be able to rule all Qin. I took his advice."

"Do you think, my lord, that your troops can resist Xiang Yu?"

"Of course not," answered Liu Bang after a pause. "But what shall I do?"

"Let me tell Xiang Bo for you that you have no intention of opposing Xiang Yu."

"How did you come to know Xiang Bo?"

"While Qin was powerful we were friends, and I saved Xiang Bo's life once when he killed a man. So he came to warn me of this danger."

"Which of you is the elder?"

"He is."

"Please ask him in. I shall address him as my elder brother."

Zhang Liang called Xiang Bo, who went in to see Liu Bang. Liu Bang offered him a goblet of wine, and pledged his word to link their families by marriage.

"Since entering the Pass, I have not touched so much as a hair," he declared. "I have kept a census of the population and sealed up the treasuries until the commander's arrival. I sent officers to guard the Pass to prevent disturbances or banditry. Day and night 1 was waiting for the commander—how dare I rebel against him? Pray tell him that I could not be so ungrateful."

Xiang Bo agreed to speak for him.

"Tomorrow, you must go early to apologize to Lord Xiang Yu in person," he said.

"I will," agreed Liu Bang.

Xiang Bo went back by night to the army and told Xiang Yu all that Liu Bang had said.

"If the Lord of Pei had not conquered Qin, you would not have been able to enter," he pointed out. "It is wrong to attack a man who has done so well. You should treat him handsomely."

Xiang Yu agreed.

The next morning Liu Bang rode up with some hundred horsemen to see Xiang Yu. When he reached Hongmen, he made his apology.

"I attacked Qin as hard as I could in co-operation with you," he said. "You fought north of the river while I fought south, but I happened to be the first to enter the Pass and conquer the land of Qin, so here we meet again. Now some mean fellow has maligned me, and made you mistrust me."

"It was your left marshal Cao Wushang," replied Xiang Yu. "Otherwise I would never have thought such a thing. "

Xiang Yu kept Liu Bang to drink with him. Xiang Yu and Xiang Bo sat facing east, the patriarch Fan Zeng faced south, Liu Bang north, and Zhang Liang, who was in attendance, west. Fan Zeng shot Xiang Yu several glances, and raised his jade pendant three times as a signal, but Xiang Yu paid no attention. Then Fan Zeng got up and went out. He summoned Xiang Zhuang and said to him: "Our lord cannot make up his mind. Go in and offer a toast. After that you can do a sword dance, and strike the Lord of Pei on his seat and kill him. Otherwise you will all become his captives. "

So Xiang Zhuang went in to offer a toast, after which he said, "Our prince is drinking with the Lord of Pei, but we have no entertainers in the army. May I perform a sword dance?"

"Very well," said Xiang Yu.

When Xiang Zhuang unsheathed his sword and started dancing, Xiang Bo did the same. Moreover, he shielded Liu Bang with his body, so that Xiang Zhuang could not hit him.

Zhang Liang went outside the gate to see Fan Kuai, who asked: "How goes it?"

"Touch and go!" replied Zhang Liang. "Xiang Zhuang is doing a sword dance, trying to get at the Lord of Pei. "

"Things are desperate!" said Fan Kuai. "Let me go in and have it out with him. "

Fan Kuai went with sword and shield to the gate of the camp where guards with crossed halberds tried to bar the way. He charged at them and knocked them down with his tilted shield. Bursting in, he lifted the curtain and stood facing west, glaring at Xiang Yu. His hair was bristling, his eyes nearly starting from his head. Xiang Yu raised himself on one knee and reached for his sword.

"Who is this stranger?" he asked.

"This is the Lord of Pei's bodyguard, Fan Kuai," answered Zhang Liang.

"Stout fellow!" said Xiang Yu. "Give him a stoup of wine. "

They gave Fan Kuai a stoup of wine. He bowed his thanks and drank it standing.

"Give him a shoulder of pork," directed Xiang Yu.

They gave Fan Kuai a shoulder of pork. He set his shield upside down on the ground, placed the pork on it, carved it with his sword, and wolfed it down.

"Stout fellow!" cried Xiang Yu. "Can you drink any more?"

"I am not afraid of death, why should I refuse a drink?" retorted Fan Kuai. "The whole world is against the king of Qin, because like a tiger or wolf he has killed more men than you can count and tortured others cruelly. So King Huai promised his generals that the first to conquer the land of Qin and enter its capital should be king. Now the Lord of Pei has conquered Qin and entered Xianyang first. But he dared not touch a single hair. He sealed up the palaces, withdrew his troops to Bashang to wait for you, and sent men to guard the Pass against bandits and other emergencies. But though he has labored so hard and achieved so much, instead of rewarding him with noble rank you listen to some mean fellow and decide to kill this hero! Such behavior is worthy of defeated Qin, but hardly of Your Lordship."

Xiang Yu had no answer ready.

"Sit down," he said.

Fan Kuai sat next to Zhang Liang. Presently Liu Bang went out to the privy, taking Fan Kuai with him.

Xiang Yu ordered his lieutenant Chen Ping to call him back.

"I have come out without taking my leave," said Liu Bang. "What shall do?"

"Where big issues are at stake you cannot trouble about trifles," said Fan Kuai. "In matters of consequence you cannot observe the minor courtesies. They are the chopper and board, we the fish and meat. Why should we take our leave?"

So Liu Bang started off, telling Zhang Liang to stay behind to make his excuses.

"What did you bring with you, my lord?" asked Zhang Liang.

"Two jade pendants for Lord Xiang Yu, and two jade cups for the patriarch Fan Zeng. As they were angry, I did not dare present them. Please do so for me."

"Very good, my lord," said Zhang Liang.

Now Xiang Yu's army was at Hongmen, while Liu Bang's was at Bashang only forty *li* away. Leaving his chariot and horses, Liu Bang rode off alone. Fan Kuai, Xiahou Ying, Jin Qiang and Ji Xin followed on foot, carrying swords and shields.

They skirted Li Mountain and took a short cut to Zhiyang.

"From here to my army is only twenty *li*," said Liu Bang to Zhang Liang. "When you reckon that I am back, you can go in again."

By the time he should have reached his army, Zhang Liang went in to apologize for him.

"The Lord of Pei had too much to drink and was unable to take his leave," he said. "He humbly sends me to present two jade pendants to Your Lordship and two jade cups to the patriarch."

"Where is he now?" asked Xiang Yu.

"Knowing that Your Highness meant to find fault with him, he left alone. He must be in his camp by now."

Xiang Yu accepted the pendants and placed them on his couch. But the patriarch put the jade cups on the ground, and drew his sword to smash them.

"Bah!" he cried. "It is no use advising a young fool. The Lord of Pei will wrest your empire from you and take us all captive!"

As soon as Liu Bang reached his army, He had Cao Wushang executed.

—From *Imperial Biography of Xiang Yu*

(translated by Yang Xianyi and Gladys Yang)

## 鸿 门 宴

沛公军霸上，未得与项羽相见。沛公左司马曹无伤使人言于项羽曰："沛公欲王关中，使子婴为相，珍宝尽有之。"项羽大怒，曰："旦日飨士卒，为击破沛公军！"

当是时，项羽兵四十万，在新丰鸿门；沛公兵十万，在霸上。范增说项羽曰："沛公居山东时，贪于财货，好美姬。今入关，财物无所取，妇女无所幸，此其志不在小。吾令人望其气，皆为龙虎，成五采，此天子气也。急击勿失！"

楚左尹项伯者，项羽季父也，素善留侯张良。张良是时从沛公。项伯乃夜驰之沛公军，私见张良，具告以事，欲呼张良与俱去，曰："毋从俱死也。"张良曰："臣为韩王送沛公。沛公今事有急，亡去，不义。不可不语。"良乃入，具告沛公。沛公大惊，曰："为之奈何？"张良曰："谁为大王为此计者？"曰："鲰生说我曰，'距关毋内诸侯，秦地可尽王也。'故听之。"良曰："料大王士卒足以当项王乎？"沛公默然，曰："固不如也。且为之奈何？"张良曰："请往谓项伯，言沛公不敢背项王也。"沛公曰："君安与项伯有故？"张良曰："秦时与臣游，项伯杀人，臣活之。今事有急，故幸来告良。"沛公曰："孰与君少长？"良曰："长于臣。"沛公曰："君为我呼入，吾得兄事之。"张良出，要项伯。项伯即入见沛公。沛公奉卮酒为寿，约为婚姻，曰："吾入关，秋豪不敢有所近，籍吏民，封府库，而待将军。所以遣将守关者，备他盗之出入与非常也。日夜望将军至，岂敢反乎！愿伯具言臣之不敢倍德也。"项伯许诺，谓沛公曰："旦日不可不蚤自来谢项王！"沛公曰："诺。"于是项伯复夜去。至军中，具以沛公言报项王。因言曰："沛公不先破关中，公岂敢入乎？今人有大功而击之，不义也。不如因善遇之。"项王许诺。

沛公旦日从百余骑来见项王，至鸿门，谢曰："臣与将军戮力而攻秦，将军战河北，臣战河南，然不自意能先入关破秦，得复见将军于此。今者有小人之言，令将军与臣有郤。"项王曰："此沛公左司马曹无伤言之，不然，籍何以至此。"项王即日因留沛公与饮。项王、项伯东向坐；亚父南向坐，亚父者，范增也；沛公北向坐；张良西向侍。范增数目项王，举所佩玉玦以示之者三。项王默然不应。范增起，出召项庄，谓曰："君王为人不忍，若入前为寿，寿毕，请以剑舞，因击沛公于坐，杀之。不者，若属皆且为所虏！"庄则入为寿，寿毕，曰："君王与沛公饮，军中无以为乐，请以剑舞。"项王曰："诺。"项庄拔剑起舞，项伯亦拔剑起舞，常以身翼蔽沛公，庄不得击。

于是张良至军门，见樊哙，樊哙曰："今日之事何如？"良曰："甚急！今者项庄拔剑舞，其意常在沛公也。"哙曰："此迫矣！臣请入，与之同命！"哙即带剑拥盾入军门。交戟之卫士欲止不内，樊哙侧其盾以撞，卫士仆地。哙遂入。披帷西向立，瞋目视项王，头发上指，目眦尽裂。项王按剑而跽曰："客何为者？"张良曰："沛公之参乘樊哙者也。"项王曰："壮士！

鸿门宴

赐之卮酒！"则与斗卮酒。哙拜谢，起，立而饮之。项王曰："赐之彘肩！"则与一生彘肩。樊哙覆其盾于地，加彘肩上，拔剑切而啖之。项王曰："壮士！能复饮乎？"樊哙曰："臣死且不避，卮酒安足辞！夫秦王有虎狼之心，杀人如不能举，刑人如恐不胜，天下皆叛之。怀王与诸将约曰：'先破秦入咸阳者王之。今沛公先破秦入咸阳，毫毛不敢有所近，封闭宫室，还军霸上，以待大王来。故遣将守关者，备他盗出入与非常也。劳苦而功高如此，未有封侯之赏，而听细说，欲诛有功之人，此亡秦之续耳，窃为大王不取也。"项王未有以应，曰："坐！"樊哙从良坐。坐须臾，沛公起如厕，因招樊哙出。

沛公已出，项王使都尉陈平召沛公。沛公曰："今者出，未辞也，为之奈何？"樊哙曰："大行不顾细谨，大礼不辞小让。如今人方为刀俎，我为鱼肉，何辞为？"于是遂去。乃令张良留谢。良问曰："大王来何操？"曰："我持白璧一双，欲献项王；玉斗一双，欲与亚父。会其怒，不敢献。公为我献之。"张良曰："谨诺。"当是时，项王军在鸿门下，沛公军在霸上，相去四十里。沛公则置车骑，脱身独骑，与樊哙、夏侯婴、靳彊、纪信等四人持剑盾步走，从郦山下，道芷阳间行。沛公谓张良曰："从此道至吾军，不过二十里耳。度我至军中，公乃入。"沛公已去，间至军中，张良入，谢曰："沛公不胜桮杓，不能辞。谨使臣良奉白璧一双，再拜献大王足下；玉斗一双，再拜奉大将军足下。"项王曰："沛公安在？"良曰："闻大王有意督过之，脱身独去，已至军矣。"项王则受璧，置之坐上。亚父受玉斗，置之地，拔剑撞而破之，曰："唉！竖子不足与谋，夺项王天下者，必沛公也。吾属今为之虏矣！"

沛公至军，立诛杀曹无伤。

——选自《史记·项羽本纪》

## 2. Jing Ke

Jing Ke was a native of Wei, whose ancestors had migrated to that state from Qi. The people of Wei called him Master Qing; but when he went to Yan he was known as Master Jing. He loved reading and fencing, and advised the Prince of We on the art of government; but the prince did not take his advice. Later, when Qin attacked Wei and annexed some of its territory as its Eastern Province, the prince's family was banished to Yewang.

Jing Ke went to Yuci to discuss the art of fencing with Gai Nie; and when the latter lost his temper and frowned at him, Jing Ke walked straight out of his house. Someone suggested that he be recalled.

"No," said Gai Nie. "Just now, when he made a slip in our discussion of fencing, I showed my displeasure; so he must have left. He will not stay here now."

When he sent a messenger to his lodging, the man reported that Jing Ke had indeed called for his carriage and left Yuci.

"Naturally," said Gai Nie. "It is because I frowned reprovingly at him."

Later Jing Ke went to Handan, where he fell out with Lu Goujian while gambling; and when Lu shouted at him he left without a word, never to see Lu again.

In the State of Yan, Jing Ke made friends with a dog-meat vender and a zither player named Gao Jianli. Jing Ke was fond of wine, and he spent his days drinking with these men in the marketplace. When they had drunk their fill, Gao would play the zither while Jing Ke sang; and so they were merry; but sometimes they became sad and shed tears as if no one else were near.

Though Jing Ke spent much time with drinking companions, he was quiet, thoughtful and studious too, and made friends wherever he went with the gallants and elders. In the State of Yan, for instance, he gained the friendship of a retired scholar named Tian Guang, who realized that he was no ordinary person.

Just at this time Prince Dan of Yan escaped from Qin, where he had been a hostage, and returned to his own state. This prince had previously been a hostage in Zhao, and since the king of Qin was born in that state they had been playmates together; after the king of Qin ascended the throne, Prince Dan went as a hostage to Qin; but, indignant at the rude way in which the king treated him, he fled. He longed to take vengeance upon Qin; but his own state was small and he was powerless. Later the king of Qin launched repeated campaigns eastwards against Qi, Chu and the three states of Jin, annexing their territory and approaching nearer and nearer to Yan. The king of Yan and his ministers were anxious because of the impending danger, and Prince Dan, who was especially troubled, asked the advice of his tutor, Ju Wu.

"Qin has expanded its territory on all sides and is now threatening the states of

Han, Zhao and Wei," said Ju Wu. "To the north it has the strongholds of Ganquan and Gukou, and to the south the fertile valleys of the Jin and Wei rivers. It controls the wealth of Ba and Han, has the mountains of Long and Shu on its west, and those of Hangu and Xiao on its east. Its population is large, its men well trained, and it possesses more than enough weapons for its troops. If the king of Qin wished to extend his borders eastwards, he can take all the land south of the Great Wall and north of the Yi River; so why risk rubbing him the wrong way just because he once slighted you?"

"What then can I do?" asked the prince.

"We will think of a plan later," replied Ju Wu.

Some time after this, General Fan Wuji of Qin offended his sovereign and fled to Yan, where Prince Dan took him in. Ju Wu advised against this.

"The king of Qin is all-powerful," said the tutor. "If he decides to vent his wrath on Yan it will be a fearful thing—enough to chill all hearts—especially if he learns that General Fan is here. This is like setting meat before a hungry tiger: only disaster can come of it. And in such a case even the best counsel will be of no avail. I advise you to send the general with all speed into hiding in the land of the Huns, while you ally with the three states of Jin in the west, with Qi and Chu in the south, and with the Khan of the Huns in the north. Only so can you take vengeance."

"It would take a long time to carry out your plan," objected the prince, "and I am in too much misery to wait. Besides, General Fan threw himself on my mercy when he had no one to turn to, and I am certainly not going to let myself be intimidated by Qin into abandoning a friend with whom I sympathize, to hand him over to the Huns. I would rather die than do such a thing. Please think again."

"This is a dangerous way of winning safety," replied Ju Wu, "stirring up trouble for the sake of peace. You are devising a shortsighted policy and increasing tension, showing concern for one man's friendship but not for the security of the state. In fact, you are increasing your own difficulties and aggravating your enemy. When you drop a goose feather on burning charcoal, everyone knows what the result will be; and when Qin swoops down like a vulture in all its fury, you do not need me to tell you what will happen. There is an old gentleman in our state named Tian Guang, who has great wisdom and courage. You might consult him. "

"Will you introduce me to him?" asked the prince.

Ju Wu assented and went to see Tian Guang to tell him that Prince Dan wished to consult him on state policy; and Tian Guang agreed to call on the prince.

Prince Dan welcomed and led him in, then knelt to dust the seat for him; and as soon as Tian Guang was seated and they were alone, the prince rose to his feet.

"Our state and Qin cannot exist together," he said. "Please consider the situation. "

"When a good steed is in its prime it can gallop over three hundred miles in one day," said Tian Guang. "But when it grows old, the poorest nag can overtake it. You have heard of the ability I possessed in my prime; but now my strength is spent. However, though I am not competent to advise on state affairs, I know a man named Jing Ke who could be of service to you. "

"Will you introduce me to him?" asked the prince.

Tian Guang agreed, then stood up to leave, and Prince Dan saw him to the door.

"What I have just told you is of the greatest consequence to our state," the prince cautioned him. "I must beg you not to disclose it. "

Tian Guang lowered his head to smile as he gave his promise, then went to plead with Jing Ke.

"Everybody here knows that we are good friends," he said. "The prince had heard of my ability, but did not know that I am past my prime; so he favored me with an audience during which he said that our state and Qin cannot exist together, and asked me to consider the matter. I made so bold as to recommend you to him, and hope you will call at the palace. "

To this Jing Ke agreed.

"I have heard that a good man's actions should be above suspicion," continued Tian Guang. "But by warning me that what he told me was of the greatest consequence to the state and begging me not to disclose it, the prince showed that he doubts my integrity. To give rise to suspicion in this way does not befit an honorable man. "

Accordingly he decided to kill himself, to spur Jing Ke on.

"Please go quickly to the prince and tell him that I am dead," he urged him. "Then he can rest assured that I will not talk."

Thereupon he killed himself. When Jing Ke called on Prince Dan and told him how Tian Guang had died and what he had said before his death, the prince bowed and knelt down, shedding tears.

"I warned him simply to ensure that my plan would succeed," said the prince after a long silence. "I did not mean him to die to prove his integrity."

After Jing Ke had taken his seat, the prince stood up and bowed.

"In spite of my stupidity, sir," he said, "Tian Guang has asked you here so that I can consult you. This shows that Heaven has taken pity on our state and will not abandon us. Now the state of Qin is insatiable in its greed and will not rest satisfied until it has seized all the lands in the world and made all the princes its subjects. It has already captured the king of Han, annexed his kingdom, and sent troops south to attack Chu and north to threaten Zhao. General Wang Jian is leading several hundred thousand men against the cities of Zhang and Ye, while General Li Xin is advancing from Taiyuan and Yunzhong. When the State of Zhao can resist no longer but surrender, then it will be our turn. We are a small, weak state, exhausted by constant warfare, so that even if we strain every nerve we cannot hold Qin at bay; and the other states are too cowed to ally with us against our common enemy. This, then, is my plan: if we can find a man of immense courage to go as our envoy to Qin and tempt the king with great gain, that avaricious sovereign will certainly fall in with our wishes. If he can be kidnapped and forced to return all the territory he has annexed in the same way in which Cao Mo compelled Duke Huan of Qi, it will be ideal. If he does not agree, our envoy can stab him to death. Then with generals commanding armies outside their borders and trouble at home, the rulers of Qin will fall out with each other; and we can seize this opportunity to form an alliance of the eastern states which will certainly defeat them. This is the great desire of my heart, but I do not know to whom to entrust this task. I hope you will consider my plan."

Jing Ke was silent for a time.

"The fate of our kingdom depends upon this," he said at last. "But my ability is of the meanest. I fear I am not fit to be entrusted with such a mission."

中国文学选读

But when the prince came up to him and bowed, begging him not to refuse, Jing Ke accepted the task. Then Prince Dan made him a noble man and lodged him in a fine mansion. He called on Jing Ke every day and presented him with delicacies, precious objects, carriages and beautiful girls, to satisfy his every wish and give him pleasure. This state of affairs went on for a long time, and Jing Ke made no move to leave for Qin. Then General Wang Jian of Qin took the capital of Zhao, captured the king of Zhao, annexed the whole state, and advanced northwards to occupy all the territory to the southern boundary of Yan. Prince Dan was thoroughly alarmed.

"The army of Qin may cross the Yi River any day now," he said to Jing Ke. " Then I shall no longer be able to entertain you, much as I would like to. "

"I was thinking of going to see you about this matter, but now you have mentioned it first," replied Jing Ke. "Unless I take some proof of goodwill, the king of Qin will not trust me. He has offered a thousand pounds of gold and a fief of ten thousand families for the capture of General Fan; so if I can have General Fan's head and the map of Dukang the king will welcome me and I should be able to carry out your plan. "

"General Fan came to me to take refuge," said Prince Dan. "I can not sacrifice him for my own ends. Please consider the matter again. "

Knowing that the prince was too soft-hearted to take his advice, Jing Ke went privately to Fan Wuji.

"The king of Qin considers you his deadly enemy," he said. "Your parents and kinsmen have been put to the sword, and now I hear a reward of a thousand pounds of gold and a fief of ten thousand families has been offered for your head. What do you mean to do?"

General Fan gazed up at the sky and sighed, then shed tears.

"The thought of this makes me burn with hatred to the very marrow of my bones," he said. "But I cannot think of any way to take vengeance. "

"I have a plan to avert danger from Yan and to avenge you," said Jing Ke. "Would you care to hear it?"

General Fan stepped forward.

"Tell me what it is," he begged.

"If I could have your head to present to the king of Qin, he would receive me with pleasure; then with my left hand I should seize his sleeve, and with my right hand stab him through the heart. You would be avenged and our prince would pay off an old score. Are you willing to help me?"

General Fan bared one arm and advanced clasping his wrists.

"This is the chance for which I have been waiting day and night, gnashing my teeth and burning with rage!" he cried. "Now you have pointed out the way."

Thereupon he killed himself.

When the prince knew of this, he hurried there to lament bitterly over the corpse; then, since there was nothing he could do, he had Fan's head placed in a sealed casket. He had been searching for a fine dagger and found one made by Xu Furen of Zhao, which cost a hundred pieces of gold. Now he made his artisans steep this dagger in poison and upon testing it found that if it drew the least drop of blood—enough to stain a thread—the result was instant death. Then Prince Dan helped Jing Ke to prepare for his journey. In the State of Yan there was a young gallant of thirteen named Qin Wuyang, who was so fierce that he killed people at will and no one dared meet his angry glance. He was chosen to assist Jing Ke.

But Jing Ke was waiting for another assistant of his own choice, who lived far away; and while making arrangements for this man to come he delayed his departure. Then Prince Dan grew impatient, suspecting that Jing Ke had gone back on his promise.

"The time is going by," he said. "Do you intend to start soon, or shall I send Qin Wuyang on ahead?"

"Why do you want to send a boy to die?" shouted Jing Ke angrily. "I am going to the powerful state of Qin armed only with one dagger. The venture is fraught with danger, and that is why I was waiting for a friend to accompany me. But since you are so impatient, I will leave now."

Thus he set out, while the prince and those who knew of the plan wore white clothes to escort him to the Yi River. After they had sacrificed to pray for success in this journey, Gao Jianii played the zither and Jing Ke sang a tragic air, at which all present wept. Then he stepped forward and chanted:

*The wind is wailing over the cold Yi River;*

*And a hero sets forth, never to return.*

After this he sang a martial air, which moved all who heard it to such anger that their eyes nearly started from their heads and their hair stood on end. Then Jing Ke mounted his carriage and drove off, without a glance behind.

Upon reaching the state of Qin, Jing Ke bribed the king's favorite minister, Lord Meng Jia, with money and gifts worth a thousand pieces of gold; and Lord Meng Jia mentioned his mission to the king.

"The king of Yan is awed by Your Majesty's might and has not the courage to oppose your troops," he said. "He begs to become your subject like the other princes and send tribute like your provinces, in order to continue his ancestral sacrifices. He dared not come in person to announce this; but he has cut off Fan Wuji's head to present to you in a sealed casket with the map of Dukang district. The envoy who brought these here is awaiting Your Majesty's orders."

The king of Qin was pleased, and displayed all his royal pomp at Xianyang Palace to receive the envoy from Yan.

Jing Ke entered first with the sealed casket containing Fan's head, followed by Qin Wuyang with a case containing the map. When they reached the steps to the dais, the ministers were surprised to see Qin Wuyang change color and tremble; but Jing Ke laughed as he stepped forward to apologize.

"This is an uncouth rustic from the barbarous north," he said. "He is overawed by his first sight of Your Majesty. Please excuse him, so that we can carry out our mission."

The king bade Jing Ke hand him the map which Qin Wuyang was holding; and when he unrolled it to the very end, the dagger appeared. Then Jing Ke seized the king's sleeve with his left hand, while snatching up the dagger to stab at the king with his right. Before he could strike him, however, the king leapt up in alarm, so that his sleeve was torn off; but when the king tried to draw his long sword it stuck fast in its scabbard, and in his terror he could not unsheathe it. He fled behind a pillar, with Jing Ke in hot pursuit; and the ministers, taken completely by surprise, were thrown into confusion. According to the law of Qin, no ministers could bear arms at court; and the royal guards in the courtyard could not enter without orders from their sovereign; but the king was too hard pressed to call for them. So while Jing Ke pursued the king, the panic-stricken ministers could only try to ward him off with their bare hands; and the king's physician, Xia Wuju, used his medical bag to beat the assassin. Terrified out of his wits, the king was fleeing round the pillar when some attendants called out:

"Pull the sword from your back, Your Majesty!"

As soon as the king did so, he was able to draw his sword and strike Jing Ke with it, slashing his left thigh. Since Jing Ke was disabled he hurled his dagger at the king, but missed him and hit the bronze pillar instead. The king struck out again and again until Jing Ke was wounded in eight places. Knowing that all was up with him, Jing Ke, squatting against the pillar, smiled scornfully and swore at the king:

"I failed because I was trying to capture you alive," he cried. "I would have forced you to agree to our prince's demands."

At that the attendants ran forward and killed him. The king brooded in silence for some time, then rewarded some ministers for their aid and punished others, giving his physician, Xia Wuju, two hundred pieces of gold.

"He is loyal to me," said the king, "for he beat off Jing Ke with his bag."

—From *Collective Biography of Assassins*

(translated by Yang Xianyi and Gladys Yang)

## 荆轲刺秦王

荆轲者，卫人也。其先乃齐人，徙于卫，卫人谓之庆卿。而之燕，燕人谓之荆卿。

荆卿好读书击剑，以术说卫元君，卫元君不用。其后秦伐魏，置东郡，徙卫元君之支属于野王。

荆轲尝游过榆次，与盖聂论剑，盖聂怒而目之。荆轲出，人或言复召荆卿。盖聂曰："曩者吾与论剑有不称者，吾目之；试往，是宜去，不敢留。"使使往之主人，荆卿则已驾而去榆次矣。使者还报，盖聂曰："固去也，吾曩者目摄之！"

中国文学选读

荆轲游于邯郸，鲁句践与荆轲博，争道，鲁句践怒而叱之，荆轲嘿而逃去，遂不复会。

荆轲既至燕，爱燕之狗屠及善击筑者高渐离。荆轲嗜酒，日与狗屠及高渐离饮于燕市，酒酣以往，高渐离击筑，荆轲和而歌于市中，相乐也，已而相泣，旁若无人者。荆轲虽游于酒人乎，然其为人沉深好书；其所游诸侯，尽与其贤豪长者相结。其之燕，燕之处士田光先生亦善待之，知其非庸人也。

居顷之，会燕太子丹质秦亡归燕。燕太子丹者，故尝质于赵，而秦王政生于赵，其少时与丹欢。及政立为秦王，而丹质于秦。秦王之遇燕太子丹不善，故丹怨而亡归。归而求为报秦王者，国小，力不能。其后秦日出兵山东以伐齐、楚、三晋，稍蚕食诸侯，且至于燕，燕君臣皆恐祸之至。太子丹患之，问其傅鞠武。武对曰："秦地遍天下，威胁韩、魏、赵氏，北有甘泉、谷口之固，南有泾、渭之沃，擅巴、汉之饶，右陇、蜀之山，左关、殽之险，民众而士厉，兵革有余。意有所出，则长城之南，易水以北，未有所定也。奈何以见陵之怨，欲批其逆鳞哉！"丹曰："然则何由？"对曰："请入图之。"

居有间，秦将樊于期得罪于秦王，亡之燕，太子受而舍之。鞠武谏曰："不可。夫以秦王之暴而积怒于燕，足为寒心，又况闻樊将军之所在乎？是谓'委肉当饿虎之蹊'也，祸必不振矣！虽有管、晏，不能为之谋也。愿太子疾遣樊将军入匈奴以灭口。请西约三晋，南连齐、楚，北购于单于，其后乃可图也。"太子曰："太傅之计，旷日弥久，心惛然，恐不能须臾。且非独于此也，夫樊将军穷困于天下，归身于丹，丹终不以迫于强秦而弃所哀怜之交，置之匈奴，是固丹命卒之时也。愿太傅更虑之。"

荆轲刺秦王

鞠武曰："夫行危欲求安，造祸而求福，计浅而怨深，连结一人之后交，不顾国家之大害，此所谓'资怨而助祸'矣。夫以鸿毛燎于炉炭之上，必无事矣。且以雕鸷之秦，行怨暴之怒，岂足道哉！燕有田光先生，其为人智深而勇沉，可与谋。"太子曰："愿因太傅而得交于田先生，可乎？"鞠武曰："敬诺。"

出见田先生，道"太子愿图国事于先生也"。田光曰："敬奉教。"乃造焉。太子逢迎，却行为导，跪而蔽席。田光坐定，左右无人，太子避席而请曰："燕秦不两立，愿先生留意也。"田光曰："臣闻骐骥盛壮之时，一日而驰千里；至其衰老，驽马先之。今太子闻光盛壮之时，不知臣精已消亡矣。虽然，光不敢以图国事，所善荆卿可使也。"太子曰："愿因先生得结交于荆卿，可乎？"田光曰："敬诺。"即起，趋出。太子送至门，戒曰："丹所报，先生所言者，国之大事也，愿先生勿泄也！"田光俯而笑曰："诺。"

偻行见荆卿，曰："光与子相善，燕国莫不知。今太子闻光壮盛之时，不知吾形已不逮也，幸而教之曰'燕秦不两立，愿先生留意也。'光窃不自外，言足下于太子也，愿足下过太子于宫。"荆轲曰："谨奉教。"田光曰："吾闻之，长者为行，不使人疑之。今太子告光曰：'所言者，国之大事也，愿先生勿泄'，是太子疑光也。夫为行而使人疑之，非节侠也。"欲自杀以激荆卿，曰："愿足下急过太子，言光已死，明不言也。"因遂自刭而死。

荆轲遂见太子，言田光已死，致光之言。太子再拜而跪，膝行流涕，有顷而后言曰："丹所以诫田先生毋言者，欲以成大事之谋也。今田先生以死明不言，岂丹之心哉！"荆轲坐定，太子避席顿首曰："田先生不知丹之不肖，使得至前，敢有所道，此天之所以哀燕而不弃其孤也。今秦有贪利之心，而欲不可足也。非尽天下之地，臣海内之王者，其意不厌。今秦已虏韩王，尽纳其地。又举兵南伐楚，北临赵；王翦将数十万之众距漳、邺，而李信出太原、云中。赵不能支秦，必入臣，入臣则祸至燕。燕小弱，数困于兵，今计举国不足以当秦。诸侯服秦，莫敢合从。丹之私计，愚以为诚得天下之勇士使于秦，窥以重利；秦王贪，其势必得所愿矣。诚得劫秦王，使悉反诸侯侵地，若曹沫之与齐桓公，则大善矣；则不可，因而刺杀之。彼秦大将擅兵于外，而内有乱，则君臣相疑，以其间诸侯得合从，其破秦必矣。此丹之上愿，而不知所委命，唯荆卿留意焉。"久之，荆轲曰："此国之大事也，臣驽下，恐不足任使。"太子前顿首，固请毋让，然后许诺。于是尊荆卿为上卿，舍上舍。太子日造门下，供太牢，具异物，间进车骑美女，恣荆轲所欲，以顺适其意。

久之，荆轲未有行意。秦将王翦破赵，虏赵王，尽收入其地，进兵北略地，至燕南界。太子丹恐惧，乃请荆轲曰："秦兵旦暮渡易水，则虽欲长侍足下，岂可得哉！"荆轲曰："微太子言，臣愿谒之。今行而毋信，则秦未可亲也。夫樊将军，秦王购之金千斤，邑万家。诚得樊将军首与燕督亢之地图，奉献秦王，秦王必说见臣，臣乃得有以报。"太子曰："樊将军穷困来归丹，丹不忍以己之私而伤长者之意，愿足下更虑之！"

荆轲知太子不忍，乃遂私见樊于期曰："秦之遇将军可谓深矣，父母宗族皆为戮没。今闻购将军首金千斤，邑万家，将奈何？"于期仰天太息流涕曰："于期每念之，常痛于骨髓，顾计不知所出耳！"荆轲曰："今有一言可以解燕国之患，报将军之仇者，何如？"于期乃前曰："为之奈何？"荆轲曰："愿得将军之首以献秦王，秦王必喜而见臣，臣左手把其袖，右手揕其胸，然则将军之仇报，而燕见陵之愧除矣。将军岂有意乎？"樊于期偏袒扼捥而进曰："此臣之日夜切齿腐心也，乃今得闻教！"遂自刭。

太子闻之，驰往，伏尸而哭，极哀。既已不可奈何，乃遂盛樊于期首函封之。于是太子豫求天下之利匕首，得赵人徐夫人匕首，取之百金，使工以药淬之，以试人，血濡缕，人无不立死者。乃装为遣荆卿。燕国有勇士秦舞阳，年十三，杀人，人不敢忤视。乃令秦舞阳为副。荆轲有所待，欲与俱；其人居远未来，而为治行。顷之，未发，太子迟之，疑其改悔，乃复请曰："日已尽矣，荆卿岂有意哉？丹请得先遣秦舞阳。"荆轲怒，叱太子曰："何太子之遣，往而不反者，竖子也！且提一匕首入不测之强秦，仆所以留者，待吾客与俱。今太子迟之，请辞决矣！"遂发。

太子及宾客知其事者，皆白衣冠以送之。至易水之上，既祖，取道，高渐离击筑，荆轲和而歌，为变徵之声，士皆垂泪涕泣。又前而歌曰："风萧萧兮易水寒，壮士一去兮不复还！"复为羽声慷慨，士皆瞋目，发尽上指冠。于是荆轲就车而去，终已不顾。

遂至秦，持千金之资币物，厚遗秦王宠臣中庶子蒙嘉。嘉为先言于秦王曰："燕王诚振怖大王之威，不敢举兵以逆军吏，愿举国为内臣，比诸侯之列，给贡职如郡县，而得奉守先王之宗庙。恐惧不敢自陈，谨斩樊于期之头，及献燕督亢之地图，函封，燕王拜送于庭，使使以闻大王，唯大王命之。"秦王闻之，大喜，乃朝服，设九宾，见燕使者咸阳宫。荆轲奉樊于期头函，而秦舞阳奉地图匣，以次进。至陛，秦舞阳色变振恐，群臣怪之。荆轲顾笑舞阳，前谢曰："北蕃蛮夷之鄙人，未尝见天子，故振慑。愿大王少假借之，使得毕使于前。"秦王谓轲曰："取舞阳所持地图。"轲既取图奏之，秦王发图，图穷而匕首见。因左手把秦王之袖，而右手持匕首揕之。未至身，秦王惊，自引而起，袖绝。拔剑，剑长，操其室。时惶急，剑坚，故不可立拔。荆轲逐秦王，秦王环柱而走。群臣皆愕，卒起不意，尽失其度。而秦法，群臣侍殿上者不得持尺寸之兵；诸郎中执兵皆陈殿下，非有诏召不得上。方急时，不及召下兵，以故荆轲乃逐秦王。而卒惶急，无以击轲，而以手共搏之。是时，侍医夏无且以其所奉药囊提荆轲也。

秦王方环柱走，卒惶急，不知所为，左右乃曰："王负剑！"负剑，遂拔以击荆轲，断其左股。荆轲废，乃引其匕首以擿秦王，不中，中铜柱。秦王复击轲，轲被八创。轲自知事不就，倚柱而笑，箕踞以骂曰："事所以不成者，以欲生劫之，必得约契以报太子也。"于是左右既前杀轲，秦王不怡者良久。已而论功，赏群臣及当坐者各有差，而赐夏无且黄金二百溢，曰："无且爱我，乃以药囊提荆轲也。"

——选自《史记·刺客列传》

中国文学选读

## Further Readings

### Feng Xuan as Retainer of Prince Mengchang

Feng Xuan, a native of Qi, being unable to support himself for his poverty, requested to be introduced to Prince Mengchang, trying to sponge a living from him. The Prince asked him, "What is your liking?" He answered, "I have none." To his question "What is your ability?" the answer was the same. The Prince smiled and condescended to accept him.

The retainers, seeing that the Prince made little of him, gave him only coarse food. After some time he leaned against a pillar, and plucking his sword, sang out his complaint: "My long sword, let's go home! I eat no fish." The men told this to the Prince, who said in reply, "Give him fish and treat him like other retainers." Before long he plucked his sword and sang again: "My long sword, let's go home! I have no chariot for travels." The others all laughed at him and told the Prince, who again said in reply, "Give him a chariot and treat him like other charioted retainers." Then he rode in his carriage, raising his sword, to visit his friends. He said, "Prince Mengchang treats me like a guest." But who could have thought that some time later he once more plucked his sword and sang: "My long sword, let's go back, for I can't support my family." The others all held him in detestation, thinking that he was avaricious and insatiable. The Prince however asked him, "Has Your Honour some dear ones?" He answered, "I have but an old mother." So the Prince had her provided for, making her want nothing. Thus Feng Yuan ceased to sing and complain.

Later Prince Mengchang issued a notice to his retainers, inquiring, "Who is well versed in accountancy and can collect debts for me from my fief in Xue?" Feng Yuan subscribed to the notice with "I can." The Prince was surprised and asked who he was. The retainers answered, "He was the man who sang, 'My long sword, let's go back!'" The Prince said smilingly, "The man must be truly capable, but I ignored him and did not give him an interview." Then Feng was conducted into his presence and he apologized, "I was taxed with my business and confused by my worries. Being timid and stupid by nature and preoccupied with State affairs, I have incurred your displeasure. Do you, not feeling mortified, really intend to collect debts for me from my fief in Xue?" Feng rejoined, "Yes indeed." Then a carriage for his convenience and an equipage carrying IOUs were ready to set out for Xue. Before departure, Feng took leave of the Prince and asked, "After I have collected the debts, what shall I buy in the market before I return?" The Prince said, "Just buy what my household lacks."

When Feng had arrived in Xue, he had the officials summon the debtors in order to check up on their IOUs. This done, Feng rose, and under the pretence of the Prince's orders, granted the repaid money to the debtors and had the IOUs burnt up. So the people shouted in a voice: "Long live the Prince!"

Feng drove all the way back to Qi and sought an interview with the Prince in the early morning. The Prince was bewildered by his quick return, and having dressed up, came out to see him, asking, "Have you collected all the debts? How soon you have returned!" Feng answered, "I collected all the debts." The Prince queried, "What did you buy in the market for my household?" Feng said, "You bade me to buy what your household lacked. I thought to myself that Your Highness had jewellery stocked in your palace, dogs and horses kept in the stalls and beautiful women wait upon you in the harem. So what your household really wanted was none other than righteousness. And I presumed to buy you righteousness." The Prince asked, "How did you buy me righteousness?" Feng answered, "Though you have the small territory of Xue as your fief, you do not love the people as your children, seeking to gain profits from them. So I made bold to tamper with your orders, and after bestowing on them the repaid money, had the IOUs burnt up. So the people acclaimed you with 'Long live the Prince!' And that was how I bought you righteousness." Much displeased, the Prince said, "Well then, let it be."

One year later the King of Qi said to Prince Mengchang, "We dare not use the premier of the late King as our own premier." The Prince took the hint and was obliged to return to his fief in Xue. When he was still a hundred *li* from the land, his vassals came all the way to greet him, leading by the hand their children and supporting their doddering aged people. The Prince looked at Feng and remarked, "I have witnessed today the result of your buying righteousness for me." Feng however gave him this advice: "A cunning hare has three holes to avert possible death. Your Highness has now one hole, which is not yet enough to ensure you absolute security. Please allow me to make you two more."

The Prince gave Feng an equipage of fifty carriages and five hundred *jin* of gold to make a westward canvassing tour to the State of Liang. The latter said to King Hui, "The King of Qi will allow his premier Prince Mengchang to position himself in any of the principalities. The one which will be the first to extend him welcome is bound to become rich and powerful. So the King of Liang vacated the premiership and made the former premier a marshal while despatching an envoy, bringing a thousand *jin* of gold and an equipage of one hundred carriages to invite Prince Mengchang. Feng drove back and gave the Prince to understand that "A thousand *jin* of gold is an enormous gift, and an equipage of one hundred carriages is a distinction fit for an eminent envoy. Now the King of Qi must have heard of this." The envoy of Liang made expressly three trips to see Mengchang, but his invitation was deliberately declined by the Prince.

When this came to the knowledge of the King of Qi, both the Sovereign and the courtiers were afraid and the imperial secretary was sent, bringing a thousand jin of gold and two painted carriages as well as a sword and a sealed letter, to visit the Prince, apologizing, "We were unlucky to have offended our ancestors who had ill fortune descend upon us. As a result we were surrounded by sycophants and incurred the displeasure of Your Highness. Although we are unworthy of your help, we wish that you would think of our ancestral temple, and return to hold sway over those thousands of people."

Feng again advised the Prince, "Would Your Highness demand the ritual vessels of the late kings and set up an ancestral temple in Xue." After the temple had been completed, Feng returned to report to the Prince, "Now that the three holes have been made, Your Highness can live in the happiness of absolute security."

Prince Mengchang was Prime Minister for dozens of years, without suffering the slightest trouble. All this was due to Feng Xuan's wise stratagems.

—From *Zhan Guo Ce* (*Warring States Records*)

(translated by Xie Baikui)

# 冯谖客孟尝君

齐人有冯谖者，贫乏不能自存，使人属孟尝君，愿寄食门下。孟尝君曰："客何好？"曰："客无好也。"曰："客何能？"曰："客无能也。"孟尝君笑而受之曰："诺。"

左右以君贱之也，食以草具。居有顷，倚柱弹其剑，歌曰："长铗归来乎！食无鱼。"左右以告。孟尝君曰："食之，比门下之客。"居有顷，复弹其铗，歌曰："长铗归来乎！出无车。"左右皆笑之，以告。孟尝君曰："为之驾，比门下之车客。"于是乘其车，揭其剑，过其友曰："孟尝君客我。"后有顷，复弹其剑铗，歌曰："长铗归来乎！无以为家。"左右皆恶之，以为贪而不知足。孟尝君问："冯公有亲乎？"对曰，"有老母。"孟尝君使人给其食用，无使乏。于是冯谖不复歌。

后孟尝君出记，问门下诸客："谁习计会，能为文收责于薛者乎？"冯谖署曰："能。"孟尝君怪之，曰："此谁也？"左右曰："乃歌夫'长铗归来'者也。"孟尝君笑曰："客果有能也，吾负之，未尝见也。"请而见之，谢曰："文倦于事，愦于忧，而性懧愚，沉于国家之事，开罪于先生。先生不羞，乃有意欲为收责于薛乎？"冯谖曰："愿之。"于是约车治装，载券契而行，辞曰："责毕收，以何市而反？"孟尝君曰："视吾家所寡有者。"

驱而之薛，使吏召诸民当偿者，悉来合券。券遍合，起矫命以责赐诸民，因烧其券，民称万岁。

长驱到齐，晨而求见。孟尝君怪其疾也，衣冠而见之，曰："责毕收乎？来何疾也！"曰："收毕矣。""以何市而反？"冯谖曰；"君云'视吾家所寡有者'。臣窃计，君宫中积珍宝，狗马实外厩，美人充下陈。君家所寡有者，以义耳！窃以为君市义。"孟尝君曰："市义奈何？"曰："今君有区区之薛，不拊爱子其民，因而贾利之。臣窃矫君命，以责赐诸民，因烧其券，民称万岁。乃臣所以为君市义也。"孟尝君不悦，曰："诺，先生休矣！"

后期年，齐王谓孟尝君曰："寡人不敢以先王之臣为臣。"孟尝君就国于薛，未至百里，民扶老携幼，迎君道中。孟尝君顾谓冯谖："先生所为文市义者，乃今日见之。"

冯谖曰："狡兔有三窟，仅得免其死耳；今君有一窟，未得高枕而卧也。请为君复凿二窟。"孟尝君予车五十乘，金五百斤，西游于梁，谓惠王曰："齐放其大臣孟尝君于诸侯，诸侯先迎之者，富而兵强。"于是梁王虚上位，以故相为上将军，遣使者黄金千斤，车百乘，往聘孟尝君。冯谖先驱，诚孟尝君曰："千金，重币也；百乘，显使也。齐其闻之矣。"梁使三反，孟尝君固辞不往也。

齐王闻之，君臣恐惧，遣太傅赍黄金千斤、文车二驷，服剑一，封书，谢孟尝君曰："寡人不祥，被于宗庙之祟，沉于谄谀之臣，开罪于君。寡人不足为也；愿君顾先王之宗庙，姑反国统万人乎！"冯谖诚孟尝君曰："愿请先王之祭器，立宗庙于薛。"庙成，还报孟尝君曰："三窟已就，君姑高枕为乐矣。"

孟尝君为相数十年，无纤介之祸者，冯谖之计也。

——选自《战国策》


## Topics for Discussion

1. *Shi Ji* gives a depiction of history. In what ways does it also represent a literary achievement?

2. Was Xiang Yu a hero? What character traits did he possess?

3. Why did Jing Ke attempt to assassinate the King of Qin?

4. Compare Xiang Yu, Jing Ke and Feng Xuan. What are some of the differences between them?

Chapter Three

# Literature in the Wei and Jin Period

## General Description

It was during the social unrest of the Wei and Jin period(魏晋 220~420) that Xuan Xue(玄学 metaphysics or neo-taoism) came to the fore. Previous Confucian influences were blended with the philosophies of Laozi and Zhuangzi to develop a broad form of thought that advocated a close relationship with nature. A basic characteristic of Xuan Xue was that, as an abstract form of thought, it did not pay attention to practical problems and hence it was inevitably criticized as "idle talk(清谈)". Xuan Xue emphasized individual freedom and encouraged an appreciation of nature's beauty, and by so doing contributed to the rise of landscape and pastoral poetry(山水田园诗). At this time the introduction of Buddhism also had a profound impact on Chinese philosophy and literature. With this new input into Chinese literature, the society began to transform into, and cultivate, an era of "self-awareness".

The poems of Tao Yuanming are an outstanding representation of the literature of the period.

This chapter highlights Tao Yuanming's masterpieces. The supplementary pieces are selected from songs in the Southern and Northern Dynasties.

# Introduction to the Works of Tao Yuanming

陶渊明

Tao Yuanming(陶渊明 365～427) was born into the home of government officials. He lived a simple and contented life, enjoying a love of nature. He voluntarily retired from his official job when he was just middle-aged and retreated to the countryside to work as a farmer. During this time his writings and thoughts were related to Xuan Xue and were intimately engaged with his daily life. He used the country theme as the material with which to write many pastoral poems. In fact, he is renowned as being the first poet to write about this subject matter from this perspective. The secluded countryside experience helped him capture his ideals in his work, enhancing his artistic creations and sharpening his writing skills.

There is no doubt that Tao Yuanming was a highly talented writer whose influence and impact have been felt by generations since. His profound five-character-line poems effortlessly present the simplicity of countryside charms.

# Selected Works from Tao Yuanming

## 1. Return to Nature( Ⅰ )

While young, I was not used to worldly cares,

And hills became my natural compeers,

But by mistake I fell in mundane snares

And thus entangled was for thirteen years.


A caged bird would long for wonted wood,

And fish in tanks for native pools would yearn.

Go back to till my southern fields 1 would.

To live a rustic life why not return?


My plot of ground is but ten acres square;

My thatched cottage has eight or nine rooms.

In front I have peach trees here and plums there;

O'er back eaves willow trees and elms cast glooms.


A village can be seen in distant dark,

Where plumes of smoke rise and waft in the breeze.

In alley deep a dog is heard to bark,

And cock crows as if o'er mulberry trees.


Into my courtyard no one should intrude,

Nor rob my private rooms of peace and leisure.

After long years of abject servitude,

Again in nature I find homely pleasure.

(translated by Xu Yuanchong)

# 归田园居(一)

少无适俗韵，性本爱丘山。

误落尘网中，一去三十年。

羁鸟恋旧林，池鱼思故渊。

开荒南野际，守拙归园田。

方宅十余亩，草屋八九间。

榆柳荫后檐，桃李罗堂前。

暧暧远人村，依依墟里烟。

狗吠深巷中，鸡鸣桑树巅。

户庭无尘杂，虚室有余闲。

久在樊笼里，复得返自然。

## 2. Return to Nature(Ⅲ)

I sow my beans'neath southern hill;

Bean shoots are lost where weeds o'ergrow.

I weed at dawn through early still;

I plod home with my moonlit hoe.

The path is narrow, grasses tall;

With evening dew my clothes wet.

To which I pay no heed at all;

If my desire can but be met.

(translated by Xu Yuanchong)

# 归田园居(三)

种豆南山下，草盛豆苗稀。

晨兴理荒秽，带月荷锄归。

道狭草木长，夕露沾我衣。

衣沾不足惜，但使愿无违。

### 3. Drinking Wine

In people's haunt I build my cot;

Of wheel's and hoof's noise I hear not.

How can it leave on me no trace?

Secluded heart makes secluded place.

I pick fence-side asters at will

Carefree I see the southern hill.

The mountain air's fresh day and night;

Together birds go home in flight

What revelation at this view?

Words fail if I try to tell you.

(translated by Xu Yuanchong)

## 饮　酒

结庐在人境，而无车马喧。

问君何能尔？心远地自偏。

采菊东篱下，悠然见南山；

山气日夕佳，飞鸟相与还。

此中有真意，欲辨已忘言。

### 4. Reading *Book of Hills and Seas*

In early summer, grass and trees grow tall,

With profuse foliage sheltering the hall.

The flocks of birds have fondest place to rest

While I love my cozy house the best.

When I have ploughed the field and sown the seed,

I, now and then, find time to write and read.

There are no deep ruts in the humble lane,

Where carriages will turn away with disdain.

Alone I taste the new spring wine in leisure

And pluck my garden vegetables with pleasure.

When gentle showers from the east draw near,

Now a pleasant breeze approaches here.

On such occasions, I leaf through *King of Zhou*,

And *Book of Hills and Seas* of long ago.

Since I can tour the whole world at a glance,

What can be better pastime than this chance?

(translated by Wang Rongpei)

## 读《山海经》

孟夏草木长，绕屋树扶疏。

众鸟欣有托，吾亦爱吾庐。

既耕亦已种，时还读我书。

穷巷隔深辙，颇回故人车。

欢然酌春酒，摘我园中蔬。

微雨从东来，好风与之俱。

泛览周王传，流观山海图。

俯仰终宇宙，不乐复何如？

## 5. The Peach Blossom Springs

In the reign of Taiyuan of the Jin Dynasty, there was a man of Wuling who was a fisherman by trade. One day he was fishing up a stream in his boat, heedless of how far he had gone, when suddenly he came upon a forest of peach trees. On either bank for several hundred yards there were no other kinds of trees. The fragrant grass was beautiful to look at, all patterned with fallen blossoms. The fisherman was extremely surprised and went on further, determined to get to the end of this wood.

He found at the end of the wood the source of the stream and the foot of a cliff where there was a small cave in which there seemed to be a faint light. He left his boat and went in through the mouth of the cave. At first it was very narrow, only wide enough for a man, but after forty or fifty yards he suddenly found himself in the open.

The place he had come to was level and spacious. There were houses and cottages arranged in a planned order; there were fine fields and beautiful pools; there were mulberry trees, bamboo groves, and many other kinds of trees as well; there were raised pathways round the fields; and he heard the fowls crowing and dogs barking. Going to and fro in all this, and busied in working and planting, were people, both men and women. Their dress was not unlike that of people outside, and all of them, whether old people with white hair or children with their hair tied in a knot, were happy and content with themselves.

Seeing the fisherman, they were greatly amazed and asked him where he had come from. He answered all their questions, and then they invited him to their homes, where they put wine before him, killed chickens and prepared food in his honor. When the other people in the village heard about the visitor, they too all came to ask questions.

They themselves told him that their ancestors had escaped from the wars and confusion in the time of the Qin Dynasty. Bringing their wives and children, all the people of their area had reached this isolated place, and had stayed here ever since. Thus they had lost all contact with the outside world. They asked what dynasty it was now. The Han they had never heard of, let alone the Wei and the Jin. Point by point the fisherman explained all he could of the world that he knew, and they all sighed in deep sorrow.

Afterwards all the rest invited him to their homes, and all feasted him with wine and food. He stayed there several days and then bade them goodbye; before he departed these people said to him: "Never speak to anyone outside about this!"

So he went out, found his boat and went back by the same route as he had come, all along the way leaving marks. When he got to the provincial town he called on the prefect and told him all about his experience. The prefect at once sent men to go with him and follow up the marks he had left. But they became completely confused over the marks and never found the place.

Liu Ziji, a scholar of high reputation from Nanyang, heard of this and enthusiastically offered to go out with the fisherman to try again. But he fell ill and died before realizing his plan. After that no one went any more to look for the way.

(translated by Yang Xianyi and Gladys Yang)

## 桃花源记

晋太元中，武陵人捕鱼为业。缘溪行，忘路之远近。忽逢桃花林，夹岸数百步，中无杂树，芳草鲜美，落英缤纷，渔人甚异之；复前行，欲穷其林。

林尽水源，便得一山。山有小口，仿佛若有光。便舍船，从口入。初极狭，才通人。复行数十步，豁然开朗。土地平旷，屋舍俨然，有良田美池桑竹之属。阡陌交通，鸡犬相闻。其中往来种作，男女衣着，悉如外人。黄发垂髫，并怡然自乐。

见渔人，乃大惊；问所从来，具答之，便要还家，设酒杀鸡作食。村中闻有此人，咸来问讯。自云先世避秦时乱，率妻子邑人来此绝境，不复出焉；遂与外人间隔。问今是何世，乃不知有汉，无论魏晋。此人一一为具言所闻，皆叹惋。余人各复延至其家，皆出酒食。停数日，辞去，此中人语云："不足为外人道也！"

既出，得其船，便扶向路，处处志之。及郡下，诣太守，说如此。太守即遣人随其往，寻向所志，遂迷，不复得路。

南阳刘子骥，高尚士也；闻之，欣然规往，未果，寻病终。后遂无问津者。

桃花源

## 6. Master Five Willows

Nobody knows where he came from or what his family name was. He is simply known as Master Five Willows after the five willow trees that grow by his house. He is a quiet man who does not talk much. He does not covet fame or wealth, and derives his pleasure from the perusal of books. He reads causally without a need for thorough understanding. Whenever he has learned something from the books, he is so happy that he often forgets his meals. He has a fondness for wine, but being poor, he cannot often afford it. His relatives and friends know about it and will invite him over for a drink. Every time he goes to their home he drinks his fill and is never satisfied until he is drunk, and then leaves without tarrying.

The walls in his house are bare, and can shelter him neither from the rain and wind, nor from the scorching sun. His cotton gown is worn to rags and he is always short of food. But he takes all this with equanimity. He often writes essays to amuse himself and to express his aspirations and interests. He spends his life in this way, disregarding personal gain and loss.

The following is my appraisal:

Qianlou said, "Neither be sad for being poor and lowly, nor be eager to seek riches and honor." Ruminating on his words, one will wonder whether he is referring to Master Five Willows and his like. Master Five Willows sips wine and composes poems to give full expression to his lofty ideals. Isn't he a common man of the ancient times of Wuhuai Shi or Getian Shi?

(translated by Luo Jingguo)

## 五柳先生传

先生不知何许人也，亦不详其姓字。宅边有五柳树，因以为号焉。闲静少言，不慕荣利。好读书，不求甚解；每有会意，便欣然忘食。性嗜酒，家贫，不能常得。亲旧知其如此，或置酒而招之。造饮辄尽，期在必醉。既醉而退，曾不吝情去留。环堵萧然，不蔽风日。短褐穿结，箪瓢屡空，晏如也。常著文章自娱，颇示己志。忘怀得失，以此自终。

赞曰：黔娄有言："不戚戚于贫贱，不汲汲于富贵。"极其言兹若人之俦乎？酣觞赋诗，以乐其志。无怀氏之民欤？葛天氏之民欤？

# Further Readings

## 1. The Tune of West Bar

Anonymous

To pick plum blossoms in West Bar I go,
To the north of Yangtze River I'll send.
I'm dressed in red like apricot aglow,
Curling my raven-black hair for my friend.
Where is West Bar, the place of rendezvous?
I'll oar to the bridge and ferry shallows.
At dusk the shrikes in nests fly out of view
When gusts of wind blow at the tallows.
The tallow trees stands before my house,
From which can be seen my jeweled head.
Stepping outdoors, I do not see my spouse,
And go to pick the lotus flowers red.
In autumn now, I go to Southern Pond,
See scarlet lotus flowers and pads in between.
I start to play with lotus seeds beyond,
Which grow in the water fresh and green.
I hold the lotus seeds in my broad sleeves,
As a keepsake for my love both day and night.
As time is longer still since my sweetheart leaves,
I look upward and see wild geese in flight.
Above West Bar wild geese fly from the north;
I go upstairs and look forward to some mail.
I see nothing as I look back and forth,
And all day long I stand with hand on rail.
By the curving handrails I stand and sigh,

中国文学选读

My hands hanging down, as white as jade.

I roll up curtains and see the boundless sky

And river waters flowing in the shade.

Eternal are the waters of the stream;

Alas for me and with man who stays afar!

If the southern wind is aware of my dream,

Please bring me in my dream to West Bar.

(translated by Wang Rongpei)

## 西 洲 曲

无名氏

忆梅下西洲，折梅寄江北。

单衫杏子红，双鬓鸦雏色。

西洲在何处？两桨桥头渡。

日暮伯劳飞，风吹乌臼树。

树下即门前，门中露翠钿。

开门郎不至，出门采红莲。

采莲南塘秋，莲花过人头。

低头弄莲子，莲子青如水。

置莲怀袖中，莲心彻底红。

忆郎郎不至，仰首望飞鸿。

鸿飞满西洲，望郎上青楼。

楼高望不见，尽日栏杆头。

栏杆十二曲，垂手明如玉。

卷帘天自高，海水摇空绿。

海水梦悠悠，君愁我亦愁。

南风知我意，吹梦到西洲。

## 2. Song of Mulan

Anonymous

Alack, alas! alack, alas!

She weaves and sees the shuttle pass.

You cannot hear the shuttle, why?

Its whir is drowned in her deep sigh.

"Oh, what are you thinking about?

Will you tell us? Will you speak out?"

"I have no worry on my mind,

Nor have I grief of any kind.

I read the battleroll last night;

The Khan has ordered men to fight.

The roll was written in twelve books;

My father's name was in twelve nooks.

My father has not grown-up son,

For elder brother I have none.

I'll get a horse of hardy race

And serve in my old father's place. "

She buys a steed at eastern fair,

A whip and saddle here and there,

She buys a bridle at the south

And metal bit for the horse's mouth.

At dawn she leaves her parents by the city wall;

At dusk she reaches Yellow River shore.

All night she listens for old folk's familiar call,

But only hears the Yellow River's roar.

At dawn she leaves the Yellow River shore;

To Mountains Black she goes her way.

At night she hears old folk's familiar voice no more,

中国文学选读

But only on north mountains Tartar horses neigh.
For miles and miles the army march along
　　And cross the mountain barriers as in flight.
The northern wind has chilled the watchman's gong,
　　Their coat of mail glistens in wintry light.
In ten years they've lost many captains strong,
　　But battle-hardened warriors come back in delight.

Back, they have their audience with the Khan in the hall,
Honors and gifts are lavished on warriors all.
The Khan asks her what she wants as a grace.
"A camel fleet to carry me to my native place."

Hearing that she has come,
　　Her parents hurry to meet her at city gate,
Her sister rouges her face at home,
　　Her younger brother kills pig and sheep to celebrate.
She opens the doors east and west
And sits on her bed for a rest.
She doffs her garb worn under fire
And wears again female attire.
Before the window she arranges her hair
And in the mirror sees her image fair.
Then she comes out to see her former mate,
Who stares at her in amazement great:
"We have marched together for twelve years,
We did not know there was a lass'mid our compeers!"
"Both buck and doe have lilting gait
And both their eyelids palpitate.
When side by side two rabbits go,
Who can tell the buck from the doe?"

# 木 兰 诗

无名氏

唧唧复唧唧，木兰当户织。

不闻机杼声，唯闻女叹息。

问女何所思？问女何所忆？

女亦无所思，女亦无所忆。

昨夜见军帖，可汗大点兵。

军书十二卷，卷卷有爷名。

阿爷无大儿，木兰无长兄。

愿为市鞍马，从此替爷征。

东市买骏马，西市买鞍鞯。

南市买辔头，北市买长鞭。

旦辞爷娘去，暮宿黄河边。

不闻爷娘唤女声，但闻黄河流水鸣溅溅。

花木兰

中国文学选读

旦辞黄河去，暮宿黑山头。

不闻爷娘唤女声，但闻燕山胡骑声啾啾。

万里赴戎机，关山度若飞。

朔气传金柝，寒光照铁衣。

将军百战死，壮士十年归。


归来见天子，天子坐明堂。

策勋十二转，赏赐百千强。

可汗问所欲，"木兰不用尚书郎。

愿借明驼千里足，送儿还故乡"。


爷娘闻女来，出郭相扶将。

阿姊闻妹来，当户理红妆。

小弟闻姊来，磨刀霍霍向猪羊。

开我东阁门，坐我西阁床。

脱我战时袍，著我旧时裳。

当窗理云鬓，对镜帖花黄。

出门看伙伴，伙伴皆惊惶。

同行十二年，不知木兰是女郎。

雄兔脚扑朔，雌兔眼迷离。

双兔傍地走，安能辨我是雄雌！


## Topics for Discussion

1. Explain why the poet Tao Yuanming chose to live a secluded life.

2. Can you relate to these poems and the poets' perspectives?

3. In your opinion does "The Peach Blossom Springs" represent a Utopian society?

4. Compare the female images in "The Tune of West Bar" and "Song of Mulan".

Chapter Four

# Poetry in the Tang Dynasty

## General Description

The Tang Dynasty(唐朝 618～907) was the most powerful dynasty in Chinese history. Historians have linked the period of the Tang and Han Dynasties together and called it the "The Prosperous Age of Han-Tang(汉唐盛世)". However, after the outbreak of the "An-Shi Rebellion(安史之乱)" in 755 AD, the power of the Tang Dynasty gradually began to decline.

Literature in the Tang Dynasty flourished, especially in the realm of classical poetry, which entered a golden age. The era, which became known as the "Tang Poem (唐诗)", was divided into four stages: Early Tang(初唐), High Tang(盛唐), Mid-Tang(中唐) and Late Tang(晚唐). Regardless of the stage, the number of poetic works that were created and the poets who wrote were as numerous and as brilliant as the countless shining stars in the sky. The book, *Complete Tang Poetry* (《全唐诗》), assembled more than 50 000 poems from over 2 200 poets, establishing a special place for poetry in the Tang era.

During this time Tang poems were divided into two styles: the "Classical Style(古体诗)" and the "Modern Style(近体诗)". The "Classical Style", also called "Gu Feng"(古风 Ancient Drift), was written with an ancient format, and had a broader content and lines of uneven length. The "Modern Style" was usually written in five-character or seven-character lines and was always restricted to four or eight lines called "Quatrains and Poems" or "Jue Ju(绝句)" and "Lü Shi(律诗)".

The two outstanding poets, Li Bai and Du Fu, are considered the two greatest poets of the Tang era.

In this chapter we will introduce the most famous poems of these two poets as well as the selected works of Wang Wei, Li Shangyin and Du Mu.

## Introduction to the Poems of Li Bai

Li Bai(李白 701~762), the genius poet, wrote during the High Tang Period. He loved to travel and make friends and he maintained a great friendship with the poet Du Fu. With his knowledge of Daoism and Confucianism, Li Bai was initially determined to make a career as an official and was treated well by the Emperor. Unfortunately he was unsuccessful and so left the capital Chang'an(长安). He carried with him a sensitive romantic nature and a liberated spirit and became known by the nickname "Poet Immortal(诗仙)". Du Fu once commented that Li Bai's poems were in a class by themselves and beyond compare. Li Bai's poems attained the peak of ancient Chinese poetry and no one can duplicate and repeat the significance of his creations.

Li Bai specialized in quatrains and in using the ancient writing style. His poems were emotional and imaginative and his ideas seemed to float freely in the air. His style became the model during the High Tang Period. Liquor and moonlight were his favorite subjects; therefore he called himself "The Immortal of Liquor(酒仙)". It is said that, being drunk, he was drawn to jump into the lake to embrace the moon.

Li Bai was not only an icon of Tang poetry; he also had a tremendous influence on subsequent generations of poets.

李白醉酒

# Selected Poems of Li Bai

## 1. Thoughts on a Silent Night

Before my bed a pool of light—

O can it be frost on the ground?

Eyes raised, I find the moon so bright;

Head bent, in homesickness I'm drowned.

(translated by Xu Yuanchong)

## 静　夜　思

床前明月光，

疑是地上霜。

举头望明月，

低头思故乡。

## 2. The Waterfall in Mount Lu Viewed from Afar

The sunlit Censer Peak exhales incense-like cloud；

The cataract hangs like upended stream, sounding loud.

Its torrent dashes down three thousand feet from high

As if the Silver River fell from azure sky.

(translated by Xu Yuanchong)

## 望庐山瀑布

日照香炉生紫烟，

遥看瀑布挂前川。

飞流直下三千尺，

疑是银河落九天。

中国文学选读

### 3. To Wang Changling Banished to the West

All willow-down has fallen and sad cuckoos cry

To hear you banished southwestward beyond Five Streams.

I would confide my sorrow to the moon on high,

For it will follow you west to the Land of Dreams.

(translated by Xu Yuanchong)

### 闻王昌龄左迁

杨花落尽子规啼，

闻道龙标过五溪。

我寄愁心与明月，

随君直到夜郎西。

李白诗《闻王昌龄左迁》

## 4. Drinking Alone in the Moonlight

Among the flowers from a pot of wine

I drink without a companion of mine.

I raise my cup to invite the Moon who blends

Her light with my Shadow and we're three friends.

The Moon does not know how to drink her share;

In vain my Shadow follows me here and there.

Together with them for the time I stay,

And make merry before spring's spent away.

I sing and the Moon lingers to hear my song;

My Shadow's a mess while I dance along.

Sober，we three remain cheerful and gay;

Drunken，we part and each may go his way.

Our friendship will outshine all earthly love;

Next time we'll meet beyond the stars above.

(translated by Xu Yuanchong)

## 月下独酌

花间一壶酒，独酌无相亲。

举杯邀明月，对影成三人。

月既不解饮，影徒随我身。

暂伴月将影，行乐须及春。

我歌月徘徊，我舞影零乱。

醒时同交欢，醉后各分散。

永结无情游，相期邈云汉。

## 5. Invitation to Wine

Do you not see the Yellow River come from the sky，

Rushing into the sea and ne'er come back?

中国文学选读

Do you not see the mirrors bright in chambers high

Grieve o'er your snow-white hair though once it was silk-black?

When hopes are won, oh! Drink your fill in high delight,

And never leave your wine-cup empty in moonlight!

Heaven has made us talents; we're not made in vain.

 A thousand gold coins spent, more will turn up again.

Kill a cow, cook a sheep and let us merry be,

And drink three hundred cupfuls of wine in high glee!

Dear friends of mine,

Cheer up, cheer up!

李白诗《将进酒》

I invite you to wine.

Do not put down your cup!

I will sing you a song, please hear,

O hear! Lend me a willing ear!

What difference will rare and costly dishes make?

I only want to get drunk and never to wake.

How many great men were forgotten through the ages?

But great drinkers are more famous than the sages.

The Prince of Poets feasted in his palace at will,

Drank wine at ten thousand a cask and laughed his fill.

A host should not complain of money he is short,

To drink with you I will sell things of any sort.

My fur coat worth a thousand coins of gold

And my flower-dappled horse may be sold

To buy good wine that we may drown the woe age-old.

(translated by Xu Yuanchong)

## 将 进 酒

君不见，黄河之水天上来，奔流到海不复回！

君不见，高堂明镜悲白发，朝如青丝暮成雪！

人生得意须尽欢，莫使金樽空对月。

天生我材必有用，千金散尽还复来。

烹羊宰牛且为乐，会须一饮三百杯。

岑夫子，丹丘生，将进酒，君莫停。

与君歌一曲，请君为我侧耳听：

钟鼓馔玉不足贵，但愿长醉不愿醒；

古来圣贤皆寂寞，惟有饮者留其名。

陈王昔时宴平乐，斗酒十千恣欢谑。

主人何为言少钱，径须沽取对君酌。

五花马，千金裘，呼儿将出换美酒，与尔同销万古愁。

# Introduction to the Poems of Du Fu

Du Fu(杜甫 712～772) was born during a tumultuous period of the Tang Dynasty. He went through the turmoil of the "An-Shi Rebellion" and suffered greatly. He resided in Chengdu(成都) for a time and endured poverty during his later years. He was displaced, and in trying to escape the war died sadly during his journey. Du Fu was deeply influenced by Confucianism. He paid a lot of attention to reality and was especially unwilling to compromise his values in a society that favored the feasting of the rich while neglecting the hungry poor. Most of his poems reflected the suffering in ordinary people's lives and displayed a great compassion for them. He wrote about the

杜甫

nation's catastrophes and focused on the pains of civilians. His poems captured events in society and aimed to depict a true reflection of social unrest and the turmoil in real life. He was addressed as "Poet Historian(诗史)" because his poems were a substitute for the absent recorded history. For his profound writing style, concern for his country, and contribution to Chinese poetry, Du Fu is acknowledged as the "Poet Sage(诗圣)".

When we talk about Tang poetry people often say "Li Du(李杜)". Although these two poets remained great friends, their personalities and poetic styles were extremely different. Du Fu's poetry was deeply emotional, his narratives very down to earth, and his language always refined. He became an example for future generations that followed.

# Selected Poems of Du Fu

## 1. Spring View

On war-torn land streams flow and mountains stand;

In towns unquiet grass and weeds run riot.

Grieved o'er the years, flowers are moved to tears;

Seeing us part, birds cry with broken heart.

The beacon fire has gone higher and higher;

Words from household are worth their weight in gold.

I cannot bear to scratch my grizzling hair;

It grows too thin to hold a light hairpin.

(translated by Xu Yuanchong)

## 春　望

国破山河在，城春草木深。

感时花溅泪，恨别鸟惊心。

烽火连三月，家书抵万金。

白头搔更短，浑欲不胜簪。

杜甫诗《春望》

### 2. Happy Rain on a Spring Night

Good rain knows its time right,

It will fall when comes spring.

With wind it steals in night;

Mute, it wets everything.

Over wild lanes dark cloud spreads;

In boat a lantern looms.

Dawn sees saturated reds;

The town's heavy with blooms.

(translated by Xu Yuanchong)

## 春 夜 喜 雨

好雨知时节，当春乃发生。

随风潜入夜，润物细无声。

野径云俱黑，江船火独明。

晓看红湿处，花重锦官城。

### 3. Good News of the Recovery of the Central Plains

'Tis said the Northern Gate has been recaptured of late;

When the news reaches my ears, my gown is wet with tears.

Staring at my wife's face, of grief I find no trace;

As I roll up verse books, my joy like madness looks.

Though white-haired, I would still both sing and drink my fill;

With verdure spring's aglow, it's time we homeward go.

We shall sail all the way through three Gorges in a day;

Going down to Xiangyang, we'll go up to Luoyang.

(translated by Xu Yuanchong)

# 闻官军收河南河北

剑外忽传收蓟北，初闻涕泪满衣裳。

却看妻子愁何在？漫卷诗书喜欲狂。

白日放歌须纵酒，青春作伴好还乡。

即从巴峡穿巫峡，便下襄阳向洛阳。

## 4. Ballad of the War Chariots

Chariots rumble

And horses grumble.

The conscripts march with bow and arrows at the waist.

Their fathers, mothers, wives and children come in haste

To see them off; the bridge is shrouded in dust they've raised.

They clutch at their coats, stamp the feet and bar the way;

Their grief cries loud and strikes the cloud straight, straightaway.

An onlooker by roadside asks an enrollee.

"The conscription is frequent," only answers he.

Some went north at fifteen to guard the river shore,

And were sent west to till the land at forty-four.

The elder bound their young heads when they went away;

Just home, they're sent to the frontier though their hair's gray.

The field on borderland becomes a sea of blood;

The emperor's greed for land is still at high flood.

Have you not heard two hundred districts east of the Hua Mountains lie,

Where briers and brambles grow in villages far and nigh?

Although stout women can wield the plough and the hoe,

Thorns and weeds in the east as in the west o'ergrow.

The enemy are used to hard and stubborn fight;

Our men are driven just like dogs or fowls in flight.

"You are kind to ask me.

To complain I'm not free.

In winter of this year

Conscription goes on here.

The magistrates for taxes press.

How can we pay them in distress?

If we had known sons bring no joy,

We would have preferred girl to boy. "

A daughter can only be wed to a neighbor, alas!

A son can only be buried under the grass!

Have you not seen

On borders green

Bleached bones since olden days unburied on the plain?

The old ghosts weep and cry, while the ghosts complain;

The air is loud with screech and scream in gloomy rain.

(translated by Xu Yuanchong)

## 兵 车 行

车辚辚，马萧萧，行人弓箭各在腰。

爷娘妻子走相送，尘埃不见咸阳桥。

牵衣顿足拦道哭，哭声直上干云霄。

道旁过者问行人，行人但云点行频。

杜甫诗《兵车行》

或从十五北防河，便至四十西营田。

去时里正与裹头，归来头白还戍边。

边庭流血成海水，武皇开边意未已。

君不闻汉家山东二百州，千村万落生荆杞。

纵有健妇把锄犁，禾生陇亩无东西。

况复秦兵耐苦战，被驱不异犬与鸡。

长者虽有问，役夫敢申恨？

且如今年冬，未休关西卒。

县官急索租，租税从何出。

信知生男恶，反是生女好。

生女犹得嫁比邻，生男埋没随百草。

君不见，青海头，古来白骨无人收。

新鬼烦冤旧鬼哭，天阴雨湿声啾啾。


## 5. The Conscripting Officer at Xin'an

Traveling through Xin'an

I heard a bellowing voice

Taking roll call, and a local official

Told me how all grown lads

Had already gone, and now the call

Was for boys in their teens, many

Short and many thin, he wondering

How such could help to defend cities;

As I stood I saw how the fat boys

Had mothers to farewell them, but how

Lone and pitiful the thin ones were;

Evening came, and I looked at the stream

Flowing east, heard the sound

Of sobbing from among green hills

Around; and thought it were best

For those mothers not to wither

Their eyes with weeping, for even

If eyes went to skin and bone, it would

Be to no avail; now our armies were

Besieging Yecheng, and soon it should fall;

How could we have thought the rebellion

Would drive the way it did, and our army

Scatter in retreat? Now our forces

Protect granaries, train new men, and dig

Fortifications that do not go down

To water, while work on tending

Cavalry mounts is not hard, and all men

Are well fed; so no need for you to weep more!

Guo Ziyi treats his men as his

Own children.

(translated by Rewi Alley)

## 新 安 吏

客行新安道，喧呼闻点兵。

借问新安吏：县小更无丁？

府帖昨夜下，次选中男行。

中男绝短小，何以守王城？

肥男有母送，瘦男独伶俜。

白水暮东流，青山犹哭声！

莫自使眼枯，收汝泪纵横。

眼枯即见骨，天地终无情！

我军取相州，日夕望其平。

岂意贼难料，归军星散营。

就粮近故垒，练卒依旧京。

掘壕不到水，牧马役亦轻。

况乃王师顺，抚养甚分明。

送行勿泣血，仆射如父兄。

# Further Readings

## 1. The Dale of Singing Birds
### Wang Wei

I hear osmanthus blooms fall unenjoyed;

When night comes, hills dissolve into the void.

The rising moon arouses birds to sing;

Their fitful twitters fill the dale with spring.

(translated by Xu Yuanchong)

## 鸟 鸣 涧
### 王 维

人闲桂花落，

夜静青山空。

月出惊山鸟，

时鸣春涧中。

## 2. Thinking of My Brothers on Mountain Climbing Day
### Wang Wei

Alone, a lonely stranger in a foreign land,

I pine for kinsfolk doubly on a holiday.

I know my brothers would, with dogwood spray in hand,

Climb the mountain and think of me so far away.

(translated by Xu Yuanchong)

## 九月九日忆山东兄弟
### 王 维

独在异乡为异客，

每逢佳节倍思亲。

遥知兄弟登高处，

遍插茱萸少一人。

### 3. On the Plain of Tombs
#### Li Shangyin

At dusk my heart is filled with gloom；

I drive my cab to ancient tomb.

The setting sun seems so sublime，

But it is near its dying time.

(translated by Xu Yuanchong)

## 乐 游 原
### 李 商 隐

向晚意不适，

驱车登古原。

夕阳无限好，

只是近黄昏。

### 4. To an Unnamed Lover
#### Li Shangyin

It's difficult for us to meet and hard to part；

The east wind is too weak to revive flowers dead.

Spring silkworm till its death spins silk from lovesick heart；

And candles but when burned up have no tears to shed.

At dawn I'm grieved to think your mirrored hair turns grey；

At night you would feel cold while I croon by moonlight.

To the three fairy mountains it's not a long way；

Would the blue bird oft fly to see you on the height!

(translated by Xu Yuanchong)

# 无　题
## 李商隐

相见时难别亦难，东风无力百花残。

春蚕到死丝方尽，蜡炬成灰泪始干。

晓镜但愁云鬓改，夜吟应觉月光寒，

蓬山此去无多路，青鸟殷勤为探看。

## 5. The Day of Mourning for the Dead
### Du Mu

The day of mourning for the dead it's raining hard;

My heart is broken on my way to the graveyard.

Where can I find a wineshop to drown my sad hours?

A herdboy points to a cot amid apricot flowers.

(translated by Xu Yuanchong)

杜牧

# 清　明
## 杜　牧

清明时节雨纷纷，

路上行人欲断魂。

借问酒家何处有？

牧童遥指杏花村。

## 6. Parting
### Du Mu

Deep, deep our love, too deep to show.

Deep, deep we drink; silent we grow.

The candle grieves to see us part;

It melts in tears with burnt-out heart.

(translated by Xu Yuanchong)

## 赠　别

杜　牧

多情却似总无情，

唯觉樽前笑不成。

蜡烛有心还惜别，

替人垂泪到天明。

## Topics for Discussion

1. What are the accomplishments of Tang poems and what place do they hold in Chinese literary history?

2. What are the artistic characteristics of Tang poetry?

3. Why is Li Bai called the "Poet Immortal" and Du Fu the "Poet Sage"?

4. Describe the differences in poetic styles between Li Bai and Du Fu.

Chapter Five

# Ci in the Song Dynasty

## General Description

Following the wars of the Five Dynasties(五代) and turmoil of the Ten States (十国), the Song Dynasty(宋朝 960～1279) again united China. Compared to the situation of the previous dynasties, the development of commerce and urban cities during the Song Dynasty was much more sophisticated. The extensive use of printing technology led to a greater dissemination of culture and the rise of an entertainment business. Although the Song history lasted for more than 300 years, it was clearly divided into two periods by the "Jingkang Incident(靖康之变)"(in 1126): the Northern Song(北宋) and the Southern Song(南宋). The Song was finally destroyed by the Yuan Dynasty.

Poetry remained very popular during the Song Dynasty, but the Song was also the time for the rise and spread of Ci(词) throughout China. It was the time when Ci reached its pinnacle of achievement, forever being associated with the Song just as Shi is with the Tang.

Ci is part of the format of Shi(poetry) and "Shi Ci(诗词)" is often combined and addressed as one concept in poetry. Ci is a type of lyric and usually it is coordinated with instruments and as such is frequently referred to as "Qu Zi Ci(曲子词)". Ci developed between the Late Tang and the Five Dynasties as a kind of new format in poetry. The major difference is that Ci, when compared to the Tang's "Ge Lü poem(格律诗 rhyming poem)" and the traditional five-character or seven-character poems, is written with uneven lengths of lines and verses. Lyrically Ci is also different from the ancient poetic style. Ci has its lyrics in a regular format and with set tunes.

Compared to Shi，Ci has a distinctive musical style and irregular lines. It is also different in its content and lyrical approach. It is said that Shi displays elegant dignity while Ci radiates the quality of enchanting charm(诗庄词媚).

During the Song Dynasty the written works of Ci were separated into two styles：the "heroic abandon school(豪放派)" and the "gentle school(婉约派)". Su Shi is representative of the "heroic abandon school" and the poetess Li Qingzhao of the "gentle school".

This chapter focuses on the works of Su Shi and Li Qingzhao. The supplementary pieces are from the works of Liu Yong and Xin Qiji.

中国文学选读

## Introduction to the Ci of Su Shi

Su Shi(苏轼 1037~1101), also known as Su Dong-po(苏东坡), was born into a well-educated family. Together with his father Su Xun(苏洵) and his brother Su Zhe(苏辙), they were known as the "Three Su", and were famous writers during the Northern Song Dynasty. Su Shi, and his poems, Ci, and prose, represented the highest literary achievements of the Northern Song. During the transition to Song Ci(宋词), Su Shi took the lead in reforming traditional concepts, creating a fresh wind to carry the new format of Song Ci.

苏轼

Prior to Su Shi, Ci was a kind of "stimulation" lyric for female singers in the entertainment business. Often it was performed in restaurants or at banquet parties with the subjects frequently being related to lust, love or sorrow. Su Shi broke the traditional boundaries between poetry and Ci, merging both genres and broadening the themes to include country scenes, landscapes of mountains and rivers, life stories, and actual events. His works extended the subject matter, added to the emotional content, enriched the vocabulary, and broadened the writing style. Su Shi's most important contribution to Ci was injecting a masculine spirit into the literature and founding a new form which became known as the "heroic abandon school".

# Selected Works of Su Shi

## 1. Niannujiao: Memories of the Past at Red Cliff

The endless river eastward flows;

With its huge waves are gone all those

    Gallant heroes of bygone years.

    West of the ancient fortress appears

Red Cliff where General Zhou Yu won his early fame

When the Three Kingdoms were in flame.

    Jagged rocks tower in the air

        And swashing waves beat on the shore,

           Rolling up a thousand heaps of snow.

To match the hills and the river so fair,

    How many heroes brave of yore

        Made a great show!

I fancy General Zhou Yu at the height

    Of his success, with a plume fan in hand,

In a silk hood, so brave and bright,

Laughing and jesting with his bride so fair,

    While enemy ships were destroyed as planned

    Like castles in the air.

        Should their souls revisit this land,

Sentimental, his bride would laugh to say:

Younger than they, I have my hair turned grey.

    Life is but like a passing dream.

O Moon, I drink to you who saw them on the stream.

(translated by Xu Yuanchong)

中国文学选读

## 念奴娇·赤壁怀古

大江东去，浪淘尽，千古风流人物。

故垒西边，人道是，三国周郎赤壁。

乱石穿空，惊涛裂岸，卷起千堆雪。

江山如画，一时多少豪杰！


遥想公瑾当年，小乔初嫁了，雄姿英发。

羽扇纶巾，谈笑间，樯橹灰飞烟灭。

故国神游，多情应笑我，早生华发。

人生如梦，一樽还酹江月。


## 2. Jiangchengzi：Hunting at Mizhou

Rejuvenated, I my fiery zeal display：

  On left hand leash, a yellow hound,

On right hand wrist, a falcon gray.

A thousand silk-capped, sable-coated horsemen sweep

  Across the rising ground

And hillocks steep.

Townspeople pour out from out the city gate

To watch the tiger-hunting magistrate.


Heart gladdened with strong wine, who cares

  About a few newly-frosted hairs?

When will the court imperial send

Me as their envoy? With flags and banners then I'll bend

My bow like a full moon, and aiming northwest, I

  Will shoot down the fierce Wolf from out the sky.

(translated by Xu Yuanchong)

## 江城子·密州出猎

老夫聊发少年狂，左牵黄，右擎苍。

锦帽貂裘、千骑卷平冈。

为报倾城随太守，亲射虎，看孙郎。


酒酣胸胆尚开张，鬓微霜，又何妨！

持节云中，何日遣冯唐？

会挽雕弓如满月，西北望，射天狼。


### 3. Shuidiaogetou: Bright Moon, When Was Your Birth

How long will the full moon appear?

    Wine cup in hand, I ask the sky.

I do not know what time of year

    It would be tonight in the palace on high.

    Riding the wind, there I would fly,

Yet I'm afraid the crystalline palace would be

    Too high and cold for me.

I rise and dance; with my shadow I play.

On high as on earth, would it be as gay?


    The moon goes round the mansions red

    Through gauze-draped windows soft to shed

    Her light upon the sleepless bed.

Against man she should have no spite.

Why then, when people part, is she oft full and bright?

Men have sorrow and joy, they part or meet again;

The moon is bright or dim and she may wax or wane.

There has been nothing perfect since the olden days.

    So let us wish that man

中国文学选读

Will live long as he can!

Though miles apart, we'll share the beauty she displays.

(translated by Xu Yuanchong)

## 水调歌头·明月几时有

明月几时有？把酒问青天。

不知天上宫阙，今夕是何年。

我欲乘风归去，又恐琼楼玉宇，高处不胜寒。

起舞弄清影，何似在人间！

转朱阁，低绮户，照无眠。

不应有恨，何事长向别时圆？

人有悲欢离合，月有阴晴圆缺，此事古难全。

但愿人长久，千里共婵娟。

苏轼词《明月几时有》

## Introduction to the Ci of Li Qingzhao

Li Qingzhao(李清照 1084～1151?) was born into an official family and was brilliant in her youth. She married a scholar, Zhao Mingcheng, and they both lived an enjoyable and happy life, embracing poetry together. Unfortunately unexpected tragedy befell her when her husband died and the imperial court fell. She lived in poverty during her escape from the war, frequently changing locations during the early Southern Song years. Finally she settled in Lin'an(临安), eking out a subsistence living. In contrast to her earlier life Li Qingzhao's later life was especially lonely and miserable.

Li Qingzhao was famous for her creative Ci works. As a result of the striking changes in her life style, before and after the war, her approach to writing also dramatically transformed. Her early stage works contained vibrant aristocratic images and her topics focused on sentimental expressions towards nature and love. Later, after moving to the south and subsequent to the disasters she encountered, her works

李清照

中国文学选读

reflected sadness and despair.

Li Qingzhao emphasized the different forms of expression in Shi and Ci. As a female poet her gentle words were made even more delicate. Through the ingenuity of her ability to express detailed descriptions of emotional states, she was able to convey subtle changes and poignant ups and downs with her vividly sentimental words.

## Selected Works of Li Qingzhao

### 1. Rumengling

Last night the wind was strong and rain was fine;

Sound sleep did not dispel the taste of wine.

I ask the maid who's rolling up the screen.

The same crab-apple tree, she says, is seen.

But don't you know,

Oh, don't you know,

The red should languish and the green must grow?

(translated by Xu Yuanchong)

### 如 梦 令

昨夜雨疏风骤，

沉睡不消残酒。

试问卷帘人，

李清照词《如梦令》

却道海棠依旧。

知否？知否？

应是绿肥红瘦。


## 2. Zuihuayin

In thin mist and thick cloud of incense, sad I stay

The animal-shaped censer I see all day.

The Double Ninth Festival comes again.

   Still alone I remain

In the curtain of gauze, on a pillow of jade,

Which the midnight chill begins to invade.


After dusk I drink wine by East Hedge in full bloom,

My sleeves filled with fragrance and gloom.

   Say not my soul

Is not consumed! Should the west wind uproll

   The curtain of my bower,

Twould show a thinner face than yellow flower.

(translated by Xu Yuanchong)

## 醉 花 阴

薄雾浓云愁永昼，

瑞脑销金兽。

佳节又重阳，

玉枕纱厨，

半夜凉初透。


东篱把酒黄昏后，

有暗香盈袖。

莫道不销魂，

帘卷西风，

人比黄花瘦。

### 3. Shengshengman

I look for what I miss:

I know not what it is.

I feel so sad, so drear,

So lonely, without cheer.

How hard is it

To keep me fit

  In this lingering cold!

Hardly warmed up

By cup on cup

Of wine so dry,

Oh, how could I

Endure at dusk the drift

Of wind so swift?

It breaks my heart, alas,

To see the wild geese pass,

  For they are my acquaintances of old.


The ground is covered with yellow flowers,

Faded and fallen in showers.

Who will pick them up now?

Sitting alone at the window, how

Could I but quicken

The pace of darkness that won't thicken!

Upon the plane-trees a fine rain drizzles

As twilight grizzles.

Oh, what can I do with a grief

Beyond belief!

（translated by Xu Yuanchong）

## 声 声 慢

寻寻觅觅，冷冷清清，凄凄惨惨戚戚。

乍暖还寒时候，最难将息。

三杯两盏淡酒，怎敌他晚来风急?

雁过也，正伤心，却是旧时相识。

满地黄花堆积，憔悴损，如今有谁堪摘?

守着窗儿，独自怎生得黑!

梧桐更兼细雨，到黄昏点点滴滴。

这次第，怎一个愁字了得!

# Further Readings

## 1. Yulinling

### Liu Yong

Cicadas chill

Drearily shrill.

We stand face to face at an evening hour

Before the pavilion, after a sudden shower.

Can we care for drinking before we part?

At the city gate

We are lingering late,

But the boat is waiting for you to depart.

Hand in hand, we gaze at each other's tearful eyes

And burst into sobs with words congealed on our lips.

You'll go your way

Far, far away

On miles and miles of misty waves where sail the ships

And evening clouds hang low in boundless Southern skies.


Lovers would grieve at parting as of old.

How could you stand this clear autumn day so cold!

Where will you be found at daybreak

From wine awake?

Moored by a riverbank planted with willow trees

Beneath the waning moon and in the morning breeze.

You'll be gone for a year.

What could I do with all bright days and fine scenes here!

Howe'er coquettish I am on my part,

To whom can I lay bare my heart?

(translated by Xu Yuanchong)

中国文学选读

# 雨 霖 铃

柳 永

寒蝉凄切，对长亭晚，骤雨初歇。

都门帐饮无绪，留恋处，兰舟催发。

执手相看泪眼，竟无语凝噎。

念去去、千里烟波，暮霭沉沉楚天阔。

多情自古伤离别，更那堪、冷落清秋节！

今宵酒醒何处？杨柳岸、晓风残月。

此去经年，应是良辰好景虚设。

便纵有千种风情，更与何人说？

## 2. Pozhenzi

### Xin Qiji

Drunken, I lit my lamp to see my glaive,

　　Awake, I heard the horns from tents to tents.

　　　Under the flags, beef grilled

Was eaten by our warriors brave.

　　And martial airs were played by fifty instruments

　　'Twas an autumn manoeuvre in the field.

　　　On gallant steed

　　　Running full speed,

　　We'd shoot with twanging bows.

Recovering the lost land for the sovereign,

Tis everlasting fame that we would win.

　　But alas! white hair grows!

(translated by Xu Yuanchong)

# 破 阵 子

辛弃疾

醉里挑灯看剑，梦回吹角连营。
八百里分麾下炙，五十弦翻塞外声。
沙场秋点兵。

马作的卢飞快，弓如霹雳弦惊。
了却君王天下事，赢得生前身后名。
可怜白发生！

辛弃疾

## Topics for Discussion

1. Why is Ci referred to as being the "only one of its kind"?

2. From the perspective of the Ci style explain the natures of the "heroic abandon school" and the "gentle school".

3. Compare the Ci works of Su Shi and Liu Yong.

4. How does Li Qingzhao express her mood in her Ci?

5. Why was Xin Qiji called the "patriotic poet"?

Chapter Six

# Essays in the Tang and Song Dynasties

## General Description

The history of Chinese literature is one of uneven development of the four literary genres(poetry, essay, novel and drama). Poetry and essay were the earliest to develop, followed later by novel and drama. Poetry began to blossom with *Shi Jing*, and its surge continued all the way through the Tang Dynasty. In contrast, the path of essay development is less clear and far more meandering. Essays written by intellectuals became popular during the Pre-Qin period. As Chinese court culture advanced and matured, it simultaneously facilitated the development of the essay, although strictly speaking, essays written by intellectuals were not generally categorized as a literary genre on their own. Subsequently, Ci Fu(辞赋) in the Han Dynasty and Pian Wen(骈文 parallel prose) in the Six Dynasties both had a strong literary sense, though their format was closer to poetry. Therefore, from the perspective of genre, we can say that prose gradually took on its own form starting in the Tang Dynasty and then grew and blossomed during the Song. There were eight remarkable prose writers during the Tang-Song period, two from the Tang and six from the Song.

During the Mid-Tang period Han Yu and Liu Zongyuan launched a movement known as the "Ancient Prose Movement(古文运动)". Although the name indicates a return to the writing style of the Pre-Qin period, the motivation was in fact to promote Confucian doctrines in literary writing, which opposed the extravagant writing style of the Six Dynasties(六朝), and hoped to separate the genre of essay from its poetic linkage. Prose came more into line with the spoken language, departing from the restrictive formats of the poetic style.

This chapter focuses on essays by Liu Zongyuan and Ouyang Xiu, with supplementary works from Zhuge Liang, Han Yu and Su Shi.

## Introduction to the Works of Liu Zongyuan

Liu Zongyuan(柳宗元 773～819 ) was a well-known writer in the Mid-Tang period, but was once banished and exiled from his government service. Devoted to Buddhism from an early age, his writing style was always partial to simplicity. Landscape essays were one of his specialties, especially those about his experiences while traveling. Although depicting landscapes had always been seen in essays, particularly after the Six Dynasties, Liu Zongyuan nevertheless was the first writer to separate travel landscape writing from the old approach, and to write about natural scenes independently.

Most of Liu's travel journals documented his life in exile in Southwest China. During his lonely solitude, traveling around the countryside became his favorite activity. Like Tao Yuanming, he retreated to a pastoral life replete with scenes of nature. Liu not only portrayed nature in his writing, but he also projected his feelings into nature. Through the scenes of mountains and rivers, he was able to describe his inner state of mind.

柳宗元

# Selected Works of Liu Zongyuan

## 1. The Snake Catcher

In the wilderness on the outskirts of Yongzhou there exists a kind of snake with black skin marked with white stripes. Any plant dies upon its touch and anyone bitten by it is doomed to die. But once it is caught and dehydrated, it can serve as an ingredient of a traditional medicine for the cure of leprosy, arthritis, swollen necks, malignant tumors, the removal of decayed flesh, and the elimination of three kinds of worms that cause illness. Since early times the court physician has ordered the people in the name of the emperor to hand in snakes twice a year. Whoever does so is exempted from taxation. People in Yongzhou are vying with one another to catch snakes.

There is a man whose surname is Jiang. His family has been enjoying this privilege for three generations. When asked, he told me with deep grief, "My grandfather was killed by a snake, and so was my father. I myself have been engaged as a snake catcher for twelve years and might have been killed many a time." I sympathized with him, saying, "Are you complaining about this work? I shall ask the official in charge to transfer you to your former work and renew the taxation on you. How would you like that?"

My words threw him into great agony. He burst into tears and said, "Do you pity me and want me to live on? But the misery I am suffering now is not at all worse than what I suffered before. If I had not taken this work, I would be in desperate straits. Three generations of my family have been living here for sixty years. Our neighbors are growing poorer day by day. In order to pay the taxes, they are compelled to hand over all the produce of their land and all the possessions in their house. They shuffle from village to village, wailing in distress, and many of them die of hunger along the way. They are beaten by wind and rain, suffering freezing cold in winter and scorching heat in summer. What's more, they have to inhale the pernicious air of deceased districts. In this way, people are dying one after another, and their dead bodies are piling up. Out of ten families that were my grandfather's neighbors, only one has survived, and out of ten families that were my father's neighbors, only two or three remain. As to the neighbors who have been living near me for the past twelve years, only four or five out of ten families have survived. Most of them are dead or have moved to other places. I luckily remain alive simply because I am a snake catcher. Whenever the relentless officers come to the village, they make a row and bully the people. The village people scream from terror. Even fowls and dogs are not left in peace. I start from my bed with fear and look into the jar. To my relief the snakes are still there. Then my mind is at ease and I return to bed. I feed the snakes with great care and deliver them to the authorities in time. Back at home, I eat the produce of the land so that I may live on till my death. I risk my life only twice a year. The rest of the time, I spend my days quite happily, unlike other village people whose lives are constantly threatened. Even if I were killed by a snake today, I would still have lived longer than my neighbors. Why should I complain?"

I feel all the more depressed upon hearing his story. I was once disbelieving of Confucius's words: "Tyrannical rule is more ferocious than a tiger." From Jiang's example I have come to realize that this saying is true. Alas! Who could have known that oppressive taxation is worse than venomous snakes? Hence I write down this story for those who are making investigations relating to the life of the common people.

(translated by Luo Jingguo)

# 捕蛇者说

永州之野产异蛇，黑质而白章；触草木，尽死；以啮人，无御之者。然得而腊之以为饵，可以已大风、挛踠、瘘疠，去死肌，杀三虫。其始，太医以王命聚之，岁赋其二，募有能捕之者，当其租入。永之人争奔走焉。

有蒋氏者，专其利三世矣。问之，则曰："吾祖死于是，吾父死于是。今吾嗣为之十二年，几死者数矣。"言之，貌若甚戚者。余悲之，且曰："若毒之乎？余将告于莅事者，更若役，复若赋，则何如？"

蒋氏大戚，汪然出涕曰："君将哀而生之乎？则吾斯役之不幸，未若复吾赋不幸之甚也，向吾不为斯役，则久已病矣。自吾氏三世居是乡，积于今六十岁矣，而乡邻之生日蹙，殚其地之出，竭其庐之入，号呼而转徙，饥渴而顿踣，触风雨，

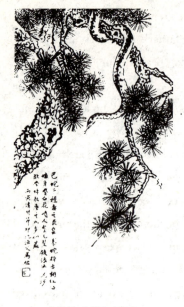

犯寒暑，呼嘘毒疠，往往而死者相藉也。曩与吾祖居者，今其室十无一焉；与吾父居者，今其室十无二三焉；与吾居十二年者，今其室十无四五焉。非死则徙尔。而吾以捕蛇独存。悍吏之来吾乡，叫嚣乎东西，隳突乎南北；哗然而骇者，虽鸡狗不得宁焉。吾恂恂而起，视其缶，而吾蛇尚存，则弛然而卧。谨食之，时而献焉。退而甘食其土之有，以尽吾齿。盖一岁之犯死者二焉；其余，则熙熙而乐。岂若吾乡邻之旦旦有是哉！今虽死乎此，比吾乡邻之死则已后矣，又安敢毒耶？"

余闻而愈悲。孔子曰："苛政猛于虎也。"吾尝疑乎是，今以蒋氏观之，犹信。呜呼！孰知赋敛之毒有甚是蛇者乎！故为之说，以俟夫观人风者得焉。

《捕蛇者说》插图

## 2. The Hillock to the West of Gumu Pond

It was on the eighth day after my discovery of Xishan Hill that I walked two hundred footsteps northwest of the mountain pass and found Gumu Pond. Upon hiking another twenty-five footsteps to the west of the pond, I came upon a fishing dike where the water was deep and the current, swift. Overhanging the dike was a hillock grown wild with trees and bamboos. Upon it, countless rocks protruded out of the earth, some standing erect, and some lying prone on the ground. They vied with one another in displaying their strange shapes. The tall overlapping ones stretching downward looked like a herd of cattle drinking from a creek. Others thrusting slantingly upwards were arrayed in a row, and looked like bears climbing up the hill face.

This hillock covered less than one mu in area, and looked so small as though it could be enclosed within a cage. I inquired after the owner, and was told, "It's apiece of deserted land belonging to the Tang family. It's on sale, but no one has come to buy it." I asked the price, and the answer was four hundred wen. I loved the place so much that I could not help but purchase it. Li Shenyuan and Yuan Keji were with me and they were very happy too, thinking it a bargain. We took to using different farming implements in turn, weeding the wild grass, chopping down dead trees and burning them off. A vision of beautiful trees and bamboos and strange rocks gradually revealed itself to our eyes. From that hillock, I observed the rising of the mountains, the floating of the clouds, and the flowing of the brook, as well as the pleasurable activities of birds and beasts, each giving its graceful performance above and below. I lay on a mat with a pillow under my head, my eyes conversing with the cool and refreshing air, my ears with the murmuring water, my spirit with the indifferent and detached ambience, and my heart with the serene and sedate atmosphere. I had unveiled two places of such unsurpassable beauty in less than ten days. Even the ancient nature goers were not so fortunate as I!

Alas! If this beautiful hillock were situated in places like Feng, Hao, Hu, Du, the nobility and the powerful would strive for its ownership. And it would not be available to them even should the price they offer rise one thousand pieces of gold each day. As it happened, nature delivered the hillock in this locality, to be disdained by passing farmers and fishermen. For years it could not find a warden, even at a price as low as four hundred wen. Shenyuan, Keji and I congratulated ourselves for having come upon it. Was it true that good fortune had alighted on this hillock?

I have had the above words inscribed on stone to congratulate the hillock for its fortune.

(translated by Luo Jingguo)

## 钻鉧潭西小丘记

得西山后八日，寻山口西北道二百步，又得钻鉧潭。潭西二十五步，当湍而浚者为鱼梁。梁之上有丘焉，生竹树。其石之突怒偃蹇，负土而出，争为奇状者，殆不可数。其嵚然相累而下者，若牛马之饮于溪；其冲然角列而上者，若熊罴之登于山。

丘之小不能一亩，可以笼而有之。问其主，曰："唐氏之弃地，货而不售。"问其价，曰："止四百。"余怜而售之。李深源、元克己时同游，皆大喜，出自意外。即更取器用，铲刈秽草，伐去恶木，烈火而焚之。嘉木立，美竹露，奇石显。由其中以望，则山之高，云之浮，溪之流，鸟兽鱼之遨游，举熙熙然回巧献技，以效兹丘之下。枕席而卧，则清泠之状与目谋，瀯瀯之声与耳谋，悠然而虚者与神谋，渊然而静者与心谋。不匝旬而得异地者二，虽古好事之士，或未能至焉。

噫！以兹丘之胜，致之沣、镐、鄠、杜，则贵游之士争买者，日增千金而愈不可得。今弃是州也，农夫渔父过而陋之，价四百，连岁不能售。而我与深源、克己独喜得之，是其果有遭乎！书于石，所以贺兹丘之遭也。

## Introduction to the Works of Ouyang Xiu

Ouyang Xiu(欧阳修 1007～1072) was the leading poetic figure during the Northern Song. He played an influential role in forming the literary style characteristic of the Song culture. He advocated implementing Han Yu's philosophy and promoting Confucian doctrines in literary writing. In his work, the promotion of moral awareness in society was favored over sentimental lyrical prose. His writing style remained with prose but occasionally he would blend in the lyrical "Pian Ti(骈体)" style so that the vocabulary would stay simple and understandable while the content lingered smooth and serene.

Written in "ancient style" prose, some of Ouyang Xiu's essays dealt with political topics, and his output of literary essays was not many either. Even so he is still recognized as the leading writer of prose of the period. His most renowned works of prose are "Zui Weng Ting Ji"(《醉翁亭记》"The Pavilion of the Drunken Old Man") and "Qiu Sheng Fu"(《秋声赋》"Ode to the Sound of Autumn").

欧阳修

# Selected Works of Ouyang Xiu

## 1. The Pavilion of the Drunken Old Man

Chuzhou is surrounded with mountains. The forests and valleys on the south-west ridge are especially beautiful. Lying in the distance, where the trees grow luxuriantly and gracefully is the Langya Mountain. Six or seven li up the mountain path, a gurgling sound grows clearer and clearer. It is from a spring that falls between two mountains. The spring is called the Wine-Making Spring. The path turns and twists along the mountain ridge, and above the spring rests a pavilion perching aloft like a bird with wings outstretched. This is the Pavilion of the Drunken Old Man. Who built this pavilion? Monk Zhixian, who lived in the mountain. And who furnished it with that name? It was the prefect, who named it after his own alias. The prefect often comes here to drink wine with his friends and he easily gets tipsy after a few cups. Being oldest in age among his companions, he calls himself "the drunken old man". The drinker's heart is not in the cup, but in the mountains and waters. The joy he gets from them is treasured in the heart, and now and then he will express it through wine-drinking.

In the morning, the rising sun disperses the forest mists, and in the evening, the gathering clouds darken the caves and valleys. This shifting from light to darkness is morning and evening m the mountains. In spring, blooming flowers send forth a delicate fragrance; in summer, the fourishing trees afford deep shades; in autumn, the sky is high and crisp, and the frost, snowy white; in winter, the water of the creek recedes and the bare bedrock emerges. These are the mountain scenes in the four seasons. Going to the mountain in the morning and returning home in the evening and enjoying the beauties of the mountain in different seasons is a delight beyond description! Carriers are singing all along the way, and pedestrians are taking rest beneath the trees. Some are shouting from the fore and are answered by others from behind. There are hunchbacked old folks, and children led by their elders. They are people from Chuzhou who have come here in an endless stream. Some are fishing by the creek where the water is deep and the fish are big. The water itself is faintly scented and the wine brewed from it is crystal clear. Upon the prefect's banquet table is a sundry layer of dishes, including the meat of wild beasts and the flavorings of edible mountain herbs. The joy of the feast lies not in the musical accompaniment of strings or flutes, but in winning the games, such as throwing arrows into the vessel, or chess playing. Wine cups and gambling chips lay scattered in blithe disarray. The revelers, now sitting, now standing, cavort madly among themselves. These are the prefect's guests, and the old man with a wizened face and white hair among them, who is half drunk, is none other than the prefect himself.

As dusk falls, one sees shifting shadows scattering in all directions. The prefect is leaving for home, and his guests are following him. The shadows of the trees are deepening, and birds are chirping high and low. The people are going home, leaving the birds free to enjoy themselves. The birds only know their joy in the wooded mountains, but are unaware of what makes the people joyful. The people only know that they are joyful on their excursion with the prefect, but are unaware that the prefect finds his joy in seeing them joyful. He, who enjoys himself with the people when drunk, and records this excursion in writing when sober, is the prefect himself. And who is the prefect? He is Ouyang Xiu of Luling.

(translated by Luo Jingguo)

# 醉翁亭记

　　环滁皆山也。其西南诸峰，林壑尤美。望之蔚然而深秀者，琅琊也。山行六七里，渐闻水声潺潺而泻出于两峰之间者，酿泉也。峰回路转，有亭翼然临于泉上者，醉翁亭也。作亭者谁? 山之僧智仙也。名之者谁? 太守自谓也。太守与客来饮于此，饮少辄醉，而年又最高，故自号曰醉翁也。醉翁之意不在酒，在乎山水之间也。山水之乐，得之心而寓之酒也。

　　若夫日出而林霏开，云归而岩穴暝，晦明变化者，山间之朝暮也。野芳发而幽香，佳木秀而繁阴，风霜高洁，水落而石出者，山间之四时也。朝而往，暮而归，四时之景不同，而乐亦无穷也。至于负者歌于途，行者休于树，前者呼，后者应，伛偻提携，往来而不绝者，滁人游也。临溪而渔，溪深而鱼肥。酿泉为酒，泉香而酒洌；山肴野蔌，杂然而前陈者，太守宴也。宴酣之乐，非丝非竹，射者中，弈者胜，觥筹交错，起坐而喧哗者，众宾欢也。苍颜白发，颓然乎其间者，太守醉也。

已而夕阳在山，人影散乱，太守归而宾客从也。树林阴翳，鸣声上下，游人去而禽鸟乐也。然而禽鸟知山林之乐，而不知人之乐；人知从太守游而乐，而不知太守之乐其乐也。醉能同其乐，醒能述以文者，太守也。太守谓谁？庐陵欧阳修也。

## 2. Ode to the Sound of Autumn

While reading at night, I, Ouyang Zi, am terrified upon hearing a sound coming from the southwest. "How strange it is!" I cry. At first it is like the pattering of the rain and the whistling of the wind, but it quickly becomes violent like the roaring of the surging waves that alarm the sleepers at night and the sudden onslaught of a storm. When it hits something, it becomes a metallic crunch like the clashing of weapons. It is also like the sound of the silent march of an army hurrying to the battlefield, should the mouth of each soldier be gagged and there be no shouting from commands. "What sound is this?" I inquire of the boy servant, "Go and find out." He comes back and says, "The moon and the stars are shining bright and the Milky Way is high up. There is no sound but that of the forest." "How sad it is!" I sigh. "It is the sound of autumn. Is autumn already here? The form of autumn is this. Its color is pale and gloomy, as the smoke has diffused and the clouds have dispersed. Its countenance is clear and bright, as the sky is high and the air is fresh with the sunshining. Its breath is piercingly cold, as it pricks people's skin and bones. Its mood is desolate and bleak, as the mountains and rivers are cheerless and silent. Thus the keynote of the sound of autumn is sad and plaintive, and at times wailing and yelling. Before autumn comes, the verdant grass and the leafy trees vie to surpass each other, and the luxuriant vegetation is delightful to the eyes. When the autumn wind blows, the grass changes its color and the leaves of the trees fall. It is the lingering mighty power of autumn that devastates the lush greenery and brings about this desolation. Autumn is the executioner. It is the season of *yin*. It is a symbol of war and corresponds with the element *jin*. It is the belligerent power of the heaven and earth, aiming to destroy and kill. The law of nature is growth in spring and harvest in autumn. Autumn can also be explained by music. In tone it corresponds with *shang* which means 'west'. In tune it corresponds with yi, which means the month of July.

*Shang* means sadness, as all things feel sad when they grow old. *Yi* means killing, as all things should be killed when they are overly abundant. Alas! Grass and trees have no feelings and they will wither in time. Man is an animal and is the paragon of all creatures. But a myriad of worries sadden his heart, and a myriad of chores exhaust his body. What affects his heart will inevitably consume his energy. And he is often troubled by the thought that he lacks the energy to achieve things that he wants to accomplish, and lacks the wisdom to comprehend things that he wants to understand. Thus his ruddy complexion is withered, like the dried up bark and his black hair turns white, like a starry sky. Since man is not made of metal or stone, how can he compete with grass and trees? Since he is the victim of his own worries, why should he blame the sound of autumn?" The boy has fallen into a doze, and is silent. Only the insects are chirping at the foot of the wall, as if they were sighing with me.

(translated by Luo Jingguo)

## 秋 声 赋

欧阳子方夜读书，闻有声自西南来者，悚然而听之，曰："异哉!"初淅沥以萧飒，忽奔腾而砰湃；如波涛夜惊，风雨骤至。其触于物也，鏦鏦铮铮，金铁皆鸣；又如赴敌之兵，衔枚疾走，不闻号令，但闻人马之行声。

余谓童子："此何声也? 汝出视之。"童子曰："星月皎洁，明河在天，四无人声，声在树间。"

余曰："噫嘻悲哉! 此秋声也。胡为而来哉? 盖夫秋之为状也：其色惨淡，烟霏云敛；其容清明，天高日晶；其气栗冽，砭人肌骨；其意萧条，山川寂寥。故其为声也，凄凄切切，呼号愤发。丰草绿缛而争茂，佳木葱茏而可悦。草拂之而色变，木遭之而叶脱。其所以摧败零落者，乃其一气之余烈。夫秋，刑官也，于时为阴；又兵象也，于行为金。是谓天地之义气，常以肃杀而为心。天之于物，春生秋实。故其在乐也，商声主西方之音，夷则为七月之律。商，伤也，物既老而悲伤；夷，戮也，物过盛而当杀。嗟乎，草木无情，有时飘零。人为动物，惟物之灵，百忧感其心，万事劳其形，有动于中，必摇其精。而况思其力之所不及，忧其智之所不能，宜其渥然丹者为槁木，黟然黑者为星星。奈何以非金石之质，欲与草木而争荣? 念谁为之戕贼，亦何恨乎秋声!"

童子莫对，垂头而睡。但闻四壁虫声唧唧，如助余之叹息。

## Further Readings

### 1. The First Memorial to the King before Setting off for War
Zhuge Liang

Your humble servant Liang begs to say:

Our late king passed away before the great undertaking founded by him was half accomplished. Now the country is divided into three kingdoms. Yizhou is drained of its manpower and resources. This is a critical juncture of life or death for our country. Bearing the late king's special favor in hearts, the officials at court who guard Your Majesty dare not slacken in their vigilance and the devoted officers and soldiers at the front are fighting bravely disregarding their personal safety. They are now repaying to Your Majesty what they have received from the late king. It is advisable that Your Majesty should listen extensively to the counsels of officials in order to carry on the late king's lofty virtues, and heighten the morale of people with high aspirations. It is injudicious that Your Majesty should unduly humble yourself, and use metaphors with distorted meanings, lest you should block the way of sincere admonition. The imperial court and the Prime Minister's Office are an integral whole. There should be impartiality in meting out rewards and punishments to officials from either administration. For both those who are treacherous and violate the law and those who are loyal and do some good deed, the same legally appointed officials should pass decision on how to punish or reward. This will make plain the equality and sagaciousness of Your Majesty's rule. There should be neither prejudice nor partiality in Your Majesty's attitude towards the officials inside and outside the court for fear that different laws be put into practice.

*Shizhong* Guo Youzhi and Fei Wei as well as *Shilang* Dong Yun are kind and honest men with a strong sense of loyalty. The late king appointed them for your sake, and I respectfully opine that all political affairs at court, regardless of magnitude, be first subjected to their inquiry before actions are taken. In this way can errors be amended, negligence avoided, and greater results attained. General Xiang

Chong is well versed in military affairs and is kind and just by nature. After evaluating his performance on a trial basis, the late king praised his talent and ability. That is why officials have elected him to be commander-in-chief. I humbly suggest that military concerns, regardless of weight, be first met with his consultation. In this way will there be harmony among the troops, and men both capable and incapable will each find his proper place in the camp. To be close to the virtuous and able officials and keep away from the vile and mean persons. That was the reason that the Western Han Dynasty was prosperous. To be close to the vile and mean persons and keep away from the virtuous and able officials. That was the reason that the Eastern Han Dynasty collapsed. When the late king was alive and talked with me about these historical lessons, he used to heave a sigh in detestation for Emperor Huan and Emperor Ling. *Shizhong*, *shangshu*, *zhangshi* and *canjun* are faithful, upright, and ready to lay down their lives for honor and fidelity. As your humble servant, I hope that Your Majesty will retain close ties to them and trust them. Then can the prosperity of the Han Dynasty be soon realized.

I was originally a commoner who had to wear clothes made of hemp, and tilled land in Nanyang. I merely managed to survive in times of turbulence and had no intention of seeking fame and position from princes. With an utter disregard of my low social status and meager fund of knowledge, the late king condescended to visit me at my thatched cottage three times to consult me about the current events of the country. I felt so grateful that I promised to serve him. Soon afterwards we suffered a military defeat. Twenty-one years have passed since I received my assignment at the time of the setback and was dispatched as an envoy at the moment of crisis. The late king knew of my prudence, and entrusted me on his deathbed with the duty of assisting Your Majesty in governing the country. Since then I have been worrying and sighing night and day lest I should do harm to the late king's illustrious fame if I fail to be effective. I was thus impelled to lead an army across the Lu River in May and went deep into the barren district. Now the whole south is under our rule and we have plenty of fighters and armaments. It is time to reward our army men and lead them northward to conquer the Central Plains. Although I am inferior in ability like a worn out horse or a blunt knife, I would do my utmost to root out treacherous evildoers, rejuvenate the Han Dynasty, and move the capital back to the old city. I owe this to the late king and wish to demonstrate my loyalty to Your Majesty.

As for government affairs such as the augmentation or repeal of certain measures, or the broadening of the way to receive exhortations, they are the duties of Guo Youzhi, Fei Wei, and Dong Yun. I hope Your Majesty would delegate to me the task of punishing the traitors and rejuvenating the Han Dynasty. If I should fail to achieve this, please punish me so as to console the soul of the departed king. If Youzhi, Wei, and Yun fail to gather exhortations for the fostering of virtues, they should be held responsible for their negligence. Your Majesty should also make the most of your resources to solicit opinions on governing a country, to judge judiciously and accept good advices, and always bear in mind the imperial edict issued by the late king prior to his death. If this can be achieved, you will have my extreme gratitude.

I will be journeying far, and my eyes are full of tears in writing this memorial upon my departure. I can hardly express what else I should say.

(translated by Luo Jingguo)

## 前 出 师 表
### 诸葛亮

臣亮言：先帝创业未半，而中道崩殂。

今天下三分，益州疲弊，此诚危急存亡之秋也。然侍卫之臣不懈于内，忠志之士忘身于外者，盖追先帝之殊遇，欲报之于陛下也。诚宜开张圣听，以光先帝遗德，恢弘志士之气；不宜妄自菲薄，引喻失义，以塞忠谏之路也。宫中府中，俱为一体；陟罚臧否，不宜异同；若有作奸犯科及为忠善者，宜付有司论其刑赏，以昭陛下平明之理；不宜偏私，使内外异法也。

侍中、侍郎郭攸之、费祎、董允等，此皆良实，志虑忠纯，是以先帝简拔以遗陛下。愚以为宫中之事，事无大小，悉以咨之，然后施行，必能裨补阙漏，有所广益。将军向宠，性行淑均，晓畅军事，试用于昔日，先帝称之曰能，是以众议举宠为督。愚以为营中之事，事无大小，悉以咨之，必能使行阵和睦，优劣得所。亲贤臣，远小人，此先汉所以兴隆也；亲小人，远贤臣，此后汉所以倾颓也。先帝在时，每与臣论此事，未尝不叹息痛恨于桓、灵也。侍中、尚书、长史、参军，此悉贞良死节之臣，愿陛下亲之信之，则汉室之隆，可计日而待也。

中国文学选读

臣本布衣，躬耕于南阳，苟全性命于乱世，不求闻达于诸侯。先帝不以臣卑鄙，猥自枉屈，三顾臣于草庐之中，咨臣以当世之事，由是感激，遂许先帝以驱驰。后值倾覆，受任于败军之际，奉命于危难之间，尔来二十有一年矣。先帝知臣谨慎，故临崩寄臣以大事也。受命以来，夙夜忧叹，恐托付不效，以伤先帝之明，故五月渡泸，深入不毛。今南方已定，兵甲已足，当奖率三军，北定中原，庶竭驽钝，攘除奸凶，兴复汉室，还于旧都。此臣所以报先帝，而忠陛下之职分也。

至于斟酌损益，进尽忠言，则攸之、祎、允之任也。愿陛下托臣以讨贼兴复之效，不效则治臣之罪，以告先帝之灵。若无兴德之言，则责攸之、祎、允等之慢，以彰其咎。陛下亦宜自谋，以咨诹善道，察纳雅言，深追先帝遗诏。臣不胜受恩感激。

今当远离，临表涕泣，不知所云。

## 2. On the Teacher

### Han Yu

In ancient times those who wanted to learn would seek out a teacher, one who could propagate the doctrine, impart professional knowledge, and resolve doubts. Since no one is born omniscient, who can claim to have no doubts? If one has doubts and is not willing to learn from a teacher, his doubts will never be resolved. Anyone who was born before me and learned the doctrine before me is my teacher. Anyone who was born after me and learned the doctrine before me is also my teacher. Since what I desire to learn is the doctrine, why should I care whether he was born before or after me? Therefore, it does not matter whether a person is high or low in position, young or old in age. Where there is the doctrine, there is my teacher.

Alas! The tradition of learning from the teacher has long been neglected. Thus it is difficult to find a person without any doubts at all. Ancient sages, who far surpassed us, even learned from their teachers. People today, who are far inferior to them, regard learning from the teacher as a disgrace. Thus, wise men become wiser and unlearned men become more foolish. This explains what makes a wise man and what makes a foolish man. It is absurd that a person would choose a teacher for his son out of his love for the child, and yet refuse to learn from the teacher himself, thinking it a disgrace to do so. The teacher of his son teaches the child only reading and punctuation, which is not propagating the doctrine or resolving doubts as the aforementioned. I don't think it wise to learn from the teacher when one does not know how to punctuate, but not to learn when one has doubts unresolved. It is folly to learn in small matters, but neglect the big ones. Even medicine men, musicians and handicraftsmen do not think it disgraceful to learn from each other. When one of the literati calls another man his "teacher" and himself his "student", people will get together and invariably laugh at him. If you ask them why they are laughing, they will say that since he is almost of the same age and as erudite as another man, it would be degrading for him to call the other man "teacher", if the other man's social rank is lower than his; and it would be flattering if the other man's social rank is higher. Alas! It is clear that the tradition of learning from the teacher can no longer be restored. Medicine men, musicians and handicraftsmen are despised by the gentlemen. How strange it is that gentlemen are less wise than these people!

The ancient sages did not limit themselves to particular teachers. Confucius had learned from people like Tanzi, Changhong, Shixiang and Laodan, who were not as virtuous and talented as Confucius. Confucius said, "If three men are walking together, one of them is bound to be good enough to be my teacher." A student is not necessarily inferior to his teacher, nor does a teacher necessarily be more virtuous and talented than his student. The real fact is that one might have learned the doctrine earlier than the other, or might be a master in his own special field.

Pan, the son of Li's family, who is only seventeen years old, but loves to study Chinese classics of the Qin and Han dynasties, and masters the six classics and their annotations. He does not follow conventions and is willing to learn from me. I appreciate his ability to act in accordance with the old tradition of learning. Therefore I dedicate this piece to him.

(translated by Luo Jingguo)

# 师　说
## 韩　愈

　　古之学者必有师。师者，所以传道受业解惑也。人非生而知之者，孰能无惑？惑而不从师，其为惑也，终不解矣。生乎吾前，其闻道也固先乎吾，吾从而师之；生乎吾后，其闻道也亦先乎吾，吾从而师之。吾师道也，夫庸知其年之先后生于吾乎？是故无贵无贱，无长无少，道之所存，师之所存也。

　　嗟乎！师道之不传也久矣！欲人之无惑也难矣！古之圣人，其出人也远矣，犹且从师而问焉；今之众人，其下圣人也亦远矣，而耻学于师。是故圣益圣，愚益愚。圣人之所以为圣，愚人之所以为愚，其皆出于此乎？爱其子，择师而教之；于其身也，则耻师焉，惑矣。彼童子之师，授之书而习其句读者，非吾所谓传其道解其惑者也。句读之不知，惑之不解，或师焉，或不焉，小学而大遗，吾未见其明也。巫医乐师百工之人，不耻相师。士大夫之族，曰师曰弟子云者，则群聚而笑之。问之，则曰："彼与彼年相若也，道相似也。位卑则足羞，官盛则近谀。"呜呼！师道之不复，可知矣。巫医乐师百工之人，君子不齿，今其智乃反不能及，其可怪也欤！

　　圣人无常师。孔子师郯子、苌弘、师襄、老聃。郯子之徒，其贤不及孔子。孔子曰："三人行，则必有我师。"是故弟子不必不如师，师不必贤于弟子，闻道有先后，术业有专攻，如是而已。

　　李氏子蟠，年十七，好古文，六艺经传皆通习之，不拘于时，学于余。余嘉其能行古道，作《师说》以贻之。


## 3. The First Ode on the Red Cliff
## Su Shi

It was on the sixteenth of the seventh month of the lunar calendar, in the autumn of the year of Renxu, that my friends and I went boating along the foot of the Red Cliff. A light breeze was blowing gently without ruffling the calm water. Wine cup in hand, I toasted my companions and recited the first verse of "The Moon Rises" from The Book of Songs. Presently the moon rose above the eastern mountain, where it hung between the Dipper and the Cowherd, whilst the river, in a white mist, merged with the moonlit sky. I let the boat drift freely as it continued its motion across the vast expanse of the river. How mighty this was! I felt like one windblown over infinite waves, not knowing where to land. And how light-hearted I was! I was beyond worldly cares, and, like a fairy, was taking flight to the sky.

We drank our wine in good cheer. I beat a rhythm on the side of the boat and began to sing, "Ah! Oars made of cinnamon wood and rudder made of magnolia wood! You are striking the crystal clear water lit by the bright moon and pushing our boat ahead against the shimmering currents. How deep my feelings are, since the person I most long for is far away on the other side of the earth." The notes of a bamboo flute in the hands of my friend accompanied my singing. The flute sounded melancholy, like someone complaining, or yearning, or weeping, or lamenting. The sound persisted long in the air as if it were an endless thin thread of silk. It discomfited the sleeping dragon that lay hidden under the water and made the widow on a lonely boat cry. I could not help but be sentimental. Straightening my clothes and my posture, I asked the flute player, "Why does the flute sound so sad?"

"'The moon is bright, the few stars are scattered and the crows fly southward,'" he quoted. "Weren't these the words of Cao Mengde? The Red Cliff faces Xiaokou in the west and Wuchang in the east and is embraced by mountains and waters. All around is a sea of greenery. Is this not the place where Cao Mengde was defeated by Zhou Yu? After Cao Mengde had seized Jinzhou and taken Jiangling, he led a naval fleet of warships linked together extending as far as one thousand lid and headed eastward down the river. His banners and pennants blotted out the sky. Holding a spear in hand, he recited poems, and sprinkled wine into the river as sacrifice. What a hero he was in his time! But where is he now? Now you and I are catching fish in the river and cutting firewood on the sandbank, with fish, prawns, and deer as company. We row a small boat on the water and drink wine from the gourd. We are like mayflies enjoying a flicker of life in this world, and as infinitesimal as a grain in the vast sea. I am sorry for the brevity of our existence and I envy the boundlessness of the Yangtze River. I wish to cling to a flying fairy and roam about with her in the sky and to be everlasting with the moon as my companion. I know very well that this dream of mine cannot be realized easily; therefore, I can only express my sorrow by playing the flute in the chilly autumn wind. "

To this lament, I dissented, "Do you know of the water and the moon? The river flows endlessly, day and night, but it seems motionless. The moon waxes and wanes, yet it never grows bigger or smaller. Therefore, seen through the eyes of change, everything in this world changes in an instant shorter than the twinkling of an eye. But when seen through the eyes of stability, everything in this world, including humanity, is eternal. Why then should we be envious of things? Everything in the universe has its owner. I will not take even a tiny bit if it does not belong to me. As to the gentle breeze on the river and the bright moon over the mountains, they are a harmonious sound to our ears if we listen to them and a pleasing sight to our eyes if we watch them. No one can prevent us from possessing them. Their supply is infinite for our use. They are an inexhaustible treasure given to us by Nature, which I may enjoy with you. "

My friends, pleased with these words, smiled happily. We rinsed the cups and helped ourselves to more wine. When the dishes and fruit had been eaten, the empty wine cups and plates were scattered about in a mess. We then reclined against one another in the boat, without knowing that dawn was breaking.

(translated by Luo Jingguo)

## 前赤壁赋
### 苏　轼

　　壬戌之秋，七月既望，苏子与客泛舟，游于赤壁之下。清风徐来，水波不兴。举酒属客，诵明月之诗，歌窈窕之章。少焉，月出于东山之上，徘徊于斗牛之间。白露横江，水光接天。纵一苇之所如，凌万顷之茫然。浩浩乎如冯虚御风，而不知其所止；飘飘乎如遗世独立，羽化而登仙。

　　于是饮酒乐甚，扣舷而歌之。歌曰："桂棹兮兰桨，击空明兮溯流光。渺渺兮予怀，望美人兮天一方。"客有吹洞箫者，倚歌而和之。其声呜呜然，如怨如慕，如泣如诉；余音袅袅，不绝如缕。舞幽壑之潜蛟，泣孤舟之嫠妇。

　　苏子愀然，正襟危坐，而问客曰："何为其然也？"客曰："'月明星稀，乌鹊南飞。'此非曹孟德之诗乎？西望夏口，东望武昌，山川相缪，郁乎苍苍，此非孟德之困于周郎者乎？方其破荆州，下江陵，顺流而东也，舳舻千里，旌旗蔽空，酾

《赤壁赋》插图

酒临江，横槊赋诗，固一世之雄也；而今安在哉！况吾与子渔樵于江渚之上，侣鱼虾而友麋鹿，驾一叶之扁舟，举匏樽以相属。寄蜉蝣于天地，渺沧海之一粟。哀吾生之须臾，羡长江之无穷。挟飞仙以遨游，抱明月而长终。知不可乎骤得，托遗响于悲风。"

苏子曰："客亦知夫水与月乎？逝者如斯，而未尝往也；盈虚者如彼，而卒莫消长也。盖将自其变者而观之，则天地曾不能以一瞬；自其不变者而观之，则物与我皆无尽也，而又何羡乎？且夫天地之间，物各有主，苟非吾之所有，虽一毫而莫取。惟江上之清风，与山间之明月，耳得之而为声，目遇之而成色，取之无禁，用之不竭。是造物者之无尽藏也，而吾与子之所共适。"

客喜而笑，洗盏更酌。肴核既尽，杯盘狼藉。相与枕藉乎舟中，不知东方之既白。

## Topics for Discussion

1. Why did Han Yu and Liu Zongyuan launch the "Ancient Prose Movement"?

2. What differences are there between Tang-Song prose and Pre-Qin prose?

3. What themes are there in Tang-Song travel landscape writing?

4. Among the pieces of prose presented, which is your favorite, and why?

Chapter Seven

# Drama in the Yuan Dynasty

## General Description

The Yuan Dynasty(元朝 1271~1368) was the first government of China where the rulers came from a Non-Han people. The Mongolian approach to governing was practical, and business was encouraged. As a result, industry and commerce developed, leading to economic and cultural prosperity. Unfortunately, during the Yuan, intellectual status was less valued and respected than it had been in the past. Consequently, instead of pursuing careers as court officials, the educated focused more on the literary arts popular among the common people. The profile of drama was raised and it outshone the other literary art forms to become the primary icon of Yuan literature. The gradual transformation from traditional literary poetry to drama and narrative fiction occurred during this time, establishing for itself a dominant position.

Yuan Qu(元曲) is also known as Yuan Za Ju(元杂剧 Yuan Drama). The basic structure of each play consisted of four acts(折 Zhe) and an opening piece(楔子 Xie Zi). Each act had its own plot and musical melody. In the opening piece the storylines were explained for the audiences.

Yuan Za Ju is similar to ancient Greek plays in that there is a combination of performing art and presentations. Furthermore Yuan Za Ju is somewhat closer to an opera performance, so that while there are dialogues between characters, the essential core of the play is set in the singing parts. Therefore art critics would evaluate not only the plot of the play but would also attach great importance to the lyrics, looking for lyrics that were elegantly written and gracefully presented. Most of the lyrics would rhyme and would be expressively presented. Dialogues were written in plain oral conversation like in a modern play.

The key characters in Yuan Za Ju included Dan(旦 a female role), Mo(末 a male role) and Jing(净 a male, often a disreputable role).

In the following chapter plays of the authors Guan Hanqing and Wang Shifu are presented. The supplementary work, *Mu Dan Ting* (《牡丹亭》*The Peony Pavilion*), is written by the playwright Tang Xianzu from the Ming Dynasty.

中国文学选读

## Introduction to *Dou E Yuan*

Guan Hanqing(关汉卿 1225～1300？) was born in the Jin Dynasty(金朝) and later lived in the Yuan Dynasty, but details of most of his life remain unclear. He was the pioneering Chinese playwright of Yuan Za Ju. He wrote many outstanding plays and was addressed as the leading dramatist of the Yuan Dynasty.

Guan Hanqing created 66 repertoires, with the most famous one, *Dou E Yuan* (*The Injustice to Dou E*, also known as *Snow in Midsummer*), having 18 versions of the script in existence. He was very good at creating a complicated plot and infusing it with a dramatic atmosphere, in addition to adding romantic expression with clear narratives. The structure of his plays was straightforward and understandable, yet the action could shift rapidly and vibrantly. He did not pay a lot of attention to polishing the detail in dialogues, but rather focused on building strong characters that reflected the reality of life in the society at the time.

关汉卿

*Dou E Yuan*(《窦娥冤》) is a famous classical tragedy about a woman named Dou E who suffers a miscarriage of justice, the truth of which is only uncovered after she has been put to death.

A poor intellectual named Dou Tianzhang(窦天章) has no money to pay for a trip to attend an official exam in the capital city. Reluctantly, he sells his daughter to the Cai family as a child bride to raise money for the trip. After the marriage, Dou E's husband passes away and she is left dependent on her mother-in-law. One day her mother-in-law, out collecting some money owed to her, encounters the rogue Zhang and his son Lü'er(张驴儿). Zhang Lü'er tries to force Dou E to marry him but she refuses. So he tries to poison her mother-in-law but by accident Zhang's father takes the poison and dies. Zhang Lü'er accuses Dou E of murdering his father.

A court official tortures both the mother-in-law and Dou E to force them to admit to the murder. In order to spare her mother-in-law further torture, Dou E admits guilt and is sentenced to death. Before the sentence is carried out, Dou E swears an oath to prove her innocence. She swears that after her death three strange events will occur: dripping blood on white ribbons, snow in the middle of summer, and a three-year drought. All of these then occur after her death. Three years later, her father Dou Tianzhang, now a government official, was sent to this city as an inspection official. He encounters the ghost of his daughter Dou E who requests that he review the case. He does and discovers the truth. He brings justice by proving his daughter's innocence at the end of the story.

*Dou E Yuan* is a characteristic and powerful tragedy that, through the perspective of a miscarriage of justice, reveals the darkness in society but also gives us the character of a kind-hearted yet unfortunate female with rebellious spirit.

中国文学选读

# Selection from *Dou E Yuan*

## Snow in Midsummer or Dou E Yuan
## Act 3

(Enter the officer in charge.)

**OFFICER:** I am the officer in charge of executions. Today we are putting a criminal to death. We must stand guard at the end of the road, to see that no one comes through.

(Enter the Attendants. They beat the drum and the gong three times; then the executioner enters, sharpens his sword and waves a flag. Dou E is led on in a cangue. The gong and drum are beaten.)

**EXECUTIONER:** Get a move on! Let no one pass this way.

**DOU E:**

*Though no fault of mine I am called a criminal,*

*And condemned to be beheaded—*

*I cry out to Heaven and Earth of this injustice!*

*I reproach both Earth and Heaven*

*For they would not save me.*

*The sun and moon give light by day and by night,*

*Mountains and rivers watch over the world of men,*

*Yet Heaven cannot tell the innocent from the guilty;*

*And confuses the wicked with the good!*

*The good are poor and die before their time;*

*The wicked are rich, and live to a great old age.*

*The gods are afraid of the mighty and bully the weak;*

*They let evil take its course.*

*Ah, Earth! You will not distinguish good from bad,*

*And, Heaven! You let me suffer this injustice!*

*Tears pour down my cheeks in vain!*

**EXECUTIONER**: Get a move on! We are late.

**DOU E**:

*The cangue round my neck makes me stagger this way and that,*

*And I'm jostled backward and forward by the crowd.*

*Will you do me a favor, brother?*

**EXECUTIONER**: What do you want?

**DOU E**:

*If you take me the front way, I shall bear you a grudge;*

*If you take me the back way, I shall die content.*

*Please do not think me wilful!*

**EXECUTIONER**: Now that you're going to the execution ground, are there any relatives you want to see?

**DOU E**: I am going to die. What relatives do I need?

**EXECUTIONER**: Why did you ask me just now to take you the back way?

**DOU E**:

*Please don't go by the front street, brother,*

*But take me by the back street.*

*The other way my mother-in-low might see me.*

**EXECUTIONER**: You can't escape death, so why worry if she sees you?

**DOU E**: If my mother-in-law were to see me in chains being led to the execution ground—

*She would burst with indignation!*

*She would burst with indignation!*

*Please grant me this comfort, brother, before I die!*

(Enter Mistress Cai.)

**MRS. CAI**: Ah, Heaven! Isn't that my daughter-in-law? This will be the death of me!

**EXECUTIONER**: Stand back, old woman!

**DOU E**: Let her come closer so that I can say a few words to her.

**EXECUTIOER**: Hey, old woman! Come here. Your daughter-in-law wants to speak to you.

**MRS. CAI:** Poor child! This will be the death of me!

**DOU E:** Mother, when you were unwell and asked for mutton tripe soup, I prepared some for you. Donkey Zhang made me fetch more salt and vinegar so that he could poison the soup, and then told me to give it to you. He didn't know his old man would drink it. Donkey Zhang poisoned the soup to kill you, so that he could force me to be his wife. He never thought his father would die instead. To take revenge, he dragged me to court. Because I didn't want you to suffer, I had to confess to murder, and now I am going to be killed. In future, mother, if you have gruel to spare, give me half a bowl; and if you have paper money to spare, burn some for me, for sake of your dead son!

*Take pity on one who is dying an unjust death;*

*Take pity on one whose head will be struck from her body;*

*Take pity on one who has worked with you in your home;*

*Take pity on one who has neither mother nor father;*

*Take pity on one who has served you all these years;*

*And at festivals offer my spirit a bowl of cold gruel.*

**MRS. CAI**(weeping):Don't worry. Ah, this will be the death of me!

**DOU E:**

*Burn some paper coins to my headless corpse,*

*For the sake of your dead son.*

*We wail and complain to Heaven:*

*There is no justice! Dou E is wrongly slain!*

**EXECUTIONER:** Now then, old woman, stand back! The time has come.

(Dou E kneels and the Executioner removes the cangue from her neck.)

**DOU E:** I want to say three things, officer. If you will let me, I shall die content. I want a clean mat and a white silk streamer twelve feet long to hang on the flag-pole. When the sword strikes off my head, not a drop of my warm blood will stain the ground. It will all fly up instead to the white silk streamer. This is the hottest time of summer, sir. If injustice has indeed been done, three feet of snow will cover my dead body. Then this district will suffer from drought for three whole years.

**EXECUTIONER**: Be quiet! What a thing to say!

(The Executioner waves his flag. )

**DOU E**:

*A dumb woman was blamed for poisoning herself,*

*A buffalo is whipped while it toils for its master.*

**EXECUTIONER**: Why is it suddenly so overcast? It is snowing!

(He prays to Heaven. )

**DOU E**:

*Once Zou Yan caused frost to appear;*

*Now snow will show the injustice done to me!*

(The Executioner beheads her, and the Attendant sees to her body. )

**EXECUTIONER**: A fine stroke! Now let us go and have a drink.

(The Attendants assent, and carry the body off. )

(translated by Yang Xianyi and Gladys Yang)

## 窦娥冤　第三折

（外扮监斩官上，云）

下官监斩官是也。今日处决犯人，着做公的把住巷口，休放往来人闲走。

（净扮公人，鼓三通，锣三下科，刽子磨旗、提刀、押正旦带枷上，刽子云）

行动些，行动些，监斩官去法场上多时了。

（正旦唱）

【正宫端正好】没来由犯王法，不提防遭刑宪，叫声屈动地惊天。顷刻间游魂先赴森罗殿，怎不将天地也生埋怨。

【滚绣球】有日月朝暮悬，有鬼神掌着生死权。天地也，只合把清浊分辨，可怎生糊突了盗跖颜渊：为善的受贫穷更命短，造恶的享富贵又寿延。天地也，做得个怕硬欺软，却原来也这般顺水推船。地也，你不分好歹何为地？天也，你错勘贤愚枉做天！哎，只落得两泪涟涟。（刽子云）快行动些，误了时辰也。

（正旦唱）

【倘秀才】则被这枷扭的我左侧右偏，人拥的我前合后偃。我窦娥向哥哥行有句言。

（刽子云）你有甚么话说？

（正旦唱）前街里去心怀恨，后街里去死无冤，休推辞路远。

（刽子云）你如今到法场上面，有甚么亲眷要见的，可教他过来，见你一面也好。

（正旦唱）

【叨叨令】可怜我孤身只影无亲眷，则落的吞声忍气空嗟怨。

（刽子云）难道你爷娘家也没的？

（正旦云）止有个爹爹，十三年前上朝取应去了，至今杳无音信。

（唱）早已是十年多不睹爹爹面。

（刽子云）你适才要我往后街里去，是什么主意？

（正旦唱）怕则怕前街里被我婆婆见。

（刽子云）你的性命也顾不得，怕他见怎的？

《窦娥冤》插图

（正旦云）俺婆婆若见我披枷带锁赴法场餐刀去呵，

（唱）枉将他气杀也么哥，枉将他气杀也么哥。告哥哥，临危好与人行方便。

（卜儿哭上科，云）天哪，兀的不是我媳妇儿！

（刽子云）婆子靠后。

（正旦云）既是俺婆婆来了，叫他来，待我嘱付他几句话咱。

（刽子云）那婆子，近前来，你媳妇要嘱付你话哩。

（卜儿云）孩儿，痛杀我也！

（正旦唱）婆婆，那张驴儿把毒药放在羊肚儿汤里，实指望药死了你，要霸占我为妻。不想婆婆让与他老子吃，倒把他老子药死了。我怕连累婆婆，屈招了药死公公，今日赴法场典刑。婆婆，此后遇着冬时年节，月一十五，有浆不了的浆水饭，澆半碗儿与我吃；烧不了的纸钱，与窦娥烧一陌儿，则是看你死的孩儿面上。

（唱）

【快活三】念窦娥葫芦提当罪愆，念窦娥身首不完全，念窦娥从前已往干家缘；婆婆也，你只看窦娥少爷无娘面。

【鲍老儿】念窦娥服侍婆婆这几年，遇时节将碗凉浆奠；你去那受刑法尸骸上烈些纸钱，只当把你亡化的孩儿荐。

（卜儿哭科，云）孩儿放心，这个老身都记得。天哪，兀的不痛杀我也。

（正旦唱）婆婆也，再也不要啼啼哭哭，烦烦恼恼，怨气冲天。这都是我做窦娥的没时没运，不明不暗，负屈衔冤。

（刽子做喝科，云）兀那婆子靠后，时辰到了也。

（正旦跪科）

（刽子开枷科）

（正旦云）窦娥告监斩大人，有一事肯依窦娥，便死而无怨。

（监斩官云）你有什么事？你说。

（正旦云）要一领净席，等我窦娥站立，又要丈二白练，挂在旗枪上。若是我窦娥委实冤枉，刀过处头落，一腔热血休半点儿沾在地下，都飞在白练上者。

（监斩官云）这个就依你，打甚么不紧。

（刽子做取席科，站科，又取白练挂旗上科）

（正旦唱）

【耍孩儿】不是我窦娥罚下这等无头愿，委实的冤情不浅。若没些儿灵圣与世人传，也不见得湛湛青天。我不要半星热血红尘洒，都只在八尺旗枪素练悬。等他四下里皆瞧见，这就是咱苌弘化碧，望帝啼鹃。

（刽子云）你还有甚的说话，此时不对监斩大人说，几时说那？

（正旦再跪科，云）大人，如今是三伏天道，若窦娥委实冤枉，身死之后，天降三尺瑞雪，遮掩了窦娥尸首。

（监斩官云）这等三伏天道，你便有冲天的怨气，也召不得一片雪来，可不胡说！

（正旦唱）

【二煞】你道是暑气暄，不是那下雪天；岂不闻飞霜六月因邹衍？若果有一腔怨气喷如火，定要感得六出冰花滚似锦，免着我尸骸现；要什么素车白马，断送出古陌荒阡？

（正旦再跪科，云）大人，我窦娥死的委实冤枉，从今以后，着这楚州亢旱三年。

（监斩官云）打嘴！那有这等说话！

（正旦唱）

【一煞】你道是天公不可期，人心不可怜，不知皇天也肯从人愿。做甚么三年不见甘霖降？也只为东海曾经孝妇冤。如今轮到你山阳县，这都是官吏每无心正法，使百姓有口难言。

（刽子做磨旗科，云）怎么这一会儿天色阴了也？

（内做风科，刽子云）好冷风也！

（正旦唱）

【煞尾】浮云为我阴，悲风为我旋，三桩儿誓愿明题遍。

（做哭科，云）婆婆也，直等待雪飞六月，亢旱三年呵，

（唱）那其间才把你个屈死的冤魂这窦娥显。

（刽子做开刀，正旦倒科）

（监斩官惊云）呀，真个下雪了，有这等异事！

（刽子云）我也道平日杀人，满地都是鲜血。这个窦娥的血，都飞在那丈二白练上，并无半点落地，委实奇怪。

（监斩官云）这死罪必有冤枉，早两桩儿应验了，不知亢旱三年的说话，准也不准？且看后来如何。左右，也不必等待雪晴，便与我抬他尸首，还了那蔡婆婆去罢。

（众应科，抬尸下）

# Introduction to *the Western Chamber*

The playwright Wang Shifu(王实甫 1230~1307? ) lived around the same time as Guan Hanqing. He was a perceptive chronicler of ordinary life, especially when it came to describing romantic affairs. Among the fourteen plays that he wrote, *Xi Xiang Ji* (《西厢记》 *The Western Chamber* ) was his most recognized masterpiece. As soon as the play hit the stage it was an immediate sensation and became an audience favorite. The critics commented that "*The Western Chamber* is the greatest play ever". In the history of drama many of the themes chosen by playwrights have been the ones that have involved romance with a happy ending. *The Western Chamber* is a play which fulfills these expectations and has become a model for all romantically themed plays.

*The Western Chamber* is based on the story *Biography of Ying-ying* (《莺莺传》) which was written during the Tang Dynasty. The author re-worked the story in order to meet the requirements of a play. The play was written on a larger scale, with twenty-one acts in five volumes. With a complicated plot and graceful language the author combined classic poetry with vivid dialogue to portray this authentic, romantic love story.

The story begins with the death of Cui, a high ranking official. His wife and nineteen-year-old daughter, Yingying(莺莺), accompany his coffin home for burial. On the journey they are trapped and have to stay at the Puji Temple(普济寺). While residing at the temple Yingying encounters a poor young man named Zhang Sheng(张生) whose parents have both passed away. Zhang, residing temporarily in the western chamber of the Puji Temple, is on his way to the capital city to attend the official exams. At first sight he falls in love with Yingying, who had already been betrothed to someone by her father when she was young.

There is a criminal Sun Feihu(孙飞虎) who hears of Yingying's beauty and gathers his gang at Puji Temple to try to force Yingying to become his wife. At the critical moment, Yingying's mother announces that she will promise her daughter's hand in marriage to anyone who can defeat the gangsters. The young man Zhang, with help from his friends, rescues Yingying from the gangsters and proposes marriage. But Yingying's mother regrets her promise and refuses to keep it, using the excuse that Yingying had been promised to someone else. She only agrees to offer Yingying as Zhang's sister. This makes the young couple suffer terribly. With the help of Yingying's maid，Hongniang(红娘)，Zhang and Yingying secretly meet each other in the western chamber nightly until the secret encounters are discovered by her mother. With persuading from Hongniang and Yingying's determination, her mother realizes that she has no reason not to keep her original promise and agrees to their marriage，but on the condition that Zhang has to first pass his official exam and build a career.

At the end of the story，Yingying bids farewell to her lover and Zhang eventually returns with the rank of an official and the two of them live happily ever after.

《西厢记》插图

# Selection from *The Western Chamber*

## The Western Chamber
## Act 3 scene 2

**Yingying enters and says:** Rose may come back at any moment. As I got up earlier than usual, I will go again to sleep for a little. (She sleeps.)

**Rose enters and says:** My young mistress ordered me to see Master Zhang and I have brought her a letter. Why don't I hear any sound of her? Has she gone to sleep again? I must go in and see.

**She sings to the tune of *PINK BUTTERFLY*:**

> *The curtains hang around*
>
> *The windows whence a fragrance of lily is spread;*
>
> *My copper rings resound*
>
> *When I open the doors painted red.*
>
> *On crimson stand with golden leaf-like plate the light*
>
> *Of silver candle is still bright.*
>
> *I gently draw aside the curtain on her bed*
>
> *And lift up the silk valance red*
>
> *So as to have a peep*
>
> *At her who's still asleep.*

**(Tune: *INTOXICATED VERNAL WIND*)**

> *I see her slanting hairpin of jade*
>
> *And her cloud of hair unmade.*
>
> *Although the sun is high in the sky,*
>
> *She has not opened her bright eye.*
>
> *How lazy she appears!*

(Yingying rises, stretches herself and sighs deeply.)

> *Sitting up and scratching her ears,*
>
> *She heaves a deep, deep sigh.*

中国文学选读

**Rose says:** In such a case, how can I give her the letter? It would be better to put it in her toilet case and let her find it herself. (She puts it there.) (Yingying makes her toilet. Rose casts a furtive glance.)

**Rose sings to the tune of UNIVERSAL JOY:**

> *Faded her rouge of previous night,*
>
> *Down falls the black cloud of her hair.*
>
> *She puts upon her face a powder light*
>
> *And arranges her locks without much care.*
>
> *She takes the letter then*
>
> *And reads it over and over again*
>
> *Without indeed a sign of weariness and pain.*
>
> *Suddenly now*
>
> *Displeased, she knits her brow*
>
> *And bends her head,*
>
> *With anger her fair face turns red.*

**Rose, revealing her sentiment by dumb show, says:** Alas! The game is up.

**Yingying says in anger:** Come here. Rose!

**Rose says:** Yes.

**Yingying says:** Where has this come from. Rose? I am the daughter of the late prime minister. Who dare to make fun of me with such a letter as this? When have I been used to reading such a thing? I shall tell my mother so that she may give you, little imp, a good thrashing on the bottom.

**Rose says:** It was you who sent me to him and he who sent me back with the letter. If you had not sent me to him, how could I have dared to ask him for it? Besides, I can not read. How could I know what he has written?

**She sings to the tune of HAPPY THREE:**

> *The fault is yours, it is quite clear.*
>
> *Why should you shift on me the blame, my dear?*
>
> *You want to make me suffer for what you have done.*
>
> *If you were not, then who is used to such a fun?*

**She says:** Do not make so much fuss, my dear young mistress! It would be better for me than for you to take this letter to your mother and tell her all about it.

**Yingying says in anger:** About what?

**Rose says:** About Master Zhang.

**Yingying, revealing her sentiment by dumb show, says:** Let me think it over, Rose. Perhaps it would be better to pardon him this time.

**Rose says:** My dear young mistress, are you afraid he will be given a good thrashing on the bottom?

**Yingying says:** I have not yet asked about Master Zhang's health.

**Rose says:** I will not tell you.

**Yingying says:** Oh, Rose, do tell me!

**Rose sings to the tune of *HOMAGE TO EMPEROR* :**

> *His face becomes so thin*
>
> *As to make me feel chagrin.*
>
> *He has no desire to drink or to eat*
>
> *And fears to move his feet.*

**Yingying says:** Why not call in a doctor to examine his illness?

**Rose says:** He has no special illness. He said himself?

**She continues to sing:**

> *I was sighing away*
>
> *For our union night and day.*
>
> *I forgot to eat and to sleep*
>
> *Till evening faded into night deep.*
>
> *I gazed at eastern wall*
>
> *And copious tears began to fall.*
>
> *My sickness would get worse*
>
> *Unless my sweat be sweetened by hers.*

**Yingying says:** You are always discreet of speech. Rose. What if others know of this? What will become of the honor of our family? Don't tell me from now on whatever he says in such language as this! The relations between us are merely those of brother and sister, and nothing more.

**Rose says:** Fine words!

中国文学选读

**She sings to the tune of *FOUR-SIDE TRANQUILLITY*:**

> *His flirting with you, you fear,*
>
> *Might lead to harm*
>
> *When it's discovered by your mother dear.*
>
> *It would create alarm*
>
> *For you and me.*
>
> *Why should you care for him under any pretense*
>
> *Since you've encouraged him to climb up the tree,*
>
> *Removed the ladder and gazed with indifference?*

**Yingying says:** Although my family is under obligation to him, how can he be allowed to do this? Hand me pen and paper so that I may write him an answer, telling him not to do in this way again.

**Rose says:** What are you going to write to him? Why should you trouble yourself again?

**Yingying says:** You do not understand, Rose. (She writes.)

**She says:** Take this letter and say to him: "When my young mistress sent me to see you, sir, it was simply a matter of courtesy between sister and brother and it meant nothing else. If you repeat what you have just done, my young mistress will be obliged to tell her mother." And Rose, you will have to answer for this!

**Rose says:** Why, my dear young mistress, are you fussing again? I will not take your letter and you need not trouble yourself for that.

**Yingying, throwing the letter on the ground, says:** How dare you, little chit! (Exit.)

**Rose, picking up the letter, sighs and says:** Ah! My young mistress, why do you show such temper?

**She sings to the tune of *DOFFING THE CLOTHES*:**

> *You maiden young*
>
> *Don't know how to restrain your tongue,*
>
> *Abusing others and making them feel sad*
>
> *By giving vent to your own temper bad.*
>
> *You think but of the scholar you cannot forget*

Instead of the example to others you've set.

**(Tune: *SMALL LIANGZHOU*)**

In his dreams you and he were twain;

When he awoke, he was single again.

For your sake he forgot to eat and sleep;

His silken robe felt cold when night was deep.

Boundless his grief appears:

In solitude his face is crisscrossed with tears.

**(Tune: *A SECOND STANZA*)**

He longed for the happy union in vain

As for the rising Wain.

I've never shut the side door

So that you two may meet no obstacle any more.

I wish you would in full bridal array be seen

While I play the role of tacit go-between.

**(Tune: *POMEGRANATE FLOWER*)**

Making your toilet in your boudoir, you're afraid

Your thin robe cannot keep out the cold when flowers fade.

Then when you heard the lute beneath the moon so bright,

Why didn't you fear the cold on dewy vernal night?

Was it because you were devoured by your flame

For the scholar so that you felt no shame?

For that sour, crazy gallant alone,

You weren't afraid of being frozen into stone.

**(Tune: *FIGHT OF QUAILS*)**

You are a flower

Thirsting for shower,

So I will be

A bearer of letters for you.

But you find fault with me

And won't reproach yourself for the folly you do.

*I can't but bear*

*What is unfair*

*Like burning scar.*

*O how crafty you are!*

*Your speech in public plausible appears;*

*In private your brows knit, your eyes are filled with tears.*

**She says:** If I do not go with her letter, she will say I disobey her. And Master Zhang is waiting for me to bring an answer. What can I do but go again to the library? (She knocks at the door.)

**Master Zhang enters and says:** So you have come, Miss Rose. What about the letter?

**Rose says:** It has failed. Don't be silly, sir.

**Master Zhang says:** My letter is a talisman to make lovers meet. How can it have failed? It must be you, Miss Rose, who were not zealous enough.

**Rose says:** Was I not zealous enough, sir? Heaven above knows the truth. It was your letter that was anything but good.

**She sings to the tune of *ASCENDING THE ATTIC*:**

*It's you who were unlucky, sir,*

*Your message I dare not defer;*

*It turned out to be your confession clear,*

*A summons for you to appear,*

*A proof I'm also concerned in this case.*

*If my young mistress should not save my face,*

*And pardon your impertinent flame,*

*E'en I should bear the undeserved blame.*

**(Tune: *PETTY SONG*)**

*From now on meetings will be hard and visits rare;*

*The moon will no more shine on western bower,*

*The phoenix will leave the Pavilion fore'er,*

*And clouds won't bring on Mountain-Crest fresh shower.*

*You may take the road high*

*And I the low.*

*I pray, sir, do not sigh:*

*The feast is o'er and guests are bound to go.*

**She says:** This is the end of the matter. You, sir, need not tell me again your innermost feelings. My mistress may be looking for me. I must return at once.

**Master Zhang says:** Miss Rose! (He remains motionless for a long time.)

(Weeping) Miss Rose, once you have gone, who can I expect to plead my cause with?

(Kneeling down) Miss Rose, Miss Rose, you must help me to have this matter put right and save my life.

**Rose says:** A learned scholar as you are, sir, can you not understand how the matter stands?

**She sings to the tune of *COURTYARD FULL OF FRAGRANCE*:**

*Don't play the cunning with a foolish air!*

*While you want to enjoy your love-affair,*

*Why not think of the torture I shall stand?*

*My young mistress may beat me, rod in hand.*

*Like a thick rope, could I*

*Go through a needle's eye?*

*If beaten, on a crutch I'd lean,*

*Could I still act as go-between?*

*If I should have my lips kept sealed,*

*How could I help you to be healed?*

**Master Zhang, still kneeling and weeping, says:** There is no other way for me. The only hope of saving my life depends on you. Miss Rose!

**Rose continues to sing:**

*You press me hard with words so sweet*

*That I can nor advance nor retreat.*

**She says:** Why should I explain to you? Here is her answer to your letter. You can read it for yourself. (She hands him the letter.)

**Master Zhang, having opened and read the letter, gets up and says smilingly:** Ah,

Miss Rose!

(Reading once more) Today is indeed a happy day. Miss Rose!

(Reading still once more) If I had known your young mistress' letter was to arrive, I should have prepared for its reception. Now it is too late so I hope I may be excused. I am sure, Miss Rose, you will rejoice too.

**Rose says:** What about?

**Master Zhang says smilingly:** Her abuse of me is all put on. In the letter she says the contrary.

**Rose says:** Really?

**Master Zhang says:** In her letter she tells me to go to the garden tonight.

**Rose says:** What for?

**Master Zhang says:** For an assignation.

**Rose says:** What is an assignation?

**Master Zhang says:** To have a secret meeting with her. Miss Rose.

**Rose says:** I do not believe it.

**Master Zhang says:** You may believe it or not as you like.

**Rose says:** Try to read me the letter.

**Master Zhang says:** There are four verses of five characters, very implicit. Wait for moonrise in western bower. Where the breeze opens half the door. The wall is shaded by dancing flower; then comes the one whom you adore. Now, Miss Rose, do you still not believe it?

**Rose says:** What does it mean?

**Master Zhang says:** Don't you understand it?

**Rose says:** I don't.

**Master Zhang says:** Well, then I will explain it to you. "Wait for moonrise in western bower" tell me the time to go to the garden. "Where the breeze opens half the door" means the door will be open for me. "The wall is shaded by dancing flowers" tell me to climb over the wall screened by the shadows of the flowers lest I should be seen. "Then comes the one whom you adore" needs no explanation. It simply means: "I am coming."

**Rose says:** Are you sure it is what she means?

**Master Zhang says:** What else can she mean if not this. Miss Rose? To tell the truth, I am a master in solving riddles, full of romance and gallantry. If it is not explained in this way, how else can it be explained?

**Rose says:** Can this be what she writes?

**Master Zhang says:** Here it is.

(Rose remains motionless for a long time.)

(Master Zhang reads the letter again.)

**Rose says:** Is it really what she writes?

**Master Zhang says smilingly:** You are absurd. Miss Rose. Here it is.

**Rose says angrily:** Then my young mistress has made a fool of me.

**She sings to the tune of *PLAYING THE CHAILD*:**

> O who has ever
>
> Seen a messenger befooled by the sender?
>
> She is so clever,
>
> Though she appears so young and tender.
>
> She tells her lover to climb
>
> Over the eastern wall for a tryst.
>
> Five words hint at the time;
>
> Four lines appeal to the lover missed.
>
> About this critical affair, O mark!
>
> I am kept in the dark.
>
> You want the cloud
>
> To bring fresh showers
>
> For thirsting flowers
>
> Rising above the crowd,
>
> But order me to use my leisure
>
> To gratify your pleasure.

**(Tune: *LAST STANZA BUT THREE*)**

> As brilliant jade her letter paper is as neat;
>
> As lily's fragrance her words are as sweet.
>
> The lines are wet

Not with her fragrant sweat

But with the rosy tear

Wept for her lover dear.

The ink is not yet dried,

Like grief of rainy spring at rising tide.

You need not doubt, sir, from now on

But do your best to win high literary renown!

Then you may do what you will of your lady fair

With golden bird on cloudy hair.

(Tune: *LAST STANZA BUT TWO*)

To him you've shown affection, my young mistress dear,

But of me you make light.

When has he become the husband you revere?

Your honeyed words would make him warm in winter's height;

E'en in mid-summer your disfavor would make me cold.

Today I'll keep a watch on you and behold

How can a metamorphosed lady fair

Attract her handsome lover with a lovely pear.

**Master Zhang says:** How can a student like me climb over a garden wall?

**Rose sings to the tune of *LAST STANZA BUT ONE*:**

The wall's not high, caressed by full-blown trees;

The door is only half-closed in the breeze.

If you attempt to steal a lady sweet,

You should have nimble hands and feet.

If you're afraid of the height of the wall,

How can you climb o'er glorious Dragon's Gate at all?

If 'mid thickset rose-bushes you're not free,

How can you pluck the flower on the laurel tree?

Make haste and have no fear!

Don't weary the longing eyes of your lady dear

Nor let her eyebrows still,

*Knit like distant vernal hill!*

**Master Zhang says:** I have already visited the garden twice.

**Rose sings to the tune of *THE EPILOGUE*:**

*Though you have been there twice,*

*this visit will be far nicer.*

*Your verse exchange was mere by-play;*

*the real thing is her letter of today.*

(Exit.)

**Master Zhang says:** Alas! All things are fated. When Rose came here, I was depressed beyond words. But who could have anticipated the happiness my young lady would send me in her letter? I am indeed a master in the art of solving riddles, full of romance and gallantry. If her verse were not interpreted in this way, how else then should it be interpreted? " Wait for moonrise in western bower" tell me the time to go to the garden. "Where the breeze opens half the door" shows me the place. "The wall is shaded by dancing flowers; then comes the one whom you adore." These lines tell me how to climb over the wall unperceived. But the damned daylight seems unwilling to depart. O Heaven! You give everything to everyone. Why won't you give me a single day! O Sun! Will you go down quickly! When I talk with a happy friend, the sun will soon westward descend. Today I am to meet my love; the sun seems glued and rooted above. It is now only midday. I must still wait for a long time. When I look again, I find everything seems against the sun's setting today. No cloud in azure sky with fragrance drifting by. Who could shorten the day, driving the sun away? Ah! The sun begins to sink in the west. I have to wait still for a long while. The sun's a golden crow In Heaven's palace high. I'd shoot it with a bow down from the western sky. Thanks to Heaven and Earth! The sun is down at last. Ah! Lamps are lit. Ah! Drums are beaten. Ah! Evening bells are ringing. I'll close the door of the library and go out. When I arrive there, I'll clasp the branch of the drooping willow tree and climb over the wall in a trice. I'll hold my young lady in my arms. O my dear young lady! I feel sorry only for you. Your letter's twenty words hide twenty pearls below; I'll pluck the fruit whose seed was sown three lives ago.

(translated by Xu Yuanchong)

中国文学选读

# 西厢记　第三本第二折

（莺莺上云）红娘这早晚敢待来也。起得早了些儿，俺如今再睡些。（睡科）

（红娘上云）奉小姐言语，去看张生，取得一封书来，回他话去。呀，不听得小姐声音，敢又睡哩？俺便入去看他。

【中吕·粉蝶儿】（红娘唱）风静帘闲，透窗纱麝兰香散，启朱扉摇响双环。绛台高，金荷小，银缸犹灿。我将他暖帐轻弹，揭起海红罗软帘偷看。

【醉春风】只见他钗单玉斜横，髻偏云乱挽。日高犹自不明眸，你好懒，懒！（莺莺起身，欠身长叹科）半晌抬身，几回搔耳，一声长叹。是便是，只是这简帖儿，俺那好递与小姐？俺不如放在妆盒儿里，等他自见。（放科）（莺莺整妆，红娘偷觑科）

【普天乐】晚妆残，乌云軃，轻匀了粉脸，乱挽起云鬟。将简帖儿拈，把妆盒儿按，拆开封皮孜孜看，颠来倒去不害心烦。只见他厌的挖皱了黛眉，忽的低垂了粉颈，氲的改变了朱颜。

（红做意科，云）呀，决撒了也。

（莺莺怒科，云）红娘过来！

（红云）有！

（莺莺云）红娘，这东西那里来的？我是相国的小姐，谁敢将这简帖儿来戏弄我？我几曾惯看这样东西来？我告过夫人，打下你个小贱人下截来！

（红云）小姐使我去，他着我将来。小姐不使我去，我敢问他讨来？我又不识字，知他写的是些甚么？

【快活三】分明是你过犯，没来由把我摧残。教别人颠倒恶心烦，你不惯，谁曾惯！小姐休闹，比及你对夫人说科，我将这简帖儿，先到夫人行出首去。

（莺莺怒云）你到夫人行却出首谁来？

（红云）我出首张生。

（莺莺做意云）红娘，也罢，且饶他这一次。

（红云）小姐，怕不打下他下截来。

（莺莺云）我正不曾问你，张生病体如何？

（红云）我只不说。

（莺莺云）红娘，你便说咱。

【朝天子】近间面颜，瘦得实难看。不思量茶饭，怕动弹。

（莺莺云）请一位好太医，着他证候咱！

（红云）他也无甚证候，他自己说来。我是晓夜将佳期盼，废寝忘餐。黄昏清且，望东墙淹泪眼。我这病患要安，只除是出点风流汗。

（莺莺云）红娘，早是你口稳来，若别人知道呵，成何家法！今后他这般的言语，你再也休题。我和张生，只是兄妹之情，有何别事？

（红云）是好话也呵！

【四边静】怕人家调犯，早晚怕夫人见破绽，只是你我何安？又问甚他危难，他只蹭掇上竿，拔了梯儿看。

（莺莺云）虽是我家亏他，他岂得如此？你将纸笔过来，我写将去回他，着他下次休得这般。

（红云）小姐，你写甚的那？你何苦如此？

（莺莺云）红娘，你不知道！（写科）

（莺莺云）红娘，你将去对他说，小姐遣看先生，乃兄妹之礼，非有他意。再一遭儿是这般呵，必告俺夫人知道。红娘，和你小贱人，都有话说也！

（红云）小姐，你又来，这帖儿我不将去，你何苦如此？

（莺莺掷书地下，云）这妮子，好没分晓！（莺莺下）

《西厢记》插图

（红娘拾书，叹云）咳，小姐，你将这个性儿那里使也？

【脱布衫】小孩儿口没遮拦，一味的将言语摧残。把似你使性子，休思量秀才，做多少好人家风范。

【小梁州】我为你梦里成双觉后单，废寝忘餐。罗衣不耐五更寒，愁无限，寂寞泪阑干。

【换头】似等辰勾空把佳期盼，我将角门儿更不牢拴，愿你做夫妻无危难。你向筵席头上整扮，我做个缝了口的撮合山。

【石榴花】你晚妆楼上杏花残，犹自怯衣单。那一夜听琴时，露重月明间，为甚向晚不怕春寒？几乎险被先生馋。那其间岂不胡颜？为他不酸不醋风魔汉，隔窗儿险化做望夫山！

【斗鹌鹑】你既用心儿拨雨撩云，我便好意儿传书递简。不肯搜自己狂为，只待觅别人破绽。受艾焙，我权时忍这番。畅好是奸。对别人巧语花言，背地里愁眉泪眼！俺若不去来，道俺违拗他。张生又等俺回话，只得再到书房。（推门科）

（张生上云）红娘姐来了，简帖儿如何？

（红云）不济事了，先生休傻！

（张生云）小生简帖儿，是一道会亲的符箓，只是红娘姐不肯用心，故致如此。

（红云）是我不用心？哦，先生，头上有天哩，你那个简帖儿里面好听也！

【上小楼】这是先生命慳，不是红娘违慢。那的做了你的招状，他的勾头，我的公案。若不觑面颜，厮顾盼，担饶轻慢，争些儿把奴拖犯。

【后】从今后我相会少，你见面难。月暗西厢，便如凤去秦楼，云敛巫山。你也赸，我也赸，请先生休讪，早寻个酒阑人散。只此，足下再也不必申诉肺腑。怕夫人寻我，我回去也。

（张生云）红娘姐！（定科）

（良久，张生哭云）红娘姐，你一去呵，更望谁与小生分剖？

（张生跪云）红娘姐，红娘姐，你是必做个道理，方可救得小生一命！

（红娘云）先生，你是读书才子，岂不知此意？

【满庭芳】你休呆里撒奸。你待恩情美满，苦我骨肉摧残。他只少手搭棍儿摩娑看，我粗麻线怎过针关。定要我挂着拐帮闲钻懒，缝合口送暖偷寒，前已是踏着犯。

（张生跪不起，哭云）小生更无别路，一条性命都只在红娘姐身上，红娘姐！

我又禁不起你甜话儿热趲，好教我左右做人难。我没来由只管分说，小姐回你的书，你自看者！（递书科）

（张生拆书，读毕，起立笑云）呀，红娘姐！

（又读毕云）红娘姐，今日有这场喜事。

（又读毕云）早知小姐书至，理合应接，接待不及，切勿见罪！红娘姐，和你也欢喜！

（红云）却是怎么？

（张生笑云）小姐骂我都是假，书中之意，哩也波哩也啰哩！

（红云）怎么？

（张生云）书中约我今夜花园里去！

（红云）约你花园里去怎么？

（张生云）约我后花园里去相会！

（红云）相会怎么？

（张生笑云）红娘姐，你道相会怎么哩？

（红云）我只不信！

（张生云）不信由你！

（红云）你试读与我听。

（张生云）是五言诗四句哩，妙也。"待月西厢下，迎风户半开。拂墙花影动，疑是玉人来。"红娘姐，你不信？

（红云）此是甚么解？

（张生云）有甚么解？

（红云）我真个不解！

（张生云）我便解波。"待月西厢下"，着我待月上而来。"迎风户半开"，他开门等我。"拂墙花影动"，着我跳过墙来。"疑是玉人来"。这句没有解，是说我至矣。

（红云）真个如此解？

（张生云）不是这般解，红娘姐你来解。不敢欺红娘姐，小生乃猜诗谜的社家，风流隋何，浪子陆贾。不是这般解，怎解？

（红云）真个如此写？

（张生云）现在——

（红定科，良久）

（张生又读科）

（红云）真个如此写？

（张生笑云）红娘姐，好笑也！如今现在——

（红怒云）你看我小姐，原来在我行使乖道儿！

【耍孩儿】几曾见，寄书的颠倒瞒着鱼雁？小则小，心肠儿转关，教你跳东墙，女字边干。原来五言包得三更枣，四句埋将九里山。你赤紧将人慢，你要会云雨闹中取静，却教我寄音书忙里偷闲！

【四煞】纸光明玉版，字香喷麝兰，行儿边湮透非娇汗。是他一缄情泪红犹湿，满纸春愁墨未干。我也休疑难，放着个玉堂学士，任从你金雀鸦鬟。

【三煞】将他来别样亲，把俺来取次看，是几时孟光接了梁鸿案？将他来甜言媚你三冬暖，把俺来恶语伤人六月寒。今日为头看，看你个离魂倩女，怎生的掷果潘安！

（张生云）只是小生读书人，怎生跳得花园墙过？

【二煞】拂墙花又低，迎风户半拴，偷香手段今番按。你怕墙高怎把龙门跳？嫌花密难将仙桂攀。疾忙去，休辞惮。他望穿了盈盈秋水，蹙损了淡淡春山。

（张生云）小生曾见花园，已经两遭。

【煞尾】虽是去两遭，敢不如这番。你当初隔墙酬和都胡侃，证果是他今朝这一简！

（红娘下）

（张生云）叹万事自有分定。适才红娘来，千不欢喜，万不欢喜，谁想小姐有此一场好事？小生实是猜诗谜的社家，风流隋何，浪子陆贾，此四句诗，不是这般解，又怎解？"待月西厢下"，是必须待得月上。"迎风户半开"，门方开了。"拂墙花影动，疑是玉人来"，墙上有花影，小生方好去。今日这颏天，偏百般的难得晚。天那，你有万物于人，何苦争此一日，疾下去波！快书快友快谈论，不觉开西立又昏。今日碧桃花有约，鳔胶黏了又生根。呀，才晌午也！再等一等，又看咱，今日百般的难得下去呵。空青万里无云，悠然扇作微薰。何处缩天有术，便教逐日西沉？呀，初倒西也。再等一等咱。谁将三足乌，来向天上阁。安得后羿弓，射此一轮落？谢天谢地，日光菩萨，你也有下去之日！呀，却早上灯也。呀，却早发擂也。呀，却早撞钟也！拽上书房门，到得那里，手挽着垂杨，滴溜扑碌跳过墙去，抱住小姐。唉，小姐，我只替你愁哩，二十颗珠藏简帖，三千年果在花园！（张生下）

## Further Readings

### An Amazing Dream

Tang Xianzu

(Enter Du Liniang with Chunxiang)

**Du Liniang:**

(To the tune of *RAOCHIYOU*)

*When I'm awakened by the orioles' songs*

*And find the springtime beauty all around,*

*I stand in deep thought on the courtyard ground.*

**Chunxiang:**

*With burnt incense*

*And silk yarns scattered here and there,*

*This spring no longer holds back maidens fair.*

**Du Liniang:**

*With the distant pass in view at dawn,*

*In my night-gown I stand forlorn.*

**Chunxiang:**

*In spring-style braid,*

*You lean against the balustrade.*

**Du Liniang:**

*That which scissors cannot sever,*

*And, sorted out, is tangled again,*

*Makes me bored than ever.*

**Chunxiang:**

*I've told the early birds*

*To meet the spring and send your words.*

**Du Liniang:**

Have you ordered the garden paths to be cleaned, Chunxiang?

**Chunxiang:**

Yes, I have.

**Du Liniang:**

Bring my mirror and gowns.

(Exit and re-enter Chunxiang with the mirror and gowns)

**Chunxiang:**

*Face the mirror when her hair is done;*

*Add the perfume to the gowns with fun.*

*Here's the mirror and gowns.*

**Du Liniang:**

(To the tune of **BUBUJIAO**)

*In the courtyard drifts the willow-threads,*

*Torn by spring breeze into flimsy shreds.*

*I pause awhile*

*To do my hairstyle.*

*When all at once*

*The mirror glances at my face,*

*I tremble and my hair slips out of lace.*

(Walks in the room)

*As I pace the room,*

*How can anyone see me in full bloom!*

**Chunxiang:**

You're so pretty today.

**Du Liniang:**

(To the tune of **ZUIFUGUI**)

*You say my dress is fine*

*And hairpins shine,*

*But love of beauty is my natural design.*

*My beauty is concealed in the hall,*

*But it'll make fish delve and birds fall*

*And outshine blooms, the moon and all.*

**Chunxiang：**

It's time for breakfast. Let's go.

(Begins to move)

Look，

*How the painted corridor shines！*

*How green the moss appears in endless lines！*

*To walk on grass I fear to soil my socks；*

*To love the blooms I want to keep them under locks.*

**Du Liniang：**

If I had not come to the garden，how could I have tasted the beauty of spring！

(To the tune of **ZAOLUOPAO**)

*The flowers glitter brightly in the air，*

*Around the wells and walls deserted here and there.*

*Where is the "pleasant day and pretty sight"?*

*Who can enjoy "contentment and delight"?*

Mom and Dad have never mentioned such pretty sights.

**Du Liniang，Chunxiang：**

*The clouds at dawn and rain at dusk，*

*The bowers in the evening rays，*

*The threads of shower in gales of wind，*

*The painted boat in hazy sprays：*

*All are foreign to secluded maids.*

**Chunxiang：**

All the seasonal flowers are in full blossom，but it's still too early for the peony.

**Du Liniang：**

(To the tune of **HAOJIEJIE**)

*Amid the red azaleas cuckoos sing；*

*Upon roseleaf raspberries willow-threads cling.*

Oh，Chunxiang，

*The peony is fair indeed，*

*But comes the latest on the mead.*

中国文学选读

**Chunxiang:**

Look at the orioles and swallows in pairs!

**Du Liniang, Chunxiang:**

*When we cast a casual eye,*

*The swallows chatter and swiftly fly*

*While orioles sing their way across the sky.*

**Du Liniang:**

It's time to leave.

**Chunxiang:**

There's more than enough to be seen in the garden.

**Du Liniang:**

No more about it.

(Du Liniang and Chunxiang begin to leave)

(To the tune of **QUASI-CODA**)

*It's true that there's more than enough to be seen,*

*But what though we visit all the scenic spots?*

*We'd better find more fun behind the screen.*

(They arrive at the chamber)

**Chunxiang:**

*I open doors of chambers east and west*

*And sit on my own bed to take a rest.*

*I put azalea in the earthen vase*

*And add incense unto the proper place.*

Mistress, please take a rest now and I'll go and see the madam.

(Exit Chunxiang)

**Du Liniang:**

(Sighs)

Back from a brief spring tour,

I know my beauty now for sure.

Oh spring, now that I love you so much, what shall I do when you are gone?

How dizzy I feel in such weather! Where's Chunxiang?

(Looks around and lowers her head again, murmuring)

Oh heavens! Now I do believe that spring is annoying. It is true indeed what is written in various kinds of poems about maidens in ancient times, who felt passionate in spring and grieved in autumn. I've turned sixteen now, but no one has come to ask for my hand. Stirred by the spring passion, where can I come across one who will go after me? In the past Lady Han met a scholar named Yu, and Scholar Zhang came across Miss Cui. Their love stories have been recorded in the books *The Story of the Maple Leaves* and *The Life of Cui Hui*. These lovely ladies and talented scholars started with furtive dating but ended in happy reunion. (Heaves a long sigh) Born and brought up in a renowned family of high officialdom, I've come of age but haven't found a fiancée yet. I'm wasting my youth that will soon pass. (Weeps) What a pity that my face is as pretty as a flower but my fate is as dreary as a leaf!

(To the tune of **SHANPOYANG**)

*Indulged in springtime passion of all sorts,*

*I'm all of a sudden roused to plaintive thoughts.*

*I have a pretty face*

*And so my spouse must be as good,*

*With a noble place. What is there to meet my fate?*

*That I must waste my youth to wait!*

*When I go to bed, who'll peep*

*At my shyness in my sleep?*

*With whom shall I lie in my secret dream?*

*Drifting down the springtime stream?*

*Tormented day by day,*

*To whom can I say?*

*About my woe,*

*About my wretched fate?*

*Only the heavens know!*

I feel dizzy. I'll lean on the table and take a short nap.

(Falls asleep and begins to dream)

(Enter Liu Mengmei with a willow-twig in his hand)

**Liu Mengmei:**

*In warm days oriole's songs ring apace*

*While man in deep affection has a smiling face.*

*I chase the fragrant petals in the stream,*

*To find the fair lady in my dream.*

I follow the footsteps of Miss Du along the path, but how is it that I lose sight of her now?

(Looks back)

Hi, Miss Du! Hi, Miss Du!

(Du Liniang rises in astonishment and greets Liu Mengmei)

I've been looking for you here and there. Now I find you at last.

(Du Liniang looks aside without a word)

I just snapped a willow-twig in the garden. Miss Du,

As you are well versed in classics, why don't you write a poem to honour the twig?

(In happy astonishment, Du Liniang is about to speak but holds back her tongue)

**Du Liniang:**

(Aside)

I've never seen this young man before. Why does he come here?

**Liu Mengmei:**

(With a smile)

I'm up to the neck in love with you, Miss Du!

(To the tune of **SHANTAOHONG**)

*For you, a maiden fair,*

*With beauty that will soon fade,*

*I've been searching here and there,*

*But alone in chamber you have stayed.*

Come with me and let's have a chat over there, Miss Du.

(Du Liniang smiles but does not move)

(Liu Mengmei pulls her by the sleeve)

**Du Liniang：**

(In a subdued voice)

Where to?

**Liu Mengmei：**

Beyond the rose grove,

Beside the mount we'll rove.

**Du Liniang：**

(In a subdued voice)

What to do, sir?

**Liu Mengmei：**

(Also in a subdued voice)

I shall unbutton your gown

And strip it down.

You'll bite your sleeve-top with your teeth,

Then make a hug and lie beneath.

(Du Liniang is shy, but Liu Mengmei comes forward to embrace her. She feigns to push him away)

**Liu Mengmei，Du Liniang：**

*Is it absurd?*

*That we seem to meet somewhere before*

*But stand here face to face without a word?*

(Exit Liu Mengmei, holding Du Liniang in his arms)

(Enter Flower God with bundled hair, dressed in red and strewn with flowers)

**Flower God：**

*The flower god looks after flowers here*

*And keeps the springtime busy year by year.*

*When petals fall from flowers in a rain,*

*The flower gazer starts to dream in vain.*

I am the flower god in charge of the prefect's back garden in Nan'an. As the prefect's daughter Du Liniang and the scholar Liu Mengmei are predestined to get married, Miss Du is so affected by her spring tour that she has enticed Liu Mengmei into her dream. I am a flower god to take care of all the beauties in this area, and so I've come here to protect her in order that she will enjoy herself to the full.

(To the tune of **BAOLAOCUI**)

*In the surge of earth and sky,*

*He swirls like a busy bee*

*And glares the flowery maiden's eye.*

*That is a meeting in the dream,*

*A wedding in the mind,*

*An outcome of the fate*

*That brings defilement of the foulest kind.*

I'll drop a flower petal to wake her up.

(Scatters some petals to the entrance of the stage)

*How can they tear themselves away from dream?*

*They'll wake up when the petals gleam.*

The scholar is still indulged in his dream, but when he wakes up, he'll see Miss Du to her chamber. I've got to go now.

(Exit the flower god)

(Enter Liu Mengmei and Du Liniang, hand in hand)

**Liu Mengmei:**

(To the tune of **SHANTAOHONG**)

*With heaven and earth as our bridal room,*

*We sleep on grass and bloom.*

Are you all right, my dear?

(Du Liniang lowers her head)

*Look at her pretty hair,*

*Loosened here and there.*

*Please never forget the day when we*

*Lie together side by side,*

*Make love for hours and hours,*

*And hug as man and bride,*

*With your face red as flowers.*

**Du Liniang:**

Are you leaving now, my love?

**Liu Mengmei, Du Liniang:**

*Is it absurd?*

*That we seem to meet somewhere before*

*But stand here face to face without a word?*

**Liu Mengmei:**

You must be tired, my dear. Sleep awhile, sleep awhile!

(Sees Du Liniang to her sleeping position, and pats her on the back)

I'm going, my dear.

(Looks back)

Please sleep awhile, my dear, and I'll come and see you again.

*She comes like gentle rain in spring*

*And wets me like clouds on the wing.*

(Exit Liu Mengmei)

**Du Liniang:**

(Wakes up with a start and murmurs)

Are you leaving, my love?

(Dozes off again)

(Enter Zhen)

**Zhen:**

*My husband holds high office here;*

*My daughter stays without much cheer.*

*Her worry comes from skirts she wears,*

*With blooms and birds adorned in pairs.*

How can you doze off like this, my child?

**Du Liniang:**

(Wakes and calls the scholar)

Oh! Oh!

**Zhen:**

What's wrong with you, my child?

**Du Liniang:**

(Stands up with a start)

Oh, it's you, Mom!

**Zhen:**

Why don't you, my child, enjoy yourself by doing some needlework or reading some books? Why are you dozing off like this?

**Du Liniang:**

Just now I took a stroll in the back garden, but I was annoyed by the noise of the birds and so I came back to my chamber. As I could not find a way to while away the

《牡丹亭·惊梦》插图

time, I dozed off for a moment. Please forgive me for having not greeted you at the door.

**Zhen:**

As the back garden is a desolate place, my child, don't go there again.

**Du Liniang:**

I'll follow your advice, Mom.

**Zhen:**

Go and study in the classroom, my child.

**Du Liniang:**

As the tutor is on leave, I have a few days off.

**Zhen:**

(Sighs)

A girl has her own emotions when she has come of age. I'd better leave her alone. As the saying goes,

*Busy for the children all her life,*

*A mother always has her strife.*

(Exit Zhen)

**Du Liniang:**

(Sighs deeply and watches Zhen leave)

Alas, heavens! I'm lucky enough today. A whimsical stroll to the back garden made me pathetic in spite of the beautiful scenery. After I came back in low spirits, I took a nap in my chamber. In my dream I saw a handsome scholar by the age of twenty. He broke a willow-twig in the garden and said to me with a smile, "Miss Du, as you are well versed in classics, why don't you write a poem to honor the twig?" I was about to reply when it occurred to me that I should not speak to him because he was a total stranger and I did not know his name yet. When I was hesitating, he came forward, spoke a few melancholy words and carried me to the Peony Pavilion. We made love there beside the peonies. With mutual passion, we stuck to each other in tenderness. When it was all over, he brought me back and said time and again, "Sleep awhile." I was about to see the scholar to the door when my mother came and startled me out of my dream. I was wet in cold sweat from my daydream. I made haste to greet my mother and then had to listen to her talk. I kept silent but was still troubled in my heart. I seemed to be sitting on pins and needles, utterly at a loss. Oh, mother, you told me to go back to my classroom, but what kind of books can bring me relief?

(Covers her eyes with her sleeve and weeps)

(To the tune of *MIANDAXU*)

*The youthful joy in love regime*

*Had reached the verge of dream*

*When Mother came into the room*

*And woke me back to my deep gloom.*

*With cold sweat that soaked my dress,*

*I was simply rooted to the ground,*

*My mind and hair in utter mess. In a sunken mood,*

*Not knowing how to sit or stand,*

*I'd go and sleep in solitude.*

(Enter Chunxiang)

**Chunxiang:**

*My make-up is undone at night,*

*With only incense burning bright.*

Your quilts have been scented, mistress. It's time to go to bed.

**Du Liniang:**

(To the tune of *CODA*)

As springtime tour has tired me out,

There is no need to scent my quilts.

Good heavens,

I wish that pleasant dreams would soon sprout.

A springtime tour from painted halls

Brings near the scent of bloom that falls.

If you should ask where lovers meet,

I say that hearts break where they greet.

—From *The Peony Pavilion*

(translated by Wang Rongpei)

# 惊 梦

汤显祖

【绕池游】（旦上）梦回莺啭，乱煞年光遍。人立小庭深院。（贴）炷尽沉烟，抛残绣线，恁今春关情似去年？【乌夜啼】（旦）晓来望断梅关，宿妆残。（贴）你侧着宜春髻子恰凭阑。（旦）剪不断，理还乱，闷无端。（贴）已分付催花莺燕借春看。（旦）春香，可曾叫人扫除花径？（贴）分付了。（旦）取镜台衣服来。（贴取镜台衣服上）云髻罢梳还对镜，罗衣欲换更添香。镜台衣服在此。

【步步娇】（旦）袅晴丝吹来闲庭院，摇漾春如线。停半晌、整花钿。没揣菱花，偷人半面，迤逗的彩云偏。（行介）步香闺怎便把全身现！（贴）今日穿插的好。

【醉扶归】（旦）你道翠生生出落的裙衫儿茜，艳晶晶花簪八宝填，可知我常一生儿爱好是天然。恰三春好处无人见，不提防沉鱼落雁鸟惊喧，则怕的羞花闭月花愁颤。（贴）早茶时了，请行。（行介）你看：画廊金粉半零星，池馆苍苔一片青。踏草怕泥新绣袜，惜花疼煞小金铃。（旦）不到园林，怎知春色如许！

【皂罗袍】原来姹紫嫣红开遍，似这般都付与断井颓垣。良辰美景奈何天，赏心乐事谁家院！恁般景致，我老爷和奶奶再不提起。（合）朝飞暮卷，云霞翠轩；雨丝风片，烟波画船——锦屏人忒看的这韶光贱！（贴）是花都放了，那牡丹还早。

【好姐姐】（旦）遍青山啼红了杜鹃，荼蘼外烟丝醉软。春香啊，牡丹虽好，他春归怎占的先！（贴）成对儿莺燕啊。（合）闲凝眄，生生燕语明如翦，呖呖莺歌溜的圆。（旦）去罢。（贴）这园子委是观之不足也。（旦）提他怎的！（行介）

【隔尾】观之不足由他缱，便赏遍了十二亭台是枉然。到不如兴尽回家闲过遣。（作到介）（贴）"开我西阁门，展我东阁床。瓶插映山紫，炉添沉水香。"小姐，你歇息片时，俺瞧老夫人去也。（下）（旦叹介）"默地游春转，小试宜春面。"春啊，得和你两留连，春去如何遣？咳，恁般天气，好困人也。春香那里？（作左右瞧介）（又低首沉吟介）天呵，春色恼人，信有之乎！常观诗词乐府，古之女子，因春感情，遇秋成恨，诚不谬矣。吾今年已二八，未逢折桂之夫；忽慕春情，怎得蟾宫之客？昔日韩夫人得遇于郎，张生偶逢崔氏，曾有《题红记》、《崔徽传》二书。此佳人才子，前以密约偷期，后皆得成秦晋。（长叹介）吾生于宦族，长在

中国文学选读

名门。年已及笄，不得早成佳配，诚为虚度青春，光阴如过隙耳。（泪介）可惜妾身颜色如花，岂料命如一叶乎！

【山坡羊】没乱里春情难遣，蓦地里怀人幽怨。则为俺生小婵娟，拣名门一例、一例里神仙眷。甚良缘，把青春抛的远！俺的睡情谁见？则索因循腼腆。想幽梦谁边，和春光暗流传？迁延，这衷怀那处言！淹煎，泼残生，除问天！身子困乏了，且自隐几而眠。（睡介）（梦生介）（生持柳枝上）"莺逢日暖歌声滑，人遇风情笑口开。一径落花随水入，今朝阮肇到天台。"小生顺路儿跟着杜小姐回来，怎生不见？（回看介）呀，小姐，小姐！（旦作惊起介）（相见介）（生）小生那一处不寻访小姐来，却在这里！（旦作斜视不语介）（生）恰好花园内，折取垂柳半枝。姐姐，你既淹通书史，可作诗以赏此柳枝乎？（旦作惊喜，欲言又止介）（背想）这生素昧平生，何因到此？（生笑介）小姐，咱爱杀你哩！

【山桃红】则为你如花美眷，似水流年，是答儿闲寻遍。在幽闺自怜。小姐，和你那答儿讲话去。（旦作含笑不行）（生作牵衣介）（旦低问）那边去？（生）转过这芍药栏前，紧靠着湖山石边。（旦低问）秀才，去怎的？（生低答）和你把领扣松，衣带宽，袖梢儿揾着牙儿苫也，则待你忍耐温存一晌眠。（旦作羞）（生前抱）（旦推介）（合）是那处曾相见，相看俨然，早难道这好处相逢无一言？（生强抱旦下）（末扮花神束发冠，红衣插花上）"催花御史惜花天，检点春工又一年。蘸客伤心红雨下，勾人悬梦采云边。"吾乃掌管南安府后花园花神是也。因杜知府小姐丽娘，与柳梦梅秀才，后日有姻缘之分。杜小姐游春感伤，致使柳秀才入梦。咱花神专掌惜玉怜香，竟来保护他，要他云雨十分欢幸也。

【鲍老催】（末）单则是混阳蒸变，看他似虫儿般蠢动把风情扇。一般儿娇凝翠绽魂儿颤。这是景上缘，想内成，因中见。呀，淫邪展污了花台殿。咱待拈片落花儿惊醒他。（向鬼门丢花介）他梦酣春透了怎留连？拈花闪碎的红如片。秀才才到的半梦儿；梦毕之时，好送杜小姐仍归香阁。吾神去也。（下）

【山桃红】（生、旦携手上）（生）这一霎天留人便，草借花眠。小姐可好？（旦低头介）（生）则把云鬟点，红松翠偏。小姐休忘了啊，见了你紧相偎，慢厮连，恨不得肉儿般团成片也，逗的个日下胭脂雨上鲜。（旦）秀才，你可去啊？（合）是那处曾相见，相看俨然，早难道这好处相逢无一言？（生）姐姐，你身子乏了，将息，将息。（送旦依前作睡介）（轻拍旦介）姐姐，俺去了。（作回顾介）姐姐，你可十分将息，我再来瞧你那。"行来春色三分雨，睡去巫山一片云。"

（下）（旦作惊醒，低叫介）秀才，秀才，你去了也？（又作痴睡介）（老旦上）"夫婿坐黄堂，娇娃立绣窗。怪他裙衩上，花鸟绣双双。"孩儿，孩儿，你为甚瞌睡在此？（旦作醒，叫秀才介）咳也。（老旦）孩儿怎的来？（旦作惊起介）奶奶到此！（老旦）我儿，何不做些针指，或观玩书史，舒展情怀？因何昼寝于此？（旦）孩儿适在花园中闲玩，忽值春暄恼人，故此回房。无可消遣，不觉困倦少息。有失迎接，望母亲恕儿之罪。（老旦）孩儿，这后花园中冷静，少去闲行。（旦）领母亲严命。（老旦）孩儿，学堂看书去。（旦）先生不在，且自消停。（老旦叹介）女孩儿长成，自有许多情态，且自由他。正是："宛转随儿女，辛勤做老娘。"（下）（旦长叹介）（看老旦下介）哎也，天那，今日杜丽娘有些侥幸也。偶到后花园中，百花开遍，睹景伤情。没兴而回，昼眠香阁。忽见一生，年可弱冠，丰姿俊妍。于园中折得柳丝一枝，笑对奴家说："姐姐既淹通书史，何不将柳枝题赏一篇？"那时待要应他一声，心中自忖，素昧平生，不知名姓，何得轻与交言。正如此想间，只见那生向前说了几句伤心话儿，将奴搂抱去牡丹亭畔，芍药阑边，共成云雨之欢。两情和合，真个是千般爱惜，万种温存。欢毕之时，又送我睡眠，几声"将息"。正待自送那生出门，忽值母亲来到，唤醒将来。我一身冷汗，乃是南柯一梦。忙身参礼母亲，又被母亲絮了许多闲话。奴家口虽无言答应，心内思想梦中之事，何曾放怀。行坐不宁，自觉如有所失。娘呵，你教我学堂看书去，知他看那一种书消闷也。（作掩泪介）

【绵搭絮】雨香云片，才到梦儿边。无奈高堂，唤醒纱窗睡不便。泼新鲜冷汗粘煎，闪的俺心悠步軃，意软鬟偏。不争多费尽神情，坐起谁忺？则待去眠。（贴上）"晚妆销粉印，春润费香篝。"小姐，薰了被窝睡罢。

【尾声】（旦）因春心游赏倦，也不索香薰绣被眠。天呵，有心情那梦儿还去不远。

春望逍遥出画堂，间梅遮柳不胜芳。

可知刘阮逢人处？回首东风一断肠。

——选自《牡丹亭》

## Topics for Discussion

1. What are the differences and similarities between Yuan Za Ju and ancient Greek plays?

2. Some say that there is no tragedy written in ancient Chinese dramas. In your opinion is *Dou E Yuan* a tragic drama?

3. Describe the personal characters of Yingying and Zhang Sheng from *The Western Chamber*.

4. Tang Xianzu and Shakespeare both passed away in the same year. Can you make comparisons between the two great playwrights?

# Chapter Eight

# Novels of the Ming and Qing Dynasties

## General Description

The Chinese word for novel, "Xiao Shuo(小说)", literally small talk, originally came from the rumors and hearsay of street gossip and from the interesting narrative works which were difficult to present properly at formal events. Later it went through transformations from the mythology of the Wei Jin Dynasty, to the legends of the Tang, to the narrative story-telling of the Song and Yuan. By the Ming and Qing the novel had developed into a major literary genre, taking its place alongside Tang Shi, Song Ci, and Yuan Qu.

During the Ming and Qing the ruling governmental feudal structures were extremely authoritarian and harsh. But, due to a growing commercial economy and the developing prosperity of urban culture, new humanitarian ideas emerged and blended in with the existing culture. In this way, traditional Chinese literature gradually turned towards a more modern direction. The development of the Ming and Qing novel(明清小说) is an example of this transition in literature. In concert with the general expansion of communication at the time, the novel generated more readers from a wider audience.

At the end of the Yuan and beginning of the Qing there were two renowned novels. These two novels, *Romance of the Three Kingdoms*(《三国演义》) and *Outlaws of the Marsh*(《水浒传》), represent the transition from the traditional Chinese fiction to the new era for novel.

*Romance of the Three Kingdoms* was the first recognized full-length novel in Chinese literary history. It is based on historical events and influenced by many incidents which, from a historical point of view, are not reliable. It is said that, from a historical point of view, the novel is based 30 percent on historical fact and 70 percent on fiction. Most of the stories and events are fabricated and exaggerated. Many powerful characters in the story have been polished or imaginatively interpreted to suit the turbulent times.

The novel *Outlaws of the Marsh* is based on folklore with many of the characters created from the vivid legends of the society. The author focused on shaping the civilian heroes with the skillful usage of colloquial language and in so doing helped to build the foundation for the development and popularization of the Chinese novel.

During the Mid-Ming, the novel *Journey to the West*(《西游记》) was based on the true historical character of Tang Xuanzang(唐玄奘), a monk who traveled to India(the west) to study and learn Buddhist Sutras. The author portrays thrillingly adventurous stories full of twists and turns and provides the reader with a highly entertaining adventure. *Journey to the West* became a very popular and compelling novel of mythical fiction. *The Plum in the Golden Vase*(《金瓶梅》*Jin Ping Mei*), a novel written in the Late Ming, opened up to another direction in the development of Chinese fiction. It shifted from legendary myths to realism, from exceptionally heroic stories to ordinary people's lives. *Jin Ping Mei* became the first novel that truly reflected the core of society.

The Qing Dynasty(清朝 1644~1911) was the last imperial dynasty in China. During this time of domestic social chaos and international turmoil, Chinese literature encountered a tremendously difficult situation. There are many who think that this complicated struggle led to *Dream of the Red Chamber*(《红楼梦》*Hong Lou Meng*), the most important Chinese literary masterpiece with the highest achievements in Chinese classical literature.

The initial Chinese novels were written with a special unique format called "Zhang Hui(章回 chapters or episodes)". Normally there would be from 80 to 120 chapters and each one would have its own topic written with two matching phrases and neat symmetry.

Although the Chinese novel is mostly a fictional narrative, lyric poetry is also often present. The poetic sections appear not only at the beginning of the chapter but also at the end with matching twin phrases. Poems are added to the content to strengthen a particular scene or a unique character. One may say that Chinese literature is the poetic literature and that the Chinese novels, full of poetry, are poetic novels.

For this chapter we have selected Chapter 27 from *Dream of the Red Chamber*. The supplementary works include legendary stories from the Tang, excerpts from *Journey to the West*, and vernacular short stories from the Ming Dynasty.

## Introduction to *Dream of the Red Chamber*

Cao Xueqin(曹雪芹 1715~1763?) was born into the family of an official. After his family fell in hard times Cao struggled and lived in poverty. It is said that "the entire family relied on eating porridge". Near the end of Cao's life he made a living by selling his paintings. During this hardship he managed to continue his writing. The novel *Dream of the Red Chamber* took ten years to complete and was revised five times. It is said about the writing of this novel that it was "word by word engraved with blood through ten years of extraordinary hardship".

曹雪芹

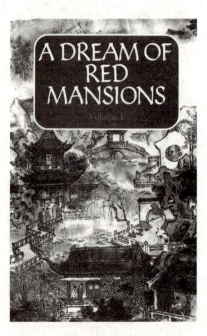

英译《红楼梦》封面

There are a total of 120 chapters in *Dream of the Red Chamber*. The first 80 chapters were written by Cao Xueqin and the last 40 chapters are believed to have been written by a follower of his. It has been said that this novel is an encyclopedia detailing the end of Chinese feudal society. Over the years, researchers and critics have gathered to form a group called "Redologist(红学家)". They specialize in and focus on meticulously studying this novel, a phenomenon rarely seen in literary history.

The novel(*Dream of the Red Chamber*) is based around four large families (surnamed Jia, Shi, Wang and Xue) and follows the tragic romantic love story of Jia Baoyu(贾宝玉)and Lin Daiyu(林黛玉). The story line surrounds the rise and fall of the Jia family, portraying the inevitable decline of this aristocratic family. In addition, the novel weighs heavily in describing the tragedy of other female characters from the Red Chamber.

The story begins with Lin Daiyu coming to live with her maternal grandmother in Nanjing after her parents pass away. When Jia Baoyu first meets his cousin Daiyu he feels like he already knows her. Soon, another female cousin Xue Baochai(薛宝钗) also moves into the Jia mansion. Although Baoyu interacts with the many women all day long, it is Daiyu with whom he is most enamored. However, because Baoyu was born carrying a piece of jade at birth and Baochai always wears a gold chain, it is thought that it is the two of them that would make a great couple. The sentimental Daiyu is not happy to hear about this potential match, so she often makes sarcastic comments to Baochai and hints to Baoyu of her interest in him. Sad and depressed, Daiyu often cries secretly and her grief only makes her health worse. Even though the sensitive Daiyu and the passionate Baoyu often argue, they continue to have deep feelings for each other.

A daughter from the Jia family, Yuanchun(元春) is canonized to become a concubine of the Emperor. She is granted a visit home and in order to welcome the returning princess the Jia family spends a fortune to rebuild the elegant and luxurious Grand View Garden(大观园). After her visit, Yuanchun arranges for Baoyu and a group of female relatives to stay in the Garden, which gives Baoyu the freedom to pass his time in seeking fun with his sisters and cousins. Among these females, Daiyu is the one with such a melancholic personality that when she witnesses falling flower petals she buries the sorrowful petals and writes a poem to express her sadness. In contrast Baoyu is not fond of books and prefers to amuse himself all day. His father is not very pleased and one time gets so mad that he beats Baoyu in punishment. During occasions in the Garden the talented girls often gather together to present their poetic specialties, to recite their own poetry, and compete with one another. In the first competition Baochai wins first prize with her poem "White Begonia". In the following competition Daiyu's charm helps her win with her poem "Chrysanthemum".

To test Baoyu's love, Daiyu's personal maid Zijuan tells Baoyu that Daiyu is returning to her hometown Suzhou for good. The news makes Baoyu quite upset and very miserable. This leads Daiyu to believe that Baoyu is truly in love with her. Many people also anticipate that they would eventually marry happily.

Although from the outside the Jia family is wealthy and famous, on the inside the family is full of conflicts and infighting with frequent accidents and unstoppable jealousy. As Baoyu grows older his father forces him to attend school. During this time some of his playmates pass away and some of them get married, making the Grand View Garden suddenly feel deserted. Daiyu hears of Baoyu's upcoming marriage and worries that no one will be able to help her speak of her own interest in Baoyu. The stress and anxiety bring her nightmares and eventually she falls ill. One day Baoyu loses his jade, the jade that had come with his birth, and he becomes very sick and unable to function. To make the situation worse, his sister, the Emperor's concubine, Yuanchun dies. It is during this chaotic time that Baoyu's grandmother makes a decision to arrange for the marriage of Baoyu and Baochai. But, she worries that Baoyu will refuse the proposal, so she lies to Baoyu and tells him that he will actually be marrying Daiyu. At soon as Daiyu is told of the impending marriage she realizes her dream is lost, her heart broken. She burns all her love poems and written works and dies while the wedding is taking place. On the wedding night Baoyu realizes his bride is not who he expected and is shocked that his lover has passed away. His melancholy drives him to the edge of ending his life.

As a result of annoying the Emperor, the Jia family is investigated, raided, and lose their entire fortune. After Baoyu's grandmother dies in grief, he gives up all his possessions and becomes a Buddhist monk.

　　　　　　　　　　　　　　　　　　中国文学选读

# Selection from *Dream of the Red Chamber*

## Tai-yu Weeps over Fallen Blossom

Let us return to Tai-yu, who had risen late after a sleepless night. When she heard that the other girls were farewelling the God of Flowers in the Garden, for fear of being laughed at for laziness she made haste to dress and go out. She was crossing the courtyard when Pao-yu came in.

"Dear cousin, did you tell on me yesterday?" he greeted her laughingly. "You had me worrying the whole night long."

Tai-yu turned away from him to Tzu-chuan.

"When you've tidied the rooms, close the screen windows," she instructed. "As soon as the big swallows come back, you can let down the curtains. Hold them in place by moving the lions against them. And cover the censer once the incense is lit."

As she said this, she walked on.

Pao-yu attributed this cold behavior to the lines he had quoted at noon the previous day, having no idea of the incident in the evening. He bowed and raised his clasped hands in salute, but Tai-yu simply ignored him, walking straight off to find the other girls.

Pao-yu was puzzled.

"Surely what happened yesterday can't account for this?" he thought. "And I came back too late in the evening to see her again, so how else can I have offended her?"

With these reflections, he trailed after her.

Tai-yu joined Pao-chai and Tan-chun, who were both watching the storks dancing, and the three girls were chatting together when Pao-yu arrived.

"How are you, brother?" asked Tan-chun. "It's three whole days since last I saw you."

"How are you, sister?" he rejoined. "The other day I was asking our elder sister-in-law about you."

"Come over here. I want to talk to you."

The pair of them strolled aside under a pomegranate tree away from the other two.

"Has father sent for you these last few days?" asked Tan-chun.

Pao-yu smiled.

"No, he hasn't."

"Oh, I thought someone told me he sent for you yesterday."

"That someone must have misheard. He didn't."

Tan-chun chuckled.

"These last few months I've saved a dozen strings of cash. I want you to take them. Next time you go out you can buy me some good calligraphy and paintings, or some amusing toys."

"In my strolls through the squares and temple markets inside and outside the city," Pao-yu told her, "I haven't seen anything novel or really well made. Nothing but curios of gold, jade, bronze or porcelain, which would be out of place here. Or things like silk textiles, food and clothing."

"That's not what I mean. No, but things like you bought me last time: little willow baskets, incense-boxes carved out of bamboo roots, and tiny clay stoves. They were so sweet, I just loved them! But then other people fell in love with them too and grabbed them as if they were treasures."

Pao-yu laughed.

"If that's what you want, those things are dirt cheap. Just give five hundred cash to the pages and they'll fetch you two cartloads."

"Those fellows have no taste. Please choose some things which are simple without being vulgar, and genuine instead of artificial. Do get me a whole lot more, and I'll make you another pair of slippers. I'll put even more work into them than last time. How's that?"

"That reminds me." Pao-yu grinned. "I was wearing your slippers one day when I met father. He asked me disapprovingly who'd made them. It wouldn't have done to tell him it was you, sister; so I said they were a present from Aunt Wang on my last birthday. There wasn't much he could say to that, but after an awful silence he commented, 'What a waste of time and energy and good silk.' When I told Hsi-jen she said: 'Never mind that, but the concubine Chao's been complaining bitterly, "Her own younger brother Huan's shoes and socks are in holes yet she doesn't care. Instead she embroiders slippers for Pao-yu." ' "

Tan-chun frowned.

"Did you ever hear such nonsense?" she fumed. "Is it *my* job to make shoes? Doesn't Huan have his fair share of clothes, shoes and socks, not to mention a whole roomful of maids and servants? What has *she* got to complain of? Who's she trying to impress? If I make a pair of slippers in my spare time, I can give them to any brother I choose and no one has any right to interfere. She's crazy, carrying on like that."

Pao-yu nodded and smiled.

"Still, it's natural, you know, for her to see things rather differently."

This only enraged Tan-chun more. She tossed her head.

"Now *you're* talking nonsense too. Of course she sees things differently with that sly, low, dirty mind of hers. Who cares what *she* thinks? I don't owe any duty to anyone except our parents. If my sisters, brothers and cousins are nice to me, I'll be nice to them too, regardless of which is the child of a wife or the child of a concubine. Properly speaking, I shouldn't say such things, but really that woman's the limit!"

"Let me tell you another ridiculous thing too. Two days after I gave you that money to buy knick-knacks, she complained to me she was hard up. I paid no attention, of course. But after my maids left the room, she started scolding me for giving my savings to you instead of to Huan. I didn't know whether to laugh or lose my temper. So I left her and went to Her Ladyship."

But now Pao-chai called to them laughingly: "Haven't you talked long enough? It's clear you're brother and sister, the way you leave other people out in the cold to discuss your private affairs. Aren't we allowed to hear a single word?"

They smiled at that and joined her.

Meanwhile Tai-yu had disappeared, and Pao-yu knew she was avoiding him. He decided to wait a couple of days for the storm to blow over before approaching her again. Then, lowering his head, he noticed that the ground was strewn with balsam and pomegranate petals.

"She's too angry even to gather up the blossom," he sighed. "I'll take these over and try to speak to her tomorrow."

At this point Pao-chai urged them to take a stroll.

"I'll join you later," he said.

As soon as the other two had gone, he gathered up the fallen flowers in the skirt of his gown and made his way over a small hill, across a stream and through an orchard towards the mound where Tai-yu had buried the peach-blossom. Just before rounding the hill by the flowers' grave he caught the sound of sobs on the other side. Someone was lamenting and weeping there in a heart-rending fashion.

"Some maid's been badly treated and come here to cry," he thought. "I wonder which of them it is."

He halted to listen. And this is what he heard:

As blossoms fade and fly across the sky,
Who pities the faded red, the scent that has been?
Softly the gossamer floats over spring pavilions,
Gently the willow fluff wafts to the embroidered screen.

A girl in her chamber mourns the passing of spring,
No relief from anxiety her poor heart knows;
Hoe in hand she steps through her portal,
Loath to tread on the blossom as she comes and goes.

Willows and elms, fresh and verdant,
Care not if peach and plum blossom drift away;
Next year the peach and plum will bloom again,
But her chamber may stand empty on that day.

By the third month the scented nests are built,
But the swallows on the beam are heartless all;
Next year, though once again you may peck the buds,
From the beam of an empty room your nest will fall.

Each year for three hundred and sixty days

中国文学选读

The cutting wind and biting frost contend.

How long can beauty flower fresh and fair?

In a single day wind can whirl it to its end.

Fallen, the brightest blooms are hard to find;

With aching heart their grave-digger comes now

Alone, her hoe in hand, her secret tears

Falling like drops of blood on each bare bough.

Dusk falls and the cuckoo is silent;

Her hoe brought back, the lodge is locked and still;

A green lamp lights the wall as sleep enfolds her,

Cold rain pelts the casement and her quilt is chill.

What causes my two-fold anguish?

Love for spring and resentment of spring;

For suddenly it comes and suddenly goes,

Its arrival unheralded, noiseless its departing.

Last night from the courtyard floated a sad song—

Was it the soul of blossom, the soul of birds?

Hard to detain, the soul of blossom or birds,

For blossoms have no assurance, birds no words.

I long to take wing and fly

With the flowers to earth's uttermost bound;

And yet at earth's uttermost bound

Where can a fragrant burial mound be found?

Better shroud the fair petals in silk

With clean earth for their outer attire;

For pure you came and pure shall go,

Not sinking into some foul ditch or mire.

Now you are dead I come to bury you;

None has divined the day when I shall die;

*Men laugh at my folly in burying fallen flowers,*
*But who will bury me when dead I lie?*

*See, when spring draws to a close and flowers fall,*
*This is the season when beauty must ebb and fade;*
*The day that spring takes wing and beauty fades*
*Who will care for the fallen blossom or dead maid?*

Pao-yu, listening, was overwhelmed with grief. To know more of this, read the next chapter.

As we saw, Tai-yu held Pao-yu to blame for her exclusion by Ching-wen the previous night. As today happened to be the occasion for feasting the God of Flowers, her pent-up resentment merged with her grief at the transience of spring, and as she buried the fading petals she could not help weeping over her own fate and composing a lament.

Pao-yu listened from the slope. At first he just nodded in sympathy, until she came to the lines:

*Men laugh at my folly in burying fallen flowers,*
*But who will bury me when dead I lie?...*
*The day that spring takes wing and beauty fades*
*Who will care for the fallen blossom or dead maid?*

At this point he flung himself wretchedly down on the ground, scattering his load of fallen flowers, heart-broken to think that Tai-yu's loveliness and beauty must one day vanish away. And it followed that the same fate awaited Pao-chai, Hsiang-ling, Hsi-jen and all the rest. When at last they were all gone, what would become of him? And if he had no idea where he would be by then, what would become of this place and all the flowers and willows in the Garden and who would take them over? One reflection led to another until, after repeated ruminations, he wished he were

中国文学选读

some insensible, stupid object, able to escape all earthy entanglements and be free from such wretchedness despite the—

*Shadows of blossom all around,*

*Birdsong on every side.*

Tai-yu, giving way to her own grief, heard weeping now on the slope.

"Everyone laughs at me for being foolish. Is there someone else equally foolish?" she asked herself.

Then, looking up, she saw Pao-yu.

"So that's who it is." She snorted. "That heartless, wretched..."

But the moment the words "wretched" escaped her she covered her mouth and moved quickly away with a long sigh.

When Pao-yu recovered sufficiently to look up she had gone obviously to avoid him. Getting up rather sheepishly, he dusted off his clothes and walked down the hill to make his way back again to Happy Red Court. Catching sight of Tai-yu ahead, he overtook her.

"Do stop!" he begged. "I know you won't look at me, but let me just say one word. After that we can part company for good."

Tai-yu glanced round and would have ignored him, but was curious to hear this "*one* word," thinking there must be something in it. She came to a halt.

"Out with it."

Pao-yu smiled.

"Would you listen if I said two words?" he asked.

At once she walked away.

Pao-yu, close behind her, sighed.

"Why are things so different now from in the past?"

Against her will she stopped once more and turned her head.

"What do you mean by 'now' and 'the past'?"

Pao-yu heaved another sigh.

"Wasn't I your play mate when you first came?" he demanded. "Anything that pleased me was yours, cousin, for the asking. If I knew you fancied a favorite dish of mine, I put it away in a clean place till you came. We ate at the same table and slept on the same bed. I took care that the maids did nothing to upset you; for I thought cousins growing up together as such good friends should be kinder to each other than anyone else. I never expected you to grow so proud that now you have no use for me while you're so fond of outsiders like Pao-chai and Hsi-feng. You ignore me or cut me for three or four days at a time. I've no brothers or sisters of my own—only two by a different mother, as well you know. So I'm an only child like you, and I thought that would make for an affinity between us. But apparently it was no use my hoping for that. There's nobody I can tell how unhappy I am. " With that, he broke down again.

This appeal and his obvious wretchedness melted her heart. But though shedding tears of sympathy, she kept her head lowered and made no reply.

This encouraged Pao-yu to go on.

"I know my own faults. But however bad I may be, I'd never dare do anything to hurt you. If I do something the least bit wrong, you can tick me off, warn me, scold me or even strike me, and I won't mind. But when you just ignore me and I can't tell why, I'm at my wits' end and don't know what to do. If I die now I can only become a 'ghost hounded to death,' and not even the masses of the best bonzes and Taoists will be able to save my soul. I can only be born again if you'll tell me what's wrong. "

By now Tai-yu's resentment over the previous evening was completely forgotten.

"Then why did you tell your maids not to open the gate when I called last night?" she asked.

"Whatever do you mean?" he cried in amazement. "If I did such a thing, may I die on the spot. "

"Hush! Don't talk about dying so early in the morning. Did you or didn't you? There's no need to swear. "

"I honestly knew nothing about your coming. Pao-chai did drop in for a chat, but she didn't stay long. "

Tai-yu thought this over.

"Yes," she said more cheerfully, "I suppose your maids felt too lazy to stir and that made them answer rudely. "

"That's it, for sure. I shall find out who it was when I get back and give them a good scolding."

"Those maids of yours deserve one, although of course that's not for me to say. It doesn't matter their offending *me*, but think what trouble there'll be if next time they offend your precious Pao-chai!"

She compressed her lips to smile, and Pao-yu did not know whether to grind his teeth or laugh.

(translated by Yang Xianyi and Gladys Yang)

## 黛玉葬花

如今且说林黛玉因夜间失寐，次日起来迟了，闻得众姊妹都在园中作饯花会，恐人笑他痴懒，连忙梳洗了出来。刚到了院中，只见宝玉进门来了，笑道："好妹妹。你昨儿可告我了不曾？教我悬了一夜心。"林黛玉便回头叫紫鹃道："把屋子收拾了，摺下一扇纱屉，看那大燕子回来，把帘子放下来，拿狮子倚住，烧了香就把炉罩上。"一面说一面又往外走。

宝玉见他这样，还认作是昨日晌午的事，那知晚间的这段公案，还打恭作揖的。林黛玉正眼也不看，各自出了院门，一直找别的姊妹去了。宝玉心中纳闷，

大观园

自己猜疑："看起这个光景来，不像是为昨日的事，但只昨日我回来的晚了，又没有见他，再没有冲撞了他的去处了。"一面想，一面由不得随后跟了来。

只见宝钗探春正在那边看鹤舞，见黛玉去了，三个一同站着说话儿。又见宝玉来了，探春便笑道："宝哥哥，身上好？我整整的三天没见你了。"宝玉笑道："妹妹身上好？我前儿还在大嫂子跟前问你呢。"探春道："宝哥哥，你往这里来，我和你说话。"宝玉听说，便跟了他，离了钗玉两个，到了一棵石榴树下。

探春因说道："这几天老爷可曾叫你？"宝玉笑道："没有叫。"探春说："昨儿我恍惚听见说老爷叫你出去的。"宝玉笑道："那想是别人听错了，并没叫我。"探春又笑道："这几个月，我又攒下有十来吊钱了。你还拿了去，明儿出门逛去的时候，或是好字画，好轻巧玩意儿，替我带些来。"

宝玉道："我这么城里城外，大廊小庙的逛，也没见个新奇精致东西，左不过是那些金、玉、铜、磁器，没处摆的古董儿；再就是绸缎、吃食、衣服了。"探春道："谁要那些作什么！象你上回买的那柳枝儿编的小篮子儿，竹子根儿抠的香盒儿，胶泥垛的风炉儿，就好了。我喜欢的什么似的，谁知他们都爱上了，都当宝贝似的抢了去了。"宝玉笑道："原来要这个。这不值什么，拿五百钱出去给小子们，管拉两车来。"探春道："小厮们知道什么？你拣那朴而不俗、直而不拙者，这些东西，你多多的替我带了来，我还像上回的鞋作一双你穿，比那一双还加工夫，如何呢？"

宝玉笑道："你提起鞋来，我想起个故事：那一回我穿着，可巧遇见了老爷，老爷就不受用，问是谁作的。我那里敢提三妹妹？我就回说是前儿我生日，是舅母给的。老爷听了是舅母给的，才不好说什么，半日还说：'何苦来！虚耗人力，作践绫罗，作这样的东西。'我回来告诉了袭人，袭人说这还罢了，赵姨娘气的抱怨的了不得：'正经亲兄弟，鞋搭拉袜搭拉的，没人看的见，且作这些东西！'"

探春听说，登时沉下脸来，道："这话糊涂到什么田地！怎么我是该作鞋的人么？环儿难道没有分例的？没有人的？一般的衣裳是衣裳，鞋袜是鞋袜，丫头老婆一屋子，怎么抱怨这些话？给谁听呢！我不过是闲着没事儿，作一双半双，爱给那个哥哥弟弟，随我的心。谁敢管我不成？这也是白气。"宝玉听了，点头笑道："你不知道，他心里自然又有个想头了。"

探春听说，益发动了气，将头一扭，说道："连你也糊涂了！他那想头自然是有的，不过是那阴微鄙贱的见识。他只管这么想，我只管认得老爷太太两个人，别人我一概不管。就是姊妹弟兄跟前，谁和我好，我就和谁好；什么偏的庶的，我也不知道。论理我不该说他，但忒昏愦的不像了！还有笑话呢：就是上回我给你那钱，替我带那玩的东西，过了两天，他见了我，也是说没钱使，怎么难，我也不理论。谁知后来丫头们出去了，他就抱怨起来，说我攒的钱为什么给你使，倒不给环儿使呢！我听见这话，又好笑又好气，我就出来往太太跟前去了。"

正说着，只见宝钗那边笑道："说完了，来罢。显见的是哥哥妹妹了，丢下别人，且说体己去。我们听一句儿就使不得了？"说着，探春宝玉二人方笑着来了。

宝玉因不见了林黛玉，便知他躲了别处去了。想了一想："索性迟两日，等他的气消一消，再去也罢了。"因低头看见许多凤仙石榴等各色落花，锦重重的落了一地，因叹道："这是他心里生了气，也不收拾这花儿来了。待我送了去，明儿再问着他。"说着，只见宝钗约着他们往外头去。宝玉

黛玉葬花

道："我就来。"说毕，等他二人去远了，便把那花兜了起来，登山渡水，过树穿花，一直奔了那日同黛玉葬桃花的去处来。

将已到了花冢，犹未转过山坡，只听山坡那边有呜咽之声，一行数落着，哭的好不伤感。宝玉心下想道："这不知是那房里的丫头，受了委曲，跑到这个地方来哭。"一面想，一面煞住脚步，听他哭道是：

　　　　　花谢花飞花满天，红消香断有谁怜？
　　　　　游丝软系飘春榭，落絮轻沾扑绣帘。
　　　　　闺中女儿惜春暮，愁绪满怀无释处；
　　　　　手把花锄出绣闺，忍踏落花来复去？
　　　　　柳丝榆荚自芳菲，不管桃飘与李飞；
　　　　　桃李明年能再发，明年闺中知有谁？
　　　　　三月香巢已垒成，梁间燕子太无情！
　　　　　明年花发虽可啄，却不道人去梁空巢也倾。

一年三百六十日，风刀霜剑严相逼；

明媚鲜妍能几时，一朝飘泊难寻觅。

花开易见落难寻，阶前闷杀葬花人；

独倚花锄泪暗洒，洒上空枝见血痕。

杜鹃无语正黄昏，荷锄归去掩重门；

青灯照壁人初睡，冷雨敲窗被未温。

怪奴底事倍伤神，半为怜春半恼春：

怜春忽至恼忽去，至又无言去不闻。

昨宵庭外悲歌发，知是花魂与鸟魂？

花魂鸟魂总难留，鸟自无言花自羞；

愿奴胁下生双翼，随花飞到天尽头。

天尽头，何处有香丘？

未若锦囊收艳骨，一杯净土掩风流；

质本洁来还洁去，强于污淖陷渠沟。

尔今死去侬收葬，未卜侬身何日丧？

侬今葬花人笑痴，他年葬侬知是谁？

试看春残花渐落，便是红颜老死时，

一朝春尽红颜老，花落人亡两不知！

宝玉听了不觉痴倒。

话说林黛玉只因昨夜晴雯不开门一事，错疑在宝玉身上。至次日又可巧遇见饯花之期，正是一腔无明未发泄，又勾起伤春愁思，因把些残花落瓣去掩埋，由不得感花伤己，哭了几声，便随口念了几句。不想宝玉在山坡上听见，先不过点头感叹；次后听到"侬今葬花人笑痴，他年葬侬知是谁？……一朝春尽红颜老，花落人亡两不知"等句，不觉恸倒山坡之上，怀里兜的落花撒了一地。试想林黛玉的花颜月貌，将来亦到无可寻觅之时，宁不心碎肠断！既黛玉终归无可寻觅之时，推之于他人，如宝钗、香菱、袭人等，亦可到无可寻觅之时矣。宝钗等终归无可寻觅之时，则自己又安在哉？且自身尚不知何在何往，则斯处、斯园、斯花、斯柳，又不知当属谁姓矣！因此一而二，二而三，反复推求了去，真不知此时此际欲为何等蠢物，杳无所知，逃大造，出尘网，使可解释这段悲伤。正是：花影不离身左右，鸟声只在耳东西。

那林黛玉正自伤感，忽听山坡上也有悲声，心下想道："人人都笑我有些痴病，难道还有一个痴子不成？"想着，抬头一看，见是宝玉。林黛玉看见，便道："啐！我道是谁，原来是这个狠心短命的——"刚说到"短命"二字，又把口掩住，长叹了一声，自己抽身便走了。

这里宝玉悲恸了一回，忽然抬头不见了黛玉，便知黛玉看见他躲开了。自己也觉无味，抖抖土起来，下山寻归旧路，往怡红院来。可巧看见黛玉在前头走，连忙赶上去，说道："你且站住。我知你不理我，我只说一句话，从今后撂开手。"黛玉回头看见是宝玉，待要不理他，听他说"只说一句话，从此撂开手"这话里有文章，少不得站住，说道："有一句话，请说来。"宝玉笑道："两句话，说了你听不听？"黛玉听说，回头就走。宝玉在身后面叹道："既有今日，何必当初？"

林黛玉听见这话，由不得站住，回头道："当初怎么样？今日怎么样？"宝玉叹道："当初姑娘来了，那不是我陪着玩笑？凭我心爱的，姑娘要，就拿去；我爱吃的，听见姑娘也爱吃，连忙干干净净收着等姑娘吃。一桌子吃饭，一床上睡觉。丫头们想不到的，我怕姑娘生气，我替丫头们想到了。我心里想着：姊妹们从小儿长大，亲也罢，热也罢，和气到了儿，才见得比人好。如今谁承望姑娘人大心大，不把我放在眼睛里，倒把外四路的什么宝姐姐凤姐姐的放在心坎儿上，倒把我三日不理四日不见的，我又没个亲兄弟亲姊妹，——虽然有两个，你难道不知道是和我隔母的？我也和你似的独出，只怕同我的心一样，谁知我是白操了这个心，弄的有冤无处诉！"说着不觉滴下眼泪来。

黛玉耳内听了这话，眼内见了这形景，心内不觉灰了大半，也不觉滴下泪来，低头不语。宝玉见他这般形景，遂又说道："我也知道我如今不好了，但只凭着怎么不好，万不敢在妹妹跟前有错处。便有一二分错处，你倒是或教导我，戒我下次，或骂我两句，打我两下，我都不灰心。谁知你总不理我，叫我摸不着头脑，少魂失魄，不知怎么样才好。就便死了，也是个屈死鬼，任凭高僧高道忏悔也不能超生；还得你申明了缘故，我才得托生呢！"

黛玉听了这个话，不觉将昨晚的事都忘在九霄云外了，便说道："你既这么说，昨儿为什么我去了，你不叫丫头开门？"宝玉诧异道："这话从那里说起？我要是这么样，立刻就死了！"林黛玉啐道："大清早起死呀活的，也不忌讳！你说有呢就有，没有就没有，起什么誓呢！"宝玉道："实在没有见你去，就是宝姐姐坐了一坐，就出来了。"

黛玉想了一想，笑道："是了。想必是你的丫头们懒待动，丧声歪气的也是有的。"宝玉道:"想必是这个原故,等我回去问了是谁,教训教训他们就好了。"黛玉道:"你的那些姑娘们也该教训教训,只是我论理不该说。今儿得罪了我的事小,倘或明儿宝姑娘来,什么贝姑娘来,也得罪了,事情岂不大了。"说着,抿着嘴笑。

　　宝玉听了,又是咬牙,又是笑。

——选自《红楼梦》第二十七回

## Further Readings

### 1. Governor of the Southern Tributary State
#### Li Gongzuo

Chunyu Fen, a native of Dongping and a well-known gallant of the Yangtse River region, was fond of drinking, hot tempered and recklessly indifferent to conventions. He had amassed great wealth and acted as patron to many dashing young men. Because of his military prowess he had been made an adjutant of the Huainan Army, but in a fit of drunkenness he offended his general and was dismissed. Then in his disappointment he let himself go and spent his days drinking.

Chunyu's home was some three miles east of Yangzhou. South of his house there was a huge old ash tree with great branches, thick with foliage, which shaded an acre of land; and under this tree Chunyu and his boon companions drank daily to their hearts' content. In the ninth month of the tenth year of the Zhen Yuan period (794 A. D. ), Chunyu got drunk, and two of his friends carried him back home and laid him in the eastern chamber. "You had better go to sleep," they said. "We shall give the horses some fodder and wash our feet. We shan't go until you feel better. "

He took off his cap and rested his head on the pillow, lying there in an intoxicated state, half dreaming and half awoke. Presently he saw two messengers come in, dressed in purple, who knelt before him and said, "His majesty the king of Ashendon has sent us, his humble subjects, to invite you to his kingdom. "

Chunyu got up from his couch, dressed and followed the two messengers to the gate, where he saw a small green carriage drawn by four horses. Seven or eight attendants who were standing by helped him into the carriage. Driving out of the gate, they set forth in the direction of the ash tree and—to Chunyu's amazement—headed down the hollow under the tree. However, he dared ask no questions. The scenery along the road—the mountains and rivers, trees and plants—looked different from the world of men. The climate too had changed. After they had traveled about ten miles, city walls came into sight, and the road began to fill with carriages and people. The footmen on the carriage kept calling out to clear the road and the pedestrians moved hurriedly out of their way. They entered a great city through a turreted red gate over which was inscribed in letters of gold "The Great Kingdom of Ashendon" The gate keepers bestirred themselves and bowed low to them.

Then a rider cantered up, calling, "As his Highness the Prince consort has traveled so far, His Majesty orders him to be taken to the East Hostel to rest." And he led the way.

Chunyu saw a gate in front swing open. He got down from the carriage and passed through the gate. There were brightly painted and finely carved balustrades and pilasters among terraces of blossoming trees and rare fruits, while tables and rugs, cushions and screens had been set ready in the hall and a rich feast laid out. Chunyu was enchanted. Presently it was announced that the prime minister had arrived, and Chunyu went to the foot of the hall steps to await him respectfully. Dressed in purple and holding an ivory sceptre, the minister approached, and they paid their respects to each other. This done, the minister said, "Though our land is far from yours, our king has asked you here because he hopes for an alliance with you by marriage."

"How can a humble person like me aspire so high?" replied the young man.

The minister asked Chunyu to follow him to the palace. They walked a hundred yards and entered a red gate where spears, axes, and halberds were displayed, several hundred officers stood still by the side of the road to make way for Chunyu, among them an old drinking friend of his named Chou. Chunyu was secretly delighted, but dared not go forward to accost him.

Then the minister led Chunyu up to a court where guards were standing solemnly in formation, showing that they were in the royal presence. He was a tall, imposing figure on the throne, wearing a white silk robe and a bright red cap. Overcome by awe, he did not look up, but bowed as the attendants told him. "At your father's wish," said the king, "We have asked you to our unworthy kingdom, to offer you our second daughter as your wife." When Chunyu kept his head bowed and dared not reply, the king told him, "You may go back to the guest house and prepare for the ceremony."

As the minister accompanied him back, Chunyu was thinking hard. Since his fa-

中国文学选读

ther was a frontier general who had been reported missing, it was possible that, having made peace with the border kingdoms, he was responsible for this invitation. Still, Chunyu was bewildered and at a loss to account for it.

That evening, amid pomp and splendor, betrothal gifts of lambs, swans and silk were displayed. There was music of stringed and bamboo instruments, feasting with lanterns and candles, and a concourse of carriages and horsemen. Some of the girls present were addressed as the nymphs of Huayang or Qingxi, others as the fairies of the upper or lower region. Attended by a large retinue, they were dressed in green phoenix head-dresses and gold cloud-like garments and decked with golden trinkets and precious stones that dazzled the eye. These girls frolicked about and played pranks on Chunyu, with such bewitching charm and clever repartee that he found it hard to reply.

"On the last Spring Purification Festival, "one girl said, "I went with Lady Lingzhi to Chanzhi Monastery to watch Yuyan perform the Brahmana dance in the Indian Quadrangle. I was sitting with the girls on the stone bench on the north side when you and your young gallants arrived, and got off your houses to watch. You accosted us and teased us and made jokes—don't you remember how Qiongying and I tied a scarlet scarf on the bamboo? Then, on the sixteenth of the seventh month, I went with Shang Zhezi to Xiaogan Monastery to listen to Monk Qixuan discoursing on the Avalokiteshvara sutra. I donated two gold phoenix-shaped hairpins and my friend one rhinoceros horn case. You were there too, and you asked the monk to let you look at the things. After admiring them and praising the workmanship for a long time, you turned to us and said, 'These pretty things and their owners surely can't belong to the world of men!' Then you asked my name and wanted to know where I lived, but I wouldn't tell you. You kept staring at me as if you were quite lovelorn— don't you remember?"

Chunyu replied by quoting the song:

> *Deep in my heart it is hidden,*
> *How can I ever forget?*

And the girls said, "Who could imagine that you would become our relative?"

Jus then three magnificently dressed men came up. Bowing to Chunyu, they announced, "By His Majesty's order we have come to be your groomsmen." One of them looked like an old friend.

"Aren't you Tian Zihua of Fengyi?" Chunyu asked him. When the other said that he was, Chunyu went forward to grasp his hand, and they talked about the past.

Asked how he came to be there, Tian replied, "On my travels I met Lord Duan, the prime minister, and he became my patron." When Chunyu asked him if he knew that Zhou was also there, he replied, "Zhou has done very well. He is now the city commandant and has great influence. On several occasions he has done me a favor."

They talked cheerfully until it was announced that the prince consort should go to the wedding. As the three groomsmen handed him his sword, pendants, robes and headdress, and helped him to put them on, Tian said, "I never thought I should be at such a brand ceremony for you today. You mustn't forget your old friends."

Several dozen fairy maids began to play rare music, piercingly tender and infinitely sad, the like of which Chunyu had never heard before. Dozens of other attendants held candles all the way down a mile-long path lined on both sides with gold and emerald-green screens vividly painted and intricately carved. Chunyu sat up straight in the carriage, feeling rather nervous, while Tian joked to put him at his ease. The girls he had seen were arriving too in phoenix-winged carriages. When he came to the gate of Xiu Yi Palace, the girls were there too, and Chunyu was asked to alight. They went through a ceremony just like that in the world of men, at the end of which screens and fans were removed, enabling him to see his bride, the Princess of the Golden Bough. She was about fifteen lovely as a goddess and well trained in the marriage ceremony.

After the wedding Chunyu and the princess came to love each other dearly, and his power and prestige increased daily. His equipage and entertainments were second only to the king's. One day the king took him and some other officials as his guards to hunt at the Divine Tortoise Mountain in the west, where there were high peaks, wide marshlands and luxuriant forests stoked with all kinds of birds and beasts. The hunters came back with a big bag of game that evening.

One day Chunyu said to the king, "On my wedding day Your Majesty said you had sent for me in compliance with my father's wishes. My father served formerly as a general at the frontier. After a defeat he was reported missing, and I have had no news of him for eighteen years. Since Your Majesty knows where he is now, I would like to call on him."

"Your father is still serving at the northern frontier," replied the king quickly. "We are in constant touch. You had better just write to him. There is no need for you to go there." The king ordered the princess to prepare gifts to send to Chunyu's father, and after a few days a reply came in his father's handwriting. He expressed his longing for his son, and wrote just as in former letters, asking whether certain relatives were still alive and what news there was so great, he said, it was difficult to send news. His letter was sad and full of grief. He told Chunyu not to come, but promised that they would meet in three years' time. With this letter in his hands, Chunyu wept bitterly, unable to restrain himself.

One day the princess asked him, "Don't you ever want to take up an official post?"

"I am used to a carefree life," answered Chunyu. "I don't understand official work."

"Just take a post," his wife said, "and I will help you." Then she spoke to the king.

A few days later the king said, "All is not well in my southern tributary state, and the governor has been dismissed. I would like to use your talents to set their affairs in order. You might go there with my daughter." When Chunyu consented, the king ordered those in charge to get his baggage ready. Gold, jade and silk, cases and servants, carriages and horsemen formed a long baggage train when he and the princess were ready to leave. And since Chunyu had mixed with gallants as a young man and never dreamed of becoming an official, he was very pleased.

He sent a memorandum to the king, saying, "As the son of a military family, I have never studied the art of government. Now that I have been given this important post, I fear I shall not only disgrace myself but ruin the prestige of the court. I would therefore like to seek far and wide for wise and talented men to help me. I have noticed that City Commandant Zhou of Yingchuan is a loyal, honest officer, who firmly upholds the law and would make a good minister. Then there is Tian Zihua, a gentleman of Fengyi, who is prudent and full of stratagems and has probed deeply into the principles of government. I have known both these men for ten years. I understand their talents and consider them trustworthy, and therefore I ask to have Zhou appointed the chief councilor and Tian the minister of finance of my state. For then the government will be well administered and the laws well kept. " The two men were then appointed to these posts by the king.

The evening of Chunyu's departure, the king and queen gave a farewell feast for him south of the capital.

"The southern state is a great province," said the king. "The land is rich and the people prosperous and you must adopt a benevolent policy there. With Zhou and Tian assisting you, I hope you will do well and come up to our expectations. "

Meantime the queen told the princess, "Your husband is impetuous and fond of drinking, and he is still young. A wife should be gentle and obedient. I trust you to look after him well. Though you will not be too far from us, you will no longer be able to greet us every morning and evening, and I find it hard not to shed tears now that you are going away. " Then Chunyu and the princess bowed, got into their carriage and started south. They talked cheerfully on the way, and several days later reached their destination.

The officials of the province, the monks and priests, elders, musicians, attendants and guards had all come out in welcome. The streets were thronged, and drums and bells were being sounded for miles around. Chunyu saw a goodly array of turrets and pavilions as he entered the great city gate, above which was inscribed in letters of gold "The Southern Tributary State". In front there were red windows and a big gate with a fine view into the distance. After his arrival he studied the local conditions and helped all who were sick or distressed, entrusting his government to Zhou and Tian, who administered the province well. He remained governor there for twenty years, and the people benefiting from his good role sang praises and set up tablets extolling his virtue or built temples to him. As a result, the king honored him even more: he was given fiefs and titles and exalted to the position of a grand councilor of state,

中国文学选读

while both Zhou and Tian also became well-known as good officials, and were promoted several times. Chunyu had five sons and two daughters. His sons were given official posts reserved for the nobility, while his daughters were married to the royal family. Thus his fame and renown were unrivalled.

One year the kingdom of Sandalvine attacked this province, and the king ordered Chunyu to raise an army defend it. Chunyu made Zhou commander of thirty thousand troops to resist the invaders at Jade Tower City, but Zhou proved proud and reckless, underestimating the enemy. His troops were routed and, abandoning his amour, he fled back alone to the provincial capital at night. Meanwhile the invaders, after capturing their baggage train and arms, had withdrawn. Chunyu had Zhou arrested and asked to be punished, but the king pardoned them both.

That same month Zhou developed a boil on his back and died. Ten days later the princess died of illness too, and Chunyu's request to leave the province and accompany the hearse to the capital was granted. Tian, the minister of finance, was appointed deputy in his place. Bowed down with grief, Chunyu followed the hearse. On the way many people wept, officers and common citizens paid their last homage, while great crowds blocked the way and clung to the carriage. When he reached Ashendon, the king and queen were waiting outside the capital, wearing mourning and weeping. The princess was posthumously entitled Shun Yi (Obedient and Graceful). Guards, canopies and musicians were provided, and she was buried at Coiling Dragon Mount some three miles east of the city. During the same month, Zhou's son Rongxin also arrived with his father's hearse.

Now though Chunyu had been ruling over a tributary state outside the kingdom for many years, he had managed to keep on good terms with all the nobles and influential officers at court. After his return to the capital he behaved unconventionally and gathered around himself many associates and followers, his power growing so rapidly that the king began to suspect him. Then some citizens reported to the king that a mysterious portent had appeared and the state was doomed to suffer a great catastrophe: the capital would be removed and the ancestral temples destroyed. This would be caused by some one of foreign birth who was close to the royal family. After deliberation the ministers decided that there was danger in Chunyu's luxury and presumption; accordingly the king deprived him of his attendants and forbade him to have any further dealings with his associates, ordering him to live in retirement.

Conscious that he had not governed badly all these years in his province, but was now slandered, Chunyu was in low spirits. The king, sensing this, said to him, "You have been my son-in-law for more than twenty years. Unhappily my daughter died young and could not live with you till old age. This is a great misfortune." Then the queen took charge of his children herself, and the king said, "You have left your home for a long time. You had better go back now for a while to see your relatives. Leave your children here and do not worry about them. In three years we shall fetch you back."

"Isn't this my home?" asked Chunyu. "What other home have I to go back to?"

"You came from the world of men," replied the king with a laugh. "This is not your home." At first Chunyu felt as if he were dreaming, but then he remembered how he had come there and, shedding tears, asked for permission to return. The king ordered his attendants to see him off, and with a bow Chunyu took his leave.

The same two messengers dressed in purple accompanied him out of the gate. But there he was shocked to see a shabby carriage with no attendants or envoys to accompany him. He got into the carriage, however, and after driving some miles they left the city behind. They traveled the same way that he had first come by. The mountains, rivers and plains were unchanged, but the two messengers with Chunyu looked so seedy that he felt let down. When he asked them when they would reach Yangzhou, they went on singing without paying any attention. Only when he insisted did they answer, "Soon."

Presently they emerged from the hollow and Chunyu saw his own village unchanged. Sadness seized him, and he could not help shedding tears. The two messengers helped him down from the carriage, through the door of his house and up the steps. Then he saw himself lying in the eastern chamber, and was so frightened that he dared not approach. At that the two messengers called his name aloud several times, and he woke up.

He saw his servants sweeping the courtyard. His two guests were still washing their feet by the couch, the slanting sun had not yet set behind the west wall and his unfinished wine was still by the east window—but he had lived through a whole generation in his dream! Deeply moved, he could not help sighing. And when he called his two friends and told them, they were equally amazed. They went out to look for the hollow under the ash tree, and Chunyu, pointing to it, said, "This is where I went in the dream."

His friends believed this must be the work of some fox fairy or tree spirit, so servants were ordered to fetch an axe and cut through the tree trunk and branches to find where the hollow ended. It was some ten feet long, terminating in a cavity lit by the sun and large enough to hold a couch. In this were mounds of earth which resembled city walls, pavilions and courts, and swarms of ants were gathered there. In the ant-hill was a small, reddish tower occupied by two huge ants, three inches long, with white wings and red heads. They were surrounded by a few dozen big ants, and other ants dared not approach them. These huge ants were the king and queen, and this was the capital of Ashendon.

Then the men followed up another hole which lay under the southern branch of the tree and was at least forty feet long. In this tunnel there was another ant-hill with small towers, which swarmed with ants. This was the southern tributary state which Chunyu had governed. Another large, rambling tunnel of a fantastic shape ran westwards for twenty feet, and in this they found a rotten tortoise shell as big as a peck measure, soaked by rain and covered by luxuriant grass. This was the Divine Tortoise Mountain, where Chunyu had hunted. They followed up yet another tunnel more than ten feet long in the east, where the gnarled roots of the tree had twisted into the shape of a dragon. Here there was a small earthen mound about a foot high, and this was the grave of the princess, Chunyu's wife.

As he thought back, Chunyu was very shaken, for all that they had discovered coincided with his dream. He would not let his friends destroy these ant-hills, and ordered that the tunnels be covered up as before. That night, however, there was a sudden storm, and in the morning when he examined the holes the ants had gone. Thus the prophecy that Ashendon would suffer a great catastrophe and that the capital would be removed was realized. Then he thought of the invasion by the kingdom of Sandalvine, and asked his two friends to trace it. They found that some six hundred yards east of his house was a river-bed long since dry and next to it grew a big sandal tree so thickly covered with vines that the sun could not shine through it. A small hole beside it, where a swarm of ants had gathered, must be the kingdom of Sandal-vine.

If even the mysteries of ants are so unfathomable, what then of the changes caused by big beasts in the hills and woods?

At that time Chunyu's friends Zhou and Tian were both in Liuho County, and he had not seen them for ten days. He sent a servant posthaste to make enquiries, and found that Zhou had died of a sudden illness, while Tian was laying ill in bed. Then Chunyu realized how empty his dream had been, and that all was vanity too in the world of men. He therefore became a Taoist and abstained from wine and women. Three years later he died at home, in his forty-seventh year, just as predicted in the dream.

(translated by Yang Xianyi and Gladys Yang)

## 南柯太守传
### 李公佐

东平淳于棼，吴楚游侠之士。嗜酒使气，不守细行。累巨产，养豪客。曾以武艺补淮南军裨将，因使酒忤帅，斥逐落魄，纵诞饮酒为事。家住广陵郡东十里，所居宅南有大古槐一株，枝干修密，清阴数亩。淳于生日与群豪，大饮其下。贞元七年九月，因沉醉致疾。时二友人于座扶生归家，卧于堂东庑之下。二友谓生曰："子其寝矣！余将秣马濯足，俟子小愈而去。"生解巾就枕，昏然忽忽，仿佛若梦。见二紫衣使者，跪拜生曰："槐安国王遣小臣致命奉邀。"生不觉下榻整衣，随二使至门。见青油小车，驾以四牡，左右从者七八，扶生上车，出大户，指古槐穴而去。使者即驱入穴中。生意颇甚异之，不敢致问。忽见山川风候，草木道路，与人世甚殊。前行数十里，有郛郭城堞。车舆人物，不绝于路。生左右传车者传呼甚严，行者亦争辟于左右。又入大城，朱门重楼，楼上有金书，题曰"大槐安国"。执门者趋拜奔走。旋有一骑传呼曰："王以驸马远降，令且息东华馆。"因前导而去。

俄见一门洞开，生降车而入。彩槛雕楹；华木珍果，列植于庭下；几案茵褥，帘帏肴膳，陈设于庭上。生心甚自悦。复有呼曰："右相且至。"生降阶祗奉。有一

《南柯太守传》插图

人紫衣象简前趋，宾主之仪敬尽焉。右相曰："寡君不以弊国远僻，奉迎君子，托以姻亲。"生曰："某以贱劣之躯，岂敢是望。"右相因请生同诣其所。行可百步，入朱门。矛戟斧钺，布列左右，军吏数百，辟易道侧。

生有平生酒徒周弁者，变趋其中。生私心悦之，不敢前问。右相引生升广殿，御卫严肃，若至尊之所。见一人长大端严，居王位，衣素练服，簪朱华冠。

生战栗，不敢仰视。左右侍者令生拜。王曰："前奉贤尊命，不弃小国。许令次女瑶芳奉事君子。"生但俯伏而已，不敢致词。王曰："且就宾宇，续造仪式。"有旨，右相亦与生偕还馆舍。生思念之，意以为父在边将，因殁虏中，不知存亡。将谓父北蕃交逊，而致兹事。心甚迷惑，不知其由。是夕，羔雁币帛，威容仪度，妓乐丝竹，肴膳灯烛，车骑礼物之用，无不咸备。有群女，或称华阳姑，或称青溪姑，或称上仙子，或称下仙子，若是者数辈。

皆侍从数千，冠翠凤冠，衣金霞帔，彩碧金钿，目不可视。遂游戏乐，往来其门，争以淳于郎为戏弄。风态娇丽，言词巧艳，生莫能对。复有一女谓生曰："昨上巳日，吾从灵芝夫人过禅智寺，于天竺院观右延舞《婆罗门》。吾与诸女坐北牖石榻上，时君少年，亦解骑来看。君独强来亲洽，言调笑谑。吾与穷英妹结绛巾，挂于竹枝上，君独不忆念之乎？又七月十六日，吾于孝感寺侍上真子，听契玄法师讲《观音经》。吾于讲下舍金凤钗两只，上真子舍水犀合子一枚。时君亦讲筵中于师处请钗合视之，赏叹再三，嗟异良久。顾余辈曰：'人之与物，皆非世间所有。'或问吾氏，或访吾里。吾亦不答。情意恋恋，瞩盼不舍。君岂不思念之乎？"生曰："中心藏之，何日忘之。"群女曰："不意今日与君为眷属。"复有三人，冠带甚伟，前拜生曰："奉命为驸马相者。"中一人与生且故。生指曰："子非冯翊田子华乎？"田曰："然。"生前，执手叙旧久之。生谓曰："子何以居此？"子华曰："吾放游，获受知于右相武成侯段公，因以栖托。"生复问曰："周弁在此，知之乎？"子华曰："周生，贵人也。职力司隶，权势甚盛。吾数蒙庇护。"言笑甚欢。俄传声曰："驸马可进矣。"三子取剑佩冕服，更衣之。子华曰："不意今日获睹盛礼，无以相忘也。"有仙姬数十，奏诸异乐，婉转清亮，曲调凄悲，非人间之所闻听。有执烛引导者，亦数十。左右见金翠步障，彩碧玲珑，不断数里。生端坐车中，心意恍惚，甚不自安。田子华数言笑以解之。向者群女姑姊，各乘凤翼辇，亦往来其间。至一门，号"修仪宫"。群仙姑姊亦纷然在侧，令生降车辇拜，揖让升降，一如人间。

撤障去扇，见一女子，云号"金枝公主"。年可十四五，俨若神仙。交欢之礼，颇亦明显。生自尔情义日洽，荣耀日盛，出入车服，游宴宾御，次于王者。王命生与群僚备武卫，大猎于国西灵龟山。山阜峻秀，川泽广远，林树丰茂，飞禽走兽，无不蓄之。师徒大获，竟夕而还。生因他日，启王曰："臣顷结好之日，大王云奉臣父之命。臣父顷佐边将，用兵失利，陷没胡中；尔来绝书信十七八岁矣。王既知所在，臣请一往拜觐。"王遽谓曰："亲家翁职守北土，信问不绝。卿但具书状知闻，未用便去。"遂命妻致馈贺之礼，一以遣之。数夕还答。生验书本意，皆父平生之迹，书中忆念教诲，情意委曲，皆如昔年。复问生亲戚存亡，闾里兴废。复言路道乖远，风烟阻绝。词意悲苦，言语哀伤。又不令生来觐，云："岁在丁丑，当与汝相见。"生捧书悲咽，情不自堪。

他日，妻谓生曰："子岂不思为政乎？"生曰："我放荡不习政事。"妻曰："卿但为之，余当奉赞。"妻遂白于王。累日，谓生曰："吾南柯政事不理，太守黜废，欲藉卿才，可曲屈之。便与小女同行。"生敦受教命。王遂敕有司备太守行李。因出金玉、锦绣、箱奁、仆妾、车马，列于广衢，以饯公主之行。

生少游侠，曾不敢有望，至是甚悦。因上表曰："臣将门余子，素无艺术，猥当大任，必败朝章。自悲负乘，坐致覆餗。今欲广求贤哲，以赞不逮。伏见司隶颍川周弁，忠亮刚直，守法不回，有毗佐之器。处士冯翊田子华，清慎通变，达政化之源。二人与臣有十年之旧，备知才用，可托政事。周请署南柯司宪，田请署司农。庶使臣政绩有闻，宪章不紊也。"王并依表以遣之。其夕，王与夫人饯于国南。王谓生曰："南柯，国之大郡，土地丰壤，人物豪盛，非惠政不能以治之。况有周田二赞。卿其勉之，以副国念。"夫人戒公主曰："淳于郎性刚好酒，加之少年；为妇之道，贵乎柔顺。尔善事之，吾无忧矣。南柯虽封境不遥，晨昏有间，今日暌别，宁不沾巾。"生与妻拜首南去，登车拥骑，言笑甚欢。累夕达郡。郡有官吏、僧道、耆老、音乐、车舆、武卫、銮铃，争来迎奉。人物阗咽，钟鼓喧哗，不绝十数里。见雉堞台观，佳气郁郁。入大城门，门亦有大榜，题以金字，曰"南柯郡城"。

见朱轩棨户，森然深邃。生下车，省风俗，疗病苦，政事委以周、田，郡中大理。自守郡二十载，风化广被，百姓歌谣，建功德碑，立生祠宇。王甚重之，赐食邑，锡爵位，居台辅。周、田皆以政治著闻，递迁大位。生有五男二女。男以门荫授官，女亦聘于王族。荣耀显赫，一时之盛，代莫比之。是岁，有檀萝国者，来伐是郡。王命生练将训师以征之。乃表周弁将兵三万，以拒贼之众于瑶台城。弁刚勇轻敌，师徒败绩，弁单骑裸身潜遁，夜归城。贼亦收辎重铠甲而还。

生因囚弁以请罪。王并舍之。

是月，司宪周弁疽发背，卒。生妻公主遭疾，旬日又薨。生因请罢郡，护丧赴国。王许之。便以司农田子华行南柯太守事。生哀恸发引，威仪在途，男女叫号，人吏奠馔，攀辕遮道者不可胜数。遂达于国。王与夫人素衣哭于郊，候灵舆之至。谥公主曰"顺仪公主"。备仪仗，羽葆鼓吹，葬于国东十里盘龙岗。是月，故司宪子荣信，亦护丧赴国。生久镇外藩，结好中国，贵门豪族，靡不是洽。自罢郡还国，出入无恒，交游宾从，威福日盛。王意疑惮之。时有国人上表云："玄象谪见，国有大恐。都邑迁徙，宗庙崩坏。衅起他族，事在萧墙。"时议以生侈僭之应也。遂夺生侍卫，禁生游从，处之私第。生自恃守郡多年，曾无败政，流言怨悖，郁郁不乐。王亦知之，因命生曰："姻亲二十余年，不幸小女夭枉，不得与君子偕老，良有痛伤。"夫人因留孙自鞠育之。又谓生曰："卿离家多时，可暂归本里，一见亲族。诸孙留此，无以为念。后三年，当令迎卿。"

生曰："此乃家矣，何更归焉？"王笑曰："卿本人间，家非在此。"生忽若昏睡，瞢然久之，方乃发悟前事，遂流涕请还。王顾左右以送生。生再拜而去，复见前二紫衣使者从焉。至大户外，见所乘车甚劣，左右亲使御仆，遂无一人，心甚叹异。生上车，行可数里，复出大城。宛是昔年东来之途，山川原野，依然如旧。所送二使者，甚无威势，生逾怏怏。生问使者曰："广陵郡何时可到？"二使讴歌自若，久乃答曰："少顷即至。"

俄出一穴，见本里闾巷，不改往日，潸然自悲，不觉流涕。二使者引生下车，入其门，升自阶，己身卧于堂东庑之下。生甚惊畏，不敢前近。二使因大呼生之姓名数声，生遂发寤如初。见家之僮仆拥篲于庭，二客濯足于榻，斜日未隐于西垣，余樽尚湛于东牖。梦中倏忽，若度一世矣。生感念嗟叹，遂呼二客而语之。惊骇。因与生出外，寻槐下穴。生指曰："此即梦中所惊入处。"二客将谓狐狸木媚之所为祟。遂命仆夫荷斤斧，断拥肿，折查枿，寻穴究源。旁可袤丈，有大穴，根洞然明朗。可容一榻。根上有积土壤，以为城郭台殿之状。有蚁数斛，隐聚其中。中有小台，其色若丹。二大蚁处之，素翼朱首，长可三寸。左右大蚁数十辅之，诸蚁不敢近。此其王矣。即槐安国都也。又穷一穴：直上南枝，可四丈，宛转方中，亦有土城小楼，群蚁亦处其中，即生所领南柯郡也。又一穴：西去二丈，磅礴空圬，嵌窦异状。中有一腐龟，壳大如斗。积雨浸润，小草丛生，繁茂翳荟，掩映振壳，即生所猎灵龟山也。

又穷一穴：东去丈余，古根盘屈，若龙虺之状。中有小土壤，高尺余，即生

　　　　　　　　　　　　　　　　中国文学选读

所葬妻盘龙岗之墓也。追想前事，感叹于怀，披阅穷迹，皆符所梦。不欲二客坏之，遽令掩塞如旧。是夕，风雨暴发。旦视其穴，遂失群蚁，莫知所去。故先言"国有大恐，都邑迁徙"，此其验矣。复念檀萝征伐之事，又请二客访迹于外。宅东一里有古涸涧，侧有大檀树一株，藤萝拥织，上不见日。旁有小穴，亦有群蚁隐聚其间。檀萝之国，岂非此耶？嗟呼！蚁之灵异，犹不可穷，况山藏木伏之大者所变化乎？时生酒徒周弁、田子华并居六合县，不与生过从旬日矣。生遽遣家童疾往候之。周生暴疾已逝，田子华亦寝疾于床。生感南柯之浮虚，悟人世之倏忽，遂栖心道门，绝弃酒色。后三年，岁在丁丑，亦终于家。时年四十七，将符宿契之限矣。

## 2. The Corpse Fiend Thrice Tricks Tang Sanzang
## The Holy Monk Angrily Dismisses the Handsome Monkey King

### Wu Cheng'en

At dawn the next day Sanzang and his three disciples packed their things before setting off. Now that Master Zhen Yuan had made Monkey his sworn brother and was finding him so congenial, he did not want to let him go, so he entertained him for another five or six days. Sanzang had really become a new man, and was livelier and healthier now that he had eaten the Grassreturning Cinnabar. His determination to fetch the scriptures was too strong to let him waste any more time, so there was nothing for it but to be on their way.

Soon after they had set out again, master and disciples saw a high mountain in front of them. "I'm afraid that the mountain ahead may be too steep for the horse," Sanzang said, "so we must think this over carefully." "Don't worry, master," said Monkey, "we know how to cope." He went ahead of the horse with his cudgel over his shoulder and cleared a path up to the top of the cliff. He saw no end of—

> Row upon row of craggy peaks,
> Twisting beds of torrents.
> Tigers and wolves were running in packs,
> Deer and muntjac moving in herds.

*Countless river-deer darted around,*

*And the mountain was covered with fox and bare.*

*Thousand-foot pythons,*

*Ten-thousand-fathom snakes;*

*The great pythons puffed out murky clouds,*

*The enormous snakes breathed monstrous winds.*

*Brambles and thorns spread beside the paths;*

*Pines and cedars stood elegant on the ridge.*

*There were wild fig-trees wherever the eye could see,*

*And sweet-scented flowers as far as the horizon.*

*The mountain's shadow fell north of the ocean,*

*The clouds parted south of the handle of the Dipper.*

*The towering cliffs were as ancient as the Primal Essence,*

*The majestic crags cold in the sunlight.*

Sanzang was immediately terrified, so Monkey resorted to some of his tricks. He whirled his iron cudgel and roared, at which all the wolves, snakes, tigers and leopards fled. They then started up the mountain, and as they were crossing a high ridge Sanzang said to Monkey, "Monkey, I've been hungry all day, so would you please go and beg some food for us somewhere." "You aren't very bright, Master," Monkey replied with a grin. "We're on a mountain with no village or inn for many miles around. Even if we had money there would be nowhere to buy food, so where am I to go and beg for it?" Sanzang felt cross, so he laid into Monkey. "You ape," he said, "don't you remember how you were crushed by the Buddha in a stone cell under the Double Boundary Mountain, where you could talk but not walk? It was I who saved your life, administered the monastic vows to you, and made you my disciple. How dare you be such a slacker? Why aren't you prepared to make an effort?" "I always make an effort," said Monkey. "I'm never lazy." "If you're such a hard worker, go and beg some food for us. I can't manage on an empty stomach. Besides, with the noxious vapors on this mountain we'll never reach the Thunder Monastery." "Please don't be angry, master, and stop talking I know your obstinate character—if I'm too

中国文学选读

disobedient you'll say that spell. You'd better dismount and sit here while I find somebody and beg for some food."

Monkey leapt up into the clouds with a single jump, and shading his eyes with his hand he looked around. Unfortunately he could see nothing in any direction except emptiness. There was no village or house or any other sign of human habitation among the countless trees. After looking for a long time he made out a high mountain away to the south. On its southern slopes was a bright red patch. Monkey brought his cloud down and said, "Master, there's something to eat." Sanzang asked him what it was. "There's no house around here where we could ask for food," Monkey replied, "but there's a patch of red on a mountain to the south that I'm sure must be ripe wild peaches. I'll go and pick some—they'll fill you up." "A monk who has peaches to eat is a lucky man," said Sanzang. Monkey picked up his bowl and leapt off on a beam of light. Just watch as he flashes off in a somersault, a whistling gust of cold air. Within a moment he was picking peaches on the southern mountain.

There is a saying that goes, "If the mountain is high it's bound to have fiends; if the ridge is steep spirits will live there." This mountain did indeed have an evil spirit who was startled by Monkey's appearance. It strode through the clouds on a negative wind, and on seeing the venerable Sanzang on the ground below thought happily, "What luck, what luck. At home they've been talking for years about a Tang Monk from the East who's going to fetch the Great Vehicle; he's a reincarnation of Golden Cicada, and has an Original Body that has been purified through ten lives. Anyone who eats a piece of his flesh will live for ever. And today, at last, he's here." The evil spirit went forward to seize him, but the sight of the two great generals to Sanzang's left and right made it frightened to close in on him. Who, it wondered, were they? They were in fact Pig and Friar Sand, and for all that their powers were nothing extraordinary: Pig was really Marshal Tian Peng while Friar Sand was the Great Curtain-lifting General. It was because their former awe inspiring qualities had not yet been dissipated that the fiend did not close in. "I'll try a trick on them and see what happens," the spirit said to itself.

The splendid evil spirit stopped its negative wind in a hollow and changed itself into a girl with a face as round as the moon and as pretty as a flower. Her brow was dear and her eyes beautiful; her teeth were white and her lips red. In her left hand she held a blue earthenware pot and in her right a green porcelain jar. She headed east towards the Tang Priest.

> *The holy monk rested his horse on the mountain,*
> *And suddenly noticed a pretty girl approaching.*
> *The green sleeves over her jade fingers lightly billowed;*
> *Golden lotus feet peeped under her trailing skirt.*
> *The beads of sweat on her powdered face were dew on a flower;*
> *Her dusty brow was a willow in a mist.*
> *Carefully and closely be watched her*
> *As she came right up to him.*

"Pig, Friar Sand," said Sanzang when he saw her, "don't you see somebody coming although Monkey said that this was a désolate and uninhabited place?" "You and Friar Sand stay sitting here while I go and take a look." The blockhead laid down his rake, straightened his tunic, put on the airs of a gentleman, and stared at the girl as he greeted her. Although he had not been sure from a distance, he could now see clearly that the girl had

> *Bones of jade under skin as pure as ice,*
> *A creamy bosom revealed by her neckline.*
> *Her willow eyebrows were black and glossy,*
> *And silver stars shone from her almond eyes.*
> *She was as graceful as the moon,*
> *As pure as the heavens.*
> *Her body was like a swallow in a willow-tree,*
> *Her voice like an oriole singing in the wood.*
> *An opening peony displaying her Charm,*
> *She was wild apple-blossom enmeshing the sun.*

中国文学选读

When the idiot Pig saw how beautiful she was his earthly desires were aroused, and he could not hold back the reckless words that came to his lips. "Where are you going, Bodhisattva," he said, "and what's that you're holding?" Although she was obviously an evil fiend he could not realize it. "Venerable sir," the girl replied at once, "this blue pot is full of tasty rice, and the green jar contains fried gluten-balls. I've come here specially to fulfill a vow to feed monks." Pig was thoroughly delighted to hear this. He came tumbling back at breakneck speed and said to Sanzang, "Master, 'Heaven rewards the good'. When you sent my elder brother off begging because you felt hungry, that ape went fooling around somewhere picking peaches. Besides, too many peaches turn your stomach and give you the runs. Don't you see that this girl is coming to feed us monks?" "You stupid idiot," replied Sanzang, who was not convinced, "we haven't met a single decent person in this direction, so where could anyone come from to feed monks?" "What's she then, master?" said Pig.

When Sanzang saw her he sprang to his feet, put his hands together in front of his chest, and said, "Bodhisattva, where is your home? Who are you? What vow brings you here to feed monks?" Although she was obviously an evil spirit, the venerable Sanzang could not see it either. On being asked about her background by Sanzang, the evil spirit immediately produced a fine-sounding story with which to fool him. "This mountain, which snakes and wild animals won't go near, is called White Tiger Ridge," she said. "Our home lies due west from here at the foot of it. My mother and father live there, and they are devout people who read the scriptures and feed monks from far and near. As they had no son, they asked Heaven to bless them. When I was born they wanted to marry me off to a good family, but then they decided to find me a husband who would live in our home to look after them in their old age and see them properly buried." "Bodhisattva, what you say can't be right," replied Sanzang. "The *Analects* say, 'When father and mother are alive, do not go on long journeys; if you have to go out, have a definite aim.' As your parents are at home and have found you a husband, you should let him fulfill your vow for you. Why ever are you walking in the mountains all by yourself, without even a servant? This is no way for a lady to behave." The girl smiled and produced a smooth reply at once: "My husband is hoeing with some of our retainers in a hollow in the north of the mountain, reverend sir, and I am taking them this food I've cooked. As it's July and all the crops are ripening nobody can be spared to run errands, and my parents are old, so I'm taking it there myself. Now that I have met you three monks from so far away I would like to give you this food as my parents are so pious. I hope you won't refuse our paltry offering. " "It's very good of you," said Sanzang, "but one of my disciples has gone to pick some fruit and will be back soon, so we couldn't eat any of your food. Besides, if we ate your food your husband might be angry with you when he found out, and we would get into trouble too. " As the Tang Priest was refusing to eat the food, the girl put on her most charming expression and said, "My parents' charity to monks is nothing compared to my husband's, master. He is a religious man, whose lifelong pleasure has been repairing bridges, mending roads, looking after the aged, and helping the poor. When he hears that I have given you this food, he'll love me more passionately than ever. " Sanzang still declined to eat it. Pig was beside himself. Twisting his lips into a pout, he muttered indignantly, "Of all the monks on earth there can't be another as soft in the head as our master. He won't eat ready-cooked food when there are only three of us to share it between. He's waiting for that ape to come back, and then we'll have to split it four ways. " Without allowing any more discussion he tipped the pot towards his mouth and was just about to eat.

At just this moment Brother Monkey was somersaulting back with his bowl full of the peaches he had picked on the southern mountain. When he saw with the golden pupils in his fiery eyes that the girl was an evil spirit, he put the bowl down, lifted his cudgel, and was going to hit her on the head when the horrified Sanzang held him back and said, "Who do you think you're going to hit?" "That girl in front of you is no good," he replied, "She's an evil spirit trying to make a fool of you. " "In the old days you had a very sharp eye, you ape," Sanzang said, "but this is nonsense. This veritable Bodhisattva is feeding us with the best of motives, so how can you call her an evil spirit?" "You wouldn't be able to tell, Master," said Monkey with a grin. "When I was an evil monster in the Water Curtain Cave I used to do that if I wanted a meal of human flesh. I would turn myself into gold and silver, or a country mansion, or liquor, or a pretty girl. Whoever was fool enough to be besotted with one of these would fall in love with me, and I would lure them into the cave, where I did

中国文学选读

what I wanted with them. Sometimes I ate them steamed and sometimes boiled, and what I couldn't finish I used to dry in the sun against a rainy day. If I'd been slower getting here, Master, you'd have fallen into her snare and she'd have finished you off. " The Tang Priest refused to believe him and maintained that she was a good person. "I know you, Master," said Monkey. "Her pretty face must have made you feel randy. If that's the way you feel, tell Pig to fell a few trees and send Friar Sand look off to for some grass. I'll be the carpenter, and well build you a hut here that you and the girl can use as your bridal chamber. We can all go our own ways. Wouldn't marriage be a worthwhile way of living? Why bother plodding on to fetch some scriptures or other?" Sanzang, who had always been such a soft and virtuous man, was unable to take this. He was so embarrassed that he blushed from his shaven pate to his ears.

While Sanzang was feeling so embarrassed, Monkey flared up again and struck at the evil spirit's face. The fiend, who knew a trick or two, used a magic way of abandoning its body: when it saw Monkey's cudgel coming it braced itself and fled, leaving a false corpse lying dead on the ground. Sanzang shook with terror and said to himself, "That monkey is utterly outrageous. Despite all my good advice he will kill people for no reason at all. " "Don't be angry. Master," said Monkey. "Come and see what's in her pot. " Friar Sand helped Sanzang over to look, and he saw that so far from containing tasty rice it was full of maggots with long tails. The jar had held not gluten-balls but frogs and toads, which were now jumping around on the ground. Sanzang was now beginning to believe Monkey. This was not enough, however, to prevent a furious Pig from deliberately making trouble by saying, "Master, that girl was a local countrywoman who happened to meet us while she was taking some food to the fields. There's no reason to think that she was an evil spirit. My elder brother was trying his club out on her, and he killed her by mistake. He's deliberately trying to trick us by magicking the food into those things because he's afraid you'll recite the Band-tightening Spell. He's fooled you into not saying it. "

This brought the blindness back on Sanzang, who believed these trouble-making remarks and made the magic with his hand as he recited the spell. "My head's aching, my head's aching," Monkey said. "Stop, please stop. Tell me off if you like. " "I've nothing to say to you," replied Sanzang. "A man of religion should always help others, and his thoughts should always be virtuous. When sweeping the floor you must be careful not to kill any ants, and to spare the moth you should put gauze round your lamp. Why do you keep murdering people? If you are going to kill innocent people like that there is no point in your going to fetch the scriptures. Go back!" "Where am I to go back to?" Monkey asked. "I won't have you as my disciple any longer," said Sanzang. "If you won't have me as your disciple," Monkey said, "I'm afraid you may never reach the Western Heaven." "My destiny is in Heaven's hands," replied Sanzang. "If some evil spirit is fated to cook me, he will; and there's no way of getting out of it. But if I'm not to be eaten, will you be able to extend my life? Be off with you at once." "I'll go if I must," said Monkey, "but I'll never have repaid your kindness to me." "What kindness have I ever done you?" Sanzang asked. Monkey knelt down and kowtowed. "When I wrecked the Heavenly Palace," he said, "I put myself in a very dangerous position, and the Buddha crushed me under the Double Boundary Mountain. Luckily the Bodhisattva Guanyin administered the vows to me, and you, Master, released me, so if I don't go with you to the Western Heaven I'll look like a 'scoundrel who doesn't return a kindness, with a name that will be cursed forever'." As Sanzang was a compassionate and holy monk this desperate plea from Monkey persuaded him to relent. "In view of what you say I'll let you off this time, but don't behave so disgracefully again. If you are ever as wicked as that again I shall recite that spell twenty times over." "Make it thirty if you like," replied Monkey. "I shan't hit anyone else." With that he helped Sanzang mount the horse and offered him some of the peaches he had picked. After eating a few the Tang Priest felt less hungry for the time being.

The evil spirit rose up into the air when it had saved itself from being killed by Monkey's cudgel. Gnashing its teeth in the clouds, it thought of Monkey with silent hatred: "Now I know that those magical powers of his that I've been hearing about for years are real. The Tang Priest didn't realize who I was and would have eaten the food. If he'd so much as leant forward to smell it I could have seized him, and he would have been mine. But that Monkey turned up, wrecked my plan, and almost killed me with his club. If I spare that monk now I'll have gone to all that trouble for nothing, so I'll have another go at tricking him."

中国文学选读

The splendid evil spirit landed its negative cloud, shook itself, and changed into an old woman in her eighties who was weeping as she hobbled along leaning on a bamboo stick with a crooked handle. "This is terrible. Master," exclaimed Pig with horror at the sight of her. "Her mother's come to look for her." "For whom?" asked the Tang Priest. "It must be her daughter that my elder brother killed," said Pig. "This must be the girl's mother looking for her." "Don't talk nonsense," said Monkey. "That girl was eighteen and this old woman is eighty. How could she possibly have had a child when she was over sixty? She must be a fake. Let me go and take a look." The splendid Monkey hurried over to examine her and saw that the monster had

> Turned into an old woman
> With temples as white as frozen snow.
> Slowly she stumbled along the road,
> Making her way in fear and trembling.
> Her body was weak and emaciated,
> Her face like a withered leaf of cabbage.
> Her cheekbone was twisted upwards,
> While the ends of her lips went down.
> How can old age compare with youth?
> Her face was as creased as a pleated bag.

Realizing that she was an evil spirit, Monkey did not wait to argue about it, but raised his cudgel and struck at her head. Seeing the blow coming, the spirit braced itself again and extracted its true essence once more. The false corpse sprawled dead beside the path. Sanzang was so horrified that he fell off the horse and lay beside the path, reciting the Band-tightening Spell twenty times over. Poor Monkey's head was squeezed so hard that it looked like a narrow-waisted gourd. The pain was unbearable, and he rolled over towards his master to plead, "Stop, Master. Say whatever you like." "I have nothing to say," Sanzang replied. "If a monk does good he will not fall into hell. Despite all my preaching you still commit murder. How can you? No sooner have you killed one person than you kill another. It's an outrage." "She was an evil spirit," Monkey replied. "Nonsense, you ape," said the Tang Priest, "as if there could be so many monsters! You haven't the least intention of reforming, and you are a deliberate murderer. Be off with you." "Are you sending me away again, Master?" Monkey asked. "I'll go if I must, but there's one thing I won't agree to." "What," Sanzang asked, "would that be?" "Master," Pig put in, "he wants the baggage divided between you and him. He's been a monk with you for several years, and hasn't succeeded in winning a good reward. You can't let him go away empty-handed. Better give him a worn-out tunic and a tattered hat from the bundle."

This made Monkey jump with fury. "I'll get you, you long-snouted moron," he said. "I've been a true Buddhist with no trace of covetousness or greed. I certainly don't want a share of the baggage." "If you're neither covetous nor greedy," said Sanzang, "why won't you go away?" "To be quite honest with you, Master," he replied, "when I lived in the Water Curtain Cave on the Mountain of Flowers and Fruit and knew all the great heroes, I won the submission of seventy-two other demon kings and had forty-seven thousand minor demons under me. I used to wear a crown of purple gold and a yellow robe with a belt of the finest jade. I had cloud-treading shoes on my feet and held an as-you-will gold-banded cudgel in my hands. I really was somebody then. But when I attained enlightenment and repented, I shaved my head and took to the Buddhist faith as your disciple. I couldn't face my old friends if I went back with this golden band round my head. So if you don't want me any longer, Master, please say the band-loosening spell and I'll take it off and give it back to you. I'll gladly agree to you putting it round someone else's head. As I've been your disciple for so long, surely you can show me this kindness." Sanzang was deeply shocked. "Monkey," he said, "the Bodhisattva secretly taught me the Band-tightening Spell, but not a band-loosening one." "In that case you'll have to let me come with you," Monkey replied. "Get up then," said Sanzang, feeling that he had no option, "I'll let you off again just this once. But you must never commit another murder." "I never will," said Monkey, "never again." He helped his master mount the horse and led the way forward.

The evil spirit, who had not been killed when hit the second time by Monkey either, was full of admiration as it floated in mid-air. "What a splendid Monkey King," it thought, "and what sharp eyes. He saw who I was through both my transformations. Those monks are traveling fast, and once they're over the mountain and fifteen miles to the west they'll be out of my territory. Any other fiends and monsters who catch them will be laughing till their mouths split, and I'll be heartbroken with sorrow. I'll have to have another go at tricking them." The excellent evil spirit brought its negative wind down to the mountainside and with one shake turned itself into an old man.

> *His hair was as white as Ancient Peng's,*
> *His temples as hoary as the Star of Longevity.*
> *Jade rang in his ears,*
> *And his eyes swam with golden stars.*
>
> *He leant on a dragon-headed stick,*
> *And wore a cloak of crane feathers.*
> *In his hands he fingered prayer-beads*
> *While reciting Buddhist sutras.*

When Sanzang saw him from the back of his horse he said with great delight, "Amitabha Buddha! The West is indeed a blessed land. That old man is forcing himself to recite scriptures although he can hardly walk." "Master," said Pig, "don't be so nice about him. He's going to give us trouble." "What do you mean?" Sanzang asked. "My elder brother has killed the daughter and the old woman, and this is the old man coming to look for them. If we fall into his hands you'll have to pay with your life. It'll be the death penalty for you, and I'll get a long sentence for being your accomplice. Friar Sand will be exiled for giving the orders. That elder brother will disappear by magic, and we three will have to carry the can." "Don't talk such nonsense, you moron," said Monkey. "You're terrifying the master. Wait while I go and have another look." Hiding the cudgel about his person he went up to the monster and said, "Where are you going, venerable sir? And why are you reciting scriptures as you walk along?" The monster, failing to recognize the key man, thought that the

Great Sage Monkey was merely a passer-by and said, "Holy sir, my family has lived here for generations, and all my life I have done good deeds, fed monks, read the scriptures, and repeated the Buddha's name. As fate has it I have no son, only a daughter, and she lives at home with her husband. She went off to the fields with food early this morning, and I'm afraid she may have been eaten by a tiger. My wife went out to look for her, and she hasn't come back either. I've no idea what's happened to them, so I've come to search for them. If they have died, I shall just have to gather their bones and take them back for a decent burial." "I'm a master of disguise," replied Monkey with a grin, "so don't try to pull the wool over my eyes. You can't fool me. I know that you're an evil spirit." The monster was speechless with fright. Monkey brandished his cudgel and thought, "If I don't kill him he'll make a getaway; but if I do, my master will say that spell. Yet if I don't kill him," he went on to reflect, "I'll take a lot of thought and effort to rescue the master when this monster seizes some other chance to carry him off. The best thing is to kill him. If I kill him with the cudgel the master will say the spell, but then 'even a vicious tiger doesn't eat her own cubs'. I'll be able to get round my master with my smooth tongue and some well-chosen words." The splendid Great Sage uttered a spell and called out to the local deities and the gods of the mountain, "This evil spirit has tried to trick my master three times, and I'm now going to kill it. I want you to be witnesses in the air around me. Don't leave!" Hearing this command, the gods all had to obey and watch from the clouds. The Great Sage raised his cudgel and struck down the monster. Now, at last, it was dead.

The Tang Priest was shaking with terror on the back of his horse, unable to speak. Pig stood beside him and said with a laugh, "That Monkey's marvelous, isn't he! He's gone mad. He's killed three people in a few hours' journey." The Tang Priest was just going to say the spell when Monkey threw himself in front of his horse and called out, "Don't say it. Master, don't say it. Come and have a look at it." It was now just a pile of dusty bones. "He's only just been killed, Wukong," Sanzang said in astonishment, "so why has he turned into a skeleton?" "It was a demon corpse with magic powers that used to deceive people and destroy them. Now that I've killed it, it's reverted to its original form. The writing on her backbone says that she's

中国文学选读

called 'Lady White Bone'. " Sanzang was convinced, but Pig had to make trouble a-
gain. "Master," he said, "he's afraid that you'll say those words because he killed
him with a vicious blow from his cudgel, and so he's made him look like this to fool
you. " The Tang Priest, who really was gullible, now believed Pig, and he started to
recite the spell. Monkey, unable to stop the pain, knelt beside the path and cried,
"Stop, stop. Say whatever it is you have to say," "Baboon," said Sanzang, "I have
nothing more to say to you. If a monk acts rightly he will grow daily but invisibly,
like grass in a garden during the spring, whereas an evildoer will be imperceptibly
worn away day by day like a whetstone. You have killed three people, one after the
other, in this wild and desolate place, and there is nobody here to find you out or
bring a case against you. But if you go to a city or some other crowded place and start
laying about you with that murderous cudgel, we'll be in big trouble and there will be
no escape for us. Go back!" "You're wrong to hold it against me, Master," Monkey
replied, "as that wretch was obviously an evil monster set on murdering you. But so
far from being grateful that I've saved you by killing it, you would have to believe
that idiot's tittle-tattle and keep sending me away. As the saying goes, you should
never have to do anything more than three times. I'd be a low and shameless creature
if I didn't go now. I'll go, I'll go all right, but who will you have left to look after
you?" "Damned ape," Sanzang replied, "you get ruder and ruder. You seem to think
that you're the only one. What about Pig and Friar Sand? Aren't they people?"

On hearing him say that Pig and Friar Sand were suitable people too, Monkey
was very hurt. "That's a terrible thing to hear, Master," he said. "When you left
Chang'an Liu Boqin helped you on your way, and when you reached the Double
Boundary Mountain you saved me and I took you as my master. I've gone into ancient
caves and deep forests capturing monsters and demons. I won Pig and Friar Sand o-
ver, and I've had a very hard time of it. But today you've turned stupid and you're
sending me back. When these birds have all been shot this bow is put away, and
when the hares have all been killed the hounds are stewed. ' Oh well! If only you
hadn't got that Band-tightening Spell. " "I won't recite it again," said Sanzang.
"Don't be so sure," replied Monkey. "If you're ever beset by evil monsters from
whom you can't escape, and if Pig and Friar Sand can't save you, then you'll think of

me and you won't be able to stop yourself from saying the spell again, my head will ache even if I'm many tens of thousands of miles away. But if I do come back to you, never say it again."

The Tang Priest grew angrier and angrier as Monkey talked on, and tumbling off his horse he told Friar Sand to take paper and brush from the pack. Then he fetched some water from a stream, rubbed the inkstick on a stone, wrote out a letter of dismissal, and handed it to Monkey. "Here it is in writing," he said. "I don't want you as my disciple a moment longer. If I ever see you again may I fall into the Avichi Hell." Monkey quickly took the document and said, "There's no need to swear an oath, Master, I'm off." He folded the paper up and put it in his sleeve, then tried once more to mollify Sanzang. "Master," he said, "I've spent some time with you, and I've also been taught by the Bodhisattva. Now I'm being fired in the middle of the journey, when I've achieved nothing. Please sit down and accept my homage, then I won't feel so bad about going." The Tang Priest turned away and would not look at him, muttering, "I am a good monk, and I won't accept the respects of bad people like you." Seeing that Sanzang was refusing to face him, the Great Sage used magic to give himself extra bodies. He blew a magic breath on three hairs plucked from the back of his head and shouted, "Change!" They turned into three more Monkeys, making a total of four with the real one, and surrounding the master on all four sides they kowtowed to him. Unable to avoid them by dodging to left or right, Sanzang had to accept their respects.

The Great Sage jumped up, shook himself, put the hairs back, and gave Friar Sand these instructions: "You are a good man, my brother, so mind you stop Pig from talking nonsense and be very careful on the journey. If at any time evil spirits capture our master, you tell them that I'm his senior disciple. The hairy devils of the West have heard of my powers and won't dare to harm him." "I am a good monk," said the Tang Priest, "and I'd never mention the name of a person as bad as you. Go back." As his master refused over and over again to change his mind Monkey had nothing for it but to go. Look at him:

*Holding back his tears he bowed goodbye to his master,*

*Then sadly but with care he gave instructions to Friar Sand.*

*His head pushed the hillside grass apart,*

*His feet kicked over the creepers on the ground.*

*He spun between Heaven and earth like a wheel;*

*At flying over mountains and seas none could beat him.*

*Within an instant no sign of him could be seen;*

*He retraced his whole journey in a flash.*

Holding back his anger, Monkey left his master and went straight back to the Water Curtain Cave on the Mountain of Flowers and Fruit on his somersault cloud. He was feeling lonely and miserable when he heard the sound of water. When he looked around from where he was in mid-air, he realized that it was the waves of the Eastern Sea. The sight of it reminded him of the Tang Priest, and he could not stop the tears from rolling down his cheeks. He stopped his cloud and stayed there a long time before going. If you don't know what happened when he went, listen to the explanation in the next instalment.

—From *Journey to the West* (Chapter 27)

(translated by W. J. F. Jenner)

## 尸魔三戏唐三藏　圣僧恨逐美猴王
### 吴承恩

却说三藏师徒，次日天明，收拾前进。那镇元子与行者结为兄弟，两人情投意合，决不肯放，又安排管待，一连住了五六日。那长老自服了草还丹，真似脱胎换骨，神爽体健。他取经心重，那里肯淹留。无已，遂行。

师徒别了上路，早见一座高山。三藏道："徒弟，前面有山险峻，恐马不能前，大家须仔细仔细。"行者道："师父放心，我等自然理会。"好猴王，他在那马前，横担着棒，剖开山路，上了高崖，看不尽——

峰岩重叠，涧壑湾环。虎狼成阵走，麂鹿作群行。无数獐钻簇簇，满山狐兔聚丛丛。千尺大蟒，万丈长蛇。大蟒喷愁雾，长蛇吐怪风。道旁荆棘牵漫，岭上松楠秀丽。薜萝满目，芳草连天。影落沧溟北，云开斗柄南。万古常含元气老，千峰巍列日光寒。

那长老马上心惊，孙大圣布施手段，舞着铁棒，哮吼一声，唬得那狼虫颠窜，虎豹奔逃。师徒们入此山，正行到嵯峨之处，三藏道："悟空，我这一日，肚中饥了，你去那里化些斋吃？"行者陪笑道："师父好不聪明。这等半山之中，前不巴村，后不着店，有钱也没买处，教往那里寻斋？"三藏心中不快，口里骂道："你这猴子！想你在两界山，被如来压在石匣之内，口能言，足不能行，也亏我救你性命，摩顶受戒，做了我的徒弟。怎么不肯努力，常怀懒惰之心！"行者道："弟子亦颇殷勤，何尝懒惰？"三藏道："你既殷勤，何不化斋我吃？我肚饥怎行？况此地山岚瘴气，怎么得上雷音？"行者道："师父休怪，少要言语。我知你尊性高傲，十分违慢了你，便要念那话儿咒。你下马稳坐，等我寻那里有人家处化斋去。"

行者将身一纵，跳上云端里，手搭凉篷，睁眼观看。可怜西方路甚是寂寞，更无庄堡人家，正是多逢树木少见人烟去处。看多时，只见正南上有一座高山，那山向阳处，有一片鲜红的点子。行者按下云头道："师父，有吃的了。"那长老问甚东西，行者道："这里没人家化饭，那南山有一片红的，想必是熟透了的山桃，我去摘几个来你充饥。"三藏喜道："出家人若有桃子吃，就为上分了，快去！"行者取了钵盂，纵起祥光，你看他筋斗幌幌，冷气飕飕。须史间，奔南山摘桃不题。

却说常言有云："山高必有怪，岭峻却生精。"果然这山上有一个妖精，孙大圣去时，惊动那怪。他在云端里，踏着阴风，看见长老坐在地下，就不胜欢喜道："造化，造化！几年家人都讲东土的唐和尚取'大乘'，他本是金蝉子化身，十世修行的原体。有人吃他一块肉，长寿长生。真个今日到了。"那妖精上前就要拿他，只见长老左右手下有两员大将护持，不敢拢身。他说两员大将是谁？说是八戒、沙僧。八戒、沙僧虽没什么大本事，然八戒是天蓬元帅，沙僧是卷帘大将，他的威气尚不曾泄，故不敢拢身。妖精说："等我且戏他戏，看怎么说。"

好妖精，停下阴风，在那山凹里，摇身一变，变做个月貌花容的女儿，说不尽那眉清目秀，齿白唇红，左手提着一个青砂罐儿，右手提着一个绿磁瓶儿，从西向东，径奔唐僧——

圣僧歇马在山岩，忽见裙钗女近前。翠袖轻摇笼玉笋，湘裙斜拽显金莲。

汗流粉面花含露，尘拂峨眉柳带烟。仔细定睛观看处，看看行至到身边。

三藏见了，叫："八戒、沙僧，悟空才说这里旷野无人，你看那里不走出一个人来了?"八戒道："师父，你与沙僧坐着，等老猪去看看来。"那呆子放下钉钯，整整直裰，摆摆摇摇，充作个斯文气象，一直的觌面相迎。真个是远看未实，近看分明，那女子生得——

冰肌藏玉骨，衫领露酥胸。柳眉积翠黛，杏眼闪银星。月样容仪俏，天然性格清。体似燕藏柳，声如莺啭林。半放海棠笼晓日，才开芍药弄春晴。

那八戒见他生得俊俏，呆子就动了凡心，忍不住胡言乱语，叫道："女菩萨，往那里去? 手里提着是什么东西?"分明是个妖怪，他却不能认得。那女子连声答应道："长老，我这青罐里是香米饭，绿瓶里是炒面筋，特来此处无他故，因还誓愿要斋僧。"八戒闻言，满心欢喜，急抽身，就跑了个猪颠风，报与三藏道："师父! 吉人自有天报! 师父饿了，教师兄去化斋，那猴子不知那里摘桃儿耍子去了。桃子吃多了，也有些嘈人，又有些下坠。你看那不是个斋僧的来了?"唐僧不信道："你这个夯货胡缠! 我们走了这向，好人也不曾遇着一个，斋僧的从何而来!"八戒道："师父，这不到了?"

三藏一见，连忙跳起身来，合掌当胸道："女菩萨，你府上在何处住? 是甚人家? 有甚愿心，来此斋僧?"分明是个妖精，那长老也不认得。那妖精见唐僧问他来历，他立地就起个虚情，花言巧语来赚哄道："师父，此山叫做蛇回兽怕的白虎岭，正西下面是我家。我父母在堂，看经好善，广斋方上远近僧人，只因无子，求福作福，生了奴奴，欲扳门第，配嫁他人，又恐老来无倚，只得将奴招了一个女婿，养老送终。"三藏闻言道："女菩萨，你语言差了。圣经云：'父母在，不远游，游必有方。'你既有父母在堂，又与你招了女婿，有愿心，教你男子还，便也罢，怎么自家在山行走? 又没个侍儿随从。这个是不遵妇道了。"那女子笑吟吟，忙陪俏语道："师父，我丈夫在山北凹里，带几个客子锄田。这是奴奴煮的午饭，送与那些人吃的。只为五黄六月，无人使唤，父母又年老，所以亲身来送。忽遇三位远来，却思父母好善，故将此饭斋僧，如不弃嫌，愿表芹献。"三藏道："善哉，善哉! 我有徒弟摘果子去了，就来，我不敢吃。假如我和尚吃了你饭，你丈夫晓得，骂你，却不罪坐贫僧也？"那女子见唐僧不肯吃，却又满面春生道："师父啊，我父母斋僧，还是小可。我丈夫更是个善人，一生好的是修桥补路，爱老怜贫。但听见说这饭送与师父吃了，他与我夫妻情上，比寻常更是不同。"三藏也只是不吃，旁边却恼坏了八戒。那呆子努着嘴，口里埋怨道："天下和尚也无数，不曾象我这个老和尚罢软！现成的饭三分儿倒不吃，只等那猴子来，做四分才吃！"他不容分说，一嘴把个罐子拱倒，就要动口。

只见那行者自南山顶上，摘了几个桃子，托着钵盂，一筋斗，点将回来。睁火眼金睛观看，认得那女子是个妖精，放下钵盂，掣铁棒，当头就打。唬得个长老用手扯住道："悟空！你走将来打谁？"行者道："师父，你面前这个女子，莫当做个好人。他是个妖精，要来骗你哩。"三藏道："你这猴头，当时倒也有些眼力，今日如何乱道！这女菩萨有此善心，将这饭要斋我等，你怎么说他是个妖精？"行者笑道："师父，你那里认得！老孙在水帘洞里做妖魔时，若想人肉吃，便是这等。或变金银，或变庄台，或变醉人，或变女色。有那等痴心的，爱上我，我就迷他到洞里，尽意随心，或蒸或煮受用；吃不了，还要晒干了防天阴哩！师父，我若来迟，你定入他套子，遭他毒手！"那唐僧那里肯信，只说是个好人。行者道："师父，我知道你了，你见他那等容貌，必然动了凡心。若果有此意，叫八戒伐几棵树来，沙僧寻些草来，我做木匠，就在这里搭个窝铺，你与他圆房成事，我们大家散了，却不是件事业？何必又跋涉，取甚经去！"

那长老原是个软善的人，那里吃得他这句言语，羞得个光头彻耳通红。三藏正在此羞惭，行者又发起性来，掣铁棒，望妖精劈脸一下。那怪物有些手段，使个"解尸法"，见行者棍子来时，他却抖擞精神，预先走了，把一个假尸首打死在地下。唬得个长老战战兢兢，口中作念道："这猴着然无礼！屡劝不从，无故伤人性命！"行者道："师父莫怪，你且来看看这罐子里是甚东西。"沙僧搀着长老，近前看时，那里是甚香米饭，却是一罐子拖尾巴的长蛆；也不是面筋，却是几个青蛙、癞虾蟆，满地乱跳。长老才有三分儿信了，怎禁猪八戒气

三打白骨精

不忿，在旁漏八分儿唆嘴道："师父，说起这个女子，他是此间农妇，因为送饭下田，路遇我等，却怎么栽他是个妖怪？哥哥的棍重，走将来试手打他一下，不期就打杀了！怕你念什么《紧箍儿咒》，故意的使个障眼法儿，变做这等样东西，演幌你眼，使不念咒哩。"

三藏自此一言，就是晦气到了，果然信那呆子撺唆，手中捻诀，口里念咒，行者就叫："头疼，头疼，莫念，莫念！有话便说。"唐僧道："有甚话说！出家人时时常要方便，念念不离善心，扫地恐伤蝼蚁命，爱惜飞蛾纱罩灯。你怎么步步行凶，打死这个无故平人，取将经来何用？你回去罢！"行者道："师父，你教我回那里去？"唐僧道："我不要你做徒弟。"行者道："你不要我做徒弟，只怕你西天路去不成。"唐僧道："我命在天，该那个妖精蒸了吃，就是煮了，也算不过。终不然，你救得我的大限？你快回去！"行者道："师父，我回去便也罢了，只是不曾报得你的恩哩。"唐僧道："我与你有甚恩？"那大圣闻言，连忙跪下叩头道："老孙因大闹天宫，致下了伤身之难，被我佛压在两界山，幸观音菩萨与我受了戒行，幸师父救脱吾身，若不与你同上西天，显得我'知恩不报非君子，万古千秋作骂名。'"原来这唐僧是个慈悯的圣僧，他见行者哀告，却也回心转意道："既如此说，且饶你这一次，再休无礼。如若仍前作恶，这咒语颠倒就念二十遍！"行者道："三十遍也由你，只是我不打人了。"却才伏侍唐僧上马，又将摘来桃子奉上。唐僧在马上也吃了几个，权且充饥。

却说那妖精，脱命升空。原来行者那一棒不曾打杀妖精，妖精出神去了。他在那云端里，咬牙切齿，暗恨行者道："几年只闻得讲他手段，今日果然话不虚传。那唐僧已此不认得我，将要吃饭。若低头闻一闻儿，我就一把捞住，却不是我的人了？不期被他走来，弄破我这勾当，又几乎被他打了一棒。若饶了这个和尚，诚然是劳而无功也，我还下去戏他一戏。"

好妖精，按落阴云，在那前山坡下，摇身一变，变作个老妇人，年满八旬，手拄着一根弯头竹杖，一步一声的哭着走来。八戒见了，大惊道："师父，不好了！那妈妈儿来寻人了！"唐僧道："寻甚人？"八戒道："师兄打杀的，定是他女儿。这个定是他娘寻将来了。"行者道："兄弟莫要胡说！那女子十八岁，这老妇有八十岁，怎么六十多岁还生产？断乎是个假的，等老孙去看来。"好行者，拽开步，走近前观看，那怪物——

假变一婆婆，两鬓如冰雪。走路慢腾腾，行步虚怯怯。弱体瘦伶仃，脸如枯菜叶。颧骨望上翘，嘴唇往下别。老年不比少年时，满脸都是荷叶摺。

　　行者认得他是妖精，更不理论，举棒照头便打。那怪见棍子起时，依然抖擞，又出化了元神，脱真儿去了，把个假尸首又打死在山路之下。唐僧一见，惊下马来，睡在路旁，更无二话，只是把《紧箍儿咒》颠倒足足念了二十遍。可怜把个行者头，勒得似个亚腰儿葫芦，十分疼痛难忍，滚将来哀告道："师父莫念了！有甚话说了罢！"唐僧道："有甚话说！出家人耳听善言，不堕地狱。我这般劝化你，你怎么只是行凶？把平人打死一个，又打死一个，此是何说？"行者道："他是妖精。"唐僧道："这个猴子胡说！就有这许多妖怪！你是个无心向善之辈，有意作恶之人，你去罢！"行者道："师父又教我去，回去便也回去了，只是一件不相应。"唐僧道："你有什么不相应处？"八戒道："师父，他要和你分行李哩。跟着你做了这几年和尚，不成空着手回去？你把那包袱里的什么旧褊衫，破帽子，分两件与他罢。"行者闻言，气得暴跳道："我把你这个尖嘴的夯货！老孙一向秉教沙门，更无一毫嫉妒之意，贪恋之心，怎么要分什么行李？"唐僧道："你既不嫉妒贪恋，如何不去？"行者道："实不瞒师父说，老孙五百年前，居花果山水帘洞大展英雄之际，收降七十二洞邪魔，手下有四万七千群怪，头戴的是紫金冠，身穿的是赭黄袍，腰系的是蓝田带，足踏的是步云履，手执的是如意金箍棒，着实也曾为人。自从涅槃罪度，削发秉正沙门，跟你做了徒弟，把这个金箍儿勒在我头上，若回去，却也难见故乡人。师父果若不要我，把那个《松箍儿咒》念一念，退下这个箍子，交付与你，套在别人头上，我就快活相应了，也是跟你一场。莫不成这些人意儿也没有了？"唐僧大惊道："悟空，我当时只是菩萨暗受一卷《紧箍儿咒》，却没有什么《松箍儿咒》。"行者道："若无《松箍儿咒》，你还带我去走走罢。"长老又没奈何道："你且起来，我再饶你这一次，却不可再行凶了。"行者道："再不敢了，再不敢了。"又伏侍师父上马，剖路前进。

　　却说那妖精，原来行者第二棍也不曾打杀他。那怪物在半空中，夸奖不尽道："好个猴王，着然有眼！我那般变了去，他也还认得我。这些和尚，他去得快，若过此山，西下四十里，就不伏我所管。若是被别处妖魔撸了去，好道就笑破他人口，使碎自家心，我还下去戏他一戏。"好妖怪，按耸阴风，在山坡下摇身一变，变成一个老公公，真个是——

白发如彭祖，苍髯赛寿星。耳中鸣玉磬，眼里幌金星。

手拄龙头拐，身穿鹤氅轻。数珠掐在手，口诵南无经。

　　唐僧在马上见了，心中欢喜道："阿弥陀佛！西方真是福地！那公公路也走不上来，逼法的还念经哩。"八戒道："师父，你且莫要夸奖，那个是祸的根哩。"唐僧道："怎么是祸根？"八戒道："行者打杀他的女儿，又打杀他的婆子，这个正是他的老儿寻将来了。我们若撞在他的怀里呵，师父，你便偿命，该个死罪；把老猪为从，问个充军；沙僧喝令，问个摆站；那行者使个遁法走了，却不苦了我们三个顶缸？"行者听见道："这个呆根，这等胡说，可不唬了师父？等老孙再去看看。"他把棍藏在身边，走上前迎着怪物，叫声："老官儿，往那里去？怎么又走路，又念经？"那妖精错认了定盘星，把孙大圣也当做个等闲的，遂答道："长老啊，我老汉祖居此地，一生好善斋僧，看经念佛。命里无儿，止生得一个小女，招了个女婿，今早送饭下田，想是遭逢虎口。老妻先来找寻，也不见回去，全然不知下落，老汉特来寻看。果然是伤残他命，也没奈何，将他骸骨收拾回去，安葬茔中。"行者笑道："我是个做虎的祖宗，你怎么袖子里笼了个鬼儿来哄我？你瞒了诸人，瞒不过我！我认得你是个妖精！"那妖精唬得顿口无言。行者掣出棒来，自忖思道："若要不打他，显得他倒弄个风儿；若要打他，又怕师父念那话儿咒语。"又思量道："不打杀他，他一时间抄空儿把师父捞了去，却不又费心劳力去救他？还打的是！就一棍子打杀他，师父念起那咒，常言道，'虎毒不吃儿。'凭着我巧言花语，嘴伶舌便，哄他一哄，好道也罢了。"好大圣，念动咒语叫当坊土地、本处山神道："这妖精三番来戏弄我师父，这一番却要打杀他。你与我在半空中作证，不许走了。"众神听令，谁敢不从？都在云端里照应。那大圣棍起处，打倒妖魔，才断绝了灵光。

　　那唐僧在马上，又唬得战战兢兢，口不能言。八戒在旁边又笑道："好行者！风发了！只行了半日路，倒打死三个人！"唐僧正要念咒，行者急到马前，叫道："师父，莫念，莫念！你且来看看他的模样。"却是一堆粉骷髅在那里。唐僧大惊道："悟空，这个人才死了，怎么就化作一堆骷髅？"行者道："他是个潜灵作怪的僵尸，在此迷人败本，被我打杀，他就现了本相。他那脊梁上有一行字，叫做'白骨夫人'。"唐僧闻说，倒也信了。怎禁那八戒旁边唆嘴道："师父，他的手重棍凶，把人打死，只怕你念那话儿，故意变化这个模样，掩你的眼目哩！"唐僧果然耳软，又信了他，随复念起。行者禁不得疼痛，跪于路旁，只叫："莫念，莫念！有话快说了罢！"唐僧道："猴头！还有甚说话！出家人行善，如春园之草，不见其长，日有所增；行恶之人，如磨刀之石，不见其损，日有所亏。你在这荒郊野外，一连打死三人，还是无人检举，没有对头。倘到城市之中，人烟凑集之所，你拿了那哭丧棒，一时不知好歹，乱打起人来，撞出大祸，教我怎的脱身？你回去罢！"行者道："师父错怪了我也。这厮分明是个妖魔，他实有心害你。我倒打死他，替你除了害，你却不认得，反信了那呆子谗言冷语，屡次逐我。常言道，'事不过三'。我若不去，真是个下流无耻之徒。我去！我去！去便去了，只是你手下无人。"唐僧发怒道："这泼猴越发无礼！看起来，只你是人，那悟能、悟净就不是人？"

那大圣一闻得说他两个是人，止不住伤情凄惨，对唐僧道声："苦啊！你那时节，出了长安，有刘伯钦送你上路。到两界山，救我出来，投拜你为师。我曾穿古洞，入深林，擒魔捉怪，收八戒，得沙僧，吃尽千辛万苦。今日昧着惺惺使糊涂，只教我回去，这才是'鸟尽弓藏，兔死狗烹！'罢，罢，罢！但只是多了那《紧箍儿咒》。"唐僧道："我再不念了。"行者道："这个难说。若到那毒魔苦难处不得脱身，八戒、沙僧救不得你，那时节，想起我来，忍不住又念诵起来，就是十万里路，我的头也是疼的；假如再来见你，不如不作此意。"唐僧见他言言语语，越添恼怒，滚鞍下马来，叫沙僧包袱内取出纸笔，即于涧下取水，石上磨墨，写了一纸贬书，递于行者道："猴头！执此为照，再不要你做徒弟了！如再与你相见，我就堕了阿鼻地狱！"行者连忙接了贬书道："师父，不消发誓，老孙去罢。"他将书摺了，留在袖中，却又软款唐僧道："师父，我也是跟你一场，又蒙菩萨指教，今日半途而废，不曾成得功果，你请坐，受我一拜，我也去得放心。"唐僧转回身不睬，口里唧唧哝哝的道："我是个好和尚，不受你歹人的礼！"大圣见他不睬，又使个身外法，把脑后毫毛拔了三根，吹口仙气，叫："变！"即变了三个行者，连本身四个，四面围住师父下拜。那长老左右躲不脱，好道也受了一拜。

大圣跳起来，把身一抖，收上毫毛，却又吩咐沙僧道："贤弟，你是个好人，却只要留心防着八戒言语，途中更要仔细。倘一时有妖精拿住师父，你就说老孙是他大徒弟。西方毛怪，闻我的手段，不敢伤我师父。"唐僧道："我是个好和尚，不题你这歹人的名字，你回去罢。"那大圣见长老三番两复，不肯转意回心，没奈何才去。你看他——

　　　　嘀泪叩头辞长老，含悲留意嘱沙僧。一头拭进坡前草，两脚蹬翻地上藤。

上天下地如轮转，跨海飞山第一能。顷刻之间不见影，霎时疾返旧途程。

你看他忍气别了师父，纵筋斗云，径回花果山水帘洞去了。独自个凄凄惨惨，忽闻得水声聒耳，大圣在那半空里看时，原来是东洋大海潮发的声响。一见了，又想起唐僧，止不住腮边泪坠，停云住步，良久方去。

——选自《西游记》第二十七回

## 3. The Courtesan's Jewel Box
### Feng Menglong

Ours tory starts with the invasion of Korea by the Japanese general Hideyoshi in the twentieth year of Wan Li period (1592). When the King of Korea appealed for help, the Son of Heave sent troops across the sea to save him; and the Board of Treasury proposed that since the grain and silver allocated to the troops were insufficient for the expedition a special tax should be raised by the sale of places in the Imperial Colleges. To this the emperor agreed.

Now this system had many advantages for those with money. In addition to having better facilities for studying and passing the examinations, the students of these colleges were assured of small official posts. Accordingly, the sons of official or wealthy families who did not want to sit for the county examination took advantage of this scheme to purchase a place in one of the Imperial Colleges. So the number of students in both the college in Nanjing and Beijing rose to over one thousand each.

One of these students was called Li Jia. A native of Shaoxing in Zhejiang Province, he was the oldest of three sons of a provincial treasurer. Although a licentiate, he had failed to pass the prefectural examination, he had purchased a place in the Imperial College at Beijing under the new system; and during his residence in the capital he went with a fellow-provincial and fellow-student, Liu Yuchun, to the singsong girls' quarter. Here he met a celebrated courtesan called Du Wei, who, because she was the tenth girl in the quarter, was also known as Decima.

*She was sweetness and loveliness incarnate;*

*Her fine eyebrows were arched like distant hills;*

*Her eyes were as clear as autumn water;*

*Her face was as fresh as dew-washed lotus;*

*Her lips were as crimson as ripe cherries.*

*Ah, the pity of it! That this lovely maid*

*Should be cast by the roadside in the dust.*

Since Decima became a courtesan she had met countless young men of rich and noble families who had not hesitated to spend all they possessed for love of her; so the other singsong girls used to say:

*When Decima is at the feast,*

*The poorest drinker drains a thousand cups;*

*When in our quarter Decima appears,*

*All other powdered faces look like ghosts.*

Though Li was a gay young fellow, he had never seen such a beautiful girl. At his first meeting with Decima he was absolutely charmed by her and fell head over heels in love. And since he was not only handsome and amiable but open-handed and untiring in his pursuit of her, the attraction soon proved mutual. Realizing that her mistress was grasping and heartless, Decima had long wanted to leave her; and now that she saw how kind and devoted Li was, she wished to throw in her lot with him. Although the young man was too afraid of his father to marry her, they fell more and more deeply in love, passing whole days and nights together in pleasure and remaining as inseparable as if they were already husband and wife. They vowed solemnly never to love anyone else.

*Their love was deeper than the sea,*

*And more sublime their faith than mountain peaks.*

After Li became Decima's lover, other wealthy men who had heard of her fame tried in vain to gain access to her. At first Li spent money lavishly on her, and the procuress, all smiles and blandishments, waited on him hand and foot. But when more than a year had sped past, Li's money was nearly exhausted. He could no longer be as generous as he would have liked, and the old woman began to treat him coldly. The provincial treasurer heard that his son was frequenting the courtesans' quarter, and sent letter after letter ordering him to come home; but the young man was so enamoured of Decima's beauty that he kept postponing his return. And later, when he heard how angry his father was with him, he dared not go back.

The proverb says that friendship based on money will end once the money is spent. Decima, however, loved Li so truly that the poorer he grew the more passionately attached to him she became. Her mistress told her repeatedly to send Li about his business and, seeing that the girl refused to do so, she began to insult him in the hope that he would leave in anger. But her insults had no effect on Li, who was naturally of a mild disposition, so she could do nothing but reproach Decima every day.

"In our profession we depend on our clients for food and clothing," she said. "As we speed one guest from the front door, another should be coming in by the back. The more clients we have, the more money and silk we shall heap up. But now that this dratted Li Jia has been hanging around for more than a year, it's no use talking about new clients—even the old ones have stopped coming. We seem to have got hold of a Zhong Kui who keeps out devils, because not a soul will come near us. There'll soon be no smoke in our chimney. What's to become of us?"

Decima, however, would not quietly submit to this. "Mr. Li did not come here empty-handed," she retorted. "Look at all the money he has spent here!"

"That was before; it's now I'm talking about. You tell him to give me a little money today for fuel and rice for the two of you. In other houses the girls are a money-tree which needs only to be shaken to shower down riches; it's just my bad luck that I've got a girl who keeps the money away. Every day I have to worry how to make ends meet, because you insist on supporting this pauper. Where do you think our food and clothes are coming from? Go and tell that beggar of yours that, if he's any good at all, he must give me some silver; then you can go off with him and I'll buy another girl. Wouldn't that suit us both?"

"Do you really mean it?" demanded Decima.

"Have I ever told a lie?" replied the old woman, who, knowing that Li had not a cent left and had pawned his clothes, thought it would be impossible for him to raise any money. "Of course I mean it."

"How much do you want from him?"

"If it were anyone else, I would ask for a thousand taels; but I'll ask a poor devil like him for only three hundred. With that I could buy another girl to take your place. But there's one condition: he must pay me within three days, then I shall hand you o-ver straight away. If he hasn't paid after three days, I'll give him a good beating with my cane, the wretch, and drive him out, gentleman or no gentleman! Nobody will be able to blame me either."

"Although he is away from home and has run out of money," said Decima, "he should be able to raise three hundred taels. But three days is too little. Can't you make it ten?"

"The young fool has nothing but his bare hands," thought the procuress. "Even if I give him a hundred days, he won't be able to get the money. And when he fails to produce it, however thick-skinned he is he won't have the nerve to turn up again. Then I can get my establishment under proper control once more, and Decima will have nothing to say."

"Well, tohumor you," she said, "I'll make it ten days. But if he doesn't have the money by then, don't blame me."

"If he can't find the money by then, I don't suppose he will have the face to come back," said Decima. "I am only afraid that if he does bring the three hundred taels, you may go back on your word."

"I am an old woman of fifty-one," protested the procuress. "I am worshipping Buddha and fasting ten days every month. How could I lie to you? If you don't trust me, I'll put my palm on yours to make a pledge. May I become a dog or swine in my next life if I go back on my word!"

*Who with a mere pint pot can gauge the sea?*

*The bawd, for all her scheming, was a fool*

*To think, because the scholar's purse was light,*

*She could so easily frustrate their love.*


That night in bed Decima discussed her future With Li. "It's not that I don't want to marry you," said the young man. "But it would cost at least a thousand taels to buy your freedom, and where can I get that now that all my money is spent?"

"I have already spoken to my mistress," replied Decima. "She wants only three hundred taels, but it must be paid within ten days. Although you have come to the end of your allowance, you must have relatives and friends in the capital from whom you can borrow. If you raise this sum, I shall be yours; and we shan't have to suffer the old woman's temper any more."

"My friends and relatives here have been cold-shouldering me because I have been spending too much time with you," said Li. "Tomorrow I'll tell them that I am packing up to leave and coming to say goodbye, then ask for money for my traveling expenses. I may be able to collect three hundred taels." So he got up, dressed and prepared to take his leave.

"Be as quick as you can!" urged Decima as he was going out. "I'll be waiting for good news." And Li promised to do his best.

On leaving the house, Li called on a number of relatives and friends, pretending that he had come to say goodbye. They were pleased to hear that he was going home, but when he mentioned that he was short of money for his journey they said nothing. As the proverb says: To speak of a loan is to put an end to friendship. They all, with good reason, considered Li as a young rake whose infatuation with a courtesan had kept him away from home for more than a year, and they knew that his father was furious with him.

"Who knows whether he is telling the truth?" they thought. "Suppose we lend him money for the journey and he spends it on girls again, when his father hears of it he will attribute the worst motives to us. Since we shall be blamed in any case, why not refuse altogether?"

"I am so sorry!" said each in turn. "I happen to be short at the moment, so I can't help you." Li received exactly the same answer from each of them, not one of his acquaintances proving generous enough to lend him even ten or twenty taels. He called at house after house for three days without succeeding in borrowing a single cent; but he dared not tell Decima this and put her off with evasive answers. The fourth day, however, found him in such despair that he was ashamed to go back to her; but after living so long with Decima he had no other dwelling place and, having nowhere else to spend the night, he went to his fellow-provincial, Liu, and begged a bed of him. When Liu asked why he looked so worried, Li told him the whole story of how Decima wanted to marry him. Liu, however, shook his head.

"I don't believe it," he said. "Decima is the most famous courtesan in that quarter and her price must be at least ten pecks of pearls or a thousand taels of silver. Her mistress would never let her go for three hundred taels. The old woman must be annoyed because you have no money left but are monopolizing her girl without paying her; so she has thought of this trick to get rid of you. Since she has known you for a long time, she has to keep up appearances and can't drive you away outright; and, knowing that you are short of cash, she has asked for three hundred taels in order to appear generous, giving you ten days in which to raise that sum. They believe that if you can't get the money in time, you won't have the face to go back; while if you do, they will jeer at you and insult you so that you can't stay anyway. This is the kind of trick such people always play. Think it over for yourself and don't let them take you in. In my humble opinion, the sooner you sever relations with them the better."

When Li heard this he was filled with misgivings and remained silent for a long time. "You mustn't make a wrong decision," went on Liu. "If you really want to go home and need money for the journey, your friends may be able to raise a few taels. But I doubt if you could get three hundred taels in ten months, let alone ten days, for people nowadays are simply not interested in their friends' troubles. Those women knew that you could never borrow such a sum: that's why they named this figure."

"I suppose you are right, my friend," said Li.

But, still unwilling to give up the girl, he continued to call on acquaintances to ask for a loan, no longer going back to Decima at night. He stayed with Liu for three days, until six of the ten days had passed, by which time Decima had become so anxious that she sent her little servant-boy out to look for him. The boy found Li on the main street.

"Mr. Li!" he called. "Our mistress is expecting you!"

Li, however, felt too ashamed to go back and said: "I am busy today. I will come tomorrow."

But the boy had his instructions from Decima and, taking hold of Li's coat, he would not let him go. "I was told to find you," he said. "You must come with me."

So Li, who was of course longing for his mistress, accompanied the boy to the courtesans' quarter. But when he saw Decima he was silent.

"What progress have you made?" asked Decima.

Li shed tears and said nothing.

"Are men's hearts so hard," she said, "that you cannot raise three hundred taels?"

With tears in his eyes, Li answered: "It is easier to catch a tiger in the mountain than to find a friend in need. I have been hurrying from house to house for six days, but I have not been able to borrow a cent; and it is because I was ashamed to come to you empty-handed that I have stayed away for the last few days. Today you sent for me, and I come feeling over whelmed with shame. It is not that I haven't done my best, but people are heartless."

"Don't let the old woman hear you," said Decima. "Stay here tonight, and we'll talk it over." Then she prepared a meal and they enjoyed the food and wine together.

In the middle of the night Decima asked: "Couldn't you get any money at all? What will become of me then?"

But Li had no answer for her and could only shed tears.

Soon it was dawn and Decima said: "In my mattress I have hidden one hundred and fifty taels of silver which I have saved up, and I want you to take that. Now that I have given you half the sum, it should be easier for you to find the other half. But there are only four days left: don't lose any time." Then getting out of bed she gave the mattress to Li, who was over-come with joy.

Ordering the servant-boy to carry the mattress for him, Li went straight to Liu's lodging, where he told his friend all that had happened that night. And when they unpicked the mattress they found in the cotton padding many silver pieces which, when weighed, totaled one hundred and fifty taels. Liu was very much impressed.

"The girl must really be in love with you," he said. "Since she is so much in earnest, you mustn't let her down. I will do what I can for you."

"If you help me now," replied Li, "I shall never forget it." Then Liu kept Li in his house, while he went round himself to all his acquaintances. In two days he borrowed one hundred and fifty taels which he gave to Li, saying: "I have done this not so much for your sake as because I am touched by the girl's devotion to you."

It was a happy Li, beaming with smiles, who came to Decima with the three hundred taels on the ninth day—one day earlier than the appointed time.

"The other day you could not borrow a cent," said Decima. "How is it that today you have got one hundred and fifty taels?" And when Li told her about his fellow-student Liu, she pressed her hands to her forehead in token of gratitude. "We must thank Mr. Liu for making our wish come true!" she cried.

They passed the night in great joy together, and the next morning Decima rose early and said to Li: "Once you have paid the money, I shall be able to leave with you. You had better decide how we are going to travel. Yesterday I borrowed twenty taels from my friends which you can take for the journey."

Li had, in fact, been wondering where he was going to get the money for their journey, but had not liked to mention this difficulty. Now he was delighted to receive these twenty taels.

As they were talking, the mistress of the house knocked at the door.

"This is the tenth day, Decima!" she called.

When Li heard this, he opened the door to invite her in.

"Thank you, aunty," he said. "I was just going to ask you over." And he placed the three hundred taels on the table.

The procuress had never thought that Li would produce the money. Her face fell and she was about to retract, when Decima said:

"I have worked here for eight years, and I must have earned several thousand

中国文学选读

taels for you in that time. This is the happy day on which I am to start a new life—you agreed to that yourself. The three hundred taels are here, not a cent less, and they have been paid on time. If you break your word, Mr. Li will take the money away and I shall immediately commit suicide. Then you will lose both the money and me, and you will be sorry."

The old woman had nothing to say to this. After long thought she finally had to fetch her balance to weigh the silver.

"Well, well," she said at last. "I suppose I can't keep you. But if you must go, go at once. And don't think you're going to take any clothes and trinkets with you." She pushed them out of the room, and called for a lock with which she padlocked the door.

It was already autumn. Decima, just risen from her bed and not yet dressed, was still wearing old clothes. She curtseyed to her mistress and Li bowed too. Then as husband and wife they left the old woman's house together.

> *Like a carp escaping from a golden hook,*
> *They scurried off, not to return again.*

"Wait while I call a sedan-chair for you," said Li to Decima.

"We can go to Mr. Liu's lodging before deciding on anything." But Decima demurred.

"My friends have always been very good to me," she said, "and I ought to say goodbye to them. Besides, they were kind enough to lend us the money for our traveling expenses the other day: we ought to thank them for that." So she took Li to say goodbye to the other courtesans.

Two of these girls, Yuelang and Susu, lived near by and were Decima's closest friends. She called first on Yuelang, who, surprised to see her dressed in old clothes and with no ornaments in her hair, asked what had happened. Decima told her and introduced Li to her. Then, pointing to Yuelang, Decima told Li:

"This is the friend who lent us the money the other day. You should thank her." And Li bowed again and again.

Presently Yuelang helped Decima to wash and comb her hair, sending at the same time for Susu. And after Decima had made her toilet, her two friends brought out all their emerald trinkets, gold bracelets, jade hairpins and earrings, as well as a brocade tunic and skirt, a phoenix girdle and a pair of embroidered slippers, until soon they had arrayed Decima in finery from head to foot. Then they feasted together, and Yuelang lent the lovers her bedroom for the night.

The following day they gave another big feast to which all the courtesans were invited; and not one of Decima's friends stayed away. After toasting the happy couple, they played wind and stringed instruments, and sang and danced, each doing her best to give the company pleasure. And this feast lasted till midnight, when Decima thanked each of her friends in turn.

"You were the chief among us," said the courtesans. "But now that you are leaving with your husband, we may never meet again. When you have decided on which day to set out, we shall come to see you off."

"When the date is settled, I shall let you all know," said Yuelang. "But Decima will be traveling a long way with her husband, and their resources are rather limited. We must be responsible for seeing that she doesn't have to go short on the way." The other courtesans agreed to this, then left, while Li and Decima spent the night again in Yuelang's room.

When dawn came Decima asked Li: "Where are we going from here? Have you any plan?"

"My father is already angry with me," replied Li, "and if he hears that I have married a singsong girl, not only will he make me suffer for it, but you will feel all the weight of his anger too. This has been worrying me for some time, but I have not yet thought of a way out."

"A father cannot help loving his son," said Decima, "so he won't be angry with you forever. But perhaps, since going straight home would offend him, we had better go to some beauty spot like Suzhou or Hangzhou for the time being. You can then go home alone and ask some relatives or friends to persuade your father to forgive you. Once you have made your peace with him you can come to fetch me, and all will be well."

"That is a good idea," agreed Li.

The next morning they said goodbye to Yuelang and went to Liu's lodging to pack their baggage. When Decima saw Liu she kowtowed to him to thank him for his assistance, and promised to repay him in future.

Liu hastily bowed in return. "You must be a remarkable woman," he said, "to remain loyal to your lover even after he became poor. I merely blew upon the fire in the direction of the wind. Such a trifling service is not worth mentioning."

The three of them feasted all day, and the following morning chose an auspicious day for the journey and hired sedan-chairs and beasts. Decima also sent her boy with a letter to Yuelang to thank her and bid her farewell. When they were leaving, several sedan-chairs arrived bearing Yuelang, Susu and the other courtesans who had come to see them off.

"You are starting on a long journey with your husband and you are short of money," said Yuelang. "So we have prepared a little gift to express our love. Please accept it. If you run short on your journey, you may find it useful." She told a servant to bring over a gilt box of the type used for carrying stationery; but since this was securely locked, its contents could not be seen.

Decima neither declined the gift nor opened it, but thanked them all. By now the chairs and beasts were ready, and the chair-bearers and grooms asked them to start. Liu offered the travelers three cups of wine in parting, and he and the courtesans saw them to Chongwen Gate where, wiping away tears, they all bid their friends farewell.

*Uncertain whether they would meet again,*
*They bade farewell, with tears on either side.*

In due course Li and Decima reached Luhe River where they were to take a junk. They were lucky enough to find an official despatch boat returning to Guazhou and, having settled the amount of their fare, they booked places on this junk. Once aboard, however, Li discovered that he had not a cent left. Although Decima had given him twenty taels, it was all gone! The fact was that Li had stayed in the courtesans' quarter until he had nothing but old clothes to wear; so as soon as he had money he naturally went to redeem a few of his gowns at the pawnshop and to have new bedding made. What was left of the silver was enough only for the sedan-chairs and beasts.

"Don't worry," said Decima, when she saw his anxiety. "The present that my friends gave us may prove useful." Thereupon she took a key and unlocked the box. Li, standing beside her, was too ashamed to look into the case as Decima took out a silk bag and placed it on the table.

"See what's in that," she said.

Li picked up the bag, which was quite heavy; and when he opened it he found it contained exactly fifty taels of silver. Decima meantime had locked the box again without saying what else it contained.

"How generous of the girls to give us this!" she exclaimed. "Now we have e-nough not only for the road but to help towards our expenses when we visit the beau-ty spots in Suzhou or Hangzhou."

Surprised and delighted, Li rejoined: "If not for your help, I should have died far from home without a burial place. I shall never forget how good you have been to me." After that, whenever they talked of the past Li would burst into tears of grati-tude, but Decima would always comfort him tenderly.

After an uneventful journey of several days, they reached Guazhou Harbor where the junk moored. Li booked another passenger boat, had their luggage put a-board and arranged to set sail the next morning at dawn. It was midwinter and the full moon was as clear and bright as water.

"Since we left the capital," said Li to Decima as they sat together in the bow of the junk, "we have been shut up in the cabin with other passengers so that we couldn't talk freely. But today we have the whole boat to ourselves and can do as we please. Now that we are leaving North China and coming to the Changjiang Valley, don't you think we should drink a little wine to celebrate and to cheer ourselves up?"

"Yes," said Decima. "I haven't had a chance to chat or laugh for a long time. I feel just as you do."

Li got out the wine utensils and placed them on the deck, then spread a rug on which they sat down together to drink to each other, until they were both under the spell of the wine.

"You had the loveliest voice in all your quarter," said Li, raising his cup to Decima. "The first time that I saw you and heard you sing so divinely, I lost my heart to you. But we have been upset for so long that I haven't heard your heavenly voice for many days. Now the bright moon is shining on the clear waves; it is midnight and there is no one about—won't you sing for me?"

Decima was in a happy mood, so, clearing her throat and tapping her fan on the deck to keep time, she sang. Her song was about a scholar who offered wine to a girl, and was taken from the opera *Moon Pavilion* by Shi Junmei of the Yuan Dynasty. It was set to the air known as "The Little Red Peach Blossom."

*As her voice reached the sky, the clouds halted to listen;*
*As her voice reached the waves, the fish frolicked for joy.*

Now on another junk nearby there was a young man called Sun Fu, who was a native of Xinan in Huizhou. He had an estate worth millions of cash, for his family had dealt in salt in Yangzhou for generations; and now, at twenty years of age, he too had entered the Imperial College in Nanjing. This Sun was a dissolute young man who frequented the courtesans' quarters in search of amusement or to buy a smile from the singsong girls: indeed, he was one of the foremost in the pursuit of pleasure.

Sun's boat was moored at Guazhou Harbour too on this particular evening, and he was drinking alone to drown his boredom when he heard a woman singing so clearly and exquisitely that not even the song of a phoenix could compare with her voice. He stood up in the bow and listened for some time until he realized that the singing came from the next boat; but just as he was going to make inquiries, the song ended. The servant whom he sent to put discreet questions to the boatman found out that the adjacent junk had been hired by a certain Mr. Li, but was unable to learn anything about the singer.

"She must be a professional, not a respectable girl," thought Sun. "How can I contrive to see her?" Preoccupation with this problem kept him awake all night.

At the fifth watch a high wind sprang up, and by dawn the sky was filled with dark clouds. Soon a snowstorm was raging.

> *Trees on the hills are hidden by the clouds,*
> *All human tracks are blotted out below;*
> *And on the frozen river in the snow*
> *An old man fishes from his little boat.*

Since this snowstorm made it impossible to cross the river, all boats had to remain in the harbor. Sun ordered his boatman to steer closer to Li's junk; and then, having put on his sable cap and fox fur coat, he opened the window on the pretext that he was watching the snow. Thus he succeeded in catching sight of Decima, for when she had finished dressing she raised the curtain of the cabin window with one slender white hand in order to empty her basin into the river. Her more than earthly beauty made Sun's head swim, and he fastened his eyes to the spot where she had appeared, hoping to gain another glimpse of her; but he was disappointed. After some reflection, he leaned against his cabin window and chanted aloud the lines by Gao Xueshi on the plum blossom:

> *Like a hermit resting on some snow-clad hill;*
> *Like a lovely girl in same glade beneath the moon.*

When Li heard someone chanting poetry in the next boat, he leaned out to look just as Sun had hoped he would. For Sun's plan was to attract Li's attention by this means in order to draw him into conversation. Now, hastily raising his hands in greeting, Sun asked:

"What is your honorable name, sir?"

After Li introduced himself he naturally asked to know Sun's name. And, when Sun had introduced himself, they chatted about the Imperial College until very soon they were on friendly terms.

"It must be Heaven's will," said Sun, "that this snowstorm should have held up our boats in order that we should meet. I am in luck. Traveling by junk is thoroughly boring, and I would like to go ashore with you to a wineshop where I can profit by your conversation while we drink. I hope you won't refuse. "

"Only meeting you by chance," replied Li, "how can I impose on you like this?"

"Oh, come," protested Sun. "Within the four seas all men are brothers. "

Then he ordered his boatman to put down the gang-plank, and told his boy to hold an umbrella for Mr. Li as he came across. He bowed to Li at the bow and followed him politely ashore.

A few paces brought them to a wineshop. They went upstairs, chose a clean table by the window and sat down. When the waiter had brought wine and food, Sun asked Li to drink; and as they drank they enjoyed the sight of the snow. After they had exchanged the usual platitudes about scholarship, Sun gradually steered the conversation around to courtesans; and now that they had found a common interest— since both young men had much experience in this field—they began to talk frankly and to exchange confidences.

Presently Sun sent his servant away, and asked in a low voice: "Who was the girl who sang on your junk last night?"

Li, only too ready to boast of his conquest, announced truthfully: "That was Du Wei, the well-known courtesan of Beijing. "

"If she is a courtesan, how did you manage to get hold of her?"

Then Li told him the whole story: how they had fallen in love, how Decima had wanted to marry him, and how he had borrowed money to redeem her.

"It must, no doubt, be very pleasant," said Sun, "to be taking home a beauty. But will your honorable family approve?"

"I have no anxiety on the score of my first wife," replied Li. "The only difficulty is that my father is rather strict, and I may have trouble with him. "

This gave Sun the opening he had been waiting for.

"Since your respected father may disapprove, where do you intend to lodge your beauty?" he asked. "Have you discussed it with her?"

"Yes, we have discussed it," replied Li with a frown.

"And does she have a good plan?" demanded Sun eagerly.

"She wants to stay for a time in Suzhou or Hangzhou," answered Li. "And when we have visited the beauty spots there, I will return home first to ask friends or relatives to talk my father round; then, when he is no longer angry, I shall fetch her back. What do you think of this plan?"

Sun looked thoughtful for a while, pretending to be very much concerned.

"We have only just met," he said at length, "and you may take offence if a casual acquaintance advises you on such an intimate matter."

"I need your advice," protested Li. "Please don't hesitate to speak frankly."

"Well then," said Sun. "Since your father is a high provincial official, he must be very jealous of your family reputation. He has already expressed displeasure because you visited low haunts: do you think he will allow you to take a singsong girl as your wife? As for your relatives and friends, they will all take their cue from your respected father. It will be useless to ask for their help: they are bound to refuse. And even if some of them are foolish enough to plead your cause to your father, once they realize that the old gentleman is against this marriage they will change their tune. So you will be causing discord in your family, and you will have no satisfactory answer to take to your mistress. Even if yon enjoy the scenery in Suzhou and Hangzhou for a time, you cannot live like that indefinitely. Once your funds run low you will find yourself in a dilemma."

Only too conscious that all he possessed was fifty taels, the greater part of which was already spent, when Sun spoke of possible financial difficulties Li nodded and admitted that such, indeed, was the case.

"Now I sincerely want to give you some advice," went on Sun. "But you may not like to hear it."

"I am very much obliged to you," said Li. "Please speak frankly."

"I had better not," declared Sun. "Casual acquaintances shouldn't come between lovers."

"Never mind about that," protested Li.

"As the ancients said, women are fickle," argued Sun. "And singsong girls in particular are likely to prove untrue. Since your mistress is a well-known courtesan, she must have friends everywhere. There may be some former lover of hers in the

south, and she may be making use of you for the journey here so that she can join another man. "

"Oh, no, I don't think so," said Li.

"You may be right," replied Sun. "But those young southerners are notorious
philanderers; and if you leave your mistress by herself, she may succumb to one of
them. On the other hand, if you take her home you will make your father angrier
than ever. In fact, there seems to be no way out for you.

"Now the relationship between father and son is sacred and inviolable. If you
offend your father and abandon your home for the sake of a courtesan, you will be u-
niversally condemned as a dissolute wastrel. Your wife will not consider you worthy
to be her husband, your younger brother will cease to respect you as his elder, and
your friends will have no more to do with you. You will find yourself a complete out-
cast. So I advise you to think this thing out carefully today. "

This speech left Li at a complete loss. Hitching his seat nearer to Sun, he demanded earnestly: "What do you think I should do?"

"I have a scheme which would be very much to your advantage," replied Sun.
"But I fear you may be too fond of your concubine to consider it, and I will have wasted my breath. "

"If you have a good plan to restore me to the bosom of my family, 1 shall be tremendously grateful to you. Don't hesitate to speak. "

"You have been away from home for more than a year, so that your father is angry and your wife displeased with you. If I were you, I would be unable to eat or
sleep for remorse. But your worthy father is angry with you only because you have let
yourself become infatuated with a courtesan and are spending money like water. You
are showing yourself unfit to inherit his property, for if you go on in this way you are
bound to bankrupt your family; so if you return home now empty-handed, the old
gentleman will vent his anger on you. But if you are willing to part with your concubine and to make the best of a bad bargain, I don't mind offering you a thousand taels
for her. With this sum, you can tell your father that you have been teaching in the
capital instead of squandering money, and he will certainly believe you. Then peace
will reign at home and you will have no more trouble: at a single stroke you will have

turned calamity into good fortune. Please consider my offer carefully. It's not that I covet your courtesan's beauty: I just want to do what I can to help you out."

Li had always been a weak character who stood in great awe of his father; so Sun's argument convinced him completely and, rising from his seat, he bowed to express his thanks.

"Your excellent advice has opened my eyes," he said. "But since my concubine has come all these hundreds of miles with me, I can't sever relations with her too abruptly. I'll talk it over with her, and let you know as soon as I gain her consent."

"Break it to her gently," said Sun. "Since she is so fond of you, she can't want to estrange from your father. I am sure she will help to restore you to your family." They went on drinking till dusk, when the wind dropped and the snow ceased.

Then Sun told his servant to pay the bill, and walked hand in hand with Li back to the boat.

> *You should tell a stranger only one third of the truth;*
> *To bare your heart to him is far from wise.*

Now Decima had prepared wine and sweetmeats on the junk for Li, but he did not come back all day. At dusk she lighted the lamp to wait for him, and when he came aboard she rose to welcome him; but she noticed that he seemed flustered and upset. As she poured a cup of warm wine for him, he shook his head in refusal and went without a word to his bed. Decima was disturbed. Having put away the cups and plates and helped Li to undress, she asked:

"What has happened today to make you so sad?"

Li's only answer was a sigh. She repeated her question three or four times until he was asleep, and by then she was so uneasy that she sat on the edge of the bed unable to close her eyes. In the middle of the night the young man woke up and heaved another great sigh.

"What is preying so heavily on your mind?" asked Decima. "Why can't you tell me?"

Li sat up, drawing the quilt around him, and tried several times to speak; but he broke off short each time and tears poured down his cheeks.

Then taking Li in her arms Decima comforted him with kind words, saying: "We have been lovers for nearly two years and won through a thousand hardships and difficulties; and you have not looked depressed once during all this long journey. Why are you so upset now when we are about to cross the Yangzi and settle down to live happily ever after? There must be a reason. As husband and wife we shall live and die together, so we should discuss our troubles together too. Please don't keep it from me."

After she had begged him several times to speak, with tears in his eyes Li said: "When I was stranded far from home you were good to me and attached yourself to me in spite of every hardship, so that I am inexpressibly grateful to you. But I have been thinking things over. My father is a high provincial official who is a stickler for convention and a very stern man. If I anger him so that he drives us out of the family, we shall be forced to wander homeless, and what will become of us then? That would mean a complete break with my father, and we could not be sure of a happy married life either. Today my friend Sun from Xinan discussed this with me while we were drinking; and now I feel quite broken-hearted."

"What do you mean to do?" asked Decima, greatly alarmed.

"A man in trouble cannot see his way clearly," said Li. "But Mr. Sun has thought out an excellent plan for me. I am only afraid you may not agree to it."

"Who is this Mr. Sun? If his plan is good, why shouldn't I agree to it?"

"His name is Sun Fu. He is a salt merchant from Xinan and a gallant young scholar. He heard you singing last night, so he asked about you; and when I told him our story and mentioned that we would not be able to go home, he offered a thousand taels for your hand. If I had a thousand taels, it would be easy for me to face my parents; and you would have a home too. But I can't bear to part with you: that's why I am sad." When he had said this, his tears fell like rain.

Taking her arms from his shoulders, Decima gave a strange laugh.

"He must be a fine gentleman to have thought out this plan," she said. "You will recover your thousand taels, and I shall no longer be an encumbrance to you if I can go to another man. What could be more reasonable and high-principled? This plan suits us both. Where is the silver?"

"Since I hadn't got your consent, my love," said Li, who had stopped crying, "the money is still with him. It hasn't yet changed hands."

"Mind you clinch with him first thing tomorrow," urged Decima. "You mustn't miss this opportunity. But a thousand taels is a lot of money; be sure it is properly weighed and handed over before I cross to the other boat. Don't let that salt merchant cheat you."

It was now the fourth watch, and since dawn was approaching Decima got up and lighted the lamp to dress herself.

"Today I am dressing to usher out an old client and welcome in a new," she said. "This is an important occasion."

She applied her rouge, powder and scented oil with great care, then arrayed herself in her most splendid jewels and most magnificent embroidered gown. Her perfume scented the air and she was a dazzling sight.

By the time she had finished dressing it was already dawn and Sun had sent a servant to their junk for a reply. When Decima stole a glance at Li and saw that he looked pleased, she urged him to give a reply at once and possess himself of the silver as soon as possible. Then Li went to Sun's boat to announce that Decima was willing.

"There is no difficulty about the money," said Sun. "But I must have the lady's jewel case as a pledge."

When Li told Decima this, she pointed to her gilt box.

"Let them take that," she said.

Then Sun, in great exultation, promptly sent the thousand taels of silver to Li's boat. When Decima had looked through the packages and satisfied herself that the silver was of the finest and the amount was correct, she put one hand on the side of the boat and beckoned to Sun with the other, so that he was transported with joy.

"May I have that box back for a minute?" she asked, parting her red lips to reveal pearly teeth. "It contains Mr. Li's travel permit which I must return to him."

Satisfied that Decima could not escape him now, Sun ordered his servant to carry back her gilt box and set it down on the deck. Decima took her key and unlocked it, disclosing a series of drawers inside; and when she told Li to pull out the first drawer, he found it filled with trinkets, pearls, jade and precious stones, to the value of several hundred taels of silver. These jewels, to the consternation of Li, Sun and the others on the two boats, Decima suddenly tossed into the river.

Then she told Li to pull out a second drawer containing jade flutes and golden pipes, and a third drawer filled with curious old jade and gold ornaments worth several thousand taels. All these, too, Decima threw into the water.

By this time the bank was thronged with spectators. "What a pity!" they exclaimed.

As they were marveling at her behavior, she drew out the last drawer in which there was a casket. She opened the casket and they saw that it was packed with handfuls of bright pearls and other precious stones such as emeralds and cat's-eyes, the like of which they had never seen before and the value of which they could not even guess at. The onlookers cried out loudly in admiration. When Decima made as if to toss all these jewels into the river too, a remorseful Li threw his arms around her and wept bitterly, while Sun came over to plead with her also. But Decima pushed Li away and turned angrily on Sun.

"Mr. Li and I suffered many hardships to come here!" she cried. "But you, to gratify your lust, lied cunningly to him in order to break up our marriage and destroy our love. I hate you! After my death, if I become a ghost, I shall accuse you before the gods. How dare you think of enjoying me yourself!"

Then Decima turned to Li.

"I led the unhappy life of a courtesan for many years," she said, "and during that time I saved up enough to support myself in my old age. But after I met you, we swore to love each other all our lives. When we left the capital I pretended that this box was a present from my friends, whereas actually it contained jewels worth over ten thousand taels of silver with which I intended to fit you out splendidly, so that when you returned to your parents they might feel well disposed towards me and accept me as one of the family. Then I could have remained happily with you ever after. But you did not trust me and were easily swayed by lies; and now you have abandoned me midway, caring nothing for my true love. I have opened this box in front of all these people to show you that a paltry thousand taels is nothing to me. I had jewels in my casket, but you, alas, had no eyes. Fate must be against me. I escaped from the bitter lot of a courtesan only to be cast aside by you. All of you here today can be my witnesses! I have not been unfaithful to him, but he has proved untrue to me!"

Then all who were present were moved to tears. They cursed and spat at Li, accusing him of ingratitude and disloyalty; while shame, unhappiness and remorse made the young man weep bitterly. He was turning to beg Decima's forgiveness when, clasping the casket in her arms, she leapt into the river. They shouted for help, but there was a thick mist over the river and the current was strong, so she could not be found. How sad that such a beautiful and famous courtesan should fall a victim to the hungry waves!

> The watery deep engulfed that lovely form;
> The river bore her from the world of men.

Gnashing their teeth in rage, the onlookers wanted to fall upon Li and Sun; and the two young men were so alarmed that they shouted to the boatmen to cast off, escaping in opposite directions. As he stared at the thousand taels of silver, Li longed for Decima; and he sat brooding all day in shame and sorrow until he lost his reason. He remained insane all his life.

As for Sun, he fell ill with fright and kept to his bed for over a month. But he was haunted day and night by Decima's ghost, who cursed him until he died a lingering death; and all men said this was a just retribution for the crime he committed on the river.

When Liu Yuchun completed his studies in the capital and packed up to return home, his boat also moored at Kuazhou; and while he was washing his face by the side of the junk, his brass basin fell into the river. He asked a fisherman to cast his net for it, but the man drew up a small casket; and when Liu opened this he found it full of priceless jewels, pearls and other treasures. Liu rewarded the fisherman well and put the casket at the head of his bed. That night he dreamed that he saw a girl coming over the waves of the river, whom he recognized as Decima. She came up to him and curtseyed, then told him how faithless Li had proved.

中国文学选读

"You were kind enough to help me with one hundred and fifty taels," she said. "I meant to repay you after we reached our destination, and although I was unable to do so I have never forgotten your great kindness. So this morning I sent you this casket through the fisherman to express my thanks. We shall never meet again." Suddenly awaking, Liu realized that Decima was dead, and he sighed for her for several days.

Later generations, commenting on this, condemned Sun for his wickedness in plotting to obtain a beautiful girl for a thousand taels of silver. Li they considered beneath contempt because, like a fool, he failed to understand Decima's worth. As for Decima, she was a pearl among women; the pity was that instead of finding a husband worthy of her, she wasted her affection on Li. This was like casting bright pearls or rare jade before a blind man, and resulted in her great love changing to hate and all her tenderness vanishing with the flowing stream.

> *Those who have never loved had best be silent;*
> *It is no easy thing to know love's worth;*
> *And none but he who treasures constancy*
> *Deserves the name of lover on this earth.*

(translated by Yang Xianyi and Gladys Yang)

## 杜十娘怒沉百宝箱

冯梦龙

话中单表万历二十年间，日本国关白作乱，侵犯朝鲜。朝鲜国王上表告急，天朝发兵泛海往救。有户部官奏准：目今兵兴之际，粮饷未充，暂开纳粟入监之例。原来纳粟入监的，有几般便宜：好读书，好科举，好中，结末来又有个小小前程结果。以此宦家公子、富室子弟，到不愿做秀才，都去援例做太学生。自开了这例，两京太学生各添至千人之外。内中有一人，姓李名甲，字子先，浙江绍兴府人氏。父亲李布政所生三儿，惟甲居长，自幼读书在庠，未得登科，援例入于北雍。因在京坐监，与同乡柳遇春监生同游教坊司院内，与一个名姬相遇。那名姬姓杜名媺，排行第十，院中都称为杜十娘，生得：

浑身雅艳，遍体娇香，两弯眉画远山青，一对眼明秋水润。脸如莲
萼，分明卓氏文君；唇似樱桃，何减白家樊素。可怜一片无瑕玉，误落
风尘花柳中。

那杜十娘自十三岁破瓜，今一十九岁，七年之内，不知历过了多少公子王孙。
一个个情迷意荡，破家荡产而不惜。院中传出四句口号来，道是：

坐中若有杜十娘，斗筲之量饮千觞。
院中若识杜老媺，千家粉面都如鬼。

却说李公子风流年少，未逢美色，自遇了杜十娘，喜出望外，把花柳情怀，
一担儿挑在他身上。那公子俊俏庞儿，温存性儿，又是撒漫的手儿，帮衬的勤儿，
与十娘一双两好，情投意合。十娘因见鸨儿贪财无义，久有从良之志，又见李公
子忠厚志诚，甚有心向他。奈李公子惧怕老爷，不敢应承。虽则如此，两下情好
愈密，朝欢暮乐，终日相守，如夫妇一般。海誓山盟，各无他志。真个：

恩深似海恩无底，义重如山义更高。

再说杜妈妈，女儿被李公子占住，别的富家巨室，闻名上门，求一见而不可
得。初时李公子撒漫用钱，大差大使，妈妈胁肩谄笑，奉承不暇。日往月来，不
觉一年有余，李公子囊箧渐渐空虚，手不应心，妈妈也就怠慢了。老布政在家闻
知儿子嫖院，几遍写字来唤他回去。他迷恋十娘颜色，终日延捱。后来闻知老爷
在家发怒，越不敢回。古人云："以利相交者，利尽而疏。"那杜十娘与李公子真情
相好，见他手头愈短，心头愈热。妈妈也几遍教女儿打发李甲出院，见女儿不统
口，又几遍将言语触突李公子，要激怒他起身。公子性本温克，词气愈和。妈妈
没奈何，日逐只将十娘叱骂道："我们行户人家，吃客穿客，前门送旧，后门迎新，
门庭闹如火，钱帛堆成垛。自从那李甲在此，混帐一年有余，莫说新客，连旧主
顾都断了。分明接了个钟馗老，连小鬼也没得上门，弄得老娘一家人家，有气无
烟，成什么模样！"

杜十娘被骂，耐性不住，便回答道："那李公子不是空手上门的，也曾费过大

钱来。"妈妈道:"彼一时,此一时,你只教他今日费些小钱儿,把与老娘办些柴米,养你两口也好。别人家养的女儿便是摇钱树,千生万活,偏我家晦气,养了个退财白虎!开了大门七件事,般般都在老身心上。到替你这小贱人白白养着穷汉,教我衣食从何处来?你对那穷汉说:有本事出几两银子与我,到得你跟了他去,我别讨个丫头过活却不好?"十娘道:"妈妈,这话是真是假?"妈妈晓得李甲囊无一钱,衣衫都典尽了,料他没处设法,便应道:"老娘从不说谎,当真哩。"十娘道:"娘,你要他许多银子?"妈妈道:"若是别人,千把银子也讨了。可怜那穷汉出不起,只要他三百两,我自去讨一个粉头代替。只一件,须是三日内交付与我,左手交银,右手交人。若三日没有银时,老身也不管三七二十一,公子不公子,一顿孤拐,打那光棍出去。那时莫怪老身!"十娘道:"公子虽在客边乏钞,谅三百金还措办得来。只是三日忒近,限他十日便好。"妈妈想道:"这穷汉一双赤手,便限他一百日,他那里来银子?没有银子,便铁皮包脸,料也无颜上门。那时重整家风,嬷儿也没得话讲。"答应道:"看你面,便宽到十日。第十日没有银子,不干老娘之事。"十娘道:"若十日内无银,料他也无颜再见了。只怕有了三百两银子,妈妈又翻悔起来。"妈妈道:"老身年五十一岁了,又奉十斋,怎敢说谎?不信时与你拍掌为定。若翻悔时,做猪做狗!"

> 从来海水斗难量,可笑虔婆意不良。
>
> 料定穷儒囊底竭,故将财礼难娇娘。

是夜,十娘与公子在枕边,议及终身之事。公子道:"我非无此心。但教坊落籍,其费甚多,非千金不可。我囊空如洗,如之奈何!"十娘道:"妾已与妈妈议定只要三百金,但须十日内措办。郎君游资虽罄,然都中岂无亲友可以借贷?倘得如数,妾身遂为君之所有,省受虔婆之气。"公子道:"亲友中为我留恋行院,都不相顾。明日只做束装起身,各家告辞,就开口假贷路费,凑聚将来,或可满得此数。"起身梳洗,别了十娘出门。十娘道:"用心作速,专听佳音。"公子道:"不须分付。"

公子出了院门,来到三亲四友处,假说起身告别,众人到也欢喜。后来叙到路费欠缺,意欲借贷。常言道:"说着钱,便无缘。"亲友们就不招架。他们也见得是,道李公子是风流浪子,迷恋烟花,年许不归,父亲都为他气坏在家。他今日抖然要回,未知真假,倘或说骗盘缠到手,又去还脂粉钱,父亲知道,将好意翻成恶意，始终只是一怪，不如辞了干净。便回道："目今正值空乏，不能相济，惭愧，惭愧！"人人如此，个个皆然，并没有个慷慨丈夫，肯统口许他一十二十两。

李公子一连奔走了三日，分毫无获，又不敢回决十娘，权且含糊答应。到第四日又没想头，就羞回院中。平日间有了杜家，连下处也没有了，今日就无处投宿。只得往同乡柳监生寓所借歇。

柳遇春见公子愁容可掬，问其来历。公子将杜十娘愿嫁之情，备细说了。遇春摇首道："未必，未必。那杜媺曲中第一名姬，要从良时，怕没有十斛明珠，千金聘礼。那鸨儿如何只要三百两？想鸨儿怪你无钱使用，白白占住他的女儿，设计打发你出门。那妇人与你相处已久，又碍却面皮，不好明言。明知你手内空虚，故意将三百两卖个人情，限你十日；若十日没有，你也不好上门。便上门时，他会说你笑你，落得一场褒渎，自然安身不牢，此乃烟花逐客之计。足下三思，休被其惑。据弟愚意，不如早早开交为上。"

公子听说，半晌无言，心中疑惑不定。遇春又道："足下莫要错了主意。你若真个还乡，不多几两盘费，还有人搭救；若是要三百两时，莫说十日，就是十个月也难。如今的世情，那肯顾缓急二字的！那烟花也算定你没处告债，故意设法难你。"公子道："仁兄所见良是。"口里虽如此说，心中割舍不下。依旧又往外边东央西告，只是夜里不进院门了。

公子在柳监生寓中，一连住了三日，共是六日了。杜十娘连日不见公子进院，十分着紧，就教小厮四儿街上去寻。四儿寻到大街，恰好遇见公子。四儿叫道："李姐夫，娘在家里望你。"公子自觉无颜，回复道："今日不得功夫，明日来罢。"四儿奉了十娘之命，一把扯住，死也不放，道："娘叫咱寻你，是必同去走一遭。"李公子心上也牵挂看婊子，没奈何，只得随四儿进院，见了十娘，嘿嘿无言。十娘问道："所谋之事如何？"公子眼中流下泪来。十娘道："莫非人情淡薄，不能足三百之数么？"分子含泪而言，道出二句：

"不信上山擒虎易，果然开口告人难。一连奔走六日，并无铢两，一双空手，羞见芳卿，故此这几日不敢进院。今日承命呼唤，忍耻而来。非某不用心，实是世情如此。"十娘道："此言休使虔婆知道。郎君今夜且住，妾别有商议。"十娘自备酒肴，与公子欢饮。睡至半夜，十娘对公子道："郎君果不能办一钱耶？妾终身之事，当如何也？"公子只是流涕，不能答一语。渐渐五更天晓。十娘道："妾所卧絮褥内藏有碎银一百五十两，此妾私蓄，郎君可持去。三百金，妾任其半，郎君亦谋其半，庶易为力。限只四日，万勿迟误！"十娘起身将褥付公子，公子惊喜过

中国文学选读

望。唤童儿持褥而去。径到柳遇春寓中，又把夜来之情与遇春说了。将褥拆开看时，絮中都裹着零碎银子，取出兑时果是一百五十两。遇春大惊道："此妇真有心人也。既系真情，不可相负，吾当代为足下谋之。"公子道："倘得玉成，决不有负。"当下柳遇春留李公子在寓，自出头各处去借贷。两日之内，凑足一百五十两交付公子道："吾代为足下告债，非为足下，实怜杜十娘之情也。"

李甲拿了三百两银子，喜从天降，笑逐颜开，欣欣然来见十娘，刚是第九日，还不足十日。十娘问道："前日分毫难借，今日如何就有一百五十两？"公子将柳监生事情，又述了一遍。十娘以手加额道："使吾二人得遂其愿者，柳君之力也！"两个欢天喜地，又在院中过了一晚。

次日十娘早起，对李甲道："此银一交，便当随郎君去矣。舟车之类，合当预备。妾昨日于姊妹中借得白银二十两，郎君可收下为行资也。"公子正愁路费无出，但不敢开口，得银甚喜。说犹未了，鸨儿恰来敲门叫道："媺儿，今日是第十日了。"公子闻叫，启门相延道："承妈妈厚意，正欲相请。"便将银三百两放在桌上。鸨儿不料公子有银，嘿然变色，似有悔意。十娘道："儿在妈妈家中八年，所致金帛，不下数千金矣。今日从良美事，又妈妈亲口所订，三百金不欠分毫，又不曾过期。倘若妈妈失信不许，郎君持银去，儿即刻自尽。恐那时人财两失，悔之无及也。"鸨儿无词以对。腹内筹画了半晌，只得取天平兑准了银子，说道："事已如此，料留你不住了。只是你要去时，即今就去。平时穿戴衣饰之类，毫厘休想！"说罢，将公子和十娘推出房门，讨锁来就落了锁。此时九月天气。十娘才下床，尚未梳洗，随身旧衣，就拜了妈妈两拜。李公子也作了一揖。一夫一妇，离了虔婆大门：

鲤鱼脱却金钩去，摆尾摇头再不来。

公子教十娘且住片时："我去唤个小轿抬你，权往柳荣卿寓所去，再作道理。"十娘道："院中诸姊妹平昔相厚，理宜话别。况前日又承他借贷路费，不可不一谢也。"乃同公子到各姊妹处谢别。姊妹中惟谢月朗、徐素素与杜家相近，尤与十娘亲厚。十娘先到谢月朗家。月朗见十娘秃髻旧衫，惊问其故。十娘备述来因，又引李甲相见。十娘指月朗道："前日路资，是此位姐姐所贷，郎君可致谢。"李甲连连作揖。月朗便教十娘梳洗，一面去请徐素素来家相会。

十娘梳洗已毕，谢、徐二美人各出所有，翠钿金钏，瑶簪宝珥，锦袖花裙，鸾带绣履，把杜十娘装扮得焕然一新，备酒作庆贺筵席。月朗让卧房与李甲、杜媺二人过宿。次日，又大排筵席，遍请院中姊妹。凡十娘相厚者，无不毕集，都与他夫妇把盏称喜。吹弹歌舞，各逞其长，务要尽欢，直饮至夜分。十娘向众姊妹一一称谢。众姊妹道："十姊为风流领袖，今从郎君去，我等相见无日。何日长行，姊妹们尚当奉送。"月朗道："候有定期，小妹当来相报。但阿姊千里间关，同郎君远去，囊箧萧条，曾无约束，此乃吾等之事。当相与共谋之，勿令姊有穷途之虑也。"众姊妹各唯唯而散。

是晚，公子和十娘仍宿谢家。至五鼓，十娘对公子道："吾等此去，何处安身？郎君亦曾计议有定着否？"公子道："老父盛怒之下，若知娶妓而归，必然加以不堪，反致相累。辗转寻思，尚未有万全之策。"十娘道："父子天性，岂能终绝？既然仓卒难犯，不若与郎君于苏、杭胜地，权作浮居。郎君先回，求亲友于尊大人面前劝解和顺，然后携妾于归，彼此安妥。"公子道："此言甚当。"

次日，二人起身辞了谢月朗，暂往柳监生寓中，整顿行装。杜十娘见了柳遇春，倒身下拜，谢其周全之德："异日我夫妇必当重报。"遇春慌忙答礼道："十娘钟情所欢，不以贫窭易心，此乃女中豪杰。仆因风吹火，谅区区何足挂齿！"三人又饮了一日酒。

次早，择了出行吉日，雇请轿马停当。十娘又遣童儿寄信，别谢月朗。临行之际，只见肩舆纷纷而至，乃谢月朗与徐素素拉众姊妹来送行。月朗道："十姊从郎君千里间关，囊中消索，吾等甚不能忘情。今合具薄赆，十姊可检收，或长途空乏，亦可少助。"说罢，命从人挈一描金文具至前，封锁甚固，正不知什么东西在里面。十娘也不开看，也不推辞，但殷勤作谢而已。须臾，舆马齐集，仆夫催促起身。柳监生三杯别酒，和众美人送出崇文门外，各各垂泪而别。正是：

他日重逢难预必，此时分手最堪怜。

再说李公子同杜十娘行至潞河，舍陆从舟。却好有瓜州差使船转回之便，讲定船钱，包了舱口。比及下船时，李公子囊中并无分文余剩。你道杜十娘把二十两银子与公子，如何就没了？公子在院中嫖得衣衫蓝缕，银子到手，未免在解库中取赎几件穿着，又制办了铺盖，剩来只勾轿马之费。公子正当愁闷，十娘道："郎君勿忧，众姊妹合赠，必有所济。"乃取钥开箱。公子在傍自觉惭愧，也不敢窥觑箱中虚实。只见十娘在箱里取出一个红绢袋来，掷于桌上道："郎君可开看之。"公子提在手中，觉得沉重，启而观之，皆是白银，计数整五十两。十娘仍将箱子下锁，亦不言箱中更有何物。但对公子道："承众姊妹高情，不惟途路不乏，即他日浮寓吴、越间，亦可稍佐吾夫妻山水之费矣。"公子且惊且喜道："若不遇恩卿，我李甲流落他乡，死无葬身之地矣。此情此德，白头不敢忘也！"自此每谈及往事，公子必感激流涕，十娘亦曲意抚慰。一路无话。

不一日，行至瓜州，大船停泊岸口，公子别雇了民船，安放行李。约明日侵晨，剪江而渡。其时仲冬中旬，月明如水，公子和十娘坐于舟首。公子道："自出都门，困守一舱之中，四顾有人，未得畅语。今日独据一舟，更无避忌。且已离塞北，初近江南，宜开怀畅饮，以舒向来抑郁之气。恩卿以为何如？"十娘道："妾久疏谈笑，亦有此心，郎君言及，足见同志耳。"公子乃携酒具于船首，与十娘铺毡并坐，传杯交盏。饮至半酣，公子执卮对十娘道："恩卿妙音，六院推首。某相遇之初，每闻绝调，辄不禁神魂之飞动。心事多违，彼此郁郁，鸾鸣凤奏，久矣不闻。今清江明月，深夜无人，肯为我一歌否？"十娘兴亦勃发，遂开喉顿嗓，取扇按拍，呜呜咽咽，歌出元人施君美《拜月亭》杂剧上"状元执盏与婵娟"一曲，名《小桃红》。真个：

声飞霄汉云皆驻，响入深泉鱼出游。

却说他舟有一少年，姓孙名富，字善赉，徽州新安人氏。家资巨万，积祖扬州种盐。年方二十，也是南雍中朋友。生性风流，惯向青楼买笑，红粉追欢，若嘲风弄月，到是个轻薄的头儿。事有偶然，其夜亦泊舟瓜州渡口，独酌无聊，忽听得歌声嘹亮，风吟鸾吹，不足喻其美。起立船头，伫听半晌，方知声出邻舟。正欲相访，音响倏已寂然，乃遣仆者潜窥踪迹，访于舟人。但晓得是李相公雇的船，并不知歌者来历。孙富想道："此歌者必非良家，怎生得他一见？"辗转寻思，通宵不寐。捱至五更，忽闻江风大作。及晓，彤云密布，狂雪飞舞。怎见得，有诗为证：

千山云树灭，万径人踪绝。
扁舟蓑笠翁，独钓寒江雪。

因这风雪阻渡，舟不得开。孙富命艄公移船，泊于李家舟之傍。孙富貂帽狐袭，推窗假作看雪。值十娘梳洗方毕，纤纤玉手揭起舟傍短帘，自泼盂中残水。粉容微露，却被孙富窥见了，果是国色天香。魂摇心荡，迎眸注目，等候再见一面，杳不可得。沉思久之，乃倚窗高吟高学士《梅花诗》二句，道：

雪满山中高士卧，月明林下美人来。

李甲听得邻舟吟诗，舒头出舱，看是何人。只因这一看，正中了孙富之计。孙富吟诗，正要引李公子出头，他好乘机攀话。当下慌忙举手，就问："老兄尊姓何讳？"李公子叙了姓名乡贯，少不得也问那孙富。孙富也叙过了。又叙了些太学中的闲话，渐渐亲熟。孙富便道："风雪阻舟，乃天遣与尊兄相会，实小弟之幸也。舟次无聊，欲同尊兄上岸，就酒肆中一酌，少领清诲，万望不拒。"公子道："萍水相逢，何当厚扰？"孙富道："说那里话！'四海之内，皆兄弟也'。"喝教艄公打跳，童儿张伞，迎接公子过船，就于船头作揖。然后让公子先行，自己随后，各各登跳上涯。

行不数步，就有个酒楼。二人上楼，拣一副洁净座头，靠窗而坐。酒保列上酒肴。孙富举杯相劝，二人赏雪饮酒。先说些斯文中套话，渐渐引入花柳之事。二人都是过来之人，志同道合，说得入港，一发成相知了。孙富屏去左右，低低问道："昨夜尊舟清歌者，何人也？"李甲正要卖弄在行，遂实说道："此乃北京名姬杜十娘也。"孙富道："既系曲中姊妹，何以归兄？"公子遂将初遇杜十娘，如何相好，后来如何要嫁，如何借银讨他，始末根由，备细述了一遍。孙富道："兄携丽人而归，固是快事，但不知尊府中能相容否？"公子道："贱室不足虑，所虑者老父性严，尚费踌躇耳！"孙富将机就机，便问道："既是尊大人未必相容，兄所携丽人，何处安顿？亦曾通知丽人，共作计较否？"公子攒眉而答道："此事曾与小妾议之。"孙富欣然问道："尊宠必有妙策。"公子道："他意欲侨居苏杭，流连山水。使小弟先回，求亲友宛转于家君之前，俟家君回嗔作喜，然后图归。高明以为何如？"孙富沉吟半晌，故作愀然之色，道："小弟乍会之间，交浅言深，诚恐见怪。"公子道："正赖高明指教，何必谦逊？"孙富道："尊大人位居方面，必严帷薄之嫌，平时既怪兄游非礼之地，今日岂容兄娶不节之人？况且贤亲贵友，谁不迎合尊大人之意者？兄枉去求他，必然相拒。就有个不识时务的进言于尊大人之前，见尊大人意思不允，他就转口了。兄进不能和睦家庭，退无词以回复尊宠。即使留连山水，亦非长久之计。万一资斧困竭，岂不进退两难！"公子自知手中只有五十金，此时费去大半，说到资斧困竭，进退两难，不觉点头道是。孙富又道："小弟还有句心腹之谈，兄肯俯听否？"公子道："承兄过爱，更求尽言。"孙富道："疏不间亲，还是莫说罢。"公子道："但说何妨！"孙富道："自古道：'妇人水性无常。'况烟花之辈，少真多假。他既系六院名姝，相识定满天下；或者南边原有旧约，借兄之力，挈带而来，以为他适之地。"公子道："这个恐未必然。"孙富道："既不然，江南子弟，最工轻薄。兄留丽人独居，难保无逾墙钻穴之事。若挈之同归，愈增尊大人之怒。为兄之计，未有善策。况父子天伦，必不可绝。若为妾而触父，因妓而弃家，海内必以兄为浮浪不经之人。异日妻不以为夫，弟不以为兄，同袍不以为友，兄何以立于天地之间？兄今日不可不熟思也！"

公子闻言，茫然自失，移席问计："据高明之见，何以教我？"孙富道："仆有一计，于兄甚便。只恐兄溺枕席之爱，未必能行，使仆空费词说耳！"公子道："兄诚有良策，使弟再睹家园之乐，乃弟之恩人也。又何惮而不言耶？"孙富道："兄飘零岁余，严亲怀怒，闺阁离心。设身以处兄之地，诚寝食不安之时也。然尊大人所以怒兄者，不过为迷花恋柳，挥金如土，异日必为弃家荡产之人，不堪承继家业耳！兄今日空手而归，正触其怒。兄倘能割衽席之爱，见机而作，仆愿以千金相赠。兄得千金以报尊大人，只说在京授馆，并不曾浪费分毫，尊大人必然相信。从此家庭和睦，当无间言。须臾之间，转祸为福。兄请三思，仆非贪丽人之色，实为兄效忠于万一也！"李甲原是没主意的人，本心惧怕老子，被孙富一席话，说透胸中之疑，起身作揖道："闻兄大教，顿开茅塞。但小妾千里相从，义难顿绝，容归与商之。得妾心肯，当奉复耳！"孙富道："说话之间，宜放婉曲。彼既忠心为兄，必不忍使兄父子分离，定然玉成兄还乡之事矣。"二人饮了一回酒，风停雪止，天色已晚。孙富教家童算还了酒钱，与公子携手下船。正是：

逢人且说三分话，未可全抛一片心。

却说杜十娘在舟中，摆设酒果，欲与公子小酌，竟日未回，挑灯以待。公子下船，十娘起迎。见公子颜色匆匆，似有不乐之意，乃满斟热酒劝之。公子摇首不饮，一言不发，竟自床上睡了。十娘心中不悦，乃收拾杯盘为公子解衣就枕，问道："今日有何见闻，而怀抱郁郁如此？"公子叹息而已，终不启口。问了三四次，公子已睡去了。十娘委决不下，坐于床头而不能寐。到夜半，公子醒来，又叹一口气。十娘道："郎君有何难言之事，频频叹息？"公子拥被而起，欲言不语者几次，扑簌簌掉下泪来。十娘抱持公子于怀间，软言抚慰道："妾与郎君情好，已及二载，千辛万苦，历尽艰难，得有今日。然相从数千里，未曾哀戚。今将渡江，方图百年欢笑，如何反起悲伤？必有其故。夫妇之间，死生相共，有事尽可商量，万勿讳也。"

公子再四被逼不过，只得含泪而言道："仆天涯穷困，蒙恩卿不弃，委曲相从，诚乃莫大之德也。但反复思之，老父位居方面，拘于礼法，况素性方严，恐添嗔怒，必加黜逐。你我流荡，将何底止？夫妇之欢难保，父子之伦又绝。日间蒙新安孙友邀饮，为我筹及此事，寸心如割！"十娘大惊道："郎君意将如何？"公子道："仆事内之人，当局而迷。孙友为我画一计颇善，但恐恩卿不从耳！"十娘道："孙友者何人？计如果善，何不可从？"公子道："孙友名富，新安盐商，少年风流之士也。夜间闻子清歌，因而问及。仆告以来历，并谈及难归之故，渠意欲以千金聘汝。我得千金，可借口以见吾父母，而恩卿亦得所耳。但情不能舍，是以悲泣。"说罢，泪如雨下。

十娘放开两手，冷笑一声道："为郎君画此计者，此人乃大英雄也！郎君千金之资既得恢复，而妾归他姓，又不致为行李之累，发乎情，止乎礼，诚两便之策也。那千金在那里？"公子收泪道："未得恩卿之诺，金尚留彼处，未曾过手。"十娘道："明早快快应承了他，不可挫过机会。但千金重事，须得兑足交付郎君之手，妾始过舟，勿为贾竖子所欺。"

时已四鼓，十娘即起身挑灯梳洗道："今日之妆，乃迎新送旧，非比寻常。"于是脂粉香泽，用意修饰，花钿绣袄，极其华艳，香风拂拂，光采照人。装束方完，天色已晓。

孙富差家童到船头候信。十娘微窥公子，欣欣似有喜色，乃催公子快去回话，及早兑足银子。公子亲到孙富船中，回复依允。孙富道："兑银易事，须得丽人妆台为信。"公子又回复了十娘，十娘即指描金文具道："可便抬去。"孙富喜甚。即将白银一千两，送到公子船中。十娘亲自检看，足色足数，分毫无爽，乃手把船舷，以手招孙富。孙富一见，魂不附体。十娘启朱唇，开皓齿道："方才箱子可暂发来，内有李郎路引一纸，可检还之也。"孙富视十娘已为瓮中之鳖，即命家童送那描金文具，安放船头之上。十娘取钥开锁，内皆抽替小箱。十娘叫公子抽第一层来看，只见翠羽明珰，瑶簪宝珥，充牣于中，约值数百金。十娘遽投之江中。李甲与孙富及两船之人，无不惊诧。又命公子再抽一箱，乃玉箫金管；又抽一箱，尽古玉紫金玩器，约值数千金。十娘尽投之于大江中。岸上之人，观者如堵。齐声道："可惜，可惜！"正不知什么缘故。最后又抽一箱，箱中复有一匣。开匣视之，夜明之珠约有盈把。其他祖母绿、猫儿眼，诸般异宝，目所未睹，莫能定其价之多少。众人齐声喝采，喧声如雷。十娘又欲投之于江。李甲不觉大悔，抱持十娘恸哭，那孙富也来劝解。

十娘推开公子在一边，向孙富骂道："我与李郎备尝艰苦，不是容易到此。汝以奸淫之意，巧为谗说，一旦破人姻缘，断人恩爱，乃我之仇人。我死而有知，必当诉之神明，尚妄想枕席之欢乎！"又对李甲道："妾风尘数年，私有所积，本为终身之计。自遇郎君，山盟海誓，白首不渝。前出都之际，假托众姊妹相赠，箱中韫藏百宝，不下万金。将润色郎君之装，归见父母，或怜妾有心，收佐中馈，得终委托，生死无憾。谁知郎君相信不深，惑于浮议，中道见弃，负妾一片真心。今日当众目之前，开箱出视，使郎君知区区千金，未为难事。妾椟中有玉，恨郎眼内无珠。命之不辰，风尘困瘁，甫得脱离，又遭弃捐。今众人各有耳目，共作证明，妾不负郎君，郎君自负妾耳！"

于是众人聚观者，无不流涕，都唾骂李公子负心薄幸。公子又羞又苦，且悔且泣，方欲向十娘谢罪。十娘抱持宝匣，向江心一跳。众人急呼捞救，但见云暗江心，波涛滚滚，杳无踪影。可惜一个如花似玉的名姬，一旦葬于江鱼之腹！

三魂渺渺归水府，七魄悠悠入冥途。

当时旁观之人，皆咬牙切齿，争欲拳殴李甲和那孙富。慌得李、孙二人手足无措，急叫开船，分途遁去。李甲在舟中，看了千金，转忆十娘，终日愧悔，郁成狂疾，终身不痊。孙富自那日受惊，得病卧床月余，终日见杜十娘在傍诟骂，奄奄而逝。人以为江中之报也。

却说柳遇春在京坐监完满，束装回乡，停舟瓜步。偶临江净脸，失坠铜盆于水，觅渔人打捞。及至捞起，乃是个小匣儿。遇春启匣观看，内皆明珠异宝，无价之珍。遇春厚赏渔人，留于床头把玩。是夜梦见江中一女子，凌波而来，视之，乃杜十娘也。近前万福，诉以李郎薄幸之事，又道："向承君家慷慨，以一百五十金相助。本意息肩之后，徐图报答，不意事无终始。然每怀盛情，恻恻未忘。早间曾以小匣托渔人奉致，聊表寸心，从此不复相见矣。"言讫，猛然惊醒，方知十娘已死，叹息累日。

后人评论此事，以为孙富谋夺美色，轻掷千金，固非良士；李甲不识杜十娘一片苦心，碌碌蠢才，无足道者。独谓十娘千古女侠，岂不能觅一佳侣，共跨秦楼之凤，乃错认李公子。明珠美玉，投于盲人，以致恩变为仇，万种恩情，化为流水，深可惜也！有诗叹云：

不会风流莫妄谈，单单情字费人参。

若将情字能参透，唤作风流也不惭。

## Topics for Discussion

1. Describe the process by which the Chinese novel developed.

2. Describe how Chinese novels contain characteristics of poetry.

3. Why did Lin Daiyu bury flowers?

4. How do you explain the "dream" of the Red Chamber?

5. Compare and contrast the characters of Sun Wukong and Zhu Bajie from *Journey to the West*.

Chapter Nine

# Modern Chinese Literature

## General Description

The Xinhai Revolution(辛亥革命) in 1911 ended more than two thousand years of imperial dynasties in China and began the modern transformation of Chinese society. Around 1919 the New Cultural Movement(新文化运动) and the literary revolution marked the end of Chinese classical literature and the birth of the modern literature.

The literary revolution aimed to promote colloquial language, abandon classical ways of writing, encourage a new modern literature, and oppose the old style literature.

The door was thrown open to advanced foreign ideas and cultures. Western philosophy and literature flowed in and vast numbers of foreign translations were introduced, competing to enter this new market. These profound changes turned Chinese literature upside down. From content to form to style, modern Chinese literature was dramatically influenced by this exposure to western literature and in response the new modern Chinese poetry, novels, drama and prose developed a fresh look distinct from traditional Chinese literature.

The process of transitioning to a modern Chinese literature was a tortuous one. On the one hand, the new movement was marked as anti-tradition, during a period of reflection leading to self-criticism of the Chinese national character as well as increased social criticism. On the other hand it was a time when the transformation was forced to cope with the harsh realities of wartime anti-Japanese sentiment, modern ideology and partisan politics. These opposing forces created many conflicts for modern Chinese writers.

This chapter introduces stories by Lu Xun and poems by Xu Zhimo. The supplementary works are by the contemporary Chinese authors Shen Congwen and Zhang Ailing.

## Introduction to the Stories of Lu Xun

Lu Xun(鲁迅 1881~1936) was the greatest modern Chinese writer. He came from a traditional family but had extensive contact with western culture, especially when it came to the theory of evolution. In Japan, Lu Xun initially studied medicine. However, he eventually abandoned the medical field to focus on literature and his desire to inform the population and help heal the ills in society.

Lu Xun's short story, *Diary of a Madman*(《狂人日记》), was the first modern Chinese vernacular work of literary fiction. His novella, *The True Story of Ah Q* (《阿 Q 正传》) is a modern work that reflects on weaknesses in the national character. His novels focus primarily on the plight of Chinese peasants and intellectuals, their spirit of survival and their struggles and conflicts, and what it reveals about the sickness underlying Chinese society. His articles are concerned with, and reflect, the reality of society. His exposition of social problems and his uncovering of critical issues for his readers provided a new direction for modern Chinese literary development.

鲁迅

In this chapter we present two stories by Lu Xun, *Kong Yiji*(《孔乙己》) and *The New Year Sacrifice*(《祝福》). The first is about the deprivation and misery of a traditional Chinese intellectual and the second is about the sufferings of an unfortunate rural woman living under the pressures of a morally restrictive traditional society.

# Selected Works of Lu Xun

## 1. Kong Yiji

The layout of Luzhen's taverns is unique. In each, facing you as you enter, is a bar in the shape of a carpenter's square where hot water is kept ready for warming rice wine. When men come off work at midday and in the evening they spend four coppers on a bowl of wine—or so they did twenty years ago; now it costs ten—and drink this warm, standing by the bar, taking it easy. Another copper will buy a plate of salted bamboo shoots or peas flavored with aniseed to go with the wine, while a dozen will buy a meat dish; but most of the customers here belong to the short-coated class, few of whom can afford this. As for those in long gowns, they go into the inner room to order wine and dishes and sit drinking at their leisure.

At the age of twelve I started work as a pot-boy in Prosperity Tavern at the edge of the town. The boss put me to work in the outer room, saying that I looked too much of a fool to serve long-gowned customers. The short-coated customers there were easier to deal with, it is true, but among them were quite a few pernickety ones who insisted on watching for themselves while the yellow wine was ladled from the keg, looked for water at the bottom of the wine-pot, and personally inspected the pot's immersion into the hot water. Under such strict surveillance, diluting the wine was very hard indeed. Thus it did not take my boss many days to decide that this job too was beyond me. Luckily I had been recommended by somebody influential, so he could not sack me. Instead I was transferred to the dull task of simply warming wine.

After that I stood all day behind the bar attending to my duties. Although I gave satisfaction at this post, I found it somewhat boring and monotonous. Our boss was a grim-faced man, nor were the customers much pleasanter, which made the atmosphere a gloomy one. The only times when there was any laughter were when Kong Yiji came to the tavern. That is why I remember him.

Kong Yiji was the only long-gowned customer who used to drink his wine standing. A big, pallid man whose wrinkled face often bore scars, he had a large, unkempt and grizzled beard. And although he wore a long grown it was dirty and tattered. It had not by the look of it been washed or mended for ten years or more. He used so many archaisms in his speech that half of it was barely intelligible. And as his surname was Kong, he was given the nickname Kong Yiji from *kong*, *yi*, *ji*, the first three characters in the old-fashioned children's copybook. Whenever he came in, everyone there would look at him and chuckle. And someone was sure to call out:

"Kong Yiji! What are those fresh scars on your face?"

Ignoring this, he would lay nine coppers on the bar and order two bowls of heated wine with a dish of aniseed-peas. Then someone else would bawl:

"You must have been stealing again!"

"Why sully a man's good name for no reason at all?" Kong Yiji would ask, raising his eyebrows.

"Good name? Why, the day before yesterday you were trussed up and beaten for stealing books from the Ho family. I saw you!"

At that Kong Yiji would flush, the veins on his forehead standing out as he protested, "Taking books can't be counted as stealing... Taking books... for a scholar.. . can't be counted as stealing. " Then followed such quotations from the classics as" A gentlemen keeps his integrity even in poverty", together with a spate of archaisms which soon had everybody roaring with laughter, enlivening the whole tavern.

From the gossip that I heard, it seemed that Kong Yiji had studied the classics but never passed the official examinations and, not knowing any way to make a living, he had grown steadily poorer until he was almost reduced to beggary. Luckily he was a good calligrapher and could find enough copying work to fill his rice bowl. But unfortunately he had his failings too: laziness and a love of tippling. So after a few days he would disappear, taking with him books, paper, brushes and inkstone. And after this had happened several times, people stopped employing him as a copyist. Then all he could do was resort to occasional pilfering. In our tavern, though, he was a model customer who never failed to pay up. Sometimes, it is true, when he had no ready money, his name would be chalked up on our tally-board; but in less than a month he invariably settled the bill, and the name Kong Yiji would be wiped off the board again.

After Kong Yiji had drunk half a bowl of wine, his flushed cheeks would stop burning. But then someone would ask:

"Kong Yiji, can you really read?"

When he glanced back as if such a question were not worth answering, they would continue, "How is it you never passed even the lowest official examination?"

At once a grey tinge would overspread Kong Yiji's dejected, discomfited face, and he would mumble more of those unintelligible archaisms. Then everyone there would laugh heartily again, enlivening the whole tavern.

At such times I could join in the laughter with no danger of a dressing-down from my boss. In fact he always put such questions to Kong Yiji himself, to raise a laugh. Knowing that it was no use talking to the men, Kong Yiji would chat with us boys. Once he asked me:

"Have you had any schooling?"

When I nodded curtly he said, "Well then, I'll test you. How do you write the *hui* in aniseed-peas?"

Who did this beggar think he was, testing me! I turned away and ignored him. After waiting for some time he said earnestly:

"You can't write it, eh? I'll show you. Mind you remember. You ought to remember such characters, because you'll need them to write up your accounts when you have a shop of your own. "

It seemed to me that I was still very far from having a shop of my own; in addition to which, our boss never entered aniseed-peas in his account-book. Half amused and half exasperated, I drawled, "I don't need you to show me. Isn't it the *hui* written with the element for grass?"

Kong Yiji's face lit up. Tapping two long finger nails on the bar, he nodded. "Quite correct!" He said. "There are four different ways of writing *hui*. Do you know them?"

But my patience exhausted, I scowled and moved away. Kong Yiji had dipped his finger in wine to trace the characters on the bar. When he saw my utter indifference his face fell and he sighed.

Sometimes children in the neighborhood, hearing laughter, came in to join in the fun and surrounded Kong Yiji. Then he would give them aniseed-peas, one apiece. After eating the peas the children would still hang round, their eyes fixed on the dish. Growing flustered, he would cover it with his hand and bending forward from the waist would say, "There aren't many left, not many at all." Straightening up to look at the peas again, he would shake his head and reiterate, "Not many, I do assure you. Not many, nay, not many at all." Then the children would scamper off, shouting with laughter.

That was how Kong Yiji contributed to our enjoyment, but we got along all right without him too.

One day, shortly before the Mid-Autumn Festival I think it was, my boss who was slowly making out his accounts took down the tally-board. "Kong Yiji hasn't shown up for a long time," he remarked suddenly, "He still owes nineteen coppers." That made me realize how long it was since we had not seen him.

"How could he?" rejoined one of the customers, "His legs were broken in that last beating up."

"Ah!" said my boss.

"He'd been stealing again. This time he was fool enough to steal from Mr. Ding, the provincial-grade scholar, as if anybody could get away with that!"

"So what happened?"

"What happened? First he wrote a confession, then he was beaten. The beating lasted nearly all night, and they broke both his legs."

"And then?"

"Well, his legs were broken."

"Yes, but after?"

"After?... Who knows? He may be dead."

My boss asked no further questions but went on slowly making up his accounts.

After the Mid-Autumn Festival the wind grew daily colder as winter approached, and even though I spent all my time by the stove I had to wear a padded jacket. One afternoon, when the tavern was deserted, as I sat with my eyes closed I heard the words:

"Warm a bowl of wine."

It was said in a low but familiar voice. I opened my eyes. There was no one to be seen. I stood up to look out. There below the bar, facing the door, sat Kong Yiji. His face was thin and grimy—he looked a wreck. He had on a ragged lined jacket and was squatting cross-legged on a mat which was attached to his shoulders by a straw rope. When he saw me he repeated:

"Warm a bowl of wine."

At this point my boss leaned over the bar to ask, "Is that Kong Yiji? You still owe nineteen coppers."

"That... I'll settle next time. He looked up dejectedly. Here's cash. Give me some good wine."

My boss, just as in the past, chuckled and said:

"Kong Yiji, you've been stealing again!"

But instead of stout denial, the answer simply was:

"Don't joke with me."

"Joke? How did your legs get broken if you hadn't been stealing?"

"I fell," whispered Kong Yiji. "Broke them in a fall." His eyes pleaded with the boss to let the matter drop. By now several people had gathered round, and they all laughed with the boss. I warmed the wine, carried it over, and set it on the threshold. He produced four coppers from his ragged coat pocket, and he placed them in my hand I saw that his own hands were covered with mud—he must have crawled there on them. Presently he finished the wine and, to the accompaniment of taunts and laughter, slowly pushed himself off with his hands.

A long time went by after that without our seeing Kong Yiji again. At the end of the year, when the boss took down the tally-board he said, "Kong Yiji still owes nineteen coppers." At the Dragon-Boat Festival the next year he said the same thing again. But when the Mid-Autumn Festival arrived he was silent on the subject, and another New Year came round without our seeing any more of Kong Yiji.

Nor have I ever seen him since—no doubt Kong Yiji really is dead.

1919

(translated by Yang Xianyi and Gladys Yang)

# 孔 乙 己

鲁镇的酒店的格局，是和别处不同的：都是当街一个曲尺形的大柜台，柜里面预备着热水，可以随时温酒。做工的人，傍午傍晚散了工，每每花四文铜钱，买一碗酒，——这是二十多年前的事，现在每碗要涨到十文，——靠柜外站着，热热的喝了休息；倘肯多花一文，便可以买一碟盐煮笋，或者茴香豆，做下酒物了，如果出到十几文，那就能买一样荤菜，但这些顾客，多是短衣帮，大抵没有这样阔绰。只有穿长衫的，才踱进店面隔壁的房子里，要酒要菜，慢慢地坐喝。

我从十二岁起，便在镇口的咸亨酒店里当伙计，掌柜说，样子太傻，怕侍候不了长衫主顾，就在外面做点事罢。外面的短衣主顾，虽然容易说话，但唠唠叨叨缠夹不清的也很不少。他们往往要亲眼看着黄酒从坛子里舀出，看过壶子底里有水没有，又亲看将壶子放在热水里，然后放心：在这严重监督下，羼水也很为难。所以过了几天，掌柜又说我干不了这事。幸亏荐头的情面大，辞退不得，便改为专管温酒的一种无聊职务了。

我从此便整天的站在柜台里，专管我的职务。虽然没有什么失职，但总觉有些单调，有些无聊。掌柜是一副凶脸孔，主顾也没有好声气，教人活泼不得；只有孔乙己到店，才可以笑几声，所以至今还记得。

孔乙己是站着喝酒而穿长衫的唯一的人。他身材很高大；青白脸色，皱纹间时常夹些伤痕；一部乱蓬蓬的花白的胡子。穿的虽然是长衫，可是又脏又破，似乎十多年没有补，也没有洗。他对人说话，总是满口之乎者也，教人半懂不懂的。因为他姓孔，别人便从描红纸上的"上大人孔乙己"这半懂不懂的话里，替他取下一个绰号，叫作孔乙己。孔乙己一到店，所有喝酒的人便都看着他笑，有的叫道，"孔乙己，你脸上又添上新伤疤了！"他不回答，对柜里说，"温两碗酒，要一碟茴香豆。"便排出九文大钱。他们又故意的高声嚷道，"你一定又偷了人家的东西了！"孔乙己睁大眼睛说，"你怎么这样凭空污人清白……""什么清白？我前天亲眼见你偷了何家的书，吊着打。"孔乙己便涨红了脸，额上的青筋条条绽出，争辩道，"窃书不能算偷……窃书！……读书人的事，能算偷么？"接连便是难懂的话，什么"君子固穷"，什么"者乎"之类，引得众人都哄笑起来：店内外充满了快活的空气。

听人家背地里谈论，孔乙己原来也读过书，但终于没有进学，又不会营生；于是愈过愈穷，弄到将要讨饭了。幸而写得一笔好字，便替人家钞钞书，换一碗饭吃。可惜他又有一样坏脾气，便是好吃懒做。坐不到几天，便连人和书籍纸张笔砚，一齐失踪。如是几次，叫他钞书的人也没有了。孔乙己没有法，便免不了偶然做些偷窃的事。但他在我们店里，品行却比别人都好，就是从不拖欠；虽然间或没有现钱，暂时记在粉板上，但不出一月，定然还清，从粉板上拭去了孔乙己的名字。

　　孔乙己喝过半碗酒，涨红的脸色渐渐复了原，旁人便又问道，"孔乙己，你当真认识字么？"孔乙己看着问他的人，显出不屑置辩的神气。他们便接着说道，"你怎的连半个秀才也捞不到呢？"孔乙己立刻显出颓唐不安模样，脸上笼上了一层灰色，嘴里说些话；这回可是全是之乎者也之类，一些不懂了。在这时候，众人也都哄笑起来：店内外充满了快活的空气。

　　在这些时候，我可以附和着笑，掌柜是决不责备的。而且掌柜见了孔乙己，也每每这样问他，引人发笑。孔乙己自己知道不能和他们谈天，便只好向孩子说话。有一回对我说道，"你读过书么？"我略略点一点头。他说，"读过书，……我便考你一考。茴香豆的茴字，怎样写的？"我想，讨饭一样的人，也配考我么？便回过脸去，不再理会。孔乙己等了许久，很恳切的说道，"不能写罢？……我教给你，记着！这些字应该记着。将来做掌柜的时候，写账要用。"我暗想我和掌柜的等级还很远呢，而且我们掌柜也从不将茴香豆上账；又好笑，又不耐烦，懒懒的答他道，"谁要你教，不是草头底下一个来回的回字么？"孔乙己显出极高兴的样子，将两个指头的长指甲敲着柜台，点头说，"对呀对呀！……回字有四样写法，你知道么？"我愈不耐烦了，努着嘴走远。孔乙己刚用指甲蘸了酒，想在柜上写字，见我毫不热心，便又叹一口气，显出极惋惜的样子。

　　有几回，邻居孩子听得笑声，也赶热闹，围住了孔乙己。他便给他们茴香豆吃，一人一颗。孩子吃完豆，仍然不散，眼睛都望着碟子。孔乙己着了慌，伸开五指将碟子罩住，弯腰下去说道，"不多了，我已经不多了。"直起身又看一看豆，自己摇头说，"不多不多！多乎哉？不多也。"于是这一群孩子都在笑声里走散了。

　　孔乙己是这样的使人快活，可是没有他，别人也便这么过。

　　有一天，大约是中秋前的两三天，掌柜正在慢慢的结账，取下粉板，忽然说，"孔乙己长久没有来了。还欠十九个钱呢！"我才也觉得他的确长久没有来了。一个喝酒的人说道，"他怎么会来？……他打折了腿了。"掌柜说，"哦！""他总仍旧是偷。这一回，是自己发昏，竟偷到丁举人家里去了。他家的东西，偷得的么？""后来怎么样？""怎么样？先写服辩，后来是打，打了大半夜，再打折了腿。""后来呢？""后来打折了腿了。""打折了怎样呢？""怎样？……谁晓得？许是死了。"掌柜也不再问，仍然慢慢的算他的账。

中秋之后，秋风是一天凉比一天，看看将近初冬；我整天的靠着火，也须穿上棉袄了。一天的下半天，没有一个顾客，我正合了眼坐着。忽然间听得一个声音，"温一碗酒。"这声音虽然极低，却很耳熟。看时又全没有人。站起来向外一望，那孔乙己便在柜台下对了门槛坐着。他脸上黑而且瘦，已经不成样子；穿一件破夹袄，盘着两腿，下面垫一个蒲包，用草绳在肩上挂住；见了我，又说道，"温一碗酒。"掌柜也伸出头去，一面说，"孔乙己么？你还欠十九个钱呢！"孔乙己很颓唐的仰面答道，"这……下回还清罢。这一回是现钱，酒要好。"掌柜仍然同平常一样，笑着对他说，"孔乙己，你又偷了东西了！"但他这回却不十分分辩，单说了一句"不要取笑！""取笑？要是不偷，怎么会打断腿？"孔乙己低声说道，"跌断，跌，跌……"他的眼色，很像恳求掌柜，不要再提。此时已经聚集了几个人，便和掌柜都笑了。我温了酒，端出去，放在门槛上。他从破衣袋里摸出四文大钱，放在我手里，见他满手是泥，原来他便用这手走来的。不一会，他喝完酒，便又在旁人的说笑声中，坐着用这手慢慢走去了。

自此以后，又长久没有看见孔乙己。到了年关，掌柜取下粉板说，"孔乙己还欠十九个钱呢！"到第二年的端午，又说"孔乙己还欠十九个钱呢！"到中秋可是没有说，再到年关也没有看见他。

我到现在终于没有见——大约孔乙己的确死了。

一九一九年

## 2. The New Year Sacrifice

The end of the year by the old calendar does really seem a more natural end to the year for, to say nothing of the villages and towns, the very sky seems to proclaim the New Year's approach. Intermittent flashes from pallid, lowering evening clouds are followed by the rumble of crackers bidding farewell to the Hearth God and, before the deafening reports of the bigger bangs close at hand have died away, the air is filled with faint whiffs of gunpowder. On one such night I returned to Luzhen, my hometown. I call it my hometown, but as I put up at the house of a Fourth Uncle since he belongs to the generation before mine in our clan. A former Imperial Academy licentiate who believes in Neo-Confucianism, he seemed very little changed, just slightly older, but without any beard as yet. Having exchanged some polite remarks upon meeting he observed that I was fatter, and having observed that I was fatter launched into a violent attack on the reformists I did not take this personally, however, as the object of his attack was Kang Youwei. Still, conversation proved so difficult that I shortly found myself alone in the study.

I rose late the next day and went out after lunch to see relatives and friends, spending the following day in the same way. They were all very little changed, just slightly older; but every family was busy preparing for the New-Year sacrifice. This is the great end-of-year ceremony in Luzhen, during which a reverent and splendid welcome is given to the God of Fortune so that he will send good luck for the coming year. Chickens and geese are killed, pork is bought, and everything is scrubbed and scoured until all the women's arms—some still in twisted silver bracelets—turn red in the water. After the meat is cooked chopsticks are thrust into it at random, and when this "offering" is set out at dawn, incense and candles are lit and the God of Fortune is respectfully invited to come and partake of it. The worshippers are confined to men and, of course, after worshipping they go on letting off firecrackers as before. This is done every year, in every household—and naturally this year was no exception.

The sky became overcast and in the afternoon it was filled with a flurry of snowflakes, some as large as plum-blossom petals, which merged with the smoke and the bustling atmosphere to make the small town a welter of confusion. By the time I had returned to my uncle's study, the roof of the house was already white with snow which made the room brighter than usual, highlighting the red stone rubbing that hung on the wall of the big character "Longevity" as written by the Taoist saint Chen Tuan. One of the pair of scrolls flanking it had fallen down and was lying loosely rolled up on the long table. The other, still in its place, bore the inscription "Understanding of principles brings peace of mind." Idly, I strolled over to the desk beneath the window to turn over the pile of books on it, but only found an apparently incomplete set of *The Kang Xi Dictionary*, *The Selected Writings of Neo-Confucian Philosophers*, and *Commentaries on the Four Books*. At all events I must leave the next day, I decided.

中国文学选读

Besides, the thought of my meeting with Xianglin's Wife the previous day was preying on my mind. It had happened in the afternoon. On my way back from calling on a friend in the eastern part of the town, I had met her by the river and knew from the fixed look in her eyes that she was going to accost me. Of all the people I had seen during this visit to Luzhen, none had changed so much as she had. Her hair, streaked with grey five years before, was now completely white, making her appear much older than one around forty. Her sallow, dark-tinged face that looked as if it had been carved out of wood was fearfully wasted and had lost the grief-stricken expression it had borne before. The only sign of life about her was the occasional flicker of her eyes. In one hand she had a bamboo basket containing a chipped, empty bowl; in the other, a bamboo pole, taller than herself, that was split at the bottom. She had clearly become a beggar pure and simple.

I stopped, waiting for her to come and ask for money.

"So you're back?" were her first words.

"Yes."

"That's good. You are a scholar who's traveled and seen the world. There's something I want to ask you." A sudden gleam lit up her lackluster eyes.

This was so unexpected that surprise rooted me to the spot.

"It's this." She drew two paces nearer and lowered her voice, as if letting me into a secret. "Do dead people turn into ghosts or not?"

My flesh crept. The way she had fixed me with her eyes made a shiver run down my spine, and I felt far more nervous than when a surprise test is sprung on you at school and the teacher insists on standing over you. Personally, I had never bothered myself in the least about whether spirits existed or not; but what

《祝福》插图

was the best answer to give her now? I hesitated for a moment, reflecting that the people here still believed in spirits, but she seemed to have her doubts, or rather hopes—she hoped for life after death and dreaded it at the same time. Why increase the sufferings of someone with a wretched life? For her sake, I thought, I'd better say there was.

"Quite possibly, I'd say," I told her falteringly.

"That means there must be a hell too?"

"What, hell?" I faltered, very taken aback.

"Hell? Logically speaking, there should be too—but not necessarily. Who cares anyway?"

"Then will all the members of a family meet again after death?"

"Well, as to whether they'll meet again or not..." I realized now what an utter fool I was. All my hesitation and manoeuvring had been no match for her three questions. Promptly taking fright, I decided to recant. "In that case... actually, I'm not sure... In fact, I'm not sure whether there are ghosts or not either."

To avoid being pressed by any further questions I walked off, then beat a hasty retreat to my uncle's house, feeling thoroughly disconcerted. I may have given her a dangerous answer, I was thinking. Of course, she may just be feeling lonely because everybody else is celebrating now, but could she have had something else in mind? Some premonition? If she had had some other idea, and something happens as a result. Then my answer should indeed be partly responsible... Then I laughed at myself for brooding so much over a chance meeting when it could have no serious significance. No wonder certain educationists called me neurotic. Besides, I had distinctly declared, "I'm not sure," contradicting the whole of my answer. This meant that even if something did happen, it would have nothing at all to do with me.

"I'm not sure" is a most useful phrase.

Bold inexperienced youngsters often take it upon themselves to solve problems or choose doctors for other people, and if by any chance things turn out badly they may well be held to blame; but by concluding their advice with this evasive expression they achieve blissful immunity from reproach. The necessity for such a phrase was brought home to me still more forcibly now, since it was indispensable even in speaking with a beggar woman.

However, I remained uneasy, and even after a night's rest my mind dwelt on it with a certain sense of foreboding. The oppressive snowy weather and the gloomy study increased my uneasiness. I had better leave the next day and go back to the city. A large dish of plain shark's fin stew at the Fu Xing Restaurant used to cost only a dollar. I wondered if this cheap delicacy had risen in price or not. Though my good companions of the old days had scattered, that shark's fin must still be sampled even if I were on my own. Whatever happened I would leave the next day, I decided.

Since, in my experience, things I hoped would not happen and felt should not happen invariably did occur all the same, I was much afraid this would prove another such case. And, sure enough, the situation soon took a strange turn. Towards evening I heard what sounded like a discussion in the inner room, but the conversation ended before long and my uncle walked away observing loudly, "What a moment to choose! Now of all times! Isn't that proof enough she was a bad lot?"

My initial astonishment gave way to a deep uneasiness; I felt that this had something to do with me. I looked out of the door, but no one was there. I waited impatiently till their servant came in before dinner to brew tea. Then at last I had a chance to make some inquiries.

"Who was Mr. Lu so angry with just now?" I asked.

"Why, Xianglin's Wife, of course," was the curt reply.

"She's gone."

"Dead?" My heart missed a beat. I started and must have changed color. But since the servant kept his head lowered, all this escaped him. I pulled myself together enough to ask.

"When did she die?"

"When? Last night or today—I'm not sure."

"How did she die?"

"How? Of poverty of course." After this stolid answer he withdrew, still without having raised his head to look at me.

My agitation was only short-lived, however. For now that my premonition had come to pass, I no longer had to seek comfort in my own "I'm not sure," or his "dying of poverty," and my heart was growing lighter. Only from time to time did I still feel a little guilty. Dinner was served, and my uncle impressively kept me company. Tempted as I was to ask about Xianglin's Wife, I knew that, although he had read that "ghosts and spirits are manifestations of the dual forces of Nature," he was still so superstitious that on the eve of the New-Year sacrifice it would be unthinkable to mention anything like death or illness. In case of necessity one should use veiled allusions. But since this was unfortunately beyond me I had to bite back the questions which kept rising to the tip of my tongue. And my uncle's solemn expression suddenly made me suspect that he looked on me too as a bad lot who had chosen this moment, now of all times, to come and trouble him. To set his mind at rest as quickly as I could, I told him at once of my plan to leave Luzhen the next day and go back to the city. He did not press me to stay, and at last the uncomfortably quiet meal came to an end.

Winter days are short, and because it was snowing darkness had already enveloped the whole town. All was stir and commotion in the lighted houses, but outside was remarkably quiet. And the snowflakes hissing down on the thick snowdrifts intensified one's sense of loneliness. Seated alone in the amber light of the vegetable-oil lamp I reflected that this wretched and forlorn woman, abandoned in the dust like a worn-out toy of which its owners have tired, had once left her own imprint in the dust, and those who enjoyed life must have wondered at her for wishing to live on; but now at last she had been swept for wishing to live on; but now at last she had been swept away by death. Whether spirits existed or not I did not know; but in this world of ours the end of a futile existence, the removal of someone whom others are tired of seeing, was just as well both for them and for the individual concerned. Occupied with these reflections, I listened quietly to the hissing of the snow outside, until little by little I felt more relaxed.

But the fragments of her life that I had seen or heard about before combined now to form a whole.

She was not from Luzhen. Early one winter, when my uncle's family wanted a new maid, Old Mrs. Wei the go-between brought her along. She had a white mourning band round her hair and was wearing a black skirt, blue jacket, and pale green bodice. Her age was about twenty-six, and though her face was sallow her cheeks were red. Old Mrs. Wei introduced her as Xianglin's Wife, a neighbor of her mother's family, who wanted to go out to work now that her husband had died. My uncle frowned at this, and my aunt knew that he disapproved of taking on a widow. She looked just the person for them, though, with her big strong hands and feet; and, judging by her downcast eyes and silence, she was a good worker who would know her place. So my aunt ignored my uncle's frown and kept her. During her trial period she worked from morning till night as if she found resting irksome, and proved strong enough to do the work of a man; so on the third day she was taken on for five hundred cash a month.

Everybody called her Xianglin's Wife and no one asked her own name, but since she had been introduced by someone from Wei Village as a neighbor, her surname was presumably also Wei. She said little, only answering briefly when asked a question. Thus it took them a dozen days or so to find out bit by bit that she had a strict mother-in-law at home and a brother-in-law of ten or so, old enough to cut wood. Her husband , who had died that spring, had been a woodcutter too, and had been ten years younger than she was. This little was all they could learn.

Time passed quickly. She went on working as hard as ever, not caring what she ate, never sparing herself. It was generally agreed that the Lu family's maid actually got through more work than a hard-working man. At the end of the year, she swept and mopped the floors, killed the chickens and geese, and sat up to boil the sacrificial meat, all single-handed, so that they did not need to hire extra help. And she for her part was quite contented. Little by little the trace of a smile appeared at the corners of her mouth, while her face became whiter and plumper.

Just after the New Year she came back from washing rice by the river most upset because in the distance she had seen a man, pacing up and down on the opposite bank, who looked like her husband's elder cousin—very likely he had come in search of her. When my aunt in alarm pressed her for more information, she said nothing. As soon as my uncle knew of this he frowned.

"That bad," he observed. "She must have run away."

Before very long this inference was confirmed.

About a fortnight later, just as this incident was beginning to be forgotten, Old Mrs. Wei suddenly brought along a woman in her thirties whom she introduced as Xinglin's mother. Although this woman looked like the hill-dweller she was, she behaved with great self-possession and has a ready tongue in her head. After the usual civilities she apologized for coming to take her daughter-in-law back, explaining that early spring was a busy time and they were short-handed at home with only old people and children around.

"If her mother-in-law wants her back, there's nothing more to be said," was my uncle's comment.

Thereupon her wages were reckoned up. They came to 1 750 cash, all of which she had left in the keeping of her mistress without spending any of it. My aunt gave the entire sum to Xianglin's mother, who took her daughter-in-law's clothes as well, expressed her thanks, and left. By this time it was noon.

"Oh, the rice! Didn't Xinglin's Wife go to wash the rice?" exclaimed my aunt some time later. It was probably hunger that reminded her of lunch.

A general search started then for the rice-washing basket. My aunt searched the kitchen, then the hall, then the bedroom; but not a sign of the basket was to be seen. My uncle could not find it outside either, until he went right down to the riverside. Then he saw it set down fair and square on the bank, some vegetables beside it.

Some people on the bank told him that a boat with a white awning had moored there that morning but, since the awning covered the boat completely, they had no idea who was inside and had paid no special attention to begin with. But when Xianglin's Wife had arrived and was kneeling down to wash rice, two men who looked as if they came from the hills had jumped off the boat and seized her. Between them they dragged her on board. She wept and shouted at first but soon fell silent, probably because she was gagged. Then along came two women, a stranger and Old Mrs. Wei. It was difficult to see clearly into the boat, but the victim seemed to be lying, tied up, on the planking.

"Disgraceful! Still..."said my uncle.

That day my aunt cooked the midday meal herself, and their son Aniu lit the fire.

After lunch Old Mrs. Wei came back.

"Disgraceful!" said my uncle.

"What's the meaning of this? How dare you show your face here again?" My aunt, who was washing up, started fuming as soon as she saw her. "First you recommended her, then help them carry her off, causing such a shocking commotion. What will people think? Are you trying to make fools of our family?"

"Aiya, I was completely taken in! I've come specially to clear this up. How was I to know she'd left home without permission from her mother-in-law when she asked me to find her work? I'm sorry, Mr. Lu. I'm sorry, Mrs. Lu. I'm growing so stupid and careless in my old age; I've let my patrons down. It's lucky for me you're such kind, generous people, never hard on those below you. I promise to make it up to you by finding someone good this time."

"Still. ." said my uncle.

That concluded the affair of Xianglin's Wife, and before long it was forgotten.

My aunt was the only one who still spoke of Xianglin's Wife. This was because most of the maids taken on afterwards turned out to be lazy or greedy, or both, none of them giving satisfaction. At such times she would invariably say to herself, "I wonder what's become of her now?"—implying that she would like to have her back. But by the next New Year she too had given up hope.

The first month was nearing its end when Old Mrs. Wei called on my aunt to wish her a happy New Year. Already tipsy, she explained that the reason for her coming so late was that she had been visiting her family in Wei Village in the hills for a few days. The conversation, naturally, soon touched on Xianglin's Wife.

"Xianglin's Wife?" cried Old Mrs. Wei cheerfully. "She's in luck now. When her mother-in-law dragged her home, she'd promised her to the sixth son of the Ho Glen. So a few days after her return they put her in the bridal chair and sent her off."

"Gracious! What a mother-in-law!" exclaimed my aunt.

"Ah, madam, you really talk like a great lady! This is nothing to poor folk like us who live up in the hills. That young brother-in-law of hers still had no wife. If they didn't marry her off, where would the money have come from to get him one? Her mother-in-law is a clever, capable woman, a fine manager; so she married her off into the mountains. If she'd betrothed her to a family in the same village, she wouldn't have made so much; but as very few girls are willing to take a husband deep in the mountains at the back of beyond, she got eighty thousand cash. Now the second son has a wife, who cost only fifty thousand; and after paying the wedding expenses she's still over ten thousand in hand. Wouldn't you call her a fine manager?"

"But was Xianglin's Wife willing?"

"It wasn't a question of willing or not. Of course any woman would make a row about it. All they had to do was tie her up, shove her into the chair, carry her to the man's house, force on her the two of them into their room —and that was that. But Xianglin's Wife is quite a character. I heard that she made a terrible scene. It was working for a scholar's family, everyone said, that made her different from other people. We go-betweens see life, madam. Some widows sob and shout when they remarry; some threaten to kill themselves; some refuse to go through the ceremony of bowing to heaven and earth after they've been carried to man's house; some even smash the wedding candlesticks. But Xianglin's Wife was really extraordinary. They said she screamed and cursed all the way to Ho Glen, so that she was completely hoarse by the time they got there. When they dragged her out the chair, no matter how the two chair-bearers and her brother-in-law held her, they couldn't make her go through the ceremony. The moment they were off guard and had loosened their grip—gracious Buddha! —she bashed her head on a corner of the altar, gashing it so badly that blood spurted out. Even though they smeared on two handfuls of incense ashes and toed it up with two pieces of red cloth, they couldn't stop the bleeding. It took quite a few of them to shut her up finally with the man in the bridal chamber, but even then she went on cursing. Oh, it was really..." Shaking her head, she lowered her eyes and fell silent.

"And what then?" asked my aunt.

"They said that the next day she didn't get up." Old Mrs. Wei raised her eyes.

"And after?"

"After? She got up. At the end of the year she had a baby, a boy, who was reckoned as two this New Year. These few days when I was at home, some people back from a visit to Ho Glen said they'd seen her and her son, and both mother and child are plump. There's no mother-in-law over her, her man is a strong fellow who can earn a living, and the house belongs to them. Oh, yes she's in luck all right.

After this event my aunt gave up talking of Xianglin's Wife.

But one autumn, after two New Years had passed since this good news of Xianglin's Wife, she once more crossed the threshold of my uncle's house, placing her round bulb-shaped basket on the table and her small bedding-roll under the eaves. As before, she had a white mourning band round her hair and was wearing a black skirt, blue jacket, and pale green bodice. Her face was sallow, her cheeks no longer red; and her downcast eyes, stained with tears, had lost their brightness. Just as before, it was Old Mrs. Wei who brought her to my aunt.

"It was really a bolt from the blue," she explained compassionately, "Her husband was a strong young fellow; who'd have thought that typhoid fever would carry him off? He'd taken a turn for the better, but then he ate some cold rice and got worse again. Luckily she had the boy and she can work—she's able to gather firewood, pick tea, or raise silkworms—so she could have managed on her own. But who'd have thought that the child, too, would be carried off by a wolf? It was nearly the end of spring, yet a wolf came to the glen—who could have guessed that? Now she's all on her own. Her husband's elder brother has taken over the house and turned her out. So she's no way to turn for help except to her former mistress. Luckily this time there's nobody to stop her and you happen to need someone, madam. That's why I've brought her here. I think someone used to your ways is much better than a new hand... "

"I was really too stupid, really... " put in Xianglin's Wife, raising her lackluster eyes, "All I knew was that when it snowed and wild beasts up in the hills had nothing to eat, they might come to the villages, I didn't know that in spring they might come too. I got up at dawn and opened the door, filled a small basket with beans and told our Amao to sit on the doorstep and shell them. He was such a good boy; he always did as he was told, and out he went. Then I went to the back to chop wood and wash the rice, and when the rice was in the pan I wanted to steam the beans. 1 called Aamo, but there was no answer. When I went out to look there were beans all over the ground but no Amao. He never went to the neighbors' houses to play; and, sure enough, though I asked everywhere he wasn't there. I got so worried. I begged people to help me find him. Not until that afternoon, after searching high and low, did they try the gully. There they saw one of his little shoes caught on a bramble. 'That's bad', they said, 'A wolf must have got him.' And sure enough, further on, there he was lying in the wolf's den, all his innards eaten away, still clutching that little basket tight in his hand..." At this point she broke down and could not go on.

My aunt had been undecided at first, but the rims of her eyes were rather red by the time Xianglin's Wife broke off. After a moment's thought she told her to take her things to the servant's quarters. Old Mrs. Wei heaved a sigh, as if a great weight had been lifted from her mind; and Xianglin's Wife, looking more relaxed than when first she came, went off quietly to put away her bedding without having to be told the way. So she started work again as a maid in Luzhen.

She was still known as Xianglin's Wife.

But now she was a very different woman. She had not worked there for more than two or three days before her mistress realized that she was not as quick as before. Her memory was much worse too, while her face, like a death-mask, never showed the least trace of a smile. Already my aunt was expressing herself as not too satisfied. Though my uncle had frowned as before when she first arrived, they always had such trouble finding servants that he raised no serious objections, simply warning his wife on the quiet that while such people might very pathetic they exerted a bad moral influence. Simply warning his wife on the quiet that while such people might seem very pathetic they exerted a bad moral influence. She could work for them but must have nothing to do with ancestral sacrifices. They would have to prepare all the dishes themselves. Otherwise they would be unclean and the ancestors would not accept them.

The most important events in my uncle's household were ancestral sacrifices, and formerly these had kept Xianglin's Wife especially busy, but now she virtually had nothing to do. As soon as the table had been placed in the centre of the hall and a

中国文学选读

front curtain fastened around its legs, she started setting out the winecups and chop-sticks in the way she still remembered.

"Put those down, Xianglin's Wife," cried my aunt hastily, "Leave that to me."

She drew back sheepishly then and went for the candlesticks.

"Put those down, Xianglin's Wife," cries my aunt again in haste, "I'll fetch them."

After walking round in the hall several times without finding anything to do, she moved doubtfully away. All she could do that day was to sit by the stove and feed the fire.

The townspeople still called her Xianglin's Wife, but in quite a different tone from before; and although they still talked to her, their manner was colder. Quite impervious to this, staring straight in front of her, she would tell everybody the story which night or day was never out of her mind.

"I was really too stupid, really," she would say, "All I knew was that when it snowed and the wild beasts up in the hills had nothing to eat, they might come to the villages. I got up at dawn and opened the door, filled a small basket with beans and told our Amao to sit on the doorstep and shell them. He was such a good boy; he al-ways did as he was told, and out he went. Then I went to the back to chop wood and wash the rice, and when the rice was in the pan 1 wanted to steam the beans. I called Amao, but there was no answer. When I went out to look, there were beans all over the ground but no Amao. He never went to the neighbors' houses to play; and, sure enough, though I asked everywhere he wasn't there. I got so worried. I begged peo-ple to help me find him. Not until that afternoon, after searching high and low, did they try the gully. There they saw one of his little shoes caught on a bramble. 'That's bad,' they said, 'A wolf must have got him.' And sure enough, further on, there he was lying in the wolf's den, all his innards eaten away, still clutching that little basket tight in his hand.... "At this point her voice would be choked with tears.

This story was so effective that men hearing it often stopped smiling and walked blankly away, while the women not only seemed to forgive her but wiped the con-temptuous expression off their faces and added their tears to hers. Indeed, some old women who had not heard her in the street sought her out specially to hear her sad tale. And when she broke down, they too shed the tears which had gathered in their eyes, after which they sighted and went away satisfied, exchanging eager comments.

As for her, she asked nothing better than to tell her sad story over and over again, often gathering three or four hearers around her. But before long everybody knew it so well that no trace of a tear could be seen even in the eyes of the most kindly, Buddha-invoking old ladies. In the end, practically the whole town could recite it by heart and were bored and exasperated to hear it repeated.

"I was really too stupid, really," she would begin.

"Yes. All you knew was that in snowy weather, when the wild beasts in the mountains had nothing to eat, they might come down to the villages." Cutting short her recital abruptly, they walked away.

She would stand there open-mouthed, staring after them stupidly, and then wander off as if she too were bored by the story. But she still tried hopefully to lead up from other topics such as small baskets, and other people's children to the story of her Amao. At the sight of a child of two or three she would say, "Ah if my Amao were alive he'd be just that size... "

Children would take fright at the look in her eyes and clutch the hem of their mothers' clothes to tug them away. Left by herself again, she would eventually walk away. In the end everybody knew what she was like. If a child were present they would ask with a spurious smile, " If your Amao were alive, Xianglin's Wife, wouldn't he be just that size?"

She may not have realized that her tragedy, after being generally savored for so many days, had long since grown so stale that it now aroused only revulsion and disgust. But she seemed to sense the cold mockery in their smiles, and the fact that there was no need for her to say any more. So she would simply look at them in silence.

New-Year preparations always start in Luzhen on the twentieth day of the twelfth lunar month. That year my uncle's household had to take on a temporary man-servant. And since there was more than he could do they asked Amah Liu to help by killing the chickens and geese; but being a devout vegetarian who would not kill living creatures, she would only wash the sacrificial vessels. Xianglin's Wife, with nothing to do but feed the fire, sat there at a loose end watching Amah Liu as she worked. A light snow began to fall.

"Ah, I was really too stupid," said Xianglin's Wife as if to herself, looking at the sky and sighing.

"There you go again, Xianglin's Wife," Amah Liu glanced with irritation at her face, "Tell me, wasn't that when you got that scar on your forehead?"

All the reply she received was a vague murmur.

"Tell me this: What made you willing after all?"

"Willing?"

"Yes. Seems to me you must have been willing. Otherwise..."

"Oh, you don't believe it."

"I don't believe he was so strong that you with your strength couldn't have kept him off. You must have ended up willing. That talk of his being so strong is just an excuse."

"Why... just try for yourself and see," She smiled.

Amah Liu's lined face broke into a smile too, wrinkling up like a walnut-shell. Her small beady eyes swept the other woman's forehead, then fastened on her eyes. At once Xianglin's Wife stopped smiling, as if embarrassed, and turned her eyes away to watch the snow.

"That was really a bad bargain you struck, Xianglin's Wife," said Amah Liu mysteriously, "If you'd held out longer or knocked yourself to death outright, that would have been better. As it is, you're guilty of a great sin though you lived less than two years with your second husband. Just think: when you go down to the lower world, the ghosts of both men will start fighting over you. Which ought to have you? The King of Hell will have to saw you into two and divide you between them. I feel it really is..."

Xianglin's Wife's face registered terror then. This was something no one had told her up in the mountains.

"Better guard against that in good time, I say. Go to the Temple of the Tutelary God and buy a threshold to be trampled on instead of you by thousands of people. If you atone for your sins in this life you'll escape torment after death."

Xianglin's Wife said nothing at the time, but she must have taken this advice to heart, for when she got up the next morning there were dark rims round her eyes. After breakfast she went to the Temple of the Tutelary God at the west end of the town and asked to buy a threshold as an offering. At first the priest refused, only giving a grudging consent after she was reduced to tears of desperation. The price charged was twelve thousand cash.

She had long since given up talking to people after their contemptuous reception of Amao's story; but as word of her conversation with Amah Liu spread, many of the townsfolk took a fresh interest in her and came once more to provoke her into talking. The topic, of course, had changed to the scar on her forehead.

"Tell me, Xianglin's Wife, what made you willing in the end?" one would ask.

"What a waste, to have bashed yourself like that for nothing," another would chime in, looking at her scar.

She must have known from their smiles and tone of voice that they were mocking her, for she simply stared at them without a word and finally did not even turn her head. All day long she kept her lips tightly closed, bearing on her head the scar considered by everyone as a badge of shame, while she shopped, swept the floor, washed the vegetables, and prepared the rice in silence. Nearly a year went by before she took her accumulated wages from my aunt, changed them for twelve silver dollars, and asked for leave to go to the west end of the town. In less time than it takes for a meal she was back again, looking much comforted. With an unaccustomed light in her eyes, she told my aunt contentedly that she had now offered up a threshold in the Temple of the Tutelary God.

When the time came for the ancestral sacrifice at the winter solstice she worked harder than ever, and as soon as my aunt took out the sacrificial vessels and helped Aniu to carry the table into the middle of the hall, she went confidently to fetch the winecups and chopsticks.

"Put those down, Xianglin's Wife!" my aunt called hastily.

She withdrew her hand as if scorched, her face turned ashen grey, and instead of fetching the candlesticks she just stood there in a daze until my uncle came in to burn some incense and told her to go away. This time the change in her was phenomenal:

中国文学选读

the next day her eyes were sunken, her spirit seemed broken. She took fright very easily too, afraid not only of the dark and of shadows, but of meeting anyone. Even the sight of her own master or mistress set her trembling like a mouse that had strayed out of its hole in broad daylight. The rest of the time she would sit stupidly as if carved out of wood. In less than half a year her hair had turned grey, and her memory had deteriorated so much that she often forgot to go and wash the rice.

"What some over Xianglin's Wife? We should never have taken her on again," my aunt would sometimes say in front of her, as if to warn her.

But there was not change in her, no sign that she would ever recover her wits. So they decided to get rid of her and tell her to go back to Old Mrs. Wei. That was what they were saying, at least, while I was there; and judging by subsequent developments, this is evidently what they must have done. But whether she started begging as soon as she left my uncle's house, or whether she went first to Old Mrs. Wei and later became a beggar, I do not know.

I was woken up by the noisy explosion of crackers close at hand and, from the faint glow shed by the yellow oil lamp and the bangs of fire works as my uncle's household celebrated the sacrifice, I knew that it must be nearly dawn. Listening drowsily I heard vaguely the ceaseless explosion of crackers in the distance. It seemed to me that the whole town was enveloped by the dense cloud of noise in the sky, mingling with the whirling snowflakes. Enveloped in this medley of sound I relaxed; the doubt which had preyed on my mind from dawn till night was swept clean away by the festive atmosphere, and I felt only that the saints of heaven and earth had accepted the sacrifice and incense and were reeling with intoxication in the sky, preparing to give Luzhen's people boundless good fortune.

1924

(translated by Yang Xianyi and Gladys Yang)

## 祝　福

　　旧历的年底毕竟最像年底，村镇上不必说，就在天空中也显出将到新年的气象来。灰白色的沉重的晚云中间时时发出闪光，接着一声钝响，是送灶的爆竹；

近处燃放的可就更强烈了，震耳的大音还没有息，空气里已经散满了幽微的火药香。我是正在这一夜回到我的故乡鲁镇的。虽说故乡，然而已没有家，所以只得暂寓在鲁四老爷的宅子里。他是我的本家，比我长一辈，应该称之曰"四叔"，是一个讲理学的老监生。他比先前并没有什么大改变，单是老了些，但也还未留胡子；一见面是寒暄，寒暄之后说我"胖了"，说我"胖了"之后即大骂其新党。但我知道，这并非借题在骂我：因为他所骂的还是康有为。但是，谈话是总不投机的了，于是不多久，我便一个人剩在书房里。

第二天我起得很迟，午饭之后，出去看了几个本家和朋友；第三天也照样。他们也都没有什么大改变，单是老了些；家中却一律忙，都在准备着"祝福"。这是鲁镇年终的大典，致敬尽礼，迎接福神，拜求来年一年中的好运气的。杀鸡，宰鹅，买猪肉；用心细细的洗，女人的臂膊都在水里浸得通红，有的还带着绞丝银镯子。煮熟之后，横七竖八插些筷子在这类东西上，可就称为"福礼"了，五更天陈列起来，并且点上香烛，恭请福神们来享用；拜的却只限于男人，拜完自然仍然是放爆竹。年年如此，家家如此，——只要买得起福礼和爆竹之类的——今年自然也如此。天色愈阴暗了，下午竟下起雪来，雪花大的有梅花那么大，满天飞舞，夹着烟霭和忙碌的气色，将鲁镇乱成一团糟。我回到四叔的书房里时，瓦楞上已经雪白，房里也映得较光明，极分明的显出壁上挂着的朱拓的大"寿"字，陈抟老祖写的，一边的对联已经脱落，松松的卷了放在长桌上，一边的还在，道是"事理通达心气和平"。我又无聊赖的到窗下的案头去一翻，只见一堆似乎未必完全的《康熙字典》，一部《近思录集注》和一部《四书衬》。无论如何，我明天决计要走了。

况且，一想到昨天遇见祥林嫂的事，也就使我不能安住。那是下午，我到镇的东头访过一个朋友，走出来，就在河边遇见她；而且见她瞪着的眼睛的视线，就知道明明是向我走来的。我这回在鲁镇所见的人们中，改变之大，可以说无过于她的了：五年前的花白的头发，即今已经全白，全不像四十上下的人；脸上瘦削不堪，黄中带黑，而且消尽了先前悲哀的神色，仿佛是木刻似的；只有那眼珠间或一轮，还可以表示她是一个活物。她一手提着竹篮，内中一个破碗，空的；一手拄着一支比她更长的竹竿，下端开了裂：她分明已经纯乎是一个乞丐了。

我就站住，豫备她来讨钱。

"你回来了？"她先这样问。

"是的。"

"这正好。你是识字的，又是出门人，见识得多。我正要问你一件事——"她那没有精采的眼睛忽然发光了。

我万料不到她却说出这样的话来，诧异的站着。

"就是——"她走近两步，放低了声音，极秘密似的切切的说，"一个人死了之后，究竟有没有魂灵的？"

我很悚然，一见她的眼钉着我的，背上也就遭了芒刺一般，比在学校里遇到不及豫防的临时考，教师又偏是站在身旁的时候，惶急得多了。对于魂灵的有无，我自己是向来毫不介意的；但在此刻，怎样回答她好呢？我在极短期的踌躇中，想，这里的人照例相信鬼，然而她，却疑惑了，——或者不如说希望：希望其有，又希望其无……人何必增添末路的人的苦恼，为她起见，不如说有罢。

"也许有罢，——我想。"我于是吞吞吐吐的说。

"那么，也就有地狱了？"

"啊！地狱？"我很吃惊，只得支吾着，"地狱？——论理，就该也有。——然而也未必，……谁来管这等事……"

"那么，死掉的一家的人，都能见面的？"

"唉唉，见面不见面呢？……"这时我已知道自己也还是完全一个愚人，什么踌躇，什么计画，都挡不住三句问。我即刻胆怯起来了，便想全翻过先前的话来，"那是，……实在，我说不清……其实，究竟有没有魂灵，我也说不清。"

我乘她不再紧接的问，迈开步便走，匆匆的逃回四叔的家中，心里很觉得不安逸。自己想，我这答话怕于她有些危险。她大约因为在别人的祝福时候，感到自身的寂寞了，然而会不会含有别的什么意思的呢？——或者是有了什么豫感了？倘有别的意思，又因此发生别的事，则我的答话委实该负若干的责任……但随后也就自笑，觉得偶尔的事，本没有什么深意义，而我偏要细细推敲，正无怪教育家要说是生着神经病；而况明明说过"说不清"，已经推翻了答话的全局，即使发生什么事，于我也毫无关系了。

"说不清"是一句极有用的话。不更事的勇敢的少年，往往敢于给人解决疑问，选定医生，万一结果不佳，大抵反成了怨府，然而一用这说不清来作结束，便事事逍遥自在了。我在这时，更感到这一句话的必要，即使和讨饭的女人说话，也是万不可省的。

但是我总觉得不安，过了一夜，也仍然时时记忆起来，仿佛怀着什么不祥的豫感；在阴沉的雪天里，在无聊的书房里，这不安愈加强烈了。不如走罢，明天进城去。福兴楼的清炖鱼翅，一元一大盘，价廉物美，现在不知增价了否？往日同游的朋友，虽然已经云散，然而鱼翅是不可不吃的，即使只有我一个……无论如何，我明天决计要走了。

我因为常见些但愿不如所料，以为未必竟如所料的事，却每每恰如所料的起来，所以很恐怕这事也一律。果然，特别的情形开始了。傍晚，我竟听到有些人聚在内室里谈话，仿佛议论什么事似的；但不一会，说话声也就止了，只有四叔且走而且高声的说：

"不早不迟，偏偏要在这时候——这就可见是一个谬种！"

我先是诧异，接着是很不安，似乎这话于我有关系。试望门外，谁也没有。好容易待到晚饭前他们的短工来冲茶，我才得了打听消息的机会。

"刚才，四老爷和谁生气呢？"我问。

"还不是和祥林嫂？"那短工简捷的说。

"祥林嫂？怎么了？"我又赶紧的问。

"死了。"

"死了？"我的心突然紧缩，几乎跳起来，脸上大约也变了色。但他始终没有抬头，所以全不觉。我也就镇定了自己，接着问：

"什么时候死的？"

"什么时候？——昨天夜里，或者就是今天罢。——我说不清。"

"怎么死的？"

"怎么死的？——还不是穷死的？"他淡然的回答，仍然没有抬头向我看，出去了。

然而我的惊惶却不过暂时的事，随着就觉得要来的事，已经过去，并不必仰仗我自己的"说不清"和他之所谓"穷死的"的宽慰，心地已经渐渐轻松；不过偶然之间，还似乎有些负疚。晚饭摆出来了，四叔俨然的陪着。我也还想打听些关于祥林嫂的消息，但知道他虽然读过"鬼神者二气之良能也"，而忌讳仍然极多，当临近祝福时候，是万不可提起死亡疾病之类的话的；倘不得已，就该用一种替代的隐语，可惜我又不知道，因此屡次想问，而终于中止了。我从他俨然的脸色上，又忽而疑他正以为我不早不迟，偏要在这时候来打搅他，也是一个谬种，便立刻告诉他明天要离开鲁镇，进城去，趁早放宽了他的心。他也不很留。这样闷闷的吃完了一餐饭。

冬季日短，又是雪天，夜色早已笼罩了全市镇。人们都在灯下匆忙，但窗外

　　　　　　　　　　　　　　　　　　　中国文学选读

很寂静。雪花落在积得厚厚的雪褥上面，听去似乎瑟瑟有声，使人更加感得沉寂。我独坐在发出黄光的菜油灯下，想，这百无聊赖的祥林嫂，被人们弃在尘芥堆中的，看得厌倦了的陈旧的玩物，先前还将形骸露在尘芥里，从活得有趣的人们看来，恐怕要怪讶她何以还要存在，现在总算被无常打扫得干干净净了。魂灵的有无，我不知道；然而在现世，则无聊生者不生，即使厌见者不见，为人为己，也还都不错。我静听着窗外似乎瑟瑟作响的雪花声，一面想，反而渐渐的舒畅起来。

然而先前所见所闻的她的半生事迹的断片，至此也联成一片了。

她不是鲁镇人。有一年的冬初，四叔家里要换女工，做中人的卫老婆子带她进来了，头上扎着白头绳，乌裙，蓝夹袄，月白背心，年纪大约二十六七，脸色青黄，但两颊却还是红的。卫老婆子叫她祥林嫂，说是自己母家的邻舍，死了当家人，所以出来做工了。四叔皱了皱眉，四婶已经知道了他的意思，是在讨厌她是一个寡妇。但看她模样还周正，手脚都壮大，又只是顺着眼，不开一句口，很像一个安分耐劳的人，便不管四叔的皱眉，将她留下了。试工期内，她整天的做，似乎闲着就无聊，又有力，简直抵得过一个男子，所以第三天就定局，每月工钱五百文。

大家都叫她祥林嫂；没问她姓什么，但中人是卫家山人，既说是邻居，那大概也就姓卫了。她不很爱说话，别人问了才回答，答的也不多。直到十几天之后，这才陆续的知道她家里还有严厉的婆婆；一个小叔子，十多岁，能打柴了；她是春天没了丈夫的；他本来也打柴为生，比她小十岁：大家所知道的就只是这一点。

日子很快的过去了，她的做工却毫没有懈，食物不论，力气是不惜的。人们都说鲁四老爷家里雇着了女工，实在比勤快的男人还勤快。到年底，扫尘，洗地，杀鸡，宰鹅，彻夜的煮福礼，全是一人担当，竟没有添短工。然而她反满足，口角边渐渐的有了笑影，脸上也白胖了。

新年才过，她从河边淘米回来时，忽而失了色，说刚才远远地看见一个男人在对岸徘徊，很像夫家的堂伯，恐怕是正为寻她而来的。四婶很惊疑，打听底细，她又不说。四叔一知道，就皱一皱眉，道：

"这不好。恐怕她是逃出来的。"

她诚然是逃出来的，不多久，这推想就证实了。

此后大约十几天，大家正已渐渐忘却了先前的事，卫老婆子忽而带了一个三十多岁的女人进来了，说那是祥林嫂的婆婆。那女人虽是山里人模样，然而应酬很从容，说话也能干，寒暄之后，就赔罪，说她特来叫她的儿媳回家去，因为开春事务忙，而家中只有老的和小的，人手不够了。

"既是她的婆婆要她回去，那有什么话可说呢。"四叔说。

于是算清了工钱，一共一千七百五十文，她全存在主人家，一文也还没有用，便都交给她的婆婆。那女人又取了衣服，道过谢，出去了。其时已经是正午。

"阿呀，米呢？祥林嫂不是去淘米的么？……"好一会，四婶这才惊叫起来。她大约有些饿，记得午饭了。

于是大家分头寻淘箩。她先到厨下，次到堂前，后到卧房，全不见掏箩的影子。四叔踱出门外，也不见，直到河边，才见平平正正的放在岸上，旁边还有一株菜。

看见的人报告说，河里面上午就泊了一只白篷船，篷是全盖起来的，不知道什么人在里面，但事前也没有人去理会他。待到祥林嫂出来淘米，刚刚要跪下去，那船里便突然跳出两个男人来，像是山里人，一个抱住她，一个帮着，拖进船去了。祥林嫂还哭喊了几声，此后便再没有什么声息，大约给用什么堵住了罢。接着就走上两个女人来，一个不认识，一个就是卫婆子。窥探舱里，不很分明，她像是捆了躺在船板上。

"可恶！然而……"四叔说。

这一天是四婶自己煮中饭；他们的儿子阿牛烧火。

午饭之后，卫老婆子又来了。

"可恶！"四叔说。

"你是什么意思？亏你还会再来见我们。"四婶洗着碗，一见面就愤愤的说，"你自己荐她来，又合伙劫她去，闹得沸反盈天的，大家看了成个什么样子？你拿我们家里开玩笑么？"

"阿呀阿呀，我真上当。我这回，就是为此特地来说说清楚的。她来求我荐地方，我那里料得到是瞒着她的婆婆的呢。对不起，四老爷，四太太。总是我老发昏不小心，对不起主顾。幸而府上是向来宽洪大量，不肯和小人计较的。这回我一定荐一个好的来折罪……"

"然而……"四叔说。

于是祥林嫂事件便告终结，不久也就忘却了。

只有四婶，因为后来雇用的女工，大抵非懒即馋，或者馋而且懒，左右不如意，所以也还提起祥林嫂。每当这些时候，她往往自言自语的说，"她现在不知道怎么样了？"意思是希望她再来。但到第二年的新正，她也就绝了望。

新正将尽，卫老婆子来拜年了，已经喝得醉醺醺的，自说因为回了一趟卫家山的娘家，住下几天，所以来得迟了。她们问答之间，自然就谈到祥林嫂。

"她么？"卫老婆子高兴的说，"现在是交了好运了。她婆婆来抓她回去的时候，是早已许给了贺家坳的贺老六的，所以回家之后不几天，也就装在花轿里抬去了。"

"阿呀，这样的婆婆！……"四婶惊奇的说。

"阿呀，我的太太！你真是大户人家的太太的话。我们山里人，小户人家，这算得什么？她有小叔子，也得娶老婆。不嫁了她，那有这一注钱来做聘礼？他的婆婆倒是精明强干的女人呵，很有打算，所以就将她嫁到山里去。倘许给本村人，财礼就不多；惟独肯嫁进深山野坳里去的女人少，所以她就到手了八十千。现在第二个儿子的媳妇也娶进了，财礼花了五十，除去办喜事的费用，还剩十多千。吓，你看，这多么好打算？……"

"祥林嫂竟肯依？……"

"这有什么依不依。——闹是谁也总要闹一闹的，只要用绳子一捆，塞在花轿里，抬到男家，捺上花冠，拜堂，关上房门，就完事了。可是祥林嫂真出格，听说那时实在闹得利害，大家还都说大约因为在念书人家做过事，所以与众不同呢。太太，我们见得多了：回头人出嫁，哭喊的也有，说要寻死觅活的也有，抬到男家闹得拜不成天地的也有，连花烛都砸了的也有。祥林嫂可是异乎寻常，他们说她一路只是嚎，骂，抬到贺家坳，喉咙已经全哑了。拉出轿来，两个男人和她的小叔子使劲的捺住她也还拜不成天地。他们一不小心，一松手，阿呀，阿弥陀佛，她就一头撞在香案角上，头上碰了一个大窟窿，鲜血直流，用了两把香灰，包上两块红布还止不住血呢。直到七手八脚的将她和男人反关在新房里，还是骂，阿呀呀，这真是……"她摇一摇头，顺下眼睛，不说了。

"后来怎么样呢？"四婶还问。

"听说第二天也没有起来。"她抬起眼来说。

"后来呢？"

"后来？——起来了。她到年底就生了一个孩子，男的，新年就两岁了。我在娘家这几天，就有人到贺家坳去，回来说看见他们娘儿俩，母亲也胖，儿子也胖；上头又没有婆婆；男人所有的是力气，会做活；房子是自家的。——唉唉，她真是交了好运了。"

　　从此之后，四婶也就不再提起祥林嫂。

　　但有一年的秋季，大约是得到祥林嫂好运的消息之后的又过了两个新年，她竟又站在四叔家的堂前了。桌上放着一个荸荠式的圆篮，檐下一个小铺盖。她仍然头上扎着白头绳，乌裙，蓝夹袄，月白背心，脸色青黄，只是两颊上已经消失了血色，顺着眼，眼角上带些泪痕，眼光也没有先前那样精神了。而且仍然是卫老婆子领着，显出慈悲模样，絮絮的对四婶说：

　　"……这实在是叫作'天有不测风云'，她的男人是坚实人，谁知道年纪轻轻，就会断送在伤寒上？本来已经好了的，吃了一碗冷饭，复发了。幸亏有儿子；她又能做，打柴摘茶养蚕都来得，本来还可以守着，谁知道那孩子又会给狼衔去的呢？春天快完了，村上倒反来了狼，谁料到？现在她只剩了一个光身了。大伯来收屋，又赶她。她真是走投无路了，只好来求老主人。好在她现在已经再没有什么牵挂，太太家里又凑巧要换人，所以我就领她来。——我想，熟门熟路，比生手实在好得多……。"

　　"我真傻，真的，"祥林嫂抬起她没有神采的眼睛来，接着说。"我单知道下雪的时候野兽在山坳里没有食吃，会到村里来；我不知道春天也会有。我一清早起来就开了门，拿小篮盛了一篮豆，叫我们的阿毛坐在门槛上剥豆去。他是很听话的，我的话句句听；他出去了。我就在屋后劈柴，淘米，米下了锅，要蒸豆。我叫阿毛，没有应，出去口看，只见豆撒得一地，没有我们的阿毛了。他是不到别家去玩的；各处去一问，果然没有。我急了，央人出去寻。直到下半天，寻来寻去寻到山坳里，看见刺柴上桂着一只他的小鞋。大家都说，糟了，怕是遭了狼了。再进去；他果然躺在草窠里，肚里的五脏已经都给吃空了，手上还紧紧的捏着那只小篮呢。……"她接着但是呜咽，说不出成句的话来。

　　四婶起刻还踌蹰，待到听完她自己的话，眼圈就有些红了。她想了一想，便教拿圆篮和铺盖到下房去。卫老婆子仿佛卸了一肩重担似的嘘一口气；祥林嫂比初来时候神气舒畅些，不待指引，自己驯熟的安放了铺盖。她从此又在鲁镇做女工了。

　　大家仍然叫她祥林嫂。

　　然而这一回，她的境遇却改变得非常大。上工之后的两三天，主人们就觉得她手脚已没有先前一样灵活，记性也坏得多，死尸似的脸上又整日没有笑影，四婶的口气上，已颇有些不满了。当她初到的时候，四叔虽然照例皱过眉，但鉴于向来雇用女工之难，也就并不大反对，只是暗暗地告诫四婶说，这种人虽然似乎很可怜，但是败坏风俗的，用她帮忙还可以，祭祀时候可用不着她沾手，一切饭菜，只好自己做，否则，不干不净，祖宗是不吃的。

四叔家里最重大的事件是祭祀，祥林嫂先前最忙的时候也就是祭祀，这回她却清闲了。桌子放在堂中央，系上桌帏，她还记得照旧的去分配酒杯和筷子。

"祥林嫂，你放着罢！我来摆。"四婶慌忙的说。

她讪讪的缩了手，又去取烛台。

"祥林嫂，你放着罢！我来拿。"四婶又慌忙的说。

她转了几个圆圈，终于没有事情做，只得疑惑的走开。她在这一天可做的事是不过坐在灶下烧火。

镇上的人们也仍然叫她祥林嫂，但音调和先前很不同；也还和她讲话，但笑容却冷冷的了。她全不理会那些事，只是直着眼睛，和大家讲她自己日夜不忘的故事：

"我真傻，真的，"她说，"我单知道雪天是野兽在深山里没有食吃，会到村里来；我不知道春天也会有。我一大早起来就开了门，拿小篮盛了一篮豆，叫我们的阿毛坐在门槛上剥豆去。他是很听话的孩子，我的话句句听；他就出去了。我就在屋后劈柴，淘米，米下了锅，打算蒸豆。我叫，'阿毛！'没有应。出去一看，只见豆撒得满地，没有我们的阿毛了。各处去一问，都没有。我急了，央人去寻去。直到下半天，几个人寻到山坳里，看见刺柴上挂着一只他的小鞋。大家都说，完了，怕是遭了狼了；再进去；果然，他躺在草窠里，肚里的五脏已经都给吃空了，可怜他手里还紧紧的捏着那只小篮呢。……"她于是淌下眼泪来，声音也呜咽了。

这故事倒颇有效，男人听到这里，往往敛起笑容，没趣的走开去；女人们却不独宽恕了她似的，脸上立刻改换了鄙薄的神气，还要陪出许多眼泪来。有些老女人没有在街头听到她的话，便特意寻来，要听她这一段悲惨的故事。直到她说到呜咽，她们也就一齐流下那停在眼角上的眼泪，叹息一番，满足的去了，一面还纷纷的评论着。

她就只是反复的向人说她悲惨的故事，常常引住了三五个人来听她。但不久，大家也都听得纯熟了，便是最慈悲的念佛的老太太们，眼里也再不见有一点泪的痕迹。后来全镇的人们几乎都能背诵她的话，一听到就烦厌得头痛。

"我真傻，真的，"她开首说。

"是的，你是单知道雪天野兽在深山里没有食吃，才会到村里来的。"他们立即打断她的话，走开去了。

她张着口怔怔的站着，直着眼睛看他们，接着也就走了，似乎自己也觉得没趣。但她还妄想，希图从别的事，如小篮，豆，别人的孩子上，引出她的阿毛的故事来。倘一看见两三岁的小孩子，她就说：

"唉唉，我们的阿毛如果还在，也就有这么大了……"

孩子看见她的眼光就吃惊，牵着母亲的衣襟催她走。于是又只剩下她一个，终于没趣的也走了，后来大家又都知道了她的脾气，只要有孩子在眼前，便似笑非笑的先问她，道：

"祥林嫂，你们的阿毛如果还在，不是也就有这么大了么？"

她未必知道她的悲哀经大家咀嚼赏鉴了许多天，早已成为渣滓，只值得烦厌和唾弃；但从人们的笑影上，也仿佛觉得这又冷又尖，自己再没有开口的必要了。她单是一瞥他们，并不回答一句话。

鲁镇永远是过新年，腊月二十以后就火起来了。四叔家里这回须雇男短工，还是忙不过来，另叫柳妈做帮手，杀鸡，宰鹅；然而柳妈是善女人，吃素，不杀生的，只肯洗器皿。祥林嫂除烧火之外，没有别的事，却闲着了，坐着只看柳妈洗器皿。微雪点点的下来了。

"唉唉，我真傻，"祥林嫂看了天空，叹息着，独语似的说。

"祥林嫂，你又来了。"柳妈不耐烦的看着她的脸，说。"我问你：你额角上的伤痕，不就是那时撞坏的么？"

"唔唔。"她含胡的回答。

"我问你：你那时怎么后来竟依了呢？"

"我么？……"

"你呀。我想：这总是你自己愿意了，不然……"

"阿阿，你不知道他力气多么大呀。"

"我不信。我不信你这么大的力气，真会拗他不过。你后来一定是自己肯了，倒推说他力气大。"

"阿阿，你……你倒自己试试看。"她笑了。

柳妈的打皱的脸也笑起来，使她蹙缩得像一个核桃；干枯的小眼睛一看祥林嫂的额角，又钉住她的眼。祥林嫂似很局促了，立刻敛了笑容，旋转眼光，自去看雪花。

"祥林嫂，你实在不合算。"柳妈诡秘的说。"再一强，或者索性撞一个死，就好了。现在呢，你和你的第二个男人过活不到两年，倒落了一件大罪名。你想，你将来到阴司去，那两个死鬼的男人还要争，你给了谁好呢？阎罗大王只好把你锯开来，分给他们。我想，这真是……"

她脸上就显出恐怖的神色来，这是在山村里所未曾知道的。

"我想，你不如及早抵当。你到土地庙里去捐一条门槛，当作你的替身，给千人踏，万人跨，赎了这一世的罪名，免得死了去受苦。"

她当时并不回答什么话，但大约非常苦闷了，第二天早上起来的时候，两眼上便都围着大黑圈。早饭之后，她便到镇的西头的土地庙里去求捐门槛。庙祝起初执意不允许，直到她急得流泪，才勉强答应了。价目是大钱十二千。

她久已不和人们交口，因为阿毛的故事是早被大家厌弃了的；但自从和柳妈谈了天，似乎又即传扬开去，许多人都发生了新趣味，又来逗她说话了。至于题目，那自然是换了一个新样，专在她额上的伤疤。

"祥林嫂，我问你：你那时怎么竟肯了？"一个说。

"唉，可惜，白撞了这一下。"一个看着她的疤，应和道。

她大约从他们的笑容和声调上，也知道是在嘲笑她，所以总是瞪着眼睛，不说一句话，后来连头也不回了。她整日紧闭了嘴唇，头上带着大家以为耻辱的记号的那伤痕，默默的跑街，扫地，洗菜，淘米。快够一年，她才从四婶手里支取了历来积存的工钱，换算了十二元鹰洋，请假到镇的西头去。但不到一顿饭时候，她便回来，神气很舒畅，眼光也分外有神，高兴似的对四婶说，自己已经在土地庙捐了门槛了。

冬至的祭祖时节，她做得更出力，看四婶装好祭品，和阿牛将桌子抬到堂屋中央，她便坦然的去拿酒杯和筷子。

"你放着罢，祥林嫂！"四婶慌忙大声说。

她像是受了炮烙似的缩手，脸色同时变作灰黑，也不再去取烛台，只是失神的站着。直到四叔上香的时候，教她走开，她才走开。这一回她的变化非常大，第二天，不但眼睛窈陷下去，连精神也更不济了。而且很胆怯，不独怕暗夜，怕黑影，即使看见人，虽是自己的主人，也总惴惴的，有如在白天出穴游行的小鼠；否则呆坐着，直是一个木偶人。不半年，头发也花白起来了，记性尤其坏，甚而至于常常忘却了去淘米。

“祥林嫂怎么这样了？倒不如那时不留她。”四婶有时当面就这样说，似乎是警告她。

然而她总如此，全不见有伶俐起来的希望。他们于是想打发她走了，教她回到卫老婆子那里去。但当我还在鲁镇的时候，不过单是这样说；看现在的情状，可见后来终于实行了。然而她是从四叔家出去就成了乞丐的呢，还是先到卫老婆子家然后再成乞丐的呢？那我可不知道。

我给那些因为在近旁而极响的爆竹声惊醒，看见豆一般大的黄色的灯火光，接着又听得毕毕剥剥的鞭炮，是四叔家正在“祝福”了；知道已是五更将近时候。我在蒙胧中，又隐约听到远处的爆竹声联绵不断，似乎合成一天音响的浓云，夹着团团飞舞的雪花，拥抱了全市镇。我在这繁响的拥抱中，也懒散而且舒适，从白天以至初夜的疑虑，全给祝福的空气一扫而空了，只觉得天地圣众歆享了牲醴和香烟，都醉醺醺的在空中蹒跚，豫备给鲁镇的人们以无限的幸福。

一九二四年

## Introduction to the Poems of Xu Zhimo

A breakthrough in the modern Chinese literary revolution was creative practical poetry. The new poetry movement liberated form, spearheading the transition from traditional classical rhyming verses to the free-style format used in the west. It created a new modern Chinese poetry—vernacular poetry.

Xu Zhimo(徐志摩 1896～1931) is an outstanding representative of contemporary Chinese poets. He studied in both England and the United States. Although he majored in Economics, he was fond of literature and was especially engaged in it and influenced by European and American romanticism and by the impact of aesthetic poetry. In 1921 he returned to China and founded a poetic association, published a poetry magazine, created and wrote many well-known poems. He died in an air-craft accident in 1931. People commented at his funeral that "he spoke poetically, acted poetically, and his entire life was full of poetry". His poems were written with clarity and harmonic rhythm; they were novel and full of imagination. His poetic style was gracefully presented, richly varied, and splendid in its pursuit of this characteristic art form.

徐志摩

# Selected Poems of Xu Zhimo

## 1. A Snowflake's Happiness

If I were a snowflake,

Drifting suavely in mid-air,

I would recognize my direction—

Soaring, soaring, soaring—

The ground below holds my direction.


Avert the cold lonely valleys,

Evade the dreary mountains,

Elude the melancholic streets—

Soaring, soaring, soaring—

My destiny it shall be!


Dancing gracefully in mid-air,

Perceiving the enchanting dwelling.

Waiting for her arrival in the garden—

Soaring, soaring, soaring—

Sigh, her pleasant aroma fills the air!


Quietly, my buoyant body floats,

Landing on her with gentle care,

Sensing her love and passion—

Fading, fading, fading—

I fade into the warmth of her heart


## 雪花的快乐

假若我是一朵雪花，

翩翩的在半空里潇洒，
我一定认清我的方向——
飞扬，飞扬，飞扬，——
这地面上有我的方向。

不去那冷寞的幽谷，
不去那凄清的山麓，
也不上荒街去惆怅——
飞扬，飞扬，飞扬，——
你看，我有我的方向！

在半空里娟娟的飞舞，
认明了那清幽的住处，
等着她来花园里探望——
飞扬，飞扬，飞扬，——
啊，她身上有朱砂梅的清香！

那时我凭借我的身轻，
盈盈的，沾住了她的衣襟，
贴近她柔波似的心胸——
消溶，消溶，消溶——
溶入了她柔波似的心胸！

## 2. Chance

I am a cloud in the sky,
A chance shadow on the wave of your heart.
Don't be surprised,
Or too elated;
In an instant I shall vanish without trace.

We meet on the sea of dark night,

You on your way, I on mine.

Remember if you will,

Or, better still, forget

The light exchanged in this encounter.

# 偶　然

我是天空里的一片云，

偶尔投影在你的波心——

你不必讶异，

更无须欢喜——

在转瞬间消灭了踪影。


你我相逢在黑夜的海上

你有你的，我有我的，方向；

你记得也好，

最好你忘掉，

在这交会时互放的光亮！


## 3. Saying Goodbye to Cambridge Again

Very quietly I take my leave,

As quietly as I came here;

Quietly I wave goodbye

To the rosy clouds in the western sky.


The golden willows by the riverside

Are young brides in the setting sun;

Their reflections on the shimmering waves

Always linger in the depth of my heart.

The floating heart growing in the sludge
 Sways leisurely under the water;
In the gentle waves of Cambridge,
I would be a water plant!

That pool under the shade of elm trees
Holds not water but the rainbow from the sky;
Shattered to pieces among the duckweeds
Is the sediment of a rainbow-like dream?

To seek a dream? Just to pole a boat upstream
To where the green grass is more verdant;
Or to have the boat fully loaded with starlight
And sing aloud in the splendor of starlight.

But I cannot sing aloud
Quietness is my farewell music;
Even summer insects keep silence for me
Silent is Cambridge tonight!

Very quietly I take my leave
As quietly as I came here;
Gently I flick my sleeves
Not even a wisp of cloud will I bring away.

## 再 别 康 桥

轻轻的我走了，
正如我轻轻的来；
我轻轻的招手，
作别西天的云彩。

那河畔的金柳，
是夕阳中的新娘；
波光里的艳影，
在我的心头荡漾。

软泥上的青荇，
油油的在水底招摇；
在康河的柔波里，
我甘心做一条水草！

那榆荫下的一潭，
不是清泉，是天上虹
揉碎在浮藻间，
沉淀着彩虹似的梦。

寻梦？撑一支长篙，
向青草更青处漫溯，
满载一船星辉，
在星辉斑斓里放歌。

但我不能放歌，
悄悄是别离的笙箫；
夏虫也为我沉默，
沉默是今晚的康桥！

悄悄的我走了，
正如我悄悄的来；
我挥一挥衣袖，
不带走一片云彩。

# Further Readings

## 1. Xiaoxiao

### Shen Congwen

Just about every day around the twelfth month, the folks at home seem to be blowing the bamboo pipes for a wedding.

Following the pipes a gaily decked bridal palanquin appears, gliding forward on the shoulders of two bearers. The girl is shut up tight inside, and even though she is wearing a festive gown of greens and reds, something she doesn't get to wear every day—she can't help sobbing to herself. For, in her heart, a young woman knows that becoming a bride and leaving her mother to become, in time, someone else's mother, means having to face a host of new and unexpected problems. It's almost like entering a trance, to sleep in the same bed with someone you hardly know in order to carry on the ancestral line. Naturally, it is somewhat frightening to think of these things, so if one is inclined to cry in such a circumstance—as so many before have cried—is it any wonder?

There are, of course, some who don't cry. Xiaoxiao did not cry when she got married. She had been orphaned, and had been sent to an uncle on a farm to be brought up. All day long, carrying a small, wide-brimmed bamboo hat, she had to look for dog droppings by the side of the road and in the gullies. For her, marriage meant simply a transfer from one family to another. So, when the day came, all she could do was to laugh about it, with no sense of shame or fear. She was scarcely aware of what she was getting into: all she knew was that she was to become someone's new daughter-in-law.

Xiaoxiao was eleven when she married, and Little Husband was hardly two years old—almost ten years

沈从文

younger, and not long ago suckling at his mother's breast. When she entered the household she called him "Sonny," according to local custom. Her daily chore was to take "Sonny" to play under the willow tree in front of the house or by the stream; when he was hungry, to give him something to eat; when he fussed, to soothe him; to pluck pumpkin blossoms and dog-grass to crown Little Husband with, or to soothe him with kisses and sweet nothings:"Sonny, now there, hush, there, there." And with that she would kiss the grimy little face: the boy would break out in smiles. In good spirits again, the child would act up once more, and with his tiny fingers, he would paw at Xiaoxiao's hair—the brown hair that was untidy and unkempt most of the time. Sometimes, when he had pulled too hard at her braid, the knot of red wool would come loose, and she would have to cuff him a few times: naturally he bawled. Xiaoxiao, now on the verge of tears herself, would point to the boy's tear-drenched face and say:"Now, now, you naughty thing, you'd better quit that."

Through fair and foul, every day she carried her "husband," doing this and that around the house, wherever her services were needed. On occasion she would go down to the stream to wash out clothes, to rinse out the diapers, but she found time to pick out colorful striped snails to amuse the boy with as he sat nearby. When she went to sleep she would dream dreams that a girl her age dreams; she dreamt that she found a cache of copper coins at the back gate, or some other place, and that she had good things to eat; she dreamt that she was climbing a tree; she dreamt she was a fish, floating freely in the water; she dreamt she was so light and lithe that she flew up clear to the stars, where there was no one, but all she could see was a flash of white and of gold, and she cried aloud for her mother—whereupon she woke up, her heart still thumping. The people next door would scold her:"You silly thing! What were you thinking of?

*Those who do nothing at all but play Wind up with bad dreams at end of day.*"

When she heard this, Xiaoxiao made no response, but merely giggled to herself, thinking of the good dreams that her husband's crying sometimes interrupted. He would sleep by his mother's side, so that it would be easier for her to breast feed

中国文学选读

him, but there were times when he had too much milk or was colicky. Then he would wake up in the middle of the night crying, and Xiaoxiao would have to get up and take him to the bathroom. This happened often. Her husband cried so much, her mother-in-law didn't know what to do with him, so Xiaoxiao had to crawl out of bed bleary-eyed and tiptoe in—brushing the cobwebs out of her sleepy eyes—to take the boy in her arms, and distract him with the lamp or the twinkling of the stars. If that didn't work, she'd peck and whistle, make faces for the child, blather on like a baby—"hey, hey, look—look at the cat"—until her husband broke out in a smile. They would play like this for a bit, and then he would feel drowsy and close his eyes. When he was asleep, she'd put him back to bed, watching over him awhile, and, hearing in the distance the insistent sound of a cock crowing, she couldn't help knowing about what time it was when she huddled back in her tiny bed. At daybreak, though she had had a sleepless night, she would flick her eyes open and shut to see the yellow-and-purple sunflowers outdoors shifting forms before her very eyes: that was a real treat.

When Xiaoxiao was married off, to become the "little wife" of a pint-sized little child, she wasn't any the worse for wear; one look at her figure was proof enough of that. She was like an unnoticed sapling at a corner of the garden, sprouting forth big leaves and branches after days of wind and rain. This little girl—as if unmindful of her tiny husband—grew bigger day by day.

To speak of summer nights is to dream. People seek the cool of the evening after summer heat: they sit in the middle of the courtyard, waving their rush-fans, looking up at the stars in the sky or the fireflies in the corners, listening to the "Weaver Maid" crickets—on the roofs of the pumpkinsheds—clicking away interminably on their "looms." The sounds from near and far are intertwined like the sound of rain, and when the hay-scented wind falls full on the face, that is a time when people are of a mind to tell jokes.

Xiaoxiao grew very tall, and she would often climb the sloping sides of the hay-stack, carrying in her arms her already sleeping husband, softly singing self-impro-vised folk melodies. The more she sang, the drowsier she felt—until she too was al-most asleep.

In the middle of the courtyard, her in-laws, the grandparents, and two farmhands sat at random on small wooden stools.

By Grandfather's side there was a tobacco-coil, whose embers glowed in the dark. This coil, made of mugwort, had the effect of repelling long-legged mosquitoes. It was wound around at Grandfather's feet like a black snake. From time to time, Grandfather would pick it up and wave it about.

Thinking about the day in the fields, Grandfather said: "Say, I heard that Old Qin said that, day before yesterday, there were a few coeds passing through town."

Everyone roared with laughter.

And what was behind the laughter? Everyone had the impression that coeds didn't wear braids; wearing the hair in the form of a sparrow's tail made them look like nuns, and yet somehow not like nuns. They wore their clothes in the manner of foreigners, yet they didn't look like foreigners. They ate, behaved in such a way... well, in a word, everything seemed out of place with them, and the slightest mention of coeds was cause enough for laughter.

Xiaoxiao didn't understand much of what was going on, and so she didn't laugh at all. Grandfather spoke again. He said:

"Xiaoxiao, when you grow up, you'll be a coed too." At this, everyone laughed once more.

Now, Xiaoxiao was not stupid when it came to people, and she figured this wasn't flattering to her, so she said:

"Grandpa, I won't become a coed."

"But you look like a coed. It won't do if you It's become one."

"No, I certainly won't."

The bystanders mined this for a laugh and egged her on:

"Xiaoxiao, what Grandpa says is right. It's not right if you don't become a coed."

Xiaoxiao was flustered and didn't know what was going on.

"All right, if I have to, I have to." Actually, Xiaoxiao had no idea what was wrong with being a coed...

The whole idea of coeds would always be thought of as queer in these parts. Every year, come June, when the start of the so-called "summer vacation" had finally arrived, they would come in small groups from some outlandish metropolis, and, looking for some remote retreat, they would pass through the village. In the eyes of the local people, it was almost as if these people had dropped down from an altogether different world, dressed in the most bizarre ways, their behavior even more improbable. On the days these coeds passed through, the whole village would come up with joke after joke.

Grandpapa was an old-timer from the region, and, because he was thinking about the carryings-on of the coeds he knew in the big city, he thought it was funny to urge Xiaoxiao to become one. As soon as he made the crack he couldn't help laughing, but he also had in mind the way Xiaoxiao felt, and so the joke wasn't totally innocuous.

The coeds that Grandfather knew were of a type: they wore clothes without regard to the weather; they ate whether they were hungry or full; they didn't go to sleep until late at night; during the day they worked at nothing at all, but sang and played ball or read books from abroad. They knew how to spend money: with what they spent in a year, you could buy at least sixteen water buffaloes. In the capital cities of the provinces, whenever they wanted to go anywhere, they'd never dream of walking, but would climb instead into a big "box," which took them everywhere. In the cities there were all sorts of "boxes" big and small, all motorized. At school, boys and girls go to class together, and, when they get acquainted, the girls sleep overnight with the boys, with no thought of a go-between or a matchmaker, or even a dowry. This is what they call being "free." They sometimes serve as district officials and bring families to their posts; their husbands are called "Masters" still and their children "Little Master." They don't tend cattle themselves, but they'll drink cow's milk and sheep's milk like little calves and little lambs; the milk they buy is canned. When they have nothing better to do they go to a theater, which is built like a huge temple, and take from their pockets a silver dollar (a dollar of their money can buy five setting hens hereabouts). With this they purchase a piece of paper in the form of a ticket which they take inside, so that they can sit down and watch foreigners performing shadow-plays. When offended, they won't curse at you or cry. By the time they are twenty-four, some still won't marry, while others at thirty or forty still have the cheek to contemplate marriage. They are not afraid of men, thinking men can't wrong them, for if they do, they take the men to court and insist that the magistrate fine them. Sometimes they spend the fine themselves, and sometimes they share it with the magistrate. Of course, they don't wash clothes or cook meals, and they certainly don't raise hogs and feed hens; when they have children they hire a servant to look after them for only five or ten dollars a month so that they can spend all day going to the theater and playing cards, or reading all those good-for-nothing books.

In a word, everything about them is weird, totally different from the lives of farmers, and some of their goings-on are not to be believed. When Xiaoxiao heard her grandfather saying all this, which explained everything, she felt vague stirrings of unrest, and took to imagining herself as a "coed". Would she behave like the "coeds" Grandfather talked about? In any case there was nothing frightful about these "coeds," and so these notions began to occupy this simple girl's thoughts for the first time.

Because of the picture that Grandfather had painted of the "coed," Xiaoxiao giggled to herself for some time. But when she had collected herself, she said:

"Grandpa, when the 'coeds' come tomorrow, please tell me. I want a look."

"Watch out, or they'll make a maidservant out of you!"

"I'm not afraid of them."

"Oh, but they read all those foreign books, recite scripture, and you're still not afraid of them?"

"They can recite the 'Bodhisattva Guanyin Dispels Disaster' sutra or 'The Curse of the Monkey Sun' for all 1 care. I'm not afraid."

"They'll bite people, like the officials; they only eat simple folk; they munch even the bones and It's spit up the remains. Are you sure you're not scared?"

Xiaoxiao replied firmly: "No, I'm not scared."

At the time, Xiaoxiao was carrying her husband, who, apparently for no reason broke out of a sound sleep crying. Daughter-in-law used the tones of a mother and, half in reassurance, half in remonstrance, said:

"Sonny, Sonny, you mustn't cry, the voracious coeds are coming!"

Her husband continued to cry, and there was no choice but to stand up and walk him about. Xiaoxiao carried him off, leaving Grandfather, who went on talking about other things.

From that moment on, Xiaoxiao remembered what "coed" meant. When she dreamt, she would often dream about being a coed, about being one of them. It was as if she too had sat in one of those motorized boxes, though she felt they didn't go much faster than she did. In her dream, the box seemed to resemble a granary, and there were ash-gray mice with little red, piggy eyes, darting all over the place, sometimes squirming through the cracks, their slimy tails sticking out behind them.

With this development, it was only natural that Grandfather would stop calling her "little maidservant" or "Xiaoxiao" and would call her "little coed." When it caught her off guard, Xiaoxiao would turn around involuntarily.

In the country, one day is like any other day in the world; they change only with the season. People waste each day as it comes, in the same way that Xiaoxiao and her kind hang on to each day; each gets his share, everything is as it should be. A lot of city sophisticates while away their summers in soft silk, indulging in good food and drink, not to mention other pleasures. For Xiaoxiao and her family, however, summer means hard work, producing ten catties or more of fine hemp and twenty or thirty wagonloads of melons a day.

The little daughter-in-law Xiaoxiao, on a summer day, must tend to her husband as well as spin four catties of hemp. By August, when the farmhands harvest the melons, she would enjoy seeing piled high in rows on the ground the dust-covered pumpkin melons, each as big as a pot. The time had come to collect the harvest, and now the courtyard was filled with great big red and brown leaves, blown from the branches of the trees in the grove behind the house. Xiaoxiao stood by the melons, and she was working a large leaf into a hat for her husband to play with.

There was a farmhand called Motley Mutt, about twenty years old, who took Xiaoxiao's husband to the date tree for some dates: one whack with a bamboo stick, and the ground would be covered with dates.

"Brother Motley Mutt, no more, please. Too much and you won't be able to eat them all."

Despite this warning, he didn't budge. It was as if, on account of the little husband's yen for dates, Motley Mutt wouldn't listen. So, Xiaoxiao warned her little husband:

"Sonny, Sonny, come over here, It's take any more. You'll get a belly ache from eating all that raw fruit!"

Her husband obeyed. Grabbing an armful of dates, he came over to Xiaoxiao, and offered her some.

"Sis, eat. Here's a big one."

"No, I won't eat it."

"Come on, just one."

She had her hands full: how could she stop to eat one? She was busily putting the hat together, and wished she had some help.

"Sonny, why It's you put a date in my mouth?"

Her husband did as he was told, and when he did he thought it was fun and came out with a laugh.

She wanted him to drop the dates so that he could help her hold the hat together while she added a few more leaves.

Her husband did as he was bidden, but he couldn't sit still, all the while singing and humming. The child was always like a cat, prone to mischief when in a good mood.

"Sonny, what song are you singing there?"

"Motley Mutt taught me this mountain song."

"Sing it properly so that I can follow."

Husband held on to the brim of the hat, and sang what he could remember of the song.

> Clouds rise in the skies, clouds become flowers;
> Among the corn stalks, plant beans for ruth;
> The beans will undermine the stalks of corn,
> And young maidens choke off flowering youth.
> Clouds rise in the skies, one after another

> *In the ground, graves are dug, grave upon grave;*
> *Fair maids wash bowls, bowl after bowl,*
> *And in their beds serve knave after knave.*

The meaning of the song was lost on husband, and when he finished, he asked her if she liked it. Xiaoxiao said she did, asking where it came from, and even though she knew that Motley Mutt had taught him the song, she still wanted him to tell her.

"Motley Mutt—he taught me. He knows lots of songs, but I... gotta grow up before he'll sing them."

When she realized that Motley Mutt could sing, Xiaoxiao said: "Brother Motley Mutt, Brother Motley Mutt, won't you sing a proper song for me?"

But that Motley Mutt, his face was as coarse as his heart; he had a touch of the vulgar about him, and, knowing that Xiaoxiao wanted a song, and sensing that she was about at the age to understand, he sang for her the ballad of the ten-year-old bride married to the one-year-old groom. The story says that as the wife is older, she can stray a bit because the husband is still an infant, not yet weaned, so leave him to suckle at his mother's breasts. Of course, little Husband understood nothing at all of this song; Xiaoxiao, on the other hand, had but an inkling. When she had heard it, Xiaoxiao put on airs, as if to indicate she understood it all. Affecting outrage, she said to Motley Mutt:

"Brother Motley Mutt, you stop that! That song's not nice."

But Brother Motley Mutt took exception: "But it *is* a nice song."

"Oh, no it isn't. It isn't a nice song."

Motley Mutt rarely said much: he had sung his song; if he had offended anyone, he wouldn't sing again, that's all. He could see that she understood a little of what he sang, and he was afraid that she would tell on him to Grandfather; then he'd really be in for it, so he changed the subject to coeds. He asked Xiaoxiao if she had ever seen coeds exercising in public and singing Western songs.

If Motley hadn't brought this up, Xiaoxiao would have long ago forgotten all about coeds. But now that he mentioned it, she was curious to know if he had seen any lately. She was dying to see them.

While he was moving the melons from the shed to a corner of the courtyard wall, Motley told her stories about coeds singing foreign songs—all of which he had originally heard from Grandfather. To her face, he boasted of having seen four coeds on the main road, each with a flag in her hands, marching down the road perspiring and singing away just like soldiers on parade. It goes without saying that all this was some nonsense he had cooked up. But the stories inflamed Xiaoxiao's imagination. And all because Motley characterized them as instances of "freedom."

Motley was one of those clownish, leering, earthy types. When he heard Xiaoxiao say (with a measure of admiration): "My, Brother Motley, but you have big arms," he would say: "Oh, but that's not all that's big!"

"You've got such a large build."

"I'm big all over."

Xiaoxiao didn't understand this at all; she just thought he was being silly, and so she laughed.

After Xiaoxiao had left, carrying her husband off, a fellow who picked melons with Motley, and who had the nickname "Mumbles" (he was not much given to talk), spoke out on this occasion for once.

"Motley, you're really awful. She's a twelve-year-old virgin, and she's still got twelve years before her wedding!"

Without so much as a word. Motley went up to the farmhand, slapped him, and then walked to the date tree to pick up the fruit that had dropped off.

By the time of the autumn melons harvest, one could reckon a full year and a half that Xiaoxiao had been with her husband.

The days passed—days of frost and snow, sunny days, and rainy days—and everyone said how grown-up Xiaoxiao was. Heaven kept watch over her: she drank cold water, ate coarse gruel, and was never sick the year round; she grew and blossomed. Although Grandmama became something of a nemesis, and tried to keep her from growing up too fast, Xiaoxiao flourished in the clean country air, undaunted by any trial or ordeal.

When Xiaoxiao was fourteen, she had the figure of an adult, but her heart was still as blithe and as unschooled as that of a child.

When one is bigger, one gets a heavier burden of household chores. Besides twisting hemp, spinning thread, washing, looking after her husband, she had odd jobs like getting feed for the pigs or working at the mill flossing silk, and weaving. She was expected to learn everything. It was understood that anyone who could make an extra effort would fit in a few chores to be done in their own quarters: the coarse hemp and spun silk that Xiaoxiao had gathered in two or three years were enough to keep her busy for three months at the crude shuttle in her room.

Her husband had long ago been weaned. Mother-in-law had a new son, and so her five-year-old—Xiaoxiao's husband—became Xiaoxiao's sole charge. Whatever happened, wherever she went, her husband followed her around. Husband was a little afraid of her in some ways, as if she were his mother and so he behaved himself. All in all, they got along pretty well.

Gradually as the locality became more progressive, Grandfather would change his jokes to: "Xiaoxiao, for the sake of freedom, you ought to cut off your braids." By this time Xiaoxiao had heard this joke; one summer she had seen her first coed. Although she didn't take Grandfather's ribbing too seriously, she would nevertheless (whenever she would pass by a pond after he made his crack) absentmindedly hold up her braid by the tip to see how good she would look without a braid, and how she would feel about it.

To gather feed grass for the pigs, Xiaoxiao would take her husband up on the dark slope of Snail Mountain.

The child did not know any better, and so whenever he heard singing he would break into song. And no sooner did he open his mouth than Motley would appear.

Motley began to harbor new thoughts about Xiaoxiao, which she gradually became aware of and that made her nervous. But Motley was a man with all the wiles and the ways of a man, strong of build, and nimble-footed who could divert and charm a girl. While he ingratiated himself with Xiaoxiao's husband, he found ways of sidling up to Xiaoxiao and of disarming her suspicions about him.

But what is a man compared to a mountain? With trees everywhere Xiaoxiao would be hard to locate. So whenever he wanted to find Xiaoxiao, Motley would stand on a rise and sing in order to get a response from the little husband at Xiaoxiao's side. As soon as Little Husband sang, Motley, after running over hill and dale, would appear face-to-face before Xiaoxiao.

When the little child saw Motley, he felt nothing but delight. He wanted Motley to make insect figures from grass, or to carve out a flute for him from bamboo, but Motley always came up with a way to send him off to find the necessary materials so that he could sit by Xiaoxiao and sing for her those songs that would bring her guard down and produce a blush on her cheeks. At times she was worried that something might happen, and she wouldn't let her husband go off; at other times it seemed better to send the boy-husband off, so that he wouldn't see what Motley was up to. Finally one day she let Motley sing his way into her heart, and he made a woman of her.

At the time, Little Husband had run down the mountain to pick berries, and Motley sang many songs which he performed for Xiaoxiao:

> Pretty maid, an uphill path leads to your door;
> If others have walked a little, I've walked more.
> My well-made sandals are worn out, walked to shreds;
> If not for you, my pretty, then who for?

When he finished, he said to Xiaoxiao "I haven't slept a wink because of you." He swore up and down that he would tell no one. When she heard this, Xiaoxiao was bewildered: she couldn't help looking at his brawny arms, and she couldn't help hearing the last thing he said. Even when he went to the outhouse, he would sing for her. She was disconcerted. But she asked him to swear before Heaven, and after he swore—which seemed a good enough guarantee—she abandoned herself to him. When Little Husband came back, his hand had been stung by a furry insect, and it was swelling up: he ran to Xiaoxiao. She pinched his hand, blew on the sting, and sucked on it to reduce the swelling. She remembered her thoughtless behavior of a moment ago, and she was dimly aware that she had done something not quite right.

When Motley took her, it was May, when the wheat was brown; by July, the plums had ripened—how fond she was of plums! She felt a change in her body, so when she bumped into Motley on the mountain, she told him about her situation, and asked what she should do.

They talked and talked, but Motley had not the faintest idea of what to do. Although he had sworn before the very heavens, he still had no idea. He was, after all, big in physique but small in courage. A big physique gets you into trouble easily, but small courage puts you at a loss as to how to work your way out.

After a while, Xiaoxiao would finger her snakelike black braid, and, thinking of life in the city, she said:

"Brother Motley, why It's we go where we can be free in the city and find work there? What do you say?"

"That won't do. There's nothing for us there. "

"My stomach is getting bigger. That won't do either. "

"Let's find some medicine: there's a doctor who sells the stuff in the market. "

"You'd better find something quick. I think—"

"It's no use running to 'freedom' in the city. Only strangers there. There are rules even for begging your bread; you can't go about it as you please. "

"You're really worthless, and you've been awful to me. Oh, I wish I was dead. "

"I swore never to betray you. "

"Who cares about betrayal; what I need is your help. Take this living thing out of my belly right away! I'm frightened. "

Motley said no more, and after a little while he left. In time, Little Husband came by from a spot where he was gathering red fruit. When he saw Xiaoxiao sitting all alone in the grass, her eyes red from crying. Little Husband began to wonder. After a while he asked:

"Sis, what's the matter?"

"It's nothing. I've got a cobweb in my eye. It smarts. "

"Let me blow it away. "

"No, It's bother. "

"Hey, look at what I've got. "

He took out of his pocket little shells and pebbles he had snatched from the near-by brook. Xiaoxiao looked at them, her eyes brimming, and managed a laugh: "Sonny, we get along so well. Please It's tell anyone else I've been crying. They might get upset. " And indeed, no one in the family got wind of it.

Half a month went by, and Motley, taking all his belongings with him left without so much as a word. Grandfather asked Mumbles (who roomed with Motley) whether he knew why Motley had left. Had he merely drifted off into the hills, or had he enlisted in the army? Mumbles shook his head, and said that Motley still owed him two hundred dollars; he had gone with not so much as a note when he left. He was certainly a no-good. Mumbles spoke his mind, but gave no indication where Motley might have gone. So the whole family buzzed about it the whole day, talking about this departure until nightfall. But, after all, the farmhand had not stolen anything and had not absconded with anything; so after a while, everyone forgot all about him.

Xiaoxiao, however, was no better off. It would have been nice it she could have forgotten Motley, but her stomach kept on getting bigger and bigger, and something inside began to move. She felt a sense of panic, and she spent one restless night after another.

She became more and more irritable; only her husband was aware of that, because she was now always harsher on him.

Of course, her husband was at her side all the time. She wasn't even very sure what she was thinking herself. On occasion she thought to herself: what if I were to die? Then everything would be all right. But then, why should I have to die? She wanted to enjoy life, to live on.

Whenever anyone in the family mentioned—even in passing—her husband, or babies, or Motley, she felt as if a blow had struck her hard on the chest.

Around October she was worried that more and more people would know. One day, she took her husband to a temple, and, making private vows, she swallowed a mouthful of incense-ashes. But as she was swallowing her husband saw her, and asked what she was doing. She told him this was good for a bellyache. Of course she had to lie. Though she implored the Bodhisattvas to help her, the Bodhisattvas did not see it her way; the child in her grew and grew just as before.

She went out of her way to drink cold water from the stream, and when her husband asked her about it, she said that she was merely thirsty.

Everything she could think of she tried, but nothing could divest her of the awful burden which she carried within. Only her husband knew about her swelling stomach; he did not dare let on to his mother and father. Because of the disparity in their ages and their years together, her husband regarded her with love mixed with fear, deeper even than his feeling for his own parents.

She remembered the oath that Motley swore, as well as what happened besides. It was now autumn, and the caterpillars were changing into chrysalises of various kinds and colors all around the house. Her husband, as if deliberately taunting her, would bring up the incident when he had been stung by the furry insect—that brought up unpleasant memories. Ever since that day, she had hated caterpillars, and whenever she saw one she had to step on it.

One day, word spread that the coeds were back again. When Xiaoxiao heard this, her eyes stared out unseeing, as if in a daze, her gaze fixed on the eastern horizon for some time.

She thought, well, Motley ran away, I can run away too. So she collected a few things, bent on joining the coeds on their way to the big city in search of freedom. But before she could make her move, she was discovered. To the people of the farm this was a grave offense, and so they tied her hands, put her away in a shed, and gave her nothing to eat for a whole day.

When they looked into the causes for her thwarted attempt at escape, they realized that Xiaoxiao, who in ten years was to bear a son for her husband to continue the family line, now carried a child conceived with another. This produced a scandal that shook the house hold and the peace and tranquility in the compound was totally disrupted. There were angry outbursts, there were tears, there were scoldings: each one had his own complaint to make. Hanging, drowning, swallowing poison, all these the long-suffering Xiaoxiao had considered desultorily, but in the end she was too young and still wanted to hold on to life, and so she did nothing. When Grandfather realized the way things were, he hit upon a shrewd plan. He had Xiaoxiao locked up in a room with two people to stand guard; he would call in her family to ask them whether they would recommend that she be drowned, or that she be sold. If it was a matter of saving face, they would recommend drowning; if they couldn't bear to let her die, they would sell her. But Xiaoxiao had only the uncle, who worked on a nearby farm. When he was called, he thought at first he was being invited to a party; only afterwards did he realize that the honor of the family was at stake, and this put the honest and well-intentioned fellow at a loss as to what to do.

With Xiaoxiao's belly as proof, there was nothing anyone could say. By rights she should have been drowned, but only heads of families who have read their Confucius would do such a stupid thing to save the family's honor. This uncle, however, hadn't read Confucius: he couldn't bear to sacrifice Xiaoxiao and so he chose the alternative of marrying her off to someone else.

This also seemed a punishment, and a natural one at that. It was normal for the husband's family to be considered the injured party, and restitution was to be made from the proceeds of the second marriage. The uncle explained all this carefully to Xiaoxiao, and then was just about to go. Xiaoxiao clung to his robe and would not let him leave, sobbing quietly. The uncle just shook his head, and, without saying a word, left.

At the time, no reputable family wanted Xiaoxiao; if she was to be sent away, someone would have to claim her, and so for the moment she continued to stay at the home of her husband. Once this matter had been settled no one, as a rule, made any more fuss about it. There was nothing to do but wait and everyone was totally at ease about the matter. At first Little Husband was not allowed in Xiaoxiao's company, but after a while they saw each other as before, laughing and playing like brother and sister.

Little Husband understood that Xiaoxiao was pregnant; he also understood that, in her condition, Xiaoxiao should be married off to someone living far away. But he didn't want Xiaoxiao to be sent away, and Xiaoxiao for her part didn't want to go either. Everyone was in a quandary as to what to do though the force of custom and circumstance dictated what had to be done and there were no two ways about it. Lately, if one asked who was making up the rules and the customs, whether the patriarch or matriarch, no one could rightly say.

They waited for a prospective husband: November came with still no one in

中国文学选读

sight. It was decided that Xiaoxiao might as well stay on for the New Year.

In the second month of the new year, she came to term, and gave birth to a son, big-eyed, with a large round head, a sturdy build, and a lusty voice. Everyone took good care of both mother and son; the customary steamed chicken and rice wine were served to the new mother to build up her strength and ritual paper money was burned to propitiate the gods. Everyone took to the baby boy.

Now that it turned out that the child was a boy, Xiaoxiao didn't have to be married off after all.

When, years later, the wedding ceremony for Xiaoxiao and her husband took place, her son was already ten years old. He could do half a man's work; he could look after the cows and cut the grass—a regular farmhand who could help with the chores. He took to calling Xiaoxiao's husband Uncle, Uncle would answer, with never a cross word.

The son was called "Herd boy." At the age of eleven, he was betrothed to a girl six years older. Since she was already of age, she could lend a helping hand and be very useful to the family. When the time for the bamboo wedding pipes to be sounded at the front door came, the bride inside the sedan chair sobbed pitiably. The grandfather and the great-grandfather were both beside themselves.

On this day, Xiaoxiao had lately given birth (the child was already three months old), and when she carried her newborn babe, watching the commotion and the festivities by the fence under the elm, she was taken back ten years, when she was carrying her husband. Now her own baby was fussing, so she sang in low tones, trying to soothe him:

"Now, there, there, look! The pretty wedding-sedan is coming this way. Look at the bride's lovely gown! How beautiful she looks! Hush! Hush! Don't act up now. Behave yourself or Mommy will get angry. Look, look! The coeds are here too! One day, when you grow up, we'll get you a coed for a wife."

1929

(translated by Eugene Chen Eoyang)

# 萧　萧
### 沈从文

　　乡下人吹唢呐接媳妇，到了十二月是成天会有的事情。

　　唢呐后面一项花轿，四个夫子平平稳稳的抬着。轿中人被铜锁锁在里面，虽穿了平时没上过身的体面红绿衣裳，也仍然得荷荷大哭。在这些小女人心中，做新娘子，从母亲身边离开，且准备作他人的母亲，从此将有许多新事情等待发生。像做梦一样，将同一个陌生男子汉在一个床上睡觉，做着承宗接祖的事情，这些事想起来，当然有些害怕，所以照例觉得要哭哭，于是就哭了。

　　也有做媳妇不哭的人。萧萧做媳妇就不哭。这小女子没有母亲，从小寄养到伯父种田的庄子上，终日提个小竹兜萝，在路旁田坎捡狗屎挑野菜，出嫁只是从这家转到那家。因此到那一天，这女人还只是笑。她又不害羞，又不怕。她是什么事也不知道，就做了人家的新媳妇了。

　　萧萧做媳妇时年纪十二岁，有一个小丈夫，年纪还不到三岁。丈夫比她年少九岁，断奶还不多久。地方规矩如此，过了门，她喊他做弟弟。她每天应作的事是抱弟弟到村前柳树下去玩，到溪边去玩，饿了，喂东西吃，哭了，就哄他，摘南瓜花或狗尾草戴到小丈夫头上，或者亲嘴，一面说，"弟弟，哪，啵，再来，啵。"在那肮脏的小脸上亲了又亲，孩子于是便笑了。孩子一欢喜兴奋，行动粗野起来，会用短短的小手乱抓萧萧的头发。那是平时不大能收拾蓬蓬松松在头上的黄发。有时候，垂到脑后那条小辫儿被拉得太久，把红绒线结也弄松了，生了气，就挞那弟弟几下，弟弟自然哇的哭出声来，萧萧便也装成要哭的样子，用手指着弟弟的哭脸，说，"哪，人不讲理，可不行！哪能这样动手动脚，长大了不是要杀人放火！"

　　天晴落雨日子混下去，每日抱抱丈夫，也帮家中作点杂事，能动手的就动手。又时常到溪沟里去洗衣，搓尿片，一面还捡拾有花纹的田螺给坐到身边的小丈夫玩。到了夜里睡觉，便常常做这种年龄人所做的梦，梦到后门角落或别的什么地方捡得大把大把铜钱，吃好东西，爬树，自己变成鱼到水中各处溜。或一时仿佛身子很小很轻，飞到天上众星中，没有一个人，只是一片白，一片金光，于是大喊"妈！"人就吓醒了。醒来心还只是跳。吵了隔壁的人，不免骂着，"疯子，你想什么！白天疯玩，晚上就做梦！"萧萧听着却不作声，只是咭咭的笑。也有很好很爽快的梦，为丈夫哭醒的事。那丈夫本来晚上在自己母亲身边睡，有时吃多了，或因另外情形，半夜大哭，起来放水拉稀是常有的事。丈夫哭到婆婆无可奈何，于是萧萧轻脚轻手爬起床来，睡眼朦胧走到床边，把人抱起，给他看月亮，看星光。或者互相觑着，孩子气的"嗨嗨，看猫呵，"那样喊着哄着，于是丈夫笑了，玩了一会，慢慢合上眼。人睡定后，放上床，站在床边看着，听远处一递一声的鸡叫，知道天快到什么时候了，于是仍然蜷到小床上睡去。天亮了，虽不做梦，却可以无意中闭眼开眼，看一阵在面前空中变幻无端的黄边紫心葵花，那是一种真正的享受。

萧萧嫁过了门，做了拳头大丈夫的小媳妇，一切并不比先前受苦，这只看她半年来身体发育就可明白。风里雨里过日子，象一株长在园角落不为人注意的蓖麻，大叶大枝，日增茂盛。这小女人简直是全不为丈夫设想那么似的，一天比一天长大起来了。

夏夜光景说来如做梦。大家饭后坐到院中心歇凉，挥摇蒲扇，看天上的星同屋角的萤，听南瓜棚上纺织娘子咯咯咯拖长声音纺车，远近声音繁密如落雨，禾花风飀飀吹到脸上，正是让人在各种方便中说笑话的时候。

萧萧好高，一个人常常爬到草料堆上去，抱了已经熟睡的丈夫在怀里，轻轻的轻轻的随意唱着那自编的山歌，唱来唱去却把自己也催眠起来，快要睡去了。

在院坝中，公公婆婆，祖父祖母，另外还有帮工汉子两个，散乱的坐在小板凳上，摆龙门阵学古，轮流下去打发上半夜。

祖父身边有个烟包，在黑暗中放光。这用艾蒿做成的烟包，是驱逐长脚蚊的得力东西，蜷在祖父脚边，就如一条乌梢蛇。间或又拿起来晃那么几下。

想起白天场上的事，那祖父开口说话：

"听三金说，前天又有女学生过身。"

大家就哄然笑了。

这笑的意义何在？只因为大家印象中，都知道女学生没有辫子，留下个鹌鹑尾巴，像个尼姑，又不完全像。穿的衣服象洋人又不是洋人，吃的，用的……总而言之事事不同，一想起来就觉得怪可笑！

萧萧不大明白，她不笑。所以老祖父又说话了。他说：

"萧萧，你长大了，将来也会做女学生！"

大家于是更哄然大笑起来。

萧萧为人并不愚蠢，觉得这一定是不利于己的一件事情，所以接口便说：

"爷爷，我不做女学生！"

"你像个女学生，不做可不行。"

"我不做。"

众人有意取笑，异口同声说："萧萧，爷爷说得划，你非做女学生不行！"

萧萧急得无可如何，"做就做，我不怕。"其实做女学生有什么不好，萧萧全不知道。

女学生这东西，在本乡的确永远是奇闻。每年一到六月天，据说放"水假"日子一到，照例便有三三五五女学生，由一个荒谬不经的热闹地方来，到另一个远地方去，取道从本地过身。从乡下人眼中看来，这些人都近于另一世界中活下的人，装扮奇奇怪怪，行为更不可思议。这种女学生过身时，使一村人都可以说一整天的笑话。

祖父是当地一个人物，因为想起所知道的女学生在大城中的生活情形，所以说笑话要萧萧也去作女学生。一面听到这话就感觉一种打哈哈趣味，一面还有那被说的萧萧感觉一种惶恐，说这话的不为无意义了。

女学生由祖父方面所知道的是这样一种人：她们穿衣服不管天气冷热，吃东西不问饥饱，晚上要到子时才睡觉，白天正经事全不作，只知唱歌打球，读洋书。她们都会花钱，一年用的钱可以买十六只水牛。她们在省里京里想往什么地方去时，不必走路，只要钻进一个大匣子中，那匣子就可以带她到目的地。城市中还有各种各样的大小不同的匣子。都用机器开动。她们在学校，男女在一处上课读书，人熟了，就随意同那男子睡觉，也不要媒人，也不要财礼，名叫"自由"。她们也做州县官，带家眷上任，男子仍然喊作"老爷"，小孩子叫"少爷"。她们自己不养牛，却吃牛奶羊奶，如小牛小羊：买那奶时是用铁罐子盛的。她们无事时到一个唱戏地方去，那地方完全象个大庙，从衣袋中取出一块洋钱来（那洋钱在乡下可买五只母鸡），买了一小方纸片儿，拿了那纸片到里面去，就可以坐下看洋人扮演影子戏。她们被冤了，不赌咒，不哭。她们年纪有老到二十四岁还不肯嫁人的，有老到三十四十还好意思嫁人的。她们不怕男子，男子不能使她们受委屈，一受委屈就上衙门打官司，要官罚男子的款，这笔钱她有时独占自己花用，有时同官平分。她们不洗衣煮饭，也不养猪喂鸡；有了小孩子也只花五块钱或十块钱一月，雇个人专管小孩，自己仍然整天看戏打牌，读那些没有用处的闲书……

总而言之，说来事事都希奇古怪，和庄稼人不同，有的简直可以说岂有此理。这时经祖父一为说明，听过这话的萧萧，心中却忽然有了一种模模糊糊的愿望，以为倘若她也是个女学生，她是不是照祖父说的女学生一个样子去做那些事？不

　　　　　　　　　　　　中国文学选读

管好歹，做女学生并不可怕，因此一来，却已为这乡下姑娘体验到了。

因为听祖父说起女学生是怎样的人物，到后萧萧独自笑得特别久。笑够了时，她说：

"爷爷，明天有女学生过路，你喊我，我要看看。"

"你看，她们捉你去作丫头。"

"我不怕她们。"

"她们读洋书念经你也不怕？"

"念观音菩萨消灾经，念紧箍咒，我都不怕。"

"她们咬人，和做官的一样，专吃乡下人，吃人骨头渣渣也不吐，你不怕？"

萧萧肯定的回答说："也不怕。"

可是这时节萧萧手上所抱的丈夫，不知为什么，在睡梦中哭了，媳妇于是用作母亲的声势，半哄半吓说：

"弟弟，弟弟，不许哭，不许哭，女学生咬人来了。"

丈夫还仍然哭着，得抱起各处走走。萧萧抱着丈夫离开了祖父，祖父同人说另外一样古话去了。

萧萧从此以后心中有个"女学生"。做梦也便常常梦到女学生，且梦到同这些人并排走路。仿佛也坐过那种自己会走路的匣子，她又觉得这匣子并不比自己跑路更快。在梦中那匣子的形体同谷仓差不多，里面有小小灰色老鼠，眼珠子红红的，各处乱跑，有时钻到门缝里去，把个小尾巴露在外边。

因为有这样一段经过，祖父从此喊萧萧不喊"小丫头"，不喊"萧萧"，却唤作"女学生"。在不经意中萧萧答应得很好。

乡下的日子也如世界上一般日子，时时不同。世界上人把日子糟蹋，和萧萧一类人家把日子吝惜是同样的，各有所得，各属分定。许多城市中文明人，把一个夏天全消磨到软绸衣服、精美饮料以及种种好事情上面。萧萧的一家，因为一个夏天的劳作，却得了十多斤细麻，二三十担瓜。

作小媳妇的萧萧，一个夏天中，一面照料丈夫，一面还绩了细麻四斤。到秋八月工人摘瓜，在瓜间玩，看硕大如盆，上面满是灰粉的大南瓜，成排成堆摆到地上，很有趣味。时间到摘瓜，秋天真的已来了，院子中各处有从屋后林子里树上吹来的大红大黄木叶。萧萧在瓜旁站定，手拿木叶一束，为丈夫编小笠帽玩。

工人中有个名叫花狗，年纪二十三岁，抱了萧萧的丈夫到枣树下去打枣子。小小竹竿打在枣树上，落枣满地。

"花狗大，莫打了，太多了吃不完。"

虽听这样喊，还不停手。到后，仿佛完全因为丈夫要枣子，花狗才不听话。萧萧于是又喊他那小丈夫：

"弟弟，弟弟，来，不许捡了。吃多了生东西肚子痛！"

丈夫听话，兜了一堆枣子向萧萧身边走来，请萧萧吃枣子。

"姐姐吃，这是大的。"

"我不吃。"

"要吃一颗！"

她两手哪里有空！木叶帽正在制边，工夫要紧，还正要个人帮忙！

"弟弟，把枣子喂我口里。"

丈夫照她的命令作事，作完了觉得有趣，哈哈大笑。

她要他放下枣子帮忙捏紧帽边，便于添加新木叶。

丈夫照她吩咐作事，但老是顽皮的摇动，口中唱歌。这孩子原来像一只猫，欢喜时就得捣乱。

"弟弟，你唱的是什么？"

"我唱花狗大告我的山歌。"

"好好的唱一个给我听。"

丈夫于是就唱下去，照所记到的歌唱：

> 天上起云云起花，
> 包谷林里种豆荚，
> 豆荚缠坏包谷树，
> 娇妹缠坏后生家。
> 天上起云云重云，
> 地下埋坟坟重坟，
> 娇妹洗碗碗重碗，
> 娇妹床上人重人。

歌中意义丈夫全不明白，唱完了就问好不好。萧萧说好，并且问跟谁学来的。她知道是花狗教他的，却故意盘问他。

"花狗大告我，他说还有好多歌，长大了再教我唱。"听说花狗会唱歌，萧萧说：

"花狗大，花狗大，您唱一个好听的歌我听听。"

那花狗，面如其心，生长得不很正气，知道萧萧要听歌，人也快到听歌的年龄了，就给她唱"十岁娘子一岁夫"。那故事说的是妻年大，可以随便到外面作一点不规矩事情，夫年小，只知道吃奶，让他吃奶。这歌丈夫完全不懂，懂到一点儿的是萧萧。把歌听过后，萧萧装成"我全明白"那种神气，她用生气的样子，对花狗说：

"花狗大，这个不行，这是骂人的歌！"

花狗分辩说："不是骂人的歌。"

"我明白，是骂人的歌。"

花狗难得说多话，歌已经唱过了，错了陪礼，只有不再唱。他看她已经有点懂事了，怕她回头告祖父，会挨一顿臭骂，就把话支开，扯到"女学生"上头去。他问萧萧，看没看过女学生习体操唱洋歌的事情。

若不是花狗提起，萧萧几乎已忘却了这事情。这时又提到女学生，她问花狗近来有没有女学生过路，她想看看。

花狗一面把南瓜从棚架边抱到墙角去，告她女学生唱歌的事，这些事的来源还是萧萧的那个祖父。他在萧萧面前说了点大话，说他曾经到官路上见到四个女学生，她们都拿得有旗子，走长路流汗喘气之中仍然唱歌，同军人所唱的一模一样。不消说，这自然完全是胡诌的。可是那故事把萧萧可乐坏了。因为花狗说这个就叫做"自由"。

花狗是"起眼动眉毛，一打两头翘"，会说会笑的一个人。听萧萧带着歆美口气说，"花狗大，你膀子真大。"他就说，"我不止膀子大。"

"你身个子也大。"

"我全身无处不大。"

到萧萧抱了她的丈夫走去以后，同花狗在一起摘瓜，取名字叫哑巴的，开了平时不常开的口，他说：

"花狗，你少坏点。人家是十三岁黄花女，还要等十年才圆房！"

花狗不做声，打了那伙计一巴掌，走到枣树下捡落地枣去了。

到摘瓜的秋天，日子计算起来，萧萧过丈夫家有一年半了。

几次降霜落雪，几次清明谷雨，一家人都说萧萧是大人了。天保佑，喝冷水，吃粗砺饭，四季无疾病，倒发育得这样快。婆婆虽生来像一把剪子，把凡是给萧萧暴长的机会都剪去了，但乡下的日头同空气都帮助人长大，却不是折磨可以阻拦得住。

萧萧十五岁时已高如成人，心却还是一颗糊糊涂涂的心。

人大了一点，家中做的事也多了一点。绩麻、纺车、洗衣、照料丈夫以外，打猪草推磨一些事情也要作，还有浆纱织布。凡事都学，学学就会了。乡下习惯，凡是行有余力的都可从劳作中攒点私房，两三年来仅仅萧萧个人分上所聚集的粗细麻和纺就的棉纱，已够萧萧坐到土机上抛三个月的梭子了。

丈夫早断了奶。婆婆有了新儿子，这五岁儿子就像归萧萧独有了。不论做什么，走到什么地方去，丈夫总跟到身边。丈夫有些方面很怕她，当她如母亲，不敢多事。他们俩实在感情不坏。

地方稍稍进步，祖父的笑话转到"萧萧你也把辫子剪去好自由"那一类事上去了。听着这话的萧萧，某个夏天也看过一次女学生，虽不把祖父笑话认真，可是每一次在祖父说过这笑话以后，她到水边去，必用手捏着辫子末梢，设想没有辫子的人那种神气，那点趣味。

因为打猪草，带丈夫上螺蛳山的山阴是常有的事。

小孩子不知事故，听别人唱歌也唱歌。一唱歌，就把花狗引来了。

花狗对萧萧生了另外一种心，萧萧有点明白了，常常觉得惶恐不安。但花狗是男子，凡是男子的美德恶德都不缺少，劳动力强，手脚勤快，又会玩会说，所以一面使萧萧的丈夫非常欢喜同他玩，一面一有机会即缠在萧萧身边，且总是想方设法把萧萧那点惶恐减去。

山大人小，到处树木蒙茸，平时不知道萧萧所在，花狗就站在高处唱歌逗萧萧身边的丈夫；丈夫小口一开，花狗穿山越岭就来到萧萧面前了。

见了花狗，小孩子只有欢喜，不知其他。他原要花狗为他编草虫玩，做竹箫哨子玩，花狗想方法支使他到一个远处去找材料，便坐到萧萧身边来，要萧萧听他唱那使人开心红脸的歌。她有时觉得害怕，不许丈夫走开；有时又像有了花狗在身边，打发丈夫走去反倒好一点。终于有一天，萧萧就这样给花狗把心窍子唱开，变成个妇人了。

那时节，丈夫走到山下采刺莓去了，花狗唱了许多歌，到后却向萧萧唱：

娇家门前一重坡，
别人走少郎走多，

铁打草鞋穿烂了，

不是为你为哪个？

　　末了却向萧萧说："我为你睡不着觉"。他又说他赌咒不把这事情告给人。听了这些话仍然不懂什么的萧萧，眼睛只注意到他那一对粗粗的手膀子，耳朵只注意到他最后一句话。末了花狗大便又唱歌给她听。她心里乱了。她要他当真对天赌咒，赌了咒，一切好象有了保障，她就一切尽他了。到丈夫返身时，手被毛毛虫螫伤，肿了一大片，走到萧萧身边。萧萧捏紧这一只小手，且用口去呵它，吮它，想起刚才的糊涂，才仿佛明白自己作了一点不大好的糊涂事。

　　花狗诱她做坏事情是麦黄四月，到六月，李子熟了，她欢喜吃生李子。她觉得身体有点特别，在山上碰到花狗，就将这事情告给他，问他怎么办。

　　讨论了多久，花狗全无主意。虽以前自己当天赌得有咒，也仍然无主意。这家伙个子大，胆量小。个子大容易做错事，胆量小做了错事就想不出办法。

　　到后，萧萧捏着自己那条乌梢蛇似的大辫子，想起城里了，她说：

　　"花狗大，我们到城里去自由，帮帮人过日子，不好么？"

　　"那怎么行？到城里去做什么？"

　　"我肚子大了。"

　　"我们找药去。场上有郎中卖药。"

　　"你赶快找药来，我想……"

　　"你想逃到城里去自由，不成的。人生面不熟，讨饭也有规矩，不能随便！"

　　"你这没有良心的，你害了我，我想死！"

　　"我赌咒不辜负你。"

　　"负不负我有什么用？帮我个忙，赶快拿去肚子里这块肉罢。我害怕！"

　　花狗不再做声，过了一会，便走开了。不久丈夫从他处回来，见萧萧一个人坐在草地上哭，眼睛红红的。丈夫心中纳罕，看了一会，问萧萧：

　　"姐姐，为什么哭？"

　　"不为什么，灰尘落到眼睛里，痛。"

　　"我吹吹吧。"

　　"不要吹。"

　　"你瞧我，得这些这些。"

　　他把从溪中捡来的小蚌、小石头陈列在萧萧面前，萧萧泪眼婆婆的看了一会，勉强笑着说，"弟弟，我们要好，我哭你莫告家中。告我可要生气。"到后这事情家中当真就无人知道。

过了半个月，花狗不辞而行，把自己所有的衣裤都拿去了。祖父问同住的长工哑巴，知不知道他为什么走路，走哪儿去。哑巴只是摇头，说花狗还欠了他两百钱，临走时话都不留一句，为人少良心。哑巴说他自己的话，并没有把花狗走的理由说明。因此这一家希奇一整天，谈论一整天。不过这工人既不偷走物件，又不拐带别的，这事过后不久，自然也就把他忘掉了。

萧萧仍然是往日的萧萧。她能够忘记花狗就好了。但是肚子真有些不同了，肚中东西总在动，使她常常一个人干着急，尽做怪梦。

她脾气坏了一点，这坏处只有丈夫知道，因为她对丈夫似乎严厉苛刻了好些。

仍然每天同丈夫在一处，她的心，想到的事自己也不十分明白。她常想，我现在死了，什么都好了。可是为什么要死？她还很高兴活下去，愿意活下去。

家中人不拘谁在无意中提起关于丈夫弟弟的话，提起小孩子，提起花狗，都像使这话如拳头，在萧萧胸口上重重一击。

到九月，她担心人知道更多了，引丈夫庙里去玩，就私自许愿，吃了一大把香灰。吃香灰被她丈夫见到了，丈夫问这是做什么，萧萧就说肚子痛，应当吃这个。虽说求菩萨保佑，菩萨当然没有如她的希望，肚子中的东西仍在慢慢的长大。

她又常往溪里去喝冷水，给丈夫见到了，丈夫问她，她就说口渴。

一切她所想到的方法都没有能够使她与自己不欢喜的东西分开。大肚子只有丈夫一人知道，他却不敢告这件事给父母晓得。因为时间长久，年龄不同，丈夫有些时候对于萧萧的怕同爱，比对于父母还深切。

她还记得花狗赌咒那一天里的事情，如同记着其他事情一样。到秋天，屋前屋后毛毛虫都结茧，成了各种好看的蝶蛾，丈夫像故意折磨她一样，常常提起几个月前被毛毛虫所螫的旧话，使萧萧心里难过。她因此极恨毛毛虫，见了那小虫就想用脚去踹。

有一天，又听人说有好些女学生过路，听过这话的萧萧，睁了眼做过一阵梦，愣愣的对日头出处痴了半天。

萧萧步花狗后尘，也想逃走，收拾一点东西预备跟了女学生走的那条路上城。但没有动身，就被家里人发觉了。

家中追究这逃走的根源，才明白这个十年后预备给小丈夫生儿子继香火的萧萧肚子，已被别人抢先下了种。这真是了不得的一件大事。一家人的平静生活，为这一件事全弄乱了。生气的生气，流泪的流泪，骂人的骂人，各按本分乱下去。悬梁，投水，吃毒药，被禁困的萧萧，诸事漫无边际的全想到了，究竟年纪太小，舍不得死，却不曾做。于是祖父从现实出发，想出了个聪明主意，把萧萧关在房里，派人好好看守着，请萧萧本族的人来说话，看是"沉潭"还是"发卖"？萧萧家中人要面子，就沉潭淹死她，舍不得就发卖。萧萧只有一个伯父，在近处庄子里为人种田，去请他时先还以为是吃酒，到了才知道是这样丢脸事情，弄得这老实忠厚家长手足无措。

大肚子作证，什么也没有可说。伯父不忍把萧萧沉潭，萧萧当然应当嫁人作"二路亲"了。

这处罚好像也极其自然；照习惯受损失的是丈夫家里，然而却可以在改嫁上收回一笔钱，当作赔偿损失的数目。那伯父把这事告给了萧萧，就要走路。萧萧拉着伯父衣角不放，只是幽幽的哭。伯父摇了一会头，一句话不说，仍然走了。

一时没有相当的人家来要萧萧，因此暂时就仍然在丈夫家中住下。这件事情既经说明白，照乡下规矩倒又像不什么要紧，只等待处分，大家反而释然了。先是小丈夫不能再同萧萧在一处，到后又仍然如月前情形，姊弟一般有说有笑的过日子了。

丈夫知道了萧萧肚子中有儿子的事情，又知道因为这样萧萧才应当嫁到远处去。但是丈夫并不愿意萧萧去，萧萧自己也不愿意去，大家全莫名其妙，只是照规矩像逼到要这样做，不得不做。

在等候主顾来看人，等到十二月，还没有人来，萧萧只好在这人家过年。

萧萧次年二月间，十月满足，坐草生了一个儿子，团头大眼，声响洪壮，大家把母子二人照料得好好的，照规矩吃蒸鸡同江米酒补血，烧纸谢神。一家人都欢喜那儿子。

生下的既是儿子，萧萧不嫁别处了。

到萧萧正式同丈夫拜堂圆房时，儿子已经年纪十岁，能看牛割草，成为家中生产者一员了。平时喊萧萧丈夫做大叔，大叔也答应，从不生气。

这儿子名叫牛儿。牛儿十二岁时也接了亲，媳妇年长六岁。媳妇年纪大，才能诸事作帮手，对家中有帮助。唢呐吹到门前时，新娘在轿中呜呜的哭着，忙坏了那个祖父、曾祖父。

这一天，萧萧刚坐月子不久，孩子才满三月，抱了自己新生的毛毛，在屋前榆蜡树篱笆间看热闹，同十年前抱丈夫一个样子。

一九二九年

## 2. Sealed Off

Zhang Ailing

The tramcar driver drove his tram. The tramcar tracks, in the blazing sun, shimmered like two shiny eels crawling out of the water; they stretched and shrank stretched and shrank, on their onward way—soft and slippery, long old eels, never ending never ending... the driver fixed his eyes on the undulating tracks, and didn't go mad.

If there hadn't been an air raid, if the city hadn't been sealed, the tramcar would have gone on forever. The city was sealed. The alarm-bell rang. Ding-ding-ding-ding. Every "ding" was a cold little dot, the dots all adding up to a dotted line, cutting across time and space.

The tramcar ground to a halt, but the people on the street ran: those on the left side of the street ran over to the right, and those on the right ran over to the left. All the shops, in a single sweep, rattled down their metal gates. Matrons tugged madly at the railings. "Let us in for just a while," they cried. "We have children here, and

张爱玲

中国文学选读

old people!" But the gates stayed tightly shut. Those inside the metal gates and those outside the metal gates stood glaring at each other, fearing one another.

Inside the tram, people were fairly quiet. They had somewhere to sit and though the place was rather plain, it still was better, for most of them, than what they had at home. Gradually, the street also grew quiet: not that it was a complete silence, but the sound of voices eased into a confused blur, like the soft rustle of a straw-stuffed pillow, heard in a dream. The huge, shambling city sat dozing in the sun, its head resting heavily on people's shoulders, its spittle slowly dripping down their shirts, an inconceivably enormous weight pressing down on every one. Never before, it seemed, had Shanghai been this quiet—and in the middle of the day! A beggar, taking advantage of the breathless, birdless quiet, lifted up his voice and began to chant: "Good master, good lady, kind sir, kind ma'am, won't you give alms to this poor man? Good master, good lady... " But after a short while he stopped, scared silent by the eerie quiet.

Then there was a braver beggar, a man from Shandong, who firmly broke the silence. His voice was round and resonant: "Sad, sad, sad! No money do I have!" An old, old song, sung from one century to the next. The tram driver, who also was from Shandong, succumbed to the sonorous tune. Heaving a long sigh, he folded his arms across his chest, leaned against the tram door, and joined in: "Sad, sad, sad! No money do I have!"

Some of the tram passengers got out. But there was still a little loose scattered chatter; near the door, a group of office workers was discussing something. One of them, with a quick, ripping sound, shook his fan open and offered his conclusion: "Well, in the end, there's nothing wrong with him—it's just that he doesn't know how to act. " From another nose came a short grunt, followed by a cold smile: "Doesn't know how to act? He sure knows how to toady up to the bosses!"

A middle-aged couple who looked very much like brother and sister stood together in the middle of the tram, holding onto the leather straps "Careful!" the woman suddenly yelped. "Don't get your trousers dirty!" The man flinched, then slowly raised the hand from which a packet of smoked fish dangled. Very cautiously, very gingerly, he held the paper packet, which was brimming with oil, several inches away from his suit pants. His wife did not let up. "Do you know what dry-cleaning costs these days? Or what it costs to get a pair of trousers made?"

Lu Zongzhen, accountant for Huamao Bank, was sitting in the corner. When he saw the smoked fish, he was reminded of the steamed dumplings stuffed with spinach that his wife had asked him to buy at a noodle stand near the bank. Women are always like that. Dumplings bought in the hardest-to-find, most twisty-windy little alleys had to be the best, no matter what She didn't for a moment think of how it would be for him—neatly dressed in suit and tie with tortoiseshell eyeglasses and a leather briefcase, then, tucked under his arm these steaming hot dumplings wrapped in newspaper—how ludicrous! Still, if the city were sealed for a long time, so that his dinner was delayed, then he could at least make do with the dumplings.

He glanced at his watch; only four-thirty. Must be the power of suggestion. He felt hungry already. Carefully pulling back a corner of the paper he took a look inside. Snowy white mounds, breathing soft little whiffs of sesame oil . A piece of newspaper had stuck to the dumplings, and he gravely peeled it off; the ink was printed on the dumplings, with all the writing in reverse, as though it were reflected in a mirror. He peered down and slowly picked the words out: "Obituaries... Positions Wanted... Stock Market Developments... Now Playing... " Normal, useful phrases, but they did look a bit odd on a dumpling. Maybe because eating is such serious business; compared to it, everything else is just a joke. Lu Zongzhen thought it looked funny, but he didn't laugh: he was a very straightforward kind of fellow. After reading the dumplings, he read the newspaper, but when he'd finished half a page of old news, he found that if he turned the page all the dumplings would fall out, and so he had to stop.

While Lu read the paper, others in the tram did likewise. People who had newspapers read them; those without newspapers read receipts, or lists of rules and regulations, or business cards. People who were stuck without a single scrap of printed matter read shop signs along the street. They simply had to fill this terrifying emptiness—otherwise, their brains might start to work. Thinking is a painful business.

Sitting across from Lu Zongzhen was an old man who, with a dull clacking sound, rolled two slippery, glossy walnuts in his palm: a rhythmic little gesture can substitute for thought. The old man had a clean-shaven pate, a reddish yellow complexion, and an oily sheen on his face. When his brows were furrowed, his head looked like a walnut. The thoughts inside were walnut-flavored: smooth and sweet, but in the end, empty-tasting.

To the old man's right sat Wu Cuiyuan, who looked like one of those young Christian wives, though she was still unmarried. Her Chinese gown of white cotton was trimmed with a narrow blue border—the navy blue around the white reminded one of the black borders around an obituary—and she carried a little blue-and-white checked parasol. Her hairstyle was utterly banal, so as not to attract attention. Actually, she hadn't much reason to fear. She wasn't bad-looking, but hers was an uncertain, unfocused beauty, an afraid-she-had-offended-someone kind of beauty. Her face was bland, slack, lacking definition. Even her own mother couldn't say for certain whether her face was long or round.

At home she was a good daughter, at school she was a good student. After graduating from college, Cuiyuan had become an English instructor at her alma mater. Now, stuck in the air raid, she decided to grade a few papers while she waited. The first one was written by a male student. It railed against the evils of the big city, full of righteous anger, the prose stiff, choppy, ungrammatical. "Painted prostitutes... cruising the Cosmo... low-class bars and dancing-halls." Cuiyuan paused for a moment, then pulled out her red pencil and gave the paper an "A." Ordinarily, she would have gone right on to the next one, but now, because she had too much time to think, she couldn't help wondering why she had given this student such a high mark. If she hadn't asked herself this question, she could have ignored the whole matter, but once she did ask, her face suffused with red. Suddenly, she understood: it was because this student was the only man who fearlessly and forthrightly said such things to her.

He treated her like an intelligent, sophisticated person; as if she were a man, someone who really understood. He respected her. Cuiyuan always felt that no one at school respected her—from the president on down to the professors, the students, even the janitors. The students' grumbling was especially hard to take: "This place is really falling apart. Getting worse every day. It's bad enough having to learn English from a Chinese, but then to learn it from a Chinese who's never gone abroad…" Cuiyuan took abuse at school, took abuse at home. The Wu household was a modern, model household, devout and serious. The family had pushed their daughter to study hard, to climb upwards step by step, right to the tip-top… A girl in her twenties teaching at a university! It set a record for women's professional achievement. But her parents' enthusiasm began to wear thin and now they wished she hadn't been quite so serious, wished she'd taken more time out from her studies, tried to find herself a rich husband.

She was a good daughter, a good student. All the people in her family were good people; they took baths every day and read the newspaper; when they listened to the wireless, they never tuned into local folk-opera, comic opera, that sort of thing, but listened only to the symphonies of Beethoven and Wagner; they didn't understand what they were listening to, but still they listened. In this world, there are more good people than real people… Cuiyuan wasn't very happy.

Life was like the Bible, translated from Hebrew into Greek, from Greek into Latin, from Latin into English, from English into Chinese. When Cuiyuan read it, she translated the standard Chinese into Shanghainese. Gaps were unavoidable.

She put the student's essay down and buried her chin in her hands. The sun burned down on her backbone.

Next to her sat a nanny with a small child lying on her lap. The sole of the child's foot pushed against Cuiyuan's leg. Little red shoes, decorated with tigers, on a soft but tough little foot… this at least was real.

A medical student who was also on the tram took out a sketchpad and carefully added the last touches to a diagram of the human skeleton. The other passengers thought he was sketching a portrait of the man who sat dozing across from him. Nothing else was going on, so they started sauntering over, crowding into little clumps of three or four, leaning on each other with their hands behind their backs, gathering around to watch the man sketch from life. The husband who dangled smoked fish from his fingers whispered to his wife: "I can't get used to this cubism, this impressionism, which is so popular these days." "Your pants," she hissed.

The medical student meticulously wrote in the names of every bone, muscle,

中国文学选读

nerve, and tendon. An office worker hid half his face behind a fan and quietly in-
formed his colleague: "The influence of Chinese painting. Nowadays, writing words
in is all the rage in Western painting. Clearly a case of 'Eastern ways spreading
Westward.'"

Lu Zongzhen didn't join the crowd, but stayed in his seat. He had decided he
was hungry. With everyone gone, he could comfortably munch his spinach-stuffed
dumplings. But then he looked up and caught a glimpse, in the third-class car, of a
relative, his wife's cousin's son. He detested that Dong Peizhi was a man of humble
origins who harbored a great ambition: he sought a fiancée of comfortable means, to
serve as a foothold for his climb upwards. Lu Zongzhen's eldest daughter had just
turned twelve but already she had caught Peizhi's eye; having made, in his own
mind, a pleasing calculation, Peizhi's manner grew ever softer, ever more cunning.

As soon as Lu Zongzhen caught sight of this young man, he was filled with quiet
alarm, fearing that if he were seen, Peizhi would take advantage of the opportunity to
press forward with his attack. The idea of being stuck in the same car with Dong
Peizhi while the city was sealed off was too horrible to contemplate! Lu quickly closed
his briefcase and wrapped up his dumplings, then fled, in a great rush, to a seat
across the aisle. Now, thank God, he was screened by Wu Cuiyuan, who occupied
the seat next to him, and his nephew could not possibly see him.

Cuiyuan turned and gave him a quick look. Oh no! The woman surely thought he
was up to no good, changing seats for no reason like that. He recognized the look of
a woman being flirted with—she held her face absolutely motionless, no hint of a
smile anywhere in her eyes, her mouth, not even in the little hollows beside her
nose; yet from some unknown place there was the trembling of a little smile that
could break out at any moment. If you think you're simply too adorable, you can't
keep from smiling.

Damn! Dong Peizhi had seen him after all, and was coming toward the first-class
car, very humble, bowing even at a distance, with his long jowls, shiny red cheeks,
and long, gray, monk like gown—a clean, cautious young man, hardworking no matter what the hardship, the very epitome of a good son-in-law. Thinking fast, Zongzhen decided to follow Peizhi's lead and try a bit of artful nonchalance. So he

stretched one arm out across the windowsill that ran behind Cuiyuan, soundlessly announcing flirtatious intent. This would not, he knew, scare Peizhi into immediate retreat, because in Peizhi's eyes he already was a dirty old man. The way Peizhi saw it, anyone over thirty was old, and all the old were vile. Having seen his uncle's disgraceful behavior, the young man would feel compelled to tell his wife every little detail—well, angering his wife was just fine with him. Who told her to give him such a nephew, anyway? If she was angry, it served her right.

He didn't care much for this woman sitting next to him. Her arms were fair, all right, but were like squeezed-out toothpaste. Her whole body was like squeezed-out toothpaste, it had no shape.

"When will this air raid ever end?" he said in a low, smiling voice. "It's awful!"

Shocked, Cuiyuan turned her head, only to see that his arm was stretched out behind her. She froze. But come what may, Zongzhen could not let himself pull his arm back. His nephew stood just across the way, watching him with brilliant, glowing eyes, the hint of an understanding smile on his face. If, in the middle of everything, he turned and looked his nephew in the eye, maybe the little no-account would get scared, would lower his eyes, flustered and embarrassed like a sweet young thing; then again, maybe Peizhi would keep staring at him—who could tell?

He gritted his teeth and renewed the attack. "Aren't you bored? We could talk a bit, that can't hurt. Let's... let's talk." He couldn't control himself, his voice was plaintive.

Again Cuiyuan was socked. She turned to look at him. Now he remembered, he had seen her get on the tram—a striking image, but an image concocted by chance, not by any intention of hers. "You know, I saw you get on the tram," he said softly. "Near the front of the car. There's a torn advertisement, and I saw your profile, just a bit of your chin, through the torn spot." It was an ad for Lacova powdered milk that showed a pudgy little child. Beneath the child's ear this woman's chin had suddenly appeared; it was a little spooky, when you thought about it. "Then you looked down to get some change out of your purse, and I saw your eyes, then your brows, then your hair." When you took her features separately, looked at them one by one, you had to admit she had a certain charm.

Cayman smiled. You wouldn't guess that this man could talk so sweetly—you'd think he was the stereotypical respectable businessman. She looked at him again. Under the tip of his nose the cartilage was reddened by the sunlight. Stretching out from his sleeve, and resting on the newspaper, was a warm, tanned hand, one with feeling—a real person! Not too honest, not too bright, but a real person. Suddenly she felt flushed and happy; she turn away with a murmur. "Don't talk like that. "

"What?" Zongzhen had already forgotten what he'd said. His eyes were fixed on his nephew's back—the diplomatic young man had decided that three's a crowd, and he didn't want to offend his uncle. They would meet again, anyway, since theirs was a close family, and no knife was sharp enough to sever the ties; and so he returned to the third-class car. Once Peizhi was gone, Zongzhen withdrew his arm; his manner turned respectable. Casting about for a way to make conversation, he glanced at the notebook spread out on her lap. "Shenguang University,'he read aloud. ' Are you a student there?"

Did he think she was that young? That she was still a student? She laughed, without answering.

"I graduated from Huaqi. " He repeated the name. "Huaqi. " On her neck was a tiny dark mole, like the imprint of a fingernail. Zongzhen absentmindedly rubbed the fingers of his right hand across the nails of his left. He coughed slightly, then continued:"What department are you in?"

Cuiyuan saw that he had moved his arm and thought that her stand-offish manner had wrought this change. She therefore felt she could not refuse to answer. "Literature. And you?"

"Business. " Suddenly he felt that their conversation had grown stuffy. "In school I was busy with student activities. Now that I'm out, I'm busy earning a living. So I've never really studied much of anything. "

"Is your office very busy?"

"Terribly. In the morning I go to work and in the evening I go home, but I It's know why I do either. I'm not the least bit interested in my job. Sure, it's a way to earn money, but I It's know who I'm earning it for. "

"Everyone has family to think of. "

"Oh, you don't know... my family... "A short cough. "We'd better not talk a-bout it. "

"Here it comes," thought Cuiyuan. "His wife doesn't understand him. Every married man in the world seems desperately in need of another woman's understanding. "

Zongzhen hesitated, then swallowed hard and forced the words out: "My wife—she doesn't understand me at all. "

Cuiyuan knitted her brow and looked at him, expressing complete sympathy.

"I really It's understand why I go home every evening. Where is there to go? I have no home, in fact. " He removed his glasses, held them up to the light, and wiped the spots off with a handkerchief. Another little cough. "Just keep going, keep getting by, without thinking—above all, It's start thinking'" Cuiyuan always felt that when nearsighted people took their glasses off in front of other people it was a little obscene; improper, somehow, like taking your clothes off in public. Zongzhen continued: "You, you It's know what kind of woman she is. "

"Then why did you... in the first place?"

"Even then I was against it. My mother arranged the marriage. Of course I wanted to choose for myself, but... she used to be very beautiful... I was very young ... young people, you know... " Cuiyuan nodded her head.

"Then she changed into this kind of person—even my mother fights with her, and she blames me for having married her! She has such a temper—she hasn't even got a grade-school education. "

Cuiyuan couldn't help saying, with a tiny smile, "You seem to take diplomas very seriously. Actually, even if a woman's educated it's all the same. " She didn't know why she said this, wounding her own heart.

"Of course, you can laugh, because you're well-educated. You It's know what kind of—" He stopped, breathing hard, and took off the glasses he had just put back on.

"Getting a little carried away?" said Cuiyuan.

Zongzhen gripped his glasses tightly, made a painful gesture with his hands. "You It's know what kind of—"

"I know, I know," Cuiyuan said hurriedly. She knew that if he and his wife didn't get along, the fault could not lie entirely with her. He too was a person of simple intellect. He just wanted a woman who would comfort and forgive him.

The street erupted in noise, as two trucks full of soldiers rumbled by. Cuiyuan and Zongzhen stuck their heads out to see what was going on; to their surprise, their faces came very close together. At close range anyone's face is somehow different, is tension-charged like a close-up on the movie screen. Zongzhen and Cuiyuan suddenly felt they were seeing each other for the first time. To his eyes, her face was the spare, simple peony of a water color sketch, and the strands of hair fluttering at her temples were pistils ruffled by a breeze.

He looked at her, and she blushed. When she let him see her blush, he grew visibly happy. Then she blushed even more deeply.

Zongzhen had never thought he could make a woman blush, make her smile, make her hang her head shyly. In this he was a man. Ordinarily, he was an accountant, a father, the head of a household, a tram passenger, a store customer, an insignificant citizen of a big city. But to this woman, this woman who didn't know anything about his life, he was only and entirely a man.

They were in love. He told her all kinds of things: who was on his side at the bank and who secretly opposed him; how his family squabbled; his secret sorrows; his schoolboy dreams... unending talk, but she was not put off. Men in love have always liked to talk; women in love, on the other hand, It's want to talk, because they know, without even knowing that they know, that once a man really understands a woman he'll stop loving her.

Zongzhen was sure that Cuiyuan was a lovely woman—pale, wispy, warm, like the breath your mouth exhales in winter. You It's want her, and she quietly drifts away. Being part of you, she understands everything, forgives everything. You tell the truth, and her heart aches for you; you tell a lie, and she smiles as if to say, "Go on with you—what are you saying?"

Zongzhen was quiet for a moment, then said, "I'm thinking of marrying again."

Cuiyuan assumed an air of shocked surprise. "You want a divorce? Well... that isn't possible, is it?"

"I can't get a divorce. I have to think of the children's well-being. My oldest daughter is twelve, just passed the entrance exams for middle school, her grades are quite good."

"What," thought Cuiyuan, "what does this have to do with what you just said?" "Oh," she said aloud, her voice cold, "you plan to take a concubine."

"I plan to treat her like a wife," said Zongzhen. "I—I can make things nice for her. I wouldn't do anything to upset her."

"But," said Cuiyuan, "a girl from a good family won't agree to that, will she? So many legal difficulties..."

Zongzhen sighed. "Yes, you're right. I can't do it. Shouldn't have mentioned it. .. I'm too old. Thirty-four already."

"Actually," Cuiyuan spoke very slowly, "these days, that isn't considered very old."

Zongzhen was still. Finally he asked, "How old are you?"

Cuiyuan ducked her head. "Twenty-four."

Zongzhen waited awhile, then asked, "Are you a free woman?"

Cuiyuan didn't answer. "You aren't free," said Zongzhen. "But even if you a-greed, your family wouldn't, right?"

Cuiyuan pursed her lips. Her family—her prim and proper family—how she hated them all. They had cheated her long enough. They wanted her to find them a wealthy son-in-law. Well, Zongzhen didn't have money but he did have a wife—that would make them good and angry! It would serve them right!

Little by little, people started getting back on the tram. Perhaps it was rumored out there that "traffic will soon return to normal." The passengers got on and sat down, pressing against Zongzhen and Cuiyuan, forcing them a little closer, then a little closer again.

Zongzhen and Cuiyuan wondered how they could have been so foolish not to have thought of sitting closer before. Zongzhen struggled against his happiness. He turned to her and said, in a voice full of pain, "No, this won't do! I can't let you sacrifice your future! You're a fine person, with such a good education... I have much money, and I want to ruin your life!"

Well, of course, it was money again. What he said was true. "It's over."
thought Cuiyuan. In the end she'd probably marry, but her husband would never be
as dear as this stranger met by chance—this man on the tram in the middle of a
sealed-off city... it could never be this spontaneous again. Never again... oh, this
man, he was so stupid! So very stupid! All she wanted was one small part of him,
one little part that no one else could want. He was throwing away his own happiness.
Such an idiotic waste! She wept, but it wasn't a gentle, maidenly weeping. She practically spit her tears into his face He was a good person—the world had gained one
more good person!

What use would it be to explain things to him? If a woman needs to turn to
words to move a man's heart, she is a sad case.

Once Zongzhen got anxious, he couldn't get any words out, and just kept shaking the umbrella she was holding. She ignored him. Then he tugged at her hand.
"Hey, there are people here, you know! Don't! Don't get so upset! Wait a bit, and
we'll talk it over on the telephone. Give me your number."

Cuiyuan didn't answer. He pressed her. "You have to give me your phone number."

"Seven-five-three-six-nine." Cuiyuan spoke as fast as she could.

"Seven-five-three-six-nine?"

No response. "Seven-five-three-six-nine, seven-five..." Mumbling the number
over and over, Zongzhen searched his pockets for a pen, but the more frantic he became, the harder it was to find one. Cuiyuan had a red pencil in her bag, but she pur-
posely did not take it out. He ought to remember her telephone number; if he didn't,
then he didn't love her, and there was no point in continuing the conversation.

The city started up again. "Ding-ding-ding-ding." Every "ding" a cold little dot,
which added up to a line that cut across time and space.

A wave of cheers swept across the metropolis. The tram started clanking its way
forward. Zongzhen stood up, pushed into the crowd, and disappeared. Cuiyuan
turned her head away, as if she didn't care. He was gone. To her, it was as if he
were dead.

The tram picked up speed. On the evening street, a tofu-seller had set his shoulder-pole down and was holding up a rattle; eyes shut, he shook it back and forth. A big-boned blonde woman, straw hat slung across her back, bantered with an Italian sailor. All her teeth showed when she grinned. When Cuiyuan looked at these people, they lived for that one moment. Then the tram clanked onward, and one by one they died away.

Cuiyuan shut her eyes fretfully. If he phoned her, she wouldn't be able to control her voice; it would be filled with emotion, for he was a man who had died, then returned to life.

The lights inside the tram went on; she opened her eyes and saw him sitting in his old seat, looking remote. She trembled with shock—he hadn't gotten off the tram, after all! Then she understood his meaning: everything that had happened while the city was sealed was a non-occurrence. The whole of Shanghai had dozed off, had dreamed an unreasonable dream.

The tramcar driver raised his voice in song: "Sad, sad, and sad! No money do I have! Sad, sad, sad—" An old beggar, thoroughly dazed, limped across the street in front of the tram. The driver bellowed at her. "You swine!"

1943

(translated by Karen Kingsbury)

## 封　锁

### 张爱玲

开电车的人开电车。在大太阳底下，电车轨道像两条光莹莹的，水里钻出来的曲蟮，抽长了，又缩短了；抽长了，又缩短了，就这么样往前移——柔滑的，老长老长的曲蟮，没有完，没有完……开电车的人眼睛钉住了这两条蠕蠕的车轨，然而他不发疯。

如果不碰到封锁，电车的进行是永远不会断的。封锁了。摇铃了。"叮玲玲玲玲玲，"每一个"玲"字是冷冷的一小点，一点一点连成了一条虚线，切断了时间与空间。

电车停了，马路上的人却开始奔跑，在街的左面的人们奔到街的右面，在右面的人们奔到左面。商店一律的沙啦啦拉上铁门。女太太们发狂一般扯动铁栅栏，叫道："让我们进来一会儿！我这儿有孩子哪，有年纪大的人！"然而门还是关得紧腾腾的。铁门里的人和铁门外的人眼睁睁对看着，互相惧怕着。

电车里的人相当镇静。他们有座位可坐，虽然设备简陋一点，和多数乘客的家里的情形比较起来，还是略胜一筹。街上渐渐的也安静下来，并不是绝对的寂静，但是人声逐渐渺茫，像睡梦里所听到的芦花枕头里的窸窣声。这庞大的城市在阳光里盹着了，重重的把头搁在人们的肩上，口涎顺着人们的衣服缓缓流下去，不能想像的巨大的重量压住了每一个人。上海似乎从来没有这么静过——大白天里！一个乞丐趁着鸦雀无声的时候，提高了喉咙唱将起来："阿有老爷太太先生小姐做做好事救救我可怜人哇？阿有老爷太太……"然而他不久就停了下来，被这不经见的沉寂吓噤住了。

还有一个较有勇气的山东乞丐，毅然打破了这静默。他的嗓子浑圆嘹亮："可怜啊可怜！一个人啊没钱！"悠久的歌，从一个世纪唱到下一个世纪。音乐性的节奏传染上了开电车的，开电车的也是山东人。他长长的叹了一口气，抱着胳膊，向车门上一靠，跟着唱了起来："可怜啊可怜！一个人啊没钱！"

电车里，一部份的乘客下去了。剩下的一群中，零零落落也有人说句把话。靠近门口的几个公事房里回来的人继续谈讲下去。一个人撒喇一声抖开了扇子，下了结论道："总而言之，他别的毛病没有，就吃亏在不会做人。"另一个鼻子里哼了一声，冷笑道："说他不会做人，他对上头敷衍得挺好的呢！"

一对长得颇像兄妹的中年夫妇把手吊在皮圈上，双双站在电车的正中。她突然叫道："当心别把裤子弄脏了！"他吃了一惊，抬起他的手，手里拈着一包熏鱼。他小心翼翼使那油汪汪的纸口袋与他的西装裤子维持二寸远的距离。他太太兀自絮叨道："现在干洗是什么价钱？做一条裤子是什么价钱？"

坐在角落里的吕宗桢，华茂银行的会计师，看见了那熏鱼，就联想到他夫人托他在银行附近一家面食摊子上买的菠菜包子。女人就是这样！弯弯扭扭最难找的小胡同里买来的包子必定是价廉物美的！她一点也不为他着想——一个齐齐整整穿着西装戴着玳瑁边眼镜提着公事皮包的人，抱着报纸里的热腾腾的包子满街跑，实在是不像话！然而无论如何，假使这封锁延长下去，耽误了他的晚饭，至少这包子可以派用场。他看了看手表，才四点半。该是心理作用罢？他已经觉得饿了。他轻轻揭开报纸的一角，向里面张了一张。一个个雪白的，喷出淡淡的麻油气味。一部份的报纸黏住了包子，他谨慎地把报纸撕了下来，包子上印了铅字，字都是反的，像镜子里映出来的，然而他有这耐心，低下头去逐个认了出来："讣告……申请……华股动态……隆重登场候教……"都是得用的字眼儿，不知道为什么转载到包子上，就带点开玩笑性质。也许因为"吃"是太严重的一件事了，相形之下，其他的一切都成了笑话。吕宗桢看着也觉得不顺眼，可是他并没有笑，他是一个老实人。他从包子上的文章看到报纸上的文章，把半页旧报纸读完了，若是翻过来看，包子就得跌出来，只得罢了。他在这里看报，全车的人都学了样，有报的看报，没有报的看发票，看章程，看名片。任何印刷物都没有的人，就看街上的市招。他们不能不填满这可怕的空虚——不然，他们的脑子也许会活动起来。思想是痛苦的一件事。

只有吕宗桢对面坐着一个老头子，手心里骨碌碌骨碌碌搓着两只油光水滑的核桃，有板有眼的小动作代替了思想。他剃着光头，红黄皮色，满脸浮油。打着皱，整个的头像一个核桃。他的脑子就像核桃仁，甜的，滋润的，可是没有多大意思。

老头子右首坐着吴翠远，看上去像是一个教会派的少奶奶，但是还没有结婚。她穿着一件白洋纱旗袍，滚一道窄窄的蓝边——深蓝与白，很有点讣闻的风味。她携着一把蓝白格子小遮阳伞。头发梳成千篇一律的式样，惟恐唤起公众的注意。然而她实在没有过分触目的危险。她长得不难看，可是她那种美是一种模棱两可的，仿佛怕得罪了谁的美，脸上一切都是淡淡的，松弛的，没有轮廓。连她自己的母亲也形容不出她是长脸还是圆脸。

在家里她是一个好女儿，在学校里她是一个好学生。大学毕了业后，翠远就在母校服务，担任英文助教。她现在打算利用封锁的时间改改卷子。翻开了第一篇，是一个男生作的，大声疾呼抨击都市的罪恶，充满了正义感的愤怒，用不很合文法的，吃吃艾艾的句子，骂着："红嘴唇的卖淫妇……大世界……下等舞场与酒吧间。"翠远略略沉吟了一会，就找出红铅笔来批了一个"A"字。若在平时，批了也就批了，可是今天她有太多的考虑的时间，她不由得要质问自己，为什么她给了他这么好的分数？不问倒也罢了，一问，她竟胀红了脸。她突然明白了：因为这学生是胆敢这么毫无顾忌地对她说这些话的唯一的一个男子。

他拿她当作一个见多识广的人看待；他拿她当作一个男人，一个心腹。他看得起她。翠远在学校里老是觉得谁都看不起她——从校长起，教授、学生、校役……学生们尤其愤慨得厉害："申大越来越糟了！一天不如一天！用中国人教英文，照说，已经是不应当，何况是没有出过洋的中国人！"翠远在学校里受气，在家里也受气。吴家是一个新式的，带着宗教背景的模范家庭。家里竭力鼓励女儿用功读书，一步一步往上爬，爬到了顶儿尖儿上——一个二十几岁的女孩子在大学里教书！打破了女子职业的新纪录。然而家长渐渐对她失掉了兴趣，宁愿她当初在书本上马虎一点，匀出点时间来找一个有钱的女婿。

她是一个好女儿，好学生。她家里都是好人，天天洗澡，看报，听无线电向来不听申曲滑稽京戏什么的，而专听贝多芬、瓦格涅的交响乐，听不懂也要听。世界上的好人比真人多……翠远不快乐。

生命像圣经，从希伯来文译成希腊文，从希腊文译成拉丁文，从拉丁文译成英文，从英文译成国语。翠远读它的时候，国语又在她脑子里译成了上海话。那未免有点隔膜。

翠远搁下了那本卷子，双手捧着脸。太阳滚热的晒在她背脊上。

隔壁坐着个奶妈，怀里躺着小孩，孩子的脚底心紧紧抵在翠远的腿上。小小的老虎头红鞋包着柔软而坚硬的脚……这至少是真的。

电车里，一个医科学生拿出一本图画簿，孜孜修改一张人体骨骼的简图。其他的乘客以为他在那里速写他对面眈着的那个人。大家闲着没事干，一个一个聚拢来，三三两两，撑着腰，背着手，围绕着他，看他写生。拈着熏鱼的丈夫向他妻子低声道："我就看不惯现在兴的这种立体派，印象派！"他妻子附耳道："你的裤子！"

那医科学生细细填写每一根骨头、神经、筋络的名字。有一个公事房里回来的人将折扇半掩着脸，悄悄向他的同事解释道："中国画的影响。现在的西洋画也时行题字了，倒真是'东风西渐'！"

吕宗桢没凑热闹，孤零零的坐在原处。他决定他是饿了。大家都走开了，他正好从容地吃他的菠菜包子。偏偏他一抬头，瞥见了三等车厢里有他一个亲戚，是他太太的姨表妹的儿子。他恨透了这董培芝。培芝是一个胸怀大志的清寒子弟，一心只想娶个略具资产的小姐，作为上进的基础。吕宗桢的大女儿今年方才十三岁，已经被培芝看在眼里，心里打着如意算盘，脚步儿越发走得勤了。吕宗桢一眼望见了这年轻人，暗暗叫声不好，只怕培芝看见了他，要利用这绝好的机会向他进攻。若是在封锁期间和这董培芝困在一间屋子里，这情形一定是不堪设想！他匆匆收拾起公事皮包和包子，一阵风奔到对面一排座位上，坐了下来。现在他恰巧被隔壁的吴翠远挡住了，他表侄绝对不能够看见他。翠远回过头来，微微瞪了他一眼。糟了！这女人准是以为他无缘无故换了一个座位，不怀好意。他认得出那被调戏的女人的脸谱——脸板得纹丝不动，眼睛里没有笑意，嘴角也没有笑意，连鼻洼里都没有笑意，然而不知道什么地方有一点颤巍巍的微笑，随时可以散布开来。觉得自己是太可爱了的人，是煞不住要笑的。

　　该死，董培芝毕竟看见了他，向头等车厢走过来了，谦卑地，老远的就躬着腰，红喷喷的长长的面颊，含有僧尼气息的灰布长衫——一个吃苦耐劳，守身如玉的青年，最合理想的乘龙快婿。宗桢迅疾地决定将计就计，顺手推舟，伸出一只手臂来搁在翠远背后的窗台上，不声不响宣布了他的调情的计划。他知道他这么一来，并不能吓退了董培芝，因为培芝眼中的他素来是一个无恶不作的老年人。由培芝看来，过了三十岁的人都是老年人，老年人都是一肚子的坏。培芝今天亲眼看见他这样下流，少不得一五一十去报告给他太太听——气气他太太也好！谁叫她给他弄上这么一个表侄！气，活该气！

　　他不怎么喜欢身边这女人。她的手臂，白倒是白的，像挤出来的牙膏。她的整个的人像挤出来的牙膏，没有款式。

　　他向她低声笑道："这封锁，几时完哪？真讨厌！"翠远吃了一惊，掉过头来，看见了他搁在她身后的那只胳膊，整个身子就僵了一僵。宗桢无论如何不能容许他自己抽回那只胳膊。他的表侄正在那里双眼灼灼望着他，脸上带着点会心的微笑。如果他夹忙里跟他表侄对一对眼光，也许那小子会怯怯地低下头去——处女风的窘态；也许那小子会向他挤一挤眼睛——谁知道？

　　他咬一咬牙，重新向翠远进攻。他道："你也觉着闷罢？我们说两句话，总没有什么要紧！我们——我们谈谈！"他不由自主的，声音里带着哀恳的调子。翠远重新吃了一惊，又掉回头来看了他一眼。他现在记得了，他瞧见她上车的——非常戏剧化的一刹那，但是那戏剧效果是碰巧得到的呢，并不能归功于她。他低声道："你知道么？我看见你上车，车前头的玻璃上贴的广告，撕破了一块，从这破的地方我看见你的侧面，就只一点下巴。"是乃络维奶粉的广告，画着一个胖孩子，孩子的耳朵底下突然出现了这女人的下巴，仔细想起来是有点吓人的。"后来你低下头去从皮包里拿钱，我才看见你的眼睛、眉毛、头发。"拆开来一部份一部份的看，她未尝没有她的一种风韵。

　　翠远笑了，看不出这人倒也会花言巧语——以为他是个靠得住的生意人模样！她又看了他一眼。太阳红红地晒穿他鼻尖下的软骨。他搁在报纸上的那只手，从袖口里伸出来，黄色的，敏感的——一个真的人！不很诚实，也不很聪明，但是一个真的人！她突然觉得炽热、快乐，她背过脸去，细声道："这种话，少说些罢！"

　　宗桢道："嗯？"他早忘了他说了些什么。他眼睛钉着他表侄的背影——那知趣的青年觉得他在这儿是多余的，他不愿得罪了表叔，以后他们还要见面呢，大家都是快刀斩不断的好亲戚；他竟退回三等车厢去了。董培芝一走，宗桢立刻将他的手臂收回，谈吐也正经起来。他搭讪着望了一望她膝上摊着的练习簿，道："申光大学……您在申光读书？"

他以为她这么年轻？她还是一个学生？她笑了，没作声。

宗桢道："我是华济毕业的。华济。"她颈子上有一粒小小的棕色的痣，像指甲刻的印子。宗桢下意识地用右手捻了一捻左手的指甲，咳嗽了一声，接下去问道："您读的是哪一科？"

翠远注意到他的手臂不在那儿了，以为他态度的转变是由于她端凝的人格潜移默化所致。这么一想，倒不能不答话了，便道："文科。你呢？"宗桢道："商科。"他忽然觉得他们的对话，道学气太浓了一点，便道："当初在学校里的时候，忙着运动。出了学校，又忙着混饭吃。书，简直没念多少！"翠远道："你公事忙么？"宗桢道："忙得没头没脑。早上乘车上公事房去，下午又乘车回来，也不知道为什么去，为什么来！我对于我的工作一点也不感到兴趣。说是为了挣钱罢，也不知道是为谁挣的！"翠远道："谁都有点家累。"宗桢道："你不知道——我家里——咳，别提了！"翠远暗道："来了！他太太一点都不同情他！世上有了太太的男人，似乎都是急切需要别的女人的同情。"宗桢迟疑了一会，方才吞吞吐吐，万分为难地说道："我太太——一点都不同情我。"

翠远皱着眉毛望着他，表示充分了解。宗桢道："我简直不懂我为什么天天到了时候就回家去。回哪儿去？实际上我是无家可归的。"他褪下眼镜来，迎着亮，用手绢子拭去上面的水渍，道："咳，混着也就混下去了，不能想——就是不能想！"近视眼的人当众摘下眼镜子，翠远觉得有点秽亵，仿佛当众脱衣服似的，不成体统。宗桢继续说道："你——你不知道她是怎么样的一个女人！"翠远道："那么，你当初……"宗桢道："当初我也反对来着。她是我母亲给订下的。我自然是愿意让自己拣，可是……她从前非常地美……我那时又年轻……年轻的人，你知道……"翠远点点头。

宗桢道："她后来变成了这么样的一个人——连我母亲都跟她闹翻了，倒过来怪我不该娶了她！她——她那脾气——她连小学都没有毕业。"翠远不禁微笑道："你仿佛非常看重那一纸文凭！其实，女子受教育也不过是那么一回事！"她不知道为什么说出这句话来，伤了她自己的心。宗桢道："当然哪，你可以在旁边说风凉话，因为你是受过高等教育的。你不知道她是怎么样的一个——"他顿住了口，上气不接下气，刚戴上了眼镜子，又褪下来擦镜片。翠远道："你说得太过分了一点罢？"宗桢手里捏着眼镜，艰难地做了一个手势道："你不知道她是——"翠远忙道："我知道，我知道。"她知道他们夫妇不和，决不能单怪他太太。他自己也是一个思想简单的人。他需要一个原谅他，包涵他的女人。

街上一阵乱，轰隆轰隆来了两辆卡车，载满了兵。翠远与宗桢同时探头出去张望；出其不意地，两人的面庞异常接近。在极短的距离内，任何人的脸部都和寻常不同，像银幕上特写镜头一般的紧张。宗桢和翠远突然觉得他们俩还是第一次见面。在宗桢的眼中，她的脸像一朵淡淡几笔的白描牡丹花，额角上两三根吹乱的短发便是风中的花蕊。

他看着她，她红了脸。她一脸红，让他看见了，他显得很愉快。她的脸就越发红了。

宗桢没有想到他能够使一个女人脸红，使她微笑，使她背过脸去，使她掉过头来。在这里，他是一个男子。平时，他是会计师，他是孩子的父亲，他是家长，他是车上的搭客，他是店里的主顾，他是市民。可是对于这个不知道他的底细的女人，他只是一个单纯的男子。

他们恋爱着了。他告诉她许多话，关于他们银行里，谁跟他最好，谁跟他面和心不和，家里怎样闹口舌，他的秘密的悲哀，他读书时代的志愿……无休无歇的话，可是她并不嫌烦。恋爱着的男子向来是喜欢说，恋爱着的女人破例地不大爱说话，因为下意识地她知道；男人彻底地懂得了一个女人之后，是不会爱她的。

宗桢断定了翠远是一个可爱的女人——白、稀薄、温热，像冬天里你自己嘴里呵出来的一口气。你不要她，她就悄悄的飘散了。她是你自己的一部份，她什么都懂，什么都宽宥你。你说真话，她为你心酸；你说假话，她微笑着，仿佛说："瞧你这张嘴！"

宗桢沉默了一会，忽然说道："我打算重新结婚。"翠远连忙做出惊慌的神气，叫道："你要离婚？那……恐怕不行罢？"宗桢道："我不能够离婚。我得顾全孩子们的幸福。我大女儿今年十三岁了，才考进了中学，成绩很不错。"翠远暗道："这跟当前的问题又有什么关系？"她冷冷的道："哦，你打算娶妾。"宗桢道："我预备将她当妻子看待。我——我会替她安排好的。我不会让她为难。"翠远道："可是，如果她是个好人家的女孩子，只怕她未见得肯罢？种种法律上的麻烦……"宗桢叹了口气道："是的，你这话对。我没有权利。我根本不该起这种念头……我年纪太大了。我已经三十五岁了。"翠远缓缓的道："其实，照现在的眼光来看，那倒也不算大。"宗桢默然，半晌方说道："你……几岁？"翠远低下头去道："二十五。"宗桢顿了一顿，又道："你是自由的么？"翠远不答。宗桢道："你不是自由的。即使你答应了，你家里人也不会答应的，是不是？……是不是？"

翠远抿紧了嘴唇。她家里的人——那些一尘不染的好人——她恨他们！他们哄够了她。他们要她找个有钱的女婿，宗桢没有钱而有太太——气气他们也好！气！活该气！

车上的人又渐渐多了起来，外面许是有了"封锁行将开放"的谣言，乘客一个一个上来，坐下，宗桢与翠远给他们挤得紧紧的，坐近一点，再坐近一点。

宗桢与翠远奇怪他们刚才怎么这样的糊涂，就想不到自动的坐近一点。宗桢觉得他太快乐了，不能不抗议。他用苦楚的声音向她说："不行！这不行！我不能让你牺牲了你的前程！你是上等人，你受过这样好的教育……我——我又没有多少钱，我不能坑了你的一生！"可不是，还是钱的问题。他的话有理。翠远想道："完了。"以后她多半会嫁人的，可是她的丈夫决不会像一个萍水相逢的人一般的可爱——封锁中的电车上的人……一切再也不会像这样自然。再也不会……呵，这个人，这么笨！这么笨！她只要他的生命中的一部份，谁也不希罕的一部份。他白糟蹋了他自己的幸福。多么愚蠢的浪费！她哭了，可是那不是斯斯文文的，淑女式的哭。她简直把她的眼泪唾到他脸上。他是个好人——世界上的好人又多了一个！

向他解释有什么用？如果一个女人必须倚仗着她的言语来打动一个男人，她也就太可怜了。

宗桢一急，竟说不出话来，连连用手去摇撼她手里的阳伞。她不理他，他又去摇撼她的手，道："我说——我说——这儿有人哪！别！别这样！待会儿我们在电话上仔细谈。你告诉我你的电话。"翠远不答。他逼着问道："你无论如何得给我一个电话号码。"翠远飞快的说了一遍道："七五三六九。"宗桢道："七五三六九？"她又不作声了。宗桢嘴里喃喃重复着："七五三六九，"伸手在上下的口袋里掏摸自来水笔，越忙越摸不着。翠远皮包里有红铅笔，但是她有意地不拿出来。她的电话号码，他理该记得，记不得，他是不爱她，他们也就用不着往下谈了。

封锁开放了。"叮玲玲玲玲玲"摇着铃，每一个"玲"字是冷冷的一点，一点一点连成一条虚线，切断时间与空间。

一阵欢呼的风刮过这大城市，电车当当当往前开了。宗桢突然站起身来，挤到人丛中，不见了。翠远偏过头去，只做不理会。他走了，对于她，他等于死了。

电车加足了速力前进，黄昏的人行道上，卖臭豆腐干的歇下了担子，一个人捧着文王神卦的匣子，闭着眼霍霍的摇。一个大个子的金发女人，背上背着大草帽，露出大牙齿来向一个意大利水兵一笑，说了句玩话。翠远的眼睛看到了他们，他们就活了，只活那么一刹那。车往前当当地跑，他们一个个地死去了。

翠远烦恼地合上了眼。他如果打电话给她，她一定管不住自己的声音，对他分外地热烈，因为他是一个死去了又活过来的人。

电车里点上了灯，她一睁眼望见他遥遥坐在他原来的位子上。她震了一震——原来他并没有下车去！她明白他的意思了：封锁期间的一切，等于没有发生。整个的上海打了个盹，做了个不近情理的梦。

开电车的放声唱道："可怜啊可怜！一个人啊没钱！可怜啊——"一个缝穷婆子慌里慌张掠过车头，横穿过马路。开电车的大喝道："猪猡！"

一九四三年


## Topics for Discussion

1. What are the "new" aspects of the modern Chinese literature?

2. How did Lu Xun include the concepts of "National Criticism" into his works?

3. Is there any artistic value in modern Chinese poetry? If so, what?

4. Some people think Shen Congwen is a so-called "homeland writer". Do you a-gree?

5. What is the theme of Zhang Ailing's short story *Sealed Off*?

Chapter Ten

# Contemporary Chinese Literature

## General Description

Contemporary Chinese literature is considered to have begun in 1949. The sixty years since 1949 can be divided into two eras, one prior to 1978 and one post 1978. The first 30 years saw frequent civil strives and a very low quantity of literary output. The last 30 years however has been a period during which China has experienced an era of major developments, policy changes and social reforms. This period, also known as the "New Time Literature(新时期文学)" period, has pushed literature towards recovery and prosperity. New genres appear like tide waves and new styles flourish, providing fresh vitality to what had been a quiet and monotonous stream.

With the unstoppable rise in the social status and education of women, the image of a male dominated field of creative writing is being replaced. A large group of female writers has started to take the lead and follow a new path towards a brighter future. In this chapter, Zhang Jie is representative of the rise of modern Chinese female writers during this transition.

The emergence of a consumer-market-oriented economy in the early 1990's significantly affected traditional literature, with the greatest challenges to traditional literary style coming from the new internet media. Inevitably, the question as to in which direction literature should head is raised. Although there is bright hope looking forward, it is also a time of uncertainty.

The main stories in this chapter are selected from Zhang Jie and Zhang Chengzhi's works. The supplementary works are written by the authors Bai Xianyong and Can Xue.

## Introduction to the Works of Zhang Jie

Zhang Jie(张洁 1937~) is an outstanding modern Chinese female author. In the half century since she started her career as a writer, she has written and published numerous novels and become very popular in China. She has won recognition at home and abroad. Her novels mainly focus on the topic of love and involve an in-depth exploration of people's spiritual worlds including the modern women's right to pursue happiness and the practical difficulties that are involved. Zhang Jie's novels are delicate, gracefully written and full of passion.

张洁

Her short story *Love Must Not Be Forgotten*(《爱，是不能忘记的》) was published in 1979, during an era without love, yet an era with a craving for love. The main male and female characters long for love, but it is a love that cannot be attained despite the suffering and torment they endure. Readers have been drawn to her novels and been profoundly touched. Her works often cover the theme of the relationship between love and marriage, an ancient theme that is still with us in real life today.

中国文学选读

## Selection from Zhang Jie's Works

### Love Must Not Be Forgotten

I am thirty, the same age as our People's Republic. For a republic thirty is still young. But a girl of thirty is virtually on the shelf.

Actually, I have a bonafide suitor. Have you seen the Greek sculptor Myron's Discobolus? Qiao Lin is the image of that discus thrower. Even the padded clothes he wears in winter fail to hide his fine physique. Bronzed, with clear-cut features, a broad forehead and large eyes, his appearance alone attracts most girls to him.

But I can't make up my mind to marry him. I'm not clear what attracts me to him or him to me. I know people are gossiping behind my back, "Who does she think she is, to be so choosy?" To them, I'm a nobody playing hard to get. They take offense at such preposterous behavior.

Of course, I shouldn't be captious. In a society where commercial production still exists, marriage like most other transactions is still a form of barter.

I have known Qiao Lin for nearly two years, yet still cannot fathom whether he keeps so quiet from aversion to talking or from having nothing to say. When, by way of a small intelligence test, I demand his opinion of this or that, he says "good" or "bad" like a child in kindergarten.

Once I asked, "Qiao Lin, why do you love me?" He thought the question over seriously for what seemed an age. I could see from his normally smooth but now wrinkled forehead that the little grey cells in his handsome head were hard at work cogitation. I felt ashamed to have put him on the spot.

Finally he raised his clear childlike eyes to tell me, "Because you're good!"

Loneliness flooded my heart. "Thank you, Qiao Lin!" I couldn't help wondering, if we were to marry, whether we could discharge our duties to each other as husband and wife. Maybe, because law and morality would have bound us together. But how tragic simply to comply with law and morality! Was there no stronger bond to link us?

When such thoughts cross my mind I have the strange sensation that instead of being a girl contemplating marriage I am an elderly social scientist.

Perhaps I worry too much. We can live like most married couples, bringing up children together, strictly true to each other according to the law... Although living in the seventies of the twentieth century, people still consider marriage the way they did millennia ago, as a means of continuing the race, a form of barter or a business transaction in which love and marriage can be separated. Since this is the common practice, why shouldn't we follow suit?

《爱,是不能忘记的》插图

But I still can't make up my mind. As a child, I remember, I often cried all night for no rhyme or reason, unable to sleep and disturbing the whole household. My old nurse, a shrewd though uneducated woman, said an ill wind had blown through my ear. I think this judgment showed prescience, because I still have that old weakness. I upset myself over things which really present no problem, upsetting other people at the same time. One's nature is hard to change.

I think of my mother too. If she were alive, what would she say about my attitude to Qiao Lin and my uncertainty about marrying him? My thoughts constantly turn to her, not because she was such a strict mother that her ghost is still watching over me since her death. No, she was not just my mother but my closest friend. I loved her so much that the thought of her leaving me makes my heart ache.

She never lectured me, just told me quietly in her deep, unwomanly voice about her successes and failures, so that I could learn from her experience. She had evidently not had many successes—her life

中国文学选读

was full of failures.

During her last days she followed me with her fine, expressive eyes, as if wondering how I would manage on my own and as if she had some important advice for me but hesitated to give it. She must have been worried by my naïveté and sloppy ways. She suddenly blurted out, "Shanshan, if you aren't sure what you want, It's rush into marriage—better live on your own!"

Other people might think this strange advice from a mother to her daughter, but to me it embodied her bitter experience. I don't think she underestimated me or my knowledge of life. She loved me and didn't want me to be unhappy.

"I don't want to marry, mother!" I said, not out of bashfulness or a show of coyness. I can't think why a girl should pretend to be coy. She had long since taught me about things not generally mentioned to girls.

"If you meet the right man, then marry him. Only if he's right to you!"

"I'm afraid no such man exists!"

"That's not true. But it's hard. The world is so vast; I'm afraid you may never meet him. " Whether married or not was not what concerned her, but the quality of the marriage.

"Haven't you managed fine without a husband?"

"Who says so?"

"I think you've done fine. "

"I had no choice... " She broke off, lost in thought, her face wistful. Her wistful lined face reminded me of a withered flower I had pressed in a book.

"Why did you have no choice?"

"You ask too many questions," she parried, not ashamed to confide in me but afraid that I might reach the wrong conclusion. Besides, everyone treasures a secret to carry to the grave. Feeling a bit put out, I demanded bluntly, "Didn't you love my dad?"

"No, I never loved him. "

"Did he love you?"

"No. he didn't. "

"Then why get married?"

She paused, searching for the right words to explain this mystery, then answered bitterly, "When you're young you It's always know what you're looking for, what you need, and people may talk you into getting married. As you grow older and more experienced you find out your true needs. By then, though, you've done many foolish things for which you could kick yourself. You'd give anything to be able to make a fresh start and live more wisely. Those content with their lot will always be happy, they say, but I shall never enjoy that happiness." She added self-mockingly, "A wretched idealist, that's all I am."

Did I take after her? Did we both have genes which attracted ill winds?

"Why don't you marry again?"

"I'm afraid I'm still not sure what I really want." She was obviously unwilling to tell me the truth.

I cannot remember my father. He and Mother split up when I was very small. I just recall her telling me sheepishly that he was a fine handsome fellow. I could see she was ashamed of having judged by appearances and made a futile choice. She told me, "When I can't sleep at night, I force myself to sober up by recalling all those stupid blunders I made. Of course it's so distasteful that I often hide my face in the sheet for shame, as if there were eyes watching me in the dark. But distasteful as it is, I take some pleasure in this form of atonement."

I was really sorry that she hadn't remarried. She was such a fascinating character, if she'd married a man she loved, what a happy household ours would surely have been. Though not beautiful, she had the simple charm of an ink landscape. She was a fine writer too. Another author who knew her well used to say teasingly, "Just reading your works is enough to make anyone love you!"

She would retort, "If he knew that the object of his affection was a white-haired old crone, that would frighten him away." At her age, she must have known what she really wanted, so this was obviously an evasion. I say this because she had quirks which puzzled me.

For instance, whenever she left Beijing on a trip, she always took with her one of the twenty-seven volumes of Chekov's stories published between 1950 and 1955. She also warned me, "Don't touch these books. If you want to read Chekov, read that set I bought you. " There was no need to caution me. Having a set of my own, why should I touch hers? Besides, she'd told me this over and over again. Still she was on her guard. She seemed bewitched by those books.

So we had two sets of Chekov's stories at home. Not just because we loved Chekov, but to parry other people like me who loved Chekov. Whenever anyone asked to borrow a volume, she would lend one of mine. Once, in her absence, a close friend took a volume from her set. When she found out she was frantic, and at once took a volume of mine to exchange for it.

Ever since I can remember, those books were on her bookcase. Although I admire Chekov as a great writer, I was puzzled by the way she never tired of reading him. Why, for over twenty years, had she had to read him every single day? Sometimes, when tired of writing, she poured herself a cup of strong tea and sat down in front of the bookcase, staring raptly at that set of books. If I went into her room then it flustered her, and she either spilt her tea or blushed like a girl discovered with her lover.

I wondered: Has she fallen in love with Chekov? She might have if he'd still been alive.

When her mind was wandering just before her death, her last words to me were: "That set... " She hadn't the strength to give it its complete title. But I knew what she meant. " And my diary... ' Love Must Not Be Forgotten... ' Cremate them with me. "

I carried out her last instruction regarding the works of Chekov, but couldn't bring myself to destroy her diary. I thought, if it could be published, it would surely prove the most moving thing she had written. But naturally publication was out of the question.

At first I imagined the entries were raw material she had jotted down. They read neither like stories, essays, a diary or letters. But after reading the whole I formed a hazy impression, helped out by my imperfect memory. Thinking it over, I finally realized that this was no lifeless manuscript I was holding, but an anguished, loving heart. For over twenty years one man had occupied her heart, but he was not for her. She used these diaries as a substitute for him, a means of pouring out her feelings to him, day after day, year after year.

No wonder she had never considered any eligible proposals, had turned a deaf ear to idle talk whether well-meant or malicious. Her heart was already full, to the exclusion of anybody else. "No lake can compare with the ocean, no cloud with those on Mount Wu." Remembering those lines I often reflected sadly that few people in real life could love like this. No one would love me like this.

I learned that toward the end of the thirties, when this man was doing underground work for the Party in Shanghai, an old worker had given his life to cover him, leaving behind a helpless wife and daughter. Out of a sense of duty, of gratitude to the dead and deep class feeling, he had unhesitatingly married the daughter. When he saw the endless troubles of couples who had married for "love", he may have thought, "Thank Heaven, though I didn't marry for love, we get on well, able to help each other." For years, as man and wife they lived through hard times.

He must have been my mother's colleague. Had I ever met him? He couldn't have visited our home. Who was he?

In the spring of 1962, Mother took me to a concert. We went on foot, the theater being quite near. On the way a black limousine pulled up silently by the pavement. Out stepped an elderly man with white hair in a black serge tunic-suit. What a striking shock of white hair! Strict, scrupulous, distinguished, transparently honest—that was my impression of him. The cold glint of his flashing eyes reminded me of lightning or swordplay. Only ardent love for a woman really deserving his love could fill cold eyes like those with tenderness.

He walked up to Mother and said, "How are you, Comrade Zhong Yu? It's been a long time."

"How are you?" Mother's hand holding mine suddenly turned icy cold and trembled a little.

They stood face to face without looking at each other, each appearing upset, even stern. Mother fixed her eyes on the trees by the roadside, not yet in leaf. He looked at me. "Such a big girl already. Good, fine—you take after your mother."

Instead of shaking hands with Mother he shook hands with me. His hand was as icy as hers and trembling a little. As if transmitting an electric current, I felt a sud-

　　　　　　　　　　　　　　中国文学选读

den shock. Snatching my hand away I cried, "There's nothing good about that!"

"Why not?" he asked with the surprised expression grown-ups always have when children speak out frankly.

I glanced at Mother's face. I did take after her, to my disappointment. "Because she's not beautiful!"

He laughed, then said teasingly, "Too bad that there should be a child who doesn't find her own mother beautiful. Do you remember in 1953, when your mother was transferred to Beijing, she came to our ministry to report for duty—She left you outside on the veranda, but like a monkey you climbed all the stairs, peeped through the cracks in doors, and caught your finger in the door of my office. You sobbed so bitterly that I carried you off to find her. "

"I don't remember that. " I was annoyed at his harking back to a time when I was still in open-seat pants.

"Ah, we old people have better memories," He turned abruptly and remarked to Mother, "I've read that last story of yours. Frankly speaking, there's something not quite right about it. You shouldn't have condemned the heroine... There's nothing wrong with falling in love, as long as you It's spoil someone else's life... In fact, the hero might have loved her too. Only for the sake of a third person's happiness, they had to renounce their love... "

A policeman came over to where the car was parked and ordered the driver to move on. When the driver made some excuse, the old man looked around. After a hasty "Goodbye" he strode back to the car and told the policeman, "Sorry. It's not his fault; it's mine... "

I found it amusing watching this old cadre listening respectfully to the policeman's strictures. When I turned to Mother with a mischievous smile, she looked as upset as a first-form primary schoolchild standing forlornly in front of the stern headmistress. Anyone would have thought she was the one being lectured by the policeman. The car drove off, leaving a puff of smoke. Very soon even this smoke vanished with the wind, as if nothing at all had happened. But the incident stuck in my mind.

Analyzing it now, I realize he must have been the man whose strength of character won Mother's heart. That strength came from his firm political convictions, his narrow escapes from death in the revolution, his active brain, his drive at work, his well-cultivated mind. Besides, strange to say, he and Mother both liked the oboe. Yes, she must have worshipped him. She once told me that unless she worshipped a man, she couldn't love him even for one day.

But I could not tell whether he loved her or not. If not, why was there this entry in her diary?

"This is far too fine a present. But how did you know that Chekov's my favorite writer?"

"You said so."

"I don't remember that."

"I remember. I heard you mention it when you were chatting with someone."

So he was the one who had given her the *Selected Stories of Chekov*. For her that was tantamount to a love letter. Maybe this man, who didn't believe in love, realized by the time his hair was white that in his heart was something which could be called love. By the time he no longer had the right to love, he made the tragic discovery of this love for which he would have given his life. Or did it go deeper even than that?

This is all I remember about him.

How wretched Mother must have been, deprived of the man to whom she was devoted! To catch a glimpse of his car or the back of his head through its rear window, she carefully figured out which roads he would take to work and back. Whenever he made a speech, she sat at the back of the hall watching his face rendered hazy by cigarette smoke and poor lighting. Her eyes would brim with tears, but she swallowed them back. If a fit of coughing made him break off, she wondered anxiously why no one persuaded him to give up smoking. She was afraid he would get bronchitis again. Why was he so near yet so far?

He, to catch a glimpse of her, looked out of the car window every day straining his eyes to watch the streams of cyclists, afraid that she might have an accident. On the rare evenings on which he had no meetings, he would walk by a roundabout way to our neighborhood, to pass our compound gate. However busy, he would always make time to look in papers and journals for her work. His duty had always been clear to him, even in the most difficult times. But now confronted by this love he became a weakling, quite helpless. At his age it was laughable. Why should life play this trick on him?

Yet when they happened to meet at work, each tried to avoid the other, hurrying off with a nod. Even so, this would make Mother blind and deaf to everything around her. If she met a colleague named Wang she would call him Guo and mutter something unintelligible.

It was a cruel ordeal for her. She wrote:

> *We agreed to forget each other. But I deceived you, I have never forgotten. I It's think you've forgotten either. We're just deceiving each other, hiding our misery. I haven't deceived you deliberately, though; I did my best to carry out our agreement. I often stay far away from Beijing, hoping time and distance will help me to forget you. But when I return, as the train pulls into the station, my head reels. I stand on the platform looking round intently, as if someone were waiting for me. Of course there is no one. I realize then that I have forgotten nothing. Everything is unchanged. My love is like a tree the roots of which strike deeper year after year—I have no way to uproot it.*
>
> *At the end of every day, I feel as if I've forgotten something important. I may wake with a start from my dreams wondering what has happened. But nothing has happened. Nothing. Then it comes home to me that you are missing! So everything seems lacking, incomplete, and there is nothing to fill up the blank. We are nearing the ends of our lives; why should we be carried away by emotion like children? Why should life submit people to such ordeals, then unfold before you your lifelong dream? Because I started off blindly, I took the wrong turning, and now there are insuperable obstacles between me and my dream.*

Yes, Mother never let me go to the station to meet her when she came back from a trip, preferring to stand alone on the platform and imagine that he had met her. Poor mother with her graying hair was as infatuated as a girl.

Not much space in the diary was devoted to their romance. Most entries dealt with trivia: why one of her articles had not come off; her fear that she had no real talent; the excellent play she missed by mistaking the time on the ticket; the drenching she got by going out for a stroll without her umbrella. In spirit they were together day and night, like a devoted married couple. In fact, they spent no more than twenty-four hours together in all. Yet in that time they experienced deeper happiness than some people in a whole lifetime. Shakespeare makes Juliet say, "I can not sum up half my sum of wealth." And probably that is how Mother felt.

He must have been killed in the Cultural Revolution. Perhaps because of the conditions then, that section of the diary is ambiguous and obscure. Mother had been so fiercely attacked for her writing; it amazed me that she went on keeping a diary. From some veiled allusions I gathered that he had questioned the theories advanced by that "theoretician" then at the height of favor, and had told someone, "This is sheer Rightist talk." It was clear from the tear-stained pages of Mother's diary that he had been harshly denounced; but the steadfast old man never knuckled under to the authorities. His last words were, "When I go to meet Marx, I shall go on fighting my case!"

That must have been in the winter of 1969, because that was when Mother's hair turned white overnight, though she was not yet fifty. And she put on a black arm-band. Her position then was extremely difficult. She was criticized for wearing this old-style mourning, and ordered to say for whom she was in mourning.

"For whom are you wearing that, Mother?" I asked anxiously.

"For a relative." Not to frighten me she explained, "Someone you never knew."

"Shall I put one on too?" She patted my cheeks, as she had when I was a child. It was years since she had shown me such affection. I often felt that as she aged, especially during these last years of persecution, all tenderness had left her, or was concealed in her heart, so that she seemed like a man.

She smiled sadly and said, "No, you needn't wear one." Her eyes were as dry as if she had no more tears to shed. I longed to comfort her or do something to please her. But she said, "Off you go."

I felt an inexplicable dread, as if dear Mother had already half left me. I blurted

中国文学选读

out, "Mother!"

Quick to sense my desolation, she said gently, "Don't be afraid. Off you go. Leave me alone for a while."

I was right. She wrote:

*You have gone. Half my soul seems to have taken flight with you.*

*I had no means of knowing what had become of you, much less of seeing you for the last time. I had no right to ask either, not being your wife or friend... So we are torn apart. If only I could have borne that inhuman treatment for you, so that you could have lived on! You should have lived to see your name cleared and take up your work again, for the sake of those who loved you. I knew you could not be a counter-revolutionary. You were one of the finest men killed. That's why I love you—I am not afraid now to avow it.*

*Snow is whirling down. Heavens, even God is such a hypocrite. He is using this whiteness to cover up your blood and the scandal of your murder.*

*I used to walk alone along that small asphalt road, the only place where we once walked together, hearing my footsteps in the silent night... I always paced to and fro and lingered there, but never as wretchedly as now. Then, though you were not beside me, I knew you were still in this world and felt that you were keeping me company. Now I can hardly believe that you have gone.*

*At the end of the road I would retrace my steps, then walk along it again. Rounding the fence I always looked back, as if you were still standing there waving goodbye. We smiled faintly, like casual acquaintances, to conceal our undying love. That ordinary evening in early spring a chilly wind was blowing as we walked silently away from each other. You were wheezing a little because of your chronic bronchitis. That upset me. I wanted to beg you to slow down, but somehow I couldn't. We both walked very fast, as if some important business were waiting for us. How we prized that single stroll we had together, but we were afraid we might lose control of ourselves and burst out with "I love you"—those three words which had tormented us for years. Probably no one else could believe that we never once even clasped hands!*

No, Mother, I believe it. I am the only one able to see into your locked heart.

Ah, that little asphalt road, so haunted by bitter memories. We shouldn't overlook the most insignificant spots on earth. For who knows how much secret grief and joy they may hide. No wonder that when tired of writing, she would pace slowly along that little road behind our window. Sometimes at dawn after a sleepless night, sometimes on a moonless, windy evening. Even in winter during howling gales which hurled sand and pebbles against the window pane... I thought this was one of her eccentricities, not knowing that she had gone to meet him in spirit.

She liked to stand by the window, too, staring at the small asphalt road. Once I thought from her expression that one of our closest friends must be coming to call. I hurried to the window. It was a late autumn evening. The cold wind was stripping dead leaves from the trees and blowing them down the small empty road.

She went on pouring out her heart to him in her diary as she had when he was alive, right up to the day when the pen slipped from her fingers. Her last message was:

> *I am a materialist, yet I wish there were a Heaven. For then, I know, I would find you there waiting for me. I am going there to join you, to be together for eternity. We need never be parted again or keep at a distance for fear of spoiling someone else's life. Wait for me, dearest, I am coming—*

I do not know how, on her death bed, Mother could still love so ardently with all her heart. To me it seemed not love but a form of madness, a passion stronger than death. If undying love really exists, she reached its extreme. She obviously died happy, because she had known true love. She had no regrets.

Now these old people's ashes have mingled with the elements. But I know that no matter what form they may take, they still love each other. Though not bound together by earthly laws or morality, though they never once clasped hands, each possessed the other completely. Nothing could part them. Centuries to come, if one white cloud trails another, two grasses grow side by side, one wave splashes another, a breeze follows another... believe me, that will be them.

中国文学选读

Each time I read that diary "Love Must Not Be Forgotten" I cannot hold back my tears. I often weep bitterly, as if I myself experienced their ill-fated love. If not a tragedy, it was too laughable. No matter how beautiful or moving I find it, I have no wish to follow suit!

Thomas Hardy wrote that "the call seldom produces the comer, the man to love rarely coincides with the hour for loving." I cannot judge them by conventional moral standards. What I deplore is that they did not wait for a "missing counterpart" to call them. If everyone could wait, instead of rushing into marriage, how many tragedies could be averted!

When we reach communism, will there still be cases of marriage without love? Perhaps... since the world is so vast, two kindred spirits may never be able to answer each other's call. But how tragic! Could it be that by then we will have devised ways to escape such tragedies? But this is all conjecture.

Maybe after all we are accountable for these tragedies. Who knows? Should we take the responsibility for the old ideas handed down from the past? Because, if you choose not to marry, your behavior is considered a direct challenge to these ideas. You will be called neurotic, accused of having guilty secrets or having made political mistakes. You may be regarded as an eccentric who looks down on ordinary people, not respecting age-old customs—a heretic. In short they will trump up endless vulgar and futile charges to ruin your reputation. Then you have to succumb to those ideas and marry regardless. But once you put the chains of an indifferent marriage around your neck, you will suffer for it for the rest of your life.

I long to shout: "Mind your own business! Let us wait patiently for our counterparts. Even waiting in vain is better than loveless marriage. To live single is not such a fearful disaster. I believe it may be a sign of a step forward in culture, education and the quality of life."

1979

(translated by Gladys Yang)

## 爱, 是不能忘记的

我和我们这个共和国同年。三十岁, 对于一个共和国来说, 那是太年轻了。

而对一个姑娘来说，却有嫁不出去的危险。

不过，眼下我倒有一个正儿八经的求婚者。看见过希腊伟大的雕塑家米伦所创造的《掷铁饼者》那座雕塑么？乔林的身躯几乎就是那尊雕塑的翻版。即使在冬天，臃肿的棉衣也不能掩盖住他身上那些线条的优美的轮廓。他的面孔黝黑，鼻子、嘴巴的线条都很粗犷。宽阔的前额下，是一双长长的眼睛。光看这张脸和这个身躯，大多数的姑娘都会喜欢他。

可是，倒是我自己拿不准主意要不要嫁给他。因为我闹不清楚我究竟爱他的什么，而他又爱我的什么。

我知道，已经有人在背地里说长道短："凭她那些条件，还想找个什么样的？"

在他们的想象中，我不过是一头劣种的牲畜，却变着法儿想要混个肯出大价钱的冤大头。这使他们感到气恼，好像我真的干了什么伤天害理的、冒犯了众人的事情。

自然，我不能对他们过于苛求。在商品生产还存在的社会里，婚姻，也像其他的许多问题一样，难免不带着商品交换的烙印。

我和乔林相处将近两年了，可直到现在我还摸不透他那缄默的习惯到底是因为不爱讲话，还是因为讲不出来什么。逢到我起意要对他来点智力测验，一定逼着他说出对某事或某物的看法时，他也只能说出托儿所里常用的那种词藻："好！"或"不好！"就这么两挡，再也不能换换别的花样儿了。

当我问起"乔林，你为什么爱我"的时候，他认真地思索了好一阵子。对他来说，那段时间实在够长了。凭着他那宽阔的额头上难得出现的皱纹，我知道，他那美丽的脑壳里面的组织细胞，一定在进行着紧张的思维活动。我不由地对他生出一种怜悯和一种歉意，好像我用这个问题刁难了他。

然后，他抬起那双儿童般的、清澈的眸子对我说："因为你好！"

我的心被一种深刻的寂寞填满了。"谢谢你，乔林！"

我不由地想：当他成为我的丈夫，我也成为他的妻子的时候，我们能不能把妻子和丈夫的责任和义务承担到底呢？也许能够。因为法律和道义已经紧紧地把我们拴在一起。而如果我们仅仅是遵从着法律和道义来承担彼此的责任和义务，那又是多么悲哀啊！那么，有没有比法律和道义更牢固、更坚实的东西把我们联系在一起呢？

逢到我这样想着的时候，我总是有一种古怪的感觉，好像我不是一个准备出嫁的姑娘，而是一个研究社会学的老学究。

也许我不必想这么许多，我们可以照大多数的家庭那样生活下去：生儿育女，厮守在一起，绝对地保持着法律所规定的忠诚……虽说人类社会已经进入了二十世纪七十年代，可在这点上，倒也不妨像几千年来人们所做过的那样，把婚姻当成一种传宗接代的工具，一种交换、买卖，而婚姻和爱情也可以是分离着的。既然许多人都是这么过来的，为什么我就偏偏不可以照这样过下去呢？

不，我还是下不了决心。我想起小的时候，我总是没缘没故地整夜啼哭，不仅闹得自己睡不安生，也闹得全家睡不安生。我那没有什么文化却相当有见地的老保姆说我"贼风入耳"了。我想这带有预言性的结论，大概很有一点科学性，因为直到如今我还依然如故，总好拿些不成问题的问题不但搅扰得自己不得安宁，也搅扰得别人不得安宁。所谓"禀性难移"吧！

我呢，还会想到我的母亲，如果她还活着，她会对我的这些想法，对乔林，对我要不要答应他的求婚说些什么？

我之所以习惯地想到她，绝不因为她是一个严酷的母亲，即使已经不在人世也依然用她的阴魂主宰着我的命运。不，她甚至不是母亲，而是一个推心置腹的朋友。我想，这多半就是我那么爱她，一想到她已经离我远去便悲从中来的原因吧！

她从不教训我，她只是用她那没有什么女性温存的低沉的嗓音，柔和地对我谈她一生中的过失或成功，让我从这过失或成功里找到我自己需要的东西。不过，她成功的时候似乎很少，一生里总是伴着许许多多的失败。

在她最后的那些日子里，她总是用那双细细的、灵秀的眼睛长久地跟随着我，仿佛在估量着我有没有独立生活下去的能力，又好像有什么重要的话要叮嘱我，可又拿不准主意该不该对我说。准是我那没心没肺，凡事都不大有所谓的派头让她感到了悬心。她忽然冒出了一句："珊珊，要是你吃不准自己究竟要的是什么，我看你就是独身生活下去，也比糊里糊涂地嫁出去要好得多！"

照别人看来，作为一个母亲，对女儿讲这样的话，似乎不近情理。而在我看来，那句话里包含着以往生活里的极其痛苦的经验。我倒不觉得她这样叮咛我是看轻我或是低估了我对生活的认识。她爱我，希望我生活得没有烦恼，是不是？

"妈妈，我不想嫁人！"我这么说，绝不是因为害臊或是在忸怩作态。说真的，我真不知道一个姑娘什么时候需要做出害臊或忸怩的姿态，一切在一般人看来应该对孩子隐讳的事情，母亲早已从正面让我认识了它。

"要是遇见合适的，还是应该结婚。我说的是合适的！"

"恐怕没有什么合适的!"

"有还是有,不过难一点——因为世界是这么大,我担心的是你会不会遇上就是了!"她并不关心我嫁得出去还是嫁不出去,她关心的倒是婚姻的实质。

"其实,您一个人过得不是挺好吗?"

"谁说我过得挺好?"

"我这么觉得。"

"我是不得不如此……"她停住了说话,沉思起来。一种淡淡的、忧郁的神情来到了她的脸上。她那忧郁的、满是皱纹的脸,让我想起我早年夹在书页里的那些已经枯萎了的花。

"为什么不得不如此呢?"

"你的为什么太多了。"她在回避我。她心里一定藏着什么不愿意让我知道的心事。我知道,她不告诉我,并不是因为她耻于向我披露,而多半是怕我不能准确地估量那事情的深浅而扭曲了它,也多半是因为人人都有一点珍藏起来的、留给自己带到坟墓里去的东西。想到这里,我有点不自在。这不自在的感觉迫使我没有礼貌、没有教养地追问下去:"是不是您还爱着爸爸?"

"不,我从没有爱过他。"

"他爱您吗?"

"不,他也不爱我!"

"那你们当初为什么结婚呢?"

她停了停,准是想找出更准确的字眼来说明这令人费解和反常的现象,然后显出无限悔恨的样子对我说:"人在年轻的时候,并不一定了解自己追求的、需要的是什么,甚至别人的起哄也会促成一桩婚姻。等到你再长大一些、更成熟一些的时候,你才会明白你真正需要的是什么。可那时,你已经干了许多悔恨得让你感到锥心的蠢事。你巴不得付出任何代价,只求重新生活一遍才好,那你就会变得比较聪明了。人说'知足者常乐',我却享受不到这样的快乐。"说着,她自嘲地笑了笑,"我只能是一个痛苦的理想主义者。"

莫非我那"贼风入耳"的毛病是从她那里来的?大约我们的细胞中主管"贼风入耳"这种遗传性状的是一个特别尽职尽责的基因。

"您为什么不再结婚呢?"

她不大情愿地说:"我怕自己还是吃不准自己到底要什么。"她明明还是不肯对我说真话。

我不记得我的父亲。他和母亲在我很小的时候便分手了。我只记得母亲曾经很害羞地对我说过他是一个相当漂亮的、公子哥儿似的人物。我明白，她准是因为自己也曾追求过那种浅薄而无聊的东西而感到害臊。她对我说过："晚上睡不着觉的时候，我常常迫使自己硬着头皮去回忆青年时代所做过的那些蠢事、错事！为的是使自己清醒。固然，这是很不愉快的，我常会羞愧地用被单蒙上自己的脸，好像黑暗里也有许多人在盯着我瞧似的。不过这种不愉快的感觉里倒也有一种赎罪似的快乐。"

我真对她不再结婚感到遗憾。她是一个很有趣味的人，如果她和一个她爱着的人结婚，一定会组织起一个十分有趣味的家庭。虽然她生得并不漂亮，可是优雅、淡泊，像一幅淡墨的山水画。文章写得也比较美，和她很熟悉的一位作家喜欢开这样的玩笑："光看你的作品，人家就会爱上你的！"

母亲便会接着说："要是他知道他爱的竟是一个满脸皱纹、满头白发的老太婆，他准会吓跑了。"

到了这种年龄，她绝不会是还不知道自己到底要什么。这分明是一句遁词。我之所以这么说，是因为她有一些引起我生出许多疑惑的怪毛病。

比如，不论她上哪儿出差，她必得带上那二十七本一套的，一九五〇年到一九五五年出版的契诃夫小说选集中的一本。并且叮咛着我："千万别动我这套书。你要看，就看我给你买的那一套。"这话明明是多余的。我有自己的一套，干嘛要去动她的那套呢？况且这话早已三令五申地不知说过多少遍了。可她还是怕有个万一时候。她爱那套书爱得简直像是得了魔症一般。

我们家有两套契诃夫小说选集。这也许说明对契诃夫的爱好是我们家的家风，但也许更多的是为了招架我和别的喜欢契诃夫的人。逢到有人想要借阅的时候，她便拿了我房间里的那套给人。有一次，她不在家的时候，一位很熟的朋友拿了她那套里的一本。她知道了之后，急得如同火烧了眉毛，立刻拿了我的一本去换了回来。

从我记事的那天起，那套书便放在她的书橱里了。别管我多么钦佩伟大的契诃夫，我也不能明白，那套书就那么百看不厌，二十多年来有什么必要天天非得读它一读不可？

有时，她写东西写累了，便会端着一杯浓茶，坐在书橱对面，瞧着那套契诃夫小说选集出神。要是这个时候我突然走进了她的房间，她便会显得慌乱不安，不是把茶水泼了自己一身，便是像初恋的女孩子，头一次和情人约会便让人撞见似地羞红了脸。

我便想：她是不是爱上了契诃夫？要是契诃夫还活着，没准真会发生这样的事。

当她神志不清、就要离开这个世界的时候，她对我说的最后一句话是："那套书——"她已经没有力气说出"那套契诃夫小说选集"这样一个长句子。不过我明白她指的就是那一套。"……还有，写着，'爱，是不能忘记的'……笔记本、和我，一同火葬。"

她最后叮咛我的这句话，有些，我为她做了，比如那套书。有些，我没有为她做，比如那些题着"爱，是不能忘记的"笔记本子。我舍不得。我常想，要是能够出版，那一定是她写过的那些作品里最动人的一篇，不过它当然是不能出版的。

起先，我以为那不过是她为了写东西而积累的一些素材。因为它既不像小说，也不像札记；既不像书信，也不像日记。只是当我从头到尾把它们读了一遍的时候，渐渐地，那些只言片语与我那支离破碎的回忆交织成了一个形状模糊的东西。经过久久的思索，我终于明白，我手里捧着的，并不是没有生命、没有血肉的文字，而是一颗灼人的、充满了爱情和痛苦的心，我还看见那颗心怎样在这爱情和痛苦里挣扎、熬煎。二十多年啦，那个人占有着她全部的情感，可是她却得不到他。她只有把这些笔记本当做是他的替身，在这上面和他倾心交谈。每时，每天，每月，每年。

难怪她从没有对任何一个够意思的求婚者动过心，难怪她对那些说不出来是善意的愿望或是恶意的闲话总是淡然地一笑付之。原来她的心已经填得那么满，任什么别的东西都装不进去了。我想起"曾经沧海难为水，除却巫山不是云"的诗句，想到我们当中多半有人不会这样去爱，而且也没有人会照这个样子来爱我的时候，我便感到一种说不出的怅惘。

我知道了三十年代末，他在上海做地下工作的时候，一位老工人为了掩护他而被捕牺牲，撇下了无依无靠的妻子和女儿。他，出于道义、责任、阶级情谊和对死者的感念，毫不犹豫地娶了那位姑娘。逢到他看见那些由于"爱情"而结合的夫妇又因为为"爱情"而生出无限的烦恼的时候，他便会想："谢天谢地，我虽然不是因为爱情而结婚，可是我们生活得和睦、融洽，就像一个人的左膀右臂。"几十年风里来、雨里去，他们可以说是患难夫妻。

他一定是她那机关里的一位同志。我会不会见过他呢？从到过我家的客人里，

　　　　　　　　　　　　　中国文学选读

我看不出任何迹象、他究竟是谁呢?

大约一九六二年的春天,我和母亲去听音乐会。剧场离我们家不太远,我们没有乘车。

一辆黑色的小轿车悄无声息地停在人行道旁边。从车上走下来一个满头白发、穿着一套黑色毛呢中山装的、上了年纪的男人。那头白发生得堂皇而又气派!他给人一种严谨的、一丝不苟的、脱俗的、明澄得像水晶一样的印象。特别是他的眼睛,十分冷峻地闪着寒光,当他急速地瞥向什么东西的时候,会让人联想起闪电或是舞动着的剑影。要使这样一对冰冷的眼睛充满柔情,那必定得是特别强大的爱情,而且得为了一个确实值得爱的女人才行。

他走过来,对母亲说:"您好!钟雨同志,好久不见了。"

"您好!"母亲牵着我的那只手突然变得冰凉,而且轻轻地颤抖着。

他们面对面地站着,脸上带着凄厉的、甚至是严峻的神情,谁也不看着谁。母亲瞧着路旁那些还没有抽出嫩芽的灌木丛。他呢,却看着我:"已经长成大姑娘了。真好,太好了,和妈妈长得一样。"

他没有和母亲握手,却和我握了握手。而那手也和母亲的手一样,也是冰冷的,也是轻轻地颤抖着的。我好像变成了一路电流的导体,立刻感到了震动和压抑。我很快地从他的手里抽出我的手,说道:"不好,一点也不好!"

他惊讶地问我:"为什么不好?"或许我以为他故作惊讶。因为凡是孩子们说了什么直率得可爱的话的时候,大人们都会显出这副神态的。

我看了看妈妈的面孔。是,我真像她。这让我有些失望:"因为她不漂亮!"

他笑了起来,幽默地说:"真可惜,竟然有个孩子嫌自己的母亲不漂亮。记得吗? 五三年你妈妈刚调到北京,带你来机关报到的那一天? 她把你这个小淘气留在了走廊外面,你到处串楼梯,扒门缝,在我房间的门上夹疼了手指头。你哇啦哇啦地哭着,我抱着你去找妈妈。"

"不,我不记得了。"我不大高兴,他竟然提起我穿开裆裤时代的事情。

"啊,还是上了年纪的人不容易忘记。"他突然转身向我的母亲说:"您最近写的那部小说我读过了。我要坦率地说,有一点您写得不准确。您不该在作品里非难那位女主人公……要知道,一个人对另一个人产生感情原没有什么可以非议的地方,她并没有伤害另一个人的生活……其实,那男主人公对她也会有感情的。不过为了另一个人的快乐,他们不得不割舍自己的爱情……"

这时,有一个交通民警走到停放小汽车的地方,大声地训斥着司机,说车停的不是地方。司机为难地解释着。他停住了说话,回头朝那边望了望,匆匆地说了声:"再见!"便大步走到汽车旁边,向那民警说:"对不起,这不怪司机,是我……"

我看着这上了年纪的人,也俯首贴耳地听着民警的训斥,觉得很是有趣。当我把顽皮的笑脸转向母亲的时候,我看见她是怎样地窘迫呀!就像小学校里一个一年级的小女孩,凄凄惶惶地站在那严厉的校长面前一样,好像那民警训斥的是她而不是他。

汽车开走了,留下了一道轻烟。很快地,就连这道轻烟也随风消散了,好像什么都没有发生过,而我,不知道为什么却没有很快地忘记。

现在分析起来,他准是以他那强大的精神力量引动了母亲的心。那强大的精神力量来自他那成熟而坚定的政治头脑,他在动荡的革命时代里出生入死的经历,他活跃的思维,工作上的魄力,文学艺术上的素养……而且——说起来奇怪,他和母亲一样喜欢双簧管。对了,她准是崇拜他。她说过,要是她不崇拜那个人,那爱情准连一天也维持不下。

至于他爱不爱我的母亲,我就猜不透了。要是他不爱她,为什么笔记本里会有这样一段记载呢?

"这礼物太厚重了。不过您怎么知道我喜欢契诃夫呢?"

"你说过的!"

"我不记得了。"

"我记得。我听到你有一次在和别人闲聊的时候说起过。"

原来那套契诃夫小说选集是他送给母亲的。对于她,那几乎就是爱情的信物。

没准儿,他这个不相信爱情的人,到了头发都白了的时候才意识到他心里也有那种可以称为爱情的东西存在,到了他已经没有权利去爱的时候,却发生了这足以使他献出全部生命的爱情。这可真够凄惨的。也许不只是凄惨,也许还要深刻得多。

关于他,能够回到我的记忆里来的就是这么一小点。

她那迷恋他、却又得不到他的心情有多么苦呀!为了看一眼他乘的那辆小车,以及从汽车的后窗里看一眼他的后脑勺,她怎样煞费苦心地计算过他上下班可能经过那条马路的时间;每当他在台上作报告,她坐在台下,隔着距离、烟雾、昏暗的灯光、攒动的人头,看着他那模糊不清的面孔,她便觉得心里好像有什么东西凝固了,泪水会不由地充满她的眼眶。为了把自己的泪水瞒住别人,她使劲地咽下它们。逢到他咳嗽得讲不下去，她就会揪心地想到为什么没人阻止他吸烟？担心他又会犯了气管炎。她不明白为什么他离她那么近而又那么遥远。

他呢，为了看她一眼，天天，从小车的小窗里，眼巴巴地瞧着自行车道上流水一样的自行车辆，闹得眼花缭乱；担心着她那辆自行车的闸灵不灵，会不会出车祸；逢到万一有个不开会的夜晚，他会不乘小车，自己费了许多周折来到我们家的附近，不过是为了从我们家的大院门口走这么一趟；他在百忙中也不会忘记注意着各种报刊，为的是看一看有没有我母亲发表的作品。

在他的一生中，一切都是那么清楚、明确，哪怕是在最困难的时刻。但在这爱情面前却变得这样软弱，这样无能为力。这在他的年纪来说，实在是滑稽可笑的。他不能明白，生活为什么偏偏是这样安排着的？

可是，临到他们难得地在机关大院里碰了面，他们又竭力地躲避着对方，匆匆地点个头便赶紧地走开去。即使这样，也足以使我母亲失魂落魄，失去听觉、视觉和思维的能力，世界立刻会变成一片空白……如果那时她遇见一个叫老王的同志，她一定会叫人家老郭，对人家说些连她自己也听不懂的话。

她一定死死地挣扎过，因为她写道：

　　我们曾经相约：让我们互相忘记。可是我欺骗了你，我没有忘记。我想，你也同样没有忘记。我们不过是在互相欺骗着，把我们的苦楚深深地隐藏着。不过我并不是有意要欺骗你，我曾经多么努力地去实行它。有多少次我有意地滞留在远离北京的地方，把希望寄托在时间和空间上，我甚至觉得我似乎忘记了。可是等到我出差回来，火车离北京越来越近的时候，我简直承受不了冲击得使我头晕眼花的心跳，我是怎样急切地站在月台上张望，好像有什么人在等着我似的。不，当然不会有。我明白了，什么也没有忘记，一切都还留在原来的地方。年复一年，就跟一棵大树一样，它的根却越来越深地扎下去，想要拔掉这生了根的东西实在太困难了，我无能为力。

　　每当一天过去，我总是觉得忘记了什么重要的事情，或是夜里突然从梦中惊醒：发生了什么事情？不，什么也没有发生，我清清楚楚地意识到：没有你！于是什么都显得是有缺陷的，不完满的，而且是没有任何东西可以弥补的。我们已经到了这一生快要完结的时候了，为什么还要像小孩子一样地忘情？为什么生活总是让人经过艰辛的跋涉之后才把你追求了一生的梦想展现在你的眼前？而这梦想因为当初闭着眼睛走路，不但在岔道上错过了，而且这中间还隔着许多不可逾越的沟壑。

对了，每每母亲从外地出差回来，她从不让我去车站接她，她一定愿意自己孤零零地站在月台上，享受他去接她的那种幻觉。她，头发都白了的、可怜的妈妈，简直就像个痴情的女孩子。

那些文字并没有多少是叙述他们的爱情的，而多半记载的都是她生活里的一些琐事：她的文章为什么失败；她对自己的才能感到了惶惑和猜疑；珊珊（就是我）为什么淘气，该不该罚她；因为心神恍惚她看错了戏票上的时间，错过了一场多么好的话剧；她出去散步，忘了带伞，淋得像个落汤鸡……她的精神明明日日夜夜都和他在一起，就像一对恩爱的夫妻。其实，把他们这一辈子接触过的时间累计起来计算，也不会超过二十四小时。而这二十四小时，大约比有些人一生享受到的东西还深、还多。莎士比亚笔下的朱丽叶说过："我不能清算我财富的一半。"大约，她也不能清算她的财富的一半。

似乎他在"文化大革命"中死于非命。也许因为当时那种特定的历史条件，这一段的文字记载相当含糊和隐晦。我奇怪我那因为写文章而受着那么厉害的冲击的母亲，是用什么办法把这习惯坚持下来的？从这隐晦的文字里，我还是可以猜得出，他大约是对那位红极一世、权极一时的"理论权威"的理论提出了疑问，并且不知对谁说过，"这简直就是右派言论。"从母亲那沾满泪痕的纸页上可以看出，他被整得相当惨，不过那老头子似乎十分坚强，从没有对这位有大来头的人物低过头，直到死的时候，留下来的最后一句话还是："就是到了马克思那里，这个官司也非打下去不可。"

这件事一定发生在一九六九年的冬天，因为在那个冬天里，还刚近五十岁的母亲一下子头发全白了。而且，她的臂上还缠上了一道黑纱。那时，她的处境也很难。为了这条黑纱，她挨了好一顿批斗，说她坚持四旧，并且让她交代这是为了谁。

"妈妈，这是为了谁？"我惊恐地问她。

"为一个亲人！"然后怕我受惊似地解释着，"一个你不熟悉的亲人！"

"我要不要戴呢？"她做了一个许久都没有对我做过的动作，用手拍了拍我的脸颊，就像我小的时候她常做的那样。她好久都没有显出过这么温柔的样子了。我常觉得，随着她的年龄和阅历的增长，特别是那几年她所受过的折磨，那种温柔的东西似乎离她越来越远了，也或许是被她越藏越深了，以致常常让我感到她像个男人。

她恍惚而悲凉地笑了笑，说："不，你不用戴。"

她那双又干又涩的眼睛显得没有一点水份，好像已经把眼泪哭干了。我很想安慰她，或是做点什么使她高兴的事。她却对我说："去吧！"

我当时不知为什么生出了一种恐怖的感觉，我觉得我那亲爱的母亲似乎有一半已经随着什么离我而去了。我不由地叫了一声："妈妈！"

我的心情一定被我那敏感的妈妈一览无余地看透了。她温和地对我说："别怕，去吧！让我自己呆一会儿。"

我没有错，因为她的确这样地写着：

你去了。似乎我灵性里的一部分也随你而去了。

我甚至不能知道你的下落，更谈不上最后看你一眼。我也没有权利去向他们质询，因为我既不是亲眷又不是生前友好……我们便这样地分离了。我恨不能为你承担那非人间的折磨，而应该让你活下去！为了等到昭雪的那一天，为了你将重新为这个社会工作，为了爱你的那些个人们，你都应该活着啊！我从不相信你是什么三反分子，你是被杀害的、最优秀者中间的一个。假如不是这样，我怎么会爱你呢？我已经不怕说出这三个字。

纷纷扬扬的大雪不停地降落着。天哪，连上帝也是这样地虚伪，他用一片洁白覆盖了你的鲜血和这谋杀的丑恶。

我独自一人，走在我们唯一一次曾经一同走过的那条柏油小路上，听着我一个人的脚步声在沉寂的夜色里响着、响着……我每每在这小路上徘徊、流连，哪一次也没有像现在这样使我肝肠寸断。那时，你虽然也不在我身边，但我知道，你还在这个世界上，我便觉得你在伴随着我，而今，你的的确确不在了，我真不能相信。

我走到了小路的尽头，又折回去，重新开始，再走一遍。

我弯过那道栅栏，习惯地回头望去，好像你还站在那里，向我挥手告别。我们曾淡淡地、心不在焉地微笑着，像两个没有什么深交的人，为的是尽力地掩饰住我们心里那镂骨铭心的爱情。那是一个没有一点诗意的初春的夜晚，依然在刮着冷峭的风。我们默默地走着，彼此离得很远。你因为长年害着气管炎，微微地喘息着。我心疼你，想要走得慢一点，可不知为什么却不能。我们走得飞快，好像有什么重要的事情在等着我们去做，我们非得赶快走完这段路不可。我们多么珍惜这一生中唯一的一次"散步"，可我们分明害怕，怕我们把持不住自己，会说出那可怕的、折磨了我们许多年的那三个字："我爱你"。除了我们自己，大概这个世界上没有一个活着的人会相信我们连手也没有握过一次！更不要说到其他！

不，妈妈，我相信，再没有人能像我那样眼见过你敞开的灵魂。

啊，那条柏油小路，我真不知道它是那样充满了辛酸的回忆的一条小路。我想，我们切不可忽略世界上任何一个最不起眼的小角落，谁知道呢？那些意想不到的小角落会沉默地缄藏着多少隐秘的痛苦和欢乐呢？

难怪她写东西写得疲倦了的时候，她还会沿着我们窗后的那条柏油小路慢慢地踱来踱去。有时是彻夜不眠后的清晨，有时甚至是月黑风高的夜晚，哪怕是在冬天，哪怕峭厉的风像发狂的野兽似地吼叫，卷着沙石噼哩叭啦地敲打着窗棂……那时，我只以为那不过是她的一种怪僻，却不知她是去和他的灵魂相会。

她还喜欢站在窗前，瞅着窗外的那条柏油小路出神。有一次，她显出那样奇特的神情，以致我以为柏油小路上走来了我们最熟悉的、最欢迎的客人。我连忙凑到窗前，在深秋的傍晚，只有冷风卷着枯黄的落叶，飘过那空荡荡的小路的路面。

好像他还活着一样，用文字和他倾心交谈的习惯并没有因为他的去世而中断。直到她自己拿不起来笔的那一天。在最后一页上，她对他说了最后的话：

> 我是一个信仰唯物主义的人，现在我却希冀着天国。倘若真有所谓天国，我知道，你一定在那里等待着我。我就要到那里去和你相会，我们将永远在一起，再也不会分离。再也不必怕影响另一个人的生活而割舍我们自己。亲爱的，等着我，我就要来了——

我真不知道，妈妈，在她行将就木的这一天，还会爱得那么沉重。像她自己所说的，那是镂骨铭心的。我觉得那简直不是爱，而是一种疾痛，或是比死亡更强大的一种力量。假如世界上真有所谓不朽的爱，这也就是极限了。她分明至死都感到幸福：她真正地爱过。她没有半点遗憾。

　　　　　　　　　　　　　　　　　　　中国文学选读

如今，他们的皱纹和白发早已从碳水化合物变成了其他的什么元素。可我知道，不管他们变成什么，他们仍然在相爱着。尽管没有什么人间的法律和道义把他们拴在一起，尽管他们连一次手也没有握过，他们却完完全全地占有着对方。那是任什么都不能使他们分离的。哪怕千百年过去，只要有一朵白云追逐着另一朵白云；一棵青草傍依着另一棵青草；一层浪花拍打着另一层浪花；一阵轻风紧跟着另一阵轻风……相信我，那一定就是他们。

每每我看着那些题着"爱，是不能忘记的"笔记本，我就不能抑制住自己的眼泪。我哭，我不止一次地痛哭，仿佛遭了这凄凉而悲惨的爱情的是我自己。这要不是大悲剧就是大笑话。别管它多么美，多么动人，我可不愿意重复它！

英国大作家哈代说过："呼唤人的和被呼唤的很少能互相应答。"我已经不能从普通意义上的道德观念去谴责他们应该或是不应该相爱。我要谴责的却是：为什么当初他们没有等待着那个呼唤着自己的灵魂？

如果我们都能够互相等待，而不糊里糊涂地结婚，我们会免去多少这样的悲剧哟！

到了共产主义，还会不会发生这种婚姻和爱情分离着的事情呢？既然世界是这么大，互相呼唤的人也就可能有互相不能应答的时候，那么说，这样的事情还会发生？可是，那是多么悲哀啊！可也许到了那时，便有了解脱这悲哀的办法！

我为什么要钻牛角尖呢？

说到底，这悲哀也许该由我们自己负责。谁知道呢？也说不定还得由过去的生活所遗留下来的那种旧意识负责。因为一个人要是老不结婚，就会变成对这种意识的一种挑战。有人就会说你的神经出了毛病，或是你有什么见不得人的隐私，或是你政治上出了什么问题，或是你习钻古怪，看不起凡人，不尊重千百年来的社会习惯，你准是个离经叛道的邪人……总之，他们会想出种种庸俗无聊的玩意儿来糟蹋你。于是，你只好屈从于这种意识的压力，草草地结婚了事，把那不堪忍受的婚姻和爱情分离着的镣铐套到自己的脖子上去，来日又会为这不能摆脱的镣铐而受苦终身。

我真想大声疾呼地说："别管人家的闲事吧！让我们耐心地等待着，等着那呼唤我们的人，即使等不到也不要糊里糊涂地结婚！不要担心这么一来独身生活会成为一种可怕的灾难。要知道，这兴许正是社会生活在文化、教养、趣味……等等方面进化的一种表现！"

一九七九年

## Introduction to the Works of Zhang Chengzhi

Zhang Chengzhi(张承志 1948～)is from the Hui ethnic group and at one time worked in archeology as a historical researcher. Currently a freelance writer, he writes and publishes works in Mongolian and Japanese languages as well as in Chinese. His early works, such as *Black Steed*(《黑骏马》1982) and *Northern River* (《北方的河》1984), incorporate themes of a young intellectual dealing with life on the grasslands, grasslands which absorb nutrients from the earth and give local life its strength and spiritual nourishment. In his later works he combines his personal ideals with his religious beliefs to undertake a spiritual search for the survival of the Hui people and their faith, such as in his novel *Inner Spirit*(《心灵史》1991). In contemporary Chinese literature Zhang is especially noted for his strong idealism.

张承志

In this chapter, Zhang Chengzhi's short story, *Green Night*(《绿夜》), poetically presents the simple and beautiful life of the grasslands and contrasts it with his reflections on, and disappointments felt towards, modern urban civilization.

中国文学选读

## Selection from Zhang Chengzhi's Works

### Green Night

After he had finally climbed up the small hill, he raised his head, drew a deep breath and gazed into the distance.

The dazzling and rich green, boundless in all directions, seemed to fill the space between sky and earth. He sensed in it a bitterness, an intimacy and an elusive melancholy. It also brought to mind myriads of recollections. His thoughts fluttered like a soundless, sentimental melody above the immeasurable expanse of grass, his body and soul transparent and tranquil.

Little Oyuna had been only eight years old then. She had sat astride the horse, her hands holding the saddle tightly. She fixed her gaze on him with pursed lips before she broke into loud crying. He had put her on the horse to divert the sorrow of their parting. Huge masses of white clouds surged from the light-blue horizon, lining up like a long formation against the azure sky. And Oyuna, this little girl of eight, what did she have on her mind? How could the light-blue line between the sky and earth produce such endless clusters of white clouds?

What a fresh feeling—giving free rein to thoughts without looking for an answer. The ocean-like emerald had filtered away the noisy, disorderly and boring yesterday. And now, here on the hilltop he could remain alone for awhile recalling the past without being disturbed. For eight full years he never again found such a serene moment. Perhaps there had not been an appropriate time or environment, though in the hustle and bustle he had often told himself: Hey, you should stop awhile to meditate carefully. Maybe, sooner or later in his life, he would be entitled to a little time for such placid, uninterrupted contemplation.

Eight years had elapsed. It was eight years before that he set out from the slope of this small hill and headed for the clamorous, bustling city along this same road with three wheel tracks. At first he often recalled Oyuna's sweet dimples and intelligent big eyes, resembling those of a baby camel. He had even published a short poem about the little girl, in which he compared her to a "joyous stream". But, oh, life—carrying coal and storing cabbages in winter, swarms of mosquitoes and flies droning in summer, machines roaring day and night in the factory beside his simple flat, the long queue before a beancurd shop... Such worldly occupations and discomforts had submerged his poem. Deep in the night he had infrequently glimpsed the flash of a star with his mind's eye, but he never recaptured the twinkling that had shaken his heart to the core.

He had left the past behind a long time ago. But now, the boundless green grassland, the winding wheel tracks and the gentle slope, were slowly taking him back in time. Here, he had been burned dark red by the sun, he had come to fierce blows with people, and he had learned the difficulties and pride of manual labor. He fixed his gaze on the limitless green. White clouds, like large boats, sailed away noiselessly in the azure sky. When the indigo shadow cast by the clouds disappeared, the three wheel tracks appeared bright and clear under the rays of the sun. This road led to his youth long gone. He seemed to hear a call from far away, and his eyes moistened as he murmured, "Oh, grassland."

This was the Xilin Gol grassland, consisting of such famous pastures as Left and Right Sunid, East and West Ujimqin, Abag and Abagnar. Now that he had finally returned, he felt an urge to open the door to his heart that had remained too long shut. His cousin had said, "May you sit steady on the gaunt back of Rocinante." Why? Because Don Quixote set out on that horse to begin his crusade against his imagined enemies, whereas he had packed his travel bag to look for his imagined pure land. He had simply cast a glance in silence at his cousin instead of disclosing his heart to him. They belonged to different generations, though he was only ten years senior. He could not bear to tell his cousin the story about little Oyuna, who was so sacred to him, for his cousin would very likely laugh in his face! Perhaps what happened eight years ago had dispersed like the clouds. But Oyuna's smile had stayed with him, the only gift left by time and life. It was also the only thing he possessed that helped him keep his dignity in front of his cousin, who would, of course, disagree with this. But then, he knew, he could find acknowledgement, sympathy, patience and condolence in the Xilin Gol grassland.

中国文学选读

He strode along the three wheel tracks, his feet brushing aside the tips of grass and his exposed chest embracing the sweeping grassland wind. He was so impatient to see the lovely girl with sweet dimples.

When he passed commune office a little while earlier, he had run into Kua Yisi, a native of Henan Province. From the crowd coming down to the long corridor of the first floor, Kua had accosted him, "Hey, brother. Come to collect folk songs? How much do you plan to reap this time? You should write a novel, making two or three thousand yuan. The last piece was worthless—how could you write about a little girl!" "Don't think everybody is like you," he had retorted, "only interested in money... " But Kua Yisi would not give in, "How about you? For just the few lines about that maiden you earned ten yuan! Would you have accepted one cent less?" The people nearby, who were leaving for home, roared with laughter. Their footsteps and cackling echoed in the dimly lit corridor. Speechless, he left the office building lonely and miserable. Why was there no communication between him and the others? Why were Kua Yisi and his cousin more popular? Did people detest the use of decent language to express sincerity, kindness and respect for the feelings of fellow beings?

That Henan rascal had shamelessly ridiculed, or worse, blasphemized his holy Oyuna. He felt as if a gush of dirty water had rushed into his heart and effortlessly invaded the tiny spot of pale-green land, which he had cherished at the innermost centre of his heart, often arousing in him tender feelings. He suddenly felt extremely exhausted.

He strode into the depths of the grassland, a little out of breath. The wide land and wild wind sweeping across it cleansed him of all artifice. Here he could forget about the many unpleasant things in the city—the smell of green onions and rotten tomatoes in the marketplace, the overcrowded twelve-square-meter flat, the noisy machines under his building, the icy-faced shop assistants, and the obscenities of that Henan rogue, Kua Yisi. Here he could bury himself in the lush grass and inhale the fresh air with immense gratitude. Only then did he come to see the necessity of returning here.

"This summer, take a trip back to Inner Mongolia," his wife had told him, her eyes on her knitting work. "You're kidding!" he replied. "How can I afford it?" He looked at her in surprise. "I'll be awarded a bonus of fifty yuan," she assured him. "We can also squeeze something out of other expenditures." "Forget about it," he said. "You are already grumbling aloud about my drinking and smoking." "This is different," she insisted, "ask for leave to go there next week." "Why?" he was perplexed. "Why not... I know, you've been looking forward to going back there." He had not expected her to see through him so easily. "But, there are the old and children at home," he hesitated. "Don't you worry about them? Just go ahead." He kissed her eyes, a wave of long forgotten warmth surging through his heart.

That night she added a dish of deep-fried peanuts to the dinner table, but he handled his chopsticks too clumsily to pick them up. He was like that when he was deep in thought, and his wife must have studied him closely at such times. In his mind's eye he saw a little girl smiling at him. She sported two upturned pigtails, like the horns of a sheep. Kua Yisi had sat on a horse and, while gesticulating wildly, was thrown to the ground. Oyuna giggled, showing her pretty dimples. At this recollection he couldn't help also laughing, and dropping another peanut on the ground. His wife, who was gently patting their baby son, smiled understandingly. That night his sleep was full of dreams, with Oyuna pestering him to translate his poem into Mongolian. He racked his brain the whole night.

After he had come to the end of the three wheel tracks, which formed an enormous curve on the grassland, and walked further, the familiar *aobao* hill gradually appeared on the horizon. The air here was imbued with the acrid smell of bitter wormwood and absinth. In the far distance he could vaguely make out a small gray speck in the middle of the broad basin. It was a dilapidated yurt from which cooking smoke was curling upwards along with the rising mist. Oyuna, my little sister, my pure stream. How have you been all these years? Do you still remember your reluctance to dismount from my horse when we were to depart? Do you remember the tearful eyes of your father, mother, and granny?

Tears welled up in his eyes. "Oyuna, it's me. Your elder brother has come back," he murmured softly.

Oh, youth, I've come to see you, because I have failed to keep you with me, though some people did so, like Pavel Korchagin. You have left me for too long. I'm unlike my cousin, who declares, "I have no yesterday." I have a yesterday and used to have my youth, which consisted of hope, difficulty, and humiliation. But there was also self-respect, derived from the hard labor to support myself. Of course, there was love, too, especially the ardent imaginings of it. His cousin once said, "Only the wretched look backwards; I only face the present reality." But his cousin lacked his experience, like singing those songs in the yurt on stormy nights or beside a bonfire. "Our flag is as red as fire/The stars and torches lead us forward." "Old uncle invites us to the orchard/Children, which one of you has made his companion cry?" "Young pioneers, we happy young pioneers! Come, let us sing a song!" "Red River Village.""Songs of the Long March" and "The Moon on the Fifteenth Day"— one song after another we sang enthusiastically. How can you, my young cousin, understand the wonderful feeling that kind of singing brought us? As we sang, we communicated with our eyes and smiles, our hearts filled with tears, aged wine and dew. .. Then all the people left. But the songs, the melody, the warmth and the feeling remained like the vestiges at the site where we pitched our tents. Those were the reminders of youth...

Granny, her hair all white now, came tottering out to meet him. She leaned on a broken lasso pole, extending a bony hand toward him. No one supported her as she walked. Her other strong and sturdy son had left the world before her. Muttering indistinctly, she held his head to her bosom and kissed his forehead with a crisp smack. That kiss, like an electric current, penetrated both his body and his soul, crushing every bit of rust that had accumulated in his heart. What would his cousin and Kua Yisi think of this picture? He, a city youth wearing a windbreaker in the embrace of an old Mongolian woman, her hair disheveled and her robe dirty and tattered. Caressing his face and shoulders, Granny mumbled that he had become too thin, and that he had suffered too much in the city during the past eight years. How strange, he thought. But then he had to admit she was absolutely right, which made his heart ache. He buried his head in her bosom, tears trickling down his cheeks despite himself.

This family still liked to spend the summer near the *aobao* hill. Everything remained unchanged: the green grass, the hill, the river, the felt rug covered with a layer of fine dung dust, the greasy pillows embroidered with golden thread, the sheep scattered on the hilly slopes like stars, and the thick yogurt emitting a cool aroma. Oyuna's sister-in-law prepared fist-sized dumplings for him. The women were kneeling on the wet, muddy ground milking the cows. The herdsmen rode on galloping horses, their postures leisurely and romantic, and their lasso poles drawing beautiful curves in the air. Homemade liquor was still more welcome than bottled liquor. Just a small half bowl made his chest burn. The evening clouds were as colorful as before and the moonlit night just as transparent. Inside the quiet, four-meters-across yurt, people from different ethnic groups and of different generations breathed evenly in their peaceful sleep. From the semicircle of a skylight he could see the bluish purple sky dotted with three bright stars, which reminded him of *A Train Ticket Studded with Stars*, a novel by Aksyonov in the 1960s.

Oyuna was not at home the day of his arrival; she was visiting a relative to the north of the *aobao* hill. He tried to visualize what she must look like after eight years. Oyuna, come back in your worn-out clothes dancing in the wind. Your little dimples made my heart ache. Come ride on my horse, my black-eyed angel, my pure stream.

The next day a young girl arrived in an ox-drawn wagon, her fluffy long hair drooping on her blue cotton robe smeared with grease, milk and wet ox dung. Without a word, she walked past him and hid behind her sister-in-law. Gone were her short, upturned braids. So were her dimples. Her skin was coarse and her eyes dim and cold. She did not even call him "A'ha"—elder brother. He was dismayed. Fumbling in his travel bag, he somehow managed to fish out a rose-colored nylon blouse, decorated with a few snow-white, wavelike stripes. With trembling hands, he handed the garment to her. "Oyuna, this is for you," he said in a quivering voice. He had dropped "little" because she was no longer a small girl. Oyuna took the blouse and walked away without a word, her head lowered. He heard her sorting out things on the ox-drawn wagon and suddenly became conscious of the eyes of his wife, his cousin and Kua Yisi staring at his back. Is this the Oyuna who was his poem, the oasis in his barren heart, the symbol of his lost youth?

中国文学选读

The basic framework of life was just like the grassland having shaken off its dreamlike gauze. Oyuna had put on the new rose blouse, but hid it underneath her blue robe. She was no longer the little angel, the joyful river of eight years ago. She sat there catching flies with her ox-dung stained hands, without the slightest touch of self-consciousness. She hid herself behind the door eavesdropping on old Mende and her mother discussing her future marriage. When her younger brother cried nonstop, she grabbed a spoon and a boot and threw them at him. She deftly kneaded dough in a basin to make noodles. She pulled a fat, one-meter tall sheep over on its side to shear its velvety summer wool. Her big eyes were filled with curiosity as she stared at the elder brother she had loved when she was eight. Then, as if struck by a sudden thought, she tossed her plait over her back and walked away. On the nights when there was no moon or stars, she would, like old Granny, howl in an extended voice to scare away wolves. She was like any other Mongolian woman, sleeping under a felt blanket on the ox-drawn wagon outside the yurt to care for the sheep. Braving wind and rain, she had grown up and matured. Her rough cheeks each had a scar, left from a bout of chilblains. Gone were the pleasant tunes produced by the small streams and springs—only a dirty inland river mutely flowed on the dry grassland.

His eyes followed Oyuna when she was busy at work. The girl had a black-speckled lamb, given to her by a relative who had gotten married in the spring. Every day Oyuna fed it milk with her little brother's bottle. At dusk, when the flock appeared on the slope, the lamb would leave the herd, bleating and running to Oyuna in the darkening or tangerine twilight. That was the happiest hour of the day for Oyuna, when she would call out to him, "A'ha! A'ha!" Her voice rang like a silver bell, sending joyful ripples into the still-water-like day. He could recognize the naive element in her voice of eight years ago and clumsily replied, "Ai—A'ha is coming! Wait a moment!" as he ran to her and the lamb. He held the milk bottle high in the air and the lamb, impatient to suck on it, stood up on its hind legs. A delighted Oyuna laughed happily, a pair of beautiful deep dimples on her red cheeks. "A'ha! A'ha!" she called to him, patting and pushing him cheerfully.

Such moments intoxicated him, because they brought back to him the eight-year-old angel, the little joyous stream. In the six years he had spent on the grassland, it was only on the last day that little Oyuna had tried to stop him from going away on horseback. As it was only on that last evening that his wife also made him feel that peculiar intimacy of the heart. For himself, during the past eight years he had enjoyed only one fleeting moment of beautiful inspiration, which he had turned into the short poem about Oyuna.

A few days later, the lame accountant Chulu, half-drunk, came to Oyuna's yurt. The lame one cast him a cold sidelong glance before dropping on to the felt rug from where he began hurling obscenities at Oyuna. Oyuna's sister-in-law was not at home and Granny was sleeping soundly in a corner. Chulu laughed raucously while pouring a bowl of wine onto Oyuna's bare feet. She dodged him and, tittering, added more wine to his bowl. The drunkard was encouraged. He pressed closer to her, tore open the collars of her blue robe and rosy blouse, pouring the wine onto her breasts.

His heart started beating wildly, but he restrained his anger. Granny mumbled something unintelligible in her dream. Oyuna's chuckling reminded him of the noisy bickering of the women workers in the factory beside his simple flat. "Imagined pure land," that's what his cousin would say with a cynical smile. He seemed to see Oyuna's rose-colored blouse and her snow-white, tight-fitting sweater soaked in Chulu's wine. He looked straight into the cripple's eyes. This sullen, ugly, fifty-year-old lame man was a tough horse-tamer. "My little girl..." As the lame one was saying this in Mongolian, he was seized with nausea. He dashed to the door, flung it open and ran out. He felt again the pain caused by the submergence of his short poem in the venomous ridicule of people such as Kua Yisi. He had a friend at the local ethnic printing house, Wu Bayir, who once told him, "As for the Mongolians, if you go to say hello, they'll kill a sheep to treat you." But things were not that simple. His memory of youth was much simpler, a memory kept in his mind despite the lapse of long years. It was like a dream, which, unfortunately, was vulnerable to the tongues of such people as Chulu and Kua Yisi.

Later he saw Oyuna supporting the drunk as he went to his horse and helping him to mount. On her way back, she darted a surprised look at him. Leaning against the felt wall of the yurt and seeing the girl pass him in a hurry, he wondered, "Oh,

Oyuna, are there no intimate and pure words even between you and me? The poem I wrote for you, not even that could cause any ripple in your heart?"

Oyuna brought a herd of cows back from the foot of the mountain. After deftly tying the cows to the milk wagon, she quickly scooped a basin of flour from the storage wagon, fetched a bucket of water, mixed the flour, kneaded the dough and made pieces of misshapen bread. From nearby she gathered some dried ox dung, using the front of her blue robe as a basket, put the dung in the stove and started a fire. As her youngest brother was still crying, she thrust a sheep's joint bone, dyed red, into his hands and cradled him in her arms while humming a lullaby. Afterwards she washed a stack of bowls, filled one with hot milk tea, added a teaspoon of butter and handed it to him. "A'ha, have some tea," she said. He took the bowl and raised his head to find Oyuna's eyes looking into his. After adding more fuel to the stove, Oyuna went to milk the cows, with one knee kneeling on the wet ground. As the stream of white milk sputtered into the bucket, the sun dipped behind the *aobao* hill. The black and white clouds all took on colors. Rays of golden red from the hilltop turned the yurt and the grassland to its west into the same gorgeous hue. Oyuna at this instant was transformed into a beauty wearing a cloak woven of the magnificent, rosy clouds.

Oh, time won't stop flowing for your sake, nor could Oyuna remain eight forever. Just like you, she needs to squarely face life, with its entire vicissitudes. It's dangerous looking for past dreams. Far better it is to keep the pure dreams in your heart only. To seek them in reality is tantamount to destroying them. Your cousin would never come to this wild grassland; he looks to Mount Huangshan and Mount Lushan, famous scenic mountains that serve but inspire no dreams. Kua Yisi worships only

《绿夜》插图

money, which is even further from your dreams. They are more realistic than you, and so are more at peace with life.

Maybe it's not so bad that his dreams were shattered, for he would then have to place his love somewhere in reality, instead of in dreams. Also he could seize the twinkling moments of beauty, when he would tell Oyuna more about that short poem, walking together with her in the sunset's glow and teasing the speckled lamb with the milk bottle. In Oyuna's pleasant chortling, he could relax both his body and emotions. What beautiful bliss!

As the days passed one by one, he finally found tranquility in the ancient, orderly and slow-paced lifestyle of the grassland—starting work early in the morning, then relaxing in the evening. He became enlightened, and began to understand Oyuna more profoundly. This is life: its tune, like some popular folk songs in northwest China and Inner Mongolia, is highly repetitive; its content is surprisingly simple. His cousin was wrong and he had been wrong, too. Only Oyuna was right. She took up her role in life calmly, no exclamation, no exasperation, no sighing. She changed water into milk tea, and milk into butter. She smiled at fate. Although she worked harder and suffered more of life's ugliness and harshness, she was happy serving hot tea and food to others, and feeding the life-sustaining milk to the speckled lamb. She was even transfigured into a stunning beauty in the crimson twilight. Why bother her, and in doing so, torture himself? No, he would enjoy the simple hours of the numbered days of his stay, just as she did every day.

His heart now beat calmly; he breathed evenly, and his eyes expressed tenderness. Riding on a stout white horse, he visited friends scattered far and wide on the grassland and at old man Mende's home he learned to sing "Gold-winged Birds." He exercised his arms and legs in the fresh morning air, and together with Oyuna, fed the speckled lamb in the crimson twilight. At night he reclined comfortably on the heavily stained embroidered pillow, while listening to comic crosstalk in Mongolian about Smoking Pipe and his wife Pipe Lighter. In the fresh, moistened air that infiltrated the yurt he slept like a baby. Reality was definitely more beautiful that what his cousin thought, but more complex and logical than what he had imagined. His body, his nerves and emotions had found peace in the serene night of vast grassland; he was totally freed from concerns for food and fuel, and there was no noise from factory machines. Wrapping himself smugly in the blanket Granny had put on him, he felt completely at one with the grassland.

That day he had drunk too much at a herdsman's tent sixty kilometers away. While swaying unsteadily on horseback on his way home, he saw the sun setting in the west, armies of dark blue clouds rolling above it.

Night fell and there were no stars. The horse trotted quickly, knowing the way well. He raised his head to sniff the damp air before the rain. More dark clouds must be gathering in the sky, he reckoned. At half past nine, almost immediately after he had crossed the Nogoon Wus River, large raindrops began spattering on the grassland.

His lined robe was soon soaked through. The cool raindrops fell on his liquor-warmed neck, from where they dripped to his equally hot chest. A half-drunk horseman does not mind riding on a rainy night at all—the darkness inspires in him a sense of bravery as if he were exploring some unknown path of life. He gave free rein to the horse, which galloped for two hours before reaching the *aobao* hill.

In the rainy darkness he saw a tiny point of light, like a jade-color pearl glowing in the night. It was from an electric torch, like the signal from a beacon on a murky sea. He urged the horse on with a whip towards the light.

There, standing outside the door, was Oyuna in a raincoat, holding the torch high. "A'ha!" She ran towards him, splashing in the puddles. She took over the reins and held his arm to help him dismount. In the pitter-patter he seemed to hear a strange strain of music. It was here that Oyuna had helped the limp accountant Chulu on to his horse. When he saw wet hair sticking to Oyuna's cheeks, that strange refrain struck his heart again. Inside the yurt a pot of noodles mixed with mutton was boiling. Oyuna's sister-in-law teased him by asking whether he had ridden the horse or whether the horse had carried him home. Granny kept scratching her silver-white hair, probably bothered by a louse. She told him there was more crosstalk on the radio about Smoking Pipe and Pipe Lighter. The hot noodle soup and aromatic mutton assured him of the comforts of home, particularly on that rainy night. On the Xilin

Gol grassland this was the only yurt that raised a light for him at night. The fire from burning ox dung warmed his bare chest as he enjoyed the noodles. He told Oyuna's sister-in-law the location of the herdsman's tent and mimicked the wedding speeches of Smoking Pipe and Pipe Lighter to amuse old Granny. He laughed, ate and talked merrily, but all the while he felt embarrassed because he was not saying what was ac-tually on his mind. He felt like crying. Someone pushed him. It was Oyuna offering him a small bowl of wine that smelled both fragrant and strong. He drained it, a fiery current slowly slipping down into his stomach. Again his heart was plucked by the mysterious refrain. "A'ha!" "Yes?" "Some more?" "Another half bowl please, Oyu-na!"

Later on he made a point of returning home late at night, and the family never asked him why. He had traveled one thousand kilometers to this felt yurt four meters in diameter—he wanted to experience again and again the ecstasy of hurrying back to this tiny dot in the grassland.

The vitality of the grassland was now hidden under the thick veil of night. All was quiet and still. Occasionally there came the distant clip pity-clop of hoofs, send-ing gentle vibrations through the earth that gently rocked his melancholy heart. The surprised chirping of birds rekindled that blissful refrain, so beautiful, so moving. He discerned in the darkness an even color, the green tone of July's grass submerged in the shade of night. In the limitless expanse of this hue there rose a bright star, the torch in Oyuna's hand. Around the light was a halo of pale green, like a firefly on the surface of a foggy lake. Oh, green night, the essence of the four seasons, the tender love of the land. The green night caressed, embraced and consoled him, encouraging him to go forward, heedless of his cousin's frowning and the jeering of people like Kua Yisi. He smiled, for he had discovered a new, wonderful melody in this green night.

Soon it was time to pack and leave. Granny gave him a small square amulet sewed with red cloth; Oyuna's sister-in-law presented him with a piece of green silk for his wife; Uncle Mende's gift was a bottle of milk wine. Other herdsmen brought cans of butter and crystalline, tinted porcelain bowls. Okabayashi Nobuyasu (a Japa-nese folk singer) once sang, "Gone are the tender feelings of the past." Sada Nasashi

中国文学选读

also sang, "You have left, your face stained with tears. " But he would not be leaving with tears; he would take within him the light Oyuna had held high for him in the green night. He knew what was gone was gone for good. Still, tomorrow, he would look back to the kindness with which they treated him today. People tend to keep in mind the most beautiful episodes of their past, and when these recollections are crushed by reality, they try to find something new to remember. Is this a weakness? Perhaps, this is how people should be. Despite repeated disappointments, there are indeed things in life that are worth recalling and cherishing.

"A'ha, quick!" Oyuna called to him in her happy laughter, just as the clouds in the west were being dyed golden red. He hurried to her. The speckled lamb was already there, jumping around her. He held up the feeding bottle. This last evening should be spent like this and, he hoped, in the beautiful picture composed of the sun, the clouds, the grassland, the lamb and Oyuna—that his own thin, small silhouette would be included.

"A'ha!" "Eh?" "Are you leaving tomorrow?" "Oh, I have to be going. " "Will you come again?" "Eh... " "Can you bring along my sister-in-law from the city?" "She? No, Oyuna, even A'ha himself doesn't know if he can come again. " "Is it very far?"... "A'ha!" "Eh?" "I want to give this lamb to you. " "Really?" "Of course! You already know how to feed it. " "My silly girl, keeping a lamb in the city is not allowed. " "Then what can I give you?" "Tonight, please raise the electric torch for me one more time, little Oyuna!"

Oyuna looked at him in surprise. He took the lamb from her and put it on the ground. It bleated and leapt back to him, sending Oyuna into a peal of merry laughter. This girl, clad in a worn-out blue robe was again transfigured into a fairy in the golden rays of the setting sun. On her rosy cheeks were two deep dimples that stirred his heart.

That night after bidding farewell to old Mende's family, he set his horse galloping back to the yurt to wait for him. Dim light sparkled on the ripples of Nogoon Wus River. A cool and fresh breeze ruffled the grass on the firm and warm soil. The July night, the green night, gently embraced him. He loosened the reins so that the horse shot forward as if it was flying.

His cousin would ask, "What did you find?" His wife would inquire, "How did you feel?" But, no, what he looked for no longer existed. He had a heavy heart, to tell the truth. But he knew for sure his experience would not become a new dream. He had planted his feet firmly on the tangible, infinite grassland. He would no longer compose naive poems as before. Like the adult Pavel Korchagin who played an accordion to amuse his lonely mother, he would sing his songs calmly, enthusiastically and with strong rhythms. He reined in the horse to a halt. In the boundless green night that wonderful refrain had gradually grown into a new, vigorous chapter. Its melody and the pure greenness of the night melted, moistened, warmed, enriched and vitalized his heart. Never before had he had such feelings. Gazing into the limitless, lovely grassland, he murmured, "Oh, grassland, farewell. Farewell, green night. Farewell, my Oyuna…"

In the far, far distance of the green night, a star burst into brightness.

1981

(translated by Zhang Siying)

## 绿　夜

他终于登上了那座小山。他抬起头来，深深地吸了一口气，向远方望去。

明亮而浓郁的绿色令人目眩。左右前后，天地之间都是这绿的流动。它饱含着苦涩、亲切和捉摸不定的一股忧郁。这漫无际涯的绿色，一直远伸到天边淡蓝的地平线，从那儿静静地等着他、望着他，一点点地在他心里勾起滋味万千的回忆。

在这一望无际的绿色上方，只有他的思绪在无声地盘旋轻飞，像是那绿中充盈的情调的旋律。他感到身心都透明般地宁静。

小奥云娜那时才八岁。她骑在马上，抓着鞍桥不肯松手。她紧闭着小嘴，牢牢地盯着他。后来她哇地嚎啕起来。本来把她抱上马背不过是为了冲淡分别的感伤。淡蓝的地平线上涌来了浩荡的白云，蓝空上排着云朵的长阵。奥云娜，这八岁小女孩的心理是怎样的呢？那天地间的一抹浅蓝中，又为什么能绵绵不尽地涌流出白白的云朵呢？

这是多么新鲜的感觉呵：可以自由地遐想，但用不着真的去寻找答案。大海般的绿色滤去了嘈杂、拥挤、热腻的昨天。此刻，在这儿，可以独自站一会儿，静静地想想过去。整整八年，他总是难得有机会这样站一会儿。也许是没有适当的时间和环境。可是在那匆忙的奔波中，他又确实常有过这样的念头：喂，该停下来，该仔细想想。也许，在人的一生中，需要留一些时间给这种独自一人的、平和的、不受干扰的思索。

八年了。八年前，他就是从这个小山坡前，顺着这条三股车辙印的道路走向那喧嚣着的、熙来攘往的都市的。最初他常常回忆。他想起过小奥云娜驼羔般聪慧的大眼睛和甜甜的酒涡。他甚至曾经发表过一首关于小奥云娜的小诗。在那首儿歌般的小诗里，他把小奥云娜称为一条"欢快的小河"。可是，哦，生活——冬天运蜂窝煤、储存大白菜，夏天嗡嗡而来的成团蚊蝇，简易楼下日夜轰鸣的加工厂，买豆腐时排的长队……淹没了诗。在深夜里，有时心里也曾闪过一眨星光，但他已经很难捕捉住那曾使他的心颤抖的一瞬。

而这一切都已离他远去。这茫无涯际的青青的原野，这弯曲的三股车辙印，这低缓的小山坡，正把他带回到昔日。在这儿他曾被晒成黑红色。在这儿他曾恶煞般和人打架。在这儿他第一次懂得了劳动的艰难和自豪。他凝望着这无边的绿色。蓝空中巨大的白船般的云朵无声地驶去了，深黛的云影移开后，那三股车道在阳光的直射下显得明亮而线条清晰。那里通向他逝去的青春。他已经听见一声遥远的呼唤。他的眼睛湿润了。"哦，草原。"他轻声说。


这里是锡林高勒。是由左右苏尼特、东西乌珠穆沁、阿巴嘎和阿巴哈纳尔等响亮的地名组成的锡林高勒草原。他终于回到了这里。他觉得自己就要打开紧闭着的、心上的门。表弟说过："祝你在洛西南特的瘦背上骑得稳。"为什么呢？"因为堂·吉诃德为寻找假想的敌人踏上征途，而你为寻找想象的净土而提起旅行袋。"他默默地看了表弟一眼。应当对属于不同世代的人闭紧心扉。他和他仅差十岁，但属于两代人。他怎么能把小奥云娜的事告诉他，再被他恣意挖苦嘲弄一番呢！不，小奥云娜是不能玷污的……也许，八年前的一切都已烟消云散，但岁月、生活和动荡的历史留给他的唯一礼物，就是小奥云娜的笑脸。他比表弟仅仅多这么一点财富。当然，表弟是不会承认这种结论的。承认他、同意他、等待和安慰他的，是这锡林高勒大草原。

他等不及捎口信给毡包。他一到公社，就大步踏上了这条三马车道。他解开衣服，草原的长风直入胸怀。草梢在脚下唰唰地分开。他渴望看到那可爱的小姑娘。他的眼前已经清晰地现出了一对甜甜的酒涡。

"老弟，这回采风，时机难得。怎么样？计划捞多少？"人流正匆匆地涌向办公楼底层那长长的楼道。河南口音的侉乙己追着他问个不休。"这回弄个长篇小说，抓它个两三千！上回那不中——咋写个小妮儿！"脚步囔囔，人流匆匆。"你别以为人人都和你一样，光想捞钱……""咋？"侉乙己恨恨地囔起来，"你咋着了！你崇高多少？你编小妮儿那几句词，还不是落了十块！少一分你能行？"一阵哄笑。原来下班的人都在满有滋味地听着。他们赞成侉乙己。楼道光线很暗。脚步声、谈笑声在墙壁上去出回音。他默默走着。孤独使人痛苦。缺乏沟通彼此的语言使人孤独。人们为什么更欣赏侉乙己的或表弟的语言呢？难道大家都讨厌用真诚的，亲切的，尊重别人感情，也使自己更纯净的语言交谈么？

这个河南侉子就这样无耻地嘲弄了，不，是侮辱了他神圣的小奥云娜。他觉得自己的心里也涌进一股污浊的脏水。这脏水居然那么轻易地冲进了他一直悄悄保留在心底的、使他的心温柔和潮润的、那一小块淡绿色的领地。他突然感到疲倦，他累得要命。

他微喘着，大步走向草原深处。这里是驰骋着自由酷烈的风儿的、开人胸襟的莽原。在这里可以不必心有城府。在这里可以把市场上大葱和烂西红柿的气味，把十二平米的家和它的拥塞，把楼下加工厂的噪音和冷冰冰的售货员，还有那河南腔的下流语言全部忘掉。在这里可以把疲惫的肉体埋在茂盛的箭草、马镰草和青灰色的艾可草丛里。他满怀感激地吞咽着这里的清爽空气。这时他才明白来到这里的必要。

"今年夏天，你回内蒙去吧。""开玩笑！哪有那么多钱？"他奇怪地望着低头织毛线的妻子。"我能领到五十块奖金。另外还可以再挤出一些。""算啦。连我喝酒抽烟你都叫唤。""不，这回不一样。你下周就请假走吧。""为什么呢？""不为什么……我觉得，你一直盼着回去一次。"她原来有一双锐利的眼睛。他迟疑了："可是家里，老人，孩子……""没关系，去吧。"他吻了吻她的眼睛，心头掠过一道生疏了的温暖的波动。

那天晚上她炸了花生米。可是他的筷子却总是夹滑。在他若有所思时总是这样。妻子也许就是常在这种时候注视着他。一个扎着两只羊角小辫的小姑娘正在对他笑。侉乙己骑在一匹马上指手画脚，马儿把他摔在地上。小奥云娜笑了，露出小酒涡。他忍俊不禁，所以又把一颗花生米掉在地上。一旁，妻子拍着襁褓中的儿子，微微地也笑了。夜里他一直在做梦。小奥云娜缠着他，要他翻译那首小诗。他绞了一夜脑汁。

他走完了三股车道在草原上画出的那个巨大的弧形。那座熟悉的熬包山从地平线下慢慢浮现出来。清凉的风带来阵阵苦蒿和艾可草的呛人苦味儿。在远处，在开阔的盆地中心，隐约能辨出一个小小的灰点。那是一座破旧的、颜色发灰的蒙古包。炊烟随着流雾，正从那里袅袅升起。小奥云娜，我可爱的小妹妹，我清澈的小河，你好么？你还记得我们分别时，你骑在我的马鞍上不肯下来的往事么？你还记得父亲、母亲，还有老奶奶流着泪水，望着我们的情景么？

　　他的眼眶里盈满了晶莹的泪。"小奥云娜，是我。你的哥哥回来了。"他轻声说。

　　哦，青春，你好！我来看你。因为我没有能留你永驻，像保尔·柯察金，像那些生命之树常青的勇士一样。我已经与你分别日久。但我也不同于表弟。表弟说："我们没有昨天。"这是他的宣言。而我却既有昨天也有你。你由憧憬、艰辛、低下地位带来的屈辱感和自尊感，真正养活自己的劳动中留下的深深脚印组成。当然，还有爱情，尤其是对它激动的想象。表弟说："没落的人才回顾过去。我们只面对现实。"但他也应该感到缺憾。至少该为他没有唱过、而且是没有在暴风雪之夜的帐篷里，在通红的牛粪火旁唱过那些歌子遗憾。"我们的旗帜火一样红，星星和火把指明前程。""老伯伯请我们来到果园。孩子们是谁呀打哭了伙伴。""少先队，我们快乐的少先队！快快来，快把歌儿唱起来！"我们起劲地、一支接一支地唱。当然，也唱《红河村》、《长征组歌》、《十五的月亮》和那个听说作者被张春桥判了十年刑的知识青年的歌。那种唱法会给人带来神奇的感受。我们唱着，传递着会心的眼神和微笑。心里盈满着泪珠、醇酒和露水……后来，人走了。但那声音、那灼烤、那旋律、那心境却和迁徙后的营盘痕迹一起，在此长留。它就是你，青春……

　　白发苍苍的老奶奶拄着一节断马杆，颤巍巍地，伸着瘦骨嶙峋的手迎面奔来。没有人扶她走。她虎背熊腰的儿子已经先她辞世。老人声音微弱地叨叨着，缓缓地跑来。她捧住他的头喷地亲了一口。这亲吻电流般击穿了他的肉体，击碎了他心上的锈垢。表弟不会理解，侉乙己不会相信，一个穿风衣的城市青年就在这片箭草地上被一个白发蓬乱、衣袍肮脏的蒙古老太婆搂在怀里。老奶奶摸索着他的脸和肩头，唠叨着说他瘦了。她坚信他八年来是在城里受苦。"多奇怪，"他想着，便却又感到老奶奶说得切中隐痛。他忍不住流下了泪。他把头埋在老人怀里。

　　这个家仍然喜欢在夏季靠敖包山居住。青草如旧。山岗如旧。小河如旧。永远沾着一层细粪末的垫毡和油腻的捻金线枕头也如旧。羊群还是在敖包山上散成一个星群。酸奶桶里舀出的奶子还是稠稠的、散发着熟悉的凉味儿。嫂子给他煮的还是拳头大的饺子。她还是把舀起沸茶的铜勺举在孩子头顶上威胁他们。女人们还是在濛濛细雨中跪在一片泥泞中挤奶。马儿在奔跑时还是在耳边掀起呼啸的风。歪着骑马的牧人还是那样姿态浪漫。套马杆子还是那么富有弹性地在空中划出弧线。酒还是散装的更受欢迎。当然，用兽医的酒精对井水也不错。一口喝掉半小碗还是烧得胸口发痛。可是老头门德如果高兴地使劲拍他的肩膀，并且瞪圆眼睛朝着脸色阴沉的瘸子乔洛吼一会《金翅小鸟》的话，再喝半碗也可以考虑。晚霞还是那么鲜艳。月夜还是那么清澄如洗。沉睡的毡包内还是那么静寂。直径四米的圆形地面上，不同民族、不同辈份的人的呼吸还是那么酣沉而平和。半圆形天窗里嵌进的那块蓝紫色的夜空，和点缀其上的三颗亮晶晶的小星，还是那么使他联想到阿克肖诺夫的《带星星的火车票》。

　　到达那天，他没有见到小奥云娜。在她赶着牛车从敖包山北的亲戚家回来以前，他想象着八年后那扎羊角辫的小女孩的模样。他心里在悄悄呼唤着她。小奥

《绿夜》插图

云娜，回来吧，你快活飞舞的破衣衫，你让人心疼的小酒涡！骑在我的马背上来吧，我的黑眼睛的小天使，我明净的小河！

第二天，一个穿着蓝布袍子的少女从牛车上下来了。她把蓬松的长发低垂在沾满油污、奶渍和稀牛粪的蓝布袍上，不声不响地从他身旁走过，躲到嫂子背后。她没有羊角似的翘小辫，没有两个酒涡。她皮肤粗糙，眼神冷淡。她甚至没有亲热地喊他一声阿哈——哥哥。他慌了。他从提包里掏出塑料袋，那是妻子跑遍全城买来的尼龙衫。玫瑰红上游着几道雪白的浪。他的手在抖。"奥云娜，"他唤道，"唀——这是给你的。"声音也在抖。他没有叫她"小奥云娜"。这不是那个"小"女孩了。少女接了过来，低着头走开了。他听见她在门外收拾牛车。他感到此刻妻子、表弟、侉乙己都在盯着自己的脊背。这是他的小诗、他干旱心田中的绿洲、他青春往事的象征、他的小奥云娜么？

生活露出平凡单调的骨架。草原褪尽了如梦的轻纱。就像肥嫩的手抓肉吃完以后，人们开始更心平气和地煮那些晒硬的肉干一样。穿上玫瑰红的尼龙衫又套上蓝布袍子的少女不会再是梳羊角辫的小奥云娜、小天使和欢乐的小河了。她满不在乎地用捧过牛粪的手挤着玫瑰红和雪白上的虱子。她躲在门外听着老门德和她母亲议论着娶她当儿媳妇的话。她抓起勺子和靴子朝哭个不停的弟弟扔去。她把满脸盆面粉拼成面条。她摔倒一米高的肥羊，骑在上面撕下滑腻的夏毛。她用大眼睛好奇地直盯着她在八岁时曾经那样留恋过的兄长。她若有所思，又猛然一甩辫子走开。她像老奶奶一样拖着长调，在没有月光和星星的黑夜里吓狼。她像每一个蒙古女人一样，睡在门外的勒勒车上，盖着一块条毡守夜。她淋着细雨，踏着泥泞，她长高了，她成熟了。她粗糙的脸庞上留着两块冬天的冻疮。小河、小溪、小泉奏出的明快儿歌已经逝而不返，浑浊的内陆河水正在干旱的大草原上无声地流。

他常常在奥云娜忙碌的时候注视着她。奥云娜有一只属于自己的青花山羊羔，那是一个亲戚家的出嫁姑娘在春季送给她的礼物。当时小羊羔只有一丁点儿大。她用弟弟的奶瓶每天给它补奶。傍晚，当归来的羊群悄悄出现在山坡上时，那只系着铃铛的青花小羊就咩咩叫着离群而来。他注视着小羊羔冲进乳青色的薄暮或是桔红的落霞，朝奥云娜奔来。这是奥云娜一天中最快活的时刻，也是他能听到奥云娜清脆的、使他感动的"阿哈！阿哈！"的喊声的时刻。水一样平静和怅惘的日子在这时掀起一层微微的喜悦的涟漪。这银铃样的喊声刺着他的耳鼓。他在其中辨出了八年前小奥云娜天真稚嫩的音素。"哎——阿哈来了！等一等！"他笨拙地答应着跑去。他把奶瓶高高地举起，小青羊羔急得直立起来。奥云娜格格地笑了，她红扑扑的脸蛋上又深深地旋出了两个甜美的酒涡。"阿哈！阿哈！"她快活地摇着他。

在这样的时刻里，他感到陶醉。因为在他发现自己失去了那个八岁的小天使和"欢乐的小河"以后，还是捕捉到了这美好的一刻。小奥云娜在他长达六年的草原生涯中，也只是在最后一天不让他上马离去。妻子也仅仅是在那个晚上使他感受到奇异的、心的亲近。他自己也一样：八年中仅仅一次产生过那样美好的情思并把它变成那首小诗。

过了几天，半醉的瘸会计乔洛来到毡包里。他也斜着醉眼，冷冷地盯了他一眼，然后栽倒在毡子上。他开始对奥云娜说出一些难听的秽语。嫂子不在家。老奶奶睡在角落里。乔洛嘎声笑着，把碗里的酒泼在奥云娜的赤脚上。奥云娜躲闪着，咯咯笑着，又给他添着酒。她鼓舞了这醉鬼。于是乔洛借着酒劲，拖着瘸腿凑过去。他推倒了奥云娜，放肆地扯开奥云娜蓝色和玫瑰红的领口，把酒咕嘟嘟地灌进她的怀里。而奥云娜却似乎十分快乐，她咯咯的笑声更清脆了。

他的心在剧烈地急跳。他抑制着怒火。白发的奶奶在一旁嘟囔着梦话。奥云娜的笑声使他联想到简易楼下那加工厂女工们的吵闹声。"想象的净土"，表弟一定正露出富有哲理的微笑。她贴身穿的玫瑰红和雪白的紧身衫一定浸透了乔洛的酒。他逼视着乔洛。这不是可以谅解的强悍的驯马手，这是一个阴沉的、五十来岁的丑恶瘸子。是讲蒙语的倨乙己。"小妮儿——"他突然恶心，想吐，他掩开小门冲到了包外。他又感到那首小诗淹没在恶毒的舌头和哄笑中唤起的痛苦之中。他在民族印刷厂有个熟人叫乌·巴雅尔，"嗨，蒙古人嘛！"乌·巴雅尔说。"你过去问一声好，他们就杀一只羊。"事实可没有这么简单。而对青青的记忆却比这简单。在岁月冲刷了很久之后．它留存下来，留在记忆里，像一个梦。可为什么又有瘸子乔洛、倨乙己呢？他们专门消灭这些梦。

后来，他看着奥云娜扶着这醉鬼走过去。在棚车那儿，奥云娜热心地把瘸子扶上马。她走回来时惊奇地望了他一眼。他斜靠着毡壁，看着姑娘从他身旁匆匆走过。哦，奥云娜，难道我们之间也没有了那种亲近和纯净的语言么？那为你写的诗句，难道竟灭不起你心上的一点波浪么？

奥云娜从山脚赶来一群乳牛。她敏捷地把牛一头头拴在车上。随即又从箱车里舀出一盆面粉。她飞快地提来一桶水。她揉好了不成形状的馒头，然后用蓝袍子前襟兜来一兜牛粪。炉火熊熊烧起来了。可是最小的弟弟在哭。她塞给弟弟一个染成红色的羊拐骨．然后拍着他，哼着催眠曲。她洗净一叠磁碗，她斟上一碗热奶茶，加上一勺黄油。她走了过来。"阿哈，喝茶啦。"她的声音平静自然。他抬起头，奥云娜黑黑的眼睛正凝视着他。他接过碗来。奥云娜添上燃料，然后走到那排乳牛跟前。她单膝跪在牛腿下的泥泞里。"嗤——嗤——"白色的奶浆喷射到木桶里。就在这时，太阳沉入了敖包山。乌云和白云都变幻了色彩。一派金红从山顶的云霞中朝这儿斜斜投来，镀红了一条狭长的草原和这座毡包。奥云娜成了一个披着红霞的、不认识的美丽姑娘。

哦，岁月不会为你而停止流逝，小奥云娜也不会为你而永远是八岁。和你一样，她也正迎面走向自己的人生，在生活的长流中浮沉。执拗地醒着去寻找逝去的梦是件可怕的事。应当让那种过于纯洁的梦永远萦绕在心头。因为在现实中追求梦境就是使梦破灭。你来到这荒莽的草原，而表弟只向往黄山和庐山，那些名胜只有服务，不会有梦。侉乙己则只向往钱，钱更不是梦。他们都比你更实际，因此也比你更安宁。

梦的破灭不是坏事，这使他将把献给梦的爱情投入现实。抓住生活中那瞬间的美，向奥云娜讲述那首小诗，和她一块走进晚霞，朝小青羊羔高高举起奶瓶，在奥云娜的笑声中，舒展开疲惫的躯体和感情，享受这美好的一瞬吧。

日子一天天过去了。他在草原古老的、日出而作的秩序中，在那循回不已的低缓节奏中平静了，感悟了。他开始更深地理解了奥云娜。生活总是这样：它的调子永远像陕北的信天游，青海的花儿与少年，蒙古的长调一样。周而复始，只有简单的两句，反复的两句。连风靡当代世界的"folk song"唱法也未离此宗。生活只是交响乐中两个主题永远矛盾的第一乐章。瘸乔洛耍的酒疯就是贝多芬著名的"命运的叩门"。正因为矛盾永恒才被人们代代咏叹，正因此，听到信天游、长调、花儿与少年才会有相似的感受。表弟错了。侉乙己错了。他自己也错了。只有奥云娜是对的。她比谁都更早地、既不声张又不感叹地走进了生活。她使水变成奶茶，使奶子变成黄油。她在命运叩门时咯咯地笑。她更累、更苦、更艰难。冲刷她的风沙污流更黑、更脏、更粗暴和难以躲避。然而她却给人们以热茶和食物，给小青羊羔以生命，给夕阳西下的草原以美丽的红衣少女。为什么要打搅她，也折磨自己呢？不，要和奥云娜和睦相处。要使这有限的几天假期更和谐和更有哲理，要使它成为人生旅途的一道清流。

他的心平静了，呼吸均匀了，眼神柔和了。他骑着大白马悠闲地串门。他去找那和善的老头门德学唱《金翅小鸟》。早晨，他在清爽的晨风中活动着筋骨；傍晚，他和奥云娜一块沐浴在红霞中喂小青羔。他舒适地枕着那个油腻黑污的绣枕，吸着透入毡墙的夏夜草原的清润空气。晚上，听完收音机里那个关于名叫烟筒的丈夫和名叫灶火的老婆的烟鬼夫妻的蒙语相声，带着忍俊不禁的神情，他香甜地睡着了。现实比表弟预言的美好，比乌·巴雅尔介绍的真实，又比他自己想象的复杂而合理。被大白菜、蜂窝煤和简易楼下轰鸣的噪音折磨得太累的肉体和他的神经、感情一起，正在这广袤的草原和如水的星夜里得到休息。他感到安慰和满足。他惬意地裹紧白发老奶奶给他盖上的毯子。他的呼吸和夜草原上牧草的潮声和谐地溶在一起。

这一天，他在六十里外的牧马人帐篷里喝了不少酒。当他歪歪斜斜地跨在马背上走向归途时，远处快要沉没的一轮红日上方正拥着一团团深蓝色的乌云。

天黑了。没有星星。马儿快步小跑着，它认识路。他抬起头，嗅到腥腥的雨气。他猜想漆黑的夜空上一定也正奔跑着、聚集着乌云。九点半钟，他刚刚涉过诺盖乌苏小河。沉重的雨点落下来了，草原上响着密麻麻的噼啪声。

夹布袍子湿透了。雨水淌过灼热的脖颈，冰凉地滑在胸脯上。微醉的骑手不会讨厌夜雨。淋着雨会产生一种空旷的、踏入人生漫漫长途时的勇敢。他纵马前行。两小时后，他催着马儿踏上了高高的敖包山。

雨丝濛濛的夜色中闪烁着一点光亮，像一颗翡翠的夜明珠。绿幽幽的，等待着他。是手电筒的灯光，是打给他的信号，就像暗夜的海洋上那灯塔的信号一样。他抽了马一鞭，向那灯光驰去。

奥云娜站在门外的雨中。披着雨衣，举着手电筒。"阿哈！"她啪啪地踏着地上的积水奔来。她接过缰绳。她扶着他的手臂。她帮助他跳下马来。雨声淅沥。这雨声中飘着一个陌生的乐句。瘸子乔洛也是在这儿被她扶上了马。他看见奥云娜面颊上紧贴着缕缕湿发。那个奇怪的乐句轻悄悄地叩着他的心弦。锅里已经煮开了香气袭人的羊肉面条，嫂子快活地问他是骑着马回来的还是马驮着他回来的。老奶奶搔着银白的乱发，可能那儿有个虱子。她告诉他今晚收音机又讲了那个烟筒丈夫和灶火老婆的有趣相声。面汤滚烫。羊肉喷香。有个家真好。倘乙已如果听见这个"家"字，一定会露出黄牙。下雨的夜里谁都往家跑。在锡林高勒的千里草原上，他在下雨时只往这儿跑。人世间只有这里在雨夜为他举起灯光。他吞着面条。牛粪火烤着赤裸的胸口。他给嫂子讲着牧马帐篷的位置，给奶奶学着烟

中国文学选读

鬼夫妻婚礼上的发言。他笑着、吃着、说着。而心里却满盛着另一些话。原来是这样：最由衷的话语是不能说出来的。说出书面语式的词汇反而使人发窘。他有点想哭。有人推他，是奥云娜端着一只小碗。酒味儿又香又烈。他一饮而尽。一股滚烫的暖流慢慢向肚肠滑去，又击响了那个轻叩心弦的神秘乐句。它不属于信天游、花儿与少年和蒙古长调。它是什么呢？"阿哈！""嗯？""还喝吗？""再倒半小碗吧，奥云娜！"

以后他有意在夜晚回家。全家也完全可以理解去找老门德学唱《金翅小鸟》的必要。他跋涉了两千里来寻找地球上一个直径四米的毡包，他还想反复体味在白天和黑夜从远方奔向大地上这一点时的深切感受。

迷濛的、潜伏着一脉生机的原野蒙着浓重的夜幕。万籁俱寂，苍穹宁静。大地的弹性从马蹄那儿传遍全身，轻摇着惆怅的心绪。他从暗夜中辨出一种均匀的色素，那是溶入夜色中的、七月青草的绿。浩淼的暗绿中亮起了一颗明亮的星，那是奥云娜为他举起的灯。那灯光也被染上了淡淡发绿的光晕，像是雾霭弥漫的拂晓湖面上跳跃着一簇萤光。蹄声惊起了宿鸟，引出了那个轻盈的乐句。那么优美，那么感人。哦，绿夜，四季的精英，大地的柔情。这绿夜抚摸着他，拥抱着他，安慰着他，使他不顾一切地朝前走。他又在编织着一个梦么？表弟已经敛起眉头。办公楼楼道的人流中已经响起哄声。但他微笑了。他已经不能承认关于两句矛盾的歌词的醒悟，因为这绿夜中有一个新奇的旋律在诞生并向他呼喊。

时间飞快地过去了。他收拾了行装。

白发老奶奶送给他一个红布缝成的小方块护身符。嫂子送给他妻子一块绿绸子。牧人们送给他一罐罐黄油和花斑透明的磁碗。门德阿爸送给他一壶奶酒。冈林信康唱过："逝去了，那往日的亲切。"左田雅志也唱过："你去了，带着脸上的泪水。"而他没有带着泪水，而是带着绿夜中奥云娜为他点燃的灯光。逝去了的已不能追还，但明天他又会怀念此刻的亲切。人总是这样：他们喜欢记住最美好的那一部分往事并永远回忆它，而当生活无情地改变或粉碎了那些记忆时，他们又会从这生活中再找到一些东西并记住它。这是一种弱点么？也许，人就应当这样。哪怕一次次失望。因为生活中确有真正值得记忆和怀念的东西。

奥云娜欢叫起来。就在此刻天空中又出现了那金红的云霞。"阿哈，快！"他忙答应着跑去。小青花羔已经在围着奥云娜蹦跳。他高高举起了奶瓶。这最后一个傍晚应当这样度过。他暗暗希望，在太阳、云层、时间、草原、小青花羔和奥云娜相会时迸射出的，那自然与人的美好画面中，也能有他瘦削的微小身影。

"阿哈!""嗯?""你明天就走么?""哦,明天不走不行啦。""还再来么?""嗯……""能带我城里的嫂嫂一块来么?""她吗?不,奥云娜,连阿哈自己也不知道能不能再来。""路很远,是么?""……""阿哈!""嗯?""我想把这只青羊羔送给你。""真的吗?""当然!你已经会喂它了。""傻瓜,城市里不能养羊。""那怎么办呢?我还能送你什么呢?""今天夜里,你再给我打一次手电光吧,小奥云娜!"

奥云娜惊讶地望着他。他从她手里抱过小青羔,把它撒在草地上。小青羔咩地叫了一声,又扑回来,朝他蹦跳着。奥云娜快活地咯咯笑了。这个身穿破旧蓝布袍子的姑娘全身通红,她鲜艳的脸颊上现出了两个深深的、动人的酒涡。

夜晚,他告别了老门德一家,纵马驰向等待着他的毡包。诺盖乌苏小河的水面上闪烁着暗淡的波光。清凉的夜风掀着流动的草浪。朦胧的、茫茫的黑土地厚实又温暖。七月的夜,绿色的夜,把他悄悄地抱入怀中。他纵开马儿,在这绿夜中飞一般疾驰着。

表弟会问:"你找到了什么?"妻子也会问:"你感觉怎么样?"不,他寻找的已不复存在。他的感情也未必轻松。但只有他自己知道:这也并非是一个新的梦。他的脚已经深深踏进了这真实的无边青草;他不会再写那样幼稚的小诗。像成年的保尔·柯察金为孤独的妈妈奏出的手风琴声一样,他也将把自己的歌唱得沉着、热情而节奏有力。他用力扯住飞奔的马儿,伫立在茫茫的绿夜中。那个神妙的乐句已经展开为一个新的、雄浑的乐章。这音乐的旋律和夜的纯净的绿色,流进了他的心。他感到这颗心从来没有这样湿润、温柔、丰富和充满着活力。他凝望着莽莽无垠的、亲爱的夜草原。"哦,别了,草原。别了,绿色的夜。别了,我的奥云娜……"他轻声说。

这时,那极远极远的绿夜深处,亮起了一颗星。

一九八一年

# Further Readings

## 1. Wandering in the Garden, Waking from a Dream
### Bai Xianyong

When Madame Ch'ien arrived at the Tou villa in the elegant Taipei suburb of Tien Mu, the road near the house was already packed on both sides with parked cars, most of them black official sedans. As her taxicab drove up to the gate, Madame Ch'ien ordered the driver to stop. The villa's iron gates were wide open, the lamps burning high above. A guard stood on either side of the gate; a man in the uniform of an aide-de-camp was busy attending to the guests' chauffeurs. As soon as Madame Ch'ien got out of the cab, the aide hurried over. A man graying at the temples, he was outfitted in a Sun Yat-sen tunic of dark blue serge. Madame Ch'ien took a calling card from her purse and handed it to him. He bowed deeply as he took it, his face all smiles, and greeted her in his northern Kiangsu accent.

"Madame Ch'ien, I'm Liu *Fukuan*. Madame probably doesn't remember me any more."

"Is that you, Liu *Fukuan*?" Madame Ch'ien glanced at him, a little startled. "Of course. I must have seen you then, at your General's residence in Nanking. How are you, Liu *Fukuan*?"

"I'm fine, thanks to Madame's blessings." Again, he bowed, and, hurrying ahead, led the way with a flashlight along a concrete driveway around the garden towards the main building.

"Madame has been well, I presume?" He turned to her and smiled.

"Quite well, thank you. And how are your General and his lady? It's been many years since I saw them."

"Madame is well; the General has been rather preoccupied lately with official business."

The garden of the Tou villa was deep and wide. Madame Ch'ien looked around her; everywhere swaying shadows of the trees and flowers and plants moved back and

白先勇

forth across each other. The garden walls were thickly lined with rows of coconut palms. A clear late-autumn moon had already risen above their lofty tops. Madame Ch'ien followed Liu the aide-de-camp around a little grove of coir palms—suddenly the two-story Tou mansion loomed up before her. The entire house, upstairs and down, was ablaze with lights, as if on fire. A wide flight of stone steps led up to a huge curved terrace. Along the stone balustrade stood pots of cassia in a neatly-spaced row—there were more than ten of them, all grown chest-high. As Madame Ch'ien stepped onto the terrace, a wave of strong fragrance enveloped her. The main doors were wide open, and inside, servants could be seen shuttling to and fro. Liu stopped at the door, bowing slightly, and extended his hand in a respectful gesture.

"This way, please, Madame."

As Madame Ch'ien entered the antechamber, Liu summoned one of the maids. "Go, quickly, and report to Madame. General Ch'ien's lady has arrived."

The only furnishings in the antechamber were exquisite redwood chairs and side tables. On the low table to the right stood a group of cloisonné vases; one, shaped like a fish-basket, held a few sprays of evergreen. Set in the wall over the table, was a large oval pier glass. Madame Ch'ien went up to the mirror, removing her black autumn evening coat; a maid hurried forward to take it from her. Madame Ch'ien stole a glance in the mirror and quickly smoothed a stray lock of hair at her right temple. At six o'clock that very evening she had gone to the Red Rose on West Gate Square to have her hair dressed, only to have the wind ruffle it as she had walked through the garden. Madame Ch'ien took a step closer to the mirror; she even felt that the color of her emerald green Hangchow silk *ch'i-p'ao* was not quite right. She remembered that this kind of silk shimmered like sea-green jade when the light shone on it. Perhaps the antechamber was not well-lit; the material looked rather dull in the mirror. Could it really have faded? She had brought this silk with her all the way from Nanking. All these years she hadn't been able to bring herself to wear it; she had dug it out of the bottom of her trunk and had it cut just for this party. If she had known, she would have bought herself a new length of silk at the Swan. But somehow she always thought Taiwan materials coarse and flashy; they hurt your eyes, especially the silks. How could they compare with Mainland goods—so fine, so soft?

"Fifth Sister, you've come after all." There was a sound of footsteps, and Madame Tou appeared. She took Madame Ch'ien's hand in hers, smiling.

"Third Sister," exclaimed Madame Ch'ien, smiling graciously also, "I'm late. I must have kept you waiting."

"Not at all. You're right on time. Dinner's just about to start."

As she spoke, she walked Madame Ch'ien arm in arm toward the main drawing room. In the corridor Madame Ch'ien cast a few glances at Madame Tou out of the corner of her eye. She couldn't help observing to herself: So, Fragrant Cassia really hasn't aged after all. The year they were to leave Nanking, she'd thrown a party at her own villa in Plum Garden, hadn't she, in honor of Fragrant Cassia's thirtieth birthday. Practically all her sworn sisters from the Terrace of the Captured Moon had come, including Fragrant Cassia's real sister, Heavenly Pepper, Number Thirteen, who was later to become concubine to Governor Jen—Jen Tzu-chiu, that is, and her own sister, Number Seventeen, Red-red Rose. The whole group had chipped in western-style, and ordered a big two-layer birthday cake, measuring thirty inches across and decorated with no fewer than thirty red candles. She must be well past forty by now, surely? Madame Ch'ien stole another glance at her old friend. Madame Tou was wearing a *ch'i-p'ao* of silver gray chiffon dusted with vermilion spangles and matching silver high heels. The ring finger of her right hand bore a diamond as big as a lotus seed, and a platinum bracelet studded with tiny diamonds twisted around her left wrist. A crescent-shaped coral pin held her hair; a pair of inch-long purple jade earrings hung below, setting off her full, pale face and making it look all the more aristocratic and dignified. In those Nanking days, she recalled, Fragrant Cassia had never had this special air about her. Then she was still a concubine, her husband, Tou Jui-sheng, a mere Deputy Minister. He's big in the government now, of course, and Fragrant Cassia has risen to be the official Madame Tou. You had to give her credit: she had sweated out all those years; now, at last, she could hold her head high.

"Jui-sheng's gone to the south to attend a meeting. When he heard you were coming tonight, Fifth Sister, he asked me specially to give you his warmest regards." Madame Tou turned to Madame Ch'ien with a smile.

"Ah," said Madame Ch'ien, "that's so thoughtful of Brother Tou." As they neared the drawing room, a swell of laughter and chatter flowed toward them from the inside. Madame Tou stopped at the entrance, again taking Madame Ch'ien's hands in hers.

"Fifth Sister, you should have moved to Taipei long ago," she said. "It's been on my mind all this time. It must be very quiet for you now, living alone in a place like that down south. You simply had to come to my party tonight—Thirteen's come, too."

"She's here, too?"

"Well, you know, as soon as Jen Tzu-chiu died, she moved out of his house." She leaned close to Madame Ch'ien's ear. "He was quite well off, and Thirteen's all by herself—you could say she's living comfortably. She was the one who clamored for tonight's party; it's the first time since we came to Taiwan. She's invited a few of her friends over from the Tien Hsiang Opera Club—gongs, drums, *sheng*, flutes, the whole works. And they all expect you to get up there and show your stuff."

"Come on, now, really, I can't do that sort of thing any more!" Madame Ch'ien hurriedly freed herself from Madame Tou, laughing and waving her hands in a gesture of deprecation.

"Don't be so modest, Fifth Sister," Madame Tou laughed. "If the famous 'Blue-field Jade' can't sing, who else would dare utter a note?" Giving Madame Ch'ien no chance to argue, she led her into the drawing room.

The main drawing room was already filled; groups of guests in dazzling evening dress were scattered here and there like clusters of flowers embroidered on silk. It was an enormous room with an alcove, furnished in a blend of Chinese and Western styles. On the left-hand side were grouped armchairs and sofas with soft cushions; on the right, tables and chairs of red sandalwood; in between, the floor was covered with a thick carpet depicting two dragons vying for a pearl. The two large sofas and four armchairs, all covered in black velvet with a design of wine-red begonia leaves, faced each other in a circle. Inside the circle on a low rectangular table stood a tall gall-bladder vase of fine blue porcelain; from the vase sprang forth a bunch of Dragon-beard chrysanthemums, their red petals veined in gold. To the right, surrounded by eight sandalwood chairs, was an Eight-Immortals table with a marble top, laden with all sorts of bonbonnières and tea things. In the alcove stood a towering ebony screen with an inlaid-mica design of bats and drifting clouds. The screen was flanked by six redwood chairs in a semi-circle, three on each side. Madame Ch'ien noticed the cymbals and stringed instruments arranged on the chairs. In front of them were two stands: one held a small drum and the other was hung with flutes and pipes all in a row. The room was resplendent. Two floor lamps were trained on a large gong, making it glitter with a golden radiance.

Madame Tou ushered Madame Ch'ien to the left side of the drawing-room, where a woman, fiftyish, wearing a pearl-gray *ch'i-p'ao* and covered with jade ornaments, was seated on a sofa.

"Madame Lai, this is Madame Ch'ien. You must have met before."

Madame Ch'ien recognized her. Lai Hsiang-yun's wife. They'd met several times in Nanking, on social occasions. At that time, Lai Hsiang-yun was an Army Commander, probably. Since coming to Taiwan, she seemed to see his name quite often in the newspapers.

"This must be His Excellency General Ch'ien's lady." Madame Lai was in the middle of a conversation with a gentleman; now she turned, looked Madame Ch'ien up and down for a moment and rose gracefully with a smile. She shook hands with her; touching a finger to her forehead, she added: "But your face does look familiar!"

She turned to the guest beside her, a stout bald-headed man with a swarthy face, attired in a long gown of royal blue silk.

"I've been chatting with the President's Staff Advisor, General Yu—I simply can't remember which opera Mei Lan-fang starred in the third time he came down to Shanghai to appear at the Cinnamon Theater No. 1. See what a memory I have!"

General Yu was already on his feet. Smiling broadly, he bowed to Madame Ch'ien.

"It's been a long time since I've had the pleasure of seeing you, Madame. That year in Nanking, at the gala performance sponsored by the Officers' Moral Endeavor Association, I had the great good fortune to be in your audience. As I recall, Madame sang in *Wandering in the Garden*, *Waking from a Dream*."

"Oh, yes!" Madame Lai put in. "I've heard so much about Madame Ch'ien's great reputation. Tonight, at last, I'll have a chance to enjoy your artistry."

Madame Ch'ien hastened to reply modestly to General Yu's compliments. She remembered he had been once to her villa in Nanking, but she also seemed to recall that he'd gotten involved in some major political scandal, been relieved of his post, and retired. Presently Madame Tou took her around and introduced her to the guests one by one. She didn't know any of the other ladies. They all looked rather young; most likely they'd arrived socially only after they came to Taiwan.

"Let's go to the other side; Thirteen and her Opera Club friends are all there."

So saying, Madame Tou showed Madame Ch'ien to the right side of the drawing room. A lady in red came mincing quickly up to greet them. She slipped her arm through Madame Ch'ien's, shaking with laughter.

"Fifth Sister," she declared, "Third Sister told me a little while ago that you were coming. I was so thrilled I yelled, 'Wonderful! Tonight we've really got the Star to come out.'"

When Madame Ch'ien first learned from Madame Tou that Chiang Pi-yueh was to be present, she had wondered whether, after being married so many years, the fiery Heavenly Pepper would have mellowed a bit. In Nanking, when the whole group was performing in the Confucius Temple District at the Terrace of the Captured Moon, Heavenly Pepper would always thrust herself into the limelight, coaxing their Master into allowing her to sing all the crowd-pleasing numbers. When she was on stage, she would look straight at the patrons, defying all the rules of their profession, her eyes reaching out like a pair of hooks all the way into the audience. The two sisters were born of the same mother, yet how different their characters were! In her worldly wisdom and generosity, Fragrant Cassia was second to none. Heavenly Pepper made the most she could for herself out of her sister's every opportunity. Jen Tzu-chiu had already presented Cassia with the betrothal gifts when Heavenly Pepper had the nerve to snatch him right from under her eyes. Surprising that Cassia could have such forbearance, she had had to wait ever so many years until finally, not without a certain sense of grievance, she had reluctantly agreed to become Tou Jui-sheng's second concubine. No wonder that every now and then Cassia would sigh: It's always your own younger sister, your flesh and blood, who'll do you in! Again Madame Ch'ien looked at Heavenly Pepper, Chiang Pi-yueh. She was all aflame in a red satin *ch'i-p'ao*. On her wrists she wore no fewer than eight gold bracelets, jingling and jangling with her every move. Her makeup was in the height of fashion: her eyelids painted with eyeshadow, the corners of her eyes heavily pencilled, her hair pouffed in a beehive, and at her temples tiny little seductive curls, like crescent hooks. After Jen Tzu-chiu died, this Heavenly Pepper, contrary to expectation, had become more vivacious than ever, even more flamboyant. On this woman you could find no trace of the war and turmoil that had been our lot these many years.

"Say! You people really have a treat in store for you. Madame Ch'ien here is the real female Mei Lan-fang!" Chiang Pi-yueh steered Madame Ch'ien toward her friends, the men and women of the Opera Club, and made the introductions. The men stood up hurriedly, bowing to Madame Ch'ien.

"Pi-yueh, It's talk nonsense. You'll make a laughingstock of me before these connoisseurs." Returning their bows, Madame Ch'ien mildly reproached her.

"Pi-yueh is right, actually," Madame Tou interposed, "Your K'unshan opera is of the true Mei School."

"Now, Third Sister,..." Madame Ch'ien murmured in protest. But when it came to K'unshan opera, even her husband, Ch'ien P'eng-chih, had said to her, "Fifth, my dear, I've heard the finest singers north and south, and I must say your voice ranks right up there with theirs."

Ch'ien P'eng-chih had told her that when he went back to Shanghai from Nanking after having heard her in *Wandering in the Garden*, *Waking from a Dream*, he thought about her day and night and simply couldn't get her out of his mind. Eventually he returned and married her. He had told her all along that if only he could have her by his side to amuse him with singing a few bars from his favorite K'unshan opera, he would be content for the remaining years of his life. She had just risen to stardom then at the Terrace of the Captured Moon. One phrase from a popular K'unshan aria in that inimitable voice of hers and she would bring down the house. The Master of the Moon Terrace had said, "Of all the singers in the Confucius Temple District, Blue field Jade is the one who must be regarded as the most classic."

"That's just what I say, Fifth Sister. Come along and meet another friend— Mrs. Hsu here is a Queen of K'unshan opera, too." Chiang Pi-yueh led Madame Ch'ien to a quietly refined young lady in a black *ch'i-p'ao*; then, turning to Madame Tou, "Third Sister," she said, "in a little while we'll have Mrs. Hsu sing *Wandering in the Garden* and Fifth Sister here sing *Waking from a Dream*. Do let's stage a grand revival of this hallowed masterpiece of K'unshan opera. Let these two great stars shine on the same stage and give our ears a big treat."

Mrs. Hsu rose at once, saying she wouldn't dare be so presumptuous. Madame Ch'ien quickly made some polite remark as well, but in her heart she was annoyed at Heavenly Pepper's lack of tact. Among all these people here tonight there probably wasn't one who didn't know opera; very likely this Mrs. Hsu beside her was a first-rate singer; later, if they actually got her to perform, she'd better not take things for granted. When it came to the techniques and skills of operatic singing, she had nothing to fear from these people; but she'd been in the south so long, and in all this time she hadn't really been in training; she wasn't at all sure of her voice. Besides, her dressmaker had been right after all: In Taipei, the long *ch'i-p'ao* has gone out of fashion. Everyone sitting here, including that old Madame Lai, her face so wrinkled it looked like chicken skin, had the hem of her gown almost to her knees, exposing a good half of her legs. In the Nanking days, a lady's gown was so long it almost touched her feet. She was sorry she hadn't listened to her tailor; she wondered whether she wouldn't look ridiculous in front of all these people if she stood up later in this long gown. When one goes onstage it's essential to create a presence instantly. In those Nanking days, when she herself gave opera dinners at Plum Garden, every time she got up to sing, her presence would hush the audience and hold it spellbound even before she uttered a note.

Smiling, Madame Tou escorted Madame Ch'ien to an officer who looked to be in his thirties. "Colonel Ch'eng, I'm turning Madame Ch'ien over to you now. If you It's take the very best care of her, I'll penalize you—you'll have to treat us all tomorrow. " She turned and whispered to Madame Ch'ien.

"Fifth Sister, you sit here and chat a while with the Colonel. He's a true opera buff. I must go look after the banquet. "

"Madame Ch'ien, this is a great honor. "

Colonel Ch'eng stood facing Madame Ch'ien and bowed smartly, military fashion. He was in dress uniform, beige gabardine, his Lieutenant-Colonel's insignia, a pair of shiny gold plum blossoms, on each lapel, his jump boots together, raven-glossy, water-smooth. Madame Ch'ien noted that his smile showed his even white teeth. He boasted a fine-chiselled face, a smooth- shaven gleaming blue chin, long slender eyes slanting upwards, with a pair of loftily raised eyebrows thrusting up into his temples. His inkblack hair was carefully brushed; his nose was straight and slender as a scallion, the tip slightly hooked. He was tall and slim, in uniform he looked extraordinarily dashing, yet Madame Ch'ien felt a touch of gentleness in the way he greeted her, without any trace of military coarseness.

"Please sit down, Madame. "

Colonel Ch'eng gave her his chair, straightening the soft cushions. He went quickly to the Eight-Immortals table and returned with a cup of jasmine tea and a bonbonnière with four kinds of candied fruit and melon seeds. When Madame Ch'ien reached for the pomegranate-red porcelain cup, Colonel Ch'eng said in a gentle voice,

"Be careful not to scald your hand, Madame."

He opened the gold-trimmed black lacquer bonbonnière; bending, he presented it with both hands to Madame Ch'ien, beaming, watching her intently, waiting for her to choose one. Madame Ch'ien took a few pine nuts, but Colonel Ch'eng hastened to dissuade her.

"Madame, those are bad for the voice. May I suggest you try one of the honeyed dates; they're good for your throat."

He fixed a honeyed date on a toothpick and handed it to Madame Ch'ien. She thanked him, popped the date into her mouth and tasted a penetrating honey-sweetness, a delightful scent. Colonel Ch'eng brought another chair and sat on her right.

"Have you been to the opera lately, Madame?" When he spoke, he leaned towards her a trifle, as if with total concentration. Again Madame Ch'ien noticed his white teeth, shining like crystals in the light.

"I haven't been for quite a while," she answered. She lowered her head and took a dainty sip of jasmine tea. "I live in the south; one rarely gets to see good opera there."

"Chang Ai-yun is playing *Nymph of the River Lo* at the National Theater right now, Madame."

"Really?" Madame Ch'ien's head was still lowered. She sipped her tea, sunk in thought for a moment, before resuming, "When I was in Shanghai, I saw her perform the *Nymph* at the Heavenly Toad Theater... That was a long time ago."

"She's still got her acting. No wonder they called her 'Peerless in the *ch'ing-i roles*.' She portrayed the love affair of Lady Fu and the poet Ts'ao Tzu-chien with great subtlety—a marvelous piece of acting."

Madame Ch'ien raised her head and met Colonel Ch'eng's eyes; immediately she averted her face. Those slender eyes of the young officer covered you like a net.

"Whose acting is so subtle and marvelous?" Chiang Pi-yueh, the Heavenly Pepper, chimed in with a laugh. Colonel Ch'eng stood up quickly and yielded his seat. Chiang Pi-yueh snatched up a handful of sunflower seeds for herself and sat down, crossing her legs and cracking the seeds open while she carried on. "Colonel, everybody says you are knowledgeable about the theater, but Madame Ch'ien is the All-

中国文学选读

Knowing First Lady of opera. If I were you, I'd stop sounding off in front of a real pro. "

"Madame Ch'ien and I have just been discussing Chang Ai-yun's *Nymph of the River Lo*. I was asking Madame Ch'ien's expert opinion," Colonel Ch'eng replied, glancing sideways at Madame Ch'ien.

"Oh, were you talking about Chang Ai-yun?" Chiang Pi-yueh chuckled. "It's all right for her to do a little opera teaching around Taiwan, but to appear as the 'Nymph of the River Lo'! Why, she couldn't pass for Lady Fu even in full costume and makeup! Last Saturday I finally made it to the National—got a seat in the back row—and all I saw were her lips moving. I couldn't hear a thing. Barely halfway through the opera her voice failed. —Well, here comes Third Sister now to invite us in to the banquet. "

Sliding doors of mahogany with carved openwork swastikas led to the banquet hall. A servant opened them and Madame Tou emerged from the magnificent room. It was pale silver, luminous as a snow cave. The two banquet tables were spread with fine scarlet linen; the plates, bowls, spoons, and chopsticks, all of silver, glowed a-gainst the scarlet. There was much standing on ceremony after the guests filed in; no one ventured to take the place of honor at the head of the table.

"I'd better take the lead. If we go on waiting for each other like this, we'll never sit down to dinner. In which case, we'd be abusing our hostess's hospitality!" That was Madame Lai, who thereupon went to the head of the first table and sat down. She beckoned to General Yu. "General, come sit next to me, why It's you. We haven't reached any conclusions about Mei Lan-fang's operas yet. "

"At your command, Ma'am!" Grinning broadly, General Yu folded his hands in an elaborate operatic salute. The guests burst out laughing and one after another took their seats. When they reached the second table, again everybody started deferring to each other. Laughing, Madame Lai called from the first table, "Madame Ch'ien, I think you'd better follow my example. "

Madame Tou came over and escorted Madame Ch'ien to the head of the second table. "Fifth Sister, please do sit down," she whispered. "If you It's take the lead, the others will have trouble getting seated. "

Madame Ch'ien looked around. The guests were all standing there watching her and smiling. She made a vague attempt to decline the honor, but at last she sat down; for a moment her heart fluttered, her face even flushed a little. It certainly wasn't as if she'd never been through this sort of high-society ceremonial, but she'd not entertained or been entertained for so long she'd become rather unused to it. When her husband was alive, nine times out of ten she would be first to take the seat of honor at banquets. Naturally Madame Ch'ien P'eng-chih would be at the head of the table; she'd never had to yield pride of place to anyone. Of all the ladies in government circles in Nanking not many could be numbered among her superiors. Of course those officials' concubines couldn't compare with her. She was Ch'ien P'eng-chih's second wife; he, a widower, had taken her in marriage with all due ceremony. Poor Fragrant Cassia hadn't even been allowed to act as hostess in her own right; hadn't *she* been the one who'd given the party for Cassia's birthday? Only since her arrival in Taiwan has Cassia dared to come out and stage such a grand spectacle, and yet she herself, when she was a singing-girl barely turned twenty, was transformed overnight into a general's lady. A singsong girl marrying into an ordinary family is enough of an event to cause comment; imagine the talk when she married one of the high and mighty! Even her own sister, Number Seventeen, Red-red Rose, had let fall a cutting remark or two.

"Sister, it's about time you cut off your braid, or when you go out for a walk with General Ch'ien people could mistake you for his granddaughter!" The year Ch'ien P'eng-chih married her he was almost sixty. She didn't care what anybody said, she was his true and honorable second wife. She understood her position, and she guarded it jealously. In the dozen or so years she was Ch'ien P'eng-chih's helpmate, she always handled banquets and such as if she were walking on eggs, smoothly, perfectly, no matter how great the occasion. Whenever she appeared in public, she carried herself with such elegance and grace that nobody would dare whisper she was the "Blue field Jade" who had sung at the Moon Terrace by the Chin Huai River.

"It must have been hard on you, Fifth," Ch'ien P'eng-chih often said to her, caressing her cheek. Whenever she heard that, she felt a twinge in her heart. There was no way she could make him see what was troubling her deep down. After all, how could she possibly lay the blame on him? She had entered the thing with her eyes open. When he married her he'd been frank with her, told her clearly that only after he'd heard her in *Wandering in the Garden*, *Waking from a Dream* had it occurred to him to take her as the companion of his old age. Well, wasn't it just the way her sister Red-red Rose had put it? Ch'ien P'eng-chih might as well be her grand daddy! What else could she have expected? It had been fulfilled after all, that ironclad prophecy made by their *shih-niang* the blind woman who was their Master's wife at the Terrace of the Captured Moon. Fifth, my girl, she told her, the best thing your sort of people can hope for is to get married to an older man who'll love you like a daughter. As for the young fellows, can you trust them? As if that weren't enough, *shih-niang*, blind as she was, had to go and take hold of her wrist and feel the bone, blinking her sightless eyes and adding with a sigh: worldly glory, wealth, position— you shall enjoy them all, Blue field Jade. Only it's a pity you've got one bone in you that's not quite right. It's just your retribution from a previous life! What else was it, if not retribution? Except for the moon, which he could not pluck from the sky, Ch'ien P'eng-chih had tried bringing her in both hands all the gold and silver and treasures of the world that would make her happy. She appreciated his thoughtfulness: he was afraid her humble origins would weigh on her mind and she'd be diffident, intimidated by the high-ranking officials and the wellborn ladies; he tried in every way to encourage her to show off her wealth, to live it up. Certainly the high style of Madame Ch'ien's parties at Plum Garden was the talk of Nanking; it was practically a sin, the number of silver dollars she tossed around at the Ch'ien residence on banquets alone. Take that birthday party she gave for Fragrant Cassia! No fewer than ten tables were laid out; for entertainment she engaged the top flutist, Wu Sheng-hao of the Rainbow Club; to preside over her kitchen she spent ten silver dollars just to transport the chef from the famed Willow Lodge at Peachleaf Ferry.

"Madame Tou, where did you find your chef?" asked Madame Lai. "It's the first time I've had such superb shark's fin since I came to Taiwan."

"He used to be Chief Cook at Minister Huang's home in Shanghai," Madame Tou replied. "Huang Ching-chih, you know. He came to us only after we got to Taiwan."

"No wonder!" General Yu put in. "His Excellency the Minister is a well-known gourmet."

"If I could borrow your chef someday to make shark's fin, it would add so much prestige to my dinner-table," said Madame Lai.

"What could be simpler?" rejoined Madame Tou. "I'd be more than happy to go out for a free meal!" This brought a laugh from all the other guests.

"Madame Ch'ien, won't you have a bowl of shark's fin?" Colonel Ch'eng ladled a bowl of the red-cooked shark's fin, adding a spoonful of Chenchiang vinegar, and set it before her. He murmured, "This is our cook's most famous dish."

Madame Ch'ien had hardly tasted her shark's fin when Madame Tou came over from the other table and proposed a toast to the guests. She made a point of telling the young colonel to refill her cup, and moving to Madame Ch'ien's side, she put her hand on her shoulder and said warmly, "Fifth Sister, it's been so long since the two of us drank to each other."

She clinked her cup with Madame Ch'ien's and downed the wine in one gulp; daintily Madame Ch'ien drank hers. As Madame Tou was leaving, she turned to Colonel Ch'eng. "Colonel, be sure you drink another round with everyone for me. Your General's not here; you'd better do the honors at this table."

Colonel Ch'eng rose to his feet. Holding a silver decanter, he bent down, all smiles, and started to pour wine into Madame Ch'ien's cup. She hastily stayed his hand.

"Colonel, why It's you serve the others. My capacity is quite limited."

Colonel Ch'eng didn't move but looked at Madame Ch'ien with a smile and replied, "Madame, this *hua-tiao* is not at all like other wines; it fades away easily. I know you'll be singing in a while, but this wine's been heated; it won't hurt your voice to drink a little."

"Madame Ch'ien's capacity is unlimited. Don't let her off!" Chiang Pi-yueh, who was seated opposite Madame Ch'ien, came around; without waiting to be served she poured herself a full cup and raised it to Madame Ch'ien. "Fifth Sister," she said, her voice ringing with laughter, "I, too, haven't had a chance to drink a cup with you for a long time."

"Pi-yueh, if we keep drinking this way, we'll get drunk." Coughing slightly, Madame Ch'ien fended off Chiang Pi-yueh's hand.

"So you won't do your little sister the honor. All right! I'll drink double. If I get drunk later, I'll just let them pick me up and carry me home."

Chiang Pi-yueh threw back her head and drained the cup. Colonel Ch'eng promptly presented her with another; she took that, swallowed it and turned the silver winecup upside down, brandishing it before Madame Ch'ien's face.

The guests applauded, "Good show, Miss Chiang!"

Madame Ch'ien had no choice but to raise her cup; she finished her *hua-tiao* unhurriedly. The wine certainly was well-heated; once down your throat it coursed like a warm current through your whole body. Still and all, Taiwan *hua-tiao* was not nearly as good as what you used to get on the Mainland, not that smooth and mellow—it felt a little scratchy on your throat. Though they say *hua-tiao* fades away easily, does it ever trip you up if you drink it down too fast! She'd never dreamed the aged *hua-tiao* she'd ordered brought directly from Shaohsing could have packed such a wallop. That night finally she fell into their trap. *The whole gang insists: How could you possibly lose your voice with a few cups of* hua-tiao? *It's such a rare occasion; it's Fragrant Cassia's special day... We sisters It's know when if ever we'll get together like this again... If you, our hostess, won't drink up, how can your guests let themselves go? Even Red- red Rose, her own little sister Seventeen, sides with them and chimes in; Sister, let's you and me drink bottoms up and be real pals for a while. Red-red Rose is arrayed in a flashing red and gold satin* ch'i-p'ao, *gorgeous as a parrot, her liquid eyes flashing this way and that. Sister, you won't do me the honor, she says. So you'll make your little sister lose face, she says. She's practically stolen the whole show, made off with all the prizes, and here she's handing me the sweet talk. No wonder Fragrant Cassia sighed: It's always your own younger sister, your flesh and blood, who'll do you in! Red-red Rose? well, granted she was young and didn't know better, but he, Tseng Yen-ching he should have known better than to join in that charade. But he, too, comes holding out a brimming cup to her, his white teeth flashing. Madame, may I also drink to you, he says. His cheeks glowing red with the wine, his eyes smoldering like two balls of dark fire, his spurred riding boots clicking smartly together, he bends down and whispers to her tenderly: Madame...*

"It's my turn now, Madame." Colonel Ch'eng rose, holding his cup high in both hands, grinning.

"Really, Colonel Ch'eng, I can't any more," Madame Ch'ien murmured, her head lowered somewhat.

"I'll drink three cups first as a token of my respect; please drink as much as you like, Madame."

Colonel Ch'eng drank the three cups one after the other; a mild glow from the wine spread over his face. His forehead began to glisten, beads of sweat appeared on the tip of his nose. Madame Ch'ien took up her wine cup and barely touched it to her lips. Colonel Ch'eng served Madame Ch'ien a wing from the Chicken à la Imperial Favorite and helped himself to a chicken head as a relish with the wine.

"My, my!" Chiang Pi-yueh trilled from across the table, "What ever are you toasting me with?" She stood up and leaned over to take a sniff of General Yu's wine. He was holding a rare gold "bird-bath" cup in his hands.

"Young lady, this here is the wine called 'Nocturnal Carousing.'" General Yu laughed roguishly; already his swarthy red face had turned liver color.

> *"Tie, fie, be off!*
> *Who is here will carouse the night with you?"*

With a grand wave of her hand Chiang Pi-yueh declaimed operatically from *The Imperial Favorite Drunk with Wine.*

"Miss Chiang," Madame Lai called from the other table, "the banquet at the Pavilion of the Hundred Flowers isn't laid yet, and here you're already 'Drunk with Wine.'" The guests burst into a roar of laughter.

Madame Tou stood up. "We'd better get ready for the show," she announced. "Will everyone move to the drawing room, please."

The guests rose, Madame Lai taking the lead. They filed into the drawing room and seated themselves here and there. The men from the Opera Club took their places on the redwood chairs in front of the screen and began tuning their instruments. There were six of them, counting the *Hu-ch'in*—one played the *erh-hu*, one played moon guitar, and one kept time with the small drum and wooden clappers. The other two performed standing, one holding a pair of cymbals, one a large brass gong.

"Madame, that Mr. Yang is superb on the *Hu-ch'in*." Sitting beside her on a leather hassock, Colonel Ch'eng pointed out the man who played the Tartar violin, whispering in Madame Ch'ien's ear. "He's also a fantastic flutist; you won't find another like him in Taiwan. You'll know the moment you hear him play."

Half reclining in the soft armchair, savoring the fresh cup of jasmine tea that Colonel Ch'eng had offered her, Madame Ch'ien followed the direction of his hand and watched Mr. Yang. He was a man of about fifty, clad in a soft silk gown the color of ancient bronze with round designs faintly woven into the fabric. His features were lean and strikingly refined; he had long, slender hands with fingers like ten panpipes of white jade.

He pulled his *Hu-ch'in* from its cotton bag, laid a pad of blue cloth over his knee and placed the instrument on top of it, adjusted the bow, and casually warmed up a little, his head inclining a bit forward and his arm extended, and suddenly the sound of the strings leaped into the air like an outflung rope. His playing of the intermezzo "Deepening Night" was clear, crisp, and plangent. The moment he finished, General Yu was first to spring to his feet, applauding, "Wonderful *Hu-ch'in*!" The other guests all clapped. Immediately the gong and drum struck up the overture "The General's Command." Madame Tou went around the drawing room inviting each guest to perform. While the guests were still politely urging each other forward, General Yu, his arm around her, had already walked Chiang Pi-yueh over to the master *Hu-ch'in*.

"May it please Your Ladyship," he announced in the shrill tones of an opera clown, "this here is the Pavilion of the Hundred Flowers."

Clapping both her hands to her mouth, Chiang Pi-yueh bent over with laughter, causing her gold bracelets to jingle without stop. The guests followed with a burst of applause, and the *Hu-ch'in* launched into the *ssu-p'ing* air from *The Imperial Favorite Drunk with Wine*. Not even turning sideways, but boldly facing the audience,

Chiang Pi-yueh began to sing. When she came to an interlude, General Yu ran off and re-entered holding aloft the gold bird-bath cup on a vermilion tray. With one hand he lifted the hem of his robe, pantomiming the role of Kao the Eunuch in a half-kneeling posture before her. "May it please Your Ladyship!" he piped, "Your slave offers wine."

Chiang Pi-yueh, on cue, assumed a drunken air, swaying from side to side and striking one operatic attitude after another. Then with a twist of her body she lunged into a "Reposing Fish" pose and lifted the cup with her teeth. Tossing it to the floor with a clang, she warbled the initial lines of the famous aria:

> Like to a vernal dream
> > is our life in this world;
> So will I for mine own ease drink
> > my measure full!

By now the guests were rolling with laughter. Madame Tou laughed till she was gasping for breath, calling out hoarsely to Madame Lai, "I think our Pi-yueh is high as a kite tonight!"

"Miss Chiang!" Madame Lai called loudly, laughing so hard she kept wiping away her tears with her handkerchief, "There's nothing wrong with being high, just be careful you It's follow the example of the Imperial Favorite and drink your fill of vinegar."

Though the guests cheered Chiang Pi-yueh on, she swaggered off and, hustling Mrs. Hsu to center stage, declared, "The Queen of K'unshan opera will now sing *Wandering in the Garden* for us; then we'll ask Madame Ch'ien, the Goddess of K'unshan opera, to follow with *Waking from a Dream*."

Madame Ch'ien looked up. She laid her cup down on the teapoy to her left and saw that Mrs. Hsu had already taken her place before the screen, her body half turned away from the audience, one hand resting on the ebony woodwind stand. She wore a black velvet *ch'i-p'ao*, and her long hair was loosely knotted at the nape of her neck. She faced outward a little, a jade-green pendant in a white earlobe showing

中国文学选读

through her hair. The trumpet-shaped floor lights shone on the drawing room like spotlights, casting her slender shadow gracefully onto the mica screen.

"Fifth Sister," Chiang Pi-yueh came over and plunked herself down next to Colonel Ch'eng. "Listen carefully and see if Mrs. Hsu's *Wandering in the Garden* can top yours," she whispered, leaning over, one hand tapping Madame Ch'ien's shoulder.

"Madame," Colonel Ch'eng also turned around and spoke smilingly. "Tonight it will be my great good fortune to have the opportunity of hearing you sing."

Madame Ch'ien looked intently at the bright gold bracelets darting and flashing on Chiang Pi-yueh's wrists; suddenly she felt dizzy, a wave of tipsiness rose to her head, and it seemed that the few cups of *hua-tiao* she'd swallowed earlier were taking their effect—her eyes felt feverish and her vision was growing hazy Chiang Pi-yueh's red *ch'i-p'ao* flared up like a globe of flame, catching Colonel Ch'eng's body in a flash, and the golden plum blossoms on his lapels started to leap forward like sparks. Chiang Pi-yueh's eyes were dancing like two balls of dark quicksilver on her glowing face, Colonel Ch'eng's long, slender eyes narrowed, shooting out threatening rays, the two faces confronting her at once, showing their even white teeth, smiling towards her, the two faces so red they shone slowly closing in on each other, merging, showing their white teeth, smiling towards her. The high and low flutes began to sound in unison, the high flute's notes like flowing water, lifting the low flute's trailing fall and carrying it into the aria set to *Black Silk Robe* from *Wandering in the Garden*:

> The glorious purples
>> the enchanting reds
>>> once everywhere in bloom
> Alas that these must yield
>> to broken wells
>>> and crumbling walls
> This joyous time
>> this fairest scene
>>> yet Heaven grants me not

> *Then in whose gardens do hearts*
>
> *by happiness delighted*
>
> *still rejoice——*

You could say these lines, sung by Tu the Beauteous Maid, are the most chal-lenging in the entire K'unshan operatic repertoire. Even the great flutist Wu Sheng-hao had said, "Madame Ch'ien, your singing of 'Black Silk Robe,' why, Mei Lan-fang himself couldn't do better. " *But why does Wu Sheng-hao play the music so high-pitched?* (*Master Wu, the girls have made me drink too much tonight; I'm not sure of my voice any more—a bit lower, please.*) *Wu Sheng-hao has said: The first thing a singer should stay away from is wine, and yet Red-red Rose, Seventeen, comes over with that cup of* hua-tiao *in her hands, saying, Sister, let's you and me drink bottoms up. She's arrayed in flashing red and gold, still there she is, saying, Sister you won't do me the honor. Don't talk like that, Sis, it's not that Sister won't do you the honor, it's that really he's the retribution in your Sister's fate. Hadn't the blind woman, our* shih-niang, *said, Worldly glory, wealth, position—Blue field Jade, only it's a pity you've got one bone that's not quite right. Oh, my retri-bution. Isn't he the retribution in your Sister's fate? Understand? Sis, it's retribu-tion. And yet he, too, comes over with a winecup in his hands and salutes: Madame. A Sam Browne belt, bright gold insignia pinned on his lapels, his waist belted tight, stance erect, his high riding boots, raven-glossy, water-smooth, with white copper spurs clicking together, his eyelids peach-pink with wine, he salutes: Mad-ame. Is there anyone who doesn't know Madame Ch'ien of Plum Garden in Nanking? Ah yes, His Excellency General Ch'ien's lady. Ch'ien P'eng-chih's lady. Ch'ien P'eng-chih's aide-de-camp. General Ch'ien's lady. General Ch'ien's aide. General Ch'ien. It must have been hard on you, Fifth, Ch'ien P'eng-chih said. Poor thing, you're still so young. As for the young fellows, how could they have kind hearts? The blind woman, our Shih-niang, said, Ah, your sort of people only the old ones can love and cherish. Worldly glory, wealth, position—only it's a pity, one bone is not quite right. Understand? Sis, he is the retribution in your Sister's fate. General Ch'ien's lady. General Ch'ien's aide-de-camp. General's lady. Aide-de-camp. Re-*

*tribution, I say. Retribution, I say. (Master Wu, a bit lower, please, my voice is failing. Oh dear, this passage set to 'Sheep on the Mountain Slope')—*

> *Spring fever*
>> *that did me by stealth surprise*
>> *I cannot send away*
> *Unspoken discontent*
>> *too suddenly*
>>> *wells all within my heart*
> *All for that I was born*
>> *a fair maid*
>>> *and have been so ever*
> *To be conjoin'd with one worthy our house*
>> *match'd to perfection*
>>> *the celestial pair*
> *Then why sweet Fortune*
>> *must my verdant spring be tossed*
>>> *so far*
> *and who is here*
>> *to see*
>>> *my sleep's affection—*

Fiercely the ball of red flame shot up again, burned till those loftily-raised eyebrows glistened dark green with sweat. The two wine-red faces were once more closing in on each other, showing their white teeth, smiling. Those fingers like jade pan-pipes flew up and down the flute. That slender shadow shimmered among the lights on the snow-green mica screen. The flutes sank even lower, grew more and more plaintive, as if they voiced all the Beauteous Maid's wistful longing. The Beauteous Maid was about to enter into her dream, and it was time her dream lover, Liu Meng-mei, appeared onstage. *But Wu Sheng-hao has said that the secret tryst in* Waking from a Dream *is the most suggestive passage. (Master Wu, a bit lower, please, I've*

drunk too much tonight. ) And yet he has to come over with a wine cup in his hands,
saluting: Madame. His riding boots, raven-glossy, water-smooth, click together,
the white copper spurs sting your eyes. His eyelids peach-pink with wine, still he
salutes: Madame. Allow me to help you mount, Madame, he said; in his tight-fitting breeches his long slender legs looked muscular, trim, like a pair of fire-tongs
clasping the horse. His horse was white, the road was white, the tree trunks were
white, and. his white horse shone in the blazing sun. They say that all along the
wayside the road to the Sun Yat-sen Mausoleum is full of white birch trees. His
white horse galloped through the birch groves like a hare darting about among stalks
of wheat. The sun beat down on the horses' backs sending up steaming white smoke.
One white. One black. The two horses were sweating. His body was stained with the
odor of horse sweat pungent to the nostrils. His eyebrows turned dark green, his
eyes smoldered like two balls of dark fire, beads of sweat came running down his
forehead to his flushed cheeks. The sun, I cried, the sun glares; I can't open my
eyes. Those tree trunks, so white and pure, so smooth, shedding their skin, layer
after layer, unveiled their tender naked flesh. They say that all along the wayside
the road is full of white birch trees. The sun, I cried, the sun has pierced my eyes.
And then he whispered in a gentle voice: Madame. General Ch'ien's lady. General
Ch'ien's aide-de-camp. General Ch'ien's—Fifth, Ch'ien P'eng-chih called, his voice
choked. Fifth, my dear, he called, his voice dying, you'll have to take care of
yourself. His hair tangled like a patch of withered white straw, his eyes sunk into
two dark holes, he stretched out his black, bony hand from under the white sheet:
Take care of yourself, Fifth. His hands shaking, he opened that gold-inlaid jewel
case. These are emeralds; he pulled out the first drawer. These are cat's eyes.
These, jade leaves. You'll have to take care, Fifth my dear, his blackened lips
quivering, Poor thing, you're still so young. Worldly glory, wealth, position—only it's a pity, you've got one bone that's not quite right. Retribution, Sis, he is the
retribution in your Sister's fate. Do listen to me, Sis, it's my retribution. Worldly
glory, wealth, position—but I only lived once. Understand? Sis, he is my retribution. Worldly glory, wealth, position—there was only that once. Worldly glory,
wealth, position—I only lived once. Understand? Sis, listen to me, Sis. But Red-

red Rose comes over with that cup of wine in her hands and says, Sister won't do me the honor, her liquid eyes flashing. So you won't give your little sister the face, she's all red and gold, flashing like a ball of fire she sits down right beside him. (Master Wu, I've drunk too much hua-tiao)—

Languishing
where may I tell
my unquiet heart
Seething
how shall I redress this life
so ill-fulfilled
except I sue to Heaven—

Right at that moment, this life so ill-fulfilled—she sits down beside him right at that moment, all red and gold, at that moment, the two wine-red faces slowly closing in on each other, right at that moment, I see their eyes: her eyes, his eyes. It's over, I know, right at that moment, except I sue to Heaven—(Master Wu, my voice.) It's over, my throat, feel my throat, is it quivering? It's over, is it quivering? Heaven—(Master Wu, I can't sing any more.) Heaven—it's over, worldly glory, wealth, position—but I only lived once—Retribution, Retribution, Retribution,—Heaven—(Master Wu, my voice.)—right at that moment, right at that moment, it's gone—Heaven—oh, Heaven—

"Fifth Sister, it's time for your *Waking from a Dream.*" Chiang Pi-yueh rose and advanced on Madame Ch'ien, beaming, stretching out her gold-bangled arms.

"Madame—" Colonel Ch'eng called softly. He rose, too, and stood before Madame Ch'ien, bowing slightly.

"Fifth Sister, please, it's your turn now." Madame Tou came over, extending her hand in an inviting gesture.

All the instruments struck up in unison—the gong, the drum, the *sheng*, and the flute—playing the codetta *Ten-Thousand-Year Jubilation.* The guests sprang up from their seats. Madame Ch'ien saw a roomful of waving and clapping hands encircling Mrs. Hsu. The winds blew with mounting intensity; raised high in the air the brass gong was struck, radiating gold in all directions.

"I can't sing now," Madame Ch'ien muttered, gazing at Chiang Pi-yueh, slowly shaking her head.

"That just won't do!" Swiftly Chiang Pi-yueh caught Madame Ch'ien's hands. "Fifth Sister, you are the star. We can't let you off tonight, no matter what!"

"My voice is gone," Madame Ch'ien sputtered. Suddenly she tore herself away from Chiang Pi-yueh's grasp; she felt all the blood in her body rush to her head, her cheeks burned, her throat smarted as if it had been slashed by a razor. She could hear Madame Tou intervene:

"Fifth Sister doesn't want to sing; let her be. —General Yu, I think we'd better have you, the 'Thunder Warrior,' for the finale tonight."

"Hurrah! Hurrah!" Madame Lai chorused from the other side. "It's been a long time since I've had the pleasure of hearing General Yu sing *Eight Great Blows.*"

Madame Lai propelled General Yu toward the gong and drums. Once onstage, General Yu clasped his hands in a salute. "My Humble Performance!" he announced. This brought forth a burst of laughter from the audience. He began to sing to the tune of "Touching Up Red Lips" for the Tartar General Wu Chu's entrance; as he sang he swept up the hem of his robe, mimed mounting a horse, and started circling the middle of the room "at a trot." His broad, fleshy face purple-red with drink, his eyes round and staring, his bushy eyebrows standing straight up, he drowned out the *Hu-ch'in* with his battle cries. Madame Lai, bent double with laughter, ran up and followed General Yu around, clapping her hands in appreciation. Chiang Pi-yueh immediately fell in behind them and kept shrilling, "Bravo, Thunder Warrior! Bravo!" Several other ladies joined in, circling around and cheering, the laughter rose higher in the drawing room, wave on wave. As soon as General Yu finished singing, maids in white jackets and black trousers appeared, bearing bowls of dragon's-eye soup cooked with red dates to soothe the guests' throats.

Madame Tou accompanied the guests outside to the terrace. The night air was dewy and chill. The guests had put on their overcoats; Madame Tou had tossed a

中国文学选读

large white silk shawl around her shoulders and walked down the terrace steps. Standing by the stone balustrade, Madame Ch'ien looked up; she saw that the autumn moon had just reached the center of the sky; it coated the trees, the garden paths, the steps with a layer of white frost. The potted cassia on the terrace sent forth a wave of fragrance even more powerful than before; it broke over her face like wet fog.

"Madame Lai's car has arrived. " Liu *Fukuan* stood at the foot of the stairs announcing the guests' cars. First to draw up was Madame Lai's brand new black Lincoln; a uniformed chauffeur jumped out of the car, opened the door with a respectful bow, and waited. Madame Lai came down the steps with General Yu and took her leave of Madame Tou. After she got into the car, she stuck her head out.

"Madame Tou," she laughed, "your opera program tonight was simply marvelous—even better than Mei Lan-fang and Chin Shao-shan in the old days. "

"Why, yes!" Madame Tou replied, half in jest. "General Yu's Thunder Warrior certainly had it all over 'Chin The Tyrant. '"

The guests on the terrace laughed and waved goodbye to Madame Lai. The second car to drive up was Madame Tou's own sedan; it carried off the group from the Opera Club. Then Colonel Ch'eng pulled up in his jeep, and Chiang Pi-yueh strutted right down; scooping up her long *ch'i-p'ao*, she tried to climb on. Colonel Ch'eng hurried round to help her in next to the driver's seat. Leaning out, she giggled, "Why, this jeep hasn't even got a door! I could get tossed out on the road any minute. "

"You'd better drive carefully. Colonel Ch'eng," said Madame Tou. She waved him over and said something in his ear. He smiled and nodded.

"Don't worry, Madame. "

He turned to Madame Ch'ien, clicked his heels and bowed deeply; he looked up at her with a smile. "Madame Ch'ien, allow me to take my leave. " He leaped nimbly into the jeep and started the engine.

"Goodbye, Third Sister! Goodbye, Fifth Sister!" Chiang Pi-yueh thrust out her hand, waving. Madame Ch'ien saw the bracelets on her arms making gold circles in the night.

"Madame Ch'ien's car?" Almost all the guests were gone; at the foot of the staircase Madame Tou spoke to Liu *Fukuan*.

"Madame," Liu stood to attention, "General Ch'ien's lady came in a taxi."

"Third Sister,..." Madame Ch'ien called from the terrace; earlier she had wanted to ask Madame Tou to get her a taxi, but there were too many guests around and she had been reluctant to speak up.

"Then as soon as my car comes back, call it in for Madame Ch'ien," Madame Tou said without hesitation.

"Yes, Madame." Liu retired.

Madame Tou turned and walked up to the terrace; in the moonlight her white shawl looked like a cluster of clouds hovering over her shoulders. A breeze brushed past, rustling the coconut palms all around and billowing Madame Tou's large shawl gently. Madame Ch'ien hurriedly pulled her coat tight; her cheeks, burning a moment ago, tingled, stung by the wind. She gave a little shiver.

"Let's go inside. Fifth Sister." Madame Tou, her arm around Madame Ch'ien's shoulder, walked with her to the house. "I'll have them make a pot of tea. Now the two of us can have a good talk together. —It's been so long since you've been here. Do you find Taipei at all changed?"

Madame Ch'ien hesitated for a moment, then she turned her head; "Oh, it has changed a great deal," she said. As they walked to the gate, she added softly, "It's changed so I hardly know it any more... They've put up so many tall buildings."

—From *Taipei People*
(translated by the author and Patia Yasin)

## 游园惊梦

### 白先勇

　　钱夫人到达台北近郊天母窦公馆的时候，窦公馆门前两旁的汽车已经排满了，大多是官家的黑色小轿车。钱夫人坐的计程车开到门口她便命令司机停了下来。窦公馆的两扇铁门大敞，门灯高烧，大门两侧一边站了一个卫士，门口有个随从打扮的人正在那儿忙着招呼宾客的司机。钱夫人一下车，那个随从便赶紧迎了上来，他穿了一身藏青哔叽的中山装，两鬓花白。钱夫人从皮包里掏出了一张名片递给他，那个随从接过名片，即忙向钱夫人深深地行了一个礼，操了苏北口音，满面堆着笑容说道：

"钱夫人，我是刘副官，夫人大概不记得了？"

"是刘副官吗？"钱夫人打量了他一下，微带惊愕地说道："对了，那时在南京到你们大悲巷公馆见过你的。你好，刘副官。"

"托夫人的福。"刘副官又深深地行了一礼，赶忙把钱夫人让了进去，然后抢在前面用手电筒照路，引着钱夫人走上一条水泥砌的汽车过道，绕着花园直往正屋里行去。

"夫人这向好？"刘副官一边引着路，回头笑着向钱夫人说道。

"还好，谢谢你，"钱夫人答道，"你们长官夫人都好呀？我有好些年没见着他们了。"

"我们夫人好，长官最近为了公事忙一些。"刘副官应道。

窦公馆的花园十分深阔，钱夫人打量了一下，满园子里影影绰绰，都是些树木花草，围墙周遭，却密密地栽了一圈椰子树，一片秋后的清月，已经升过高大的椰子树干子来了。钱夫人跟着刘副官绕过了几丛棕榈树，窦公馆那座两层楼的房子便赫然出现在眼前，整座大楼，上上下下灯火通明，亮得好像烧着了一般；一条宽敞的石级引上了楼前一个弧形的大露台，露台的石栏边沿上却整整齐齐地置了十来盆一排齐胸的桂花，钱夫人一踏上露台，一阵桂花的浓香便侵袭过来了。楼前正门大开，里面有几个仆人穿梭一般来往着。刘副官停在门口，哈着身子，做了个手势，毕恭毕敬地说了声：

"夫人请。"

钱夫人一走入门内前厅，刘副官便对一个女仆说道：

"快去报告夫人，钱将军夫人到了。"

前厅只摆了一堂精巧的红木几椅，几案上搁着一套景泰蓝的瓶樽，一只观音尊里斜插了几枝万年青；右侧壁上，嵌了一面鹅卵形的大穿衣镜。钱夫人走到镜前，把身上那件玄色秋大衣卸下，一个女仆赶忙上前把大衣接了过去。钱夫人往镜里瞟了一眼，很快地用手把右鬓边一绺松弛的头发抿了一下，下午六点钟才去西门町红玫瑰做的头发，刚才穿过花园，经风一撩，就乱了。钱夫人往镜子又凑近了一步，身上那件墨绿杭绸的旗袍，她也觉得颜色有点不对劲儿。她记得这种丝绸，在灯光底下照起来，绿汪汪翡翠似的，大概这间前厅不够亮，镜子里看起来，竟有点发乌。难道真的是料子旧了？这份杭绸还是从南京带出来的呢，这些年都没舍得穿，为了赴这场宴才从箱子底拿出来裁了的。早知如此，还不如到鸿翔绸缎庄买份新的。可是她总觉得台湾的衣料粗糙，光泽扎眼，尤其是丝绸，哪里及得上大陆货那么细致，那么柔熟？

"五妹妹到底来了。"一阵脚步声，窦夫人走了出来，一把便握住了钱夫人的双手笑道。

"三阿姊，"钱夫人也笑着叫道："来晚了，累你们好等。"

"哪里的话，恰是时候，我们正要入席呢。"

窦夫人说着便挽着钱夫人往正厅走去。在走廊上，钱夫人用眼角扫了窦夫人两下，她心中不禁觇敲起来：桂枝香果然还没有老。临离开南京那年，自己明明还在梅园新村的公馆替桂枝香请过三十岁的生日酒，得月台的几个姊妹淘都差不多到齐了——桂枝香的妹子后来嫁给任主席任子久做小的十三天辣椒，还有她自己的亲妹妹十七月月红——几个人还学洋派凑份子替桂枝香订制了一个三十寸双层的大寿糕，上面足足插了三十根红蜡烛。现在她总该有四十大几了吧？钱夫人又朝窦夫人瞄了一下。窦夫人穿了一身银灰洒朱砂的薄纱旗袍，足上也配了一双银灰闪光的高跟鞋，右手的无名指上戴了一只莲子大的钻戒，左腕也笼了一副白金镶碎钻的手串，发上却插了一把珊瑚缺月钗，一对寸把长的紫瑛坠子直吊下发脚外来，衬得她丰白的面庞愈加雍容矜贵起来。在南京那时，桂枝香可没有这般风光，她记得她那时还做小，窦瑞生也不过是个次长，现在窦瑞生的官大了，桂枝香也扶了正，难为她熬了这些年，到底给她熬出了头了。

"瑞生到南部开会去了，他听说五妹妹今晚要来，还特地着我向你问好呢。"

窦夫人笑着侧过头来向钱夫人说道。

"哦，难为窦大哥还那么有心。"钱夫人答道。一走近正厅，里面一阵人语喧笑便传了出来。窦夫人在正厅门口停了下来，又握住钱夫人的双手笑道：

"五妹妹，你早就该搬来台北了，我一直都挂着，现在你一个人住在南部那种地方有多冷清呢？今夜你是无论如何缺不得席的——十三也来了。"

"她也在这儿吗？"钱夫人问道。

"你知道呀，任子久一死，她便搬出了任家，"窦夫人说着又凑到钱夫人耳边笑道："任子久是有几份家当的，十三一个人也算过得舒服了。今晚就是她起的哄，来到台湾还是头一遭呢。她把'赏心乐事'票房里的几位朋友搬了来，锣鼓笙箫都是全的，他们还巴望着你上去显两手呢。"

"罢了，罢了，哪里还能来这个玩意儿！"钱夫人急忙挣脱了窦夫人，摆着手笑道。

"客气话不必说了，五妹妹，连你蓝田玉都说不能，别人还敢开腔吗？"窦夫人笑道，也不等钱夫人分辩便挽了她往正厅里走去。

正厅里东一堆西一堆，锦簇绣丛一般，早坐满了衣裙明艳的客人。厅堂异常宽大，呈凸字形，是个中西合璧的款式。左半边置着一堂软垫沙发，右半边置着一堂紫檀硬木桌椅，中间地板上却隔着一张两寸厚刷着二龙抢珠的大地毯。沙发两长四短，对开围着，黑绒底子洒满了醉红的海棠叶儿，中间一张长方矮几上摆了一只两尺高青天细瓷胆瓶，瓶里冒着一大蓬金骨红肉的龙须菊。右半边八张紫檀椅子团团围着一张嵌纹石桌面的八仙桌，桌上早布满了各式的糖盒茶具。厅堂凸字尖端，也摆着六张一式的红木靠椅，椅子三三分开，圈了个半圆，中间缺口处却高高竖了一档乌木架流云蝙蝠镶云母片的屏风。钱夫人看见那些椅子上搁满了铙钹琴弦，椅子前端有两个木架，一个架着一只小鼓，另一个却齐齐地插了一排笙箫管笛。厅堂里灯火辉煌，两旁的座灯从地面斜射上来，照得一面大铜锣金光闪烁。

窦夫人把钱夫人先引到厅堂左半边，然后走到一张沙发跟前对一位五十多岁穿了珠灰旗袍，戴了一身玉器的女客说道：

"赖夫人，这是钱夫人，你们大概见过面的吧？"

钱夫人认得那位女客是赖祥云的太太，以前在南京时，社交场合里见过几面。那时赖祥云大概是个司令官，来到台湾，报纸上倒常见到他的名字。

"这位大概就是钱鹏公的夫人了？"赖夫人本来正和身旁一位男客在说话，这下才转过身来，打量了钱夫人半晌，款款地立了起来笑着说道。一面和钱夫人握手，一面又扶了头，说道：

"我是说面熟得很！"

然后转向身边一位黑红脸身材硕肥头顶光秃穿了宝蓝丝葛长袍的男客说：

"刚才我还和余参军长聊天，梅兰芳第三次南下到上海在丹桂第一台唱的是什么戏，再也想不起来了。你们瞧，我的记性！"

余参军长老早立了起来，朝着钱夫人笑嘻嘻地行了一个礼说道：

"夫人久违了，那年在南京励志社大会串瞻仰过夫人的风采的。我还记得夫人票的是《游园惊梦》呢！"

"是呀，"赖夫人接嘴道，"我一直听说钱夫人的盛名，今天晚上总算有耳福要领教了。"

钱夫人赶忙向余参军长谦谢了一番，她记得余参军长在南京时来过她公馆一次，可是她又仿佛记得他后来好像犯了什么大案子被革了职退休了。接着窦夫人又引着她过去，把在座的几位客人都一一介绍一轮。几位夫人太太她一个也不认识，她们的年纪都相当轻，大概来到台湾才兴起来的。

"我们到那边去吧，十三和几位票友都在那儿。"

窦夫人说着又把钱夫人领到厅堂的右手边去。她们两人一过去，一位穿红旗袍的女客便踏着碎步迎了上来，一把便将钱夫人的手臂勾了过去，笑得全身乱颤说道：

"五阿姊，刚才三阿姊告诉我你也要来，我就喜得叫道：'好哇，今晚可真把名角儿给抬了出来了！'"

钱夫人方才听窦夫人说天辣椒蒋碧月也在这里，她心中就踌躇了一番，不知天辣椒嫁了人这些年，可收敛了一些没有。那时大伙儿在南京夫子庙得月台清唱的时候，有风头总是她占先，扭着她们师傅专拣讨好的戏唱。一出台，也不管清唱的规矩，就脸朝了那些捧角的，一双眼睛钩子一般，直伸到台下去。同是一个娘生的，性格儿却差得那么远。论到懂世故，有担待，除了她姊姊桂枝香再也找不出第二个人来。桂枝香那儿的便宜，天辣椒也算捡尽了。任子久连她姊姊的聘礼都下定了，天辣椒却有本事拦腰一把给夺了过去。也亏桂枝香有涵养，等了多少年才委委屈屈做了窦瑞生的偏房。难怪桂枝香老叹息说：是亲妹子才专拣自己的姊姊往脚下踹呢！钱夫人又打量了一下天辣椒蒋碧月，蒋碧月穿了一身火红的缎子旗袍，两只手腕上，挣铸铜钻，直戴了八只扭花金丝镯，脸上勾得十分入时，眼皮上抹了眼圈膏，眼角儿也着了墨，一头蓬得像鸟窝似的头发，两鬓上却刷出几只俏皮的月牙钩来。任子久一死，这个天辣椒比从前反而愈更标劲，愈更怫挞了，这些年的动乱，在这个女人身上，竟找不出半丝痕迹来。

"哪，你们见识见识吧，这位钱夫人才是真正的女梅兰芳呢！"

蒋碧月挽了钱夫人向座上的几位男女票友客人介绍道。几位男客都慌忙不迭站了起来朝了钱夫人含笑施礼。

"碧月，不要胡说，给这几位内行听了笑话。"

钱夫人一行还礼，一行轻轻责怪蒋碧月道。

"碧月的话倒没有说差，"窦夫人也插嘴笑道，"你的昆曲也算得了梅派的真传了。"

"三阿姊——"

钱夫人含糊地叫了一声，想分辩几句。可是若论到昆曲，连钱鹏志也对她说过：

"老五，南北名角我都听过，你的'昆腔'也算是个好的了。"

钱鹏志说，就是为着在南京得月台听了她的《游园惊梦》，回到上海去，日思夜想，心里怎么也丢不下，才又转了回来娶她的。钱鹏志一径对她讲，能得她在身边，唱几句"昆腔"作娱，他的下半辈子也就无所求了。那时她刚在得月台冒红，一句"昆腔"，台下一声满堂彩，得月台的师傅说：一个夫子庙算起来，就数蓝田玉唱得最正派。

"就是说呀，五阿姊。你来见见，这位徐经理太太也是个昆曲大王呢，"蒋碧月把钱夫人引到一位着黑旗袍，十分净扮的年轻女客跟前说道，然后又笑着向窦夫人说："三阿姊，回头我们让徐太太唱《游园》，五阿姊唱《惊梦》，把这出昆腔的戏祖宗搬出来，让两位名角上去较量较量，也好给我们饱饱耳福。"

那位徐太太连忙立了起来，道了不敢。钱夫人也赶忙谦让了几句，心中却着实嗔怪天辣椒太过冒失，今天晚上这些人，大概没有一个不懂戏的，恐怕这位徐经理太太就现放着是个好角色，回头要真给抬了上去，倒不可以大意呢。运腔转调，这些人都不足畏，倒是在南部这么久，嗓子一直没有认真吊过，却不知如何了。而且裁缝师傅的话果然说中：台北不兴长旗袍喽。在座的——连那个老得脸上起了鸡皮皱的赖夫人在内，个个的旗袍下摆都缩得差不多到膝盖上去了，露出大半截腿子来。在南京那时，哪个夫人的旗袍不是长得快拖到脚面上来的？后悔没有听从裁缝师傅，回头穿了这身长旗袍站出去，不晓得还登不登样。一上台，一亮相，最要紧了。那时在南京梅园新村请客唱戏，每次一站上去，还没有开腔就先把那台下压住了。

"程参谋，我把钱夫人交给你了。你不替我好好伺候着，明天罚你作东。"

窦夫人把钱夫人引到一位三十多岁的军官面前笑着说道，然后转身悄声对钱夫人说："五妹妹，你在这里聊聊，程参谋最懂戏的，我得进去招呼着上席了。"

"钱夫人久仰了。"

程参谋朝着钱夫人，立了正，利落地一鞠躬，行了一个军礼。他穿了一身浅泥色凡立了的军礼服，外套的翻领上别了一副金亮的两朵梅花中校领章，一双短筒皮靴靠在一起，乌光水滑的。钱夫人看见他笑起来时，咧着一口齐垛垛净白的牙齿，容长的面孔，下巴剃得青亮，眼睛细长上挑，随一双飞扬的眉毛，往两鬓插去，一杆葱的鼻梁，鼻尖却微微下伛，一头墨浓的头发，处处都抿得妥妥帖帖的。他的身段颀长，着了军服分外英发，可是钱夫人觉得他这一声招呼里却又透着几分温柔，半点也没带武人的粗糙。

"夫人请坐。"

程参谋把自己的椅子让了出来，将椅子上那张海绵椅垫挪挪正，请钱大人就了坐，然后立即走到那张八仙桌端一盅茉莉香片及一个四色糖盒来，钱夫人正要伸出手去接过那盅石榴红的瓷杯，程参谋却低声笑道：

"小心烫了手，夫人。"

然后打开了那个描金乌漆糖盒，伛下身去，双手捧到钱夫人面前，笑吟吟地望着钱夫人，等她挑选。钱夫人随手抓了一把松瓤，程参谋忙劝止道：

"夫人，这个东西顶伤嗓子。我看夫人还是尝颗蜜枣，润润喉吧。"

随着便拈起一根牙签挑了一枚蜜枣，递给钱夫人。钱夫人道了谢，将那枚蜜枣接了过来，塞到嘴里，一阵沁甜的蜜味，果然十分甘芳。程参谋另外搬了一张椅子，在钱夫人右侧坐了下来。

"夫人最近看戏没有？"程参谋坐定后笑着问道。他说话时，身子总是微微倾斜过来，十分专注似的，钱夫人看见他又露出了一口白净的牙齿来，灯光下，照得莹亮。

"好久没看了，"钱夫人答道，她低下头去，细细地啜了一口手里那盅香片，"住在南部，难得有好戏。"

"张爱云这几天正在国光戏院演《洛神》呢，夫人。"

"是吗？"钱夫人应道，一直俯着首在饮茶，沉吟了半晌才说道，"我还是在上海天蟾舞台看她演过这出戏——那是好久以前了。"

"她的做工还是在的，到底不愧是《青衣祭酒》，把个宓妃和曹子建两个人那段情意，演得细腻到了十分。"

钱夫人抬起头来，触到了程参谋的目光，她即刻侧过了头去。程参谋那双细长的眼睛，好像把人都罩住了似的。

"谁演得这般细腻呀？"天辣椒蒋碧月插了进来笑道，程参谋赶忙立起来，让了座。蒋碧月抓了一把朝阳瓜子，跷起腿嗑着瓜子笑道："程参谋，人人说你懂戏，钱夫人可是戏里的'通天教主'，我看你趁早别在这儿班门弄斧了。"

"我正在和钱夫人讲究张爱云的《洛神》，向钱夫人讨教呢。"程参谋对蒋碧月说着，眼睛却瞟向了钱夫人。

"哦，原来是说张爱云吗？"蒋碧月噗哧笑了一下，"她在台湾教教戏也就罢了，偏偏又要去唱《洛神》，扮起宓妃来也不像呀！上礼拜六我才去国光看来，买到了后排，只见她嘴巴动，声音也听不到，半出戏还没唱完，她嗓子先就哑掉了——嗳唷，三阿姊来请上席了。"

一个仆人拉开了客厅通到饭厅的一扇镂空口字的桃花心木推门。窦夫人已经从饭厅里走了出来。整座饭厅银素装饰，明亮得像雪洞一般，两桌席上，却是猩红的细布桌面，盆碗羹箸一律都是银的。客人们进去后都你推我让，不肯上座。

"还是我占先吧，这般让法，这餐饭也吃不成了，倒是辜负了主人这番心意！"

赖夫人走到第一桌的主位坐了下来，然后又招呼着余参军长说道：

"参军长，你也来我旁边坐下吧。刚才梅兰芳的戏，我们还没有论出头绪来呢。"

余参军长把手一拱，笑嘻嘻地道了一声："遵命。"客人们哄然一笑便都相随入了席。到了第二桌，大家又推让起来了，赖夫人隔着桌子向钱夫人笑着叫道：

"钱夫人，我看你也学学我吧。"

窦夫人便过来拥着钱夫人走到第二桌主位上，低声在她耳边说道：

"五妹妹，你就坐下吧。你不占先，别人不好入座的。"

钱夫人环视了一下，第二桌的客人都站在那儿带笑瞅着她。钱夫人赶忙含糊地推辞了两句，坐了下去，一阵心跳，连她的脸都有点发热了。倒不是她没经过这种场面，好久没有应酬，竟有点不惯了。从前钱鹏志在的时候，筵席之间，十有八九的主位，倒是她占先的。钱鹏志的夫人当然上座，她从来也不必推让。南京那起夫人太太们，能僭过她辈分的，还数不出几个来。她可不能跟那些官儿的姨太太们去比，她可是钱鹏志明公正道迎回去做填房夫人的。可怜桂枝香那时出面请客都没份儿，连生日酒还是她替桂枝香做的呢。到了台湾，桂枝香才敢这么出头摆场面，而她那时才冒二十岁，一个清唱的姑娘，一夜间便成了将军夫人了。卖唱的嫁给小户人家还遭多少议论，又何况是入了侯门？连她亲妹子十七月月红还刻薄过她两句：姊姊，你的辫子也该铰了，明日你和钱将军走在一起，人家还以为你是他的孙女儿呢！钱鹏志娶她那年已经六十靠边了，然而怎么说她也是他正正经经的填房夫人啊。她明白她的身份，她也珍惜她的身份。跟了钱鹏志那十几年，筵前酒后，哪次她不是捏着一把冷汗，任是多大的场面，总是应付得妥妥帖帖的？走在人前，一样风华蹁跹，谁又敢议论她是秦淮河得月台的蓝田玉了？

"难为你了，老五。"

钱鹏志常常抚着她的腮对她这样说道。她听了总是心里一酸，许多的委屈却是没法诉的。难道她还能怨钱鹏志吗？是她自己心甘情愿的。钱鹏志娶她的时候就分明和她说清楚了。他是为着听了她的《游园惊梦》才想把她接回去伴他的晚年的。可是她妹子月月红说的呢，钱鹏志好当她的爷爷了，她还要希冀什么？到底应了得月台瞎子师娘那把铁嘴：五姑娘，你们这种人只有嫁给年纪大的，当女儿一般疼惜算了。年轻的，哪里靠得住？可是瞎子师娘偏偏又捏着她的手，眨巴着一双青光眼叹息道：荣华富贵你是享定了，蓝田玉，只可惜你长错了一根骨头，也是你前世的冤孽！不是冤孽还是什么？除却天上的月亮摘不到，世上的金银财宝，钱鹏志怕不都设法捧了来讨她的欢心。她体验得出钱鹏志那番苦心。钱鹏志怕她念着出身低微，在达官贵人面前气馁胆怯，总是百般怂恿着她，讲排场，耍派头。梅园新村钱夫人宴客的款式怕不噪反了整个南京城，钱公馆里的酒席钱，"袁大头"就用得罪过花啦的。单就替桂枝香请生日酒那天吧，梅园新村的公馆里一摆就是十台，摁笛的是仙霓社里大江南北第一把笛子吴声豪，大厨师却是花了十块大洋特别从桃叶渡的绿柳居接来的。

"窦夫人，你们大师傅是哪儿请来的呀？来到台湾我还是头一次吃到这么讲究的鱼翅呢。"赖夫人说道。

"他原是黄钦之黄部长家在上海时候的厨子，来台湾才到我们这儿的。"窦夫人答道。

"那就难怪了，"余参军长接口道，"黄钦公是有名的美食家呢。"

"哪天要能借到府上的大师傅去烧个翅，请起客来就风光了。"赖夫人说道。

"那还不容易？我也乐得去白吃一餐呢！"窦夫人说，客人们都笑了起来。

"钱夫人，请用碗翅吧。"程参谋盛了一碗红烧鱼翅，加了一匙羹镇江醋，搁在钱夫人面前，然后又低声笑道：

"这道菜，是我们公馆里出了名的。"

钱夫人还没来得及尝鱼翅，窦夫人却从隔壁桌子走了过来，敬了一轮酒，特别又叫程参谋替她斟满了，走到钱夫人身边，按着她的肩膀笑道：

"五妹妹，我们俩儿好久没对过杯了。"

说完便和钱夫人碰了一下杯，一口喝尽，钱夫人也细细地干掉了。窦夫人离开时又对程参谋说道：

"程参谋，好好替我劝酒啊。你长官不在，你就在那一桌替他做主人吧。"

程参谋立起来，执了一把银酒壶，弯了身，笑吟吟便往钱夫人杯里筛酒，钱夫人忙阻止道：

"程参谋，你替别人斟吧，我的酒量有限得很。"

程参谋却站着不动，望着钱夫人笑道：

"夫人，花雕不比别的酒，最易发散。我知道夫人回头还要用嗓子，这个酒暖过了，少喝点儿，不会伤喉咙的。"

"钱夫人是海量，不要饶过她！"

坐在钱夫人对面的蒋碧月却走了过来，也不用人让，自己先斟满了一杯，举到钱夫人面前笑道：

"五阿姊，我也好久没有和你喝过双盅儿了。"

钱夫人推开了蒋碧月的手，轻轻咳了一下说道：

"碧月，这样喝法要醉了。"

"到底是不赏妹子的脸，我喝双份儿好了，回头醉了，最多让他们抬回去就是啦。"

蒋碧月一仰头便干了一杯，程参谋连忙捧上另一杯，她也接过去一气干了，然后把个银酒杯倒过来，在钱夫人脸上一晃。客人们都鼓起掌来喝道：

"到底是蒋小姐豪兴！"

钱夫人只得举起了杯子，缓缓地将一杯花雕饮尽。酒倒是烫得暖暖的，一下喉，就像一股热流般，周身游荡起来了。可是台湾的花雕到底不及大陆的那么醇厚，饮下去终究有点割喉。虽说花雕容易发散，饮急了，后劲才凶呢。没想到真正从绍兴办来的那些陈年花雕也那么伤人。那晚到底中了她们的道儿！她们大伙儿都说，几杯花雕哪里就能把嗓子喝哑了？难得是桂枝香的好日子，姊妹们不知何日才能聚得齐，主人尚且不开怀，客人哪能尽兴呢？连月月红十七也夹在里面起哄：姊姊，我们姊妹俩儿也来干一杯，亲热亲热一下。月月红穿了一身大金大红的缎子旗袍，艳得像只鹦哥儿，一双眼睛，鹃伶伶地尽是水光。姊姊不赏脸，她说，姊姊到底不赏妹子的脸，她说道。逞够了强，捡够了便宜，还要赶着说风凉话。难怪桂枝香叹息：是亲妹子才专拣自己的姊姊往脚下踹呢。月月红——就算她年轻不懂事，可是他郑彦青就不该也跟了来胡闹了。他也捧了满满的一杯酒，咧着一口雪白的牙齿说道：夫人，我也来敬夫人一杯。他喝得两颧鲜红，眼睛烧得像两团黑火，一双带刺的马靴啪哒一声并在一起，弯着身腰柔柔地叫道：夫人——

"这下该轮到我了，夫人。"程参谋立起身，双手举起了酒杯，笑吟吟地说道。

"真的不行了，程参谋。"钱夫人微俯着首，喃喃说道。

"我先干三杯，表示敬意，夫人请随意好了。"

程参谋一连便喝了三杯，一片酒晕把他整张脸都盖了过去了。他的额头发出了亮光，鼻尖上也冒出几颗汗珠子来。钱夫人端起了酒杯，在唇边略略沾了一下。程参谋替钱夫人拈了一只贵妃鸡的肉翅，自己也挟了一个鸡头来过酒。

"嗳唷，你敬的是什么酒呀？"

对面蒋碧月站起来，伸头前去嗅了一下余参军长手里那杯酒，尖着嗓门叫了起来，余参军长正捧着一只与众不同的金色鸡缸杯在敬蒋碧月的酒。

"蒋小姐，这杯是'通宵酒'哪。"余参军长笑嘻嘻地说道，他那张黑红脸早已喝得像猪肝似的了。

"呀呀唪，何人与你们通宵哪！"蒋碧月把手一挥，操起戏白说道。

"蒋小姐，百花亭里还没摆起来，你先就'醉酒'了。"赖夫人隔着桌子笑着叫道，客人们又一声哄笑起来。窦夫人也站了起来对客人们说道：

"我们也该上场了，请各位到客厅那边宽坐去吧。"

客人们都立了起来，赖夫人带头，鱼贯而入进到客厅里，分别坐下。几位男票友却走到那档屏风面前几张红本椅子就了座，一边调弄起管弦来。六个人，除了胡琴外，一个拉二胡，一个弹月琴，一个管小鼓拍板，另外两个人立着，一个擎了一对铙钹，一个手里却吊了一面大铜锣。

"夫人，那位杨先生真是把好胡琴，他的笛子，台湾还找不出第二个人呢，回头你听他一吹，就知道了。"

程参谋指着那位操胡琴姓杨的票友，在钱夫人耳根下说道。钱夫人微微斜靠在一张单人沙发上，程参谋在她身旁一张皮垫矮圆凳上坐了下来。他又替钱夫人沏了一盏茉莉香片，钱夫人一面品着茶，一面顺着程参谋的手，朝那位姓杨的票友望去。那位姓杨的票友约莫五十上下，穿了一件古铜色起暗团花的熟罗长衫，面貌十分清癯，一双手指修长，洁白得像十管白玉一般，他将一柄胡琴从布袋子里抽了出来，腿上垫上一块青搭布，将胡琴搁在上面，架上了弦弓，随便咿呀地调了一下，微微将头一垂，一扬手，猛地一声胡琴，便像抛线一般窜了起来，一段《夜深沉》，奏得十分清脆嘹亮，一奏毕，余参军长头一个便跳了起来叫声："好胡琴！"客人们便也都鼓起掌来。接着锣鼓齐鸣，奏出了一支《将军令》的上场牌子来。窦夫人也跟着满客厅一一去延请客人们上场演唱，正当客人们互相推让间，余参军长已经拥着蒋碧月走到胡琴那边，然后打起丑腔叫道：

"启娘娘，这便是百花亭了。"

蒋碧月双手捂着嘴，笑得前俯后仰，两只腕上几个扭花金镯子，铮铮锵锵地抖响着。客人们都跟着喝彩，胡琴便奏出了《贵妃醉酒》里的四平调。蒋碧月身也不转，面朝了客人便唱了起来。唱到过门的时候，余参军长跑出去托了一个朱红茶盘进来，上面搁了那只金色的鸡缸杯，一手撩了袍子，在蒋碧月跟前做了半跪的姿势，效那高力士叫道：

"启娘娘，奴婢敬酒。"

蒋碧月果然装了醉态，东歪西倒地做出了种种身段，一个卧鱼弯下身去，用嘴将那只酒杯衔了起来，然后又把杯子当啷一声掷到地上，唱出了两句：

> 人生在世如春梦
> 且自开怀饮几盅

客人们早笑得滚做了一团，窦夫人笑得岔了气，沙着喉咙对赖夫人喊道：
"我看我们碧月今晚真的醉了！"

赖夫人笑得直用绢子揩眼泪，一面大声叫道：
"蒋小姐醉了倒不要紧，只要莫学那杨玉环又去喝一缸醋就行了。"

客人们正在闹着要蒋碧月唱下去，蒋碧月却摇摇摆摆地走了下来，把那位徐太太给抬了上去，然后对客人们宣布道：

"'赏心乐事'的昆曲台柱来给我们唱《游园》了，回头再请另一位昆曲皇后梅派正宗传人——钱夫人来接唱《惊梦》。"

钱夫人赶忙抬起了头来，将手里的茶杯搁到左边的矮几上，她看见徐太太已经站到了那档屏风前面，半背着身子，一只手却扶在插笙箫的那只乌木架上。她穿了一身净黑的丝绒旗袍，脑后松松地挽了一个贵妃髻，半面脸微微向外，莹白的耳垂露在发外，上面吊着一九翠绿的坠子。客厅里几只喇叭形的座灯像数道注光，把徐太太那窈窕的身影，袅袅娜娜地推送到那档云母屏风上去。

"五阿姊，你仔细听听，看看徐太太的《游园》跟你唱的可有个高下。"

蒋碧月走了过来，一下子便坐到了程参谋的身边，伸过头来，一只手拍着钱夫人的肩，悄声笑着说道。

"夫人，今晚总算我有缘，能领教夫人的'昆腔'了。"

程参谋也转过头来，望着钱夫人笑道。钱夫人睃着蒋碧月手腕上那几只金光乱窜的扭花镯子，她忽然感到一阵微微的晕眩，一股酒意涌上了她的脑门似的，刚才灌下去的那几杯花雕好像渐渐着力了，她觉得两眼发热，视线都有点朦胧起来。蒋碧月身上那袭红旗袍如同一团火焰，一下子明晃晃地烧到了程参谋的身上，程参谋衣领上那几枚金梅花，便像火星子般，跳跃了起来。蒋碧月的一对眼睛像两丸黑水银在她醉红的脸上溜转着，程参谋那双细长的眼睛却眯成了一条缝，射出了逼人的锐光，两张脸都向着她，一齐咧着整齐的白牙，朝她微笑着，两张红得发油光的面庞渐渐地靠拢起来，凑在一块儿，咧着白牙，朝她笑着。笛子和洞箫都鸣了起来，笛音如同流水，把靡靡下沉的箫声又托了起来，送进《游园》的《皂罗袍》中去——

原来姹紫嫣红开遍
似这般都付与断井颓垣
良辰美景奈何天
赏心乐事谁家院——

杜丽娘唱的这段"昆腔"便算是昆曲里的警句了。连吴声豪也说：钱夫人，您这段《皂罗袍》便是梅兰芳也不能过的。可是吴声豪的笛子却偏偏吹得那么高（吴师傅，今晚让她们灌多了，嗓子靠不住，你换枝调门儿低一点儿的笛子吧。），吴声豪说，练嗓子的人，第一要忌酒；然而月月红十七却端着那杯花雕过来说道：姊姊，我们姊妹俩儿也来干一杯。她穿得大金大红的，还要说：姊姊，你不赏脸。不是这样说，妹子，不是姊姊不赏脸，实在为着他是姊姊命中的冤孽。瞎子师娘不是说过：荣华富贵——蓝田玉，可惜你长错了一根骨头。冤孽啊。他可不就是姊姊命中招的冤孽了？懂吗？妹子，冤孽。然而他也捧着酒杯过来叫道：夫人。他笔着斜皮带，戴着金亮的领章，腰杆扎得挺细，一双带白铜刺的长筒马靴乌光水滑地啪哒一声靠在一起，眼皮都喝得泛了桃花，却叫道：夫人。谁不知道南京梅园新村的钱夫人呢？钱鹏公，钱将军的夫人啊。钱鹏志的夫人。钱鹏志的随从参谋。钱将军的夫人。钱将军的参谋。钱将军。难为你了，老五，钱鹏志说道，可怜你还那么年轻。然而年轻人哪里会有良心呢？瞎子师娘说，你们这种人，只有年纪大的才懂得疼惜啊。荣华富贵——只可惜长错了一根骨头。懂吗？妹子，他就是姊姊命中招的冤孽了。钱将军的夫人。钱将军的随从参谋。将军夫人。随从参谋。冤孽。我说。冤孽，我说。（吴师傅，换枝低一点儿的笛子吧，我的嗓子有点不行了。哎，这段《山坡羊》。）

中国文学选读

没乱里春情难遣

蓦地里怀人幽怨

则为俺生小婵娟

拣名门一例一例里神仙眷

甚良缘把青春抛的远

俺的睡情谁见——


那团红火焰又熊熊地冒了起来了，烧得那两道飞扬的眉毛，发出了青湿的汗光。两张醉红的脸又渐渐地靠拢在一处，一齐咧着白牙，笑了起来。笛子上那几根玉管子似的手指，上下飞跃着。那袅袅的身影儿，在那档雪青的云母屏风上，随着灯光，仿仿佛佛地摇曳起来。笛声愈来愈低沉，愈来愈凄咽，好像把杜丽娘满腔的怨情都吹了出来似的。杜丽娘快要入梦了，柳梦梅也该上场了。可是吴声豪却说，《惊梦》里幽会那一段，最是露骨不过的。（吴师傅，低一点儿吧，今晚我喝多了酒。）然而他却偏捧着酒杯过来叫道：夫人。他那双乌光水滑的马靴啪哒一声靠在一处，一双白铜马刺扎得人的眼睛都发疼了。他喝得眼皮泛了桃花，还要那么叫道：夫人。我来扶你上马，夫人，他说道，他的马裤把两条修长的腿子绷得滚圆，夹在马肚子上，像一双钳子。他的马是白的，路也是白的，树干子也是白的，他那匹白马在猛烈的太阳底下照得发了亮。他们说：到中山陵的那条路上两旁种满了白桦树。他那匹白马在桦树林子里奔跑起来，活像一头麦秆丛中乱窜的白兔儿。太阳照在马背上，蒸出了一缕缕的白烟来。一匹白的，一匹黑的——两匹马都在淌着汗。而他身上却沾满了触鼻的马汗。他的眉毛变得碧青，眼睛像两团烧着了的黑火，汗珠子一行行从他额上流到他鲜红的颧上来。太阳，我叫道。太阳照得人的眼睛都睁不开。那些树干子，又白净，又细滑，一层层的树皮都卸掉了，露出里面赤裸裸的嫩肉来。他们说：那条路上种满了白桦树。太阳，我叫道，太阳直射到人的眼睛上来了。于是他便放柔了声音唤道：夫人。钱将军的夫人。钱将军的随从参谋。钱将军的——老五，钱鹏志叫道，他的喉咙已经咽住了。老五，他喑哑地喊道，你要珍重吓。他的头发乱得像一丛枯白的茅草，他的眼睛坑出了两只黑窟窿，他从白床单下伸出他那只瘦黑的手来，说道，珍重吓，老五。他抖索索地打开了那只描金的百宝匣儿，这是祖母绿，他取出了第一层抽屉。这是猫儿眼。这是翡翠叶子。珍重吓，老五，他那乌青的嘴皮颤抖着，可怜你还这么年轻。荣华富贵——只可惜你长错了一根骨头。冤孽，妹子，他就是姊姊命中招的冤孽了。你听我说，妹子，冤孽呵。荣华富贵——可是我只活过那么一次。懂吗？妹子，他就是我的冤孽了。荣华富贵——只有那一次。荣华富贵——我只活过一次。懂吗？妹子，你听我说，妹子。姊姊不赏脸，月月红却端着酒过来说道，她的眼睛亮得剩了两泡水。姊姊到底不赏妹子的脸，她穿得一身大金大红的，像一团火一般，坐到了他的身边去。（吴师傅，我喝多了花雕。）

迁延，这衷怀那处言
淹煎，泼残生除问天——

就在那一刻，泼残生——就在那一刻，她坐到他身边，一身大金大红的，就是那一刻，那两张醉红的面孔渐渐地凑拢在一起，就在那一刻，我看到了他们的眼睛：她的眼睛，他的眼睛。完了，我知道，就在那一刻，除问天——（吴师傅，我的嗓子。）完了，我的喉咙，摸摸我的喉咙，在发抖吗？完了，在发抖吗？天——（吴师傅，我唱不出来了。）天——完了，荣华富贵——可是我只活过一次，——冤孽、冤孽、冤孽——天——（吴师傅，我的嗓子。）——就在那一刻，就在那一刻，哑掉了——天——天——天

"五阿姊，该是你《惊梦》的时候了。"蒋碧月站了起来，走到钱夫人面前，伸出了她那一双戴满了扭花金丝镯的手臂，笑吟吟地说道。

"夫人——"程参谋也立了起来，站在钱夫人跟前，微微倾着身子，轻轻地叫道。

"五妹妹，请你上场吧。"窦夫人走了过来，一面向钱夫人伸出手说道。

锣鼓笙箫一齐鸣了起来，奏出了一支《万年欢》的牌子。客人们都倏地离了座，钱夫人看见满客厅里都是些手臂交挥拍击，把徐太太团团围在客厅中央。笙箫管笛愈吹愈急切，那面铜锣高高地举了起来，敲得金光乱闪。

"我不能唱了。"钱夫人望着蒋碧月，微微摇了摇两下头，喃喃说道。

"那可不行，"蒋碧月一把捉住了钱夫人的双手，"五阿姊，你这位名角儿今晚无论如何逃不掉的。"

"我的嗓子哑了。"钱夫人突然用力甩开了蒋碧月的双手，嘎声说道，她觉得全身的血液一下子都涌到头上来了似的，两腮滚热，喉头好像让刀片猛割了一下，一阵阵地刺痛起来，她听见窦夫人插进来说：

"五妹妹不唱算了——余参军长，我看今晚还是你这位黑头来压轴吧。"

　　"好呀，好呀，"那边赖夫人马上响应道，"我有好久没有领教余参军长的《八大锤》了。"

　　说着赖夫人便把余参军长推到了锣鼓那边。余参军长一站上去，便拱了手朝下面道了一声"献丑"，客人们一阵哄笑，他便开始唱了一段金兀术上场时的《点绛唇》；一面唱着，一面又撩起了袍子，做了个上马的姿势，踏着马步便在客厅中央环走起来，他那张宽肥的醉脸胀得紫红，双眼圆睁，两道粗眉一齐竖起，几声呐喊，把胡琴都压了下去。赖夫人笑得弯了腰，跑上去，跟在余参军长后头直拍着手，蒋碧月即刻上去加入了他们的行列，不停地尖起嗓子叫着："好黑头！好黑头！"另外几位女客也上去跟她们喝彩，团团围走，于是客厅里的笑声便一阵比一阵暴涨了起来。余参军长一唱毕，几个着白衣黑裤的女佣已经端了一碗碗的红枣桂圆汤进来让客人们润喉了。

　　窦夫人引了客人们走到屋外露台上的时候，外面的空气里早充满了风露，客人们都穿上了大衣，窦夫人却围了一张白丝大披肩，走到了台阶的下端去。钱夫人立在露台的石栏旁边，往天上望去，她看见那片秋月恰恰地升到中天，把窦公馆花园里的树木路阶都照得镀了一层白霜，露台上那十几盆桂花，香气却比先前浓了许多，像一阵湿雾似的，一下子罩到了她的面上来。

　　"赖将军夫人的车子来了。"刘副官站在台阶下面，往上大声通报各家的汽车。头一辆开进来的，便是赖夫人那辆黑色崭新的林肯，一个穿着制服的司机赶忙跳了下来，打开车门，弯了腰毕恭毕敬地候着。赖夫人走下台阶，和窦夫人道了别，把余参军长也带上了车，坐进去后，却伸出头来向窦夫人笑道：

　　"窦夫人，府上这一夜戏，就是当年梅兰芳和金少山也不能过的。"

　　"可是呢，"窦夫人笑着答道："余参军长的黑头真是赛过金霸王了。"

　　立在台阶上的客人都笑了起来，一齐向赖夫人挥手作别。第二辆开进来的，却是窦夫人自己的小轿车，把几位票友客人都送走了。接着程参谋自己开了一辆吉普军车进来，蒋碧月马上走了下去，捞起旗袍，跨上车子去，程参谋赶着过来，把她扶上了司机旁边的座位上，蒋碧月却歪出半个身子来笑道：

　　"这辆吉普车连门都没有，回头怕不把我甩出马路上去呢。"

　　"小心点开啊，程参谋。"窦夫人说道，又把程参谋叫了过去，附耳嘱咐了几句，程参谋直点着头笑应道：

　　"夫人请放心。"然后他朝了钱夫人，立了正，深深地行了一个礼，抬起头来笑道：

"钱夫人，我先告辞了。"

说完便利落地跳上了车子，发了火，开动起来。

"三阿姊再见！五阿姊再见！"蒋碧月从车门伸出手来，不停地招挥着，钱夫人看见她臂上那一串扭花镯子，在空中划了几个金圈圈。

"钱夫人的车子呢？"客人快走尽的时候，窦夫人站在台阶下问刘副官道。

"报告夫人，钱将军夫人是坐计程车来的。"刘副官立了正答道。

"三阿姊——"钱夫人站在露台上叫了一声，她老早就想跟窦夫人说替她叫一辆计程车来了，可是刚才客人多，她总觉得有点堵口。

"那么我的汽车回来，立刻传进来送钱夫人吧。"窦夫人马上接口道。

"是，夫人。"刘副官接了命令便退走了。

窦夫人回转身，便向着露台走了上来，钱夫人看见她身上那块白披肩，在月光下，像朵云似地簇拥着她。一阵风掠过去，周遭的椰树都沙沙地鸣了起来，把窦夫人身上那块大披肩吹得姗姗扬起，钱夫人赶忙用手把大衣领子锁了起来，连连打了两个寒噤，刚才滚热的面腮，吃这阵凉风一逼，汗毛都张开了。

"我们进去吧，五妹妹，"窦夫人伸出手来，搂着钱夫人的肩膀往屋内走去，"我去叫人沏壶茶来，我们俩儿正好谈谈心——你这么久没来，可发觉台北变了些没有？"

钱夫人沉吟了半晌，侧过头来答道：

"变多喽。"

走到房子门口的时候，她又轻轻地加了一句：

"变得我都快不认识了——起了好多新的高楼大厦。"

——选自《台北人》

## 2. Hut on the Mountain

### Can Xue

On the bleak and barren mountain behind our house stood a wooden hut.

Day after day I busied myself by tidying up my desk drawers. When I wasn't doing that I would sit in the armchair, my hands on my knees, listening to the tumultuous sounds of the north wind whipping against the fir-bark roof of the hut, and the howling of the wolves echoing in the valleys.

"Huh, you'll never get done with those drawers," said Mother, forcing a smile. "Not in your lifetime."

"There's something wrong with everyone's ears," I said with suppressed annoyance. "There are so many thieves wandering about our house in the moonlight, when I turn on the light I can see countless tiny holes poked by fingers in the window screens. In the next room, Father and you snore terribly, rattling the utensils in the kitchen cabinet. Then I kick about in my bed, turn my swollen head on the pillow and hear the man locked up in the hut banging furiously against the door. This goes on till daybreak."

"You give me a terrible start," Mother said, "every time you come into my room looking for things." She fixed her eyes on me as she backed toward the door. I saw the flesh of one of her cheeks contort ridiculously.

One day I decided to go up to the mountain to find out what on earth was the trouble. As soon as the wind let up, I began to climb. I climbed and climbed for a long time. The sunshine made me dizzy. Tiny white flames were flickering among the pebbles. I wandered about, coughing all the time. The salty sweat from my forehead was streaming into my eyes. I couldn't see or hear anything. When I reached-home, I stood outside the door for a while and saw that the person reflected in the mirror had mud on her shoes and dark purple pouches under her eyes.

"It's some disease," I heard them snickering in the dark.

When my eyes became adapted to the darkness inside, they'd hidden themselves—laughing in their hiding places. I discovered they had made a mess of my desk drawers while I was out. A few dead moths and dragonflies were scattered on the floor—they knew only too well that these were treasures to me.

"They sorted the things in the drawers for you," little sister told me, "when you were out." She stared at me, her left eye turning green.

"I hear wolves howling," I deliberately tried to scare her. "They keep running around the house. Sometimes they poke their heads in through the cracks in the door. These things always happen after dusk. You get so scared in your dreams that cold sweat drips from the soles of your feet. Everyone in this house sweats this way in his sleep. You have only to see how damp the quilts are. "

I felt upset because some of the things in my desk drawers were missing. Keeping her eyes on the floor, Mother pretended she knew nothing about it. But I had a feeling she was glaring ferociously at the back of my head, since the spot would become numb and swollen whenever she did that. I also knew they had buried a box with my chess set by the well behind the house. They had done it many times, but each time I would dig the chess set out. When I dug for it, they would turn on the light and poke their heads out the window. In the face of my defiance they always tried to remain calm.

"Up there on the mountain," I told them at mealtime, "there is a hut. "

They all lowered their heads, drinking soup noisily. Probably no one heard me.

"Lots of big rats were running wildly in the wind," I raised my voice and put down the chopsticks. "Rocks were rolling down the mountain and crashing into the back of our house. And you were so scared that cold sweat dripped from your soles. Don't you remember? You only have to look at your quilts. Whenever the weather's fine, you're airing the quilts; the clothesline out there is always strung with them. "

Father stole a glance at me with one eye, which, I noticed, was the all-too-familiar eye of a wolf. So that was it! At night he became one of the wolves running around the house, howling and wailing mournfully.

"White lights are swaying back and forth everywhere. " I clutched Mother's shoulder with one hand. "Everything is so glaring that my eyes blear from the pain. You simply can't see a thing. But as soon as I return to my room, sit down in my armchair, and put my hands on my knees, I can see the fir-bark roof clearly. The image seems very close. In fact, every one of us must have seen it. Really, there's somebody squatting inside. He's got two big purple pouches under his eyes, too, because he stays up all night. "

Father said, "Every time you dig by the well and hit stone with a screeching sound, you make Mother and me feel as if we were hanging in midair. We shudder at the sound and kick with bare feet but can't reach the ground. " To avoid my eyes, he turned his face toward the window, the panes of which were thickly specked with fly droppings.

"At the bottom of the well," he went on, "there's a pair of scissors which I dropped some time ago. In my dreams I always make up my mind to fish them out. But as soon as I wake, I realize I've made a mistake. In fact, no scissors have ever fallen into the well. Your mother says positively that I've made a mistake. But I will not give up. It always steals into my mind again. Sometimes while I'm in bed, I am suddenly seized with regret: the scissors lie rusting at the bottom of the well, why shouldn't I go fish them out? I've been troubled by this for dozens of years. See my wrinkles? My face seems to have become furrowed. Once I actually went to the well and tried to lower a bucket into it. But the rope was thick and slippery. Suddenly my hands lost their grip and the bucket flopped with a loud boom, breaking into pieces in the well. I rushed back to the house, looked into the mirror, and saw the hair on my left temple had turned completely white."

"How that north wind pierces!" I hunched my shoulders. My face turned black and blue with cold. "Bits of ice are forming in my stomach. When I sit down in my armchair I can hear them clinking away."

I had been intending to give my desk drawers a cleaning, but Mother was always stealthily making trouble. She'd walk to and fro in the next room, stamping, stamping, to my great distraction. I tried to ignore it, so I got a pack of cards and played, murmuring "one, two, three, four, five..."

The pacing stopped all of a sudden and Mother poked her small dark green face into the room and mumbled, "I had a very obscene dream. Even now my back is dripping cold sweat."

"And your soles, too," I added. "Everyone's soles drip cold sweat. You aired your quilt again yesterday. It's usual enough."

Little sister sneaked in and told me that Mother had been thinking of breaking my arms because I was driving her crazy by opening and shutting the drawers. She was so tortured by the sound that every time she heard it, she'd soak her head in cold water until she caught a bad cold.

"This didn't happen by chance." Sister's stares were always so pointed that tiny pink measles broke out on my neck. "For example, I've heard Father talking about the scissors for perhaps twenty years. Everything has its own cause from way back.

Everything."

So I oiled the sides of the drawers. And by opening and shutting them carefully, I managed to make no noise at all. I repeated this experiment for many days and the pacing in the next room ceased. She was fooled. This proves you can get away with anything as long as you take a little precaution. I was very excited over my success and worked hard all night. I was about to finish tidying my drawers when the light suddenly went out. I heard Mother's sneering laugh in the next room.

"That light from your room glares so that it makes all my blood vessels throb and throb, as though some drums were beating inside. Look," she said, pointing to her temple, where the blood vessels bulged like fat earthworms. "I'd rather get scurvy. There are throbbings throughout my body day and night. You have no idea how I'm suffering. Because of this ailment, your father once thought of committing suicide." She put her fat hand on my shoulder, an icy hand dripping with water.

Someone was making trouble by the well. I heard him letting the bucket down and drawing it up, again and again; the bucket hit against the wall of the well— boom, boom, boom. At dawn, he dropped the bucket with a loud bang and ran away. I opened the door of the next room and saw Father sleeping with his vein-ridged hand clutching the bedside, groaning in agony. Mother was beating the floor here and there with a broom; her hair was disheveled. At the moment of daybreak, she told me, a huge swarm of hideous beetles flew in through the window. They bumped against the walls and flopped onto the floor, which now was scattered with their remains. She got up to tidy the room, and as she was putting her feet into her slippers, a hidden bug bit her toe. Now her whole leg was swollen like a thick lead pipe.

"He," Mother pointed to Father, who was sleeping stuporously, "is dreaming it is he who is bitten."

"In the little hut on the mountain, someone is groaning, too. The black wind is blowing, carrying grape leaves along with it."

"Do you hear?" In the faint light of morning, Mother put her ear against the floor, listening with attention. "These bugs hurt themselves in their fall and passed out. They charged into the room earlier, at the moment of daybreak."

I did go up to the mountain that day, I remember. At first I was sitting in the cane chair, my hands on my knees. Then I opened the door and walked into the white light. I climbed up the mountain, seeing nothing but the white pebbles glowing with flames.

There were no grapevines, nor any hut.

1985

(translated by Ronald R. Janssen and Jian Zhang)

# 山上的小屋
### 残 雪

在我家屋后的荒山上，有一座木板搭起来的小屋。

我每天都在家中清理抽屉。当我不清理抽屉的时候，我坐在围椅里，把双手平放在膝头上，听见呼啸声。是北风在凶猛地抽打小屋杉木皮搭成的屋顶，狼的嗥叫在山谷里回荡。

"抽屉永生永世也清理不好，哼。"妈妈说，朝我做出一个虚伪的笑容。

"所有的人的耳朵都出了毛病。"我憋着一口气说下去，"月光下，有那么多的小偷在我们这栋房子周围徘徊。我打开灯，看见窗子上被人用手指捅出数不清的洞眼。隔壁房里，你和父亲的鼾声格外沉重，震得瓶瓶罐罐在碗柜里跳跃起来。我蹬了一脚床板，侧转肿大的头，听见那个被反锁在小屋里的人暴怒地撞着木板门，声音一直持续到天亮。"

"每次你来我房里找东西，总把我吓得直哆嗦。"妈妈小心翼翼地盯着我，向门边退去，我看见她一边脸上的肉在可笑地惊跳。

有一天，我决定到山上去看个究竟。风一停我就上山，我爬了好久，太阳刺得我头昏眼花，每一块石子都闪动着白色的小火苗。我咳着嗽，在山上辗转。我眉毛上冒出的盐汗滴到眼珠里，我什么也看不见，什么也听不见。我回家时在房门外站了一会，看见镜子里那个人鞋上沾满了湿泥巴，眼圈周围浮着两大团紫晕。

"这是一种病。"听见家人们在黑咕隆咚的地方窃笑。

等我的眼睛适应了屋内的黑暗时，他们已经躲起来了——他们一边笑一边躲。我发现他们趁我不在的时候把我的抽屉翻得乱七八糟，几只死蛾子、死蜻蜓全扔到了地上，他们很清楚那是我心爱的东西。

"他们帮你重新清理了抽屉，你不在的时候。"小妹告诉我，目光直勾勾的，左边的那只眼变成了绿色。

"我听见了狼嗥，"我故意吓唬她，"狼群在外面绕着房子奔来奔去，还把头从门缝里挤进来，天一黑就有这些事。你在睡梦中那么害怕，脚心直出冷汗。这屋里的人睡着了脚心都出冷汗。你看看被子有多么潮就知道了。"

我心里很乱，因为抽屉里的一些东西遗失了。母亲假装什么也不知道，垂着眼。但是她正恶狠狠地盯着我的后脑勺，我感觉得出来。每次她盯着我的后脑勺，我头皮上被她盯的那块地方就发麻，而且肿起来。我知道他们把我的一盒围棋埋在后面的水井边上了，他们已经这样做过无数次，每次都被我在半夜里挖了出来。我挖的时候，他们打开灯，从窗口探出头来。他们对于我的反抗不动声色。

吃饭的时候我对他们说："在山上，有一座小屋。"

他们全都埋着头稀哩呼噜地喝汤，大概谁也没听到我的话。

"许多大老鼠在风中狂奔。"我提高了嗓子，放下筷子，"山上的砂石轰隆隆地朝我们屋后的墙倒下来，你们全吓得脚心直出冷汗，你们记不记得？只要看一看被子就知道。天一晴，你们就晒被子，外面的绳子上总被你们晒满了被子。"

父亲用一只眼迅速地盯了我一下，我感觉到那是一只熟悉的狼眼。我恍然大悟。原来父亲每天夜里变为狼群中的一只，绕着这栋房子奔跑，发出凄厉的嗥叫。

"到处都是白色在晃动，"我用一只手抠住母亲的肩头摇晃着，"所有的东西都那么扎眼，搞得眼泪直流。你什么印象也得不到。但是我一回到屋里，坐在围椅里面，把双手平放在膝头上，就清清楚楚地看见了杉木皮搭成的屋顶。那形象隔得十分近，你一定也看到过，实际上，我们家里的人全看到过。的确有一个人蹲在那里面，他的眼眶下也有两大团紫晕，那是熬夜的结果。"

"每次你在井边挖得那块麻石响，我和你妈就被悬到了半空，我们簌簌发抖，用赤脚蹬来蹬去，踩不到地面。"父亲避开我的目光，把脸向窗口转过去。窗玻璃上沾着密密麻麻的蝇屎。"那井底，有我掉下的一把剪刀。我在梦里暗暗下定决心，要把它打捞上来。一醒来，我总发现自己搞错了，原来并不曾掉下什么剪刀，你母亲断言我是搞错了。我不死心，下一次又记起它。我躺着，会忽然觉得很遗憾，因为剪刀沉在井底生锈，我为什么不去打捞。我为这件事苦恼了几十年，脸上的皱纹如刀刻的一般。终于有一回，我到了井边，试着放下吊桶去，绳子又重又滑，我的手一软，木桶发出轰隆一声巨响，散落在井中。我奔回屋里，朝镜子里一瞥，左边的鬓发全白了。"

"北风真凶，"我缩头缩脑，脸上紫一块蓝一块，"我的胃里面结出了小小的冰块。我坐在围椅里的时候，听见它们叮叮当当响个不停。"

我一直想把抽屉清理好，但妈妈老在暗中与我作对。她在隔壁房里走来走去，弄得踏踏地响，使我胡思乱想。我想忘记那脚步，于是打开一副扑克，口中念着："一二三四五……"脚步却忽然停下了，母亲从门边伸进来墨绿色的小脸，嗡嗡地说话："我做了一个很下流的梦，到现在背上还流冷汗。"

　　"还有脚板心，"我补充说，"大家的脚板心都出冷汗。昨天你又晒了被子。这种事，很平常。"

　　小妹偷偷跑来告诉我，母亲一直在打主意要弄断我的胳膊，因为我开关抽屉的声音使她发狂，她一听到那声音就痛苦得将脑袋浸在冷水里，直泡得患上重伤风。

　　"这样的事，可不是偶然的。"小妹的目光永远是直勾勾的，刺得我脖子上长出红色的小疹子来。"比如说父亲吧，我听他说那把剪刀，怕说了有二十年了。不管什么事，都是由来已久的。"

　　我在抽屉侧面打上油，轻轻地开关，做到毫无声响。我这样试验了好多天，隔壁的脚步没响，她被我蒙蔽了。可见许多事都是可以蒙混过去的，只要你稍微小心一点儿。我很兴奋，起劲地干起通宵来，抽屉眼看就要清理干净一点儿，但是灯泡忽然坏了，母亲在隔壁房里冷笑。

　　"被你房里的光亮刺激着，我的血管里发出怦怦的响声，像是在打鼓。你看看这里，"她指着自己的太阳穴，那里爬着一条圆鼓鼓的蚯蚓。"我倒宁愿是坏血症。整天有东西在体内捣鼓，这里那里弄得响，这滋味，你没尝过。为了这样的毛病，你父亲动过自杀的念头。"她伸出一只胖手搭在我的肩上，那只手像被冰镇过一样冷，不停地滴下水来。

　　有一个人在井边捣鬼。我听见他反复不停地将吊桶放下去，在井壁上碰出轰隆隆的响声。天明的时候，他咚地一声扔下木桶，跑掉了。我打开隔壁的房门，看见父亲正在昏睡，一只暴出青筋的手难受地抠紧了床沿，在梦中发出惨烈的呻吟。母亲披头散发，手持一把条帚在地上扑来扑去。她告诉我，在天明的那一瞬间，一大群天牛从窗口飞进来，撞在墙上，落得满地皆是。她起床来收拾，把脚伸进拖鞋，脚趾被藏在拖鞋里的天牛咬了一口，整条腿肿得像根铅柱。

　　"他，"母亲指了指昏睡的父亲，"梦见被咬的是他自己呢。"

　　"在山上的小屋里，也有一个人正在呻吟。黑风里夹带着一些山葡萄的叶子。"

　　"你听到了没有？"母亲在半明半暗里将耳朵聚精会神地贴在地板上，"这些个东西，在地板上摔得痛昏了过去。它们是在天明那一瞬间闯进来的。"

那一天，我的确又上了山，我记得十分清楚。起先我坐在藤椅里，把双手平放在膝头上，然后我打开门，走进白光里面去。我爬上山，满眼都是白石子的火焰，没有山葡萄，也没有小屋。

一九八五年

## Topics for Discussion

1. Describe the differences between the two periods of contemporary Chinese literary development that took place during the last 60 years.

2. The female character under Zhang Jie's pen is described as a "painful idealist". Explain why.

3. What is the unique artistic characteristic of Bai Xianyong's fictions?

4. Some have commented that Can Xue's stories are "bizarre". What is your opinion?

# Appendix

## I  Glossary

### Feng Sao（风骚）

"Feng" comes from "Guo Feng". Fifteen Guo Feng were a major portion of the content of *Shi Jing*. So "Feng" represents *Shi Jing* while "Sao" refers to *Li Sao*, which itself represents *Chu Ci*. Putting the two words, "Feng" and "Sao" together connect the two major works that symbolize the beginning of the great tradition of Chinese poetry.

### Han Fu（汉赋）

This was a common writing style during the Han Dynasty, with sentences part way between poetry and prose, and a neat length arranged in longer verses. Although it contained lyrical expression, it mostly depicted objective matters. The authors often used a large number and variety of words in the pursuit of an aesthetic beauty.

### Xuan Xue（玄学）

A way of thought formed during the Wei-Jin Dynasties, it was a philosophy that pursued the very nature of being. It was strongly influenced by Lao-Zhuang and deeply absorbed the elements of Buddhist philosophy. It advocated a respect for nature, the pursuit of freedom and a sense of beauty, all of which had a tremendous impact on Wei-Jin literary development.

### Pian Wen(骈文)

A written style very popular during the Six Dynasties. The style, similar to Han Fu, is part way between poetry and prose. It adopted a format of four or six characters per line, emphasized matching verses and lyrical rhymes, and used metaphoric and flowery vocabulary. It pursued beauty with its form, but in the end, when taken to the extreme, it became a format enamored with form over content.

### Six-Dynasty Zhi-Guai(六朝志怪)

A style of literary sketches produced during the Six Dynasties. Written with classical language and a relatively short length, Zhi-Guai mostly depicted unusual tales that permeated the society, with many of the characteristic themes involving immortals and ghosts. The style depicted stories with a simple formality and became the initial form for fictions.

### An-Shi Rebellion(安史之乱)

In 755, An Lushan(安禄山), a Tang Dynasty general, joined with Shi Siming (史思明) and together they mobilized a revolt against the Tang Emperor. The unrest and turmoil lasted for eight years and swept across the northern part of China. Although the rebellion was eventually put down, it greatly weakened the Tang, and thereafter its strength gradually declined.

### Tang Legends(唐传奇)

These are popular classical Chinese short stories written during the Tang Dynasty, the content of which focused mostly on peculiar surreal matters or out of ordinary outlandish tales. Compared to Six-Dynasty Zhi-Guai, Tang legends paid greater attention to real life and possessed a more conscious awareness of literary creation.

### Tang-Song the Great Eight(唐宋八大家)

This term refers to the eight greatest essay writers of the Tang and Song Dynasties. Han Yu and Liu Zonguan were from the Tang and Ouyang Xiu, Zeng Gong, Wang Anshi, Su Xun, Su Shi and Su Zhe were from the Song.

中国文学选读

### Song-Yuan Narratives（宋元话本）

These were the base scripts which were used during local folk singing or story-telling performances. They were oral depictions transferred into printed form, allowing the published results to be edited and modified. This was the beginning of Chinese fiction written in a vernacular style.

### Jingkang Incident（靖康之变）

In 1126 the Jin Dynasty invaded the Song and surrounded the capital of Bianliang (today's Kaifeng). The Song Emperor did not dare to fight and instead intended to make peace by giving away land. However, the Jin army abducted the Emperor, along with many members of the imperial court. The Song Dynasty was forced to move their capital south and thus ended the era known as Northern Song and began the era known as Southern Song.

### Dan, Mo, Jing（旦、末、净）

These are the main characters in a Yuan Za Ju (a Yuan-Dynasty drama). Dan is a leading female role, Mo an upstanding male role, and Jing, also known as painted faces, is typically a disreputable male role.

### Xinhai Revolution（辛亥革命）

Under the leadership of Sun Yat-sen's party, a democratic revolution broke out in 1911 (in the year of Xinhai on the lunar calendar). It was aimed at overthrowing the autocratic rule of the Qing Dynasty and establishing a republic.

### National Criticism（国民性批判）

It is the key theme of modern Chinese literature and also a main topic of Lu Xun's novels. National criticism seeks to raise awareness, to generate questions and to reflect the values of traditional Chinese culture. Furthermore it promotes modern concepts such as science and democracy to reform society and improve life.

### Young Intellectuals(知青)

Zhi Qing(short for "young intellectuals") specifically refers to the generation who finished high school or higher education during the 1960's and 1970's. The government arranged and advocated for this young generation, some voluntarily and some forcibly, to resettle in the rural areas to be re-educated in hard life. During the late 1970's most of these young intellectuals returned to the city.

# II  Chronological Table and Major Literary Events

| Chronological Table | Major Literary Events |
|---|---|
| 周朝建立（Founding of the Zhou Dynasty 1046 BC） | 《诗经》（*Shi Jing* or *Book of Songs* 1100—600 BC） |
| 春秋时期（The Spring and Autumn Period 770—476 BC） | |
| 孔子（Confucius 551—479 BC） | |
| 战国时期（The Warring States Period 475—221 BC） | 庄子（Zhuangzi 369 BC—?）<br>屈原（Qu Yuan 339—278 BC?） |
| 秦统一中国（Qin unification 221 BC） | |
| 秦朝灭亡（Fall of the Qin Dynasty 206 BC） | 《战国策》（*Zhan Guo Ce* or *Warring States Records*） |
| 西汉（Western Han 206 BC—25） | 司马迁（Sima Qian 145—87 BC） |
| 东汉（Eastern Han 25—220） | |
| 佛教传入中国（Buddhism introduced into China） | |
| 三国（Three Kingdoms 220—280） | 诸葛亮（Zhuge Liang 181—234） |
| 两晋（Western and Eastern Jin Dynasties 265—420） | 陶渊明（Tao Yuanming 365—427） |
| 南北朝（Southern and Northern Dynasties 420—589） | |
| 隋朝（Sui Dynasty 581—618） | |
| 唐朝建立（Tang Dynasty founded in 618） | |
| 初唐（Early Tang 618—713） | |
| 盛唐（High Tang 714—765） | 王维（Wang Wei 701—761）<br>李白（Li Bai 701—762） |

| Chronological Table | Major Literary Events |
|---|---|
| 安史之乱（An-Shi Rebellion 755—763）<br>中唐（Mid-Tang 766—835） | 杜甫（Du Fu 712—762）<br>韩愈（Han Yu 768—824）<br>柳宗元（Liu Zongyuan 773—819）<br>杜牧（Du Mu 803—853）<br>唐传奇（the Tang Legends） |
| 晚唐（Late Tang 836—906）<br>唐朝灭亡（Fall of the Tang 906）<br>北宋（Northern Song Dynasty 960—1126） | 李商隐（Li Shangyin 813—858）<br><br>柳永（Liu Yong 987—1053）<br>欧阳修（Ouyang Xiu 1007—1072）<br>苏轼（Su Shi 1037—1101） |
| 靖康之变（The Jingkang Incident 1126）<br>南宋（Southern Song Dynasty 1127—1279）<br>元朝（Yuan Dynasty 1271—1368）<br><br>明朝（Ming Dynasty 1368—1644） | 李清照（Li Qingzhao 1084—1151）<br>辛弃疾（Xin Qiji 1140—1207）<br>关汉卿（Guan Hanqing 1225—1300?）<br>王实甫（Wang Shifu 1230—1307?）<br>吴承恩（Wu Cheng'en 1501—1582）<br>汤显祖（Tang Xianzu 1550—1616）<br>冯梦龙（Feng Menglong 1574—1646） |
| 清朝（Qing Dynasty 1644—1911）<br>辛亥革命（The Xinhai Revolution 1911） | 曹雪芹（Cao Xueqin 1715—1763）<br>"五四"新文化运动（the May 4th New Cultural Movement in 1919）<br>鲁迅（Lu Xun 1881—1936）<br>徐志摩（Xu Zhimo 1896—1931） |
| 民国（The Republic 1912—） | 沈从文（Shen Congwen 1902—1989）<br>张爱玲（Zhang Ailing 1920—1995）<br>张洁（Zhang Jie 1937—） |
| 中华人民共和国成立（Founding of the People's Republic of China 1949—）<br>"文化大革命"（"The Cultural Revolution" 1966—1976）<br>改革开放（Reformation and Opening up to the outside world 1978） | 白先勇（Bai Xianyong 1937—）<br>张承志（Zhang Chengzhi 1948—）<br><br>残雪（Can Xue 1953—） |

# Ⅲ   Acknowledgments

*Chinese Literature: A Reader* has been developed from teaching materials used in the Chinese Literature course offered by East Asian Studies at Renison University College, University of Waterloo, Canada. Composed in both Chinese and English, this textbook is targeted at the teaching of Chinese literature to overseas students and combines a survey of the history of Chinese literature with selected readings. It can be used as a textbook for teaching Chinese literature overseas, as well as a source for reading materials to provide a taste of Chinese literature.

The compilation of this book is one of a series of ongoing steps in the development of the Confucius Institute, a cooperation between the University of Waterloo and Nanjing University which began in 2007. The Chinese Literature course, which has been taught at Renison University College since 2001, has provided a solid foundation and a rich accumulation of experiences for the generation of this textbook. With generous support from Nanjing University, the combined efforts of the two editors have been brought to fruition.

We would like to express our heartfelt thanks to Prof. Aimin Cheng, Director of the Institute for International Students, Nanjing University, for writing the preface and for his unending encouragement in support of the publishing of this book.

We would also like to express our sincere thanks to Sue-Anne Tu and Chris Hubberstey for their helpful contributions in the process of putting together this book.

We also sincerely appreciate the valuable opinions and consultations offered by Prof. Zhangcan Cheng, Department of Chinese Language and Literature at Nanjing University, and Miss. Yilin Gu at Jin Tan, Nanjing.

Finally, we would like to give special thanks to all the authors and translators of the works selected for this book, whose creative contributions were indispensable. The warm feedback and love expressed by readers is the best gift in recognition of their hard work.

September 2009